Midwest Book Review

calls *BEFORE* by J. Kilburn
"A deftly crafted blending of Crime Fiction
and Coming-of-Age…. recommended…."

InD'tale Magazine says:

"Mr. Kilburn is a master at writing character development!"

Independent Book Review says:

"The tension is thick….
And the characters are exceptionally well written."

Readers' Favorite calls Kilburn's characters

"…mischievous, everyday kids who turn out to be
anything but…. Kilburn breathes life into them
with some hilariously awkward scenes…."

Brittany Wendell's coming-of-age adventure brings a few unexpected twists and turns...

BEFORE, a Novel by J. Kilburn takes your average teenagers, gives them family and community, and then plausibly and seamlessly drops them into international intrigue in a small college town. These teenagers go about their sweet and sordid adventures blissfully unaware of their role in larger and more complicated regional events. *BEFORE, a Novel* is a coming-of-age story, but it's also a story about international Organized Crime and the role that small-town folks, your neighbors, your loved ones, and even the Honors Student next door might play in that dark and dangerous world.

WHAT REVIEWERS ARE SAYING ABOUT

BEFORE by J. Kilburn

"…especially and unreservedly recommended for community library General Fiction collections."
- Julie Summers in *Reviewer's Bookwatch* by MIDWEST BOOK REVIEW, May 2022

"…the dialogue is... probably among the top one percent in its sarcasm and authenticity."
- Jamie Michele for *READERS FAVORITE*, January 2022
- 5 stars!

"Kilburn weaves this teenage story with threads of secrets.... With a slow but tantalizing pace, this coming-of-age story is going to be tough to put down for fans of character-driven fiction."
- Manik Chaturmutha for *INDEPENDENT BOOK REVIEW*, April 2022

"…each and every one of the characters he creates in this story are well thought out…."
- Jennifer Shepherd for *IND'TALE MAGAZINE*, April 2022
- 3 stars!

before

a   novel

Crime and Coming-of-Age Fiction
for Adventurous Readers

by
J. Kilburn

Sometimes the line between Sweet Sixteen
and Hardened Criminal is uncomfortably
hard to discern....

James K. Mossman III
Publisher

Northfield, Vermont, USA
www.cerealnovel.com

BEFORE, a Novel by J. Kilburn

Copyright 2021, 2022 James K. Mossman III

Kindle Direct Publishing Paperback Edition
Copyright 2022 James K. Mossman III - All Rights Reserved
Independently Published in Northfield, Vermont, USA

ISBN# 978-0-578-37918-0
Printed and Distributed by Amazon / KDP

07132022:2115

Publisher's Cataloging-in-Publication Data

Names: Kilburn, J., author. | Huntress, Ardelia, illustrator.
Title: Before : a novel / by J. Kilburn ; illustrated by Ardelia Huntress.
Description: Northfield, VT : James K. Mossman, III, 2022. | Series: Heaven's door series ; book 1. | 14 b&w illustrations. | Summary: Follows the drama, mayhem and romance encountered by some young people as they grow up against a backdrop of international intrigue in a small college town. These teenagers go about their adventures and misadventures completely unaware of their role in larger and more complicated regional events.
Identifiers: ISBN 9780578379180 (pbk) | ISBN 9781005477080 (epub)
Subjects: LCSH: Teenagers – Fiction. | Parenting – Fiction. | Organized crime – Fiction. | Career development – Fiction. | Moral development – Fiction. | BISAC: FICTION / Action & Adventure. | FICTION / Coming of Age. | FICTION / Crime.
Classification: LCC PS3611.L42 B44 2022 | 813 K55—dc22

This tale contains violence, romance, nudity, sex, drugs, tobacco and alcohol use, and lots of other ill-advised or maladaptive behavior. There is no Rock-'n-Roll.

AUTHOR'S RESPONSE TO THE CONTENT WARNING:

There is some cussin' and some fight'n and more than a little ethically-questionable behavior in these pages. I found it best to keep the vernacular and activities of my young characters authentic. I hope you will find them likeable... in spite of their mis-steps.

Concerned about teen substance abuse, domestic violence, or risk-taking behavior?

Visit www.topdogsnovel.com/resources to find links to helpful community organizations.

ILLUSTRATIONS

I am once again indebted to Ardelia Huntress for sharing her artistic talents and literary criticisms. She makes my little world complete.

COVER ART

Cover design by James K. Mossman III

Thanks to Sven Lachmann for posting the beautiful streamscape picture on Pixabay.
Thanks to Patrick Pascal Schaub for all of that money – also on Pixabay.
Pixabay is a Royalty-Free image sharing website.

Thanks to SmartSign LLC for manufacturing the custom road sign, as well as for permission to reproduce a photograph of it.
SmartSign can meet all your custom sign needs!

MUSIC
Music referenced in this book includes:

"Baby It's Cold Outside" written by Frank Loesser (1944) - Frank Music Corp. / MGM

"Constant Craving" written by K.D. Lang and Ben Mink (1992), performed by K.D. Lang on the her album Ingenue / Sire Records

"Careless Whisper" written by George Michael ad Andrew Ridgeley (1984), performed by George Michael and the group WHAM! on the album Make It Big / Columbia Records

Many heroes inspired this tale...

We tend to think in terms of charging into burning buildings or battling foreign enemies, but sometimes the things Heroes are made of, and from, are smaller and more mundane - yet still brave, profound, and self-sacrificing. My first book was inspired by someone who lost his life for Doing the Right Thing.

This second book is a story about someone who kept a secret and gained a life. The world is better for it.

**He saw her for the first time up at Hattie Wendell's place.
But so much happened before that moment... and after.**

CHAPTER ONE

Beginnings...

There's this deep and dark ravine just up out of Collegeville, on the Mill Village end of town, and that's the place where they found all that money.

Just this side of the abandoned bridge at the bottom of that tiny valley there's a little gravel cul-de-sac created by drivers swinging the car wide as they turn around to leave the dead-end where the road now stops. Nobody ever goes up there anymore, except to fish, or maybe to park and fornicate. But back in the late 'Eighties everyone passed through there - that gravel spot was smack-dab on a busy road between town and the Outside World. In those days it was just a little pull-off to one side of the old state route that snaked up through that ravine to the new Interstate Highway. Used by snowplows, postal route drivers and school busses turning around to go back town, it was wide and wheel-worn. If a driver backed up too far, they'd end up in the hole that was once the basement of a stately gothic carriage barn... someone did, once, before the trees grew up enough to prevent it. It's all still up there, right past the empty, broken-windowed, falling-down mansion and its little orchard of gone-wild apple trees, the whole of it gradually disappearing into encroaching forest.

In 1991, during the old state road's last year in that wet gully, some folks from Mill Village were driving through there on the way to the interstate one warm and sunny late-fall day, when suddenly there was this drifting CLOUD of greenbacks on the road... like they were driving through a pile of fallen leaves! They looked back and all these dollars were swirling in the air behind the car, spiraling into two vortexes on either side, then dropping and scattering just like the foliage. They probably wouldn't have noticed but for the fact that fallen leaves aren't uniform rectangles, green on one side and grey on the other and covered with faces of dead presidents. Well of course they stopped, right at that very gravel pull-off, parked the big old Pontiac Lemans wagon with the hazards on, and bailed out to start chasing bills just as fast as they could go. They paused to count now and again, as their hands filled up.

"Oh, Wow! They aren't all ones, either!"

"Yup, I've got three hundred already! Here's a bunch more, look in that ditch over there...."

So they picked up a couple thousand dollars, just like that.

There's probably some of that money, still unfound, rotting in the leaf-litter up there to this very day.

But back to those town folks: they turned around and took the money they'd picked up down to the police department. The cops working that day were absolutely delighted to take the money off their hands. They told those good citizens that some guy over in Stone City had reported losing his wallet off the roof of his car somewhere on that very road, just yesterday. Ya, I bet. Those folks from Mill Village were law-and-order types and didn't dream of asking for a finder's fee, or how the hell that much money fit into a wallet. It wouldn't have. A paper shopping-bag, maybe.

Those folks were just part of the history in that ravine, a sum of events both long past and recent. Some of this history would be germane to a certain young man from Ontario in his unknown and not-too-very-distant future, in ways that you or I or he could not even have imagined. And you'll see that money again here and there in this tale and others - you can count on it.

***

As much as the Interstate Highway up there at the top of the hill was a step forward in time, the old soon-to-be-abandoned state road was a step back: this ravine had welcomed travelers to town since the days of the Concord Coach. In the old days - the really old days - the roads had gone from Quebec City to Boston over the tops of the ridges. There was an inn up there, back in 1800, not too far from where the superhighway exit is now - funny how the main road is right back on top of the ridges, two hundred years later. Two centuries back, travelers to town would get dropped at the inn by a stagecoach. Once fortified by a night's sleep they would hire a local team to bring them down through that ravine in a four mile trip to the bustling little mill town just getting started at the river below. The little pike never got wider or straighter when first the Model A, then the Model T, then the Edsel and the Mercury took over. Instead, it just got gravel and then stone and then blacktop in ever deeper layers that couldn't hide the sags in the downhill edge as the whole thing moved towards its destiny. When the Interstate superhighway and heavy trucks came, it was the beginning of the end for the little road down to town. You could peer over the guardrail - the old creosoted wooden post and steel cable kind - and see four, eight, ten feet down the layers and layers of asphalt and stone from previous repairs slowly sliding down the clay hillside and towards the brook far below. After they built that new interstate access highway it wasn't five years before the old road - the whole thing, they say - slid one hundred and fifty feet down, in one piece, to the bottom. The few remaining telephone poles with their old blue glass insulators, the wooden guardrails with their many steel cables, and even the signs followed the pavement to the bottom too.

That road is sitting there as you read this, on the bottom of the ravine, right next to the brook: a series of long level spots gradually growing a green carpet of thick moss that obscures the now-undisturbed sections of pavement that once welcomed a young man named Bruce Sutton to Collegeville as he embarked on the adventure that would bring him to meet the makers, givers and takers of all that money.

***

Okay, here goes… "I think I should go to The Academy."

In a kitchen in a suburb of Toronto, Ontario, Canada, a year or two before those folks in the neighboring country were chasing around clouds of loose money, a boy just becoming a young man made a case for where he wanted to spend the next four years of his life. The kitchen could have been any one of tens of thousands of kitchens across North America where this same discussion, or versions of it, were playing out during this time of year. So unremarkable and mundane, this years-ago beginning of great and terrible things....

Just voices, at first, there in that suburban Toronto kitchen: two of them older, but not too old, male and female, and a younger voice that was resonant, earnest, deepening by the day. The words spoken by the teenager idealistic but the mind behind them growing up even as he spoke, coming to resolve and resolution. It could have been your own kitchen, thirty years ago, with its dark cupboard doors, light, bright windows, steel sink and Formica-covered counters with cookie jars, crockery and tinware lining the wall in the back.

The female voice filled the kitchen suddenly, with a strident, urgent, demanding question: "Where?!?" Bruce's mother stared at him, open-mouthed, her finger motionless in the air, pointing at his father and her husband to emphasize some now-forgotten point she had been making.

Bruce's father's voice was deep, but softer than his wife's - caught off-guard, almost tentative: "Huh?" The man hung momentarily and uncharacteristically slack-jawed, his expression a mixture of surprise at his son's remark and irritation that was carried over from thirty seconds before.

"The Academy. In Vermont. The States..." Bruce turned to address his mother - *she'll be the Hard Sell...* "They have a great Architecture program, a football team that will make for kind of a nice atmosphere on weekends, and it's in the mountains. I'd like to be someplace different, for a while. Kind of a small-town place. Quaint, white houses and church steeples and all..." He looked back and forth between his parents, an eager smile on his face. "A nice place for you guys to visit, eh?" He rummaged behind his back for a second and brought a pamphlet out of his pocket. "I've got a catalogue right here..."

Bruce Sutton could have been any young nearly-man, but the high-school Senior in this kitchen, on this long-ago late-fall evening, was muscular and tall, easygoing, still just a kid. A boy with the typical hockey-player's mop of even-length, just-below-the-ears and go-everywhere brown hair gathered into unruly and defiant locks that reminded his mother of a garden gone awry.

His mother recovered first. Gloria Sutton looked the glossy brochure in her son's outstretched hand warily, almost in horror. "In the STATES?!? Do they even HAVE a hockey program down there?" She wasn't quite that naïve, but she placed hockey - and her son's place on a team - right up there with straight A's on the report card.

"Yah, Mom, a good one. Top of their league a couple of times recently. Nice rink. Lotta championship banners, eh?"

His father's eyes narrowed as he, too, chimed in to agree with, if not echo, his wife's concerns: "It's kind of a SMALL school, isn't it?"

Bruce knew what his father was getting at. "Ya, about a thousand or so, eh?" He held outstretched hands up, palm out. Wait. "But I'll get to PLAY there. A LOT!"

Wise parents were both talking at once again:

"There won't be any scholarships for hockey at a school THAT small, will there?" Dad, ever the accountant.

"But I THOUGHT you were going to go to Michigan! Just across the lake, eh?" Mom, the hockey fan and mother who didn't want her only son too very far away.

Bruce sighed while he waited for them to finish, then pressed his argument: "Look. I could go to Michigan, or McGill, or maybe I could still get into Cornell or Northeastern, and I MIGHT even get a scholarship...."

His mother nodded furiously. Those were large schools with big hockey programs.

Bruce continued: "...But I wouldn't get to PLAY, not 'til I'm third year or a Senior."

His mother's head unconsciously shook in the negative and her mouth started to open....

Bruce ignored her expression and soldiered on: "They're BIG programs and I'm NOT THAT GOOD." *I might not even GET a scholarship to one of those teams....* Bruce Sutton did not think in terms of which college he was applying to - he thought in terms of where he would play hockey. *Same difference*, or so he thought.

Gloria Sutton shook her head even more vigorously now, a grim set to her mouth and a crease between her eyes reflecting her inner assumption as well as her belief: *Don't sell yourself short with false modesty, son, it's unbecoming. Best damned hockey player in the family!*

Pete Sutton frowned, considering what he already kind of suspected. He also knew enough not to agree with his son in front of his hockey-mom of a wife.

Bruce continued: "At a smaller school, I'll be on the ice NEXT YEAR, as a freshman! It's a small team. I'll get ice time. At The Academy, they'll hear about me two, maybe three years in a row." Here in this household, it went without saying that THEY were the professional hockey scouts. He looked back and forth at his parents.

His father looked grim. "It seems wasteful to throw away the chance at scholarships, Bruce." *Kid might just get one....* Pete Sutton's hand had wandered, as it habitually did when he was concerned about money, to rest on the lip of his wallet pocket, as if to protect his hard-earned wealth from snatching fingers in a crowd. He was unaware of the habit.

Bruce hid the smile that arose from genuine affection. He knew that his father's concern about money was born of real hardship. The man had reportedly gone to college with a suit, one set of everyday clothes, and a bicycle, and then he had earned everything else. Bruce was aware that what he was doing was an affront to the man's sensibilities. *I'll have to tread very carefully to win him over.* "It's a good program, Dad." He held out the brochure again. "The people at that school are workers. The students AND the professors. At one of the big schools, I'm not going to see a professor at eight o'clock at night in a study room. They'll be driving their Mercedes off to some social function or play racquetball as soon as it hits five o'clock, eh? At this school in Vermont, I'm telling you, the DEPARTMENT HEAD is right there with his sleeves rolled up, tutoring students at ten o'clock at night! In the Engineering school, too, full professors hanging out in the office with the DOOR OPEN, no secretary, and kids are WORKING in there, doing their homework IN HIS OFFICE, I've SEEN it!" He sealed his argument with a bright, engaging, eye-brows high smile.

His parent's differences showed, briefly.

His father immediately assumed marketing was at work. "Yes, those videos are slick, and that's what they want you to think, but that's why they send them to your high school." Calm, almost condescending.

His mother frowned. "You've been to VERMONT?!?" Anxiety crept into her voice. 'When? When did you go to Vermont, Brucie?"

His mother was right this time, *but why does she have to worry so much?* "DAD, I've BEEN there!"

His mother both nodded - *I knew it* - and shook her head - *Oh, the betrayal* - at the same time. *Won't even tell us when he's off to a foreign country, he's too independent already, this one....*

Bruce caught his breath - *best not to be seen as arguing.* There was a big difference between having a discussion and having a fight. In this house, they only had discussions. He was glad of that right now, and would strive to keep it so. Bruce lowered his voice. "I took a trip with Scott last year... August. That weekend we went to Montreal. It was fine, just a hundred, hundred-fifty miles South... No big deal."

Gloria Sutton certainly seemed to think it was a big deal, alright: "You went to a different COUNTRY and didn't even TELL us you were GOING?" She punctuated her admonishment with an angry scowl.

Whups, eh? Bruce shrugged an eyebrow and tried to look a little meek about it, even though he didn't actually feel that way.

His father's response was more measured: "How long have you been thinking about this?"

Bruce's voice rose a little as he forgot himself in his frustration. He wasn't getting his intended point across. "It was FINE. I'm a citizen in BOTH countries, remember?"

Born in Detroit while visiting Grandma, to one parent who'd emigrated North across the lake and another parent whose people had lived on the North Shore since the days of the Hudson's Bay Company, Bruce Sutton was a citizen of a continent, able to legally migrate North and South the same as the geese. This fact would figure into his future in a very important and unanticipated way some day soon.

He continued: "No sweat at the border. Next year, I'll be living there, on my own." Actually, he'd be in a dormitory with two hundred other young men, and be heavily supervised and mentored, but that was a fine distinction. "It was no big deal to check it out... AND it was a good idea." Bruce looked pointedly at his father. *See, I'm mature, thinking things through, checking them out... capable of making a good decision.* "YES, I know that this will cost a lot of money. NO, it wouldn't be a good idea to go just because I want to play hockey there. BUT, it's a good place for me to make a name for myself on the ice, have fun doing it, and the program there is GOOD, so I'll have something to fall back on if I don't make it on the ice. Hockey might not-"

His mother interrupted: "Oh yes you will!" *Make a successful hockey career? Of course!* "You just need confidence, Honey!"

Bruce waited so that he would not be talking over her. He wanted to be heard. "Look, it's part of the plan, eh? It's a good plan. MY plan. I go to school, play hockey. If I get picked up...."

His mother muttered under her breath, "You will...."

"THEN I'll play pro until I can't anymore and then I'll design stadiums with my fame from the ice to sell me. If I DON'T get picked up...."

Bruce's parents both started to open their mouths....

Bruce shook his head vigorously and turned up his volume a notch: "WHICH IS A POSSIBILITY, THEN I've got a nice comfy skill with which to support me into old age and I'll be able to afford a house and a car and a dog and all that stuff..."

His parents responded nearly in unison:

"We'll discuss it."

"We'll have to talk about it."

On that most important of things, they were agreed.

Bruce Sutton left the kitchen unmoved and muttering under his breath. *They can "discuss" it all they want.* He smirked. He already knew where he was going to school next year. He'd gotten his Provisional Notice of Early Acceptance in the mail just last week, and had already signed and mailed the check from his summer's savings account, just to make sure. *I'll break it to them after they've had some time to mull it over....* He smiled. Some kids - pretty good hockey players - went off to college to be in a hockey program. Once there, they practiced a lot and mostly warmed a bench at game time. HE was going off to school to PLAY hockey. *THAT's worth the six thousand dollars I put up in the last five summers. Mom and Dad will cough up the rest when they see the place!*

***

Bruce was the only student in his secondary school who had visited all five potential colleges on his list before he'd even started his Senior year. He hadn't left his parents out of it intentionally; he just knew what needed to be done, so why make a big production out of it?

During his explorations, he saw a lot of soaring brick architecture, a lot of ivy climbing up walls, and a lot of wow-factor amenities meant to impress parents with tight fists around big checkbooks. He also saw a falling-down wooden ice rink, some grand and new and uninspiring cement ones, and one that looked like a community rink. That one, especially, did not inspire thoughts of memories made or of legends born. He quickly crossed off some schools from his list.

At each school he'd called ahead the Thursday before. Said he was a hockey player, looking at schools, and wondered if the Admissions Department could give him directions. He already had those from course catalogues and mailings, of course, but they didn't need to know that... One admissions counselor gave him directions and then hung up. A couple told him what time to arrive to catch regularly scheduled tours. The Academy was different.

***

The Academy salesperson on the other end of the phone asked him where he played hockey. Not where he went to high school, even though it amounted to the same thing. She asked about his league, its record. She asked about his coursework. She asked when he thought he might be on campus, and then told him how to get to the rink and how to get to Admissions. She said she would see him Saturday. It was personal, human and genuine.

Bruce's friend Scott was sponsoring the weekend road-trip with his brand-new driver's license and car in exchange for the cost of admission for the two of them into the Parc Safari open-air zoo up near Montreal. Scott was hoping to major in engineering or something responsible and lucrative like that, but he also wanted to summer in the wilds of an undiscovered continent where he would sedate large animals for hands-on, close-quarters study. His plans were not as fully-formed as Bruce's. Scott hoped that there would be some attractive and available female biologist also involved in this same work, sharing a tent with him on the unexplored savanna. Bruce figured his friend's wide and ever-present smile and rocker-length curly yellow hair would make the female company likely, but he wasn't sure about an engineering job with annual summer vacations to the lands watched over by Kilimanjaro. Scotty had some things to figure out.

Early on the second day of their road-trip weekend they checked out of the motel and headed east out of Montreal on Bruce's errand. Scott drove them towards the Eastern Townships on the Autoroute, then south on a major Quebec artery. Two hours into their trip they crossed through U.S. Customs into Vermont with little trouble. Bruce had the college brochure with him for the Inquisitors at the Line, but didn't need it. They got waved through after a cursory interrogation and headed South on an "Interstate" multi-lane divided highway.

Scott looked over at Bruce: "Hmmm. Culture shock, eh? The highways are different."

They weren't.

Bruce shrugged. "It's still drive-on-right. Go south on Route Ninety-One. Follow one of these foreigners so you don't get all confused, eh, you being new to driving and all...."

"Maybe someday your parents will let you get a moped, eh?"

"Asshole." Bruce snickered. "Taking Dad's Audi on dates next month…"

"See it when I believe it." Scotty laughed. "AND it's still your DAD'S, not YOURS."

"Asshole." Bruce said it with a smile and looked out the window to reflect on that problem for a bit. His own savings were going into first-year tuition costs, to make his choice -whatever it finally was - more likely to stick with certain opinionated parents. *Got to make it a matter already settled....*

The landscape didn't seem immediately different: farms and cows and fields and woods bordered the highway. The houses here were more bland: white and trimmed in deep green or black instead of the gaudy, fluorescent pinks, bright greens, aquas and harvest golds used on residences in the flatlands to the south and east of Montreal. Mountains appeared. The wide valley and farms of the St. Lawrence River region were behind then for good, apparently. Brick buildings materialized beside the highway, then gas stations and a strip... the outskirts of a New

England city, perhaps? The city never appeared. The white frame houses and farms and woods returned, along with a tree-lined ever-wider river that meandered southwards with the highway.

About two hours later Scott stopped the car at the bottom of a long, down-sloping exit ramp, right in front of a stop-sign that marked a narrow, barely two-lane road frugally paved in cracked, sun-bleached macadam. Three official-looking signs scare-crowed from the far edge of the narrow road, but nothing else at all to indicate that this place was somewhere, anywhere:

GAS 5.0 >

THE ACADEMY 4.0 >

MILL VILLAGE 5.0 >

Scott looked left and right. Blacktop disappearing under the throughway bridges to the right, the same road plunging down a hill and disappearing around a forested bend to the left. "You sure about this? Like the middle of NOWHERE, eh?"

Bruce pointed: "It says there's at least ONE gas station, too! Drive, Scotty!"

"You say so... should have named it Middle-Of-Nowhere-Vill." Scotty sighed, grimaced, and shifted the car into drive.

"Let's just see it. You biologists make judgements on empirical evidence, right? Let's get some data on this Academy."

A skeptical Scott turned the car to the right.

They went under the expressway bridges, passed a long-ago farm, and then entered thick forest on a steep side-hill. The car fell down a road designed more for bobsled or luge, with twisting, plunging descents and hard corners. Shortly the pavement tipped into a deep ravine where all daylight seemed to be left behind.

The road the boys were slaloming down would be gone before Bruce even returned to actually attend school. Construction was already starting: equipment was parked here and there along the side of the road, piles of stone and boulders lined both shoulders in a wide spot not too far from the highway interchange, orange signs shouted "WORK ZONE" at regular intervals. By the time Bruce was an Academy Cadet the state had finally re-located the numbered highway off of the collapsing and ever-under-repair side of what was really a very tall stream-bank and instead put it straight over the top of the hill on the other side of the brook.

Some strange things happened in that ravine those boys were falling into, in those few decades after after the Interstate came, but before the road was relocated. Perhaps Scotty felt it as he piloted their descent to town on that sinking road, but he merely assigned his tension to the narrow lanes and bumps and curves and crazy forty-five mile-per-hour posted speed which he couldn't seem to make half of in the car's pitching and bucking ride. Bruce didn't know about any of those things as he and Scott passed over the soon-to-be-abandoned bridge at the bottom of the ravine, but who knows? Maybe he heard about all that cash later. It's possible... that money was touched by just about everyone who would end up central to his story, though he had yet to meet any of them. For now, he and Scott bounced over that same bridge, passed the gravel pull-off, the orchard, the falling-down mansion, and went on their innocent and merry way, none the wiser about the history of the place other than a brief shiver that tickled the passenger's spine and shoulders.

Bruce put that flicker of chill down to the creepy old apple trees and the forlorn, falling-in mansion that looked straight out of a child's Halloween book.

Scotty pointed at the decaying, once-opulent home as they went by. "Nice. That must be the Academy President's house…"

The road emerged into daylight on a flat plateau dotted with well-pruned apple trees on one side and Holstein cows on the other. They drove through - yes, literally right down the middle of - a barnyard on this major numbered state highway. Scott had to stop for a cat and a tractor, in that order. They gawked at blue silos that castled over the barn and yard, and then they made a short downhill pitch through someone's flower garden to a stop-sign in an idyllic little village of less than twenty houses.

"Must be for all the academy staff, eh? All ten of them." Scotty waggled a finger over the steering wheel.

"Asshole. Go right, eh? College is about two miles down the road."

They arrived at the Academy campus a couple of hours earlier than Bruce had anticipated. He was relieved to find that it was big and brick and permanent and bordered by a store and gas station complex on one end and a village center on the other. The square, cookie-cutter architecture and paint scheme seemed to dominate around a mown-grass green fenced by granite posts and heavy black chain. One end of the green was right by the road. Bruce found it easy to pick out college-owned property that spilled along the road to the left and right of the end of the fenced lawn by the red and gold paint and the pine-green trim on the buildings. He had Scott drive past the Admissions Office so he could get his bearings and then they went to scope out the town.

Scott had only a passing interest; his college ambitions lay elsewhere at the moment. They ate a late breakfast at a little café on the town green surrounded by brick and wooden storefronts and churches, with a well-kept train station on one end of the block and a wide river bordering the other end. Much to Scotty's surprised indignation, small New England towns seemed to have chain grocery stores, hardware stores, and gas stations just like Canadian towns did.

As they drove past a couple of freshly-painted mansions and many well-kept homes on the way back to campus, Bruce pointed randomly and announced: "Academy President's house… Academy President's OTHER house… President's SUMMER house…"

Scotty admitted defeat. "Ya, yay, yes, eh?" He shrugged, as much as his grip on the steering wheel allowed. "So it's a real hopping place. YES, it looks NICE here. Ya, ya, it's a real college. But do they have hockey, like REAL HOCKEY, eh?" He knew that was the litmus test for his friend.

"Let's go see." Bruce gestured. "Out to the main road, go in on the other end of the campus…"

Hopping place? Yes, then, in Bruce's sixteenth year. Not later, though.

***

In twenty years the college, the dorms, the bustle of academia, the young minds… nearly all of it would be gone, memorialized only in a few buildings of common architecture here and there converted to apartments, starter-business space, a thrift shop. Bruce would be forever gone from this place, too. He'd be dead in eight years, mourned in nine, and found in eleven. What little remained - bones, threads that the crime lab didn't destroy in testing, a wide-grinned and empty skull missing two teeth - these would be officially interred in their own designated perpetual crypt: a drawer in the walk-in safe in the Evidence Room at the Vermont State Police lab. They have to do that, you know, when they realize that they won't solve a case. The remains still have to be kept, perpetually. In case. The evidence - what little there is of it - must be available for the jury at trial. Murder has no Statute of Limitations.

But so much happened before that. Bruce had not the faintest idea that he would be meeting The Reaper in so short a time, or here, or that before he did, he himself would send two men off to meet Death before him. What a change a few years makes in a young man. Or in his prospects. Could Scotty have stopped him, put an restraining hand on his arm and said, 'Hey, there, slow down a minute, eh?' If he'd known, had any inkling of what lay beyond the mouth of that dark door, would he have told his friend, 'Don't go in there?' Would Bruce have heeded the warning? Suddenly knowing even everything, would Bruce have turned around, foregone his plan and his dreams, and retreated to safe obscurity in some sporting goods store in Toronto? Or would he have at least changed his Academic Advisor, stayed with his original major, stayed on his imagined and planned trajectory? Maybe not, had he known all. Change one thing, change everything. By the end, Bruce Sutton had so much to lose. But he had so much, too.

Those that survive him and remember him know that well.

***

This trip occurred in the innocent and carefree days before all that.

In the here and now of two boys ready to seize the future, back in those days where the future held only promise, they found the rink, unaware of the doom hanging over the campus and the young man. The rink was across a set of railroad tracks and down on the bottoms by the wide, meandering river. The arena was old. Brick crumbled on one corner, while a battered wooden front double door provided an impossibly mundane and window-less entrance. The facade seemed uninspiring. A handmade sign had been set into the brick over the double doors:

THE STABLE

painted carefully in black block letters on a small piece of white plywood that had seen better days.

When Bruce tried to open it, this doorway to his near future, it was locked. But not secured quite fast in all dimensions through which we flit - the door handle had an electric effect on the boy-man. Time stopped. He saw a body - a man - fall to the street in front of him, a single whisp of gun-smoke curling up between them. A girl pranced through his vision - a beautiful, wide, smooth, smiling face with full lips and green eyes and a sea of black curls floating around it. He felt the weight of a burbling child on his knee before he saw the top of the boy's head, as they sat on a sun-laced bench under the branches of a low tree... and then it was gone already. Shadows and green around him, instead. He felt a strange blow to his solar plexus, another, his breath left him and he saw the world rise around and over him as his knees buckled. A strange thought intruded as he worked his mouth like a beached fish, trying to get air back in - *I'm just too damned tired to do this today.*

He let go of an ancient black door-handle as he fell, his stomach lurched, and found that he was standing in front of an aging hockey rink in Collegeville, Vermont, in the United States, his hand just off the same... *no, this one is different, a different door-handle, bronze and different.... Whoah!*

Scott, not a hockey player but a fair judge of the inspiring, looked dubious. "You sure, Bru?" Perhaps he'd seen his friend's face. Or maybe it had all been too quick.

Bruce shrugged. He felt a lingering slight nausea, but the flash-forward was already dismissed as a flash-back. *Must have been that damned acid I took last month. Absolutely no more of that shit, ever.* He shook his head to clear it.

"Good call." Scott put a hand on his shoulder. "Drive you anywhere else you want to go check out while we're down here, eh?" *This one's a wrap.* Boston, maybe?

A truck pulled up. A guard in a blue uniform jumped out. "Help you gentlemen?"

Bruce and Scott smirked at each other. Gentlemen.

Ah, what the heck, we're here... Scott spoke up: "My friend here plays. Hockey. He's good. Maybe coming here someday." *Not likely, but* "can he see the rink?"

The guard sized them up. He looked at their car, squinted casually at the license plate. "Sure." The man walked over, flourished a keyring with myriad keys on it, picked one seemingly at random, and opened the door. "Give you the guided tour. I get called away, just don't trip on anything and make sure you push the door shut behind you so it re-locks. Take a minute to get the lights up… I'll be right back." He disappeared into a cavernous dark space behind another set of double doors.

The guard returned and gestured them inside these inner doors, into some sort of small lobby.

Ice was near - Bruce could smell it in the air as he took in his surroundings. There were small pictures of the Academy teams from over the ages arrayed around the room. The early ones in black-and-white, with five, six, ten players in them. The most recent in color, with twenty or so players, a couple of coaches, and a few other staff-people. Some photos featured an additional team member: a big plastic-headed mascot in an oversized, many-buttoned military uniform with sweeping coat-tails and an oversized foam Stetson for a hat. Beyond the next set of double doors a hockey rink was slowly forming out of the gloom as the big overhead lights warmed up. The campus guard opened the double doors and gestured them through as the dim brown-ness became sodium orange.

Every hockey rink has a different smell. Wet ice. Wood. Cement. Paint. Sweat. Leather. Mildewed padding. Tape. Each arena combined those elements into a distinct bouquet that, in Bruce's mind, immediately identified the place. *This one smells like games won.* Wide wooden beams stretched across the cavernous space above them. Small sets of wood-plank bleachers on either side framed the rink.

"I know it doesn't look like much, but those guys fill this place, every game, and they play HARD." The guard made a sweeping gesture up at championship banners hung on the high wood beams above center ice. Other schools vanquished. League tournaments won. "It's a very competitive league, Division Three, with no clearly superior school, so they usually duke it out into the late season. You should come see a game. New rink coming soon - some pictures in the lobby, if you want to check it out."

Bruce stood with his hands on his hips, looking up at the championship banners. "I've seen what I need to see." He turned to look at Scotty, while speaking to the guard. "Architecture building? Is it far away?"

"Right up the hill. I've got to check on a couple of things and get the lights. I'll meet you out by your car in a couple of minutes."

Ten minutes later the guard came out of the rink, shaking the door behind him with a rattle to check that it was locked. Bruce and Scott started to get into the car.

The guard pointed - no need. "Right up these stairs here. It's that building right up there." He was already heading up the hill on many-stepped cement stairs, ascending at something between a run and a trudge, keys and belly swinging back and forth.

The boys followed and quickly caught up.

Pooof, poof, whooof, "Whew! I love this campus, but I HATE all these stairs!" The panting guard looked florid.

They crossed a small campus road and started up another flight of stairs through a tall pinewoods on a steep hill behind a row of brick buildings. They summited the stairs at a service road that seemed to go to the back of each building. The guard bent over and put his hands on his knees. "Too many damned donuts." He looked up and grinned, still red-faced from his climb. "Anyways, this is the back." He pointed to a door. "Architecture and Art. Started this program about ten years ago, converted the building… Go ahead and walk around while I check doors." The guard had recovered enough to stand up and fish around for yet another of the hundred or so keys he carried on two large rings. "I'll meet you out front, two floors up, at the other end of the building." He unlocked the door, waved them through, pulled the door shut behind them, and flicked a door-side light switch. "Out front. That way." He pointed toward some obscure spot down the corridor and beyond the ceiling. "You'll find it." With that, he took off down a corridor, shaking office doorknobs on his way.

Bruce looked around. He and Scott were standing in a large room full of cubicles. Tops of things were visible sticking up over the tops of the uniform cubicle walls or hanging from the ceiling: plush toy animals, airplane models, the top of a skyscraper with a furry stuffed gorilla on it, numerous aluminum painter's lamps. Bruce walked into the middle of the maze. Each cubicle contained a large desk with a sloped surface. Tee-squares, protractors, and clamps were a built-in part on each of the desktops. The work surfaces were mostly empty, but Bruce could imagine them full of blueprint paper marked up with building plans and soaring dreams. The room had a comfortable, lived-in feel, even in the midst of summer. He turned. Scott was over in one of the cubicles, thumbing through a photo album. Bruce went and looked over his friend's shoulder at the album, open to a picture of a female student holding a beer and wearing a T-shirt that said "Design-Build Ball 1989." She menaced the camera with a cardboard-and-tinfoil sword. Scott turned the pages. The back of someone's head, as they hunched over one of the desks with a building elevation coming to life under their hand. Three guys in formal wear, two ladies in prom-gowns squatting daintily in front of them, each holding some oversized mockup of a drafting tool: a very realistic slide rule, almost as tall as the standing students; a four-foot pen; a protractor cut out of cardboard or plywood; a drawing square made of two-by-fours and plywood. Fred Flintstone appeared in one picture, live and in-person, holding a beer, flanked by a VERY scantily-clad Wilma and... a female Charlie Chaplin? What looked like a presentation: starched shirts, ties, grey military uniforms, an easel. Bruce thought the uniforms looked especially good on the curvy members of the class. *Wow! Imagine sitting next to all those filled-out uniforms every day!* Another picture showed students standing behind a formal podium with a large projection of building plans in the background. Bleary-eyed students at workstations, windows black in the background, one uniformed student pointing to the clock, the moment frozen forever at two-forty-four in the morning. A black-and-white picture, a close-up of a set of smooth legs in roller blades, supporting a very female backside clad in tight leather shorty-shorts. *Nice architecture.*

Bruce decided he could like it in here, and it wasn't even a hockey rink. "What do you think, eh?"

Scotty surveyed the room around them and said, "Yeah. Yeah." To himself or to Bruce, he wasn't sure. *This place is... interesting.*

Bruce wondered if the people in the photo album were even in school anymore. Had they graduated, moved on into the real world outside, grown up, gotten jobs, made families already? Would he meet some of them in the fall, a year in the future? *Wonder if I'll meet the owner of that nice rear end on the roller blades?*

The guard was waiting when the two boys emerged out front of the building. Bruce and Scott pushed the door shut behind them and followed the blue-uniformed man on a brick walkway across an oblong square promenade. The marching-ground was bordered on all sides by a row of tall, stately trees with brick buildings set back in orderly rows on both sides behind the promenade and the trees. The guard gestured broadly with a sweep of his arm: "Dormitories. Classrooms. Okay, you two, what else do you want to see?"

Bruce tossed his head towards his friend. "Scott here wants to save the whale. Biology program?"

The guard turned to Scott. "You want to see the Wetlab?"

"Huh?"

"Wet Lab. Where they keep the critters."

"Lab mice?"

"Oh, no, a lot more than that. It's like a jungle in there...." The man in the blue uniform grinned. *The Wet Lab always snags future bio majors.*

Scott perked up. "Yah! Like, show the way, eh?"

The guard took them down a short road and into the front of a cluster of brick buildings that all looked like they belonged at different institutions: an old-fashioned, traditional brick academic building with large windows on one side, a taller, angled and more modern structure with few windows and garish stripes of white and dark red brick making a bold statement that the building DOES NOT BELONG on the other. In the middle, connecting these two, was a flat brick facade with row upon row of tiny windows and all manner of ivy growing in such thick bunches on the walls and over the windows to the extent that Bruce wondered if some jungle experiment had gone wrong.

The guard keyed in and held open a door. "Good time to be here, gentlemen. Lots of changes. This is getting renovated, too, with a new wing. Plans have a built-in greenhouse that you'll walk through on the way into the building. It's a standard pre-grad school biology program. A little local research here and there, mostly solid foundation for whatever your frien..." The guard turned towards them. "What's your name?"

"Scott."

"Scott. Well, Scott, for whatever you're going to do in grad school after your undergraduate, if you're planning to go that far. Some of the engineering and geology classes tie in, I've heard, soils and natural history of the continent, glaciation - the college is built on a glacial feature - like I said, good basic program for a well-rounded pre-whatever-you-end-up-doing. Down these stairs."

They jogged down two flights of stairs, the guard's keys jingling and clanking to mark time with the steps. The guard paused at a plain wooden office door, and announced like a train conductor, "Okay, Wet Lab!" He put a key in the doorknob. "Please don't pick anybody up, I don't know what kind of experiments anybody might be in the middle of... handling might be bad. I don't really know." He opened the door.

A dense wave of humidity hit them from a large room cobbled into a basement alcove with uneven angles a smooth grey floor. It smelled like a pet store, or a teenaged boy's bedroom. Wet wood shavings. Crickets. Mouse piss. Stale water. Green things. Fish poop.

Scott walked into the room with bugged-out eyes and a wide grin.

The room was monopolized by a large blue kiddy-pool right in the center, water swirling in and out of it, hoses going this way and that, some sort of large pump driving it all. Something that looked like a contractor's lamp hung from the ceiling, casting a warm red glow over the little indoor pond. A turtle the size of a small plate was basking on a low rock in the middle. Around the edges of the room, at the walls and on a few makeshift shelves, were glass tanks that contained a frog or a toad sitting despondently in an inch of water. There were living aquariums: bubbly, colorful, exotic, and also the requisite and more bland feeder-fish aquariums. One tank contained cascading moss and creeping plants on rocks and old wood - water spilled down the moss into a shallow sump, where it was forever and again pumped back up to the top of the moss. A salt-water aquarium in one corner had Scott's attention: a starfish creeping across the glass over a few waving fronds of sea-plant provided an almost alien show. One side of the room was occupied by mice and white rats in glass and wire cages. There was a lot of water on the painted and sealed floor: overspray and drips from the various pumps. A few frogs hopped around loose here and there, in and out of the puddles.

Bruce watched a toad stalk and eat a cricket near one wall. He grimaced as he followed the puddles and extension cords criss-crossing across the floor. *Good business for the undertaker*. He wondered how many little critters were electrocuted in the course of a schoolyear.

Behind it all, looking out of place in this wet and wild room, a desk and a bookcase occupied the far wall. Binders and papers lay randomly in piles. Bruce walked over towards the academic and bureaucratic island to inspect some sort of colorful lizard with suction toes. The lizard, free, was climbing the wilds up the side of a plastic coffeemaker.

The guard muttered nervously: "I… think I'd… better call Tanya." Then, louder, to the boys: "I don't think they're usually this… FREE, in here. The lab director hasn't been around for a while… vacation." He looked over at the auto-perk coffee pot. "Gecko-piss coffee. Mmmmm."

Bruce and Scott stepped gingerly around the basement room, trying to inspect the various furry and scaly creatures without stepping on any of them, while the guard used the phone on the desk to call someone at home about the escapees.

"Plants?" The blue uniformed guy looked around the room. "Yah… Yes, Ma'am, they look watered." Pause. "The colored ones?" He looked over at a glass terrarium with colored frogs inside, right where they were supposed to be, clinging to mossy sticks or the inside of glass panels. "They're there." Silent, peering closely at the terrarium, then: "Yes, five." He listened for a minute, then got an impish smile. "Sure. Welcome back! Thanks, Tanya, bye." He put the phone down and turned around. "You gentlemen want to round up some wildlife? Wash your hands in the sink o'er there, rinse off REAL well, and then corral some of these frogs, if you can." He stepped over to a sink near the desk without waiting for an answer, and by example started scrubbing, just like a surgeon. "And wash up, when you're done, too, before you leave the room. First wash is to protect them, the second to protect you when you eat your lunch." The guard went to the desk and picked up the gecko by sliding a finger up under it, between the legs, then he carried it over to a covered glass tank with a heat-lamp above it.

Bruce shrugged and joined Scott, who was already at the sink scrubbing up. The boys started chasing frogs. It took a while.

The man in the blue uniform smirked. It was quite a picture, the two kids-not-quite-adults crouched down, peering under counters and cabinets, hopping around after frogs and toads who were themselves hopping around after loose crickets. Who knew what the crickets were chasing? The guard thought to himself once more, watching his new animal control deputies: *if this room doesn't bring the aspiring biologist here, I don't know what will!* "Just put them in the kiddy pool with the turtle, if you catch any. They'll probably stay put in there."

Scott carefully dropped a leopard frog into the pool. "What happened?"

"A welcome-back surprise for the lab tech coming back from her vacation. I'm kind of sorry we screwed it up." The guard thought for a moment. He went back over to the gecko cage and carefully slid his finger under the lizard once again. He carried the little creature over to the desk and set it right back where he had found it, on the coffee-maker. He dipped his fingers under the faucet and sprinkled some drops of water on the gecko. They disappeared into the skin. "He'll be alright. She comes back tomorrow. You gentlemen didn't see a thing, right?"

***

Bruce met with Julie from Admissions later in the morning. Scott decided to join them, on a whim. She showed up in jeans and a sweatshirt. The grey hoodie was brand-new and proudly sporting the Academy logo, of course, but Julie looked informal, friendly, welcoming. Not like other stiff-and-starched or stenciled rugby-shirt admissions personnel Bruce had met. Their guide covered the course catalogue, the athletic programs, the facilities, the costs, and the local attractions and amenities. All this while on a walking tour of the campus, pointing to the various buildings as she described the purposes and contents. She briefly described the history of The Academy and explained the regimental dorm-life that descended from the founding into the present-day structure of the student body at this private school with a gunrack in each room and its own militia.

Bruce had a bit of an idea already, from the course catalogues and brochures he'd researched, but most of this information was new to Scott.

Huh?? As the woman talked and pointed, Scott looked around for tanks, soldiers, guns. *Well, maybe they're all off in the Gulf.* He'd seen a tank, just the one, guarding the rugby pitch. *These people must REALLY take their "football" seriously.* Americans were a strange bunch.

***

The Academy was founded in the early 1800's as a place to form young men into learned, capable leaders for a new country that needed surveyors, architects, builders, and leaders. Local boys from around Vermont and New Hampshire - still considered the wild frontier in those early days of the new nation - were polished on the twin stones of disciplined military training and advanced education: sciences, mathematics, military history, classic literature. For nearly two hundred years, the fortunes of this small and elite school waxed and waned with the coming and goings of war: skirmishes on the ever-westward moving frontier of the nation, the Civil War, the Spanish-American War. The school became a specialized Cavalry training ground, where graduates would be accepted immediately into military service as officers. The ever-progressive leadership of the school made sure cavalry training progressed from a stable of horses to trucks to early tanks by World War One, the Great War, the War to End All Wars, certainly the last time the country would need The Academy's graduates. That hockey rink that Bruce and Scott toured was actually the stable, built in the late 1800's when the school was bulking up for the Spanish-American War. The school nearly closed after the Versailles Treaty at the end of World War One, for lack of interest. There was no future in war, now that the greatest and most horrible of them had been fought. Other, more traditional college programs far away and in the wider world distracted area youth from the benefits of a military college lifestyle in sleepy little hamlet beside the river dividing New Hampshire and Vermont. Then came World War Two, and The Academy once again became a busy place. Every time the country needed warriors, leaders, and well-regulated troops, the nation turned once again to the graduates of the tiny university in the remote hills of New England. Wars and conflicts and D-M-Z's caused enrollment to tick back up again. The Korean conflict. Vietnam. Every peace brought a gradual contraction.

After Vietnam, the Academy became a special training ground for another, quieter kind of warrior. There were courses on Chinese culture, immersion courses in Russian language, engineering classes that focused on trajectories and ballistic coefficients and orbital physics. A graduate might head off towards Basic Training, but on completion immediately be sent to a foreign land, out of touch and also out of uniform. Some of the faculty kept an eye out for especially promising students and carefully steered their careers towards a particular branch of service or government office.

That little quad of four brick dormitories on the side of Vermont Route 5 quietly provided leader-warriors to the country for generations. Read your histories: Bull Run, Clark's Creek, Antietam, San Juan Hill, Verdun, Belleau Wood, Iwo Jima, the Solomon Islands, Tunisia, Normandy… Academy graduates were there. They were there in histories that you won't read, too: histories quietly summarized in publications carefully filed away from public view, histories that sometimes ended with an anonymous star on a wall in a discrete Three-Letter Agency lobby in Langley, Virginia.

For the Academy, the end of the Cold War became the end of many other things. Bruce and his classmates entered a school with declining enrollment, too many expenses, too much room, and more than one disaster looming. They did not know that they were to be the last traditional class to graduate. By the time they were Sophomores, the Academy was accepting civilian students. The year after they graduated, the college accepted community members to a new slate of evening classes. Five years after Bruce graduated, all new students had single, private rooms by default, because there simply were not enough bodies enrolled to fill the dorms. The next decade came, and with it a catastrophic fire that jumped across alleys and streets, from building to building. They called it the Hanover Fire, after the name of the dorm where it started. Suddenly the college was gone to history. As was Bruce by then.

But that was later.

***

Julie asked if there was anything in particular they wanted to see, or any building they wanted to tour. "So far, I've just shown you a lot of front doors... Do you want to take a look at the rink?" *This kid will jump at that!*

"No, I've seen what I need to."

Scott was ready to go, too. "All set here, eh."

Julie put on a smile, but inwardly she shrugged. *The hockey players always want to see the rink if they're seriously interested in the school.* She guessed that neither this one, nor his friend, would be showing up in a year's time.

***

That visit to Vermont gave both young men a lot to think about. Bruce and Scott visited a couple of other schools that happened to be convenient to the Great Lakes region, but the Academy was the only one that got a second visit. They came back one more time during the next schoolyear, to see a hockey game, of course. That night after the game they walked around the campus again, from riverfront athletic fields to hilltop brick administration building. They wound through long brick boxes of classrooms, through bustling dormitories, into and out of quiet office-lined hallways. Wandering on their own this time - uninhibited by escorts or sales staff, eager to see what college life was really like on this American campus with its long military history.

***

Boys that age are as changeable as an April wind. That next year, as they were pushing through their Senior year of secondary school, both of the young men had applied to The Academy in far away Vermont.

Scott had suddenly decided to major in Architecture, so that he could design public zoos and aquariums.

Bruce had settled on business, so that in his retirement he could manage that pro hockey team that he would assuredly be playing for between now and then. Or maybe he would work as a sales rep for one of the better equipment companies. Or maybe he would run a stadium... Director of Facilities. One thing for sure: He would spend the next ten or twenty years on the ice. *THAT will never change!*

And that is how Bruce Sutton ended up in the family kitchen one night, trying to convince his parents that he should attend a military college in far away Vermont.

***

Bruce had a predictably stellar final year of Secondary School, that last winter in Toronto, both academically and on the ice. His district's team, the Maples, won three, four, six, then eight games by wide margins. Bruce didn't take many shots on goal, but when the puck was behind the opposing net, somehow he always seemed to be there with his stick curling impossibly around the post and behind the goalie's heavily padded legs. SCORE! He seemed unstoppable, he felt invincible. SCORE! He and his teammates skated their way to the regional finals, where Bruce and two of his defensemen carried the rest of the team to a final showdown with a much larger school. Sutton

SCORES! Bruce swooped back and forth across the ice, always there when the puck was near the opposition's net, always near his goalie when the puck was deep in their own zone. Late in the last game of his secondary-school hockey career, he even took a chance at a slapshot from mid-ice right before the first-period ending buzzer. HE SCORES!

They lost that last game, but not by much, and they put on a good show against a much larger school with a deeper pool of talent on the team. Some of those guys were going on to the BIG hockey schools, on scholarship. There was pain, but no shame, in a two-point loss, six-to-four, in the finals against a school that had the championship five years out of every decade. He'd been sure that a final-game win would propel him into early fame - a Sports Section front page expose on this rising talent heading off to college in the States. The interview and article never came. His school hockey career faded into mediocrity and obscurity with the loss, and with it hopes of early notice by Pro recruiters evaporated into hard reality. That didn't change his plans: Bruce knew where he was going to start… he just didn't know where he was going to finish.

In just a few years, Bruce would forever Lie In State in an oversized brown paper shopping bag closed with tamper-proof evidence tape, dated and signed and then locked inside a vault consecrated by procedure, the Rule of Law, and a brief prayer service. That somber event would occur thirteen years to the day from the young man's first visit to the state, county and very town where he would die. The small ceremony would be complete with an attending Vermont State Police Color Guard of one, a Chaplain, a weary ex-Governor, a regretful Father-In-Law, and two parents who would forever wonder: *What the hell happened to our little boy?*

You, Dear Reader, are about to find out.

Chapter Two

THE PIPELINE

There is a North-South public works project through Vermont, built in the late Nineteen-Sixties and early 'Seventies with Federal Department of Transportation dollars as part of a larger, national project. The legislation authorizing this grand scheme was named the "National Civil Defense Highway Authorization Act," which was loosely conceived as a way to move Army National Guard tanks around between the fifty states in case of a Red Communist invasion of the United States mainland, or a way for city folks to beat it away from the bullseye in case of a forewarned nuclear exchange between the Superpowers. The real, unstated reason for this nationwide frenzy of construction was much simpler: citizens wanted to hop in their automobile and get cross-country quickly. But it was expedient to use the Cold War to get the funds rolling. In those times, nothing stirred hearts, minds and Federal coffers like the threat of Communist aggression. Thus, the modern interstate highway system was born.

The Soviet and Cuban invaders never materialized, and mass exodus from coastal cities is more likely to be prompted by a hurricane warning than a Global Launch Threat Assessment. But a dangerous and disruptive invader did arrive in Vermont, and it came on those very interstate highways that were built as part of the larger national network.

In the 'Seventies members of the Topdogs Motorcycle Club from all over the nation started gathering every summer at Miles Pond up in the hard-scrabble landscape of northeastern Vermont. Locals from the area remember long lines of motorcycles - all Milwaukees or homemade jobs - parked by the dozen at intersections, exhaust pipes thundering and booming. Astride them were strangers, Outsiders: men wearing black leather jackets and denim vests with snarling three-headed dogs sewn onto the back. These TOPDOGS fellows provided an exciting and imposing presence that shattered the atmosphere of that idyllic little tourist spot on the side of a formerly quaint and quiet pond. They brought naughty four-lettered words, anti-social messages embroidered onto small personal patches on their riding clothes, and sometimes behavior to go with the words and messages. This merry, angry mix of motorcyclists caroused freely, apparently jobless or on endless vacation, partying on into late hours of the night when the farmers were just getting up for the Early Milking. Cursing, giggling, howling... the locals couldn't figure out if these bikers were Happy Hippies or angry sons of the very Devil himself. The bikers usually came with camping gear or rudely-clad women or both on the back of the big motorcycles, as well as hair that resembled rumors of the Wild Man of Brighton Bog. They'd flock in to Miles Pond for about a week every August in a cacophony of noise and a riot of color - the flat, matte sheen of black leather and bright indigo of denim were splattered and splashed with reds and browns and royal blues announcing the common thread of the visitors. The wide and bold "TOPDOGS" ribbon running shoulder-to-shoulder told folks exactly WHICH band of outlaws had descended on the normally-quiet little spot. Wide lower patches shouted the foreign names of far-off, alien places: "Albany," "Hartford," "Scranton," "Pensacola," "Seattle."

There was a combined motor-court and campground on the eastern end of the pond. Rustic, maybe a few decades out of touch, with fire rings and picnic tables right by the water, individual tent sites, and ten cabins by the road for rent too. That's where these wild and carefree motorcyclists gathered, at first. They'd fill the place right up to overflowing, then take over the woods and fields across the road, as well.

Anybody that had overlapping reservations would be wise to leave - they'd get pushed out or become part of the party otherwise.

By the early 'Eighties it had gotten bigger: the entirety of Miles Pond, all the way around, hosted one big party for half of August. Motorcyclists from all over the nation and the world descended on that little puddle like noisy, barking, migrating geese. They came for social discourse, late-night fun, and meetings about club business. Patches began to speak of international ambitions: "Saranac," "Portland," "Trenton," but also "Montreal," "Mexicali," "Caracas," "Manchester," "Liverpool," "Copenhagen," "Sao Paolo." The locations seemed endless. All of them Topdogs. With them came groupies, girlfriends, wives and pickup trucks full of beer. In later years they were followed by strippers, hookers, car trunks full of imported and not necessarily legal liquor, and big vendor-owned refrigerated beer trucks. Lots of marijuana came with these bikers, and also "California Drugs:" acid, psilocybin, angel dust, cocaine, speed, heroin.

The local community mostly welcomed them. Nothing these bikers did was overtly harmful to those wise enough to get the hell out of the way. Sales of gas and beer, cigarettes and meat at the local general store boomed in August. Campgrounds made a year's worth of revenue in two weeks, every lot booked or double-booked.

There was talk, though: some of the local young men skulked around the edges of these many-day parties, developing a taste for marijuana. Some of the town's daughters delivered babies in April and May and folks speculated on the timing. Stuff disappeared.

In the mid-Eighties it stopped. One summer, the annual migration never came. Life returned to normal, except that the horde of loud, laughing, angry and merry motorcyclists had themselves become the new normal, for two or three weeks each summer. And then they were gone. The campground faltered - by this time, culture had changed and folks were buying pull-behind campers and going to far-away National Parks for the summer instead of driving twenty or fifty miles down the road to the shore of a quiet little "lake." The pond-side motor inns with their tiny cottages, no amenities and 1920's feel became quiet and empty year-round. Vacationers packed up the car, hopped on the interstate, and drove all the way to salt water now. Quiet summer getaways on the shores of buggy little far-away ponds were no longer the Going Thing. Trees grew up through fire-rings. Paint, then boards, fell off the cabins. Miles Pond became as a ghost town. Even the once-busy mainline railroad faltered and died. The paved roads cracked and reverted to gravel.

The Topdogs found someplace else to go, too, as they became a part of the little pond-side burg's history. The bikers and their retinue congregated for the last time in August of 1984, then disappeared like dissolving whisps of smoke. They left a legacy, though. Some of the folks in that area had a really strong appetite for coke and potent British Columbia weed and un-taxed Canadian whiskey. These and other illicit items flowed up and down the north-south interstate highway through Vermont and New Hampshire in an international flood of wealth and ills that caused regional police agencies and their officers to give their stretch of this nationwide highway system its own local nickname: "The Pipeline."

***

"Oh, they're still around. They run around Quebec like they own the place, and they've got a big presence in Connecticut. They've GOT to be here, or going back and forth. We're just not seeing them. Sure seeing the problems, though...."

The man speaking sat at the head of a long, dark, highly-polished conference room table. With his short haircut and blue suit and cuff links, he could have been a banker or an IBM executive. His tie-tack gave away his real authority. It was green and gold and in the shape of a tiny badge. Vermont Department of Public Safety. The man to his right, also in a blue business suit, was the state's chief State Trooper.

The man to his left was from the Department of Liquor Control. He was responsible for taxing all of the wine and spirits sold in the state of Vermont. Each bottle for which the tax was paid was "sealed" with an adhesive strip over the cap, on which was stamped the DLC logo and a code. Hard liquor was heavily regulated in Vermont, and could only be sold at state-granted franchises - roughly ten per county - that maintained a monopoly on the business. Liquor is expensive in the Green Mountain State. The bureaucracy keeps it that way.

The man to the left of the Liquor Control inspector was retired from an amorphous, unspecified, and little-discussed Federal job where he was frequently posted overseas. His last posting in the foreign service had been to a Central American country, where he was carried on the books as a "Literacy Instructor." When he'd retired from "teaching," he'd joined the Vermont State Police, where he'd risen to the rank of Troop Commander before retiring again. Now, he was a college professor who lectured military college students on Constitutional Law, Criminal Procedure, and Law Enforcement, among other weighty subjects.

To the left of all of them sat an agent of the Federal Drug Enforcement Administration. Like the rest of the people here, his suit jacket was also blue. It seemed to be the color of the day, or of the work.

"And when they're going back and forth, spill-over crime drops off the pipeline."

"Do you KNOW that?"

"These drugs are coming from somewhere. Cocaine doesn't grow this far north, but it might as well. They sell it by the pound, and weed by the BALE around here, some times of the year."

This was back when having an ounce of weed was hush-hush stuff, back when it could get you in really BIG trouble. Now, with the Legalization Push, nobody gives a shit. Back then, you could end up In The System over just a little baggie and a pack of wrapping papers. Jail was a possibility, maybe even prison.

The professor grimaced. He'd had a brush with someone in that business, just recently. He'd grounded her until she turned twenty.

"And whiskey revenues are off by several tens of thousands. There's Canadian whiskey out there, but it's not moving through the sanctioned franchises. We think they're bringing it in on the lake. Or in trucks. We're not really sure." The Liquor Control man sighed and shrugged, hands open to the heavens.

The Trooper leaned forward. "Last fall, a biker - a REAL one, one of those Topdog fellows - well, they showed up at the You-Save Store near the state capitol, a bunch parked the bikes right out front, and this guy, he advertised the biker uniform right there in the front of that chain store for four hours. We have the surveillance tapes - he just STOOD in that ONE spot, right by the registers, turning a clockwise circle the whole time, one r.p.m. by the watch, by the way." He sat back. "Making their presence known."

The college professor grimaced again. He lived about twelve miles from a You-Save. He wondered if his own community was marked and owned territory, now, too.

That statement also caused the DEA man to sit up. "You mean somebody was pitching a flagpole."

"Ya, I think they're marking turf."

"Right in the damned capitol city..."

"For a southward expansion... of those Quebec ones."

"Yes."

"Be nice to have a view from the street, as it's happening."

"Yes. Or maybe right from behind the handlebars."

"Where'd they come from originally?"

Shrugs.

"They've always just kind of been around."

***

No one knows the origins of the Topdogs Motorcycle Club. They just appeared, one summer in the late Fifties, in groups of twos and threes and tens, on streets and highways in port cities on the East Coast. By the mid-sixties, the Topdogs rode here and there in packs of twenty-five or fifty on some weekends. There were rumors that they were disillusioned war veterans who were unable or unwilling to fit back into civil society. There were other rumors that said the bikers were former Mafia middlemen, under indictment, Italians or Sicilians who'd traded their silk suits for denim and were hiding in plain sight. The most credible stories said that the first Topdogs were simply hippies who liked motorcycles, didn't like authority figures, and were fiercely aggressive in asserting their personal freedoms. The truth was probably a combination of the rumors... or something else entirely. The Topdogs were a mystery.

The Topdogs seemed, as a general rule, to like freedom, drugs, liquor, women, fighting, anything with an engine but especially motorcycles, assembling in large groups for raucous and dangerous-looking parties, and summer. They bought what they could pay for, were rumored to take what they needed when they did not have money, and seemed to live by a code more common to the Western Territories of the 1870's. In the north these Topdogs disappeared into the woodwork in the crueler months. Here one day and gone the next, like a migrating herd of predators.

They were met with instant fear or admiration - depending on who was looking - everywhere they went.

***

Bruce Sutton arrived on the Academy campus on a breezy late-summer day that stretched the national flags and many regimental banners tight on their nylon ropes. He and two hundred other young men and women frowned nervously as they dropped luggage into unceremonious piles in front of each assigned dorm. They did not realize it, but they would not be seeing these personal effects again for many months. The incoming recruits bid goodbye to parents, loved ones, or taxi-drivers and then were lined up in orderly rows to be marched off to a barber, a uniform quartermaster, and a retinue of academic advisors. Bruce and his new classmates were sworn in en-masse in a ceremony where distant parents could only wave at their offered sons and daughters from the back of a large and crowded auditorium. After those hurried affairs, the new students were rushed into newly assigned dormitories where angry third-year students alternately berated and encouraged them as they changed into uniform athletic outfits loudly silk-screened with their dormitory name front and back. Bruce was now known simply as "Sutton / Hanover" in bold green-on-grey vinyl font. He disappeared into the anonymity of a new military recruit participating in a hundred-and-seventy-year-old academic tradition meant to build minds, character, servants to the needs of the nation, and leaders.

***

"We're NOT sending him to the wolves without a sidearm."

Another Task Force meeting: more voices, more faces, more agendas. The Blue Suits present at this meeting were arguing back and forth over the prospect of equipping their hypothetical cross-border cop with a firearm. Too many voices in this room and in the argument: U.S. Federal Drug Enforcement Agency, Vermont State Police Drug Task Force, U.S. Customs and Border Protection, New Hampshire State Police. Canadian authorities would join eventually, too: the Royal Canadian Mounted Police and Surety Du Quebec, probably, maybe some of the Canadian Customs and "CIC" Immigrations people from the border. Each U.S. agency had its own training, its own certification rules, and its own procedures for arming agents and - very rarely - informants. They hadn't checked to see what the procedures in Canada were like, yet... worse, probably.

"We feel that he will best serve all our interests in an informant capacity, as a private person." The DEA man had the most experience with undercover operations of this type, the widest jurisdiction, and also the most legal procedures and headaches. A civilian was easier.

The Vermont State Police representative stirred. "Better he's a cop. Civilians usually take bigger risks. And he should be able to protect himself."

The New Hampshire State Police Major sat back. "Soooo. I don't see THAT working. He puts his gun ON when he's on THIS side of the border, and then takes it OFF right before he crosses the line? Aren't his new friends going to NOTICE?"

The DEA guy had an easy answer: "Isn't that what they all have to do anyway? WE sure aren't going to let someone cross without declaring a weapon, and handguns are generally prohibited in Canada..." *Not that I'd want Joe-the-Squeal-Civilian armed!* He passed that sentiment on with a shrug.

The Customs and Border Protection Agent snorted. "You know how many people we pat down at the border? Less than one percent. Only eleven percent of motorists are required to get out of their cars. Dog is only going to smell it if we're checking." He deflated, resigned to the truth: "Guns coming and going all the time." A rare, but honest admission of defeat from the man.

The DEA agent started to speak again, but the CBP Agent held up his hand as he straightened back up. "And as to the OTHER side, I see it all the time: those bikers, the Topdogs, they just drive RIGHT AROUND the gate sometimes. The guys on the Canadian side of the line don't even try to stop them. I don't know if it's a day-of-the-week thing, or a personnel thing, or a directive, but I wouldn't assume anything... " He held up a hand as the room stirred: wait. "As a matter of fact, I would be VERY CAREFUL about involving Canadian law enforcement until we have a damned good handle on this thing, and then I would keep them VERY Out Of The Loop as to the identity and location of the agent. We've had some experience there. It wasn't good."

"Really." Uh-oh. The Vermont State Police Major had a sudden case of acid stomach. "So we're going to run somebody up there without..."

The DEA guy spoke up. "Technically, you can't. That's illegal. To run an agent of the government across the border without the notification, advice, and approval of the appropriate agency on the other side of the line... that's an invasion of sorts."

The Three-Letter Agency man - retired to school-teaching for real, now - nodded as he clarified: "Not an invasion, legally. A covert intelligence agent."

The DEA man waved his hand in the air dismissively and continued: "That's why we think a civilian would be a better choice."

The Federal Prosecutor didn't like that option. "Usually, a civilian witness can be impeached. Juries are less likely to believe them anyway, and often there is something in their history that comes up during the trial and it kills any credibility they might have. It's GOT to be a law officer."

The former-oversees-agent-turned-college-professor commented on that: "Can't he be impeached just by the mere fact that he was operating across the border as an undeclared and therefore illegal agent? "

"Shit." Various other mild curses. A loud slap as a folder thrown down in disgust hit the table. One nod. Stone-faced disapproval of the mere professor from the government lawyer who hadn't thought of the very same issue. Silent frustration filled the room.

The college professor liked that people tended to forget that he had once been a Player on a more dramatic stage. "Complicated, isn't it?" His voice was as merry as his smile.

The Vermont State Police Major looked at the table. "Well, that's why we've got this little round-table going. We've got to hash this stuff out."

They argued the merits of it for another two hours, made very little progress on logistics, and then tabled the discussion until next month's meeting.

***

The old Academy stable no longer echoed with the pounding of hooves on compacted dirt. It now echoed with the slap of sticks on ice, the hiss of skates coursing back and forth, the scratchy sound of a player making a fast acceleration or stop. The coaches stood up in the Official's box, watching this season's talent from on high, while the junior coaching staff of assistants worked the players through a practice scrimmage below.

Every player rotated to another position after each whistle. Every face-off, all the players would be in a new position - even the team veterans, Seniors and fifth-year students with well-known habits and long track records.

Whistle. Hustle over to the puck-drop at Center. Face-off. Heavy action on the ice. Icing, or more embarrassing, the assistant staff would call a penalty. Switch to Left Wing. Face-off happens to your right. Chasing - or better, bringing - the puck up and down the ice. Shot on goal. Whistle. Switch to Right Wing. And so on, all the way back through the Defensive Line and into the Goalie's Box. Yes, Head Coach even rotated his players through the imposing box in front of the net for the first week of the season. He wanted to see all the strengths and weaknesses in each position, and he wanted them to know what each player on the ice was up against. Plus, you never knew when you might want to pull your goalie to make up for a man in the Penalty Box.

On this team, a player who had spent his high-school years on defense might suddenly find himself in goal, or playing wing, come game-time. New recruits were brought in, assessed, broken of all the bad habits that inadequate coaching had encouraged, and then sent out where their natural abilities gave the team an edge. Lower-echelon coaching staff at the secondary schools often missed a player's real natural strengths. Head Coach was a big believer in developing skill sets. He could take an athlete - any athlete - put them on skates, give them a skill set, and make them into a hockey player. But the magic, in any arena, was combining advanced skill sets with the best use of a player's natural talents. Then, in a little change-up, his own little personal tweak on the game: come game-time, he would have players rotate subtly on the ice. The Left Wing who is covered by the opposing team's wing subtly drifts back during play and takes over defense. The defensive line shifts ever so slightly and a player on the other side of the ice scoots forward. The ersatz center player moves left. Suddenly, the opposing team's players are covering the wrong guy. Usually it didn't work. But when it DID, you could flummox the whole line for just long enough to let a player break deep and uncovered. It was beautiful. Natural ability, skill-set, surprise.

Head Coach gestured at the ice. His assistant followed his gaze. They discussed one of the new ones, fresh talent from Toronto. He looked good if you read over his high-school career. He looked bad on the ice, here. The guy was small - well, average. Head Coach liked 'em big.

"He's fast." The Assistant Coach, by very nature of his position an underdog himself, found himself rooting for the kid.

"Yep. There is that."

"He reads the puck well."

"Umhmm. Sure does." Head Coach remained non-commital.

They stood in the way of coaches everywhere: arms crossed, scowling, a hand occasionally going up to rest on a chin.

The assistant conceded: "He's small, though." I get that. Best to be on the right side of Head Coach's decision.

The head coach winced as he grumbled, "And outside of three feet from the net, he wails around with that stick like it's a polo mallet or something." *A skate-in scorer, if that. Never in a million years going to make Pro*, but "maybe useful here, IF he gets some stick-work."

The assistant shook his head. "The guy has no SHOT." On THAT they agreed.

"So what do we do with him?"

"Train him up a shot?"

Head Coach bit a knuckle. "Put him with Larry. See if he can learn. And send him to the weight room."

***

The conference room needed to be a little bigger this time. The Federal folks had brought a couple of assistants, and also a back-row piece from this chess-board of ever-changing, frequently-in-conflict mess of local, state, and national interests. The New Hampshire State Police arrived with a couple of Captains who would actually be handling field operations, if they ever got that far. The Border Patrol wanted more agents to sit in. A U.S. Border Patrol Internal Affairs Investigator wanted a seat at the table, for some reason. A few of the police chiefs from around Vermont came, wanting skin in the game.

They decided to discuss talent.

The DEA guy started: "So, since you've elected to go with a sworn officer, for credibility reasons... we haven't figured out all the logistics yet, but that's where you're headed... we've got to discuss WHO exactly you're looking for." He looked around the room and made a Keep Your Seats gesture with his hands, palms down.

He needn't have bothered. The people were all managers, not Operations, and no one in their right mind would have volunteered for this assignment anyway.

They had people that did this: Older cops who could still pass for thirty or so and had the street-savvy and balls to go into harm's way on a daily basis. Cops who'd already sown a family and the marriage was a bit thin now, so they didn't mind not being home so much. Cops who fed on the excitement of being Behind Enemy Lines two or three hundred days a year.

A hundred and twenty-five thousand in line-of-duty life insurance courtesy of the Department of Justice helped with any residual worry about workplace "accidents." That was a nice kite for a family left behind but it would suddenly seem like a woefully inadequate pittance if the check were ever actually written. This was dangerous, seat-of-the-pants work for a cop who had nerves of steel and not much to lose. Part of the reason they were together here was simple and terrible: each of the agencies represented had lost a case, an operation, or even an informant to the world they were trying to expose. They were discussing issuing someone a one-way ticket to Hell. Everyone at the table was cognizant of that.

"The multi-state nature of this alleged 'pipeline' of yours, as well as its operational and international implications, suggest that a strong presence by cooperating or even leading Federal agencies will be a useful and conviction-enhancing asset to a unique and multi-jurisdictional investigation like the one you aspire to initiate and prosecute."

A member of the Vermont delegation leaned over to whisper to his New Hampshire counterpart: "What did he just say? There were so many long words...."

New Hampshire grinned and spoke out of the side of his mouth in reply: "They want to scoop you. Imagine that."

The DEA man scowled in their general direction and then continued, walking over to a white-board on an easel. The white-board would be erased, and then erased again, and then wiped down with methanol, it would go WITH him and into the trunk of his car, where it would be squirreled away against prying eyes that might try to decipher the smears into useful information. Not necessary really. Someone in this very room would probably blab to someone else, and so on, and before the information was repeated very many times at all, the bikers would know more about this meeting than the DEA man would remember. Their counter-intelligence was very good, somehow. *Probably too many assholes gossiping at the water cooler.* He picked up his green marker.

ATTRIBUTES:

Dependable.

He tapped the whiteboard next to this proclamation. "We all want someone who will see this through to the end. We're going to invest SIGNIFICANT time and resources into this operation, and it would seem a shame if our efforts are not fruitful. In addition, there will be several years of court cases where access to testimony from our penetration agent will be crucial to prosecutorial success. Our man HAS to be DEPENDABLE. Not someone who's going to change his mind and go jetting off to retire in Brazil or make a mid-life career swap into the Culinary Arts. He has to KNOW that he's in it for the LONG HAUL, and understand the implications."

The DEA man paused for comment.

One of the Senior Troopers from Vermont leaned over and whispered to his compatriot. Maybe they had someone in mind.

The DEA Agent wrote on the board again, underneath the last:

STABLE

He began talking while he was still scrawling: "This goes with dependable, but it's a little different. One of the key problems with putting an officer into undercover work... by nature, human beings rise - or fall - to the common denominator of the people around them." He gave a little jab at the rest of the room, since he still disagreed with the direction they were going in: "That's why a citizen informant is often more useful. They've already fallen as low as they're going to go. I mean..." He chuckled. "They're a RAT. You know their capabilities, and their limits. It gives you a leg up, and when they fuck up you can just distance yourself and find somebody else. There's always SOMEBODY with an axe to grind. Anyway..." He tapped the board again, next to STABLE.

A New Hampshire State Police Captain leaned over and whispered to his Vermont counterpart: "Sounds real dependable to me."

The Senior Trooper smirked, then quickly dropped into an interested perusal of the two items on the whiteboard when the DEA man turned towards them as he continued speaking.

"But you seem to want a sworn officer...." He shrugged, gave a rueful shake of his head to indicate how he really felt about that, and then gestured at the whiteboard again. "A stable individual is already fully-formed in his personality, confident in who they are, not needing affection or approval of their peers, and unlikely to be negatively influenced by the personalities in the group that they are trying to infiltrate." The government man held up a finger: This is important. "He can APPEAR to be go-with-the-flow, but he is anything BUT. He calculates each move, each activity, and does NOT absorb unsavory behavior by osmosis. We find that officers who fit this description are usually a little older, with family attachments to keep them grounded, and a long history of positive accomplishments to fall back on for self-esteem purposes." He looked around the room.

Nods, interest, impartial looks, a couple of audible "yeps."

One of the New Hampshire police managers muttered "sociopath with family and community ties" to the general room. That received grunts, laughs, and a couple of serious nods.

The college professor snickered at some private thought.

"So next we have EXPERIENCE." The DEA man wrote it up on the board, in big block letters:

EXPERIENCED

"You're... We're going to need to use someone who can perceive the hazards and the advantages in any given situation or opportunity, who can quickly and effectively decide on a given course of action in stressful and possibly even threatening circumstances. The best at this usually have a long history of such decisions and behaviors, are practiced at optimizing these situations, and have the experience - there's that word again - to be able to recognize threats and opportunities as they arise. This person is also usually a person with ten or tens of years in street-level law enforcement, topped off with a year or two of investigation and a few months of informal, low-risk undercover work." He looked around the room.

"So you're looking for somebody about forty."

A discussion ensued:

"Guy who's that age is one of us."

"So we're looking for a mid-life cop, content to remain on the streets or without aspirations to management level."

"Married."

The Customs and Border Protection supervisor was making a list on a yellow legal pad, jotting down everything everyone was saying.

Professor Wendell made his own list. It looked different. He shook his head minutely, a reflex.

The DEA man continued: "Experience on the street. ALSO..." He tapped next to EXPERIENCED again and spoke with careful, louder emphasis on some of his words: "The officer must have a long history of court testimony behind him. THAT is ESSENTIAL. The officer or agent MUST be presentable, credible, understandable, and unflappable on the witness stand. These GANGS of bikers, not clubs, they're GANGS, they're criminal conspiracy enterprises... well anyway, they hire private investigators to come up with information that will discredit or diminish witnesses, INCLUDING police officers. These GANGS hire the best lawyers, laundering drug and prostitution and gambling receipts RIGHT THROUGH COUNSEL in the process, money is no object, they get the best and then these EXPERIENCED lawyers tear officers of the law apart on the witness stand, they absolutely FLAY them. A successful undercover operation uses a penetration officer that is highly capable, confident, and reliable on the witness stand. THOSE qualities come with EXPERIENCE. We DO NOT want some rookie cop who's never prosecuted anything more than a speeding ticket TESTIFYING on behalf of a multi-agency, multi-million dollar budget undercover operation. Convictions WILL BE LOST by INEXPERIENCE." He sat back down.

There was quiet muttering around the table, whispering amongst representatives of the little fiefdoms.

"So... We want someone who's spent a lot of time in court?"

"Yah, someone they've SEEN testifying. That's gonna help."

Snickers.

"Multi-million dollar, huh?"

Looks around the table.

"How's a married cop going to keep his pecker clean when he's surrounded by biker chicks every night?"

"Oh, this is our gay biker candidate."

"Affirmative action."

"Who's getting millions?"

"I still think we should use an informant. Squeeze someone."

One of the Vermont men leaned over towards his wing-mate, a career prosecutor from the Vermont Attorney General's Office. "Multi-million? I've only seen numbers for three, four hundred thousand..."

"Oh, don't worry. You'll never see it. The Feds will spend it before you even have boots on the ground.... They'll buy a bunch of cars, a new radio system, Border Patrol will get some fancy gadgets.... They're already billing for their time, hell they've probably got you on the books somewhere and they're billing for OUR time." He shook his head. "We'll be lucky if we see a hundred grand to cover two hundred in overtime."

The political lawyer might have said this a hair too loud - the DEA man's scowl swiveled in his direction.

The Senior Trooper shrugged and nodded, to the amusement of the prosecutor next to him and the consternation of the DEA man.

Several voices muttered at once:

"Who elected the DEA to be lead on this anyway?"

"It's where the money is coming from, gets the prize."

"He who holds the purse-strings..."

The college man near the far end of the conference-room stood up, throwing his legal pad into his open briefcase. He looked towards the Vermont delegation. A Senior Trooper in a blue State-issue blazer nodded his head minutely.

The hubbub got louder. Some took this as a sign that the meeting was breaking up.

Professor Wendell shut his briefcase and began talking, quietly but authoritatively, while closing and latching it. "So that's a really nice list." He looked up. "Your hypothetical penetration agent, your UNDERCOVER, will be identified by counter-intelligence assets... probably EXPERIENCED ones, possibly formerly employed and TRAINED by a government or quasi-government agency, by the way. Your operation will be toyed with, information you receive will be false or tailored to cause you to take actions that will meet the objectives of, even BENEFIT your very target, and you will possibly get to watch as your undercover operative is left on the side of the road with his pants around his ankles." His eyes flared with something between jovial merriment and danger. The look on his face and his tone were incongruent.

The room got very quiet.

The chief DEA man remained seated, out of force of will. He asked, lightly, "WHO, exactly, are you?"

The Vermont Senior Trooper answered for the upstart. "That is Professor Walter Wendell. He teaches Criminal Justice Procedure and also some diplomacy courses at The Academy."

"He's a civilian?" The DEA man seemed to find this incredulous. "You brought a civilian?!"

Someone un-seen and un-identifiable quietly said, "OOOOoooo! Diplomacy!"

Smiles.

The Trooper smiled, too. "He's a citizen. Of the country we work for. He has some unique insights." The Trooper waved a finger. He indicated the retinue of subordinate bureaucrats on either side of the DEA man. "You brought a few people, yourself. You should see what he has to say."

The DEA man stood and started to pack his briefcase. His entourage took the cue to start gathering their own things into cases and folders. Someone picked up a rag and some solvent.

Professor Wendell smiled pleasantly, pointed, wagged his finger and shook his head: No. Leave the list.

The lackey paused, rag in mid-air, looking back and forth between his boss and the academic.

Professor Wendell's expression changed. The mirth of his eyes increased, but his face suddenly became stony, like the sun had passed behind a cloud. His head shook again, minutely, once left a centimeter, once right two centimeters, back to center. He flicked his hand gently, and it came to rest in a loose fist down at his side, the index finger not quite pointing at the floor.

The government people sat back down, except for the head DEA man. He remained standing at his open briefcase as he looked around the room, trying to figure out how and when he'd lost the baton.

Walter Wendell sat back down, slumping back in his seat, tipping back, one elbow on the arm of the chair. The index finger of that hand pointed beyond the DEA Agent, at the whiteboard list behind.

A couple of the assembled law enforcement professionals and political appointees realized that this - formerly - unassuming man had the only comfortable chair in the room. An office chair for some desk nearby had found its way into the room, and this professor had grabbed it.

Now he leaned back and lectured from it, quietly but firmly: "Your list up there, that's pretty typical, isn't it?" He didn't wait for an answer. "I mean, for any real, deep-cover operation. Male, probably white, forties, a little standoffish but eager to please, predictable, well-behaved, put-together... dependable, stable, experienced, married..." He nodded. "You think they don't know that? WHO do you think they're SUSPICIOUS of? Let me guess: You've run some operations, or tried to, but it takes YEARS to even get NEXT to these people, they always keep you at arm's length. Keep your friends close, but your enemies closer. Or you've had a few good informants, maybe even people you've used before, and suddenly they just up and disappear on you. Sound familiar? Counter-intelligence. You know who the biggest employers of government-trained former intelligence agents are? Criminal enterprise. Mafia. Russian mob. Street gangs. Bikers. Private security firms, legitimate ones, who will do work for any of the above." He shook his head. "You fuckers don't stand a chance against a counter-intelligence operative trained by a nation-state. WE are the VARSITY and the varsity squad's services are FOR SALE when players get bored of politics and some of the varsity already work for your adversary and THAT is who you're up against."

Silence in the room. The DEA Agent sat back down. He tried to seem mildly interested, but actually, he was stricken. Three or four things, bad experiences with even worse endings... they suddenly made sense.

Walter Wendell stood up. "I spent five years in the U.S. Military, two of them posted somewhere-else-not-here and not in uniform. There was no OFFICIAL war with that country. Unofficially... We acted like it. Under the Rules of the Hague... that's the Geneva Conventions on War, to which these United States of America are a signatory, by the way... an officer of the military of a country at conflict may be SUMMARILY EXECUTED if discovered behind enemy lines while out of uniform in a time of war." He paused to let them draw the conclusion. He couldn't be more specific, and didn't need to be. "After my Active Duty, I went to school and then I took a job for a couple of years with a department of the U.S. government as an information-gathering employee. I traveled a lot. Some of the places I visited had a dim view of Americans. Some of them had a dim view of capitalism. Informants frequently disappeared. I lost... tools. Human ones. A competitor from another team, a friendly team, lost the race during one of my trips. It could have been any one of us. The opposing team had high motivation to prevent... touchdowns. And low motivation to play by any of the conventional rules. Sound familiar?" He started circling the room, slowly, around the backs of the chairs. "There are somewhere upwards of eleven thousand retired intelligence agents, field agents, in Europe alone. How many here? How many in other countries on other continents? How many of those, do you think, have squirreled away enough money to run off to the beach for the rest of their lives when the game ends or their wall falls? How many of them miss the excitement of the chase, the risk, the game? What number of them have criminal proclivities? What percentage are sociopaths? How many work for organized crime, right now?"

Some of the Federal people looked sick.

Walter Wendell walked up to the white board and tapped it with his finger, hard. "This list, it is exactly who they're looking for. For increased scrutiny. For danger to their organization." He tapped the whiteboard again. "You want somebody the OPPOSITE of this list. Someone young, free, un-inhibited, willing to take risks, or appearing so. Someone a-typical: NOT typical. Someone they KNOW we would NEVER throw at them. You want someone they won't even see coming."

***

The Head (paid) and Assistant (not really paid very much, but equally valuable) coaches were watching the films and doing a critique of the first week of practice and scrimmages. From this session, they'd pick the positions and the composition for each of offensive and defensive lineups - but to do that, they had to watch practice tapes, over and over, tape after tape. Hours of it.

There was one new player they were still unsure of: that kid from Ontario. They were glad to have Bruce Sutton at The Academy, as this new student from Canada had real talent and on-ice presence for a freshman right out of the gate. They were even flirting with the idea of giving him some game time, early on, to further assess him. But now they had to shape him for the next four years, to get the most out of his talents. Just because he was scoring goals for his high school didn't mean The Academy might not find him useful somewhere else on the line.

The Head Coach thought it all depended on the puzzle: the other players on the team that determined where each athlete fit.

The Assistant thought it was a pain in the ass. He was more concerned with un-teaching all the bad habits these kids had learned on the ice in high school, and then seeing who they really were without the amateur habits. *This is college. It's a different game.*

Head Coach's eyebrows rose away from their natural scowl for a second. "He's got sense. Good sense. He knows where the puck is going to be and he can GET there. And his passing's okay... He's willing to pass." This kid's stock had gone up in this man's opinion.

"But he's not going to be able to bully his way into the zone, and he sure isn't going to slap one in from mid-ice!" The Assistant flinched.

On the tape he could see it: The puck moved faster from his wrist-flick passes than it did from his slap-shot.

"I dunno. We have a few more practices before we have to figure anything out. He's definitely playing. Definitely." Head Coach nodded unconsciously. *This year, maybe.* "But to me, he looks like a really spry Defenseman."

The Assistant Coach had a thought. "You know, that's a really killer wrist flick. No wind-up, just fwooop! And the puck is across the ice. It's pretty fast. Set it up about halfway to the net, I bet no one sees him coming."

***

The next month's meeting was smaller. Just seven at the table.

One of them stood. "I'm Captain Johnathan Evers, Vermont State Police." He gestured to his right. "This is Trooper Robert Greenway, Vermont State Police, and to my left, New Hampshire State Police Barracks Commander Anthony Calzotti." He gestured. "You remember Professor Wendell, I suspect. And over here, Agent Sid Wyczinski, US Border Patrol. At the head of the table, we're going to have someone from the U.S. Attorney's office, Burlington, sitting in, today that's Marsha Westerman, hello, and next to her is a Deputy U.S. Marshall, Ed Price." He sat.

Trooper Greenway scraped back his chair and stood up. "This is our executive working group. We'll add agencies and personnel as need be, ONLY if need be. I expect at some point we'll add local departments, when we have to, if we have a specific operation going on in a specific location. A few of the police chiefs who have been bitching around about spillover crime, they're the ones who got this whole thing started, they may join us after we firm things up. That's about it."

Professor Wendell asked, "Feds bail on you?"

U.S. Attorney Westerman answered that one: "They are going to invest in an operation that the combined Federal government agencies have more control over. I'm... WE," she gestured back and forth between her and the Deputy Marshall, "are here as a... courtesy. You're running something in two states and it likely pokes into Canadian citizens, too. Uncle wants to know what's going on with this 'Pipeline Project,' as you call it."

Trooper Greenway's head moved around. "That's fair. I get it. Maybe we'll make a team."

Commander Calzotti wanted to know more about the game plan. "We going to be able to do this, just us?" He looked around the room with a skeptical scowl, studiously avoiding the Feds over at the far end of the table.

Professor Wendell grinned and answered that question. "You'll do it BETTER. Less administrative trouble. You have the sanction of both governors, right?"

Evers and Calzotti both exchanged a look and nodded in unison.

"So let's go talk to the Canadians. I hear through my own grapevine that they're maybe a little compromised, at the actual government level, so here's how I want to do that..."

People around the table listened as they wondered about this grapevine that the good Professor referred to.

Marsha Westerman listened to the man's lecture for a few minutes and then held up a finger to interrupt. "I'm sorry... WHO are you?"

Walter Wendell smiled. "I'm your Clandestine Operations Consultant."

"Our what?"

"This here party is going to be running an agent of the government in more than one country, under aliases?" He shrugged. "That's clandestine operations."

Trooper Evers stood up. "He's got some experience in doing this sort of thing. We might need to see how he goes about it."

Agent Wyczinski chipped in: "Half of each criminal incident is happening across the line. We have GOT to get up there. Whether they want us to, or not."

"Ya, the Pipeline starts in one country and ends up in another. Hell, you could follow it all the way from Montreal to Florida! How do you deal with that effectively without seeing both ends?"

"Montreal, Quebec City, and Europe too, the way I hear it...."

Marsha Westerman slid back from the table. "You're talking about ACTUALLY running around in a FOREIGN COUNTRY?!? On the ground?"

Trooper Evers made a hands-down, it's-okay gesture from his chair. "He's not going to be a FEDERAL agent, whoever our boy turns out to be, and from that side of the line, he's just going to be a witness. If they don't want a piece of it."

Professor Wendell added, "We need to go feel them out."

Marsha Westerman looked skeptical. "I suspect that's against the law, running an investigation up there, if they don't want to participate. You can't just GO there. It's an international bord-"

"So?" Agent Wyczinski smiled like the Cheshire Cat. "Let me tell you a story. Few years back, I was working something out in the Dakotas. Now, there was this road, all washed out and impassable, on our side of the line. Another road, a logging road, but passable, that followed the Canadian side of the line. I used to cruise that Canadian road once in a while. In my official car."

The Deputy Marshal found that incredulous. "Didn't they stop you at the border?"

"Yah, long enough to look uncomfortable and tell me that I couldn't have a gun in Canada. I told em, You didn't see it." He shrugged. "So our boy pokes his nose over the border. So it comes out in court? The jury isn't going to care, and it's not going to make an International Incident unless Pierre Canada-man on trial turns out to be the Prime Minister."

The U.S. Attorney scowled. "We'll see."

Trooper Evers shared a look with his New Hampshire counterpart.

The New Hampshire lawman grimaced. *This isn't going well.*

***

Bruce Sutton's freshman year at school began well enough for the new Academy Recruit. The campus was small, so he'd been able to find all his classrooms quickly. No wandering around all morning, lost, giving up, and then showing up as a new student on the second day of lectures. Bruce's classes were demanding but not tedious, for the most part. He hadn't expected first-year business coursework to be especially intriguing, and he discovered that he wouldn't find out until next year anyway - first year instruction covered math, writing, history, and general electives. Courses tailored to his major would arrive with next year's semesters.

The military aspect of the school was ever-present, but not overbearing. Bruce and his classmates were yelled at a lot by upperclassmen - and a few women - in olive-green T-shirts and felt campaign hats, and he found that intimidating at first, but by the second week he found it amusing. Judging by the sound of their scratchy voices, he suspected it was more work doing the yelling than listening to it. In spite of the hazing and the pointless chores, he decided he'd made a good choice of college.

He found some of his fellow students especially interesting - the women in uniform looked exotic and intriguing with their hair up every day, their uniform caps just-so over their brows and braids.... It gave him a mild thrill to see an un-related female in the hallway in a bathrobe in the morning, scooting off to or from the Women's Latrine. That interest also gave him a headache - the Upperclassmen and Regiment Officers kept rapping him on the back of the head. "Two demerits for staring, Sutton!" "Eyes to the front, Recruit, you've seen your own mother every day of your life!" "Drop for push-ups, Sutton, and don't take your eyes off the tiles 'til you hear that girl's door close!" Apparently they were supposed to get used to proximity without fraternity or familiarity - some sort of military thing, he supposed. That would change next year, Bruce sincerely hoped... he'd heard some rumors, and he caught a few appraising looks from young women in his First-Year Scramble.

Bruce decided he'd also made a good choice of where to go to develop his hockey talents. Practices and actual scrimmage games started only a few short weeks into the schoolyear. *Thank God - ice time!*

His life resumed the rhythm he'd grown accustomed to in high school, with a few added twists: Wake. Dorm chores - while getting yelled at. (He sometimes grinned ruefully as he scrubbed a sink with a toothbrush and thought to himself, *well, I did pick a military college!*) Assembly - get yelled at a lot while standing in formation. PT, actually a pretty good warm-up for hockey practice. Scramble back into the dorm to get ready for hockey. Hit the ice, if it was available, for informal scrimmages nevertheless attended - or even played - by the coaching staff. Get cleaned up. Breakfast. Go to school. Do schoolwork. Hit the ice again in the afternoon, this time for a formal, coached practice session and wind-sprints and pushups on the ice and stick practice and maybe even a little hockey. Shower. Schoolwork. Supper in the cafeteria while sitting at attention and counting your chews (chew each fork-full thirty-three times by regulation). Do more schoolwork, and oh, by the way, also memorize the state's history, the school's history, and also the five hundred and seventy-two individual rules that members of the Academy Regiment must live by on pain of shun and shame. Shine your shoes. Shine your boots. Shine the upperclassmen's boots. Shine the upper-classwomen's boots. Dorm chores, all while being harassed. Make your bed, perfectly. Make your bed again, it wasn't right. Make your bed three more times for practice. Now UN-make it, and get into it. Lights out at midnight. Oh, we're getting you up early, the entire regiment is going for a two-mile run in the morning, first hundred to finish get an hour of liberty on Saturday, so go right to sleep. Finally, drifting off, just getting to sleep... the dormitory fire alarm goes off, sending students spilling out into the cold air of night in regulation pajamas or bathrobes and standing at attention while all hands are accounted for.

They're trying to kill us.

That was the collective suspicion among new recruits.

***

Their Clandestine Operations man organized a little brain-storming session for the blue-suited lawmen. He chose the general location, but did not attend. "You want this little session of yours someplace that's laundered, far from where you're actually doing the job, just in case the opposition has penetrated the folks you're talking to. They'll know you're laying something on - don't say WHEN - but they won't know WHERE. They'll assume it will be in that area. You can knock some things back and forth without totally tipping your hand. Just in case. And I'm not law enforcement. I have no place at that meeting. I'd sure like to hear about it, though. Later."

So Vermont State Police Troopers Evers and Greenway traveled west, by commercial airline commuter hop, to Ottawa, Ontario, Canada, to attend a regular annual international meeting of U.S. and Canadian law enforcement professionals. While there, they mingled and networked with law officers from both sides of the border. They hoped to find professionals of a similar mind among their contemporaries to the north - it would be good to know the folks on the other side of the fence, even if they didn't end up working the investigation. At the Ottawa conference the two Vermont policing professionals made a short list of Canadian counterparts with sufficient authority and jurisdiction and then found a Mountie who seemed to be eager enough to host a second, smaller, more focused gathering a little further west.

***

That second, smaller meeting was in Thunder Bay, Ontario, two weeks after the international conference. Thunder Bay back then was a small port city, really a large town, with a couple of four-lane roads and a few long business strips. Instead of tall buildings downtown, there were immense steel grain elevators standing sentinel over the docks and wharves along Lake Superior. Long, ocean-sized ships waited in orderly rows for their turn at the elevator nipple.

This smaller meeting was billed as a round-table discussion on cross-border criminal investigation, all in the hypothetical. Thunder Bay sits on an International Body of Water, and is also only fifty short miles north of the U.S. border. The Vermont delegation was supposedly there to observe how the Big Boys ran such an operation, if there ever was one in their neck of the woods... Vermont has a border and a lake, right? The U. S. Feds and the Mounties had something going on in Minnesota or Michigan and Ontario, and it could be used as a model someday, maybe?

Getting a committee to agree on anything - let alone a cross-border operation with international implications - is, was and always has been contentious, nit-picking, boring work.

On day two, Evers and Greenway were trying to hammer out something useful about authority and jurisdiction, as well as the mechanics of multi-jurisdictional prosecution. All without letting on that actually THEY were the ones running the meeting - the agency with actual iron in the fire. So they had some proxies and some patsies acting for them.

Like in the early meetings back in Vermont, each agency present had its own idea of what the ideal undercover officer should be and also which agency should supply the candidate: Michigan State Police, the FBI, Royal Canadian Mounted Police, Surete du Quebec, Ontario Provincial Police, CIC (the Canadian customs agency), the New York State Police, and also the U.S. Coast Guard, because of those big lakes.

Also in attendance, ostensibly because of its location, was the Minnesota State Patrol. That agency had been invited as a bit of mis-direction by the Vermont folks, and was aware of its role in that, but nevertheless also interested in how such a hypothetical operation in their neck of the woods would work. Someday some of these same law enforcement agencies would hold a roundup like this in Vermont, to perform a misdirection of their own.

The Michigan State Patrol was there because they split those big lakes just about in half. A lot of places to smuggle and hide things along an international line so porous as that, and Vermont had a couple of lakes, too... a similarity there that could prove instructive.

The Illinois Bureau of Criminal Investigation sat at the table with four Management-level police officers representing that high-profile agency. Illinois representatives were invited to muddy the waters, but were unaware of their true role.

The U.S. Federal Drug Enforcement Agency was back at the table with a different set of faces and egos for the same set of problems.

The Canadians who were hosting this multi-agency, multi-national meeting were friendly but reserved. Mostly they were willing to let the U.S. state and federal agencies toss ideas back and forth while they listened and made notes. The Canadians didn't seem especially aggressive about cross-border crime. Then again, most of the contraband was flowing SOUTH into the United States. The Canadians had less incentive to cut the head off the snake, as they seemed to have the more docile end of the beast.

Too many agencies, too many agendas, but the meeting was set up with a separate, secret agenda of its own, and the Vermont cops kept subtly returning to it.

"You guys shouldn't send a cop up there without a piece." Trooper John Evers was emphatic about that. "A cop is a cop is a cop. All the time. They need protection. Tools of defense and apprehension."

These DEA folks still wanted to run the show, even here at a Canadian meeting, and they still wanted to play the stage with a civilian.

No surprise there - echoes of their own recent meetings back east.

"We feel that he will best serve all our interests in an informant capacity. A private citizen does not need, nor are they entitled to possess, a weapon, here or there." *Constitution be damned.* If you were non-sworn personnel who hadn't completed a Required Course of Fire for Qualification, then you weren't going to carry a weapon, period.

A Minnesota State Patrol officer argued that: "Well he's not. He's a cop. Well, maybe a former one, but none-the-less a cop. Should be, at any rate. He's going to have to protect himself... ESPECIALLY if he's recognized." The Minnesota folks had been instructed to lay it on very thick. Walter Wendell had placed a phone call to an old friend, and had asked for that delegation to argue the operation like it was their own. Mis-direct. Confuse. Cloud.

The RCMP functionary leaned forward. "Soooo. He puts his gun ON when he is on YOUR side of the border, and then he takes it off when he crosses to our sovereign country of Canada, eh? Our biker friends aren't going to notice that?" He grinned. *Ridiculous!*

A different Minnesota law officer responded. "Well, he can't cross the border with it, anyway. He stashes it. Somewhere. But I still think he should be a sworn officer on BOTH sides of the border."

"You're thinking a dual citizen... Is that even possible?"

The variety of accents in the room created an air of international mystique and intrigue to the proceedings.

Trooper Johnathan Evers smirked to himself. If they only knew... we're about to lay on a sort of a spy-thriller back home!

As if prompted by his unspoken thought, a commander from Surete du Quebec, the province-wide police force, answered that in his thick French-Canadian-sprinkled English. As he did so, he improbably added 'H' sounds in front of his consonants and especially his 'W's, while dropping those same 'H's where they were expected: "Oui, zhet is true. He is a citizen of both countries, oui, zhet would be possible, certainment, certainly, zhet he may be an officer of both, also oui... yes. Such an interesting prospect, oui!" He smiled. "We have checked. Zhet would work, eh."

It was difficult for some of those assembled to understand him.

He thought the same of speech from those with thick Yankee accents from Vermont and upstate New York.

An Illinois law enforcement executive scowled. He was trying to catch up: "But if he is an officer of the S.Q., or a Mountie, he is a CANADIAN agent. You have to give the boy a job... can we? Last I checked, I can't hire outside a Naturalized citizen...." Chicago was a jurisdictional nightmare, but at least it was all one country.

The DEA man leaned forward. "So let me understand this." He looked around the conference table. "He is, hypothetically, born on one side of the line, grew up on the other, parents either-slash-or, so he technically is a dual citizen by nature of birth versus parent country of residence?

"Oui, oui. Yes." The Quebec man sat back. He found the prospect amusing. Hypothetically, it would work. In reality, it would be a jurisdictional nightmare. *No man can serve two masters.* "C'est possible, chu amusee... forgive me, possible, more or less, yes, but practical? Interesting, at best, when a man must serve two masters, is it not?" He might have had a little experience there, judging by his pained grin.

Trooper Evers pitched in: "That's about the size of it, what you have to do? Find somebody who is a citizen of both countries, get him hired and schooled by both forces? He wears one hat on one side of the border, and one hat on the other?" He paused, put two fingers of each hand in the air. "Figuratively." He kept up one finger: wait. "Oh, and he's never voted or signed a petition." A certain college professor had schooled him in the necessary requirements. Now for the mis-direction, again, just in case: "Where the hell in Minnesota are you going to find somebody who's all of that?"

One of the Mounties offered his opinion: "I think there's a slim chance that would work... we wouldn't object to it, sir. It would make it much easier to establish cross-border drug conspiracies if we could have the same officer testify to activities that occurred on both sides of the border, eh? I like it." He already had someone (from his own force, of course) in mind, someone who would be sufficiently malleable to keep the politicians happy. "Ottawa would be very happy to have some convictions, I'm sure we can help with that."

One of the Surety du Quebec officers raised an eyebrow at his distant colleague. *Really? You sure about that?* Sitting back with his arms crossed perhaps telegraphed more of his prejudices than he intended - everyone at the table could tell he did not like his Mountie compatriots very much.

Turf wars are a constant problem in all things political, including law enforcement.

The Minnesota delegation brought the argument around again. "Then he's GOT to have a gun. He's certified on both sides, he's a cop on both sides, he's got to have a firearm."

Some of these policing and politics professionals probably slept with their department-issue service weapons tucked under their pillows. Some of the DEA agents and administrators probably actually needed to, especially if they worked cases near the border. The thought of sending an actual Federal agent - or even a local police officer - into a den of thieves, unarmed, was enough to cause indigestion or outright revolt, depending on the person contemplating the trip.

"You can't ask a cop to-"

A DEA man interrupted: "We wouldn't need this discussion if we used a civilian informant who can jump the border without all these issues. We were really hoping the role here would…"

Another DEA man interrupted his fellow to re-iterate to the group: "It's how we do it, usually."

Trooper Evers cut in: "Well, this guy's goose is still cooked if they finger him for an informant, isn't it? Same thing."

New Hampshire State Patrol Commander Anthony Calzotti had followed his Vermont compatriots, ostensibly here to observe how a hypothetical DEA/Canadian operation might liaison with state and local law enforcement, should such an operation ever happen back East. He put in his own two cents now. "This is a really unique opportunity you guys have here, to put a law enforcement officer, the same one officer, on both sides of the border. Informants are great, but they aren't COPS. That's always been the problem, hasn't it? The law stops at the border. Maybe not now."

Someone from the Illinois delegation leaned forward. "Someone should work up the crimes and elements required for conviction in all the various jurisdictions - Ontario, Illinois, Michigan, Minnesota, U.S. Special Maritime Jurisdiction for the lakes... oh, Canada too. We've got to make sure we lay the right charges for the right activities in the right place." The Illinois cop stopped. "Like a spread-sheet or something. Help us keep it straight. Otherwise the badge doesn't mean boo."

Nods around the table.

A Surety du Quebec administrator slid his chair back and stood up to begin pacing. "Okay. We make him a cop." The word in his mouth sounded like 'cup.' He squinted, thinking. "One of ours. Special commission, under zhe seal of zhe Crown, so-to-speak." He stopped his pacing and looked over toward the Midwestern contingent: Minnesota, Michigan, Illinois. "'How is zhet going to produce anything in less zhen deux, trois... two or three years, eh?" He nodded. "I like it, mais parce que... Forgive me." He shrugged at his lapse. "I like it, but because of schooling, training, certification... it is a long process, no?" He sat back down. "Two countries, maybe a state and a province, too... that could take some time, for zhis man to go to all zhis cop school." He grinned and spread his hands wide, in measure of the problem.

One of the Michigan officers answered that: "I don't know, we've got some Federal park rangers over our way that come up in just a few weeks.... I think it's two hundred, three hundred hours, plus a week of firearms, and then they're good to go." He turned to look around the room. "That sound about right?"

Shrugs.

Someone from the DEA spoke: "Only good in the park, or on the Special Maritime or Exclusive Jurisdiction. That means Federal Reservations, such as Indian Affairs, wildlife management areas, that sort of thing." He scowled. "No jurisdiction."

A Minnesota cop spoke up: "And they're Peace Officers, technically - they actually are barred by law from independently investigating a felony, aren't they?"

A Drug Enforcement man replied: "Which is ninety-eight percent of what we're doing: investigating state and federal major crimes. Even just gathering intelligence, that could be viewed as a violation of the enabling legislation that validates the commission."

One of the DEA men grumbled: "Yah, to do investigations, you've got to go through Flet-sie..." He looked over at the Canadian Delegation. "Federal Training Center... that's close to a six-month show." He smirked disdainfully. "That makes you a REAL cop." *Park Rangers issue parking tickets for sitting on the flowers...* "Not some wet-behind-the-ears Nature Nugget with a badge for show."

Trooper Evers shrugged. "Wow. Sounds complicated." He nodded in the direction of the Midwest Section DEA entourage. "Better it be a civilian, if he's not a fully-certified police officer with wide jurisdiction and authority, like you guys say."

"Do you Feds ever get one officer a commission from more than one agency?" Trooper Greenway was trying to very carefully steer the group's discussion in useful directions without giving too much away.

One of the Minnesota police officers responded: "I started out at Isle Royale, up on Lake Superior. I had a commission from the Department of the Interior, National Park Service. Because there was a lot of boat traffic coming and going, a guy from Customs showed up my second week and handed me a commission from them. No training or anything, other than showed me how to do a Port-of-Entry Inspection. Some of the Rangers at other parks had commissions from local or state jurisdictions, depending on the violation they'd wear one hat or the other, I met a Ranger who had Department of the Interior papers AND a commission from that Commonwealth of Massachusetts, AND he was also an appointed Assistant County Prosecutor.... he worked out on the Cape, and he switched hats about every five minutes."

Evers and Greenway both sat up. THIS was interesting....

A Michigan policing administrator asked the question for them: "Wow. Wasn't it hard to dance to separate tunes?"

The Minnesota officer/administrator shrugged. "Not really. The goals of the agencies didn't conflict much." He looked around the room furtively. "Here...." State and Federal agencies were well known for competing with each other. He shrugged again, with a grimace this time.

Trooper Evers brought them back to it, again. "So we're back to square one. Law Officer with maybe more than one employer. Or not. Civilian. Or not. Couple a years of training, then, that case. But he'd still need a gun? Or not?"

One of the Feds scowled at this backwoods Vermont law officer so full of questions. "You really like this kid, don't you?"

Evers held up both hands, palm-out: Don't lay that on me.... "I don't even know him, and won't ever, but I DON'T like the idea of sending a cop out into the wild without all the tools of the trade." He grinned. "Not even a Midwest cop. And I wouldn't dream of sending a Trooper on this kind of gig. The Governor would retire me to the State Manure Pit."

The room filled with laughter.

"It is a unique opportunity." The lead RCMP man sighed. "I think he should probably be armed, if it can be made... legitimate. We have lost a few informants, too, here and there. You've convinced me."

The DEA man scowled. "Alright. Fine. He's an international cop, our man, sworn in two countries, armed in two countries. Great. Now how are we going to handle the border?"

Minnesota ran the ball again: "He'll have two? Stashes for each, just over the border?"

"Besides the obvious safety and legal issue, won't that look suspicious, for a new guy, just showing up all complicated like that?"

Trooper Greenway forgot himself for a moment, and hammered down a point: "We'll figure something out. For now, he's a dual citizen, employed by an agency or agencies on each side of the border, and as such is authorized to enforce the laws of the respective countries - wherever he is at the time - and authorized to carry a firearm."

Silence, nods, looks back and forth around the table. Heads nodding now, grudging assent or general assent, depending on the agency.

"Now, what about the take? How do you get a conviction for crimes where the elements are all met, but individual elements of each charge are committed in more than one jurisdiction?"

The meeting descended into a cacophony of diverging opinions, hypothetical what-ifs, speculation, and not-so-well-informed case studies. The Federal agency representatives started - or maybe continued - infighting and chest-puffing that began to dominate the meeting.

New Hampshire State Police Commander Anthony Calzotti leaned over toward his Vermont counterparts and gestured at the Feds with his chin. "We should have brought more lawyers."

The Surete du Quebec administrator overheard this and his jovial smile changed subtly to a sigh and a nearly-hidden eyeroll. He winked at his neighbors from across the international line as his face resumed its usual merriment.

The meeting continued for hours, back and forth with no progress made. At one point Commander Anthony Calzotti leaned over towards his Vermont counterpart and whispered, "I miss New England."

Trooper Greenway responded to the room in general: "You guys aren't making any progress here."

The discussion shortly descended into a squabble about just which agency had the most credibility, authority, and jurisdiction over the infractions likely to be identified by the investigation - a controversy compounded by the differences in law from one side of the border to the other. Evers and Greenway listened to all manner of agency banner-waving, hypotheticals, and bad ideas and then went home unsure of what they were going to do. Inter-agency cooperation was tricky enough... cross-border cooperation was going to be exponentially more difficult.

They hadn't even brought the prosecutors into the discussion yet.

***

During the four days Evers, Greenway, and Calzotti were at the Thunder Bay mini-conference, all hell broke loose in Quebec: thirteen people were killed in drug- and gang-related violence in small Canadian cities just North of Vermont. Magog, Sherbrooke, Megantic, LaColle became biker-against-biker war zones.

Evers and Greenway were surprised to find that the Governor himself received them when they reported back to the Department of Public Safety headquarters on Tuesday morning.

In his suit-coat and tie, formal as always, Vermont's chief executive met with them in a hallway, then steered them towards a suddenly-empty conference room. Greenway mingled with the Governor's retinue outside while Evers and the Governor were introduced to each other by the Director of Public Safety, who closed the door as he withdrew.

The Governor eyed the long table in the middle of the room, went to half-perch on the dubious structure, then changed his mind. It wasn't the heavy and sturdy furniture he was used to in the Executive Conference Room at the Pavilion. He crossed his arms and stood behind a chair at the head of the table instead. "I see an awful lot of bikers with patches on their backs, sometimes a whole darn posse of them, when I drive through Stone City these days. At least one every time I go through. WE do NOT want them here. Not like they are in Quebec. There's a bomb going off up there once a month, and now...." He raised an eyebrow in reference to recent events. "THAT is NOT how we're going to live." The state's governor was direct as always: "The Director of Public Safety tells me you're doing something about it. What do you need?"

Evers summarized it. "Thankyou, Sir. We have some reports from police chiefs around the state, they're seeing indications, so we tried to put together a Pipeline Thing. New Hampshire wants to come on board with us, so does the Border Patrol, maybe, so we've got a task force ginned up. Unfortunately the Feds got the purse and then backed out. They're going to do their own operation."

"What do YOU want to do?"

It was incredibly unusual - unheard of - to have direct access to the Governor from this level. Trooper Evers was shocked and also glad to find that the Chief Executive of the State of Vermont didn't micro-manage. He was not law enforcement, but he'd been known to ditch his Security Detail and carry his own weapon, on occasion. That made him One Of The Boys, after a fashion.

Evers knew this was his shot, so he thought for twenty seconds - an eternity - and then pitched it big: "We want to hire one or two folks that will fit in, make them law officers, and then have them grow hair and follow - or ride with - the bikers back and forth across the border. We want to find a way to make that legal, or at least tacitly acceptable, and we'll need that person or persons to have a Get Out Of Jail Free card, because they'll probably have to be naughty to be credible, and we'll need about three, maybe four hundred thousand dollars a year or so to make it all work. A couple hundred directly to the operation, through Public Safety, and the rest for supporting departments, as it's needed."

The Governor's eyebrows went up a fraction.

Trooper Evers plowed on, afraid to lose this once-in-a-career opportunity: "Plus whatever the AG needs for prosecution and pre-trial incarceration, probably a lot more than what we'll need. And we'll need it to be more hush than 'Rosie the Riveter's Loose Lips Sink Ships,' because some folks think they've got professional counter-intel - that's former spies, think Double-Oh-Seven - working for them, and we've heard that some Canadian agencies may be compromised. It's got to be quiet, and then come with a hammer." *There. I've said my piece, what he does with it is up to him.*

The Governor was quiet for a moment. Evers could see him replaying the entirety of the requirements back inside his head. Finally, the politician and administrator answered: "Done. It's not going to happen right away. Appropriations will have to fund some grant money for local departments, which you two will be on a committee to hand out quietly as you need to. The Department of Public Safety will get a boost next year, too, one that you two can grab. That's all a year away, though.

I have to quietly sell it for the next seven months, and then the fiscal year will start four months after that. Think this can wait that long?"

"Well, we'll get busy on our end, and then we will find out. Probably take that long to get the train rolling, anyway. Thank you, Sir."

"No problem." The Governor's formal posture relaxed for a moment as he related a personal story: "My dad played banjo in the State Championships every year up to Craftsbury. It was a big thing, back then. They had to kill the festival for ever more after the Topdogs showed up and mauled the place two years running. Nice that they like music and all, but we don't want them back here." He shook his head. "Dad had fun at that show. It broke his heart."

Trooper Evers flinched, and sucked his teeth in a grimace. *That explains the interest from the top.* "That's unfortunate. We'll do our best."

"That's all we can do." The Governor turned away and was absorbed by the two members of his Protective Detail - one of them a cop and one of them a press aide. With a gun and a bulky new brick of a cellphone between them, they could probably keep the state's top bureaucrat safe from just about any of the daily hazards he was likely to encounter.

Trooper Greenway sidled over to Evers. "How'd it go?"

"We got a green light. About a year. Probably about the same amount of time it will take to set it up."

Actually, in the end, it would take four years before they had an agent on the ground.

***

Bruce liked college hockey, but by the second week of practices he was worried. The formal practices were in the afternoon, so he didn't have to get up at some un-Godly hour of the morning to go use a rink in the dark of morning before high school. The locker room was the same, the pads were the same, the ice was the same… But everything had changed.

It was FAST. And no longer easy. In secondary school hockey, he was among the best in his class. Here at college, Bruce played with some of the best of the class - Eastern Conference, Division Three. Even in the practices he was suddenly challenged to keep up. You could fall off the back of a team like this. There would be more Rookies next year. He dug in, and worked harder.

The Academy Regimentals were a young team this year. A very well-developed team had nearly all graduated last year, leaving a lot of room for fresh talent, right away. That was to Bruce's advantage, because even though he wasn't as good as he had (just last year) thought he was, the coaching staff put him on the ice at game time. Defense.

His new on-ice boss and mentor was just now explaining the change, though he didn't really need to. Mostly to soften the blow. "We rotate it around, so since you've played offensive line in the past, you're our Ringer on your line. DO NOT try to slapshot until we improve that. You're too slow. Work on the accuracy of that wrist-flick you pass with. THAT is going to put some in the net when you come forward from the defensive zone." The assistant coach handed Bruce a stack of VHS tapes. "Watch these. We've got the guys wearing colored jerseys, different colors, to help you see who is moving where. It's a counter-clockwise rotation. It confuses the hell out of some teams." He tapped the stack of tapes in Bruce's hands. "Watch. The last one's a game tape."

At practice the next day, Head Coach patted Bruce's shoulder. "Congratulations. You're a hockey player. Learn quick. You're going to need to. WE are going to need you to. You've got a good read on the game, you seem to know what's going to happen before the action gets there, so you can use that to defend the zone." He patted Bruce on the helmet, pat-pat-pat and sent him over to the Defensive Staff, who were in reality two of last year's players who were still in the area, working for accommodating employers, and also still had an itch to be near the ice.

***

The starting Center and Team Captain was a Sophomore, a big, brawny African-Italian guy named Curtis. He had an easy manner, a killer set of arms and could make an effortless slap-shot with no wind-up - a slap with his stick that would send the puck rocketing across the rink on an seventy-mile-an-hour, three-inch-over-the-ice hover that usually made it all the way into the net. Bruce couldn't match it on his best day. Bruce liked Curtis immediately, even if he was a little jealous of the guy's talent and muscle. All the players liked him - that's why he was the Captain. Curtis had the ability to be both the best on the team and to inspire the best from his wingmen and his teammates. Curtis set an example by the way he could effortlessly and casually vault out of the box onto the ice to join a hustle when a tired man steered in, by the way he got worked up for a road game, by the way he hustled to practices early.

Everyone was sure he'd go Pro before graduation. Even the coaches worried about it, a little - Curtis had been first-string for three years. Curtis knew better. He'd watched enough Pro games to know that even though he was talented, he wasn't THAT talented. He'd be stuck in an "Enforcer" role and spend the rest of his hockey career starting fights on the ice. He was there to play the game. *I wanted to be a boxer, I'd 'ave gone to BOXING school!* Curtis was headed off to manage a store or warehouse or sell insurance or whatever else he could drum up with a business degree.

The first game of the academic year was 'Away,' at another New England school. Bruce and his teammates were getting on a bus at three in the afternoon on Friday and heading off to Maine for a Saturday night game. They'd be at a hotel in Portland by eight that evening, and practicing on game ice the next day. Unusually, the team had a brief lunch in the campus cafeteria a couple of hours before getting on the bus. Most of the Away Game meals were on the road or served up at some hockey fan's big kitchen on the way out of town.

Curtis talked a lot over lunch. The coaches weren't around. "These guys, I hear they're good. 'Couple a these Mainers, I hear they got recruited outta high school, scholarships and all, but they went Division Three because they wanted to actually get out on the ice."

Bruce looked down at his plate and grinned. *Yah, just like me.*

"We got some work ahead of us. Good thing it's a fun job. So let's just get on this bus and get to work." He looked around the several tables. "No need to be nervous, it's the same hockey game you been playing since you was five. We're just getting on a bus and going to work." He grinned. "Maybe we'll even have some FUN kickin' their asses."

Curtis was so RELAXED. No pre-game jitters, no ass-kicking threats, no insults to the motherless bastards on the other team, no wasted energy. He saved it all for the game, all for the opposing net. Coach talked of strategy, effort, discipline. Curtis brought them attitude, confidence.

The Regimentals lost a hard-fought game against a bigger school by four points. It would be one of only two losses for the season.

***

"I think I have a prospect." Professor Wendell leaned back in his office chair at the college and held the phone to his ear to hear the reply.

Pause.

"No... for the Pipeline thing."

He listened again.

"Year, huh? Really?!" He scowled and smiled at the same time. "This will probably take a little longer…"

Pause.

He frowned. "No, he's worth waiting for. One of the hockey players... might be just right for our own little game."

Pause.

"He's a dual citizen. Potentially, he could work for both countries, be sworn in each one. He's kind of young, but I'm going to start grooming him."

A long pause as he listened to a lengthy point on the other end.

He smiled. "Ya, that's what I think. Best situation, actually, if you can find an agency up there that will sponsor him. One you can trust. He might be able to work it from one end to the other if we get it right."

Another pause.

Walter Wendell frowned. "No, this is going to take a while. I'm going to steer him in the right direction, but I don't think it's appropriate to put your hooks into him too early. Let him come to it on his own."

He chuckled as the person on the other end spoke.

"Oh, I'll give him a kick in the right direction." He laughed, listened, then laughed some more. "He's a new student. I'd say… Two or three years."

Professor Wendell had to pull the phone away from his ear while it yelled at him. A person across the room could have heard the tongue-lashing.

He sighed and put the phone back to his head once the noise stopped. "You tell the Governor that's how long it usually takes. You can only get information if you have an agent in place. It takes TIME to get one in there at the start."

Pause.

Frown. "No, I think this is a real possibility. He's the right age, has both flags, and I've done a little checking in the guise of his Academic Advisor and found a few things that tell me he's our boy. He's focused but also fun-loving. Quite the Lady's Man in high school. Independent. His parents don't quite know what to do with him, so they're letting him forge his own path." *Wow, that sounds familiar: Brittany.* He discarded the irrelevant, errant thought. "I'll watch him and steer him, and keep my eye out for any others, but..."

Pause.

He stretched back in the chair as he listened for a moment. "Look, the whole citizenship thing... I checked, and if he hasn't voted, this one's definitely our boy. This is gift-wrapped for what you need."

Pause. Laughter.

"Well, I'm going to try not to like him. Where he's going, well, he'll do okay or he'll be fucked up for life or behind bars or maybe dead. Those are the three choices, pretty much."

Pause. More laughter, a little forced this time. Some questions.

"Yes, I survived it. Different stakes, though."

Pause.

"Okay... Do that. I'll give you a call in six months or so with a thumbs-up or thumbs-down. I'll know by then."

Professor Wendell put down the telephone. He felt a little giddy, though his poker face showed only pleasant satisfaction. *Fifteen years out of it, and I'm going to lay on an operation!* From the distant view and safety of his academic office in a little college town in New England. *Even better!*

***

Amazing to think that only twenty years have gone by. Collegeville is so different today. History lives on, but the campus quad is now a quiet grassy park frequented most often by squirrels and blue jays. Families live in the tiny, house-like staff dorms that are left here and there around the edge. The bigger buildings, the barracks, are all gone to the fire and the wrecking-ball. The academic cluster is now an office-park for starter-companies. A tiny community college monopolizes the former science complex. Cross the railroad tracks and venture down by the river to see the long-planned new rink and you'll be disappointed - the new one never came to fruition and in the end the refrigeration equipment building was scrapped along with the old stable. They were torn down to make way for a flour mill expansion.

You can still see the lines of the campus, though, in the regular size and shape and design of those remaining brick buildings scattered up and down the street. The empty spaces between them that were once filled with tall and grand academic buildings now just large lawns and small neighborhood parks.

Visit, if you must see it for yourself: just take Route Five northwards two exits from where I-89 and I-91 meet. The Academy, what's left of it, is right there were Route 5 takes a hard yink through Collegeville.

Walter Wendell lives someplace else, works somewhere different, and wakes each day wondering if he should have the power to turn back time, where would he start?

The hockey player from Toronto spent three years more than the sum of his living years in that town, but his bones were carried away, complete with the dirt and litter underneath them, before the biggest changes came to Collegeville and the campus. Even now he's still interred at the State Crime Lab, a sterile and cold place where those bones will probably rest for as long as anyone who knew Bruce Sutton remains alive to miss him.

Chapter Three

The new helper at Hattie Wendell's place....

It wasn't exactly clear when breakfast at the farmhouse became a tradition. One day the team was headed off in the bus for a holiday tournament out of state. The campus cafeteria was closed on the account of school being out in-between the semesters. The team usually met at the downtown pizza place when this happened, but this time they had to be on the road early so they could haul ass across three states and still get to the hosting rink in time for an afternoon practice on the game ice.

Hattie Wendell overheard the coaching staff wondering about stopping off at a Smiley's Restaurant or some such place. She wasn't normally one to eavesdrop, but since she was RIGHT THERE and offended by the thought of her favorite hockey team being stuffed up with fast-food right before the most important game of the year... "Well, why don't you bring everybody up to the farmhouse for breakfast? We sure as hell have enough room, why that kitchen used to feed THIRTY on holidays when I was their age!"

Hattie convinced everyone that her kitchen and dining room were up to the task, and then she convinced everyone that SHE was up to the task. The rest of the Hockey Booster Club thought it would be a fun, one-time thing, and arranged for a few helpers to show up just in case it was too much for Hattie. The team bus parked at the end of the pavement up in The Hollow, and the boys trooped up the steps of a great, hulking farmhouse and ate a truly nutritious pre-game breakfast. They won every game in the tournament.

Next time, it was lunch, and again they won. And again. Gradually, most of the "helpers" stopped showing up as they realized that Hattie had things well in hand, plus there were twenty eager pairs of hands ready to help out if she needed anything done. So it became a tradition for the Regimentals, before many of the road trips to an away game, especially when the campus was shut down for a holiday or break: eat pancakes and home-fries, pie and sausage, or carrots and a pot-roast with Hattie Wendell from the Hockey Booster Club, win the away game.

By the time Bruce became involved with Academy hockey, Hattie's place was an old game-day tradition. But something changed at the Wendell farmhouse in the summer between his Sophomore and Junior years: when the team showed up for a booster-club pre-game breakfast in the Fall of Bruce's third year of college, Hattie Wendell had a full-time helper. One he couldn't take his eyes and thoughts away from.

Brittany was tall, with wildly curly black hair, a rosy complexion and green eyes that hinted at the stormy shores for which she was named. She was uncommonly beautiful, in the way that a classical painting by one of the great masters draws the eye, even the eye of those unschooled in art. Brittany Wendell had confident, squared-up shoulders and a regal bearing which made her seem even taller and older than her sixteen years - none of that ungainly, awkward, hyperactive, uncoordinated movement associated with many teens.

Because she was beautiful and self-assured, smart, graceful, mature for her years, and noticed by all the boys, all of the girls at her school hated her, or so she inferred and assumed. The boys, they all liked her, too much, and had been following her every mood and move since she was thirteen. Brittany had learned to remain aloof from her peers for these reasons, which of course made them resent her, or want her, even more. It might not have been that simple, but schools are sometimes hard places, and this young person didn't trouble herself to try to learn and follow the unwritten rules, which slight made the hallways and classrooms full of peers all the harder towards her.

***

Even three years before, Brittany's mother had taken to giving her sweet-faced, black-haired daughter a hard time about it, being the social jitterbug that she herself was: "I just don't understand why you don't spend more time with your FRIENDS."

What friends, Mom. Everybody hates me. Brittany stared back, placid, eyes revealing nothing because she could say nothing that would turn this woman from her course.

"It's not good for you to sit around by yourself in your bedroom all the time!" And so on. The social butterfly that had birthed her had a thousand versions of the advice. Worse, later, when the woman presented a solution, already implemented: "I invited over Cessy and Margaret, and I asked them to bring their daughters along. I do hope you'll be nice and spend some time with them."

Oh, THANKS, Mom. That was very nice of you, setting up a play-date for your thirteen-year-old daughter and making her look TOTALLY like a RETARD. Thanks a LOT.

Of course, the girls got to the Wendell house with their mothers, cast jealous and hostile stares at Brittany during her token appearance, and immediately departed for the downtown just a short walk away. By themselves.

There were other incidents, schisms between mother and daughter. An aborted modeling effort. Unwelcome lessons on makeup, housekeeping. A party planned for months and hosted by the mother, with Brittany disappointing because she was in the midst of a bad case of the flu and only wobbling downstairs in sweats to get orange juice and aspirin for her fever. Brittany refusing to join the right groups, damning herself by neglecting to attend the prescribed events, shaming the mother with independence and selfish thoughtlessness. Squandering her mother's good advice.

Brittany's poor mother! She only had ONE daughter to raise right, and this headstrong thing just plunged right past her good advice, over and over again. *That ungrateful, troublesome child!*

Sometimes parents are hostile to what they don't understand, and mothers are almost always overly critical of the oldest daughter at some point or other in their upbringing. At the same time, it often seems that as much as a teen CAN'T get along with their parents, they can form very close bonds with a grandparent. The grandparent has a wider perspective born of more years of experience. As in, "Well, his or her mother went through that or this, and they turned out fine, more or less, so it'll be alright." It's less personal; The grandparent CARES, but in a more relaxed and objective way. So it was with Brittany and Hattie Wendell.

***

Brittany talked to her dad one night in the spring of her fifteenth year, after she and her mother had spent most of the afternoon fighting. Walter Wendell sat at his desk, grading papers, and Brittany stood in the open doorway as teens do, close by a quick exit, leaning on the wooden doorframe and fiddling with her cotton sweatshirt absentmindedly with one hand. Her mother and his wife was out running errands. The little brother was terrorizing some other neighborhood at the moment. They could be frank.

"Why does she treat me like I'm a BAD kid?"

Walter Wendell looked at his daughter skeptically. "Your mother?" Walt figured this dust-up would pass. They all had, more or less. Finally: "Does she really?"

Brittany thought for a moment. "No… She treats me as if… Like I won't come home at night or do my homework or eat breakfast unless SHE tells me to, first. Like I… Like I have to be a CERTAIN WAY or she's not happy. Like I have to friends with HER friends."

"She's treating you the way she thinks she has to. She's treating you like you're a child, because she can't see that you're NOT anymore. And she's worried about you. You're DIFFERENT, different than what she expects." *A lot different than she was at that age, I'd expect.* Walter hadn't really known Robin until he'd come back to town after his first hitch with Uncle Sam. He sighed. "Sometimes I think it would be easier if you came home too late, smelling of beer and cigarettes and boys, missed doing all your homework for a month, and failed a test here and there. THAT IS NOT PERMISSION, YOUNG LADY." He smiled. "It's what she expects." He emphasized: "It's what she's equipped to

UNDERSTAND." Walt settled back a bit, thought for a moment. "But you're different. You're older, wiser, and smarter than we ever were at your age." He winced, inwardly. "And your mother doesn't know how to deal with that. We APPRECIATE it, but we don't know how to PARENT it. And it's not in your mother's nature to just sit back and watch. She loves you, you know that, right?"

Brittany nodded, quickly, up and down, as tears started to stream down her cheeks. "I FEEL like she HATES me. I KNOW that she doesn't, but I FEEL it!"

Walt then-and-there decided that the four thousand dollars they'd spent on the year of weekly counseling for Britt had been his best investment ever. At the time, he had simply thought, *why wait until she's thirty and miserable and divorced to start fixing her family-of-origin baggage?* Now it was paying off. *Thank GOD I had that lightbulb go off!* "I know, honey. I know. Thankyou for making the distinc-"

"And she's ALWAYS trying to get me to be like her friend's girls, all cheery and cheeky and fake, and she has NO IDEA how fu… fully MESSED UP some of them are. I mean, you DON'T WANT TO KNOW what goes on at that school. You really DON'T. And she wants me to BE LIKE THEM?!?" The tears were gone. Angry defiance had taken it's place.

Brittany's arms were crossed in front of her now. Her elbows were just a bit higher than they were last year, because she was filling out.

She was a grown-up now, this little girl he had helped to raise. Walter Wendell sighed. *More problems on the horizon.* He imagined his wife, lecturing Britt: 'You don't have enough friends' would become 'You have too many BOY friends.' He really felt for this young woman. But he was powerless to help her in her struggles with her mother. He loved them both, and the two of them would have to sort it out.

As it turned out, Brittany already had a solution. "So I've been thinking about Grammy Wendell. Up there in that big farmhouse, all alone and all…"

Walt thought she was changing the subject. *Gosh, what a great kid.* "You're worried about your grandmother… I think someday maybe she'll come to live in town." *Robin will have a fit, giving up her cardio room, right there by the front door… I'll probably have to build an addition…* "We'll cross that bridge when we come to it." He suddenly brightened. "Hey! You two get along pretty well... Maybe you can help us convince her? When the time comes."

"Actually, I had another idea." Brittany fiddled with a drawstring on the hoodie she was wearing. She looked up, straight at him, and held eye contact: I'm serious. "You know I plan to go to college here in town, right?"

"Huh? Yah. That's a ways off yet, tiger." The Academy had tuition trade with lots of schools. As a faculty kid, she could go to just about any college or university in the Northeast. "Whataboutit?" He turned his attention back towards the papers in front of him, only half-listening, conversation closed. Or so he thought.

"Don't get mad."

Walt's head came back up.

Brittany still looked across and down at him, composed, serious. "I think Id like to try living with Grammy. At the farmhouse. Now. Before Mom and I kill each other. It gets really bad when you aren't here."

He started to try to ask about that, but the level and unwavering green eyes and a brisk and minute shake of the girl's head told him no.

"And I could stay there while I'm in college, save on dorm fees, or rent or whatever. 'Cause there's NO WAY I'm living with Mom while I'm in college, could you IMAGINE that?!?"

He could. Walt unwittingly let the pictured turmoil cross his face for just a flicker of a second.

"See! You agree with me!" Brittany quieted, then continued, calmly. "So why not now? I could help Grandma, not that she really seems to NEED much help now, but I'd be there for later... If she did. And it would be good for ME. Very good for me..."

Walter Wendell remained silent. Britt was old beyond her years: stable, dependable, hard-working, smart, and not at all frivolous. But did she know what kind of commitment an aging relative could become? How busy she might be with college, where he was quite sure she would have a very active social life, especially with the boys. (*God forbid, just don't think about it, Walt.*) How to explain all that to a fifteen year old girl...

"Dad?" Pleading, almost.

He had never heard hear plead for anything before, ever. Something she wanted, they gave it to her or they said no and maybe she went out and figured a way to work for it and get it herself. Babysitting, mowing lawns, saving, scheming, that unwise experiment in a sales career... Never whining. "You know that someday she might need more from you than you have time to give?"

"I'd be around more than the Home Health nurses and Meals on Wheels. YES, I may get busy in college, but can you see me changing THAT MUCH between now and then? Anyways, I think Grammy Wendell would make a GREAT college roommate!" Her tone turned serious, and she lowered her voice. "And it gets me out from under Mom." She looked up with begging eyes. "I've been thinking about this for a long time. You know I'm up there all the time already. More, lately." Unconsciously, she put her hands on her hips.

Jesus, this little girl has HIPS now. And resolve. He could see it in the set of her, as she quietly argued her point. *She's going to find a way to go, whether we want her to or not...*

"Let me do it while I can, while she's still up there for me."

Walt sighed. "Let me talk it over with your mother... No, you KNOW I have to do that, sweetheart. And someone should probably ask your grand-"

"She's had a room set up for me all winter. Somehow she knew this was coming before I did."

Walt looked at the girl sharply.

"NO, she did NOT put the idea in my head. But when I asked... She knows it's time. Dad, I REALLY want to go." Brittany walked over to the desk, moved a book, and sat down in The Chair, a little shaker chair that the children used to sit in when they helped Daddy correct papers. She didn't fit on it anymore - people were smaller two hundred years ago. She looked over at her father evenly, seriously. "How often does your kid get to be safe and warm and fed and in school and in touch when they run away from home?"

Walter Wendell was so surprised that his chair barked on the floor when his head whipped around. He knew she must have chosen those words very carefully. *Jesus. She is more miserable, and more desperate, than I've realized...* and she had hit a nerve, knowingly or not.

The Wendell family already had experience with a runaway... well not that, exactly.

Walt's older brother had gone missing in 1976, never to be heard from again.

A dark and empty hole opened up for just a moment. *Paul would be... forty-four now? Forty-five? Fare thee well, brother, wherever the winds have taken you.* The empty hole loomed, then Walter by force of will pushed it closed and shook his head to clear it.

He stood up, opened his arms, and she stepped up and forward off the little chair and into his warm hug. He had to be careful where he put his hands. *Jesus, she's growing up too quick! She's crying again, too. Wow.* Walt sighed again. It was easier with Brian. *His mother expects him to be a little shit, and he is. No, that isn't fair.* He was a typical teenager, that's all. *Britt, she hasn't been a teen since she was twelve.* He let go and sat back against the desk with his arms folded, resolute, uncomfortable, and probably in for a hard time with Robin. "I'll talk to your mother." *Shit. How did it get this bad without me noticing?* "Hang in there, kid." Except she wasn't. Not anymore - she was making plans to fly. *Hopefully not in the way of the father that preceded her.*

***

So they tried it. Just for the summer. That Fall, Brittany got the rest of her stuff from her parent's place in the village and started riding the rural-route bus to school. Her sixteenth birthday was also a send-off party of sorts. As best as she could , Brittany Wendell tried to be an independent adult with a very cool older housemate for the rest of her high-school years.

And that was how Brittany Wendell came to be at the hockey breakfast at the old farmhouse way up above town on the day Bruce saw the Love of His Life for the very first time.

But that is a story for later.

***

The farmhouse was built in typical fashion of New England settlement homes: on a gently-sloping hillside up in a south-facing hollow above what would eventually become town. First a small, square house built for the settling family while they cleared fields of stones and stumps, then a shed attached to that, then a barn off the end of the shed, and then, once the farm was cleared and attended to, a large two-story house appended to the other end of the first small cabin. Eventually a porch, another larger and detached barn (fires were common disasters, best not to lose it all in one hard-luck day), maybe a smoke-house or sugaring shack. The first little house with the sleeping loft tucked up under the low roof became the kitchen, the loft became storage for dried goods - hams, shelled beans, cabbages, apples. Anything that needed it cold and dry could be reached with a small ladder that went up through the ceiling. Cold-storage items - butter, milk, meat - went into the refrigerated cellar of the main house, which was invariably built over a cold spring, and thus kept at a nearly constant forty to fifty degrees, winter and summer. The first barn, the smaller attached one, became a garage when the auto entered history. The shed held chickens, bicycles, an old and gothic-looking baby carriage, a corn-crib, a row of drying firewood. In the wintertime, one could range from the parlor in the Big House, into the warm kitchen and past the wood-fired range, out into the shed - air only a little frostier here - and all the way out to the garage to start a car warming, a trip of almost a hundred and fifty feet, all without ever taking a single step out into the twenty-below zero air or blowing snow.

Brittany reveled in it. The wood-fired cooking, the chicken-tending, the kerosene lamps, all of this provided her a sense of continuum with Wendell family all the way back to the first Colonial farmers that settled the area before the year Eighteen-Hundred-and-One. She felt attached to her history, here in this place.

***

Brittany settled in with her grandmother quickly. In a month it was like they'd been housemates all along. Hattie offered parenting in the form of gentle questions, short bits of advice, or a comforting pat on the shoulder - almost never in the form of direction. Brittany made sure to be respectful and cheery, even when they had a disagreement, and chose to hide it as best she could when she did not take her Gram's advice. In most things that was not necessary, as they had been bonding on and off previously for years in that old farmhouse kitchen. In times past, Brittany had a way of showing up on her bicycle after school, a habit that had started somewhat worryingly not long after her training wheels came off. (Walt had learned to swing by up there - three miles out of his way - on the way home from work in most weather, because more likely than not, he would be collecting a bicycle and a girl to bring back to the village with him.)

Brittany and her grandmother became peas in the same pod, or as close to it as a young girl and a woman sixty years her senior can be in such circumstances.

Brittany spent that first summer she was up there full-time working, just the same as she'd spend much of the previous summers: baby-sitting, mowing lawns. She had a daily, weekly, and annual routine, and all three schedules already revolved around spending as much time with Grandma Wendell and the chickens and the farmhouse as possible. She added haying to her list of jobs that summer by the simple expediency that she was interested in the work and it paid.

***

The farmer just up the road from her grandmother's farmhouse finally threw up his hands and let an Outside Girl work on the place because he was tight for help - something chivalry and decorum would have prevented just a generation or two before. Gender roles up there in the Hollow got kind of iffy as boys kept disappearing - first to World War Two and Korea, then to Vietnam, later to college and to summer jobs "away." The landscape, both physical and social, was changing. The farmer's eldest daughter, herself soon to leave with a husband emigrating to far-away Oregon, spent the third week of June teaching the young Wendell girl to drive a John Deere tractor.

An aside, here: the farmer's remaining sons, two lads named Jeffrey and Clay, considered themselves the luckiest little sumbitches in the Northwoods on baling day, as they ran the baler and following wagon but also spent an inordinate amount of time watching their new neighbor at work. Brittany ran an ancient kerosene tractor back and forth across their fields, tedding hay a short section ahead of the baling crew and the always-impending late-afternoon thunderstorm.

They put her on the tractor because, frankly, she was a bit small to be heaving sixty-pound bales up ten, twelve feet to the top of a hay-wagon. Their father was pragmatic about it: "Pay her less for driving, I s'pose, but somebody ought ta do it. Tractor don't drive for shite by isself no madder how much I pay it."

Brittany didn't mind the easy work: clad in a bikini top, she used the high perch on the tractor seat - and the haying weather - to tan up a bit. A swimsuit on under her Haying Clothes served another entirely practical purpose, too - she could, with perfect decency and decorum, peel off her dusty and hay- and chaf-filled clothes at the end of the day to shake them out beside a cold brook right there at the field. Then she would plunge into the teeth-chatteringly cold water for an immediate and refreshing bath before she hopped on her bicycle to pedal home. Those boys quickly developed an intense interest in the brook.

***

She stayed busy, between all the jobs. Brittany had few bills of her own to pay, but needed to save for college expenses and her future, as well as a few expenses at the farmhouse. She was not going to freeload off Grandma Wendell, if she could help it.

Brittany got regular rides into town for babysitting and lawn-mowing, from her father and with another Academy professor who lived a mile or so further up the Hollow road from Hattie Wendell's farmhouse. The other professor drove in every morning to keep office hours and teach summer school, then went back up through the Hollow every afternoon at three or four. A perfect schedule for Brittany. He seemed absolutely tickled pink to have the company, and didn't bother to try to hide it. But he never put a hand on her leg and he was a gentleman and looked away when she had to lean in through the window and reach back down to the seat to retrieve something fallen or forgotten.

Brittany was pragmatic about that: *so what if being around me makes some ancient fifty-year-old smile?* He'd never hit on her, not once, even if he was as smitten by her Thousand-Ships-face as every other boy, young and old, that she'd ever run into - she was getting used to that by then. Brittany got a kick out of it herself - the elevated mood he got into when she was in the car was kind of catching. *Not a bad effect to have on people*, she supposed, *as long as they aren't deluding themselves into thinking they're maybe going to get a piece.* Unfortunately, Brittany had seen enough around town and school by the age of fifteen-going-on-twenty to already be somewhat jaded about these things.

Or to perpetuate them. She was a hit at mowing lawns in town. Hardworking, energetic, serious, dependable. And a lot of the older folks in town were amused to have a GIRL for a Yard Boy, how unique and progressive was that! Of course, there were other reasons she was a hit: all summer, young eyes followed her. The first spring, she wore an old pair of jeans that had gotten so many patches of red and blue bandanna material under the holes that the pants looked like a quilt. By midsummer she'd cut the legs off and used them for shorty-shorts. Over those couple of summers they frayed so much that they ended up smaller than some swimsuit bottoms. There was a thong of denim, faded almost to white where it got the most sun, a zipper, one pocket in the rear, and pretty much the rest of it was patches in the rough approximation of a pair of shorts. Brittany looked back and down. *Whole lotta patches.* Good thing, too, because she was getting bigger and the original, long-favored pair of jeans would have been far past fitting over her backside. Those patches added material. *I suppose I'll have to get a new pair, soon....* In the meantime, she looked damn good, she was sure, bent forward while pushing on a lawnmower handle in the hot sun. She made sure to mow up- and down-slope instead of cross-slope, so that her legs would get a good workout and be up to the exposure they were getting. Brittany wore a baggy white t-shirt most of the time, so that she wouldn't look slutty. *Best not to show too much at once* - she'd figured that one out already. She was the talk of the town the first time she mowed on Main Street, nevertheless.

"She's doing WHAT?!" Brittany's mother was absolutely incensed, fumes coming right out of her ears, steam in her nostrils and various four-letter words in reference to the situation. "What kind of fucking little harlot does she think she is, flaunting herself around in front of the whole damned town like that?!?" She bitched and smoldered to anyone who would listen - anyone except the daughter in question, for some reason. No one in earshot ever mentioned that Robin usually sunned herself while wearing next to nothing on the FRONT lawn of their downtown house. ("Oh, it's got better exposure.") Or that she was known to wear some pretty deeply-cut - and braless - dresses to social functions.

Robin wasn't too impressed with her daughter's summer career choices, either: "MOWING LAWNS like some well-endowed TOMBOY?!?" Her voice went up a pitch. "PAINTING BARNS out there in her ALTOGETHER so folks can just ooogle up the ladder at her BUNS all day?" The woman's voice went up a whole octave this time: "BALING HAY in a BIKINI?!? It's just NOT right, Walt!"

"What did you expect her to do for work?"

"I don't know! The supermarket, a Four-H counselor, or something! She's the talk of the town! Or her ASS is." Robin seemed to have very strictly defined roles for her oldest child.

Maybe you shouldn't have bought her all that slinky underwear when she was still a child, either. "Well, everyone's TALKING about her, apparently, but I don't see anyone TOUCHING her. Not ONE boy, as far as I can tell. That's pretty good for sixteen. And I don't think my mother would put up with any shenanigans up there."

Robin stamped her foot. "It would be OKAY if it was ONE boy! I think it would be FINE if she had a boyfriend. But not on display in front of the WHOLE GODDAMNED TOWN! It's just not RIGHT, Walt!"

"Why?"

Robin glared at him, but she couldn't articulate her reasoning.

Walt thought it was maybe a good thing that their daughter had gotten away. Since his wife could no longer take it out directly on Britt, he was seeing a side of her that he hadn't ever fully appreciated. He was glad to be Robin's husband, most of the time. He was equally glad that he wasn't Robin's daughter. Walt thought back to Brittany's fourteenth birthday party. Well, Robins party, really. Last time he'd thought about that, Brittany was asking to move out. He tried not to think about it much. *Fourteen for Chrissakes!*

***

The party was planned, though of course larger than expected. The gifts were a surprise - to nearly everyone - and largely unwelcome.

There had been sheer presents, and then lacey presents, then skimpy presents. All from Brittany's own mother. Brittany turned pink, then flushed angry red, then retreated behind a wall of grey stoicism appropriate to the large guest list of Robin's friends.

Walt was the only guy there, besides her little brother, and Walt had become embarrassed, and then concerned, and soon mad with anger. He finally left the table on pretense: to go out back and split a beer with his son. He didn't want to see the rest of it, and didn't think a little brother should, either. He could tell that some of the neighbor women were a little uncomfortable about it, too. *Holy cow, she's only just fourteen, not getting MARRIED tomorrow or something! Jesus, Robin!*

So Walt grabbed Brian by the elbow and said, "Hey, lets go to the fridge." Then the two male Wendells went out back with a bottle of Coors. Walt twisted the cap off and offered Brian the first sip. "You're twelve now, you might as well. Don't go blabbing it around town and get your dad arrested, and NEVER without me, little man." *It gets the boy out of the kitchen, at least, and got his little mind off the girl-things he most definitely should NOT have seen.* Walt absolutely smoldered as he passed the beer bottle back and forth.

Brian smirked and realized he HAD SOMETHING on his Dad now. Brian still had a hazy memory of the man coming home in a Trooper uniform way back when he was still playing with his blocks on the living room floor. No, he wouldn't actually blab... but it was nice to share a secret, one with consequences, with a grownup. *Wow.* "If you were still the State Police, would you have to turn yourself in?"

Walter Wendell grimaced. *How do you explain 'sworn to serve' and 'don't believe in this law' to a twelve year old?* "Duck if you see a cop." He tousled the boys hair. *Not the best parenting, but what the hell are the only two guys at a fucking UNDERWEAR PARTY for a LITTLE GIRL going to do after seeing THAT?!?* As far as Walt was concerned, they BOTH needed a beer. *Fucking Robin! No need to push the girl into the arms of the local varsity jacket stud club. Jesus!*

So father and son sat out back by the cooling grill, sharing a misdemeanor. "You probably shouldn't bring this little too-doo in there up again. YOU shouldn't even have SEEN it - that's serious Woman Stuff. Your mother should have waited until she was in college." *Or later.* "Your sister will probably throw them in a drawer and forget all about them. How's the beer?" He said it curtly. He was angry, still.

Much later Walt came back into the kitchen. He'd set his son to weeding the in the flowers out back - something safe enough for a kid to do 'til the beer was off his breath. All of Robin's friends were in the kitchen cleaning up while smoking and chatting. She had probably invited them without mentioning it to Brittany. He looked through to the next room: the dining room table was a mess of wrapping paper, boxes, tissue, silk, and lace. Brittany, fourteen years old for about seventeen hours now, sat in the middle of it. Shell-shocked.

Walt stood in the doorway. "Need some help? I'll get the trash. You can pick up... those... clothes."

"Why does she DO that?"

Oh, boy. He grimaced. *Guess we're doing this right now, with company in the house. But best not to put her off...* "Britt... you know this was HER party, right? Not yours? She THINKS she was doing it for you. She really does. But these things aren't really... appropriate for you."

Brittany stayed seated, but her mood was rising. "Makes me SIT here FOUR FUCKI... FOUR HOURS with her chatty-catty friends who I don't even LIKE and open UNDERWEAR for a b-b-BRIDE?!?" The tears were going now.

So was the company. Walt registered doors opening and shutting behind him, the rustle of coats and many steps of shoes, the commotion of a group exit. *Smart women. Party's over, ladies.* Brittany had done real well to keep the tears and anger at bay until the end, he figured. She'd done more to keep up appearances - a gift to Robin - than Robin would ever appreciate. She must have been embarrassed, frustrated, mortified. Angry. "Yes, Britt. Four fucking hours, Sweetie. It's okay. You did great to humor her. More great than you needed to, maybe."

He balled up tissue and boxes.

Brittany made a stack of folded lingerie.

Robin was nowhere to be seen.

Walter Wendell had a thought: "You going to return any of this? I don't see why you can't..."

"No, Dad, I'm going to throw it all in a drawer and try to forget about it." She sighed.

Hmmmph. "Can I ask you a question?"

Brittany looked up at him through her curly bangs. "No. I haven't. I haven't found the right boy to do it with." She was turning the same scarlet red as the racy, lacy nightgown which she was absent-mindedly folding.

"That's good to hear, Honey, 'cause I think you're a little young for that sort of thing by about ten years, but that wasn't actually my question..."

She turned even deeper red as she giggled nervously. "Ooooops." She paused. "You know, I think I might tell you when I did."

Walt kept a stoic face, but inwardly he was screaming: *Don't give me a stroke, kid! I just can't wait for THAT conversation... Why the hell would she tell ME? Why can't ROBIN handle all this shit like a good mother is SUPPOSED TO?!?* What he said, after he was sure of his composure, was: "Okay... well, that's up to you. Don't tell me before you're older." *A lot older. In fact, don't tell me at all. I'll probably be able to figure it out from the moony grin on whatever boy you come home with someday...* "What I want to know is... Well, I'm curious, if it had been some of YOUR friends" (although he'd never seen her have any friends, actually, and a brief flicker of concern passed his brow as he filed that thought for later consideration) "...who'd given you all of this stuff for your birthday, how would you have felt about it?"

Brittany thought for a moment, while her hands absently folded and re-folded a tiny teddy-style bodysuit.

Walt thought the underwear looked just perfect for something out of a raunchy romance novel, and not something he'd ever thought he'd see his daughter holding as they had a conversation over the table. *Incongruous.* And then the light bulb went off, and he realized HE was her friend. And immediately he wasn't sure that was really such a good thing. *I'm setting her up for older men. Shit. I'm gonna have to ask some questions with someone about this.* He made a mental note to look up a professional from Social Services, *preferably one who knows kids real well.... Maybe I can get a referral for-*

"Friends..." Brittany bit her lip as her eyes searched around in her head for a scene from another life, in another dimension, one where she had friends. Finally, she focused on her father, across the table. "I think I would have liked it. I sure as hell would have hidden it from you two. But I would have liked it. We would have talked about boys, and girl-things." A single tear ran down her cheek one more time, but she was smiling now, at the imaginary and impossible world where that might happen.

"Good. Good, Britt. Let's you and I talk about boys, just once."

Her features clouded.

"Please. This is important, Britt." *Not like her mother is going to talk with her about it constructively...* The girl-woman in front of him closed her eyes.

She steeled herself, then stood, pulled out a chair, and patted the seat. "Sit, Dad."

He slumped into the chair, curious, but smirking. *This is a role reversal…*

Brittany stood beside him, facing him, arms folded, leaning against the heavy dining room table. "I already know… What I need to know." She colored again.

Walt found himself uncomfortable to sit there at eye-level with the girl's heaving bosom. There were places where he avoided letting his eyes transit, now. *She's too young to look like some heroine in a Civil War romance novel*, but here she was: *This little girl is growing up.* "Do you?" He shook his head ruefully. "Your mother should be explaining this, but…"

Brittany nodded, tightly, and her eyes became wet again.

Shit. Gone and made her cry again. "I'm sorry. Forgive me while I do my best. You are…" He grimaced, looked at the floor, and scratched the back of his head. "No, you don't need to go wearing those things there… to get noticed." Walt gestured backhandedly at the table. "Women don't even need those to… make them pretty. And they don't really cover you, either. I'm doing a really bad job of this." He sat forward with his elbows on the table and put his palms up on his forehead. *Watch out for the boys. How do I say it?* "What I mean, is…"

"Dad?" As usual, Brittany grabbed the conversation - and the problem - by the horns. She tilted her head.

He removed his hands from his own head and looked up.

"Why do… ladies wear these?" She gestured absently and dismissively at the pile of elastic and satin and sheer things.

Walt's head wobbled and he grimaced as he tried to figure out how to explain THAT to this girl. "Ahhh, so they won't be TOTALLY uncovered. Decent."

"But you can SEE right THROUGH this!" She giggled. "It's so short!" She picked up and held a sheer… *THING*… in front of her form.

Walt cringed and had an Errant Thought: *I don't even know the names for most of this underwear….*

The girl gestured to another silky item nearby: "I wouldn't go meet the Postman wearing THIS housedress!"

Walt colored angry and blushed at the mere sight of it, and then thought, *I suppose THAT depends on how unhappy you are.* He discarded that irrelevant thought. "I suppose it's about power, in a way…" *Here you go, have a look, but you can't HAVE it unless I give it to you. How do I explain that to her?*

"Power?"

Oh, boy. "You'll see someday." He pushed back from the table to stand up. "God gave you that body and you have made it into a beautiful person. But that body, as you grow up and become a woman, gives you power. Power over boys… and men. You've noticed that?"

Brittany nodded.

Walt looked out the window and continued formulating his thoughts as he spoke them. "It's not your fault that they get all moony over you. It's NATURAL. Birds, bees… whales."

Brittany giggled a wet, snotty laugh at that.

"They all do it. It's not really THEIR fault, either. The boys… young men." He sighed. "The good ones want… to spend time around you, and know that, and work around it. Or ask you out. How they FEEL about you is just something that happens. But it's THEIR problem, and THEIR responsibility, not yours. How they ACT around you, what they DO, they have control of. The young ones, or the selfish ones, or the bad ones, they won't CARE about controlling their actions, or know how. The rest of them, well, they'll treat you all the more carefully because of it. Because of the birds and the bees and whales." He paused again. He was struggling. "Look, I'm doing a really bad job of this. It's just that… Don't show more than you're willing to give away, but don't be ashamed of your body, either." *Jesus, this little girl has CURVES, now.* "Just… try to keep them, I mean it, decently covered." He pointed to the pile of less-than clothing. "THAT is not decently covered. It's a gift for someone special, or for yourself, or… tools, to create… a mood." *Should I have told her that?*

"Dad?"

"What?" He braced himself for the real, probing, hard-to-answer questions that her mother should really be answering.

"Boobs. Butts. Are they PRETTY?"

Shit. Walt looked out the sliding glass door, at the back yard. He answered quickly, and it was only half a lie, far less damaging than a father trying to explain a word like SEXY to his young teen-aged daughter. "Yes, sometimes... Boys are going to find them... interesting."

"Daddy?" A pause. "Am I pretty?"

Now how the hell do I answer that, in context? Safe enough just to be honest, he supposed. "Of course. Of course… I'm not supposed to notice. I'm just supposed to keep the boys away from you and make sure you come home at a decent hour in the evening…. And don't get caught wearing THIS stuff around until you're already married."

The girl turned, gave Walter Wendell a kiss on the cheek as she rushed by his chair, and then disappeared in a peal of laughter. She was out of the dining room and up the stairs in a flash. She turned halfway up the stairs to yell back down towards the kitchen: "That's the LAST time, Daddy! You're a married man and I'm a GROWN WOMAN now!"

Walt had sat at the table, wondering if he'd conveyed ANYTHING important or appropriate to this barely fourteen-year-old girl who thought she was teetering on the edge of womanhood.

***

Sixteen-year-old Brittany Wendell had a rule about babysitting: The mother drove her home. It made things less awkward. Because even when the father-type wasn't a cheating prick, it was still uncomfortable. Some men and boys of all ages got strange around her, even the ones that weren't looking to get lucky. They seemed to fall into two broad categories: those that got smiley and talkative, and those who got tense and quiet. She supposed the problem was the same, regardless of what made it to the surface, or whether the man actually acted on their delusional appetites.

It happened, once, a man, a father and husband, he'd asked her if she wanted to go home 'the long way.' She was disturbed, but also mildly amused, and declined simply, without excuses: "I'd rather go right home, if you don't mind." She worried a little bit about what would have happened had the man minded, and she also wondered exactly what it was that she was doing to so addle all these awkward boys-at-heart. So it was just easier to have the mother drive her home. Brittany made that point up front, now, during the scheduling, just so there would be no misunderstandings. She decided to just let them think whatever they were going to about it. She supposed she could imagine the gossip:

Was she raped?

Did some husband DO something to her?

Is she a SLUT that knows she can't keep her little hands off a married man if she's left alone in the car with him?

Is she uncomfortable riding with men, because she WANTS her FATHER FIGURE?

Brittany snorted by way of reply to her own imagination. *Let them think what they will.* Some of the mom-types probably appreciated her rule, if they knew their husbands even the tiniest little bit…

Right now Brittany was riding up to Grandma Wendell's with her dad, because she had been babysitting for the Sevigny boys. Their mother wasn't available to drive Brittany home on account of having caught her husband, their father, with the last babysitter. Mrs. Sevigny had up and flown the coop to her old high-school boyfriend's place, that man's wife having gone to live with a former lover in an unrelated small-town drama. Soap opera plots had a way of perpetuating themselves, thought Brittany. She also thought she needed a car, so she could avoid these complicated situations altogether. Maybe a steadier job, too. *Hmmmm… How do I get all that fixed in one whack?*

"…going up there?" Walter Wendell intruded on her thoughts.

"Fine, Dad. We're getting along great." She was distracted, still working on The Problem in her mind. "I'm a lot happier." She grimaced. "Sorry. You know what I mean."

"Less yelling?"

"No yelling."

"Your grandmother says you've taken on a cut of the bills?"

Brittany shook her head. "Not very much. I never went up there to free-load." She laughed - a snort, really. "A SMALL cut. Less than I cost in hot water, probably. But I wanted to make the point."

You are. He sighed. "I miss you, kiddo."

"I'm around, Dad. Now. Here." She pointed down at the seat she was sitting in to emphasize. "Thanks for the ride. It really makes things… easier. That I can call anytime."

"Of course you can." He paused. He had a question, and was something between curious and concerned, and very much wanted to know the answer, but he wasn't really sure it was his business, *but wait, I*

AM playing the father role for a while, still… So he asked as calmly and lightly as he possibly could, "Didn't want to ride home with Eric?"

Brittany giggled, then swallowed it, and became serious. "It's not funny, really. His wife left, caught him with the babysitter LAST night." She leaned over and said quietly, confiding it as an aside, "It's all over school…" She sat back up and continued: "So tonight he had some THING he had to do and couldn't get out of… and needed a different sitter."

Brittany's dad went very quiet for a mile. Finally: "So… You thought maybe you didn't want to ride home with him because…?"

Peals of Brittany's laughter rang out in the truck. "No. NO! He COULDN'T give me a ride home, not unless his own KIDS chaperoned from the back seat!" More seriously, she continued: "His wife LEFT him, Dad. Last night. He's a single father now, until they fix their shi… problems. Or whatever. The boys were in bed by seven, and I didn't want to get them up to go for a ride into the sticks in the middle of the night." She giggled again. "And no, Mr. Sevigny doesn't fu… ornicate with EVERY sitter, just Trudy. And yes, Trudy fornicates with EVERY dad she can, she's got a thing for them." She looked over at her father, who looked a little tense and maybe pale, though it was impossible to tell for sure in the green glow of the dash lights. Brittany lifted a mischievous eyebrow, probably unseen in the dark of the cab. "Want Trudy's phone number?"

"That's NOT funny! In my day, people weren't sneaking around like that all the time!" Incensed shock and distaste graveled his voice.

Brittany laughed all the way through the next mile. "Oh, yes they were, Dad! You're just too goody-two-shoes to know about it!" She was laughing so hard she had to hold her stomach. She coughed, then kept laughing.

"We need to find you a different job. You're getting exposed to family problems you shouldn't know about until you're divorced yourself."

"You're just too sheltered, Dad." Brittany turned serious. "Daddy, I think we have to talk about boys. And girls. Just once…"

"Smarty-pants." He said it with a grudging smile.

They were quiet for a couple of miles. Walt considering just how many OTHER family problems his little girl might have been exposed to, and Brittany already moving on and worrying about the problems right in front of her: those of a teenager in need of a license and insurance and oh, yes, a car. The troubles of a young woman who hasn't yet learned to navigate the social caste system in her school. The concerns and crisis's of a girl who is sure every one of her classmates hates her.

***

Walt got a phone call the next day.

He swiveled away from his open office door. "Oh, hello. How goes it in the world of green and gold?"

Pause.

"Just doing my part to prepare young minds…"

Pause.

Walter Wendell sat up. "Really."

Pause.

He scratched his head. "That would keep Oppseck. Sorry. Operational Security. I mean, that would be IDEAL, in the BEST of ways. A very small pool of need-to-know personnel. Shit, YOUR OWN COP might not even KNOW he was in the operation until…"

Pause.

"EXACTLY."

Pause.

"The only trouble I see with it, too. No one knows about it, then he's all Up The Creek by himself if the shit hits the fan."

Pause.

"Yah, it's probably safer than the whole world knowing. You going to figure out a way to cover him?"

Pause.

"Well, that's your problem. You want to throw him in for a while, I've got a buddy retired into policing in Albany, he could show him some…"

Pause.

Walt laughed. "Yah, same gig, safer environment. Well, maybe. More than two blocks from the cop-house and he'd probably feel safer in East Talazak-has-been, some nights. I can touch base, see how he'd feel about a puppy for a while."

Pause.

"Bob, look, I gotta say it: Don't send up anyone you like... He's not likely to come back the same guy you knew. You probably won't get him back in uniform. My guy, he said, and this is the STABLE, OLDER ones, he said around forty percent come back alcoholics or a drug problem, and about half of those end up serving time."

Pause.

"Yes, that's right. Prison."

Pause.

"That's what my guy said. Cited some DOJ paper, said he knew a couple went South. 'Don't fuck up somebody you think is going somewhere' is how he put it. Send someone you don't like. You may have to jack him up yourself, too, at the end... Just a word of advice from a buddy-o-mine named Seavey."

Pause.

"Dig around, see what you find out."

Pause.

"Maybe we can get a pardon from the Governor." He laughed.

Pause.

"Yah, do that."

Pause.

"I don't really know. Foreign Service guys, a couple of them stayed in-country. Liked the bush better, I guess. Could happen to your guy. Our guy. Different stakes, though."

Pause.

He shrugged. "I don't know... We'll see, I guess."

Pause.

"Next week? Okay."

Pause.

"Yah. You, too."

Walt leaned back and savored it, for just a moment. He nodded to himself and smiled. *Hope whoever the asshole is, he keeps his hat on straight.* He shrugged. *Oh well.* He smiled again. *TWO potential agents... Yep, we got an Op on!*

CHAPTER FOUR

Tabitha

There WAS one student at school who was genuinely nice to Brittany: a tiny little wren of a girl with a nose-ring and short, uncombed red hair. She was cute, unique, energetic, tomboyish and also unabashed, which Brittany found especially interesting. This girl participated in school sports and seemed especially fond of hockey. The young woman showed some amount of athletic talent as well as what were considered passing good looks and thus was one of the ones who all the jocks literally swooned over, even if they knew she was unobtainable.

Brittany thought that Tabitha probably treated her nicely for the same reasons that the boys sometimes did. Brittany didn't care, and chose to give this classmate some minor amount of attention. They had a couple of classes together, and so shared a computer in one and became lab partners in another. Their classmates looked on with a mix of jealousy and snickers. It was good to have a friend. *Let them talk.*

The boys still followed Brittany's every move, waiting for her to trip and fall into somebody's arms, she supposed. On this particular day, a smirk crossed Brittany's mind, chasing the thought. *I guess I'll have to humor one of them soon, just to see what all the hoo-ha is about... and to get the REST of them off my back!* The boy who was in the general direction of her gaze was getting all moony-eyed now, and... *Oh, wow. Coming up to SAY something to me?!? This could be precious!* Brittany considered the likely and usual proposals: I want to take you for a ride in my car. I want to be your prom date. I want to take you out and forget to bring you home on time. I want a set of your underwear. I want a quickie. I want I want I want I...

"Brittany. I. Want. You. To. Know." The boy - one of the Sophomores - rushed through the rest in a frantic effort to get it all out without babbling: "That you have the most beautiful eyes in the whole school!" And then in an undertone, and more composed because he had gotten the hardest part done, careful that nobody else would overhear: "I really hope that we can be friends someday..."

Brittany suddenly felt strange, all a-quiver, in the most unfamiliar way. His voice seemed very close in her ear, like she could feel his breath against her very spine.

He leaned in further. "Because it would make my life wonderful for the rest of time." And then he scampered away to the safety of his friends and fellow jocks, who had much to say about it:

"WOW, you finally TALKED to her!"

"Way to go Jeffer!"

"What did you SAY to her?"

"She didn't say NUTHIN' that's a STRIKE, dude, but good try..."

Jeff got high-fives all around, but he wouldn't give anyone the scoop on what he'd said to their hot classmate.

Brittany stood there, her expression suddenly serious, all the mirth and skepticism drained from her face. *Oh!*

***

It was corned beef again at the farmhouse this mid- September night, the end of a cut which had lasted all week, with carrots and potatoes from the garden. Soon it would be time to cover the remaining root crops and greens with deep layers of straw so that Hattie Wendell, and now Brittany, would have fresh vegetables come spring. Most of the tomatoes were already in the cellar, hanging green or in various stages of red, right on vines which had been pulled out of the ground and hung from nails on the sides of the overhead beams. The onions were braided and hanging in bundles from the same beams. Half the carrots were in peat moss in large tubs in the shed. Brittany had helped her grandmother plant the turnips in boxes of sand in the cellar. Every day Hattie would pull dried beanstalks from the garden shed and then the two would spend an hour after supper shucking the beans into a tin pail beside the kitchen range, where the ever-present heat from the wood cooking fire finished the drying.

Brittany loved learning about these age-old traditions of survival, these cycles of planting and harvest and preservation. Humans had been putting up food for maybe thousands of years, and storing beans, onions and tomatoes in this very same way for hundreds. People had forgotten all about it in two or three generations of electricity. Brittany vowed not to be one to forget.

Brittany and her grandmother were in the kitchen, sitting at the small everyday table, and shucking this evening's beans. Just a few dim lights were on. The room was dark in the early night of fall, but felt cozy. Everything Brittany was interested in - the supper on her plate, Grandma Wendell, the clock, the wood-fired range, the counter where all the meals were made and had been made for four generations before and maybe would be made for generations to come - all of that was well enough lit to see. The walls, the dark doorways to other rooms, and the floor were not lit at all, and could hardly be seen. It made Brittany wonder what this house had been like back in the day, not so long ago, when kerosene lamps and tallow candles and distillate lanterns lit up the place. She felt like she was floating in time. Through time. Unanchored by Einstein's rules. She smiled. Brittany wanted to share it, show it to someone who had not seen these... *possibilities*. Sharing the possibility of the past and present intertwined.

"Gram?"

"Yes, dear?"

Brittany seemed to be holding a conversation with the kitchen at large as the voices floated back and forth in the near-dark. "How do you feel about pajama parties?"

Her grandmother smiled and reached for another shell bean. "Just you and me, or are we having company?"

"Company. Well, just one." She turned her head to address her grandmother directly. "Can I have someone over for the weekend?"

"I wondered about that, so far away from town up here... Why, of course, Brittany!" Brittany's grandmother had a sudden thought. "Who's coming?"

"A friend. From school."

"Should I make up a room, or.... Oh dear... what do you want for dinner?" Hattie experienced a flicker of anxiety, there and then gone. "I haven't had company in some time...." No one staying over, at any rate. *Not since before Walt's father died, actually*, she reflected. She didn't consider Brittany company, and never had.

"Room? No. Peejay parties pretty much rule out sleeping, so we can hang out in my room. You know: Homework, talking, cards..." Brittany looked down at the table and mumbled, "Beer, drugs. That stuff." Brittany paused and looked at her grandmother expectantly.

"Either you're pulling my leg, or it's going to be the shortest sleepover in the history of cotton flannel pajamas. Dinner menu?"

Brittany pointed to her own ears. "Well, you've still got your good looks AND your hearing, too! Whatever for dinner. From the garden, please, not store-made, if that's alright. Can we help make it?"

Her grandmother smiled. "Sure, sweetheart. I really like having you up here, you know that?"

"Thanks, Gram."

***

So on Friday afternoon, two of them got off the bus in front of the old farmhouse. It was the first time Brittany had ever had an overnight guest in years, at either of the places she had lived, all of two of them, and it was also the first time that Brittany and Tabitha had spent any lengthy time together outside of school.

Hattie Wendell was pleased to see that she knew Brittany's friend through the hockey booster club.

Tabitha was a somewhat unique and much regarded player who had elbowed her way out of her figure-skating tutu and onto the BOYS hockey team when she was eleven, and was now turning heads and schooling opposing team players as a member of the Varsity squad. Big? No, a shrimp. But fast and scrappy.

"Well Tabitha! What a surprise! How nice to see you!" She hugged the girl. "Going out for hockey again this year?"

They talked of the upcoming hockey season as they made a supper: sweet, dry, dark squash that had already been halved and baked over bacon strips in the wood-fired oven; potatoes that they boiled on the stovetop; shell beans that had soaked all day and now were boiling on the stovetop with bacon crumbled and thrown in; apples from the orchard above the house, the first picking of the year, gathered by Brittany and Tabitha while the beans were cooking, then made into a thick, shortbread-crusted pie that cooked while they ate dinner. The aromatic and spicy pie was then served for dessert with heavy whipped cream on top and thick slices of aged cheese on the side.

Their visitor remarked after the meal: "Misses Wendell, I'm not going to fit into my hockey pads this winter if I come back here!"

After dessert, the girls helped with the dishes and the cleanup on the counters, and then retired to the parlor to do homework on the big table in that quiet room. Hattie was impressed that they got right to homework on a Friday night. She smiled and thought for a few minutes, and then stirred together some dry ingredients so she could have muffins going first thing in the morning.

***

Hattie was up well before dawn broke, as was her habit, coating a muffin-pan with bacon fat so she could make cornmeal muffins for breakfast. She ground coffee, set it perking on the wood-fired range, got the muffins in the oven, started new bacon frying, went out to get more wood, and when she came back inside was surprised to find that the smells hadn't lured the girls down. *No matter- I'll carry breakfast up the stairs, right to the peejay party!* She reached for a large wicker serving tray.

And THAT was how Hattie Wendell suffered her first attack of angina.

***

Hattie Wendell stood against the counter sipping a cup of weak tea as the girls came into the kitchen at eleven on Saturday morning, finally lured out of bed by the smell of coffee (reheated), corn muffins (heated up again, very carefully, so that they wouldn't dry out), and bacon (a fresh batch, you could only cook it for so long, the almost-burned batch would go into the week's baked beans). She regarded the girls speculatively and almost warily.

"MMMMmmmm. Thanks, Grandma!" Brittany leaned close to Tabitha's ear. "You're going to LOVE her muffins!" Brittany broke a piece off one and popped it into Tabitha's mouth.

Hattie looked on silently over the rim of her teacup. *You certainly seemed to love HER muffin earlier this morning!* She had to close her eyes and steel herself to concentrate for a moment to clear the picture from its repeat loop on the back of her eyeballs.

Brittany mistook her grandmother's quiet demeanor. "Oh, sorry we're up so late… We can still help with fall chores, can't we?" Brittany poured two mugs of coffee. She turned to Tabitha. "I don't USUALLY stay in bed this late; Grandma will vouch for me."

Yes, usually you're up-and-at-em. Of course, you WERE, after a fashion, this morning. A flicker of horror mixed with rueful mirth crossed her strained face.

Brittany turned. "Grandma? Are you feeling alright this morning? You're a little pale…"

Actually, the woman was grey, almost green. But the aspirin she'd taken, or perhaps just the passage of time, had eased her chest pain somewhat. Hattie supposed she would survive the shock, this time. "Oh, I'm fine." She turned. "Tabitha? How did you sleep last night?" *Not much, I'd reckon. If I was your mother, Brittany dear, I'd make you sleep in different bedrooms. Maybe I should....*

"Oh, fine Misses Wendell." Tabitha took a sip of coffee. Her cheeks were very pink as the hot coffee hit her mouth. "Mmmmm… Thankyou very much, Ma'am."

Hattie regarded the girls. She couldn't tell, not down here. "You're welcome. I've got a nice little breakfast nook all set up for you two on the porch." The woman shoo'd them out towards the sunlight and fresh air and a little card table she had put out there, once she'd recovered. She started loading up plates - the same plates she'd almost dropped earlier, during her attack of chest pain - with bacon and apple slices, put the muffins in a towel-lined wicker basket, and followed them to the porch. "Here you go, dears." She steeled herself to keep a straight face, and then asked Tabitha, "Are you staying tonight?"

Silence for a moment, and then Brittany said, "Could she? We're not imposing?"

No, just remember that I'm old and I need my sleep. "Of course not!" *Just don't be noisy.* "It's a big old empty farmhouse. The more the merrier!" *Well, let's hope it's not TOO many more. We'll have to talk about that. Good grief! Do I SAY anything?*

Tabitha blushed, for sure this time, and smiled at Hattie. "Thankyou Misses Wendell." She turned to Brittany and her blue-grey eyes flared avidly.

Hattie could see it now. Tabitha didn't have the sangfroid that her granddaughter seemed to possess. *My Brittany seems to have made that little girl very happy during their little intercourse.* "Call me Grandma Wendell. We're all like family up here." *Apparently some more than others...* As she entered the doorway to the house, she turned. *Let them know they're safe, at least.* "Don't go running off to Vegas, or anything like that." *One runaway in the family is enough.*

Hands stopped with food halfway to open mouths. Brittany was facing her grandmother, while Hattie could only see the back of Tabitha's head now. A blush started on the back of the red-headed girl's neck, under that short hair. Brittany looked like she was bemusedly waiting on a thunderclap that might or might not crack the windows.

Hattie continued: "You're both younger than you think. You don't have to hide anything here, but do remember that I'm old and I need to sleep, even if you young-uns don't." *There, that will keep them quiet, at least.* Hattie didn't want a chance in hell of HEARING them, now that she knew what all last night's carrying-on and giggling was about. Especially not until she had this figured out. "Enjoy breakfast, you two." She withdrew into the kitchen.

The two girls looked at each other for a beat, Brittany turned pink, and then the porch filled with hushed giggles and one excited utterance that might have come from either one of them. "Oh, shit!"

They ate their breakfast on that beautiful, clear, warm early Fall morning while enjoying almost summer-like temperatures, with just a hint of the sharp syrupy acid odor of a few early fallen leaves in the air. A little vase of roses right in the middle of the little table-for-two completed their intimate outdoor brunch. That vase was the subject of much discussion.

"How nice! They're BEAUTIFUL!" Brittany smiled. *Nobody can say my grandmother doesn't have a sense of humor....*

"Where on EARTH did she get those, this time of year?" Tabitha turned her head back and forth, looking for a rosebush in bloom somewhere in the yard.

It was too late in the year, of course.

Brittany waved a dismissive hand. "Oh, they're definitely from downtown."

"How? Did she get them yesterday, like she KNEW I was...?"

"Going to put the moves on me?" Brittany picked up another piece of bacon. "She has her ways. She probably made a phone call this morning. She has a lot of friends that pass by, drop things off." Brittany flourished a bite from a stiff piece of bacon and chewed before continuing: "It's definitely a message. Breakfast for the lovers. Don't worry over it." Brittany smirked. "Subtle." She chewed on more bacon absentmindedly. "I wonder how she knows... She likes you, by the way."

Tabitha's head went back in a skeptical scowl. "How do you know that?"

"She talked about it, openly, and..." Brittany wiggled her bosom. "More tonight." She grinned. "Grandma didn't assign you a separate bedroom..."

Tabitha blushed and leaned forward to reach across the small table to swat her friend. Then she got a worried look on her face. "But you WILL, won't you?"

"May-be...." Brittany grinned in a way that she hoped was coy and then batted her eyelashes in the general direction of her friend.

***

In the afternoon, all three of them went out back to pick up drops in the orchard. The worst of these would be run through the small press for cider, while the best of them would be cut up for pies for the next couple of weeks. The rest of the apples waited on the tree for a hard frost to set them ripe. Later, Brittany and Tabitha would split firewood for the next week and stack it in the little shed between the house and garage while the chickens dodged between their legs. The farmhouse - even without a working farm around it - still required a regular amount of work.

Hattie looked out the window as she peeled and quartered the drop apples at the kitchen counter. She smiled to herself. The young women worked together well, even though Tabitha was unfamiliar with the tasks. They were having fun, out there in the long-quiet farmyard. Calm, assured, happy, mildly intimate… *as in-love as two young people can be after only one brief night of… HAD it been only one? Did those two already know each other, before, in that way?* Hattie thought of past days when the farm was still operating, of how cows in the herd - all females - would mount the one who was ready and needing for the bull to come... a strange intercourse that was unremarked and mildly amusing, but useful behavior back in that day: Time to inseminate that cow. *Is that what's going on with those two girls, after a fashion? Are they ready for boys?* Now THERE is a frightening thought! As Grandma watched from the kitchen, she had another thought, and wondered idly: *What would it have looked like if it had been a boy up here to dinner? Heaven forbid! Separate bedrooms, that's what! So is that what I should do now?* Unbidden images stalked her mind as she tried to make the pie crust: cows mounting cows, those girls together, cows, girls, cows, girls, cows.... She put a hand over her stomach, just below her breastbone, and eyed the cabinet where she kept remedies. *I suppose I should see a doctor soon....* Patrick Walter Wendell, her husband of almost thirty-one years, had died not long after his first angina set in. Hattie continued her tasks with a grim set to her mouth.

On Saturday evening the three of them sat down to winter squash and beans from the previous supper. Hattie had freshened it up with a side of pork: a thick loin slow-simmered in water with a pinch of pickling spices. The boiled meat was and moist and tender and surprisingly sweet.

Hattie spooned out squash and made a comment about "eating your own leftovers" that entirely passed the girls by. They didn't realize that to her surprise, education, and brief horror, Brittany's grandmother had not just inferred their relationship.

Tabitha gushed about the meal, complained about her hockey pads fitting again, and then asked, "Can I move in, too?"

Brittany's grandmother put down her fork. "I don't think so. I think you two should take it a little more slowly than that." She was frowning, but her eyes were full of mirth, even if her digestion was still a little off.

Tabitha looked up quickly. "I meant for the food, Ma'am." More quietly, as she looked at her lap: "I'm sorry." She turned pink again.

"You shouldn't be. Call me Grandma Wendell." She turned to Brittany. "Are they all this quick?" She turned to Tabitha. "I KNOW what you meant, dear. Don't eat too much, you're going to be stuffed." *It always bothered me to have relations when I was on a full stomach.*

Brittany looked at her grandmother, searching. Finally: "Grandma, are you TEASING us?"

"Why, no, child. I AM hoping to sleep, tonight, though. Now that I know what all that giggling was about, it isn't quite as... cute. It's... concerning." *What are the rules supposed to be?* It hadn't even occurred to Hattie that her granddaughter would bring someone home. *Especially THAT kind of someone!* "You two...." *Less complicated that it's a girl, but also more.* "You're awfully young."

Brittany raised her eyebrows, shrugged, and winked at Tabitha, whose face was now as red as her own hair.

Hattie turned to Tabitha. "You don't need to be ashamed. It's just awkward. I don't know whether to put you two into a room further away from mine, make you keep the door open, or put you into separate bedrooms." She saw Tabitha's eyes go into veiled alarm at that. "It's more complicated than last time I had teenagers living here." *Or maybe just more open? Who knows?* She thought of a child, long gone to the winds. What did HE get up to in this house? *Something... proof of it right here at this table, I suppose. And now gone sixteen years....* Pain crossed her face.

Something in the room had changed, though the girls didn't know what it was. They finished the meal in silence.

While Hattie ruminated on these matters, the girls spent the rest of the evening doing homework at the kitchen table.

Tabitha wondered - and worried - about whether she might be put in a spare bedroom, away from that curly, curvy prize she had just won over.

Hattie Wendell spent a great deal of time trying to figure out of this "sleep-over" - or more like "not-sleeping while over" - meant that she didn't need to have "The Talk" with Brittany, or if it meant that she had better HURRY UP and have the discussion.

Finally, Hattie decided to consult the two girls involved. "You two ready for a break? Good. Let's have pie." She got out plates and put a fat slice of apple pie and a big peak of home-whipped cream on top of each one. "So do you two need The Talk?" *There. Direct. That's always best.*

Forks clinked to the table.

Tabitha finally spoke: "Well I certainly don't need it!" She winked at Brittany - a new step.

Ahhh. She's becoming more comfortable in who she is. That's a good thing, I suppose. Hattie decided to wait them out.

Tabitha became serious. "They tell us about it in school in our seventh grade, anyways. Diseases and babies and all that. Just in case a kid has their head stuck in the sand."

Brittany followed up. "I went to the same seventh grade. I think I caught you LOOKING at me during that class, Tabitha!" She giggled. "And I've seen how a mommy cat gets knocked... PREGNANT and pretty soon her life is all about the kittens. We're okay, Grandma." She waited a beat, and then added as an afterthought, "Not much chance of that THIS time!"

Dear God? Do I stop them? Do I send the girl home? Cruel to separate her from her friend... apparently her ONLY friend. Cruel to the girls, too, just when they're deciding who they are.... They'd do it anyway, just in some uncomfortable bushes instead of safe in the bedroom upstairs. Even if it was a boy, it would be hard to stop her... risky to try. Do I ask them to hide it better? Well, I was the one who opened the door... literally and figuratively! Well now what the blazes do I do with this child? Hattie shook her head, not seeing the girls in front of her. *Tread carefully, here, Hattie. She's so much like Paul....*

Grandma Wendell seemed preoccupied, so the two girls went back to their schoolwork.

***

Sunday morning came and the three of them sat around the kitchen table sharing a stack of pancakes fresh from a cast-iron griddle on top of the wood-fired range. Hattie turned to Brittany. "Pass the syrup, dear.... Thankyou." She regarded her granddaughter coolly. *My, someone sure was talking to God a lot last night.*

Brittany put her hand in front of her mouth, her eyes sparkling while she glared at Tabitha.

Ah, she hears me. Hattie wasn't done. She turned towards Brittany's friend. "Tabitha," *I think you've made a convert.* "...it's been a lovely weekend. Are you going to come often?"

Brittany threw her fork down. "Grandma! PLEASE!"

Well, if I can't get any sleep when you have a FRIEND over, then you two can't pretend nothing happened. "Really, if you don't want to be teased, then don't let me hear you. Bite a pillow." She leaned in conspiratorially towards Tabitha. "You must be very good. I'm so GLAD you're a girl. I don't know WHAT I'd have to do if I caught a boy in her bedroom. It wouldn't be pretty." *And you are. I can see why she likes you. One of many reasons, I'm quite sure.* "Pass the cider, please." *My God, what do I do with these two?*

***

On Monday night, as Brittany folded laundry in the darkening gloom of the parlor, Grandma Wendell stuck her head in the doorway from the bright kitchen, where she was putting up a squash into individual pie fillings destined for the freezer. "She's a nice girl."

Brittany remained quiet. Unfocused eyes looked past the laundry as the teenager stood folding and thinking. She nodded automatically, only half participating.

"A little tomboyish. Nothing wrong with that. I can see why people think she's cute." Hattie came into the parlor to be face-to-face with her granddaughter. "Brittany, do you think you'll have her up here again? Often?" *And just what do I do about THAT?*

Brittany stopped folding. "I don't think so." She sighed. "I think I'll probably break her heart."

Hattie looked stricken. "Well, that will be less complicated..." She unconsciously put her hand to her breast. "I mean, as far as what I do about ... how sleeping arrangements go." She paused, and smoothed her apron while she thought. "Why, Brittany?"

"I wanted to see what it was like. With somebody else there. She's liked me for a while.... She's about the only friend I have at school, too." She looked up. "You know I've never even been kissed, before? I'm sixteen years old, Grandma."

"Aren't you using her, then?"

"Oh, she wanted to be used... She's kind of got the same problem I do, I think."

Hmmmm. Hattie sensed trouble in that, but left it alone. "So what do you think?"

Brittany nearly growled it: "I want MORE."

Hattie grimaced. "Oh boy."

Brittany smiled. "Yes, I think. Boy!"

Hattie suddenly had to go back into the kitchen. *Dear Lord help me to be a good almost-parent! Give me the wisdom of Solomon and the patience of the Saints!* She eyed the refrigerator, where she'd found her long-dead husband's old jar of nitro. *It won't help me.* The years-old little pills in the brown glass bottle were supposed to be hard white circles. The wet mess at the bottom told enough. *Long gone, like Pat. I wonder what HE would have made of this? Not much, likely - he probably would have thrown the both of them out!* She headed over to the cupboard for an aspirin.

***

The following Tuesday evening over dinner, Hattie Wendell had to ask her granddaughter some questions. She wasn't one to beat around the bush.

"Brittany? So are you planning to have any BOYS up here to the house?" She was silent for a beat. "For a slumber party?"

"Oooohhhhh, I don't think we'd be sleeping!" Then, quickly: "I AM kidding, Grandma! No. I'm sure you have to draw the line somewhere, and I wouldn't want to put you in… a difficult position. I mean, I guess I sort of already have. Sort of… Sorry. We just got carried away." Her eyes flared. *She's a REALLY good kisser!*

"I'm still not sure if I should have made up a second room this weekend? Not something an old folk like me has had to think about before, you know." She smiled. "I like her, Brittany. I really do. But it was a… surprise." *You have NO idea just how much!* "Should we at least maybe have some rules about boys?"

"I don't think you have to worry yourself too much, right away. I promise not to have any boys in my bedroom. Besides, it would lead to talk. A lot of it!" She paused.

Hattie thought THIS little sleepover might lead to a lot of talk, if folks saw them together down at school. *There is something BETWEEN those two, now.*

A mischievous lift appeared on one corner of Brittany's mouth, and she turned to look out the back window. "Maybe the hayloft, though… There's still some old hay up there, right?"

Hattie didn't know what to say, or whether her new housemate was serious. She decided to say nothing, and she was biting her lip too hard anyway. The amusement made it up to her eyes as she cast an appraising look at Brittany, who had now turned back to the table and started eating again. She sat and chewed with carefully staged disinterest on her face. Hattie thought about the girl's mother. *No wonder she is living up here!* She shook her head. *Tough one to parent, this girl. Good child, but about ten years older than most of them. Another Willful Child. There can be trouble in that....* Pain crossed her face and her heart.

Hattie made a mental note to keep more track of what was going on out in the barn.

***

Brittany didn't invite Tabitha to stay over again. ("Well, Grandma, I don't want to tease her.") But she and the girl did become fast friends and they frequently spent evenings together doing homework. Tabitha had the use of her father's aged boat of a sedan in the evenings, now that she was sixteen. She had a regular route from the village to the farmhouse and back.

It made Hattie happy, as she remarked to Brittany one day later that fall. "It's nice she still comes around - her heart can't be too thoroughly broken. You're a kind soul to let her down gentle, you know."

"Oh, well, I think she still holds out hope. And besides, we're lab partners in the Advanced Biology class."

"Oh, how appropriate!" No one could say that Brittany's grandmother didn't have a sense of humor.

Brittany ignored her remark. "And we're friends. It works."

Late some evenings after homework, Tabitha, on her way to the door, would look at Brittany with hungry, fluttering, pleading eyes. She did not bother to hide her angst and desire from an amused but concerned Hattie Wendell.

Brittany was firm, as always: "You had your turn. Go find a nice girl to settle down with."

***

"Sylvia, how are you, dear? It's Hattie." Hattie was on the antique telephone in the kitchen.

A long pause.

"I'm glad to hear that. Look, would you stop by for a cup of tea on your way home sometime next week?"

She listened to the response.

"Yes, Wednesday would be fine. Thankyou."

She listened again.

"Oh, no. Everything is wonderful up here! Actually, I have a new housemate I want you to meet."

Hattie listened with interest and then amusement.

"Oh, younger. MUCH younger. And she's a girl. Sorry to disappoint."

Hattie paused again.

"You'll see Wednesday. Thanks, Sylvia! See you then!"

***

Sylvia lived a few miles up the Hollow from Hattie. She usually took a different, shorter way home that involved more pavement and fewer ruts and lower risks of getting stuck in one season or bounced off the roadway in another, but every few weeks she stopped by to check up on Hattie, or to drop off something from town. Usually it was some grocery item that the older woman had forgotten during her regular shopping trip with the "town Wendells" (her son's family). Sometimes the chickens needed more feed or Hattie was out of new sealing lids for her canning jars. Once it was a strange request for a dozen roses - delivery revealed no Mystery Car in Hattie's driveway, but the woman was obviously laying on a breakfast for two. Hattie gave no clues - she was absolutely mum about the affair. Sylvia suspected that the old woman was lonely more often than she was really out of something, so she made sure to drop by as often as she could to have some of her dinner-plate sized molasses-ginger cookies and a cup of tea. They always had relaxed, pleasant visits and frequently played a hand or two of cribbage if time allowed.

Hattie knew Sylvia through the hockey Booster Club - both women were rabid hockey fans, and they often sat together during games at the Academy. Hattie chose not to go to Away games ("that's a long haul on the bladder at my age") and relied upon Sylvia to give a lengthy and full report the next day after the Academy Boys played on someone else's ice. If it was a win, they toasted there at the farmhouse with two glasses of cream sherry and cookies or a plate of wonderfully moist chocolate cake with butter-cream frosting from Misses Folsom's bakery downtown. If it was a loss, it was two small shots of the worst kind of whiskey. They had a mantra, those two: "Only the sting of hard liquor can get the bitter taste of defeat out of your mouth!" It was their tradition, and just about the only time that Hattie drank alcohol any more.

Sylvia also sometimes dropped by the night before an Away Game to help with preparations for a Team Breakfast at the farmhouse, though lately she'd been too busy at home. Hattie seemed to have things well in hand, on that front, anyway.

Sylvia worked for the state. She was a mid-level functionary in the social services central office in Montpelier. The hockey games were a good distraction for the large and sometimes frustrating agenda at the Agency of Health and Human Services, Department of Social Welfare, through which Sylvia had come to know a lot of the kids around the county.

Hattie figured Sylvia would be a good person to go to for advice.

Wednesday turned into one of those gifts of a fall day in the Hollow: white-frosted grass in the low spots on the lawn in the morning, a ground-frost that stayed almost 'til noon. Later on, a sudden balmy note to a fresh breeze on this already sunny mid-October afternoon brought temperatures up to the seventies. Hattie worked up a sweat putting squash out on the lawn on scattered pieces of plywood to cure the rind in the heat and sunlight. She'd have to rotate them once an hour over the course of the short afternoon and then after the bus came by Brittany would help her put them away in the bins in the shed. Sun-cured squash was worth the several days of effort, and some years Hattie was still serving her own winter squash from the year before as she and the grandkids were starting the next year's seeds in egg-cartons. And now one of those grandchildren was living here, eager to learn all the tasks that went with the other end of the growing season. Hattie thanked her lucky stars.

The day was just drawing to a close as Hattie and Brittany lugged the last of the heavy Hubbard and Butternut squash back into the shed. They picked up squares of plywood in the near-dark as pastel blues and oranges and pinks gradually washed out of the sky low in the notch to the west of The Hollow. Hattie went in to make tea.

A manual transmission whined in the driveway, headlights swung across the lawn, then a vehicle door shut with a hollow clunk. Hattie looked out the window and saw Sylvia's very old and spartan four-wheel drive pickup parked under the carriage lamp down at the bottom of the steps. "Oh, good!" Hattie scurried out to the porch to meet her friend. Brittany was off doing homework in a well-lit parlor on the other side of the house by now. Hattie would have some private time with Sylvia, she hoped. "Sylvia! It's good to see you! It's been a few weeks, almost a month!" Their visits were less frequent in the summer and fall, outside of hockey season.

Sylvia mounted the last step and swung onto the porch to sweep her friend into a hug. "Hello, Hattie! It's that time of year! Soon we'll be having sherry and chocolate cake nearly every weekend!"

"We will, or those boys will answer to ME! They're looking awfully young this year, though!" Hattie missed 'her' Seniors. A couple of them had sent notes to let her knew where they had ended up after college.

"We'll see. They've pulled a few out of the hat, before."

Hattie took Sylvia's arm. "Let's go for a walk, if you don't mind."

They strolled up past the house in the dark, through the garden, and up towards a bench at the back of the orchard. Hattie leaned a little bit on Sylvia's arm on the tricky spots, but they both knew the path well enough that the darkness wasn't an issue. Trees passed - or rather, they passed them - as grasping, reaching arms sensed rather than seen. Not threatening to Hattie... embracing. Familiar. Hattie had been born here, the daughter of hired help. She had played in these trees when they and she were smaller, and she supposed her mother had traipsed through them daily for years before that. She had married Patrick Wendell, and raised his children. Now another generation: Brittany.

Hattie gathered her thoughts and then talked as they slowly made their way up through the dark orchard, her voice disembodied and ethereal. "Thankyou for coming. My granddaughter, Brittany, moved in up here a couple of months ago. Well, right at the beginning of summer, actually. Time does fly!"

Ah! The Mystery Car! "Yes it does...." *But I wonder why the roses?* Sylvia gave her friend an appraising look that was unseen, there in the shadow-filled orchard.

Hattie continued: "She's a dear. And we've always gotten along so well... It's nice to have some company around the place." Hattie leaned in closer to her friend. "I've been alone up here for twelve years, you know."

Sylvia didn't know. Hattie had been a fixture, single and spry, for all the eight years that Sylvia had been going to see Academy hockey. Hattie's husband had never come up in anything more than passing, in all that time. Sylvia wondered what this was all about, but was patient by nature and by training.

The two women made themselves comfortable, side-by-side, on an old, mossy wooden bench under a leafless apple tree. Snow would be in the air soon, and geese, but this evening was merely crisp, with a delicious tang to the air - the sappy smell of freshly-fallen leaves. The sounds of still-falling aspen leaves intruded every time the light breeze settled down on this cloudless, quiet night. Sylvia wondered what kind of issues had brought about this new domestic situation. *Hattie's health, maybe?* She'd know soon enough.... They silently soaked in the descending night, the shapes resolving in the darkness around them as their eyes adjusted, the seasonal change in the air.

After a time, Hattie began speaking again. "Brittany is sixteen. She's old for her age, I suspect. Not frivolous. Good report card... earns it I think. She does a lot of homework at that kitchen table in there." Hattie paused. "She left home because of minor trouble."

Sylvia's mind suddenly churned. *WALTER?!?* She was a mandatory reporter. *Am I in this context?* Legally, yes, she was obligated to report any and all danger to the welfare of a child that she became aware of. *In this place, here in this orchard, on this bench with my friend? Yes, even here.* "With her father?" It popped out, aloud.

Hattie chuckled. Then she turned acidly serious. "His oysters would see the sharp side of my splitting axe. No. Her mother, actually. Too hard on her, I think. They just aren't the same type." *Or maybe they're both EXACTLY the same type.... Time will tell, I suppose.*

Sylvia was embarrassed. "I'm sorry. I asked that question three times already today." *A necessary habit.* "I guess work has made me a bit jaded...." She sighed and then thought for a moment. "As to the other... Mothers and daughters often don't get along at some point. It will pass." Sylvia was relieved that she wouldn't have to figure out how to protect a girl and keep a friendship all under the same family roof.

Hattie chuckled. "Oh, I don't think so. She's up here for the duration, she says, and I think I believe her. She's kind of all grown up and moved out, if you know what I mean. That's why I asked you to come up, actually. I am by circumstance somewhat old-fashioned." Hattie paused again. Finally: "What do I do about BOYS? I'm not really a parent here, but I don't want to be neglectful or encourage Brittany to be a delinquent, either. Can you tell me the facts of life as they apply to raising a teenager, Sylvia? A mature one? In this day and age?"

Sylvia smiled. "I don't think you have much to worry about. They learn most of what they need to know in school now, either in class or from their classmates. Most of them" - *no, that's not fair* - "MANY of them are sexually active at younger ages than your granddaughter. They learn a lot from each other, sometimes the wrong things, but almost all of them are AWARE. Sixteen? She's legally an adult, at least in that way, right now. The age of consent in Vermont is sixteen... well, unless he's older." She shook her head as she brushed that thought away. *Not an assumption I need to worry about in this context....* "That means she can knowingly and with full understanding of the consequences, at least in the eyes of the law, engage in sexual activity. She could also get married, though that might be a bit more tricky - she'd have to be emancipated, by court order, first." Sylvia paused. *I don't know why I said that.* She collected her thoughts and continued: "What I'm trying to say is that you don't have to worry about being held responsible. I wouldn't ENCOURAGE her, but you don't need to protect her virtue. The law says that's up to her, now. Be there to guide her, carefully, to try to steer her away from unhealthy situations and twenty-five-year-olds, and to give her a comfortable shoulder to lean on when her heart gets broken."

"What about... Here?" Hattie gestured to the yard, the house, the orchard. "She is no longer a child living with her parents. She LIVES here, now. She pays on some of the bills, for goodness sake! Do I chaperone? Do I worry about what's going on up here when I'm down at the rink?"

Sylvia thought for a minute. "I would have a talk with her about what you are comfortable with. She's still in high school, and you two should keep up some appearances. She'll probably do whatever she's going to do anyways, she'll just be careful about hiding it from you if she thinks she's not supposed to be doing it." Sylvia chuckled. "Yes, Brittany will probably have a boy up here while you are down at a game. That would be the perfect time to do that sort of thing - a predictable time slot, night-time, the bedroom is available. They can be sneaky. There are pressures. From the body. From peers."

Hattie let out a big sigh. "Something I hadn't really thought about when she moved in. She's not nine anymore, making cookies and snuggling with a blanket."

"In a way, it's easier on you that you're not her parent. You're not her Guardian?"

Hattie shook her head. No.

"And you said she's pretty mature and responsible? She seems grown up?"

"Yes, thank God! I think she came here so that she wouldn't come to a bad end. Things were that bad with her mother. I just don't want it to happen anyways."

"Hattie, sexual activity is not a bad end. Pregnancy might not even be a bad end. She has a VAGINA. She knows it, the boys know it. She feels it now. She - and probably someone else, too - will most likely EXPERIMENT with it soon, if she hasn't already. Have a talk. Ask her to be smart, to use a condom as well as other birth control, be discrete, and come to you if she has any sort of trouble at all." Sylvia paused... "Tell her that alcohol can make her too easy, even a victim. I think the rest will take care of itself. Really. People have been doing this for thousands of years, even young people. You two will be okay, especially if she's as smart as you say she is."

"Thanks, Sylvia."

"YOU call me if YOU have any questions. I think it's WONDERFUL that you have some COMPANY up here! And you two really get along okay?"

"Like peas in a pod, most of the time!"

"Because you're permissive, or because she's respectful?"

Hattie thought for a moment. "A little of both, I think. I CAN be permissive, as you put it, because she IS respectful. I view Brittany as a housemate. Not a guest. Not a child. Because she doesn't act like one."

"That's the best way it can work. You'll do okay... No, you'll do GREAT! Look how you did with Walt!"

Yes, well Walt wasn't humping a furrow into some girl when he was sixteen. At least, I don't think he was.... "Thankyou, Sylvia." *If he was, I wasn't serving the two of them breakfast afterwards.* "I feel better." *Sort of.*

Sylvia stood up. "Well, when do I get to meet her?"

"How about now? Let's go have that cup of tea?"

As they walked slowly and gently back down through the orchard and into the yard, a full moon broke into the black sky over the top of a far-away ridge. The orchard was bathed in alien blue-grey daylight.

Sylvia could almost feel the heat from this last full moon of the summer. She leaned in towards Hattie as they walked, and said in a low voice: "You know, it could be a girl, too. Her romantic interest, I mean. Young people have more… choices… than we used to at that age."

"Oh, thankyou!" Hattie's step hitched as she felt a tickle of residual chest pain dance up the inside of her sternum, into her neck, and out through her left arm. Then it was gone. "That thought hadn't even crossed my mind!" *Until I walked in on those two, nose-to-tail so-to-speak, and gave myself the beginnings of a heart attack!*

"Just something to consider. It could make pajama parties, you know… Sleep-over rules, ahhh, a little COMPLICATED, if you were the conservative type." Sylvia noticed that her friend, her aged face pale grey in the moonlight, was trying to stifle a nervous laugh as they went up the back steps into the house, and thought that perhaps those kind of relationships were probably a little out of Hattie Wendell's experience.

Chapter Five

Working Girl

Brittany ducked into the Nurse's Office.

Mrs. Miller had been School Nurse when Brittany's father attended, and speculation was that the steel-grey haired woman had come with the building when it was built several generations before that. She walked with a slight stoop, probably from frequent attendance to small and sitting children sporting scrapes and bruises and sore throats. Mrs. Miller also had what she herself considered a perpetual smile that was nevertheless as quickly replaced with a scowl when she disapproved of behavior that she didn't consider appropriate. MOST of the behavior she witnessed in the school system now she considered VERY inappropriate, and as a result, the scowl was taking ever-increasing precedence over her smile. Her white uniform was perpetually covered with a blue sweater worn threadbare at the elbows, and her shoes made all the girls shudder - they promised themselves to study harder or primp longer before school so they would not be forced to work as a nurse and wear those horrible, clunky white shoes with the regulation one-inch heels and stiff leather uppers.

On this day the aged nurse looked up with a stained-toothed smile, happy to greet one of the ones that was Going Somewhere in life: Brittany Wendell. Mrs. Miller made sure to peruse the file drawer in the front office whenever she had the chance, to help her make such distinctions. She closed her book and was about to ask how she could help, her mouth opening to form the words, when she saw Brittany veer *straight to that God-damned bowl all the Loose Ones go to!* Her smile turned to a toothy rictus of disbelief. *I expected better of THIS one.*

***

The Bowl contained little foil packages of latex that disturbed the aged nurse and most of the parents, but not as much as a pregnancy would have. It was a recent addition, going on the counter just a couple of years back when the Powers-That-Be at the school realized that Mill Village was a college town, and college boys might have diseases or leave babies behind. (It went without saying that none of the local boys had diseases, and none of them would ever impregnate a local girl and then leave town, even though a few older souls remembered that young Brittany Wendell herself was proof enough that sometimes the young buck would jump ship for warmer ports....) Folks in town, when pressed, grudgingly admitted that some of these college boys were probably sleeping or maybe even Not Sleeping with their daughters when they could pull the skirts up over the victims' heads, probably with the assistance of a little liquor. These poor girls needed to be protected! The Selectmen invited the Police Chief to a weekly meeting and presented the problem.

The Police Chief said, roughly, "How in the Hell am I gonna do THAT?!?" Keeping the boys and girls apart in this town was NOT his job, as far as he was concerned. *Not unless they give me enough men - and maybe a couple of token women now, too, I suppose - to surround the campus in a blue line three bodies deep!*

It became the School Board's problem next. The Good Health and Abstinence classes weren't working, that was fairly obvious. At every School Association meeting, there was a pair of thirty-two year old parents bemoaning their innocent daughter, just turned fifteen or seventeen not eleven months ago and now showing front-and-center and blown up like she was carrying around a womb-infesting Space Alien that would disrupt their lives and eat their finances and wreak havoc on their very culture.

The Police Chief, who was required to sit these Godawful waste-of-time School Association meetings, listened and figured about one in eight of those was carrying her own daddy's one-in-the-same baby and grand-baby, two in eight were carrying an unwanted child from non-consensual sex resulting from actual or threatened violence, three in eight were pregnant as a result of being passed-out drunk at a party and might never know exactly which one of her classmates was the daddy, and the other two were probably perfectly happy to be knocked up and leaving school for motherhood. He thought maybe there were OTHER solutions to the teen pregnancy problem: A yearly lecture for the boys and girls on the hazards of mixing excessive alcohol and bush-parties. No longer rewarding the jocks for winning an away game by letting the cheerleaders ride home with them in the darkened bus (the cheerleading squad van going home empty, those nights). Slowing down the literal flood of alcohol out the back door of the convenience store on nights that the blonde kid closed alone. Lastly, and maybe firstly, maybe some of these parents should actually TALK to these kids, or do something with them on Friday nights instead of turning them loose with the car keys.

Instead, by formal edict of the combined Selectboard and School Association, Solutions were obtained. They didn't even have to schedule a separate meeting, since the members of both boards were exactly the same people, and only the Chair differed.

And so, the Nurse's Office began handing out Solutions. The Bowl, as it was universally known, was a popular stop. Condoms were expensive. Nurse Miller was prohibited from making a report regarding who was stopping in, so there were no social hazards other than her angry stare. Anyone who could brave that had earned a rubber twice over.

***

Brittany took her time. A pile of pamphlets, tidied up hourly by the good nurse, occupied the space next to the bowl. She ignored those. *Hmmmmm.* Lubricated. Unlubricated/Mint Flavored. Ultra-Sensitive Spermicidal. *Hmmmm.* She took her time. *Well, better grab three of each!* She caught sight of Mrs. Miller's angry frown in the background and winked at her before she turned and walked out the door.

Mrs. Miller decided to retire at the end of the next schoolyear, *Social Security age brackets be damned to hell.*

***

Brittany mowed her last lawn of the summer after school on a sweltering, late-October day that reached seventy-nine degrees by three-O'clock.

She excused herself from her afternoon study-hall by simply picking up her books and walking out shortly after signing in. *What are they going to do, bring me up before a judge on truancy? For missing STUDY HALL?!?* She went to her locker, got her backpack, walked past the Front Office and the Principal's lair, and traipsed right out the front door of the school. Brittany hopped on her too-small one-speed bicycle with the banana seat and high handlebars, then pedaled her way down the hill and over to Main Street. She'd decided to have a little fun with it, and she was in a hurry anyways, so she hadn't changed out of her short wool skirt and stockings before leaving school. Once at the customer's house, she pulled Mrs. Chase's mower out of the grey carriage shed in the back, unbuttoned her blue oxford blouse and tied it loosely closed with a knot over her midriff, and went to work in the dimming fall sun.

There was a regular parade out front of the house after school - cars going by three and four times. The boy's Varsity soccer team jogged by in loose formation.

Strange, the practice field is on the other side of town… Word gets around.

More cars went by. Some of the cars stopped, right in the street, while drivers and passengers took an extra-long look. Now some College Boys were running laps around Mrs. Chase's block.

The yard was almost done. Brittany's hard work in the heat had caused her to sweat her shirt wet with dark stains where it gathered against her skin.

The right car stopped.

Brittany stopped, too, and shut off the mower. She stretched her arms, arched her back, and looked back over her shoulder right at the street and her new spectator. Jeff turned off the car and leaned his tawny head out of the window. His sedan blocked the street, but he didn't really care at the moment, and no one in traffic that day was going to bother a boy who stopped for a couple of minutes to talk to THAT pretty girl wearing THAT getup while she mowed. Formal, prim, brief, hard-working, and a knock-out. Wow!

The police car went by on the side of the street closest to Brittany, the lane that was still moving. Now that the Chief knew what the traffic jam was all about, he really didn't give a shit. *Twenty years ago and I'd a-stopped, fershure!* He took a look at Brittany as he passed, silently whistled to himself as he quickly averted his gaze, and filed that one as one of the "happy to be knocked-ups." He thought she and that Jeff kid would *probably make a good couple once they're all growed up, and those two'll tough it out okay in the meantime until they do.*

Jeffrey waited until the police car was well out of the way and then yelled across the street. "Brittany! Need a ride home?" He hardly expected any answer, let alone a yes, but circumstances - her legs, mainly - required that he make a public offer.

Brittany walked to the edge of the sidewalk. "Jeffrey, right?"

"Yat's me! So… You need a ride up to your grandmother's place?" Not a chance in Hell, but can't hurt to ask…

Brittany carefully strolled out in the road to Jeffrey's car, timing her foray into the road so that the cars in BOTH lanes had to stop, and conscious that half the town was looking at her now or would be hearing about it later. She leaned in close to the window, so that no one else would hear. "I'm hot. Take me to the river. I'll be done here in a couple of minutes."

Jeffrey's mouth opened, but nothing came out.

Brittany waited.

Someone about ten cars back on her side honked.

Brittany stepped back onto the sidewalk and pointed to the driveway that led between houses to the carriage shed. "Maybe you should let all these other cars get going?"

"Uhyut." Jeffrey snapped out of it, started up the car, and cut in front of traffic that had just started moving again to pull into the driveway. He stretched back with his arm around the back of the empty passenger seat. "I'll be waiting. However long it takes." The boy was all smiles now! *Swimming! The possibilities!* He also wasn't convinced she wasn't putting him on.

Brittany went back to the mower, fired it up with a tremendously dramatic pull on the starter cord, then mowed the last two passes up the middle. As she went by the car to put the mower back in the shed, she asked Jeff to put her bike and bookbag in the trunk.

The bike didn't fit all the way. Jeff fiddled with a bungee cord and left a handlebar sticking out in the end. It helped him to have a task to concentrate on, though. *Hoya shit, I guess she's seriously going to come for a ride!*

When she got in the car, Jeffrey announced a problem: "Ah, Brittany? Ah... I... Need to go to my house. Didn't expect to swim in October, ya know?"

"Oohhhh, I don't think we'll need swimming suits. You can find a place like that, can't you? Can't WAIT to hit the water, it feels like a HUNDRED DEGREES today!"

Jeffrey suddenly felt hot, too. He didn't waste any time getting to a suitable swimming hole, that was sure!

Twenty minutes later, Brittany stood in still summer-warm river water up to her armpits. Her breasts bobbed on the water in front of her. She looked at Jeffrey, who was Not Swimming in the water about ten feet away. Mostly, he'd been watching her while he pretended to Get Ready To Dive In. *Hmmmm. I guess I didn't need any of those things from the bottom drawer, did I?* She smirked, and then took a deep breath. "Jeffrey? Do you want to? You CAN, if you want to. I actually wish you would." She wriggled her shoulders, just the tiniest bit, and bit her lower lip into her mouth. "Would you go get my backpack out of the trunk, Jeffrey? There's something we need out of it."

Brittany enjoyed a long and curious look at Jeffrey's naked, chiseled and youthful body as he scrambled out of the water, into his unlaced sneakers, and up the bank to his car. *Hmmmrrrgggh!* She suddenly wanted to sink her fingers and teeth into him. *Oh! So we're really going to do this...* Brittany was nervous as all Hell, but she wasn't going to show it. And this boy was making it easier, letting her call the shots. In control. She immersed herself one more time and then Jeffrey was there on the bank, naked and muscular and hard, holding her bag, and she was coming out of the water to meet him.

Jeffrey's eyes bugged out.

"Unzip the little pocket in the front. Yes, that one. Grab two of them."

Jeffrey quivered as Brittany fussed with the condoms. She'd never done this before, so it took a minute.

"Come back in the water, please." Brittany backed up until she was submerged to the armpits again. "And Jeff? The less this gets around, the more likely it will happen again. Okay?" Brittany held out her arms for him to step into. "Now come here."

***

"WELL, how was it?"

Tabitha was full of questions that Brittany wasn't sure she should actually answer.

"Are you SURE you want to hear about all of this?"

Tabitha nodded avidly and quickly in wide-eyed near-horror. Her face softened. "Well, who else are you going to tell, and how else am I going to know how it is with those boy-parts involved?" She made a show of bracing herself, teeth clenched, eyes squinted squeamishly, head pulled back away. "Soooo?"

Brittany sighed, closed her eyes, and drew a deep breath. She nearly growled out the last word: "It was AWWWWSOME!!!" She composed herself. "Oh, I have GOT to have that again!" She calmed down a little more and inspected her friend to see how she was holding up.

Tabitha looked more than a bit crestfallen. "THAT good?"

"Well, it hurt a little at first. We did it in the water. I've heard that helps a bit. Not sure, there... kind of sore, still, actually. But it was WORTH it, oh, Tabitha you've GOT to try it!!"

Tabitha's red hair stood in counterpoint to her face, which had paled behind her veil of freckles. The girl's mouth skewed sideways like she was contemplating a put-off chore. "I'll pass." She wondered briefly about tetanus or rabies or leeches, there in the river. She shivered. "Ick." She got the squeamish expression again. "So did he, you know... IN you?"

"Yah." Brittany got a distant look in her eye and laughed. "I thought we were going to fall over and drown!"

"Aren't you worried about being pregnant?"

Brittany chuckled. "Hell, no. I got him to wear two of those things, in case one leaked or broke."

Tabitha frowned. "TWO?!? I've heard you can't get a boy to wear ONE of them, let alone TWO! They HATE those things!"

Brittany smiled seductively. "I didn't negotiate. I told him he'd last longer. Get to hold me longer. Be against my naked body longer. Be IN me longer. I convinced him!" Brittany smiled a victorious smile.

"You've convinced me!" Tabitha gnawed on her lip for a moment. "Puh-LEASE?" She eyed her friend with hunger.

"No, you had your turn. More times than anyone else has or probably will. I'm sorry girlfriend, I really am."

Tabitha sighed.

***

Brittany and Tabitha were doing Tuesday evening homework on the kitchen table at the farmhouse as an early-Fall snow gently swirled down outside. The sudden change of weather was surprising every time it happened, but normal. Sometimes snow came down even before all the leaves were gone from the trees. This year the weather had been hot as all Hades right up 'til Halloween, then the Arctic had descended on them. Grandma Wendell had made them a warm and filling wintertime supper of Shepard's Pie and then the girls had helped clean up the kitchen and went out to the shed to split some firewood. Now they were hitting the books by the warm wood-fired cookstove while Hattie put up a new batch of gingerbread cookies. Good to be available nearby for taste-testing on an evening like that....

Hattie held a kitchen curtain aside, looking out the window at the growing storm. "It's picking up out there, Tabitha. They don't take very good care of this road at night, you know…"

Brittany looked up from a textbook. "I'm not even sure they have the PLOWS on yet." She was referring to the town road trucks. Last she knew, the large, detachable wing-plows were all lined up in a row down at the municipal garage, awaiting colder days. Sometimes they went on before Halloween, sometimes they went on the first of December.

Hattie let the curtain drop. "Well, colder days seem to have arrived!"

Brittany chuckled ruefully. *Not bicycling weather anymore! Shit....*

A voice came out of the mop of red hair bent close over an anthology of literature: "Just a few more sections, Grandma Wendell.

Then I should probably go…" She didn't yet have snow tires on that big boat of a car her father let her use. The snow probably wouldn't amount to much, but the road down to the village WAS curvy and she didn't want to chance slippery corners. At the same time, the Wendell kitchen was a cozy place to do homework, with a ready supply of coffee or tea and snacks such as the cookies that were just coming out of the oven built into the side of the ancient woodstove. There was also the side benefit of ready access to her pretty, if no-longer available lab partner. Tabitha felt comfy here, and was loathe to leave.

Hattie wondered what Tabitha's kitchen was like. Was it hard being a school-aged lesbian in her home? Were her parents angry? Supportive? Disappointed? Worried about grandchildren someday? Unaware? *Are there other reasons why she's up here so much?* Hattie didn't really know Tabitha's people. She decided to ask around at the next Blue Line club… *No. That might expose secrets.*

"Tabitha?"

The girls kept doing their homework. Tabitha answered distractedly: "Yeup?"

"Is your home safe for you? To be… yourself in, I mean?"

Both girls put down their homework.

"You mean, do my parents know I like girls? Yes. They can't figure out whether it's cute or gross, but they're glad I'm not going to be getting pregnant on a date. They think it will pass when I meet the Right Boy, later."

"Will it?"

"I don't think so. Mom and Dad will probably have a bit of a fit when they realize that. But yes, I'm safe. I'm lucky, I guess. There's another… Someone else in town who is grounded, literally locked in her bedroom, until they find a boy in there with her."

"Oh dear."

While Hattie sat in her rocker by the wood-fired range and thought about that, the girls went back to doing homework. The clock in the parlor tick-tocked, pencils and highlighters scratched, chairs creaked, the fire in the range popped. The lights flickered a couple of times, as they often do on rural electrical services.

A little later, Brittany's grandmother had more questions. "May I pry?"

Tabitha winced a little, preparing. She expected a question about "what's it like," or "what do you do," or something voyeuristic like that. She nodded, and steeled herself.

Hattie Wendell unfortunately knew EXACTLY what THOSE TWO did, or at least far more about it than she wanted to. She'd just been to the doctor in the village and gotten her own prescription for various cardiac medicines related to that little incident. "You're up here an awful lot. That's why I wondered. Are you two… a couple?"

Tabitha colored a little. She smiled, but she looked pained. Brittany looked at her friend expectantly.

Tabitha took a deep breath and kept her eyes carefully on Grandma Wendell as she answered. "It's a nice place to do homework. But I could do homework at my house. I love her. Brittany. LOVE her. She won't give me the time of day anymore, and I know that, but I still want to be around her. Every minute of every day. So we have this instead. Homework. It's enough." She turned towards Brittany. "It's nice, actually. Uncomplicated. In a complicated sort of way. I'm hoping for a miracle, though. You already knew that."

Brittany took Tabitha's hand. "Sorry, girlfriend. Boys are just WHERE IT'S AT for me. If I didn't like chest hair and beard stubble and penises (Grandma you didn't hear that), then you'd be the first one to know, I think. But we still wouldn't date. Not like that. I'm not that kind of girl. Coupled, I mean."

A horrified Hattie was suddenly very sorry she had brought the matter up. Tabitha was sad, and Brittany had just given both of them much more information than maybe they wanted to have. She wondered if Tabitha already knew all that.

Tabitha smiled at her friend. "I know." She sighed, and started gathering up her things. "I think it's time to go."

Tabitha was in the middle of stuffing her backpack - hurriedly - when Brittany stopped her and took the backpack away to set it in a chair so she could give her friend a long hug, then a kiss on the cheek. She stepped back, held Tabitha at arm's length, and said, "You're just smitten with me 'cause I'm HOT. The next pretty girl comes along, you'll forget all about me and I'll be doing homework alone up here ever after."

Tabitha replied, high-pitched and tight-voiced, "Probably!" She giggled, even as she wiped a single tear out of the corner of an eye. She put on her coat and grabbed her backpack, gave Hattie a brief hug and then sprinted to the kitchen door, where she stopped short with her hand on the doorknob. "Oh SHIT!"

Tabitha's car lay half-buried in the yard, a wind-blown drift piled up high against the driver's door and hood.

Tabitha turned her head back to the kitchen with wide eyes. "It's a frigg… erated BLIZZARD out there!"

Hattie and Brittany came over to look out adjacent windows.

Brittany thought it was funny. "Oooops!"

"Oh dear. THIS wasn't in the forecast at all…" Hattie turned to Tabitha. "I think you'd better spend the night, Tabitha. The couch, or should I make up another bedroom upstairs?"

Tabitha giggled. "The couch will be fine. Almost like old times!"

Hattie reconsidered. "Yes, I guess it better be the couch, down here where I can keep an eye on you…"

Brittany squinted over at her red-headed friend. "You PLANNED this, didn't you?!? Well, just because you got lucky, don't think you're getting LUCKY!" She held out her arm primly and then she and Tabitha walked off arm-in-arm to the linen closet in the front of the house.

Hattie yelled after them: "Tabitha, don't forget to call your folks, they'll worry!"

***

The three of them had a very nice pee-jay party in the living room watching television. By mutual accord they treated it like a Saturday, instead of a school night. Hattie wasn't even sure they'd have school tomorrow. Tabitha was already tucked in sideways on the couch, under a thick layer of wool blankets. Brittany sat on the floor in front of her, leaning up on the couch. Hattie was in a rocker pulled up by Tabitha's head. She was sitting up with them, nursing a small glass of sherry and seeing late-night television for the first time in six or eight years. She was the one who had invited Tabitha to stay over, after all.

Sometime after ten the power went out.

Hattie was ready for that. She already had candles and matches handy. There were three glass-and-tin candle-lanterns by her chair.

"Here you go, girls. That's our signal to hit the hay! Brittany, can I have a hand up the stairs?"

A questioning look flickered across Brittany's face and was gone. "Sure, Grandma. Give me a couple of minutes?" Brittany went to brush her teeth.

Hattie loitered by the couch for a minute. "Tabitha, do I need to protect her virtue? Make up a couple of rules?" Her voice was stern but shaky - she was quaking with laughter at the strangeness of it. But inside, she also felt genuinely bad for this nice and nearly heartbroken young girl. She didn't want the night to get... *complicated.*

Tabitha thought it was embarrassment that caused the woman's voice to get all tremulous. "No, don't worry. She's a GOOD friend and I won't screw that up."

"Do not ask for more before saying thankyou for what you have received. Old proverb." Hattie went over to the darkened TV, unplugged it, and then turned off the switch at the now-dark lamp. "It'll be nice to have you around for breakfast. I miss cooking for your appetite!" She gave the girl a pat on the shoulder through the blanket, and turned.

Brittany came back into the room, kissed Tabitha primly on the top of the head, and then helped her grandmother up the stairs to bed.

***

Sometime in the night Tabitha was woken up by her own smile... her mouth stretched so wide and big it hurt her cheeks. She must have been dreaming, of course. Then Brittany's breath was close in her ear.

Brittany whispered again: "Tabitha, wake UP."

Tabitha opened her eyes and saw a flannel nightshirt hovering in the dark above her. She came more awake and realized that Brittany was standing by the arm of the couch, bent low over her. Tabitha sat up. The house loomed dark around them. She whispered, "Am I getting lucky?"

In a low voice, Brittany replied, "I want to dance. Help me with the chairs."

"Huh?" But Tabitha got up and helped Brittany carry the couch back from the television.

"On THREE. One, two, THREE."

The heavy couch was hard work. It thumped and scraped a couple of times on the way across the polished hardwood floor.

"Here's good. Let's scoot these chairs back..."

Now they had a ten-by-ten space in front of the fireplace (which was now the TeeVee place, the chimney having been stuffed with insulation and capped years ago). Brittany went over to the old Hi-Fi record player in the corner and reached underneath for the cord. "Power's on." She clicked on a small lamp and searched a rack of records until she found what she was looking for.

Tabitha came up behind her to follow Brittany's finger across the spines of the record sleeves. "Should I put on some clothes?" Having been un-prepared, her peejays for this sleep-over consisted of yesterday's bra and underwear.

"Dancing will keep us warm." Brittany pulled a record out of its sleeve and put it on the turntable. She set both their candle-lanterns, still burning, on the high mantle, where they cast a warm orange glow through the immediate area. Brittany switched off the little lamp, and the recesses of the room faded to brown as she carefully dropped the needle of the Hi-Fi onto the spinning record. "Grandma has some really great old records."

The music started, quiet and low and tinny. A brass big-band opening spilled onto their candle-lit dance floor. Brittany grabbed Tabitha's hand and pulled her to the center of the room.

Tabitha tried to follow her friend's lead to the unfamiliar music, and then suddenly the corner of her mouth went up as she recognized "Baby It's Cold Outside." *That old song by Frank Leosser....* It's a crooning duet, one about seduction - or maybe coercion - that people always sing around Christmas, for some reason. *Frank Leosser. No shit.* Under her breath, she muttered, "You have GOT to be KIDDING me." But she was all smiles now.

Brittany remained silent, aloof, businesslike, apparently more interested in the music and their choreography than anything else.

They held each other and spun apart and together and twirled through the night and the candlelight and the storm.

***

When Hattie Wendell came down in the morning, the blankets were neatly folded and stacked on the couch. She went over to the kitchen door, flipped on a lamp, and peeked under the curtain to check the yard. Tabitha's car was still there, still buried. There was no sign of either girl. Hattie turned on the radio and shortly heard the expected: no school just about everywhere. It looked like her Brittany already knew that, or she'd be up now. The woman made a batch of her farmhouse muffins, and while they were baking in the wood-fired oven she put on some bacon and eggs and coffee. The scents filled the kitchen.

No girls.

Well I'm not making THAT mistake again! Hattie set breakfast up to keep for a while and found projects to keep her busy - there were plenty of those at the farmhouse that morning, mostly involving firewood, snow, and suddenly-cooped up chickens who protested from inside the far end of the the shed.

Finally, an hour later than usual, Brittany literally slunk into the kitchen in a sweatshirt, a sheepish grimace on her face. She stopped at a cupboard for glasses and then went to the fridge so she could pour two cups of cider.

Hattie briefly speculated to herself on a lot of things, including whether her granddaughter was parading around in that extra-long sweatshirt without anything decent on underneath. *That girl!*

"When in Rome, Grandma!" Brittany winked and started back towards the stairs.

Hattie shook her head. *No shame, that one.* She sighed. *Nothing to be done about it now.* She yelled after the retreating figure, almost sternly: "I am afraid I am a BAD influence! I should chase both you girls out of that room and into some chores RIGHT NOW!" She sighed again, laughed, and then yelled at her granddaughter's receding back: "Are you two hungry yet?"

The voice wafted back from the front of the house, musically: "Sure am now that I smelled it!"

"Mmmmmmm Hmmm." *That DOES seem to be how it worked out. How do I put a stop to it now? I should have never let that girl sleep over the first time, if I'd known?* She sighed again.

"Sorry!"

Hattie could tell from the muffled echo that Brittany was ascending the front stairs. She talked up through the register, that open screen in the ceiling that let heat from the kitchen go into the upstairs hallway. They sometime used it as an intercom. "I'll lay out breakfast!"

The response chimed down through the register in stereo: "We'll be right down!"

"Scoot along! You two will need the fuel! You have a lot of shoveling ahead of you!"

They came into the kitchen a moment later.

Hattie furtively scrutinized them: Tabitha looked a bit tousled - *but who doesn't in the morning* - and a little embarrassed. She was wearing one of Brittany's sweatshirts, over-large on the smaller red-head, and she was wearing *(or NOT wearing) God knows what or not underneath* - the hem came down to the young woman's knees. Brittany reached down into the fridge and bent over to... Hattie looked at a spot somewhere else, then realized it had never mattered when her granddaughter had come down in a morning sweatshirt on any other day. "Good lord." Hattie held out a basket of muffins, while theatrically turning her head sideways. "I just don't know about you two." She closed her eyes to steel herself and then decided to start the morning over again: "Tabitha, I'll assume you found the couch uncomfortable."

Tabitha eyed the treasure in the heavy wicker muffin-basket and carefully scrutinized the contents before selecting just the right muffin. "Yum. Thankyou!" She took a plate from the table and then wandered over to look out the window at the already-half-shoveled front walk. The snow-shovel was stuck haphazardly into a snowbank down by a white pile that probably contained her car.

Hattie smirked. "Well, young lady, you certainly got lucky, didn't you?" She shook her finger at Brittany: "Don't you get any BOYS snowed in up here...."

Brittany was politely holding a porcelain plate in one hand - to catch crumbs - and a piece of muffin in the other, chewing, grinning, and trying to avoid Tabitha's eye.

"You'll have your work cut out for you to get that car out. Tabitha, do you want to borrow some boots?" Hattie scowled at the naked legs on display and tried not to think of those same limbs twined together there under the sheets up there this morning. Then she realized she was making rather a big assumption. *What if it WAS just a sleep-over this time? Is Brittany just twisting my tail? So confusing, these two!*

Brittany spoke around a mouthful of muffin. "Don't worry. We're confused, too."

Tabitha reached for another piece of muffin. "How do you two do that? Yes, I'm going to have to, I think." The snow was two feet deep, even where it hadn't piled up against walls and mailboxes and cars.

Brittany's grandmother said, "Runs in the family." She paused. "Don't give the farmhouse a reputation, girls." *I didn't mind bare legs BEFORE I knew they were sleeping together....*

The girls ate a very light breakfast, drank coffee, and then headed back upstairs to get into clothing they could shovel in. As they left the room, Brittany affectionately grabbed Tabitha's hand and held it up close behind her own back to pull her friend along. Brittany yelled back to her grandmother in the kitchen as they reached the front stairs: "Just pretend we're Danish!"

A little while later, as Brittany's grandmother pondered what on Earth "Danish" had to do with it, she heard someone drawing water for a bath. There was a lot of sloshing and splashing, and some giggling, and then she heard the tub drain for a minute. They'd overfilled it, apparently. Then more splashing as one of them (*or probably both of them knowing Those Two*) got in. *My, those girls are taking a THOROUGH turn through Rome! Oh, dear goodness.* Hattie had a brief moment of panic when she really thought to herself about it. *HOW on EARTH did I end up running a BORDELLO for that young...* No, that wasn't true. Tabitha was the ONLY person that spent the night. And it had started innocently enough. Being housemates with a teen was fraught with moral dilemmas.

What if Brittany was doing all that up there with a BOY? Hattie needed a second to get THAT unbidden picture out of her head. *Less of a heart-attack, I suppose....* Her step hitched as she had a sudden realization: *Well, she doesn't seem to have LASTING relationships with THAT gender. Or does she? Is that what I'd approve of? At this young age? But why is it okay for my granddaughter to be up here writing the New Arabian Nights with a GIRL, when I'd be having a FIT if there was a BOY up there?* She started walking again, and then realized she didn't remember where she'd been headed. The old woman shrugged. *No matter. I'll...* She frowned again. *It doesn't make SENSE. It all started with that sleep-over... Was I supposed to break them up right in the middle, that first time? Does THAT happen often at sleep-overs these days? My God!*

Hattie thought back to 'Bundling', as it used to be called, and one eyebrow twitched up. There was a day, long before her own time, when early settlers used to throw young people into the same bed for the night - fully dressed, and they'd better be fully dressed when they got out in the morning. A common rite of courtship or matchmaking. Ostensibly to visit, and then sleep. The more conservative households threw a wide board between the two young people. The households that didn't have a board to spare? More layers of clothing? Who knows? What happened in the dark, in the wee hours of the night, was a matter of speculation, but it was a socially-accepted way of encouraging courting and pairing for people about this very age, in some regions of Colonial America.

And now? Now that there are more than five houses in a county? Now that young people seem to fall in love with whoever? Too complicated to suss it all out! Hattie put her hands on her hips, unconsciously, and sighed. *I'll let Brittany be Brittany and just enjoy having young people in the house again. However they come.* Hattie giggled. *WHY did I put it THAT way?*

Hattie couldn't figure out whether to be horrified or amused, so she simply accepted her new reality. Nothing up there offended her sensibilities too awfully much, even if it wasn't "proper" by the standards she was raised on. There really WAS love there, even if Brittany was too young to know it. And her granddaughter was a nearly-grown working woman now, out of the house and earning money, even if it was only from mowing lawns and babysitting. *A lot more responsible than many of them, even if she was still in the school system. Is she an adult?* It was best that she didn't have to outright HIDE anything here, where she lived and ate and slept. And now loved. *Poor, clueless girl.* Hattie wasn't even sure that Brittany knew she might be getting in romantic trouble.

She heard giggling, and the sound of water running through the pipes as the tub drained. She yelled up through the register, "Ask Tabitha if she can help you shovel the porch roof, too…" *Useful, having young people around again.* Last winter, during a couple of storms that the rest of the Wendell family missed due to being out of town, Hattie had to hire a boy to shovel the porch roof and in front of the shed. *Jeffrey, I think his name was. Nice boy. Hmmmph.* At least it WASN'T Jeffrey, or any other boy, here now. Hattie was sure that BOTH of them - her and Brittany - would be in trouble with certain folks down in the village if the girl DID get pregnant. *No chance of that here. Don't fret yourself into a funk, Hattie. Don't borrow trouble!*

***

The heavy snow went away in a week of alternating rain and cold sun, but the frost stayed around and sometimes the rain froze to the ground. Color left the Hollow, as even the yellow leaves of the popples blew away. The world was now a palette of muted greys and browns and dead straw-yellows. Night came early, often before Brittany pedaled one of her bicycles into the yard. Hattie Wendell worried about that.

So did Brittany, for different reasons. She had two bikes (her childhood one-speed and a mountain-bike with gears and brakes that she'd bought with her own money, there was a Story there, and she tried not to think about THAT too much). She supposed she could put lights, front and back, on one of them. Probably the mountain bike, since it was more versatile and easier on her legs when she was coming back up the steep road out of town.

Unfortunately, Brittany wanted a job down the valley at the Junction, in the commercial strip. She pictured a waitressing job at Pizza Place or Chummie's or some busy restaurant like that. She was sixteen. She could work after school and on weekends. She could drive. But she lacked two things: a car, and a license to operate it. Brittany had passed the Driver's Ed class at school last year, WITHOUT doing a single mile of out-of-school practice on her learner's permit. She was fairly confident she could pass a road test if she was familiar with the car. The problem was the car. If she could get the car, she could practice on the back roads up in the Hollow and then she could get Grandma Wendell to accompany her to the local D.M.V. office to take her license exam.

A car, even a twelve-year-old and rusted-out junker, was an expensive item for a girl whose sole source of legitimate income up to this point had been yard work, baby-sitting, and roof-shoveling. Brittany was not quite sure she wanted to clean out her savings, even if a car would get her down the road to a more regular job with more regular money. She'd worked HARD and at some amount of risk to get that money in the bank - *there's that Story again*, and she smiled to herself in spite of all the negative that lurked in that place. *So that's where THAT money ought to stay for the time being....*

Brittany drummed her fingers on the kitchen table.

"Everything alright, dear?" You're awfully quiet, tonight…"

"I'm working on a problem." Brittany's math textbook lay open in front of the girl's unfocused eyes. She hadn't touched her pencil in fifteen minutes.

Hattie took it at face value. On her way out of the room and up to bed she rested her hand on the top of Brittany's head. "Don't fry your brain."

"Thanks, Grandma. You want an arm on the stairs?"

"No, thankyou, dear. I'm having a good day."

"You SURE?"

"Positive as pie. Goodnight." Hattie stepped slowly off into the recesses of the house.

Brittany listened intently for the five minutes it took her grandmother to navigate the length of the darkening house, shutting off lamps and closing curtains as was her habit, and then shuffle carefully up the stairs, one step at a time. Step, rest. Step, rest. Step, rest. Fourteen creaks. She refused help five times for every once that she asked for it. Brittany dreaded what she would hear some time when her grandmother refused help on an evening she needed it. The house noises stopped. Grandma Wendell had settled in.

A car. Tap, tap, tap went the fingers. Brittany squinted. Smiled. Squinted back into deep thought. Her eyebrows went up as the solution gelled. She nodded her head and spoke aloud: "Michael Frey…."

Brittany had a PLAN. NOW she could finish her math homework!

***

Brittany Wendell's 'Plans-with-a-P," as she called them, usually worked to her expectation, after a fashion. They also often resulted in a Grounding - she'd be limited to school and her bedroom for a week or two.

Her most locally well-known and notorious "Plan" had resulted in a noisy and dramatic rescue by gleeful members of the Collegeville Fire Department, and was a good illustration of how things usually went awry:

When Brittany was eleven, she took a dare from a classmate named Livvy, the dare turned into a Plan, and the Plan turned into an adventure that left Brittany stranded overnight in the deep, dark cellar of a crumbling mansion on the outskirts of Collegeville.

She'd snuck out of her own safe and comfortable home and into the falling-down, rotting mansion because nobody was EVER going to call her a chicken, and also because Livvy was cool and intriguing and Brittany really wanted to impress her and maybe even be friends! The first part of the adventure went exactly according to the Plan: Brittany climbed into the falling-down house through a missing window and carved her initials into the now-substantial tree that was growing up right through the living room and out a hole in the roof, all as planned.

After that was when things started to go awry on her. As she backed up to admire her work with a flashlight, she'd gone through a soft spot in the floor. She hit her head on the way through and been quite knocked out by the sudden end of her little trip.

Brittany Wendell came-to in a dark and dank dirt-floored void and discovered that the living room was over a VERY deep cellar. The stairs had long-ago rotted away, the few boards and tree-trunks were all too slippery or steep to climb, and the rock walls shifted and crumbled whenever she tried to put any real weight on them. She had the good sense to give up trying to claw her way out, lest she fall again or cause the decaying foundation to cave in on top of her, and had spent the rest of the night in the pitch-black, haunted gloom of a large house gone back to nature.

Her parents had discovered her missing in the morning, interrogated her friend, uncovered the dare, and gone looking for their adventurous daughter. Walt found his daughter and was headed back home to get a ladder when word got out - probably via Livvy's family - and the whole town suddenly reacted in pure manic-panic-joy. The fire siren went off with a long and deep wail - Brittany, still in her dungeon two miles away, had heard that. Ten minutes later, Walter Wendell - on his way back up with a ladder strapped to the roof of his car - had to pull over to let the Collegeville fire truck go by. He followed the fire truck as it went bounding and swaying up the access road, through a farm, and to the mansion. After ten minutes of commotion and all manner of discussion and arguing and hand-wringing and excited posturing, the volunteer fire crew eventually lowered a ladder down to the floor of Brittany's gloomy trap.

The farmer spent the rest of the day rounding up his cows - the fire truck's screeching up-and-down siren and flashing lights made sure of that. They'd bulled right through the farmyard just when the cows were lined up in the road to enter the Milking Parlor.

The Fire Department boys retired to the local VFW and regaled themselves with all the technical prowess and close calls involved in lowering a ladder to a child stuck in a cellar-hole. (It's not their fault, really. Collegeville had been having an exceptionally good run of luck, and short of an insurance-fraud arson, there hadn't been a rippin' good structure fire for several years. Those poor men were bored out of their minds!)

Brittany spent the first day of her freedom (from the cellar) confined (to her room), alternately getting cuts and scrapes examined and re-cleaned or getting chewed out by whichever of her parents were maddest at that particular moment.

Her father ended up meting out Brittany's punishments after several hours of turmoil at the Wendell house: she was grounded for a week for sneaking out, and she was grounded for two MORE weeks for not leaving a note saying where she was sneaking TO and when she'd be back. Ever the pragmatic one, Walter Wendell. He had to be - by the time this little girl was the tender age of eleven, he'd become well-acquainted with the disasters that resulted from her little "Plans-with-a-P." He could tell it would get worse - *best to leave her some wiggle-room that will hopefully assist in future rescues, if it comes to that.*

NOW Brittany had another plan in the long line of carefully mapped-out misadventures. This particular scheme would have massive downstream implications for Brittany, and for others as well. Some of them would be welcome... others not so much.

***

Michael Frey was one of those boys who could build a car out of the random collection of junk in someone's yard - and had. His cars looked GOOD, too. They were wire-brushed and sanded and Bond-O'd and primed and painted and buffed and painted again and polished and generally worked over until they gleamed. You would never know it, but each of those cars started as a rusted-out junker in somebody's field.

Michael rebuilt the first one the summer before he got his Learner's Permit, so he could drive around in style while his mother or his father supervised from the seat beside him. Michael did all his practice driving on a powder-blue Plymouth with a jacked-up back end and headers, whatever they were. Usually only a few like-minded individuals could understand most of what he said when he talked cars: his father and older brothers and maybe some of the local car mechanics. His father and his big brother helped him out on that first one, and then Michael Frey was off on his own, building and selling about two a year. He'd drive a finished project for a month or two, then sell it to the buy the parts he needed for the next "rescued rig" from someone's field or barn - many of which he managed to get for free, or near to it. As far as cars and car parts went, he was born as shrewd a dealer as they ever came.

He reminded Brittany very much of a little weasel. Something about his pinched nose and the placement of his eyes and his small stature just looked... weasel-ish. At least to her. And he acted the part, in her opinion. Brittany couldn't STAND him in school, even though he was two grades ahead of her and rarely in her orbit. She found that for some strange reason she also couldn't stop looking at him whenever he circled by. Unfortunately, even though she disliked him thoroughly and completely, she WANTED the boy - she'd figured out that much. Ever since she was fourteen. He'd come into sight and she'd get all stupid and mushy inside. *It's SO UNFAIR that the total ASSHOLES always make you want to wrap your arms and legs around them right where they are whenever you pass them standing in the hall by their locker!* She would do ANYTHING for five minutes of kissing him - she'd either eat him alive, face-first, or swoon into repose right there on the floor with him, she wasn't sure which - and he didn't know and probably didn't care. Brittany hadn't said word one to him the whole time they were in school, and she doubted he noticed her. She'd been relieved when he started going off to the vocational school for part of the day in his Junior year.

He's going to notice me NOW, though! Or so she hoped. She had a PLAN, one that tied in well with a different, bigger plan.

Michael was now a Senior in the Auto Trades program (big surprise there) at the regional vocational school. This month he was driving a restored shining green 1950's pickup with big chromed vertical exhaust pipes behind the cab and a custom stake-bed with a couch built into it, probably for the little drive-in fifteen miles down the road. For his next project car he was working on a four wheel drive truck.

Neither of those are really ME, but I can probably convince him to start some other project if I ask just right....

***

Brittany coasted down the Frey family's driveway on her bicycle one crisp, mid- November morning just a week later.

Michael's house wasn't hard to find: look for a big two-story, three-bay garage with all the trimmings behind a small, unadorned, single-story manufactured home.

Michael was in the garage re-installing the hood on a large four-by-four pickup. He looked up at movement in the driveway outside. "Wh... Ahh, hi. Brittany, right?"

Brittany had decided to play coy. "Ahuh." She dismounted her bike, laid it down, and stood with her legs twisted across at the ankles and her hands behind her back. "Watcha doin?" Girlish. Innocent. Flighty.

"Workin' on this truck. New, well, rebuilt actually, engine." He put his wrench down on a cart and stood up to size her up. "Little nipple-ee for bikin' by now, ain't-tit?" He leered at the curve of her legs right where they disappeared up under her plaid shirt.

Oh, good! Keep looking, you horny little shit.... "Just a little!" She crossed her arms behind her back again, and swayed side-to-side. "I was kind of hoping you could help me with that..."

"You want to buy a car? Well, the Chevy 'll be for sale in about three months when I finish with this here mud truck..."

"Actually, I was thinking more of a trade... And sooner."

Michael scowled. "There's a good used car lot up to the Jones place. I know it looks like a junkyard, but there be treasure up there, trust me. I could go with you if you're worried about finding something decent..." He laughed at her. "I don't think they take ten-speeds in trade."

"Michael?" She stopped and waited until she was sure he was paying attention. "I would do ANYTHING for a car. Well, anything for YOU."

Michael looked at her with a little more interest now. Something in the tone of her voice... He noticed she was wearing a couple of flannel shirts, but those weren't pants. He realized she was wearing very tight black leggings instead. *Bet there's a real nice ass there somewhere there under the tail of those long shirts.... Hmmmmm.* But Michael Frey was also scowling a bit still. He didn't think he'd heard right... *or maybe I'm misunderstanding something?* His eyebrows went up. *Maybe SHE doesn't understand what she's getting into!*

Brittany filled the silence in the garage: she left coy behind and laid it out straight: "I want a car. Nice enough to get me through two more years of school and back and forth to a job, probably on the strip down at The Junction. Doesn't have to be stellar, like the ones you work over normally, but DEPENDABLE is a must."

Michael had already ducked back under the hood of the truck as *this greedy-needy little philly went blah, blah, blah. Yah, whatever.* He clicked a socket onto his wrench. "Heard that a million times before." *I'm not the state welfare agency for spoiled little-* "whatever."

I'll fix THAT in a hurry. Brittany smirked lecherously. "I'll give you four hours. I'll do ANYTHING you want me to. ANYTHING. To you. Four hours only."

Michael hit the back of his head on the hood of the truck. He held his tongue, though, because he suddenly sure wanted to hear the rest of THIS!

"Then you put me together a car. When the car is finished, you call me, and I'll pick it up, and I want the title, too, and then I'll give you four more hours. And you can do ANYTHING you want to me. ANYTHING."

She had his shocked-silent, open-mouthed attention NOW.

"Just please don't hurt me too much, and be gentle, if you can, because I'm new at this. Do you think that would maybe work out for us, Michael?" Brittany crossed her arms behind her back again, and bounced on her feet as if in anxiety. Her small curves put on a show with all the added bouncing, even under the two heavy flannel shirts.

Michael finally found his speech. "JESUS, girl!"

"No, I don't think Jesus has very much to do with this. Don't make me regret it later." Brittany looked Michael up and down. "Are your parents home?"

Michael shook his head. His weaselish smirk was back, but the corners of his mouth were WAY higher than Brittany had ever seen them before.

"Michael, you're DIRTY. Let's go take a shower. Your four hours start when you're CLEAN." She walked up and give him a wet and lingering kiss on the least-greasy of his two cheeks. "Ready?"

Oh yeah. He was ready!

***

That little car deal would come back to haunt Michael in a short few years.

Michael got a job in the local car dealership after he was all done with school. There, he gradually came to realize that he didn't like working on OTHER people's cars. Salt and slush and road-grime raining down on you when the winter tires were going on and coming off. Filthy engines. Even dirtier interiors, with boogers on the stick shift and on the side of the seat and God-knows-what on the steering wheel.

On the fifth-year anniversary of his graduation from high school, Michael Frey took the police exam for the Fall Class at the Vermont Police Academy. He'd heard that the State Police and some of the city departments liked their new hires to be a little older, a little more experienced in the outside world, and to have a "real" career under their belts. One they could fall back on if things didn't work out in the world of policing. No harm done, no hurt feelings, no pressure; that kind of thing. Well, Michael had the car business to fall back on, and now he was ready to try something new.

He sat the exam with one hundred and three other hopefuls, young and old, realistic and pipe-dreaming and a few maybe clinically delusional. Some men and women were sitting the test for the Game Warden I and II positions (those were mostly the ones in jeans, boots, and flannel shirts, he'd bet). Some were sitting for municipal police openings, and who knows how many were sitting for State Police openings, like Michael. He'd sure like to be a Trooper! Michael wasn't above admitting that he liked to drive fast, and he'd heard that sometimes a Trooper would drive forty, fifty, seventy miles to get to an incident. That, and the salary of forty to fifty thou' a year had piqued his interest. Twice what he made in cars....

He was seated next to a forty-something-year-old guy with a potbelly, flabby arms, and bad B.O. This man wore a black "Darth Vader rules" t-shirt and dirty sweatpants with highly polished black leather military boots underneath them. The man-boy's fingers were still stained from the recent application of blacking spit-shined onto the boots. *One of the delusional ones, maybe? Yessireee!*

On his other side, one of the flannels: a woman with long braids and a blackwatch plaid shirt. She eyed the polished black boots and dirty sweatpants stuffed into them over there on Michael's neighbor and then raised an eyebrow minutely in Michael's direction.

He covered his mouth and nodded furtively.

A Test Proctor banged on a little bell to call them to order.

The exam was a thirty-question "Vermont Law Enforcement Candidate Exam" with questions that exposed your proficiency in math, logic, and problem-solving. Michael was done in five minutes. The prospective Imperial Trooper next to him scribbled and figured and worried for the full twenty-one minutes allotted.

The next exam was a pile of paper seven-hundred questions long. Some sort of psychological weed-out multiple-choice, one of the computer-scanned ones with all the ovals next to the responses. Seven hundred and twenty-three questions, somewhere upwards of twenty-nine hundred little ovals, like the SAT on steroids. *That will take care of stinky there*, sitting next chair up, already breathing fast and furiously erasing and re-erasing while setting his name and social on the top of the test.

It was a timed test. They were supposed to hurry. It still took most of two hours. Michael did not have time to go back and review his answers on the few questions he left blank "for later," against the test instructions. Sloth-and-polish to his left didn't get all the way to the last page of waiting ovals.

Finally, the last test. Well, no. Not a test, actually. "Background Investigation Application and Information." *Hmmmm.* Michael started filling in boxes and lines. A lot of the required information was stuff that he didn't know off the top of his head, like "postal address and telephone number of the two nearest neighbors at your last five addresses" and "street address of your elementary school(s)." He left blanks. They'd hit him up for it again, later, he figured. *Uh-oh.* Question number twenty:

Have you ever paid for sex? (Yes 0 / No 0)

Oh SHIT!!! Yes, or no. Only two choices. Fuck! Well, ya. And what good fucks it was! But he had no idea it was going to screw his career choice five years or more down the road... Shit!

Michael left it blank, with an asterisk. Down below, next to another asterisk he placed on the bottom of the page, he wrote: "Barter." He was feeling pretty glum when he left the exam.

It came up again at the polygraph.

***

They'd called this guy in for an exam, partly because the pool of candidates just wasn't that good, and partly because they were vicariously and professionally interested in just what kind of barter you could make for sex in rural Vermont. On a per-hour basis, polygraphs are surprisingly expensive, but they justified the time and cost as investigatory: Maybe there was some sort of weird new-age criminal enterprise trading maple syrup for sex or some wild thing like that? They couldn't imagine, but thought it would be amusing and possibly professionally enlightening to find out.

Michael was surprised and relieved when the Vermont State Police called him in early July. He'd just about given up on it.

And now here he was, on the appointed day, tied by five or six electrical leads and a blood-pressure cuff to this machine that was going to determine his future. He was relaxed. He'd never stolen much of anything past sixth grade, hadn't smoked a whole lot of dope in school, and remembered everything he'd done when drunk. What could they really find to fault? It's not like he'd killed anybody or anything.

Question number nine from the stern Examiner: "Have you ever paid for sex?"

The pen-tips hooked to those needles on the machine jumped all OVER the paper.

"SHIT!" Michael couldn't figure out whether to shrink in or bolt from the chair. Half of his body gripped the arm of the heavy institutional chair, the other half tensed in readiness for flight.

The examiner frowned, hiding a victorious smile that made it to his eyes as he looked past Michael Frey at someone else who was loitering in the doorway. "A yes or no answer, please."

"I'm not sure. More like a TRADE, maybe?"

The technician glowered at him. There was now another cop in the room, one in uniform, who was trying to hide a smirk.

Michael suddenly recognized the cop as one of the locals from his hometown. *Oh, CRAP! They're going to interrogate me and then ARREST me! It's been set up since the exam!* The needles worried and slew wildly up and down the paper. Michael slumped in defeat in the examination chair.

The technician turned off the machine.

The paper strip stopped rolling. The needles with their tiny ink-pen tips squiggled in place and time with Michael's thoughts, leaving dark black marks on Michael's record.

"Mr. Frey, why don't you tell us about it."

Oh, what the hell, here goes. "I worked on cars when I was younger. All through high school. Sold some, mostly when I was through witt'em an' ready for a bigger projet." Michael paused to straighten his posture and his backwoods English, which he'd veered into as he thought of his youth. "Took junks out of somebody's back past-yee and made them into rodders and that kind of thing. Never got a ticket, by the way." He thought that was important to point out. "So there was this girl…" *A lot of sad stories start that way,* Michael realized right away. He slumped again, but kept his diction proper to the moment this time. "She came to me and said she wanted a car. Not the one I was working on. Wanted something made up just for her. She told me she'd give me eight hours in the sack for a car and title. So I ah… got cleaned up and I ah… completed the transaction." He looked up.

"Did you know the girl?"

"Went to school with her, she was a couple of, well maybe one or two years behind me."

The Collegeville police officer behind him spoke up. "How old was she?"

Michael flinched. "Seventeen, I think. Well, first car… Maybe a Junior or a Sophomore. Old enough to need a car." *There. That puts her safely at sixteen.* He actually had no idea.

"Would you have had sex with her anyway, regardless of the 'transaction,' as you call it?"

Michael thought of what was revealed when the shower came on and the flannel shirts came off. "In a heartbeat." He colored.

"Eight hours, you said?"

"Four hours right when she put it to me and four hours when the car was done and the title was in her hand. She timed it with a damned wristwatch alarm, both times!" He'd said more than he intended to.

The cops exchanged a look. They were both wondering if that watch had created any sort of performance anxiety. They didn't ask.

"Did you tell anyone about it?"

"I... ah... Well, ya. Not about the car, though. Folks knew my work. They... kind of drew their own conclusions."

The examiner was curious, now, and mildly frightened. He had a daughter coming of age soon, and he considered her somewhat more liberal than he was comfortable with. "What kind of car did this young lady end up with?" He wondered what a little girl's virtue was worth...

Michael brightened. He sat up straight as he considered it. "It was a real piece of work, actually. Little shorty Ford Pinto that wasn't in too bad-a-shape when I found it. I put thirteens on the front, jacked up the back a little so its ass was in the air " - *Just like hers!* - " and put wide fifteens back there. Chrome rims. Painted it sort of a sea green with a pink squiggle for the wiggle... kind of an inside joke." He laughed, looked left and right at the two law enforcement officers, and then remembered where he was. "Er... Punched a sunroof in the top of it. Didn't do too much engine work, except to give it enough zip to turn the fifteens around on the stock tranny and rear-end... Well, had to bore it out a little for that, squeeze twin carbs under there, that was a job!" He leaned back in the chair and seemed briefly annoyed, then embarrassed to be restrained by his arm, the Velcro, and the wires. He continued sheepishly: "Put a boost on the air a little bit - there's a kit a guy at the NAAP store found for me, bolted right on, made for a different car but I built a plate and it fit sorta good enough... Got six pounds at four thousand, 'nuff to scare it a little... Made it a bitch to get the mix right, that's why I had to stuff in the twin carbs, one for idle and one for when the boost started to kick in..." Michael completely forgot where he was again, reclined back, and tried to put his arms behind his head, but was stopped when the various cords and sensors attached to him got in the way. He sat forward with his elbows on the table instead. "Gave her a second set of rims, too, with narrower tires, studded snows on them. Girl lived way the hell back up in that Hollow, didn't want her in the ditch come the first storm. Heard about the gas tank problem those Pinto hatchbacks had, put on a funky bumper, a lot of light metal pipe in it, but strong, all welded together with gussets and angles... Made it low to the ground and covered it with a plastic cowling I had-ta bend-t'under with a couple a salamanders pointed at it 'til it got soft... Looked like it belonged. Gave 'er some weight back there over the tires and I figured it would take care of her if she was rear-ended. Good little car. She was still driving it when she went west."

The cops exchanged another look. The examiner cop asked, carefully, "How much do you think that car was worth, once you were done with it?"

Michael slumped back down a bit. "Oh, I dunno, maybe three or four thousand?" Sheepishly: "Well, maybe more at auction." A lot more, he suspected. Three or four thousand was what he had into it. This one was his best build yet, and he'd already sold one car for a price in the low five figures.

The Examiner sat back. "So, that's about five hundred an hour? Or more?" *Much more, from the sounds of it....* He waited a bit with a raised eyebrow. "She must have been good!" The examiner was having a little fun at Mr. Frey's expense.

Michael sank further into his chair.

"Mr. Frey, I'm going to instruct you to respond 'No,' regarding that question, 'Have you ever paid for sex.' Now, and also if it comes up again in the future, as pertains to this specific incident only. I believe the correct term is 'barter.'" He sat forward, flicked a switch, and the paper started turning again. "Have you ever PAID for sex?"

The tiny pens fluttered all over the graph paper strip again. "No."

***

"Whadayathink?"

The Trooper-examiner and the town cop stood together over a conference room table where the paper was rolled out and taped down at intervals sufficient to keep it there. The examiner was making little colored marks with a grease-pencil. Michael Frey was long gone.

"I think he sure liked her a lot. Still does, by the look of this thing. Did you see how it squiggled every time he thought of the car or her?

Right THERE to THERE to THERE and THERE. Heart-rate." The examiner chuckled. "He's got the hots for both of them!"

They shared a laugh.

The Trooper-Examiner continued. "And I think that girl was a piece of work. Know her?"

"Brittany Wendell. Yah. She went out to Wisconsin or someplace out on the prairie about... some time last year, I guess." He grimaced when he remembered WHY she had fled. "Sounds like her style, actually." He smiled. "She WAS a piece of work." *Didn't know about THIS particular line of... 'work.' Wonder if Bruce knows?* He disregarded it. *That boy's got to be dirtier than a used sock, now, too.*

"Too bad you couldn't talk to her..."

"I don't think I need to. I know I'm still payin' for sex I ain't had for eight years, to the tune of two-eighty-five a month. We all pay in one way or another. Thanks, Dennis."

They shook hands and the Collegeville cop went back to start a background investigation so he could maybe hire himself a new police officer.

***

His hometown eventually offered Michael Frey a policing job. The Staties hadn't come calling yet, so he took the Chief of Police up on the offer.

The Chief had just one bit of advice for Officer Frey after he swore him in: "Kid, keep your side businesses legit. You know, receipts and all that shit. Nothing you can't put on a slip."

'Nuff said.

But all that was much later.

***

It took Michael a few weeks of non-stop work, but in mid-December, Brittany would drive her new car eleven miles over the hill to the local "strip" that lined both sides of the State Route where the department stores and the auto dealerships were. She'd waltz in the front door of a busy establishment on a school-night and be working tables by herself by that weekend. It seems there was a sudden opening on the waitstaff roster that week.

***

Chapter Six

Back in the early 90's, there was a new waitress at the local Smiley's Restaurant for just a couple of months in the fall of one year. She was pretty and young and engaging, and she only worked every other Friday and most Saturdays and a few Sunday mornings here and there, because she was still in school and her folks didn't want her mucking her grades all up on account of a little spending money.

The Manager of this Smiley's franchise, a late-middle aged guy with neatly trimmed hair and no known personal life, he looked her, watched her for a bit, and thought she was going to be a Sure Thing. Everyone knows it's the waitstaff and not the food that really keeps a sit-down place full. The young woman said she knew half of everyone from over the hill and seemed to, she was pretty and well-mannered and quick, and she had the right sort of banter and smile no matter how frantic the pace was, even on her very first night. So that manager was confused when he noticed the weekend numbers were starting to drop off. He was even more shocked when he realized that folks were LEAVING, getting right up out of their seats and hoofing it out of there before they'd even had an appetizer or a cup of coffee! Whole families coming in, sitting down, and then heading for the door as soon as they got their menu.... He couldn't figure it out, for a while, and worked over the specials and made sure the waitstaff paid extra attention to clean tables and clean seats and no more fingerprints on the water glasses EVER!

It turned out that when certain husbands and wives and their two-point-five kids, mostly the ones from up to Collegeville way, settled in for some nice family-style dining at Smileys, one or three out of ten of them didn't want Trudy Jones as their waitress. They'd be seated and then look up for the menu and there was Trudy, smacking her gum with her pad and pencil out, ready to take their orders. The husband would color a little, or maybe just look uncomfortable. Trudy would smile a tight little smile. And suddenly, Misses Whoever would get up, grab the kids by the arm and the husband by the ear, and drag the whole family out of there in a huff.

This happened over and over again for about a month. The manager asked Trudy to stop smacking her gum. He asked her to stop chewing gum altogether. He gave her breath mints. He looked for effluvia hanging out of her nose when it shouldn't be. And then, finally, that family-dining manager started asking questions:

He'd run out into the parking lot after departing families: "Can I help you?" "Is there something Smiley's needs to change?"

The kids would be whining, crying, or bitching. The husband would be mute as a clam under a withering sun. The wives, always angry, would invariably answer: "We just aren't hungry anymore." Meanwhile, the children would be protesting loudly that yes, they very well WERE hungry. The husband would have no opinion in the matter.

Trudy. Always with Trudy. Always with families from over the hill.

***

Brittany and Tabitha heard one of these exchanges one Wednesday night in mid-December when they were getting out of Brittany's new car for a couple of Smiley Sundaes. Brittany was scoping out WHICH establishment she wanted to try to work at, and picking up applications. The raven-haired girl and her red-headed friend ate appetizers at the Central Grill, salads at Pizza House, a main course (burgers) at Fast Fry, and finally, dessert was going to be at Smiley's ice cream counter.

"But Brittany, I'm FULL!" Tabitha wailed in-between belches.

"This is the last one for tonight, really." She turned to open her door as she said, over her shoulder, "Hey! YOU are the one who's been pestering me for a date!" She smiled a big, beaming come-hither smile at her friend... and then ruined the moment by saying, "If I get you full enough, you'll forget all about trying to get me to put out."

Tabitha pouted. "You're DEVIOUS and you're USING me."

"And you like it."

Tabitha shut her door with perhaps a bit more force than she intended. "Sorry.... No, I like your company. Damn good thing, or you'd be plowing through all this food ALONE."

As they made their way across the frozen slush in the parking lot, they saw a family sullenly and brisky trudging to the family station wagon: the kids throwing a subdued fit, the father rolling his eyes in exasperation and carrying an extra coat, the woman grimly leading the way with pursed lips and squinted eyes and folded arms. She was apparently hot enough under the collar that she didn't need her jacket - or maybe just in too much of a hurry to bother with it.

Some guy in a starched shirt and tie came running out of the restaurant, waving his arms in the air. The man wore a busboy apron that was at once incongruous with his outfit and also comedic as he ran past Tabitha and Brittany yelling: "Hold on a minute, please. Please! I just want to ask you a couple of questions… about your visit, really!" The manager - that had to be who he was - was drawing even with the family. "Please, Ma'am!"

The two girls stopped and turned to watch this drama unfold in the unashamed way that teenagers sometimes have of absorbing the world around them.

The mother-type was already behind the open passenger door of the car, about to get in. She whirled at the Smiley's manager. "What the hell do YOU want?!?"

He straightened, lowered his still entreating index finger, and said as firmly as he could muster in the face of this woman's ire, "I would LIKE to know WHY everyone keeps LEAVING before they even get a glass of WATER!" He shifted on his feet, and resorted to pleading: "Please... Ma'am, is there something wrong with my restaurant?"

The woman squinted in anger, knuckles twisting, already on physical attack in the deepest most reptilian folds of her mind. "MAYBE you should ask your WAITRESS!" Then she dropped into her seat and slammed the door.

The husband just shrugged. "Come along kiddos." He shooed his children - their children - into the back seat of the car, and then gave a resigned sigh. He looked like he was afraid to get into the car. Finally, he opened his door, handed in the extra coat, and squeezed in.

Through the open door the two girls heard the mother: "...wouldn't BE hungry if your FATHER wasn't such a..." The door closed.

Brittany and Tabitha looked at each other, then followed the slumping form of the weary, tie-wearing man into the restaurant. They sat up on tall stools at the long dessert counter and waited for menus, so they could pick out their ice-cream topping arrangement. They both saw her at the same time. The manager was in the back, talking to... TRUDY! The girls exchanged a glance. Brittany bit her lip.

Tabitha's quiet musical voice belied the awfulness of the situation. "Hmmmmm. I guess we know that Trudy's babysat for the Bertranski's some time in the past three years..."

They both burst out laughing.

They ate their ice cream, watched customers come and go and waitstaff bustle around, and then Brittany asked for the check and a job application. The two of them got an appraising smile and then change along with two standard institutional applications.

They had a silent and thoughtful ride home.

Tabitha, thinking about how quiet and uneventful and probably loveless her life would soon be, with Brittany working and over there.

Brittany, wondering whether she could clear her plate and work the weekend. A lot depended on what the restaurant decided to do with Trudy. If they figured it out.

As Tabitha got out of the car, Brittany leaned over to look up and ask her a question. "You think maybe Smiley's will be hiring soon?" She couldn't hide the merriment in her voice.

Tabitha looked down sadly. "I think I'm going to miss you once you're working all the time."

***

Brittany went back the next evening, ready to work. She talked her way into an hour in the kitchen with the dishwashing staff as an extended interview, and she was on the payroll and covering tables with an experienced waitress by her side well into the evening on the day after that.

Trudy ended up on the weekend/opening schedule (the Manager's choice, not hers). This didn't work out very well, because she liked sleeping in on weekends, and in protest Trudy ditched her Christmas Day shift. Within a month after that she was all moved on (her choice, not the Manager's, or so she thought). The manager still didn't quite understand the problem, but he had a pretty good idea that Trudy would be a better fit somewhere else.

***

That same week that Brittany got a waitressing job, her father got another call from an office at the Department of Public Safety.

"Next Tuesday?" He turned and looked at his calendar. "That should... No, not that early. I've got a class... they still make me teach, you know." He waited while the Senior Trooper on the other end consulted his own desk-blotter calendar. He listened for a moment, frowned, and then said, "Yah, that will work. Tuesday, five. How about Montpelier? Easier for me...scare up some office space somewhere?"

They wouldn't risk a meeting in one of the restaurants, even if it was busy and noisy.

"Pavilion? That works."

***

Two weeks later, on a Tuesday evening, representatives of regional law enforcement descended on a post-modern cement and glass office complex in the Vermont state capitol. The building that looked decidedly out-of-place next to a turn-of-the-century wood and brick hotel that actually fronted the street on that block. From this anonymous and utilitarian five-story building would spring forth a project that would tie up lives - and ultimately take some - for years into the future.

This meeting involved a larger assembly of the small task force that had met a few times already: Representatives from New Hampshire, again; the Border Patrol; the U.S. Attorney for the district; some U.S. Marshalls; a single representative from the DEA; a very few suits from the Vermont Department of Public Safety; a couple of police chiefs from Vermont and New Hampshire; a lone college professor. The Feds outnumbered state and local law enforcement roughly two-to-one, now. They suffered introductions and then discussed logistics, funding that would be arranged out of the Governor's offices in Vermont and New Hampshire, training, and support services.

The man - a man this time, the face kept changing, much to the group's general and collective discomfort - from the U.S. Attorney's office stood to give a brief presentation on authority and jurisdiction. He essentially told the group that since too many jurisdictions were involved, the hypothetical lawman they were planning for couldn't possibly exist or function - the Federal government simply didn't have the framework to issue law enforcement credentials to cover this situation. "Look, we're under the Major Crimes Act here, which only applies to United States Special Maritime and Territorial Reservations... Your guy sees a murder over on the Fort Drum Military Training Area, yah, he can pull his federal shield and make an apprehension. Same thing if it's off the coast, or out on the lake, I suppose. He - or she - sees the same crime, right here in this room, and there's no Federal interest. It's not against Federal law to snuff someone right here. That's STATE law. That's why those guys up at the border have to let the drunk drivers through. YES, it's dangerous, and YES, they have authority to enforce Federal law, but the Feds don't have jurisdiction up there, YOU do."

From that simple lesson the discussion devolved into a many-voiced interrogation of no one, everyone:

"You're saying it should be a local cop?"

"No, that won't work. We're going to be charging this biker riff-raff with offenses from all over the U.S. Code... Section Sixteen, Eighteen, Twenty-One, Forty-Two.... You need a Federal officer."

"I thought you said you didn't have jurisdiction."

"Won't that help, he doesn't have jurisdiction? He won't have to butt in and stop anything that a local officer is sworn to apprehend...."

"Which crimes are more important?"

"Federal crime does Federal time. State crime does state time."

Someone butted in: "Time is time...."

"So what are all your DEA guys up to, if they can't apprehend outside of special jurisdiction?"

"Can't you just refer the charges, once you have the evidence?"

"Yah, this blockhead did this here, you take that, he did that over there, we'll stuff him for that, et cetera...."

"But what if the evidence needs to be used in more than one trial.... Doesn't Double Jeopardy apply?"

"Not really. Plenty of precedent, as long as the elements of each charge are satisfied."

"Who goes first? Arresting authority? Most serious charge? The biggest trial budget? Won't that create conflict for our little task force?"

And so on.

Heads shook. Eyes rolled around the table.

They changed subjects, or rather, expanded the problem. The Border Patrol Supervising Agent brought up the Canadian Problem, as they were calling it. What do we do about activities, that taken as a whole, meet all the elements of a state or Federal crime, but are committed partly here and partly in another country? What about jurisdiction then?

They went around and around like this for half an hour, and then the Federal folks and the Border Patrol left the meeting.

Walter Wendell waited until the doors shut down the hall. Then he waited thirty more seconds. Finally: "Cagey of you not to mention that you have a potential solution on the way..."

One of the Vermont cops replied: "You said keep it small. We're bouncing ideas, but anyone outside of this very small group is kept out of the sharper picture."

Professor Wendell nodded. "Good. Nothing worse than hearing about your own operation by way of the coffee-urn rumor mill. Good way to lose one. Let's talk about equipment. That's a biggie." He stood up and began pacing. "You've all got a lot of standard-issue, regulation equipment. It's probably bought in lots, so it's got sequential serial numbers, it's recognizable to folks with the right friends, it's got records attached to it somewhere." He stopped. "You know, Smith and Wesson has a service... you send them the serial of a firearm, and they tell you its complete history, as far as they've got it. You being anyone. Joe blow wants to know."

That little gem caused uncomfortable looks.

Professor Wendell smiled wolfishly. "Yah. That easy." He stabbed the conference room table with his finger. "CLEAN. Any equipment, any weapons, any tools, any cars, any radios..." He shook his head. Bad idea. "ANYTHING you give to our guy, it has to be CLEAN. THEY will spot it, THEY will wonder about it, THEY will CRUCIFY him with it." He turned and looked at Senior Trooper Evers. "Do you plan on equipping him with anything?"

Trooper Evers answered sheepishly: "Well, he's got to have a sidearm... IF that's approved, but I mean, he might carry it anyways, even if it ISN'T approved, that's what I'd do..."

Trooper Greenway chipped in, a little more firmly. "Radio... maybe not... or one of those new cellphone things. Easy enough to get. Motorcycle. We'll have to find one."

The New Hampshire Trooper, Calzotti, had input on that: "Go to an auction, buy it with a cashier's check, it'll be washed out."

Professor Wendell thought about this for a moment. "I like that..." He shrugged. "There's TWO ways to do this: One, you give him something that is out of regulation, not part of a bid-lot buy. Cashier's check, sure. You equip him with it, train him with it, make sure it doesn't end up in any paperwork." He smiled. "Or TWO, you set everyone up. Figure out what you want him to have, NOW. Our guy isn't going to hit the street for two years. Issue the tools - gun, motorcycle, whatever - to the program NOW, keep all the paperwork in place right where it's supposed to be, dot all the I's and Tee's, and then report the stuff stolen, one at a time, over the next few months."

"Like it's had time to percolate." Trooper Evers grinned. "They check it, they find out..."

Trooper Greenway slapped the table. "Possession of Stolen Property! I like it!"

Professor Wendell became effusive, a rare thing. "THAT, gentlemen, is how we're going to create a penetration agent who will get you into the..." He dropped his voice to a quiet, almost reverent tone to finish with a single, ominous name: "Topdogs."

***

Brittany was a busy girl, right from the start. Business picked back up at Smiley's Family Dining. The Manager put a quarter-page ad in the paper, complete with photo: MEET OUR NEW WAITSTAFF. THEY ARE EAGER TO SERVE YOU! Some of the families from over the hill came back. New diners started showing up pretty regularly. Younger, mostly. Groups of boys. College men from the prestigious Ivy-League campus across the river in New Hampshire. Academy students, from that little military school up the valley, who came through with their parents and grandparents, and then came again later in groups of scratchy-faced young men with short haircuts and long stares at the new waitress. They were unusually well-behaved and spent money, so it seemed like a net gain, even if the demographic was changing.

The Manager breathed a sigh of relief. *Things are picking up!*

***

Hattie Wendell had some questions, that December. Her granddaughter's job was a surprise. She thought it best to open with the easy one, over supper, on one of Brittany's nights off.

Brittany absent-mindedly ate some of the the last of the brussels sprouts from the summer's garden while she tried to fit schoolwork into her busy new schedule. She and Hattie had dug the vegetables out from under the snow a few weeks ago, in a flurry of late-season, last-minute gardening, then baked batches of them in the oven, halved, over bacon crumbles. They put them up in small bags in the large freezer as ready-made meals for later evenings. Now she was eating them as a side to her homework.

Brittany's grandmother watched the young woman while her nose followed text from side to side in a thick and battered textbook that Hattie recognized from when Walt was in school (it still had his name scrawled on the edge of the closed pages, proof of an early and abandoned flirtation with delinquent tendencies). She grimaced. *This might not be easy.* "Brittany? You're working quite a lot, aren't you?"

"Oh, Grandma, I'm sorry." Brittany looked up from the ancient schoolbook, food poised halfway to her mouth. "Are my late nights getting to you?" She put down her fork and carefully folded shut the book. "I know I make a lot of noise when I come home. I'm sorry, I'll…"

"No, it's not that, dear. I worry about YOU. Don't tire yourself out. And your homework. And friends. I worry."

"My homework's fine. Really. And yes, I am tired when I come home. More than I thought I would be. But I'm doing this NOW, while I can. It's good practice for college." She knew this would somewhat placate her grandmother. "Work, work, work, study, work, study. Same thing. Don't worry. REALLY."

"How long are you going to keep this up?"

"For a few months, until they realize I'm an indispensable part of the Smiley's National Corporation, and I have them wrapped around my finger. Then I can set my own schedule. No more than twenty hours or so a week. I promise."

If that was supposed to give her grandmother comfort, it didn't. *Twenty! Plus all the driving to and fro…* "Brittany, I really hate to do this. But… I want to see your report card, next time. And the last one. I want to be able to make a comparison." *Be careful here, Hattie. Don't make her fly the coop….*

Aaaaarrrrrgh! "Grandma, OOOOOoooooh!" Brittany stamped her foot under the table in frustration.

"See, dear? You're working too much already and you've become short with me."

There wasn't much Brittany could say to that. "Shit."

"And cursing. Now, I didn't tell you that you COULDN'T work. That's not up to me. I just want to see your report cards. We always worked here on the farm when we were in school, but things were… different, back then."

"Ooo-KAY!" Brittany gripped the table and took a breath to calm herself. "I'm sorry. But REALLY, it's NOT going to be a BIG DEAL. Sherry has a KID and works at the mill, NIGHTS, and makes all her classes and passes all her tests…" Brittany knew immediately that was a bad example on several counts.

Her grandmother settled for the most obvious: "Don't you think you can do better than 'pass'?"

"I do, Grandma. I do." Brittany went to her purse, hanging from the coat-rack by the door. She pulled out a yellow piece of carbon-paper. "Here. Here's the last one."

Hattie put on her glasses. She smoothed the wrinkled paper and pored over the marks, squinting. "A bee-plus in Physical Education. When I was a girl, we weren't allowed to TAKE physical education. It was only for the boys. I guess a Bee-plus will do." She looked over her reading glasses at her granddaughter and smiled.

Hattie didn't mention, but everyone in the family and half the town besides knew that in spite of this handicap in her education, Hattie had still made the United States Olympic Ski Team one year. That she had no medals was probably more a result of world politics than any lack of athletic ability or determination.

"Now, for the things that matter: Why did you get an A-minus in Home Economics when you got an A-plus in every other academic course?"

Brittany was frustrated by the implied criticism. "It's not MY fault that no one will cooperate with me when we have to bake a stupid cake! It's all PARTNER stuff, and APPARENTLY I don't work well with others."

"You don't need to yell. I'm not your mother. Why not?"

"I'm sorry, Grandma. No, you're definitely NOT. The other girls in class hate me because I have all A's even though I hardly ever work at it. I just pay attention in class and do my homework in study hall and don't pass notes and don't chatter all the time. And they hate me because I'm pretty and because their boyfriends pay attention to me and…" She'd started to raise her voice again. She stopped with a sneer on her face.

"And that eats at you all the time, just like this?" Hattie suddenly realized there might be several larger issues here than work and grades.

Brittany nodded, quickly, as a drop streamed down one cheek. "I WANT to get along… But it doesn't seem to work."

"I never thought Home Economics was something that should be taught in school, in the first place. If you can't read a recipe book and bake a cake by the time you're out of the sixth grade…!" Hattie smiled at Brittany, a careful, gentle smile. "It's a very nice report card. Make sure you keep it that way, as best you can." She went over to the other side of the table and put her hand under Brittany's chin, gently pulled her face up, and looked into her eyes. "Don't tire yourself out, dear. You're so young, so much to DO in life!"

"Work is good for me, Grandma." Brittany wiped the side of her nose and put her arm around the old woman standing beside her. "They treat me better over there, even the other kids my age. I might actually make… well, not FRIENDS, but…. Did you know that I went out to the Burger Binge with the waitstaff and the dishwasher the other night and we all had milkshakes after work? Besides Tabitha, those are the ONLY people my age I've ever gone ANYWHERE with, who weren't hostile or trying to get in my pants. Well, I guess Tabitha doesn't count there…" She smirked. "That Tab…" She looked up at her grandmother. "It's good. For me. As a person." Brittany put her arm back and gave the older woman a squeeze.

Well. "It sounds like maybe it IS, dear." Hattie gave her granddaughter a double pat on the shoulder and shuffled back to her own chair at the other side of the table. Her gait had nothing to do with ill health, and everything to do with dread. "Now." She sat and took a deep breath. "There's one other thing."

Brittany cringed. *Oh, KRAP! She's going to start MOTHERING me! Things have been going SO well up here… and now THIS!*

Hattie came out with it firmly and directly: "Brittany Wendell, what's up with that CAR? I'm hearing ALL SORTS of rumors down in town…. Do you know what people are saying about you?"

Whups! Brittany sighed. *Oh, crappolla.* She slumped, the surprise leading to resignation. "Yes, Grandma, some of the RUMORS are true, probably." She shuffled her bottom on the chair, sat up primly, took a deep breath, and asked, "What do you want to know?"

I'm really sorry to ask this, and I'm quite sure it isn't true, but "Have you… you should know…." *Oh, just say it, Hattie!* "Brittany, they're saying you slept with that boy for a car!" *Let's just start with the most alarming and juicy and obviously WRONG and INCORRECT tidbit and let her know WHAT PEOPLE ARE SAYING ABOUT HER and be done with it and relieved! Poor dear needs to know -*

"Well, we didn't sleep. It was more of a daylight thing. His parents are around too much in the evening." She shrugged.

Hattie's chair shrieked back an inch and the old woman looked mortified as she thought about THAT in stunned silence. Finally: "Oh, honey, what an AWFUL thing to do! Why on EARTH would you do that?" The poor woman was thunderstruck for a moment. "We... Your... Walt and I, we would have HELPED you, you know." Hattie shook her head. *I can't have heard right.* Disbelief. Horror. *Do I KNOW this girl, this... sixteen-year-old who has WHORED herself?* "You didn't HAVE to do THAT." Anger rose. "How could you DO that to yourself?!" *What a terrible, awful, horrible end this girl has come to!*

"No, Grandma." Brittany held her ground, proudly. "I didn't HAVE to do it at all. I have some money in the bank." *Quite a bit, actually...*

Hattie had reared back in horror and shock. "You...." *What do I say?*

Brittany's eyebrows went up. *But I don't think I'll tell her THAT story!* "But I wanted something RELIABLE, and I didn't want to spend my savings."

"Brittany Wendell, you've made yourself into a prostitute!"

"No, Grandma, I've made myself into a WAITRESS. With transportation." Brittany sat before her grandmother proud and resolved, defiant and unashamed.

Hattie opened her mouth to say something, but Brittany shook her head and held up a hand: Wait, let me finish.

"Now I COULD have let him date me, and let him grope me under the bleachers and plunge around in me in the back seat of one of his other cars for a few months, and let him parade me around like a trophy, and doted on his every whim and urgent need for a few years..."

Hattie started to come out of her chair, her mouth opening. "YOU-" her eyes flared as the old woman stuffed a quick succession of mean words here before she continued - "are a USER of people! First Tabitha, then that boy, how many oth-"

Brittany simply raised her volume, to keep the floor. "...and then MAYBE he would have married me, and maybe he would have left BEFORE he gave me children and maybe he would have left AFTER he gave me children, but I'm sure somewhere in there he would have, at some time, given me a car for my trouble, and maybe child support, too. Or maybe not. THIS way, it was quick and painless and simple and honest. He got me six times"

Hattie went wide-eyed with shock. *Who IS this wild girl?!?* Her mouth started to open again to say something, but she was having trouble catching her breath....

"and then we were done. I didn't have to put up with his groping or his drunken behavior when we're around other boys, or laugh at his stupid jokes or have sex under a lab table after school four times a week as my token duty."

Brittany's grandmother sat back down, heavily. *Oooof. Sometimes this girl can be so coldly logical and calculating that it's frightening. Oh. Her father.* Hattie flashed to other arguments with a different teen, here in this kitchen. She suddenly felt very tired. "YOU are SCARY!" She looked around the kitchen for help. There was none. "I'm going to have to think about this." She grimaced. *Be careful here, Hattie, with this child. Don't drive her the way of Paul.... Goodness, she's the worst of her mother and father and Walt put together: a randy secret agent seductress on the hustle!* "I'm going to have to think on this... not too much, I hope." She squinted shrewdly at Brittany. "What ELSE do you need?"

"Don't worry Grandma. I'm really not going to do THAT very often." She leaned over the table conspiratorially. "Do you want to know a secret?" She lowered her voice. "This is a REALLY BIG secret. Do you?" Brittany grinned at her like the Cheshire cat.

"Oh, boy. I think I might as well." *What on Earth else is this girl up to?*

"It's only happened once before..."

Well, Hattie thought, *isn't THAT a relief! Or not. So this ISN'T the FIRST time!*

"I traded sex for a ride to a swimming hole. First sex. Someone I really wanted. Well, first boy sex." She looked across at her grandmother. "Do you really want to hear this?"

Hattie Wendell was looking extremely uncomfortable, perhaps even ill. "I think I'd better." *This is a Willful Child, Hattie. Be careful here... they are so easy to loose to the four winds! Hear her out and bite your tongue and think on it before saying anything!*

"There's a boy. I liked him. He said things that made me... nice inside. It was time. I had him take me swimming. In the buff. Nature took its course, but it took a while - he was a nice boy. I think he would have just watched me swim all afternoon!"

Hattie was wondering if this young man was still a 'nice boy,' or if after a taste of Brittany, he was chasing every tail in the county. *Poor young man probably didn't know what he was getting into with THIS one...*

"But I don't want to have to DATE and have to do all the right things and say all the right things and be someone's little showpiece and wear their stupid varsity jacket and put my aa- tail in the air on a schedule. Are you alright?"

Hattie's face went a little ashen as she felt a sudden heavy indigestion percolating. She nodded her head. "Being a housemate has more to it than I'd bargained for." *Especially with a girl - a young woman - in today's age. My goodness.* "I'm alright. Go on." Hattie steeled herself. *Patience, Hattie, don't lose another one.*

"The boy that built the car? I liked him, too. In a different way. Since I was WAY TOO YOUNG. But I hate him. He's a jerk. But I WANT him. Or did. And now I've HAD him, and it's out of the way, and I GOT SOMETHING for it. Something USEFUL, that will LAST a while." She smiled. "Not flowers or some dumb varsity jacket or a bunch of dates out. Or a baby. I got a CAR. And I got HIM out of my system. So people talk?" Brittany stood up to put the rest of her dinner in a Mason jar for breakfast. "They already talked. Now they just have something to talk ABOUT. Something that's actually true, for a change." Brittany laughed. "And I've had a lot less time in the sack than most of the girls who are dating. They have to Put Out to keep their boy, most of them. I'm a Free Woman."

Anger came to Hattie Wendell again: "Brittany, you're thinking thoughts that shouldn't occur to a girl until she's twenty-five!" She relaxed a little, by force of will. "I'll have to think on all this for a while." *A long while.* Hattie paused. "What are we going to do when your mother finds out?"

Brittany laughed outright. "Remind her that I was born exactly four months after she was married." She looked pointedly over at her grandmother. "Four months after her eighteenth birthday. And that she still looks fondly at every young buck that walks by the front yard when she's out sunning herself in her all-together and that she's certainly the talk of the town on Tanning Days." Brittany giggled. "Those two weren't saints, at my age."

"You ARE scary." *And no, they weren't saints... but one of them was an angel. So she still doesn't know.... So much like him, though.* Hattie's pain crossed her face. She still harbored a little anger. Now at Brittany, too. But she was smiling, if sternly, by force of will. *A living Wendell child... a treasure, this.* "Let's have some tea and a scone and let me think this through for a couple of days." Hattie got up and went towards the wood range to put the teakettle on a hotter section of the top.

"I'm sorry, Grandma. I'm not as scary as some of them, trust me."

"I do believe you're probably right." She turned. "Is being a girl very complicated, these days?" *But she's not a girl anymore, is she, this lover and user of men.... What do I do with her?* Hattie eyed the fresh-from-the-oven scones and decided to pass. She wasn't hungry anymore.

"VERY complicated. Very." Brittany sighed at the mere thought of it. There was nothing to do for it, so she dismissed thoughts of the complications waiting at school and helped herself to half a cranberry scone.

***

Hattie Wendell remained convinced that there was more than one reason the girl was so comfortable here at the farmhouse. Apparently she didn't know it, and certainly wouldn't remember, but Brittany had lived at the Wendell farm as a baby and toddler.

Walter Wendell married a pregnant Robin after he came back from his first hitch in the service. A two year enlistment, back then. He hadn't been home in those two years. Walter had stepped in for his older brother Paul, who'd fled town as soon as the pregnancy news broke and the shit hit the fan in the Wendell household. When Walt re-enlisted for his Second Act in government service, the young new mother and recent bride had herself flown the coop for a bit - left her new baby and the farm and Walter's boyhood bedroom in a huff one night and not returned. But she had not flown in the same direction as Walt. The "father" of the now-abandoned child was not where he could be easily reached, and there was some discussion that maybe Hattie and Patrick would become "Mother" and "Father" for all intents and purposes.

Robin had come to her senses, or run out of other options, eventually, and returned to her parents' home in the village. The baby daughter, now a vivacious and energetic toddler, was re-united with mother some months later, very shortly before Walter returned on leave from his second hitch of overseas service.

Hattie sat in the dark in her rocker with a cup of tea and ruminated on the strange twists and turns of these many years. "Girl has come home and she doesn't even know it!" *And she is just as smart and driven and opinionated and sure of herself as her father was.* Paul had been sure enough of himself - or dead enough - to leave his entire family behind almost twenty years ago without ever a single glance back. They never talked about him. Walt was Brittany's father now, and Brian's too, and that was that. *And that's nearly the end of us and the Wendells, if Brittany goes the way of Paul....* She thought of a house in the village, and a boy who lived in it: *I wonder what Brian will be like?* Her thoughts returned to Brittany's wild confession. *She's a chip off the old block, isn't she! Almost seventeen years Paul's been gone now - gone without a word, without a trace! Phillip gone nineteen and Patrick gone fifteen... Suzy gone eighteen years. Oh, how nice it would be if this old house was still full.... My God, how this farm has been cruel to Wendells! I do hope that Brian makes it through the hard years alright....* She wasn't sure that Brittany quite had, now that she knew the girl better.

***

Time and fate had not been kind to the Wendells.

Hattie sat in her rocker in that staid and sturdy kitchen that had been on this hillside for a century-and-a-half and she thought about family and memories - something she had avoided for some decades. She rocked and reflected more and more often, now. Sometimes she would become so immersed in her past that she would be surprised when she came out of her reverie and discovered a different season, a different year on the calendar, items thirty-five years out of place, venison and potatoes boiling away on the wood range. Today she went back to the boisterous time after World War Two, when life on the farm held nothing but renewed promise right up until that bad winter....

A tough flu year in the 'Fifties took out Patrick Wendell's sister and the woman's new baby. Her young husband went silent and then bitter and then he wandered away into the Outside World. The same bad year finished his own aging parents and many of the old folk around town.

Hattie's mother and father lived on the farm as the Hired People - that's why Hattie had grown up there, and how she'd met Patrick. Her mother and her siblings had all died over that same winter - the children of the flu bug, the mother of a broken heart. Hattie's father began drinking and managed to drown his sorrows for good as a homeless and decrepit rag-man who lived in vacant boxcars parked at the neighboring Junction.

Hattie and Patrick had children of their own by then, and they were haunted with fright that winter and the next. Those two New Parents breathed a sigh when their own flock all seemed to escape the reaper... or so they thought.

Daughter Suzy had died in a farming accident the year she turned fifteen. Tragic, but common enough in those days. Also proof enough, so said the more conservative neighbors, that girl children belonged in the kitchen, the garden and maybe the chicken coop, but nowhere else. Maybe true for all the long-haired children, boy or girl, in this new age of tractors. The elder Wendell had not blamed himself, thankfully. That child had never been so happy as when she was driving the team of horses or working the line of stanchions in the milking parlor. A tear spilled down Hattie's wrinkled cheek, even now. *Suzy would have taken over the farm, I'm sure of it* - her boy from up the road was already with them for holidays by then. *They would have raised cows and children together right here.* Instead, that long beautiful braid of black hair wound around the shaft and That Was That. Hattie shook her head with an unnoticed tear ready to fall from her chin.

Son Phillip managed to escape the Draft that took so many of his generation off to the other side of the world. He went to Maine Maritime Academy, graduated, and joined the Merchant Marine - only to meet his end in a supposedly safer occupation aboard a ship that plied back and forth across a great inland sea. He'd died in a freak storm on Lake Superior. They still sang songs about the shipwreck on the radio like it was some sort of ancient maritime disaster and not her curly-haired son. She couldn't bear to hear about it. Hattie didn't listen to the radio much for a few years.

Paul had started dying - or disappearing - first, though he was the last to actually go. He received his draft notice in 1968. He'd opened it there in the kitchen in front of them, thrown it in the trash and flitted away that very minute, then had the gall to come back months later to a raving and shamed and shaming father. He worked around the farm while Patrick Wendell tried to decide whether to call the police or not, then flitted away again after weeks of shouting came to a head. The boy-now-man had returned to work and hide at the farm for a winter, then disappeared again in the summer.... over and over. Even by the time the war was over and arrest wasn't likely, he kept disappearing - he seemed to have something going on somewhere, that boy. Back and forth to some other life, on an annual cycle, for years. Hattie shook her head at the thought of it. *He migrated like a goose, that one.* Another winter here, got the young girl from town pregnant, and then when he found out he'd gotten her In Trouble he flew the coop for good so fast he'd shed his feathers. Just said, cryptically, "a man can't have two masters, nor two Queens, either." He stepped out of the room for a minute and the next thing they knew, he'd got in his car and left like he was going to the store, leaving poor Robin standing there in the kitchen with her own father and his parents. Never to be seen again, that man: clothes all upstairs, suitcase under the bed, shaving kit on the counter, coat hanging in the hall.

Still alive? Probably. Maybe. Hattie came back to the kitchen, back to the present. *Where ARE you?*

***

Right now the man was downtown in the bustling city of Montreal, dealing with headaches: the kind that come with helping to run a rowdy gentlemen's club on a busy night when the owners, the customers and the trouble might all be one in the same.

"No, no, no! You would put those guests over there, eh?" The club manager nearly pulled his hair out in frustration. Two of the waitresses had bailed, three of the dancers had walked out in the middle of the last evening, and now his new Hostess was trying to seat the High Rollers - big spenders, obvious by their dress and manner - in the cheap seats at a table, instead of in one of the plush leather money-doubling private booths.

"Ouess, ouess, je regret." The Hostess grimaced, then turned to the party with a bright smile. "Allons 'y! This way, gentlemen! Only the best pour vous!"

Paul watched her walk away, the well-dressed tourists in tow. He sighed. *She's going back into the floor rotation or out the door.* He felt a heavy hand clap his shoulder.

The owner of the hand gave a merry laugh. "Bet jou wish jou were still the Busboy! Jou've been up here so long, jou're beginning to sound like one of us!" The man turned and faded into the dark spaces of the club, the three pairs of bright canine eyes on the back of his vest the last to disappear in a dance and weave that followed the man's steps.

Thoughts of the farm and parents were the furthest thing from Paul's mind on this and every night. He was a Canadian businessman now, and that was that.

***

"Hi, Mom, it's Walt."

Walter Wendell had waited a couple of days to make this phone call. But then the fifth of his co-workers had brought it up at lunch, acting all concerned, but really just fishing lecherously into the sex life of his very pretty young daughter. And it didn't sound good, *even if the gossip mill HAS probably blown whatever it was all out of proportion.*

"I'm sorry, what was that, Mom?"

Hattie thought maybe the connection was bad - it often was on her rural telephone line. "I SAID, HOW'S LIFE DOWN IN THE VILLAGE THESE DAYS?"

"You don't have to shout. Good, good."

Boy, something is sure bothering Walt, now, isn't it? "Been a while since you've been up, I was beginning to think you'd skipped the country with some little thing from the office!"

"You watch too much TeeVee."

Actually, Hattie watched less television than her son did. She decided to ask about family. "So how are you, and how are my daughter-in-law and grandson?"

Walt didn't even hear his mother. "What's up with that CAR?" *There. It's out.* He already felt better. *There's a simple explanation and a whole bunch of groundless speculation going on. That's it.*

Hattie sighed as she responded. It came out as a poorly-hidden groan: "You heard."

Uh-oh. "I heard some things. Well, more or less the same thing a bunch of different times. You know how the rumor mill works in this town. That's a score." He flinched. *Shit. Poor choice of words.*

Hattie was glad her son couldn't see the smirk on her face. *Ironic, the way he put that... Kind of Freudian, actually. Shit. He knows.*

Silence on the phone line. ....

Her son finally had to ask, "Have you heard them, too?" *Just rumors. Must be. They say such terrible things about each other at that age....*

Hattie snorted. *Well, yes, and SEEN it, unfortunately, but not with the one you're talking about. Good God, my mind is in the gutter tonight.* "What, exactly, have you heard, Walt?" All innocent-like, she hoped.

"Well, it SOUNDS like my daughter is a budding little Hollywood madam with a taste for fast cars. Or something like that." Walt didn't actually want to say the words, words like 'fornication' and 'prostitution' and 'money' and especially not 'sex.' He didn't want to offend his poor mother's sensibilities, she being a Puritan. All old ladies, and especially mothers, are.

Hattie held the phone to her heart for a moment as she steeled herself and slumped back into the rocker. *He got it just about right. The Brittany situation, that is. She humped some boy until he was so addled he gave her just about two or three or five thousand dollars worth of car. Must have been some long, wild ride. I wonder what an hour or two of me was worth, back in my day, so long ago?*

"Mom?" The silence concerned Walt. *Jesus, did I give my own mother a heart attack?* "You alright?"

"Oh. Well. You can't always believe what you hear." *And now I'm covering for her. Good grief.*

"It's a pretty nice little car." *Just how DID she afford it?* Walt had reasons to be concerned, and he knew a few things about Brittany that his mother didn't. *Brittany can be... willful. Independent. Creative in a scary sort of way.* "Very nice...." He was fishing.

"Yes, it IS! She took me for a ride in it when she went to get her license! You should come up for dinner, and we can all go cruzin, as they say, around the Hollow!" *And avoiding the subject. Shame on me.*

"Ya, Mom, that'd be just great." Walt rushed to get back to the subject. "Now how did she PAY for that car? Did you help her?"

Not on your life. I don't think my aged ass would have been good for the boy's arousal, even if I'd kept my clothes on. "She mowed a lot of lawns this summer, didn't she? I think the boy gave her a deal. He was kind of sweet on her." *If not before she jumped his bones, then definitely after.*

"She's not acting wild, is she, out every night 'til eleven, that sort of thing?" Walt was relieved. He had a feeling that if his daughter was up to mischief, his mother would have noticed. *She's old-fashioned but not entirely naïve - she'd trip onto it if something was UP.* He was glad he'd gotten it all out in the open.

Hattie was thinking, *more like twelve midnight, after she works all evening and closes and then goes out on the town with her new friends from work....* "Oh, NO! She works pretty hard, Walt. No time to be out carousing in the evening for that one." *At least, not 'til later.* "I really don't think you need to worry yourself." *I'll worry for both of us.*

"So how's it going with you two? She any trouble?"

YOU try raising a teen. That's right. NOT raising. Well, you've still got one at home. I hope he gives you an easy time.... "We're HOUSEMATES, Walt!" *Ooof. Got more than you bargained for, Hattie. But she's sweet and* "No trouble at all. She's a wonderful child, and I'm very lucky you put her up to staying with old, doddering Grandma."

"We didn't put her up to it."

Hattie knew that. "Why don't you come up for dinner next Sunday night?" (Brittany never worked Sunday nights, so far, that was scramble-to-get-your-schoolwork-done night in this farmhouse, and there was usually a redhead around, too...) "You can see how it's going for yourself." She got a momentary picture of trying to eat dinner with Walt and Robin and Grandson Brian while Brittany and her friend were having a noisy romp in the bedroom upstairs. She snorted again.

"Godblessyou. You coming down with something? I'll check and get back to you. That sounds really great, Mom. Thanks for telling me what's been going on. Bye, now." Walter Wendell hung up the phone, already relieved and moving on to other worries.

That hurt. At least I didn't tell him any OUTRIGHT lies. I just worded everything very carefully. Like a kid would do.... Hattie hung up the phone. "BRITTANY WENDELL YOU ARE A VERY BAD INFLUENCE!!"

The reply floated back on the air through darkened rooms, distant and musical. "Sorry!" They must be studying by kerosene lamplight in the front room. That girl burned through lamp oil like it was the next up-and-coming trend! It was Brittany's one weeknight off, and she and Tabitha were doing homework.

"TABITHA, WOULD YOU LIKE TO COME UP FOR DINNER NEXT SUNDAY NIGHT?" *There, THAT would throw some confusion into the works, at least. Anybody could see it, and if they were blind, they could hear it. I wonder if it's unethical to use the girl as 'cover' for my granddaughter?*

The red-headed teen's brief answer wafted back on the currents of the old house. "Yum!"

"BRITTANY's FAMILY IS COMING UP FROM TOWN FOR A LITTLE SIT-DOWN AND LOOK-SEE. THAT ALRIGHT, YOU TWO?"

Silence. They were probably discussing it. Giggles. They'd reached a conclusion.

In a moment, in unison:

"Yyyyeeepp!"

"Yuuuupp!"

And now I'm misleading her parents and yelling around the house like a teenager! "A VERY, VERY BAD INFLUENCE!!!"

Giggles chimed back through the night-filled hallways.

***

A few days later, Hattie Wendell decided she'd calmed down enough to Have A Talk with her granddaughter. She turned from the counter, took a deep breath, and plunged into a very careful lecture.

"Brittany, I've had my think. And now I want to have my say, so I can put it out of my mind."

Brittany looked up from her breakfast expectantly.

"You're a good girl. But you did a BAD thing. You weren't CHEAP, I'll say THAT for you. But sex is about more than purchasing power. It was wrong. And I'm mad about that. Disappointed is a better word, I suspect."

"That makes two of you. I don't think Tab will ever forgive me, either." Brittany seemed downright sad about that part.

"Should I have broken you two up, that weekend, would that have prevented all this?"

"No. It would have just HIDDEN it. And nothing BAD happened." *Either time.* She looked sideways into the further reaches of her head for a moment. "YES, it was WRONG. But that doesn't mean I shouldn't have done it. Big picture, Grandma."

"You want a big picture, how about all the rumors in town? Your FATHER has certainly heard them. I covered for you. I'm not sure I should have done that."

Brittany sighed. "There were ALWAYS rumors. Since I was about thirteen." *Some of them worse than this. Now, at least, a couple of them are true.* "And yes. Michael has a bit of a mouth. I was HOPING he would have more… discretion. But I wasn't counting on it."

"But Brittany, people SEE the CAR!"

"Yes, and if I'd paid for it the conventional way, with MONEY that I actually HAVE IN THE BANK, unlike most of my loose-lipped schoolmates by the way, they STILL would have been saying that I'd fucked my way into it, unquote!" Brittany gazed back, chin up, a righteous set to her eyes and mouth.

Hattie took note. "Would they really?"

"Yes."

"Shit. Excuse my French."

"Wow, Grandma. Exactly! Shit!"

"Damned if you do, damned if you don't?"

"Yep."

Ooooff. That's TERRIBLE! "Get along to school, sweetie. I've made you late. DON'T SPEED. I'm going to try to forget about this whole thing." *The sooner, the better!* "You've gotten yourself a very nice car, by the way." *Good God, how do I argue with her?*

"Thanks. It kicks butt in the corners when you're haul-assing it to school 'cause you're late." She grabbed her backpack and coat and ran out of the kitchen, giggling. A moment later she reappeared, struggling to put a backpack strap over one shoulder while keeping her purse strap on the other. It wasn't working. Her wool coat was too big for the adjustment of either strap. "I'm kidding!" Her voice came up out of her hair as she placed both bags on the floor to adjust the straps for Winter wear. "No foolin' around on that slippery old road today!"

The day was crisp and typical for December. A mix of last night's rain and snow, a lot of fallen wind-blown branches, and a coating of cold, dry snow on top of all of that covered the road, the walk, the yard, and Brittany's car. The puddles had a skim of ice over the top. This hard freeze would stay with them right through the New Year, by the looks.

Brittany flung open the front door, ran down the steps, and promptly threw her feet up in the air for some unexplained reason. The backpack landed first, then her elbows, then her bottom. "OW!GODDAMMOTHERFUCKINHURTSMOTHERFUCKER!" She got up, brushed off her bottom, and then inspected her elbows to make sure they were whole.

Hattie watched in horror and amusement from the kitchen window. *Got to take care of that butt before she checks to see if her arms are broken. My hard-screwing, hard-swearing little sailor-girl!* Hattie stuck her head out the door. "ARE YOU SURE YOU'LL BE CAREFUL DRIVING, AT LEAST?"

"I will now! Bye, Grandma!"

Hattie watched her granddaughter get into that little car. She couldn't figure out whether it was awful or nice, but she was glad the girl had the sense enough to bring it back to that boy and get studded tires put on. *I wonder how much THAT had cost!* As Brittany backed into the road, Hattie noticed the pink squiggle-stripe for the first time. *Hhhmmmmm. Ahhh. Just like the pants commercial: 'PUT A LITTLE SQUIGGLE ON YOUR WIGGLE!' I wonder if she knows?*

Hattie closed the door and stepped back into the recesses of the house shaking her head.

***

Two days later, another phone call repeated the last one.

Hattie really poured on the sugar. "Oh, HI! It's SO GOOD to hear from you! How ARE-"

"WHAT the HELL is GOING ON up there?!?" Brittany's mother wasn't one for pleasantries.

Hattie looked around the kitchen. "Stripping the last of the shell beans from the pods into Mason jars?"

"Don't you beat around the bush with me! That little brat's turned into a real TRAMP since she moved up there with you!"

Maybe you shouldn't have thrown her a sexy underwear party when she was only thirteen going on fourteen. "I don't know WHAT you're talking about. We're having a great time of it up here and-"

"FIRST she was FRIGID, then she started dyking out with some TOMBOY-GIRL-SOMETHINGOROTHER like some LESBIAN and"

"Are you coming up for dinner on Sunday?"

"NOW she's whoring herself out to EVERY BOY that comes along ASKING?!?!? I don't know WHICH is WORSE! Every time she embarrasses me, she seems to find a way to TAKE IT UP A NOTCH!!!!"

Hattie held the phone about eight inches from her ear now -the handset almost wouldn't reach her mouth. *Take a Tylenol, Robin. Or a Midol. Or Prozac. Whatever will work, if anything.* "Yes, I think she's dating now." *There, that was nice and neutral.*

"WELL I HOPE YOU'RE DOING SOMETHING ABOUT ALL THIS!!!"

I notice you aren't volunteering any help, mother-of-the-troubled-daughter. "It's a phase they go through. Spreading rumors about each other, I mean."

"DID YOU HEAR ME?!? SHE FUCKED SOME GUY FOR A CAAAAARRRRRR!!!! JESUS, BRITTANY!!!"

"Robin, you don't have to shout. And yes, if she was in the room, or anywhere near it, she would have heard you. But she's at work.

There are OTHER ways to get a car, you know." *Save your own eardrums: try to change the subject.* "So are you all coming for dinner?"

"YoubetchorassIam. I want to SEE that little troublemaker."

Check your gun at the door. "That will be very nice." *You should try therapy.* Inspiration struck. "She's bringing a friend!"

Suddenly, Hattie's daughter-in-law was all honey and purrs. "Oooooo! That's wonderful! A FRIEND... I can't wait to meet him!"

Oh boy. "See you at four. Don't forget your husband and son." But the phone was already down on the other end. *There's something really wrong with that woman.*

A bit later, Hattie got on the phone again:

"So, Tabitha, I invited you, and I kind of had... ULTERIOR motives. Alright, fraudulent." She explained her predicament.

"Of course she thinks Britt's bringing a boy." Tabitha wasn't the least bit surprised. "She couldn't IMAGINE anything else for her perfect little 'family moment.'"

"She hasn't even met you and she was calling you names. I just wanted you to know.... To be prepared."

"We've already talked about it. I kind of know what it's all about, I think."

"Tabitha, are you two... is your... Do people KNOW?"

Tabitha smiled ruefully, though Hattie couldn't see it. "Well, we do homework together. And I won't go out with boys, even though some of them REALLY want me to. That pretty much GUARANTEES we're doing terrible, horrible, UNSPEAKABLE things to each other, including whatever they can imagine (and believe me, they spend a LOT of time imagining it), and all that was BEFORE we ever... ah... Had... Were..."

"That's really awful."

"Yes, it is. Welcome to high school. We'll be fine. I've been to her house to do homework, a couple of times when we were waiting for a ride. The woman HAS actually met me. We'll play it by ear. I'm tough. And you know Britt."

"Thankyou, Tabitha."

"For what?"

"For being one of the Good Ones."

***

Brittany got just a few private minutes with her father while Hattie was suffering her daughter-in-law's help with setting the table and putting the last little touches on dinner. Brittany and her dad were bringing in a little more firewood from the shed for the kitchen range.

"Dad, I did."

"That's nice. What?"

"I told you I would tell you when I did. I did. Recently." She was all smiles.

Walt realized ALL the rumors were true: *girls, boys, cars, trucks, the men's AND women's college hockey teams, the teacher after school. Oh shit!* He dropped his armful of firewood on his foot. Clunk-a-thunk-whump-"OWGODDAMMIT!"

"No, it wasn't THAT bad." She smiled sweetly as she balanced her wood on one arm while helping her dad pick up his dropped bolts. "I wanted you to know."

"Er... Thanks." *I think. Not really.* "Do you need to, ah... uuuuuugghh!" He was straightening back up with much too big an armload of split cordwood.

Neither of them moved towards the farmhouse.

"Ah... need to talk about it?"

"No. Don't believe everything you hear. But I suppose you might as well believe some of it. Thanks for telling me about power." She was already starting up the back steps to the farmhouse.

Walt stood dumbfounded in the yard, his arms full of firewood. *Oh, SHIT!*

Eventually, he recovered enough to join his family in the warm house.

The evening was a smashing success on outside appearances. Festive, the kitchen already decorated with holly and wreaths (Christmas was just a week away), also fun, friendly... and fake. Tension radiated and rebounded and set the air all a-quiver. Everyone was waiting for her to blow her top. It went without saying who HER was... Robin had a reputation.

Supper was great, as all meals in the Wendell farmhouse are. Pork slow-roasted in a broiling pan with onions and fennel harvested earlier in the year from the garden out back. Potatoes dug just this afternoon, out of a barrel of peat moss in the basement. Gravy from the roast juices (*take your new cholesterol medicine later, Hattie*) slathered on the potatoes. Coleslaw from the last of the fresh cabbage and carrots from the cold-storage crate in the shed, with home-dried parsley chopped up and mixed in. Homemade rolls, lovingly mixed and kneaded and turned and patted down and double-risen before being turned onto a baking sheet by Brittany and Tabitha. Lively conversation about school, work, harvest, relatives, friends, and upcoming hockey. A seasonal pre-Christmas cake heavy with prunes and candied fruit (their own, from citron and watermelon grown all summer in a cold-frame and preserved in mid-September in a marathon canning, pickling, and freezing session). They all treated Tabitha as a member of the family, for the most part. Everyone is family around the table at mealtime - at least that is the appearance kept.

Tabitha did notice that Brian kept looking at her, watching closely how she interacted with his older sister. Like he was trying to figure something out. *Ah. He's heard about it, too.*

Robin finally cornered her daughter in the kitchen, after the apple pie. She leaned in low, and mean, so close that as she shook her finger at her daughter it actually sternly poked the air behind the girl.

Brittany saw her mother's arm moving beside her and knew exactly what the finger was doing - she'd seen it enough before. She felt each stab in her breastbone as the bile-filled woman drove her words home into the empty air beside her.

The woman nearly hissed at her daughter: "WHAT are you THINKING, girl?!"

Brittany thought her mother sounded remarkably like an evil witch. *Come on, lets have the rest of it, crone. Might as well get it over with.*

"I mean, COME ON, a LESBIAN now? Not to mention ending up with some PIMP'S car, I don't want to know WHAT you did for that!"

"He's not a pimp. He reconditions cars. I liked his work."

Yelling now, forgetting or not caring to hold it back: "THAT is what EVERYONE in town is saying. You have NO shame!"

Walt's father's voice boomed in from the other room: "GET IN HERE, YOUNG MAN." Mother and daughter looked up to see Brittany's younger brother Brian scurrying out of the doorway and high-tailing it back to his chair at the table. An eavesdropper.

"Jesus! CAN'T YOU CONTROL EITHER OF YOUR KIDS, WALT?!?"

Walter Wendell took a deep breath and let that one pass. He'd volunteered for the job and that was that. To his son: "Sit. Snooping is unbecoming behavior, Mister."

Gee, she is just being a bitch to EVERYBODY tonight. Brittany forced herself to smile, but got the wording wrong: "Are you done, Mom?"

"NO I'M NOT! You watch your TONE, you little SLUT!" She wasn't bothering to hide her venom, either, now. "AND HUMPING A GOD-DAMNED LESBIAN, FOR CHRIST'S sake!" She made sure her voice broke on the last word.

Great. Brittany was resigned to it. *A nice little soap opera for the whole family to hear. And guest. After-dinner entertainment. Sorry, Tabitha.*

Her mother's fists balled up. "What I just don't understand is HOW you could DO THIS to me!"

Quietly, seriously, Brittany said the first thing that came to her mind, without filter. "Actually, I did it to Tabitha."

WHAP!!

It was the first time her mother had slapped her, but it hurt far, far less than all those things the older woman had said over these too many years.

Chairs scraped. Running footsteps from the other room.

Brittany finally raised her own voice: "THAT, BITCH, is the LAST time you are EVER going to touch me." She glared at her mother coolly, up on her toes, nose to nose.

There were other people in the room now, hands on arms, pushing, pulling. Neither woman really noticed.

Brittany's tone became very quiet. But she'd learned her mother's venom well - she squinted the words out of her mouth: "If you so much as FART in my direction in the next two years, I'm emancipating in COURT! How'd THAT be for the TALK OF THE TOWN?!"

Robin had a raised finger and a mouth open to speak, but she was stopped in her tracks.

"I work a job. I've got all A's and B's and I'll have them for the rest of school. I already live outside the parent's home. I checked with Legal Aid. I can initiate the process against your wishes. Legal Aid thinks I'm likely to win. SO FUCK YOU! Now get out of my house." Brittany smiled, sweetly. "The rest of you can stay for card games. Even YOU, Brian! I'll give you all a ride down the hill later, in my NEW CAR!" She'd gone gleefully manic now.

Her mother's lip was quivering ever so slightly. The women were still toe-to-toe, still being held and shoved by unnoticed restraining hands, but one of them was shrinking, ever so slightly. The mother tried to hold her ground, couldn't, and then turned and let herself be pulled from the kitchen and back into the dining room from which she'd-

"FLOWN IN ON HER FUCKING BROOM!" Brittany cranked up the volume again for the parting shot.

Brittany's grandmother spoke quietly from behind her. "That's enough, Brittany. Let them go." She leaned in close to the young woman's ear. "Always let the asshole leave if they've been knocked down." *You did good, Dear.* Hattie released Brittany's right arm and relaxed her hold on her waist.

Brittany stayed rooted in place in the middle of the kitchen floor. There was a commotion of hats and coats and car keys and then they were gone.

"JesusandMaryandtheSaintsabove! I am SO sorry, Brittany. I... I won't do that again." Hattie patted her granddaughter on the arm. "Your grandmother really 'fucked up.'"

Brittany hadn't moved, but she was shaking now. Uncontrollably, apparently. She sat down, right there in the middle of the kitchen floor where she'd been standing. Her legs trembled as she sat, trembled so hard that one of her knees kept hitting the floor. Knock-knock-knock-knock.

Hattie's eyes went wide. *Oh shit!* "TABITHA! TA-BITH-AAAA!! Are you HEEEEERRRRE, Girl!?!" She was suddenly afraid to leave Brittany. She'd seen this before.

Tabitha came into the kitchen thirty seconds later, head high, eyes red and wet. "Holy SHI- Hey Brittany, it's OKAY, they're GONE now, girl Jesus, what do..."

Grandma knew just what to do. "Go get a blanket! And hurry your buns up!" Hattie was down on the floor now, holding her trembling granddaughter, whose dazed green eyes were no longer entirely focused.

Tabitha came flying back with a puke-green wool blanket from the couch.

"She's in shock." Hattie shook her head. "Help me here." Grandma wanted one more thing, as she arranged the blanket around Brittany. "Who smokes?"

Tabitha looked down in puzzlement. "Huh?"

Hattie threw her hands in the air. *No sense I'm making, I'm myself rattled!* "We need a cigarette, girl!"

Tabitha bounded out of the room, out of the house, and down the front steps, slipping only once on ice. She came back in a flurry of cold air, with a pack of Winstons held high. By way of explanation: "Dads."

"God loves us tonight. Here, Sweetie." Hattie knocked a smoke and the lighter out of the pack in one smack and lit up like a champion emphysema candidate. She stuck the cigarette between Brittany's lips. It promptly fell out on account of the whole-body shaking. Tabitha picked it up, gave her hand a brief disbelieving and disgusted look, and then held it up to her panicked friend. Brittany took a big drag, way too big, coughed, shook, coughed, spasmed in shakes again, and got the hang of it.

Tabitha HAD to: "Grandma Wendell, you're a BAD influence!"

The three women, one old and two just becoming, sat on the floor together laughing while Brittany shook and smoked and cried and choked and giggled - sometimes all at once.

Sometime after the cigarette burned out, Hattie felt that it was time to get all of them up off the floor. "Who's up for a shot of brandy? I know I am, after that disaster!" Hattie looked at the two very young women. Winced. "Maybe that's not such a good idea. I'll tough it out." She saw Tabitha's crestfallen look. "Oh, stop your pouting. I have to be careful SOMEWHERE. When you're both eighteen. That'll be good enough for me." She turned to look at Brittany, still in her arms on the floor. "Isn't it enough for one day that I got you smoking?"

Brittany giggled again, snot poking in and out of her nose. She felt better, except a little sick and light-headed. She hadn't smoked since she was thirteen (which had lasted a whole week). Tabitha leapt up and grabbed a handful of paper towels. Brittany blew her nose.

Hattie sighed. "I am SO, so sorry." She shook her head back and forth in time with her words. "Stupid, stupid, stupid, stupid."

Brittany's voice still quivered. "S'okay, Grandma. Gives me a chances to gave her a piece of my minds." Brittany still wasn't quite straight in the head, apparently.

"Gave ME a chance to SEE it." Tabitha smiled at Brittany, then gave her a fake shot to the jaw. "You go, Girl."

Hattie stood up and regarded them both. Tabitha was doing the holding now. Brittany looked measurably better, her eyes were focused now at least. Grandma smiled at peace restored. "You two are really precious, you know."

When Brittany could finally get up, they all went to the living room and plopped down on the couch. Brittany slid off, back onto the floor, and scooted over in front of Tabitha to lean back against her friend. They watched Tee-Vee for a bit while Tabitha combed Brittany's wavy black hair with her fingers.

Hattie looked at the clock on the mantle. "Girls, do you have work to do for tomorrow?" Sunday night WAS a school-night, after all, even if you've just thrown water on a witch, so-to-speak.

Tabitha got up and shuffled awkwardly, one steadying hand on top of the waist-high head in front of her, to step around her classmate. She stood up straight and stretched. "I SUPPOOOOOZZE!"

Brittany looked up speculatively. "We could ride in, together, tomorrow, and I could take the bus home. I'm not working."

Tabitha's face lit up as if the very Heavens had parted.

Brittany turned to look up at the couch behind her. "Do you mind, Grandma? I know it's a school-night, but…"

"Get some SLEEP, you two. I mean it. Tabitha, call your parents first, see how they are about school-nights."

Tabitha went to the kitchen to use the phone.

Brittany gave her grandmother a long hug. "Thankyou, Grandma. For giving me a place to go."

"I wouldn't want to live there, either." *I had no idea how bad it was. SOMETHING was brewing, the way Brittany went up on her toes like that.....* " I'm sure she'll feel bad later."

"I doubt it."

The girl is probably right. Hattie sighed, and turned off the tee-vee. It would do Brittany some good if she could have company tonight. Hattie couldn't stay up half the night processing the evening with her daughter. That was a job for another teenager.

Tabitha came back into the room. "They're fine. Mom said, I quote, 'No hanky-panky all night, it's a school-night.' AS IF, after all of that!"

Brittany, finally standing up, scrutinized her friend. "They… know you pretty well, don't they?"

"Oh, they think I'm 'randy as an old goat' is how Mom put it, once." She looked towards Grandma Wendell with an embarrassed smirk. "I don't know what would give them that idea...."

(Tabitha was very matter of fact about her preferences in front of her parents - she was one of the lucky ones who'd progressed easily from innocent childhood exclamations: "that girl is pretty!" onward to heartfelt expressions of desire mainly learned from the boys: "God, that new neighbor, she's a DISH!!")

Tabitha winked at Brittany and then gave a sidelong glance at Grandma Wendell. "Your grandmother must tell secrets."

Hattie ignored that. "Well it IS a school-night. It's good advice." Hattie was mildly unnerved. *So they know. What goes on here. Oooof!* She shooed the two young women with the backs of her hands. *I wonder if that implicates me, somehow?* "Take your homework up with you. Goodnight, you two. I've got some cleaning up to do in the kitchen." She hurried them off over their protests. They wanted to help with the dishes from the disastrous night. *No good leaving them in the residue of it.* It would pass by morning, the shock and strain of it... quicker if they got away from the kitchen and up in a bedroom to - hopefully - do some homework. *Did I just send them off to bed together?! Whups!* She shrugged. *Not germane to the bigger evening, I think.* Hattie was proud of her granddaughter: she'd run away from the venom, and when it followed her, she carefully vanquished the source with strong and measured words - and also research, apparently. Hattie didn't know that the poor girl had been to see Legal Aid. That part surprised her. *Such complicated lives, these children!*

Hattie Wendell set about rinsing plates, washing silver, and putting leftovers into cold storage on the porch or in the fridge. She'd do the lion's share of the dishes in about six hours, when she got up at four in the morning. They'd keep for the night, rinsed, just this once. She overheard Brittany admonishing Tabitha as the two very young women went up the stairs:

"Don't get any ideas, Girl. And it's only for tonight. Just this one time."

The red-head's musical voice floated in from the front hall, growing fainter, and then came through the register as they summited the stairs. "It always is, Brittany." A creak overhead. "It always is."

***

Hattie had the dishes done and a fresh batch of cornbread muffins and bacon ready for the girls when they came down in the morning. If she didn't know they were sometimes lovers, she would have felt like she had two granddaughters in the house. She couldn't figure out if it mattered. They loved each other, maybe not each the same way, but enough. Their behavior was matter-of-fact and appropriate to time of day and situation; they kept their hands mostly to themselves in mixed company, except for affectionate or friendly pats and caresses that could pass between any couple of intimate friends. The line was so blurred with these two.... Here they were, lurching into the kitchen sleepy-eyed, open hands seeking coffee mugs, Brittany's sweatshirt dangling to Tabitha's knees, Brittany in a wool sweater - that must be scratchy - and Super-Hero themed underwear bottoms. *Am I perpetuating sin, letting these two consort under this roof? ARE they still, or has that passed?* Hattie shook her head and decided that it was none of her business. *We drove one away... let this one be who she will be, Hattie.*

There WAS something else that was her business, though. "Do I need to take away that pack of cigarettes, Tabitha?" She held out her hand.

Tabitha reared back, eyes wide. "They're not mine, I swear!"

Hattie sighed. "The thing you young folks never understand when you get started is that cigarettes are MEDICINE, and just like any other they are ADDICTIVE. Habit-forming medicine is useful, but dangerous. Any idiot can take up a bad habit. Like nose-picking."

Both girls said

"IIIIIIICKK!!!!"

"EEEWWWWWWW!!!"

at just the right time.

"So, the key is NOT when you WANT to. ONLY if you NEED to." Grandma Wendell started putting dishes from the night before away in cupboards, but she was still lecturing. "And not too many folks really NEED to, most of the time. You saw a good example just last night in the kitchen, someone who needed to. Car accident witnesses, too, if it's bad."

"That was certainly a car wreck, alright."

"Thankyou Tabitha, we hadn't noticed. I am SO, so sorry. Brittany, Dear, are you okay?"

Brittany waved her hand dismissively. "Teen-aged super-hero vanquishes one more evil villain. Had to happen sometime, I suppose."

***

Insert a perky male 1940's radio-drama announcer's voice:

AND YESTERDAY EVENING, WHEN THE WENDELL FAMILY GOT HOME!!

Now read on:

"What the hell was THAT?!?" Brittany's father seethed through clenched teeth; he looked like a bull terrier gone human.

He'd done well to wait until Brian was out of the car - like a shot, once they were home, the boy didn't even say anything, just bolted into the house and left his parents to have it out. Brian had suffered a long, silent ride down from the farmhouse and wanted to get the hell away from whatever was coming. Walt didn't blame him. Now here it was, the boy was gone, and he could let loose.

Robin had other ideas - she was ready for Round Two: "THAT was our DAUGHTER running WILD while you and your MOTHER act like she's some sort of sainted NURSE up there!" Brittany's Mother felt some amount of injustice that she was blamed for the fights. She always was.

"She's a TEENAGER, Robin. That's what they DO."

They hadn't even bothered to get out of the car yet.

"Maybe if you SUPPORTED me a little bit…" Robin made sure her voice broke a little there at the end. Sometimes it helped.

"I CAN'T support you now that you've jumped down her throat like some Goddamned bible-thumping drill Sergeant! Jesus, Robin! NOW... I can't say a THING about any of it now, because I HAVE TO BE THE LOVING PARENT here! What the hell were you thinking, attacking her like that?"

"Well, SOMEONE has to bring her under control!" Robin dabbed at her eyes with a tissue. *Jesus, Walt, you worry more about her than you do about ME.*

"NOT that way. And now, since you've gone over the top with…"

Robin whirled in the front seat. The whole car rocked. "I SUPPOSE you want me to CONGRATULATE her on being a TEEN WHORE?!?"

Walt sighed. He was giving up, actually. "No. I want you to set limits and get her to think about consequences, and parent her in a POSITIVE way. But you can't do that, can you? And that's why she's up at"

"But WALT! Think about THOSE THINGS she's been DOING!!! She's OUT OF CONTROL up there! I can't help it if I come off bitchy, SOMEONE'S got to keep her IN LINE!!!!" The tears were coming for real, this time. Frustration. Self-pity. Habit.

"You said it, not me! But you're right. You ARE a bitch to her." He raised his voice, because her mouth was opening and he wanted to finish: "AND ONE OF US HAS TO BE SUPPORTIVE AND SAY ALL THE RIGHT THINGS, SO THAT MEANS I CAN'T SAY A GODDAMNED THING TO HER ABOUT ANY OF THESE… allegations." Walt got out of the car and started pacing in the frosty driveway. Walter Wendell wasn't high-strung, but he'd been holding back an awful long time. Just trying to be pleasant got old tonight.

Robin was out of the car, too, but not headed into the house. "OH! So let's just BLAME IT ON THE BITCH! RIGHT?!?" Her voice gelled in the frosty air, spewing like smoke.

Apparently she wants a scene. Right here in the driveway. So be it. "You know what, Robin? YES. LET'S. You've TOTALLY SCREWED UP any chance we had of talking to her about this, this THING. THESE things. And if you weren't"

"But WALT..."

"IF YOU WEREN'T SO AWFUL TO HER, she wouldn't be up with my Mother." He was tempted to say, AGAIN, but didn't. "She didn't go up there to play nurse. She went UP THERE to get AWAY from YOU! And I don't really blame her."

Robin stood rooted to her spot while Walt paced up and down the driveway. She didn't like to give up on a good fight. Duke it out long enough, you'll win, that was her motto. But Robin was running out of arguments. "Fuck you, Walt."

"Hmmph." He paced faster; He was getting good and worked up, and it put him over the top this once. He took a deep breath and leaned into it, careful to keep well back from his wife. "SO, MISSES WENDELL, what YOU are going to DO, is be POLITE and RESPECTFUL and treat her like an adult, and you know what, why don't you just treat her like she's NOT your kid and maybe it'll work better for you, and if you CAN'T do any of that then when you're around her why don't you just KEEP YOUR MOUTH SHUT and look PLEASANT or BRITTANY won't be the ONLY one EMANCIPATED from you?" He turned with carefully-staged wild and gleeful eyes. "How bout THAT?!?"

Robin stood stock-still in the driveway, leaning slightly forward to make a forgotten point, her mouth a frozen O.

She looked to Walt like a landed fish. *Good. I've got her attention. Finally can't think fast enough to come up with a retort.* "So the NEXT TIME you see Brittany, EVEN IF she's got a WHOLE GANG OF BADASS BIKERS BANGING HER, IF SHE LIKES IT, THEN YOU LIKE IT, AND YOU SMILE AT HER! I SEEM TO REMEMBER THAT YOU LIKED GETTING NAILED AT ONE TIME IN YOUR LIFE, AND TOSSED YOUR LITTLE TUSH OUT THERE

FOR A FEW FAVORS AT AROUND THAT AGE, YOURSELF!" *And that car of Brittany's is certainly more sensible than putting a few thousand dollars worth of blow up your nose during your abbreviated out-of-town college career!* But of course he didn't need to say that.

He was talking to her back, anyway. The front door slammed so hard the glass fell out.

***

BBBBBRRRRINGGGGG. BBBBBBBRRRRRINNNGGG. The sharp, tinny cups of a phone with real bells - two of them on the front, staring like eyes into the farmhouse kitchen - rang out.

Hattie lifted the handset on the shelf below the honey-colored wooden box. "Brittany! Phone's for you, Dear!" Hattie Wendell held out the ancient iron-and-ceramic handset that usually cradled on the side of the wood box.

Amazing it still worked, but the line voltage for telephones hadn't changed since Alexander Graham Bell had patented the first local exchange: fifty volts for a carrier, two hundred volts to ring. The one concession to modernity: there was no operator to ring up and connect them, so they'd had to install a little in-line dialer that hung just below the phone box.

Brittany looked up from the bowl full of walnuts she was gradually running through the old hand-cranked meat-grinder that was bolted to a low shelf in one corner of the kitchen. She was loath to leave her task. She was having fun baking in that hundred-and-forty-year-old kitchen. "Boy or girl?"

"Your father."

"Hmmmmm. Neither. In that context, I mean."

Brittany and Hattie shared a laugh as the girl got up to take the phone.

"What are you two giggling about?" Walter Wendell tried to sound stern.

Brittany knew better. "Girl stuff. Makeup, tampons, that kind of stuff."

"Forget I asked. Ahhh, Brittany, about the oth…"

"Are you lecturing or commiserating?

Silence.

Brittany took a deep breath, counted to five, and tried again. "I'm sorry, Dad. That was… Me being defensive. You were saying something. Areyoumad?" She rushed it out and grabbed the counter beside her, trying somehow to hold herself from interrupting again, bracing herself for what was sure to come.

"As I was saying. The other night was… awful. I just wanted to see if you were alright."

Brittany slid down against the cupboards until she was sitting on the floor. She had to angle the phone handset away from her mouth to reach - the old cords didn't stretch. She gave a thumbs-up to her grandmother. "I'm good. Okay, really. How is… she?"

"Not good. She's really upset. About how it went. Sorry, of course."

Brittany thought to herself that *if my mom was REALLY sorry, she would have been the one calling*, not her dad.

"…and she's convinced herself she did something wrong as a mother. The usual. Has she always treated you that way?"

"You mean behind closed doors, when you weren't around?" *Yes. Just like that. Except* "she's never slapped me before…"

"Did you ever stick up for yourself before?"

"Well…. Not that much. Dad? Was I wrong?"

"No, honey. She was wrong." He sighed. "No parent should resort to name-calling. I'm really sorry about that."

"YOU don't have to be."

Now he was nervous. "But, ah… Honey? Can you maybe take it down a notch or two? I mean, she said it the wrong way, but I've… people... heard…"

"But what? What exactly have you HEARD, Dad?"

"Well, that you have a parade of boys following at your heels…"

"And that's MY fault?!" She grinned.

He could hear the grin, so that allowed him to try to continue. "And that maybe, ah, well, ah… Yu… Shit. Never mind. It's none of my business anyways, and you're pretty much a grown woman now."

"Ah, thanks?" Brittany was a little disappointed. She'd kind of wanted to see where this was heading. "Now. Really. What do you want to know? Ask it."

There was a whole lot of silence on the telephone line.

Walt was thinking, fast: *So what exactly did you DO to that boy to end up with a few thousand dollars worth of car for it, anyways? Are you practicing safe sex? Are you sleeping with that little Lesbian girl who came to dinner? Is it true that you mowed a lawn on MAIN STREET in a MINI-SKIRT and a WET T-SHIRT? How much does my mother know about all this, and how much of it is going on UP THERE at the farmhouse? Do you even OWN a swimsuit anymore?* What he SAID, was: "Are you living life in the way that YOU really want to, Brittany?"

Wow. Score one for Dad. He must be DYING to ask something a little more juicy than THAT! "Yes, Dad, I am. Looking back, I wouldn't change a THING."

Humph. Confident little girl. Not one thing, huh? Well, that itself will probably change with a little aging, but what the hell. How can you argue with someone as certain of herself as that? And really, she IS the most focused and… OLD little girl I know of… But I worry about you, girl, because "You're not as old as you think you are. Have fun, but PLEASE make it to twenty in one piece, sweety."

"Oh, jeez, Dad, I'll consider it a victory just to make it to seventeen, why worry about something as far away as twenty?"

He could hear the laughter in her voice, so he didn't panic. "And try not to give your mother and me a stroke. OR your grandmother, for that matter. How is SHE dealing with all this?"

"All of WHAT, Dad? You're such a drama queen. We're having a real good time. I've introduced her to beer and dope and girls and the MTV channel. You should come up on a Saturday night sometime! Make sure you knock first…"

Well that answers that. She IS sleeping with the Lesbian. "Your grandmother watches MTV?"

"Ah, she wants to talk to you now. Dad - don't worry about a thing. And thanks for checking up on me. Bye!"

A short scuffle ensued on the Farmhouse end of the phone line.

"YOU go AWAY and let me talk to my SON, young lady! Walt, what kind of lies are she spinning? There's no MTV up here!"

Mother and son had a nice talk about everything but the other night.

***

Christmas at the Wendell family farmhouse was a subdued affair. Robin couldn't make it for some reason. Brittany, either - she had to work, all day, a rare double shift. Walt and Brian came up and sat down to a somewhat smaller meal than usual, and then, once the one-o'clock dinner had settled somewhat, went out behind the shed to uncover the wood-splitter and finish the last of the ten cords of wood that Hattie and Brittany would need to see them through the winter - a little unconventional, if very practical Christmas gift. They returned to the village at dark, their ears ringing, fingers cold, and backs sore. Walt thought about having ready-made firewood delivered next year. The load of logs dropped a year ahead was getting to be too much work. His daughter, though not a polished-nails, oh-don't-get-me-dirty type, probably wasn't going to be running a chainsaw any time soon, even if she did have the time.

***

Walt and Robin had a rough few weeks, and then, in the New Year, decided to patch it up with a date. Robin looked through the movie section in the paper and found a nice Hollywood romance about a couple of forty-somethings and their wayward children. It was playing in the little theater over in the county seat, not too far away. Walt said he'd take them out to eat on the cheap on the way, some place quick. Nothing fancy - he wanted to keep it light. In those days, frugal and fancy meant Smiley's, the chain restaurant over on the strip.

Robin was excited about their date, almost hyper: "And let's not spend a MINUTE thinking about OUR family!" She shouted it almost gleefully.

Like it's that bad. He let it pass. *We are trying to make up.* "Sure, Robin, as long as the movie folks don't have a fourteen-year-old boy and a sixteen-year-old daughter who's living with her grandmother..." He could imaging THAT scene: His wife getting up and storming out of the theater, cursing all the way. He grimaced.

"If THAT happens, I'm LEAVING." She grabbed her purse off the coatrack by the door and slung the little sack over her shoulder. Its strap probably outweighed it two-to-one. Walt wondered how she could fit anything besides her driver's license in there. *Probably she can't. Same with the skirt and top, actually.*

"You SURE that's the movie you want to see?" He sized her up: *I wonder what she'd be wearing if we were going out to someplace expensive...* "You look good, Robin."

"Well, it's either that or the one about gun-slinging goblins, or that really STUPID movie about the two women who run off on a crime spree together."

You should try it. You might like it. Get you out of the house, at least. Stop it, Walt, you're trying to be nice. Deep breath. "Making up is much nicer, Robin. Let's go catch a movie, Babe!" He put on a smile. *If I act like I'm having fun, it'll BE fun.* He went out to start the car. It being mid-January, his wife would throw a FIT if the seats were cold when she got in and plastered the backs of her naked thighs against the vinyl. *But she sure does look good in that short skirt she's slipped into!*

Robin strutted across the icy parking lot and into Smiley's on Walt's arm like she was still an eighteen-year-old college football cheerleader. A few heads turned. A couple old farts tried to get a better look at her butt when she sat down. It wasn't hard. There are swimsuit bottoms out there that cover more than that little black pleated skirt did. Robin liked to flaunt it, and she still HAD it for a thirty-five year old. Folks in the restaurant were thinking, *Wow... she must be SOME COLD when she's getting out of that car!*

Walt and Robin were seated and looking at the on-every-table Specials Menu when a crisp-voiced girl cleared her throat and asked if they were ready to order drinks and appetizers.

Walt felt his wife jerk to attention beside him. He looked up from his menu to see their daughter standing next to the table, holding a pitcher of water and two glasses. She was dressed... *like a waitress. Oh, shit.*

"I don't FUCKING BELIEVE THIS GODDAMNED SHIT!!" And then, after she'd taken a good, deep breath, even louder: "CAN'T YOU LEAVE US ALONE FOR ONE FUCKING NIGHT?!?" Robin was already up off the red plasti-leather bench seat and around her daughter and on her way down the aisle towards the exit. Her coat was still there on the bench beside Walt, probably left as a statement.

Brittany's dad didn't know what to do, for a second. "So you got a job?" *Maybe THAT's how she got the car.* "I'll talk to you later, when you're not working. Sorry about this." Walter gathered up both coats and scooted out past his daughter, who was still holding the water glasses and pitcher and whose expression was inscrutable. "Good for you, kiddo. Don't work TOO hard." And then he was gone.

The dining floor was very quiet. Brittany stood rooted to the floor in front of the empty table. A glass clinked. There were silverware noises, and then the murmur of talking started. Brittany looked at the Manager and shrugged, then headed for the dish-room window with the unnecessary glasses.

Every patron in the place could hear the yelling out in the parking lot, right through the commercial plate-glass windows.

Roger, the manager, was holding his head. *Oh, crap! Not AGAIN!*

***

Early January found Hattie Wendell in a state of flurry! The first Away Game for her treasured Academy hockey team was coming up tomorrow, and with all that had been going on at the farmhouse with her new roommate/granddaughter, she hadn't even given it a thought! But now a bus full of hungry hockey players was on the way in just twenty-four hours. Those boys were going to win - they'd better - and Hattie was going to do her part!

Brittany worked a lot - more than ever, it seemed - so Hattie was on her own for cleaning up and making pies on Friday morning, even with school still out for the Christmas and New Year holidays. That was fine with her - Hattie had been doing it mostly by herself all along. In the morning she popped the top on a couple of quart jars of home-canned blueberry preserves for making pie filling, went through the apple bins and selected a half-bushel that were starting to dry out or fade, and then took five packs of bacon and some paper-wrapped packages of locally-cured "cuts" out of the freezer. She rolled out four pie-crusts and set them in tins, with two pre-woven top-crusts all laid out on waxed paper, ready to go on top of the blueberry preserve pies. Hattie commenced with those two first. She'd peel and chop the apples while the first of the pies with the prepared fillings baked in her wood-fired range. *No chance of the house being cold today!* She got the apple mix ready, polished the chopping block and kitchen table with a little bit of oil, worked the two surfaces over with a dry rag, and then cleaned up here and there around the kitchen and parlor.

Her friend Sylvia called, from work, at noon. Sylvia was President of the hockey booster club this year. "Do you need any help up there tomorrow, Hattie?"

"Oh, I don't think so. You're always welcome, of course, but I already have a helper for the morning, and I hear she's already got some waitressing experience! Thankyou, though. Kitchen will be crowded enough once they all arrive!"

"Okay... Glad to hear it actually, kind of a thin weekend for help around here... Everyone interested seems to be going to a hotel over there tonight. The club's making kind of a thing of it."

"Oh, that sounds fun!" Hattie didn't travel, so she wasn't concerned about missing the game and the weekend's festivities in far western New York. *What a long ride - no thankyou to that!* "You going?"

"No... I've got some fresh faces staying with me a while, and Hank is on-call tomorrow, so I think I'll be staying around. I'm more than happy to come over..."

"Well, you can if you want to, of course, but we're fine." Hattie lowered her voice to a conspirator's street-corner hustle: "What you COULD do is stop by the store on your way home...."

"Oh, sure! What do you need?"

"Pie crusts. Don't tell!" She chuckled.

"Sure. I'll be on my way through the usual time. How many?"

"Oh, four, I think. I didn't want to ask Walt."

"It will be our little secret."

Hattie said, somewhat defensively, "EIGHT pies IS a lot of work, you know. That's SIXTEEN crusts that have to be rolled out, for fruit pies..."

Sylvia smirked, and her voice responded over the tinny antique phone handset with musical mirth: "They'll never know."

Sylvia stopped at the farmhouse at six that evening to drop off the frozen pie crusts. She had hedged and brought eight, and she also thoughtfully included a large can of coffee, several boxes of pre-made oven-bake hashbrowns from the frozen section, and two more cartons of eggs, in case Hattie was short. They visited for a bit while Hattie rolled out the top-crusts for the frozen bottom crusts that were now thawing on the counter. (Everything had to be the same temperature when it went in the oven, or Bad Things would happen.) Sylvia eventually took her leave and went home to attend her own ever-changing flock - her Sitter could only stay so late.

Fostering was not part of Sylvia's job - in fact, it often created a conflict of interest. She couldn't directly work a case involving one of her "boarders." That made for some complicated footwork within her department and its umbrella agency, so most often she took in children from other counties. Juggling a job, an ever-fluctuating mix of traumatized personalities, a marriage, and a little farm complete with ten chickens and a sheep... Hattie didn't know how the woman did it. She considered Sylvia and her husband Hank to be angels.

By ten that night, the last of the pies were out of the oven. Hattie went out to check the crates of cold goods in a corner of the unheated shed, up against the stone foundation of an outside wall of the farmhouse kitchen... yes, cold but not freezing. They'd be alright for the night. All the orange juice, milk, cream, eggs, and potatoes that Walt had brought up on Thursday night were safely tucked there and still as cold as when they'd left the store. She went in to bank the range for a quick start to the morning's cooking fire.

God, I love cooking for these hard-charging and hungry young men! Now give them a WIN tomorrow!

Brittany came home from work in the dark of night to a house that smelled of just-baked pies: the smokey smell of hot lard and flour; the rich, buttery aroma of well-done crust; the fruity perfume that announced blueberries; the tangy, cidery, spicy aroma of baked apples and cinnamon and cloves. There was a note on the table:

NOPE! TOMORROW MORNING AND NOT TIL THEN

Brittany smiled. She did sneak a peek at them, though. *Wow! Eight. Yum! I hope there's a slice left for me!*

***

Hattie Wendell let Brittany sleep in until five that next morning and then brought her up a cup of hot black coffee, right to the bedroom. *It's a little early for her hours, but she's young and she can sleep later this morning, after they're gone. I need the help!* Brittany's grandmother was by nature caring, but also practical.

Brittany bounded down the stairs a few minutes later, fresh-faced and a little nervous. She'd served a whole lot of college boys while waitressing at work, but this was different. They were all coming to her HOME.

"Just treat it like your restaurant, Dear." Brittany's grandmother spoke over her shoulder as she stirred up batter for muffins. She spoke out of context in an aside: "Can you grease those tins with bacon fat? Thankyou." Once her granddaughter was on task, she continued. "That's what we are to them, at least until their stomachs are full!"

Thanks, Grandma. "How come I've never thought of coming up to help you with this before?" Brittany was making up pancake batter now, using one of Grandma Wendell's notes from some other past hockey breakfast, made for some other past helper.

"Well, some other folks from the Booster Club drop by to help now and again. There's not much to it, really, except the dishes. Those boys do use up every bit of china in the place!"

"Don't worry about the dishes, I'll do them..."

Hattie looked appraisingly at her granddaughter's backside. "Oh, I think you'll have a helper or ten." The girl had come down in a pleated school-girl skirt she'd been wearing since she was fourteen - it's a wonder it still fits her at all - and a form-fitting oxford shirt. *Oh, dear.* "I suspect they'll be delighted to assist you."

Brittany thought about that for a minute. She'd dressed up in her best school clothes this morning - she wanted to look nice for company. Now she looked back and down at herself for a moment, scowling, calculating. *Hmmmm...* She'd just bought the skirt, a doppelganger for the one it had replaced, because the last one certainly no longer covered her decently - it pulled up too much in back. She'd thought this new one certainly was proper attire... She frowned. *Still too small to drape over it right?* IT being her increasingly filled-out hips which supported a very different bottom than the one she'd had at fourteen. *Hmmmmm.*

Hattie thought that she looked cute, just standing there thinking about her own bottom. Brittany's deep concentration on the problem - her own butt - caused her mouth to go crooked in a right-leaning smirk and her eyebrows to pucker. Stage expressions, and the poor girl didn't even know it. *The Academy boys will find this young lady irresistible,* she'd wager. *Oh, dear.*

Brittany came back to the moment with a broad smile. *Problem solved.* "I'll just wear sweats!" She started for the kitchen doorway.

"Brittany Wendell! Have you LOOKED at yourself in those sweatpants?!? It doesn't matter WHAT you wear, this kitchen is going to be full of WOLVES today. Don't worry about it. They're BOYS and you're a GIRL." Hattie Wendell looked at Brittany shrewdly. "I think you'll probably be able to handle them."

Brittany took one last look down at herself, front and back, then shrugged and rolled up her sleeves. "Where do I start?"

Hattie stirred up a two-gallon bowl of pancake batter and then set Brittany to cooking some ahead of time on the griddle. "They'll be here soon. Try to get about twenty ahead, and put them in the turkey roaster as they're done. Keep the cover on, they'll stay moist. Set it on the back corner of the range over there on the trivet..."

Brittany poured and flipped pancakes for a bit, on a liberal puddle of bacon grease on top of the wood fired range. The kitchen got smokey after a time. "Should I crack the door?"

"Good idea." Hattie looked at the clock as she waved away the dense kitchen aromas and haze. "Quarter to seven. They'll be here soon. Remember: You're a waitress, not a resident. They don't even know you live here. You're just a volunteer on the Booster Club, today."

Brittany steeled herself with a sigh and squared her shoulders.

And then the team bus was stopping right out front.

***

Not surprisingly, Brittany Wendell replaced food as the center of attention at breakfast:

Where'd SHE come from? Woooooowhooooowouldyalookatthat!

Lotta White Meat on THAT girl! CAAAAYUUUUTE!

She related to THAT old thing?!?

Vermont's finest Blue-Ribbon!

Five bucks I can get in her pants this week!

Wow, pretty!

Would ya look at THAT sculpture!

What's your number, baby?

Oh My God I've Died And Gone To Heaven!!

Wow, that girl is FINE!

That one's GOT to be CHERRY, dudes!

WHERE can I get a PICTURE POSTER of this?!

She's got a nice dumper, eh?

Who else is IN LOVE!

And various other comments, most rude even if intended to be complimentary, some not so rude, exclamations frequently awe-inspired, all unspoken, but never-the-less communicated and understood back and forth around the large dining room table and several sturdy old kitchen tables brought into the Wendell farmhouse from the old shed for the occasion of Hockey Breakfasts. Communicated with quick looks, furtive gestures, winks, subtle fork-pointing, and exaggerated wide-eyed expressions carefully staged only when both female backs in the room AND the coaching staff's heads were turned.

Brittany was ever the efficient waitress, bringing pancakes, drinks, pies, and bacon back and forth through the house. Hattie hardly had to lift a finger, other than taking things in and out of the oven. Hockey players looked up dreamily when their waitress dangled over the table to put down food. Some stole sideways glances at the front of her shirt when she brushed by them to retrieve an empty serving dish. A few scooted minutely back when she leaned forward over the table, ostensibly to pass a greeting to some other player also leaning back to be seen, but of course checking out this new doe's ass, conveniently between them while they conversed.

Someone with less polished social graces looked at the bacon and said, out loud, "Perdue's finest!"

"It's PORK, not CHICKEN, you shi… Er, POOP-head!"

Another nearby player rapped the offending loudmouth in the back of the head.

A few minutes later: "Wow. Quite the apple pie.... Love that cheddar!" Apparently this enthusiastic young man liked the apple pie and cheese slice combination that remained on the rim of his plate once he'd finished his eggs and potatoes.

Coach knew exactly what was being said. "MANNERS, gentlemen." *Jesus. Idiots are going to get the whole team thrown out, along with trashing our Away winning streak....*

Those Academy hockey players - well, actually nearly the whole male three-quarters of the student body - had devised a unique rating system for those of the other gender. All of it based on fine cheeses, for which New England in general and Vermont in particular were famous. Cheddar, cottage, blue, Romano, Roqueforte... their creativity and imagination were amazing, boundless and sometimes cruel. A "cheddar" was a sharp-looking girl. Good dresser, took care of herself, always at her best, a blue ribbon girl. Went well on anyone's arm, fancied up whatever they were with, good to bring to social functions. There were a lot of breakdowns in this locally-produced category: An AGED Cheddar was a perfectly desirable and delicious older woman - someone else's still-hot mother, for instance. A Blue-Ribbon Wisconsin Cheddar was a particularly fine Midwestern girl. Blue-Ribbon Vermont Aged Cheddar was most often Professor Wendell's wife, who was a real hottie in spite of being thirty-something, and who was both from the Vermont and frequently on display on sunny spring and fall days, possibly even specifically for passing Academy students. Coach knew about that, too, and made sure his own wife's chaise was set up in a comfortably-appointed private nook out in the BACK of their house. He'd even gone to the expense and trouble of putting in a pool right there to make sure the tanning chair was likely to STAY there, along with any scantily-clad wife and daughters that might be enjoying the sun. He was quite aware that these young Regimentals were WOLVES. As he looked around the dining room and into the adjoining parlor, he watched roughly twenty heads turning back and forth in time with the young woman's movements. *Shit, these guys are FOR SURE going to screw up our winning-streak breakfast spot....*

Somehow, Brittany remained oblivious to the stir. Ever-efficient, she worked the kitchen and the serving while her grandmother continued to cook batches of eggs in an extra-large and ancient cast-iron skillet.

One player just kept his gaze on Brittany's beautiful, wide, curl-framed face every time she floated through the dining room. This young man's looks were chaste and appraising and appreciating and frank. Eye contact. Averting his gaze to her hair - fascinating - or his plate whenever she draped herself down next to him to refresh a plate or take away an empty bowl. Brittany's fair complexion, green eyes and cascading, unruly hair were his own personal Vermeer. He drank in this newfound art whenever he could steal a glance at her.

Hattie put up with all of this behavior for a while, the chaste and the boorish, until it became clear that these players were beginning to neglect their food. She couldn't have the boys trying to win on empty stomachs! So she sighed and went to the head end of the table between the dining room and the parlor, the two "feed" rooms for the day.

"Boys!" No effect on the hubbub. "BOYS!" A couple of the hockey players closest to Hattie looked up now. *Hmmmm.* "Brittany, could you come over here for a minute, dear? Thankyou." *Well, NOW they're paying attention to me. Well, no. At least they are all looking in the right direction.* Hattie put her arm around Brittany. "THIS is my granddaughter. Brittany. Yes, she's very pretty, isn't she? No, you may not date her. Or entertain the thought. She's very young. Too young for any of you! And therefore, NOT available! Treat her like your sister..." Hattie squared herself up as well as her seventy-something year old form would let her. "And if I find out any one of you has engineered a rendezvous with her, even a date? He will meet a bitter end, that one." She smiled gently at Brittany, who's now-rosy cheeks made her even more beautiful, and thus more dangerous to these forewarned young bucks. "Don't get any of these fine hockey players killed, dear. Coach needs each and every one of them to win." She patted the girl's shoulder. "You can go back to work, now."

The coaching staff talked it over in the bus on the way back down to the main road. Head Coach had lived in the community long enough that he'd heard the stories about Hattie that still circulated from way back at the start of World War Two, when Roosevelt cancelled the Winter Olympics: supposedly the woman had briefly threatened the statesman's life. He and his staff had also heard about other little dust-ups here and there. The general consensus was that the sweet little old lady up there in the farmhouse might just be serious. Uh-oh.

Head Coach stood up, there in the aisle, as the bus gathered speed on the wide State Route. "Guys! Hey - GENTLEMEN! A word!" He waited until the hubbub quieted to the point where the loudest noise was now the throaty rumble of the diesel bus engine. "BENCHED! BENCHED is what the poor sonofabitch is going to find himself that pisses off Hattie Wendell!" He shook his finger at them. "Not a one of you is going to screw up our going-away breakfast WINNING tradition. I find out one of you is banging that little girl, who is ONLY SI... FIFT... FOURTEEN... FOURTEEN YEARS OLD by the way, YOU'RE BENCHED! RIDING THE PLANK until your little brother's kids graduate from medical school. GOT THAT?" Head Coach sat back down. And worried.

***

The Academy team members crowded into the Visitor's locker room at Adirondack State U., just North and East of Syracuse, some seven hours later. Some players were hyper, jovial. Others were a little nervous, or business-like. Everyone had their own pre-game personality, their own pre-game ritual, a mood unique to them.

Curtis, the Captain, taped up his ankles before his skates went on, wrapping over and around the back of his foot over and over again with cloth medical tape. When the pre-game bustle of the locker room went quiet for a moment, he looked up, and offered this bit of advice about the young girl who was still being discussed, even a state away: "Like Misses Wendell says, SISTER." He looked up with a merry scowl. "Pretty sister, but all you Pretty Boys related!"

An anonymous and muffled voice somewhere in the locker room replied to that: "She MY sister, I'd STILL do 'er, she be some EXTRA FINE gouda, that girl up there!" The speaker straightened up from lacing his own skate and looked around the locker room with a grin.

Then he ducked, quickly. He didn't mean it, of course. Still, he was met with a flurry of thrown orange peels and mouth-guards and one water-bottle hurled hard enough to dent anyone but a hockey player, as well as a flurry of cat-calls, boos, and insults:

"That's disgusting."

"Knew you were from Pennsylvania!"

"Is that why your feet are webbed?"

"You are a sad, sad case, dude."

Curtis shut them off with a stern reminder: "Decorum, gentlemen!" Then announced, "Okay, enough of this foolin' around. Let's have a practice so we can go snow these dudes tonight!"

The Hockey Cadets won the first away game of the season, eight to five, that evening, in a hard-fought series of three skirmishes that went the Home Team's way for the first two periods. Bruce played defense, but amazingly enough, he scored a one-in-a-million goal in the third period when they were one-down on the OTHER team's Power Play. That Academy team captain, he'd been thrown into the box on a whistle, head hanging as he skated over to sit out his penalty and thus leave his team a man down.

***

"Thanks, Brucie! You-all saved my ASS!"

"Yah, Coach would have KILLED you if we'd gone belly-up in the third on the CAPTAIN'S penalty. Wouldn't want to lose you so early in the season, now, eh?"

"I wouldn' want to miss the next Hockey Breakfast up at the old lady's just on account o' being DEAD. Thanks."

"Yeh, that apple pie was something.... And so's the helper." Bruce got a faraway look in his eye.

"Yah, you be careful, man... that be Cottage Cheese. Be risky even if she didn't have a Grandma...."

'Cottage Cheese' was from town. There were dangers in that: age, pregnancy, sudden demands, 'accidental' meetings with family. Ensnarement. Entrapment. Complications. There were also a fair number of marriages among Alumni that had started as Cottage Cheese affairs. Most of the young men swore they would never be so entangled, but many of them later graduated with local women and their families in attendance. Cottage Cheese could be tricky - it was something that rarely came one slice at a time - and you might end up with a whole lot on your plate!

Bruce shook his head and played it cool. "Just one of many in the dairy case, eh." *I can't stop thinking about her, though.*

As Bruce, Curtis, and the rest of the team furtively discussed that Wendell woman's new helper on the bus ride back from upstate New York, those hockey players were all quite certain about one thing. This new Brittany girl they'd seen up at the weekend's Breakfast: *that chick, she HAS THE RIND ON.* A betting pool started.

One of the more outspoken Cretins on the bus was stunned by his own sudden insight, and loudly exclaimed to the whole bus in general: "You suppose she and that old woman are sitt'n around talkin' 'bout which one of us was the finest meat?"

***

The Smiley's Manager thought about adding more staff, but then in February, his new Waitress, Brittany, came to him to ask for a favor...

She had her report-card in hand and told it out all in a rush: "So... I have all A's and high B's, well, only one of those, and I need the money and business seems REALLY good right now, so can I work maybe three nights a week and sometimes BOTH days on the weekend?" Brittany batted her eyelashes.

The man's cramped and crowded hospitality industry office did have one perk, rear-and-center, in the form of a tall upholstered office chair. Other than the restaurant seating, the stools at the ice cream counter, and an over-turned five-gallon pail just inside the back door, his was the only chair in the place. He leaned back in it now, to consider. "That's a lot of work for a schoolkid, Brit. Don't burn yourself out. Your parents could raise a stink if your grades go down because I let you over-work."

Brittany didn't waver. "I don't live with them anymore. I'm OUT. And they won't. My grades, I mean. I'm in the home stretch in a jock school where college prep means soccer, basketball or hockey, and then baseball, in that order. I already bust the grading curve. They'll be glad to have me 'normal' for a few semesters."

The manager sat silently and raised his eyebrows. *A whole lot of information there... is that so? YOU think so, or that's how it really is?* His eyes narrowed as he filed all of that away for later consideration.

Her boss gave her a look: Really? Brittany remained quiet, holding her ground.

Finally, he sighed and sat forward. "We'll try it for a month." The Smiley's manager was a good guy. He didn't have any kids of his own - that was a long story that he didn't burden anyone at work with. These employees were his kids. A new crop every year or two. "And I want to talk to your Guidance Counselor. Soon. Let him or her know that I'm going to be calling and instruct them to go ahead and talk to me straight. Okay?"

Brittany rolled her eyes. "Oooookayy. When can I sign up for more shifts?"

"AFTER I talk to your school." He scooted the chair back. End of conversation. He stood up to reach for some ledger on a tall set of shelves beside his desk, but then turned, hand in the air, as Brittany's back was already to him. "Brittany? How long have you been out of the house?"

Brittany paused, then spoke over her shoulder: "About six months." She waited for the question. A lurid question, the leering glance, the wrong assumption. A pitch.

"Call me Roger. No more of this Mister shit. You're out of the house, you're one of the grown-ups, here."

***

Paul Wendell looked out the window as he waited for traffic to move. His short commute - just in from a luxury condominium up in Outremont - took forty minutes longer than it should, on average. He lived less than fifteen miles from Club Castor et Chat. *I just don't understand it... everyone else is headed OUT, why should it take me so long to get IN to this city?!* He drummed his fingers on the steering wheel of the fleet sedan that came with his job. *Oh good. We're moving. All of the length of two cars.* Traffic stopped again. A distant memory was knocking at his mind.... *oh! Yes... just like trying to send one cow INTO the barn when all the others are coming out.* That disastrous milking was his first one alone - his father was at the dairy association, negotiating their future. *Funny how I should end up groomed to manage affairs at a business that also depends so heavily on fine mammary glands....* He peered out the side window, up at the tall glass facade of a large retailer's store-front billboard. There, three stories above traffic, heavily-bundled workmen cleaned the glass with anti-freeze as relatively scantily-clad Art Directors and paper-hangers worked on staging on the inside. This upcoming fashion ads were going up. *Poor cold bastards out there... they must HATE the divas on the warm side of all that glass!* He checked traffic to his front - *still stopped dead* - and then eyed the block-long wall of glass that towered above the street. *Pity we can't have a billboard like that down in Vermont... we'd be full-to-overflowing even on a Tuesday!*

* * *

They were still talking about her three weeks later. Someone lacing up his skates or putting on shoulder pads in the locker room before practice would shake his head in wonder as he quietly reflected, "Wow. Can't wait for that next Away Game breakfast."

"I know, man. Scenery up there is amazing."

"That be some FINE block of all-American dairy product up there, dude. "

"Absolute CREAM of the cheese!"

"Hind with rind...."

"I've seen her somewhere else." That was met with sharp and inquiring looks, to which the speaker only replied with a grin. When pressed, he dug in fast: "Nope. I ain't saying."

"You going to keep that fine little Gouda all to yourself, you pig?"

Gouda was the most sought-after cheese. She was soft and ripe, spreadable if you were persistent or got it to the right temperature with a little heat.

"Hmmmm." The lucky teammate thought about it for a moment. "That fits. And, yes. Yes, I hope to." Actually, he was worried for the guy from Toronto. He spent FAR too much time giving that girl the puppy-dog eyes last time they were up there. No sense encouraging him - he was going to get in some trouble with THAT one, you could tell. He flicked his head in the general direction of Bruce: "Brain-gone-soft over there be stalking her if he finds out where she be evenings."

Bruce smirked and didn't look up from cleaning his mouth-guard with blue mouthwash solution and a toothbrush. *Damn right. I'd follow her to Death's door! Why the fuck did I put it like that?* "She's alright...." He shrugged.

"Hey...." Curtis threw a roll of tape at Bruce to get his attention. "HEY! You be careful. That be sticky real quick. She be Cottage Cheese, Brucie."

Another anonymous player yelled across the locker room to everyone in general: "Yah, she be Hind With The Rind... all sorts of complications there, man!"

Someone unseen muttered, "Holy grail, man...."

Someone else replied: "Holy hell of a lotta problems! Find yourself some Swiss on campus and forget about it."

Curtis scowled. "Less girls, more hockey!" He pointed at the doorway. "We've got pressing business at hand. We be about to hit the ice, gentlemen!"

***

About a week later, after a brief phone call, Brittany's school-appointed Guidance Counselor came over for a complimentary dinner with his wife and young kids in tow. Rick Garland had started just a decade ago as a gym teacher, dropped everything to go back and get an M.S. in Education, met a wife while in his second round of school, and then returned to his hometown to raise his own kids and mentor a few hundred others of various ages. While the rest of the Garland family munched their Smiley-Starter appetizers, Rick went over to the empty dessert counter with the Manager of the Smiley's Franchise, Roger Sterling. They already knew each other socially and professionally. Now they sat on the stools and talked about the school and Brittany over a couple of cups of coffee.

Roger came to the point after a little small talk. "Some kids get their shit straight one time, bring that report card in, and then it goes right back into the toilet once they're working too much." He saw it all the time. Kids hurrying to be adults, kids hurrying to get that car, kids hurrying to work for more beer. "Brittany - she one of those?"

Rick shook his head. He chewed on his thoughts for a minute, and then washed them down with a sip of coffee. "She's one of our really stellar ones. I expect big things from her...." He grimaced. "She'd be a shoo-in for one of the Ivy Leagues if she'd round out a bit. I'm kind of disappointed she's not going out for one of the Varsity sports...." *Never a real team player, though, that girl.* Rick looked up in puzzlement. "How's she get along with the customers?"

"Great. Business is up. BIG up. She's pretty, personable. Brings in the boys. Pleasant. Families like that. Real formal. The grandma-types eat that up."

"How about with the other staff, her co-workers…?"

"No complaints. Keeps to herself, but pitches in on all the work. Moves around, helps out without being asked, everyone appreciates that. Good kid."

"Yes, she is. Try it. Make her give you a copy of her report card every quarter; that way you'll know. Brittany will probably make it work. Smart kid, and focused."

"Is she really out on her own, now?"

Rick the Guidance Counselor's head came up a little at that. "That what she told you?" He considered. "Maybe it's mostly true. She lives with her grandmother, I guess they sent her up there to help out the old woman. Nice of her to do it. Most girls Brittany's age would KILL to live in the village." His head shook. "She's not emancipated. Mom and Dad still sign her report card."

"Hmmm." Roger filed that away. He'd been fed misinformation before. So far, Brittany's seemed half-true and not much of a stretch. *And he only has an outsider's view of the story, however noble Rick's intentions.* "She wants to work an awful lot. Almost thirty hours... that's an awful, awful lot for a teenager, what with movies and dances and boys and sports and homework and all that."

Rick laughed. "Brittany isn't one of those. You'll see. She'll be alright. Give her what she wants for hours and she'll probably cut back herself if it's not working out. Call me anytime if you have concerns."

"Thanks, Rick. I will. Now…. Ahh, what can you tell me about a girl from over your way, name of Trudy Jones?"

Long pause.

"Not very much." He clammed up, but forced a professional smile onto his face. As Rick continued some inward debate the corners of his mouth began working, matched by alternating fear and merriment in his eyes.

Roger looked on grimly, then said, "Aw, it doesn't matter anyways. She's gone now, and that's that."

Rick suddenly smiled. "Well, not as a school employee, but as a father and husband, I CAN tell you that she babysat for us a couple of times in the past. I made my WIFE drive her home the second time." And then, in an undertone: "She made a pass at me. Determined girl." He grinned. "If I was twenty years younger…! Frightened the shit out of me, she did."

"THAT is starting to make SENSE." The manager told Rick what things were like earlier that winter, before he'd hired Brittany.

"Yah, that does make sense, doesn't it? A lot of commotion over there, since she's been babysitting. Too bad you couldn't keep her on. I'd hate to see it start up again…"

They stood up and shook hands, and Rick went back to his family at the table. He made a mental note to refer Trudy to the once-a-week school counselor again. Maybe it would save a few marriages. *Or not. Too many husbands eager to drive a babysitter home. Probably that's how it all started.*

Rick's thirty-two-year-old wife was wiping dipping sauce off the front of their four-year-old. "Hey, sweetie. Welcome back. They REALLY loaded up on this appetizer platter! I think the kids are going to be full…. What was that all about?"

He sat down in the booth and reflexively straightened the mess of food on the table in front of his four-year-old, who was trying and failing to eat finger-food with a fork. "THAT was about a sixteen-year-old going on twenty-five." He had some questions for Brittany, next time they met. *All this work for instance… the girl hardly needs to save for college. Keep those grades up by paying attention to school, pick up a sport, and she'll have a scholarship to an out-of-state school, one of the big ones, for sure.* And *is she adequately supervised up there at her grandmother's house?* Hattie was known as a bit of a… trend-setter, and there had been rumors. A LOT of rumors. "Roger and I have a Common Concern working here."

His wife's head swiveled in confusion. "Huh?"

"Student stuff." Rick then pointed at the children. "How about we get those two a couple of ice cream sundaes and call that a meal? We'll make them eat vegetables all day tomorrow?" He eyed the carnage of leftovers on the platter warily as the waitress brought the big people's dinners to the table. *Oh, thank goodness!*

"Sounds like a good idea." She winked at him. "Eat light... you've got a workout coming later. I'm calling this Date Night, you stud!"

***

"Hey, Bruce! How goeszit, eh?"

Bruce and Scott stopped on a walkway as they passed between classes. With busy schedules and ever-widening circles, they were becoming more like acquaintances than best friends. That was okay; they were comfortable enough with their history and their friendship that they knew they would be something like family for the rest of their lives.

Bruce stopped, and hung his head. "How is going? Terrible, eh? I can't get that GIRL out of my head."

"Which girl?" Actually, Scotty had a pretty good idea. His friend hadn't stopped talking about that Town Girl since he'd first seen her.

"Her." Like that would explain it. Bruce added some clarification: "Up there."

Scotty snickered. *Toast.* "Lust at first sight, huh?"

"Something like that." Bruce smiled. He saw her beautiful green eyes, that fair circle of face, those pursed lips looming in close as she reached down in front of him to put down a plate or a pie...

"...THAT little piece of Camembert!" *Fucker's not hearing me...* "Bruce! BRUCIE!!!" Scott waved his hand in front of his friend's face. "You've got a problem, eh?"

Bruce came-to and focused on Scott for a moment. "There are like NINE HUNDRED chicks at this place, including that amazing little number from the Sciences Department that hangs out with you..." Bruce shook his head to clear it. "And all I can think about now is this chick at that farmhouse... and now she's in my head, all the time, eh? What the FUCK do I do?!?"

"Go find yourself some Pub Swiss and get it out of your system, that's what you do. She's like HALF your age and from TOWN and you are just MOONY!"

"All I want in the world is just to TALK to her again."

"You talked?"

Bruce shrugged. "Well, she asked me if I wanted more sausage...."

Scotty raised an amused and skeptical eyebrow. *Really?* "She was SO screwing with you!" He shook his head and grimaced in quiet exasperation. *No help for him, but...* "I can help you, buddy."

Bruce made dismissive facial expressions at his own shoes. *Nobody can help me.*

A female Academy student named Cynthia passed by, furtively checking out Bruce. Dituscano/Paine Hall presented the Gold Standard of unattainable Imported *Fromage*: a Third-Year student from Montreal who was trendy, sophisticated, and rumored to be just a little older and more worldly than the rest of the young women on campus. Mysterious and exotic because of a little bit of an accent and her unusually regal carriage. Cynthia played Varsity lacrosse and she was fit for it: big-boned, muscular, strong. Yet she was also soft, feminine, perfectly hourglass proportioned... and frequently dressed to show off her figure and the skin it was in. She took in the back of her uniform shirts just a hair on the sides to preserve her figure-eight shape - no one but a roommate knew that. She turned young heads everywhere she went, and that was just the way she wanted it!

Cynthia crossed the campus at a demure and languid pace at odds with her dress and the day's weather - she was in Lycra shorty-shorts and jog-bra, with an open warm-up coat over them as her only concession to the frigid winter weather. As this self-appointed Siren strutted by the two Canadian boys on her way to the gym, she beamed her best angelic smile at them. Her eyes might have briefly closed dreamily, or maybe it was a wink, or maybe she was just so tired from third-year coursework in Business Admin that all her bodily functions, even her winking, were in slow motion. The corners of her full and red lips turned up just a flicker as she caught Scott watching her every move and sway and ripple and jiggle, as best he could see them under and around the un-zipped jacket. Cynthia spent a lot of time on those lips, and on her body, getting everything Just So every time she was going anywhere further than down the hall to the bathroom. One day soon she was going to SHARE those lips and that body, and when she DID, she wanted her partner to be good and hungry. *That Bruce guy, the hockey player... he'd be a good candidate. The other one, nice that I caught his attention, I'm still Doing It Right, but that hockey player....* She ran fingers through her hair and made sure she jutted out her bottom lip as she did so. *Chu TRES interessant! I would be fromage Cordon Bleu pour toi, mon ami!*

A few years hence, Bruce and Cynthia would recognize each other in a vastly different venue. They would each be shocked at the unexpected apparent career choice of the other. Here, now, Bruce didn't even notice the voluptuous woman passing and preening for their attention.

Scott was transfixed for long enough to forget his friend. *THAT girl is a walking calculus lesson!* He appraised the mystery-shrouded woman's receding curves for another second and then he turned back to his friend and... *Oh, shit!* Bruce was still staring at his own shoes. Scotty's eye's widened. *Guy is TOAST, eh! EVERYONE notices Cynthia!* "Dude, that Quebec wheel just rolled by, that absolute TASTY creme-de-la-Camembert of a DISH, she just walked by, did you even SEE her?!?" He pointed at the retreating derriere: exhibit A. "Like I said..." He knocked Bruce in the side of the arm. "Yoo-hoo, eh? I can help you." He leaned in close. "I've heard about her." Word travels fast on a small campus. "She lives with her grandmother up in the woods outside of town."

Bruce's head came up. "She LIVES there? What ELSE do you know?" Scott suddenly had Bruce's full attention.

"One of my classmates is a townie. I've heard some things." Scott wisely decided to let Bruce settle out the truths and the rumors for himself. *CAN'T be true - not the half of them.* "She waits tables over at Smiley's, on the strip. Bunch of us go over on Friday sometimes... Better food than the mess hall, and stellar scenery, eh? Might be a couple of us basically just go and watch her work, I guess. Supermodel material, that one...." *Tricky, though... still in school. Oh, well. He's a grown man, he can make his own decisions.* He tried to give half-hearted warning: "Maybe her family will rope you down and you'll spend the rest of your life here, eh?"

Bruce didn't even hear his friend. "Smiley's, eh? Scott, THANKS. Thanks a lot." Bruce turned and hurried away, already moving towards his next class.

"No problem! Five bucks says you GET IN HER PANTS WITHIN THE WEEK!" Scot was yelling now, because Bruce was jogging away in his haste to get on with his day so he could get through to dinnertime. Scott turned to go the other way and immediately felt like a Boer. "Uh, excuse us, ahm, me. Ma'am." *Shit.*

Professor Roberts eyed *the little Cretan* with disdain as she passed, then closed her eyes and sighed. *We are hosting a Breeding Colony here.* She smirked. *And now he's probably checking out MY legs and sniffing my Granny Undies.* She shook her head minutely and cringed. *I should have taught Biology at a Women's School.*

Scott stepped aside to let one of the professors pass. He spied an abandoned and familiar-looking backpack at his feet. *His mom would KILL me if I let him fail out of school just 'cause he's all moony over some Town Girl!* Scott stooped to get Bruce's forgotten backpack and as he bent down he gave a sidelong glance at the passing legs of That Hot Professor from the Biology Department, the one who was pretty darned good looking in spite of her doctorate and title. *Another set of pants - well, a uniform skirt, today - that me or Bruce can maybe... well, probably not.*

Scott trotted off to an afternoon class with two backpacks.

Bruce found his missing backpack waiting when he went over to Scott's dorm early that evening. He'd dropped by to ask if he could borrow a car - Scott's or Scott's roommate's or ANYONE'S. Bruce was a Man With A Mission.

Chapter Seven

"Hi, welcome to Smiley's, I'm Brittany and I'll be your Server, would you like to start with an appetizer or…"

"I know. We've met."

The table menu dropped away from his face, and there he was. *Ah, THAT one.* Brittany squinted dubiously at him. "Well, would you like to order?"

"At the farmhouse. Hockey Breakfast." Bruce looked up expectantly.

"That's nice. You want the same thing you had then?" Brittany gave him a sassy smile and threw out one hip for both show and effect.

"Sure. Why not, eh?"

Five minutes later, Brittany returned with coffee and orange juice. Seven minutes after that she came with a slice of (factory-made) apple pie and five deep-fried cheese sticks. Fifteen minutes later she put a platter in front of him. "Sorry. No-Go on pancakes at seven in the evening. Senior Special, okay?" She was already making her way back towards the kitchen, looking over her shoulder at him with a sparkle in her eye.

Bruce looked down. Coleslaw, baked beans, mashed potatoes, and a hotdog-bun combination that was already cut up into bite-sized pieces. He dug right in. It wasn't that much different than a busy-night dinner at home when he was growing up (except his folks hadn't sliced his hotdog up for him for years, of course). Familiar. It felt comfortable already.

Brittany didn't say another thing to him all night. That was fine with Bruce. He liked to watch her work the tables.

***

"Thanks for the car, man."

"No problem, Bruce. So, you get a piece?"

"Yes." Scott was just picking up his arm for a high-five when Bruce continued: "Apple. Pie. With mozzarella sticks. They didn't have any block cheddar."

"Huh?"

"She served me as close as she could come to a farmhouse breakfast. Pie, cheese sticks, beans, hotdogs instead of sausage, mashed potatoes instead of tater-wedges." He got a faraway look in his eye. "I don't know why it wasn't fries..."

Scott eyed his friend, thunderstruck. This conversation wasn't going the way he'd expected.

Bruce didn't notice his friend's consternation. "Oh, and coleslaw. Came with the Special." Bruce wiggled his fingers up in the air for quotation marks. "Breakfast." He smiled widely. "I think it's a good omen."

Scott wasn't sure what that meant. Or why Bruce was acting so happy about it. "You're batty, eh?"

"Well, I figure it can't be going TOO bad. I've already had breakfast with her. Twice."

Scotty thought about that for a moment. *You call that BREAKFAST?* "You poor, poor man. Go do your homework."

***

One day after New Year's Eve, when the event was sufficiently removed, Tabitha brought up the horrible "family night" dinner again, during Study Hall. Mister Garland, "Rick" to his students, was subbing-in. He was a pushover: students talked all they wanted, the general level of hubbub rose, and by the end of the period it felt like a bustling restaurant on a Friday night. Social Hour. Nobody got any work done when Rick subbed, much to the Principal's dismay and the students' general delight.

Rick was NOT a pushover. He was the Guidance Counselor, which also made him the school's social worker. He eaves-dropped from the proctor's desk whenever he got a study hall. If he kept his mouth shut long enough, the students forgot he was there. He learned all manner of important things about these kids from what he heard directly as well as what he heard repeated. Sometimes he'd follow up, carefully. He also suspected that some of the students knew what he was up to, and so would rotate their seating, as well as the topic, as a way of passing on information that needed to come to his attention.

Tabitha knew. She had just manipulated Brittany into a chair right near the desk. "I just thank my lucky stars that MY mother isn't like that. I mean, can you IMAGINE? With me... Well, how I am?" Genuine fear crossed her face for a moment. Tabitha appeared to have put a lot of thought into her friend's situation - trauma by proximity and association. "I mean, I don't even have a place to go..." She turned to Brittany. "No, I mean I'd have to stay and be who they wanted me to be or live in a constant screaming match." She shook her head and looked like she was going to be sick. "It would be awful. Being in your situation. I'm glad you got out."

"Well, you'd be spending a lot of time at my house." Brittany stretched in her chair and kissed her friend on the cheek, then looked around and realized that probably wasn't appropriate here. *Oh, well.* "You'd have a place to go." She wiggled her eyebrows, more for everyone who was suddenly looking at them.

Rick looked up and frowned. Making Out in Study Hall was NOT part of his plan.

"Yes, but not like you." Tabitha was almost envious, even though she didn't need to be. She put her hand on Brittany's arm, and raised her voice just a little to add emphasis. "I just mean, I'm glad you have a place to go." She saw a few classmates wringing their hands and fluttering eyelashes at each other, thought about it, and decided it didn't matter. Boys and girls hooked up at school all the time, when they could get away with it.

"Well, it was either the farmhouse or 'Go West, Young Girl.'"

Tabitha shivered and stage-whispered, "Yah. Maybe I can see that. What IS it with you two?"

Brittany looked around the study-hall. Over her shoulder, out of the corner of her eye, she could see Rick with an ear turned towards them. She turned her head, met the educator's eye, and replied loudly: "Later. No talking. We have homework."

***

Opportunity came on a snowy Monday when school let out early on account of the weather.

"So, you ready for story-time?"

They were at Tabitha's house this afternoon. There was an early-February blizzard going on, one that even the town plows couldn't navigate. Brittany made it down out of The Hollow in the gloom and thickening drifts, but by eleven school was let out early and by twelve they were sending every bus behind a town plow. By the second time a bus got stuck it was one o'clock, the Hollow Road was closed to traffic and nobody in their right mind would go out anyway. And thus, Brittany was marooned. Tabitha put on as straight a face as she could muster and invited her friend to sleep on the couch at the Bayer house.

Brittany's eyebrow went up skeptically, but she accepted. She called work (no way to get over there with the roads piled high, and she doubted anyone but state plow truck drivers would be in tonight, anyway), and then tried to call Grandma, but the phone lines were apparently down. Probably wiped out when one of the busses or plow trucks crashed. Grandma would figure it out.

Tabitha's mother had a ready solution. "I really don't want her to worry. I know I would. Tabitha's uncle is a town-truck driver. I'll have him stop by your house, whenever they finally punch through."

"Thanks. That's a nice idea." Brittany was tickled pink that this woman called it 'her' house.

"Can you kids help me get the driveway clear about four o'clock?" She turned to Tabitha: "Your father will be coming home, and if we can get the car tucked away in the garage 'til all this is over, it would be a good thing…"

"Sure, Ma'am."

"Thankyou." Mrs. Bayer turned to Brittany. "I'll feed you for your trouble." She smiled. "I would anyway, of course."

"Give us a call, Mom. We'll be upstairs. There's some juicy gossip Brittany and I didn't get to finish yesterday."

Her mother eyed the two girls speculatively. Finally: "Door open?"

Brittany blushed.

Tabitha wheeled, laughing. "Mo-om!" Then she scowled quizzically at Brittany. *I don't think I've ever seen THAT before!* "Brittany... you're PINK!"

"Shoe's on the other foot, I guess." Brittany grabbed her friend's hand, and headed for the stairs. "Call us!"

Brittany settled on Tabitha's narrow, quilt-covered bed, pointedly looked the narrow width of it from one side to another, and then frowned at her friend.

"Flirt." Tabitha eyed the open door with distaste.

"Just as well." Brittany bounced up, found a super-large teddy bear from a small rocker-chair in the corner, and placed him - or it - in front of the open bedroom door as a door-prop. The bear watched the bed from the floor.

Brittany settled back on the bed cross-legged, and patted the quilt beside her. "Teddy there will chaperone. I'm wise to your tricks."

Tabitha rolled her eyes and settled beside her friend, then scooched back suddenly. "So WHAT is UP with your MOM?"

Snow silently swirled by the window behind them as Brittany gathered her thoughts. "Good question. She hates me more every day. That's the short answer."

Tabitha folded her legs under her and waited.

"You look cute." Brittany's face changed. "These are my best days, living with Grandma, spending time with you. But..." She sneered, then continued: "Living with my mother…" Brittany suddenly looked mad. "Those were my worst days. And hers, too, I think. She's getting older. I'm young. She wants what I have." Brittany got up. "Wait here."

Brittany skipped down the stairs, breezed past Tabitha's mother, and went out into the Bayer family garage through a covered walkway. The snow blew in over her bare feet and at the door to the garage she had to step in a deep pile that brushed under her skirt above her knee. She shivered, but didn't really care. It wasn't the first time she'd been on an errand in the snow with bare feet. She found Tabitha's car - Mr. Bayer's old car - unlocked in the garage, as she expected, and rooted around in the glove box for a moment. On her way back, she paused in the breezeway for two minutes to smoke a cigarette. By the time she flicked it away, the bottoms of her feet were frozen and the snow was no longer melting when it hit the tops of her toes. *Oh, well.* She wiped her feet as best she could on the scratchy broom-straw mat inside the house door (she could hardly feel it with the cold-hard feet), shivered, and skipped back towards Tabitha's bedroom.

Tabitha's mother passed in the hallway, sniffed the air, turned, and looked at Brittany's receding back as she went up the stairs. *No shoes. Wow.* She shook her head. *Couldn't-a-been.*

Brittany came back in the bedroom, patted the doorstop on the head, and hopped back on the bed next to Tabitha. She swiveled and put her cold, damp feet on Tabitha's lap, then burrowed them under the girl's legs.

"Brrr… SHIT those are COLD!" Tabitha jerked back. She lowered her voice before continuing: "Grandma would SWAT you if she smelled that… This isn't an emergency."

Brittany answered grimly: "It will be." She sighed. "We used to go to the beach for part of a week every summer. You know, the wonderful American family vacation. They do movies about us. Well, my family's version was a little different." Brittany smelled her own sleeve. "Yuck. Grandma's going to kill me."

Tabitha had a simple solution: "Then stop."

"In a few days."

"Ahuh." Tabitha leaned back sideways and gave her friend a stern scowl. "I'm not going to let you leave smokes in my glove box anymore."

"Ya, ya, I've got my own car. It's got a glove box. I'll make sure I drive from now on. Anyways, we'd go to the beach and Dad and I and Brian would build sand castles and pick up shells and sea-creatures and... Mom would pick up, ah... other things." Brittany laughed. "For as long as I can remember, she used to rip the foam pads out of her bikini tops. Said they were scratchy. Now I'm older, I understand it. She might as well have gone topless. I bet folks used to look at her to figure out the temperature of the water! And she looked GOOD! Even as a child I knew it. Everyone on the beach checked her out, and kept checking." Brittany wasn't in Tabitha's bedroom anymore, not even in cold, snowy Vermont. Behind her eyes she was somewhere on a beach on the coast of New England and it was ninety-five degrees and her mother is there, a little ways down the beach, wearing a tiny little set of strings with bright stripes saying, "Here I am, look at me! That's what all her beach clothes were, and she's got the figure to make even those straight stripes curl up, you know?" Brittany was back in the room looking to see if her friend understood.

Tabitha nodded. *Who could miss it?*

Folks around town well knew that Mrs. Wendell (the younger, *aaahhh, TRENDY* one that lived in the village) would be out on her front lawn on the main street on the first day it passed for seventy degrees in the sun, fifty degrees would do if it was April and she could maneuver the chaise chair out onto a firm enough snow-pile. There she'd be, dressed in next-to-nothing or maybe less. Tanning. Preening. On Display.

And yes, Tabitha had used the woman's poking nipples as a thermometer once or twice - *Oh, it LOOKS like a nice day, but there must be a chill breeze, that woman's hard as a rock out there....* "She'd curl MY stripes if I didn't know her..."

Brittany pushed her friend away in mock disgust. "Ya. You know. So she'd be wrestling in the surf with some hunked-out beach-bum volleyball player, or a bunch of college-boys, just having the time of her life being oo-oogled and felt-up while Dad was feeding us supper or reading us bed-time stories or tucking us in. He didn't seem worried. He said it was her Special Kind Of Vacation. She always came home. I think." Brittany scowled. "Well, there was once." She paused, thinking it through. "She fell asleep on the beach. What she said over breakfast, anyway. Funny. She didn't LOOK sleepy, the last time we saw her the night before, grabbing beers from the fridge to take down to a bonfire..."

Brittany sighed. "Now that I'm… older, I understand her VACATIONS a lot more."

Tabitha wasn't shocked, but she WAS perplexed: "What about your DAD, Brit? Didn't he get PISSED?!" She didn't know very much about Walter Wendell, but she did know that he used to carry a gun at work. *You don't screw with a guy who carries a gun, or with his wife… everyone knows that!*

"He hid his feelings well. I knew vacations made him sad, and made Mom happy. I never knew what was really going on, and my Dad never gave us any reasons to ask." She turned to look her friend square in the eye. "You know, I'm not even sure he's my DAD?"

Tabitha's eyes got wide. "Nofuckinway…."

"I was born FIVE months after they were married. I mean, I know I look like him, but… I've heard stories around." Brittany shrugged. "If I DIDN'T look like a Wendell, I'd sure wonder."

"Holy shit, Girl!" Tabitha shook her head vigorously to clear it of THAT uncomfortable thought. "Didn't they fight? You know, when she'd finally roll in during her 'vacations' as you put it?"

"No, Tab. Unlike YOU, my father isn't very possessive. He was glad she was happy, but sad that it took 'vacations' to do it. He said that once. Before I knew what it meant. We don't talk about it now…."

"That woman's a piece of work! And your dad is…" Her head shook. "Too understanding." Tabitha still wasn't sure she understood the connection. "What's this got to do with YOU, Britt? Why is she so angry at YOU?"

"There's a lot to it, I think." Brittany squared her shoulders to deliver it direct: "At some certain age, the lusty young bucks that she still wants started looking at ME, instead of HER."

Tabitha's eyes saucer-ed and she sat bolt upright to respond with a booming "OH, GODDAMNEDFUCK'NSHIT!"

Mrs. Bayer, downstairs, stopped chopping cassolette ingredients long enough to tip back her head and yell, "Language, girls!" *I wonder what that was all about?* She grinned. *They doing the little strips and just found out they got each other pregnant?*

Brittany nodded. "Yes. Oh shit. And I'm getting more… available, while she's getting older. Oh, shit, indeed."

"You moved out so you wouldn't be competing."

"Yep."

They sat in silence for a while. A plow truck scraped and quaked by. More silence. Brittany picked up a corner of the quilt and fiddled with it. Tabitha rubbed Brittany's frozen toes.

Brittany dropped the quilt. "That's not all of it. It's REALLY"

Tabitha's mother went by in the upstairs hallway.

Brittany lowered her voice for a word: "...fucked UP." She resumed her normal tone. "She wants me to be JUST LIKE her, and then she resents me for it if I am. My fourteenth birthday - you missed a good one - she gave me all this slinky stuff. Teddies. Lacey-racy. Tried to make me into a teen whore." She wrung her hands. "I DON'T get that one." She peered off into the void for a moment, then shrugged. "I know she hates me because of some other things, too. College." Brittany turned to look at Tabitha squarely again. "Did you know I lived with Grandma for about a year after I was born?"

Tabitha shook her head, wide eyed.

"She won't talk about it. Gram, I mean. I've asked. Just says, 'Your mother was away in college and a new baby was a little much.' I know she and Dad got married before she was eighteen. She must have been a star student, already in college?" *I'm not sure, actually....* Brittany shrugged. "She dropped out, but not because of grades, I would guess. I probably get blamed for that. A lot of young bucks there, she missed out on, once she dropped out. I probably get blamed for that, too. I don't think she's a happy woman." Brittany stood up. "I told Dad, well, more or less, I told him it was move up here or run away."

"Holy shit. I'm sorry I brought it up." Tabitha started to tear up for her friend. Tabitha was overtaken by sudden fear: "Would you have?"

Brittany ignored the question. "Don't be. I'm glad you asked - I want you to know. But I don't want to talk about her again. There aren't enough smokes in that there glove box for all the scary stories I've got about that woman." Brittany grabbed her friend's hand and said, with stage-cheer: "LET'S GO MAKE SOME MOLASSES COOKIES!" She looked Tabitha square in the eye - a pained, tragic, thirty-years-too-old look. "I'm tired of this shit."

Tabitha, nodded quickly, silently, mortified by the sudden emptiness in those beautiful green eyes.

On the way out of the room, Brittany grabbed the bear and tucked it under her arm.

Once the cookies were on black steel sheets and the mixing bowls washed up, Tabitha's mother took over watching the progression of cookies through the oven so that the two girls could go do the shoveling. Two feet of heavy snow and a huge pile out at the road made for slow work.

Tabitha's father came home early and arrived before they were done. They took turns: Mr. Bayer relieving his daughter and her friend alternately as the three of them shared two coal scoops.

When the car was safely tucked into the garage and Mr. Bayer was headed into the house, Brittany got a sudden strange look on her face. "Want to go do another one?"

"One what?"

Brittany leaned on the shovel, exhausted. "Driveway."

"Oh!" *No, not really, I'm sore and my feet are cold and I'm exhausted and my fingers feel like they're going to fall off, but* "sure!" *Fair is fair.* Tabitha put on an smile she didn't feel.

"Wait here a sec...." Brittany skipped into the Bayer garage for a moment, then returned with her arm out. "Let's go surprise my poor, poor brother, shoveling all cold and alone over there...."

Tabitha smiled. *How thoughtful.* Sometimes she wondered if Brittany remembered she HAD a brother. *And now here she is, headed to help him out.... Is this 'being a grown-up?'*

When the young women arrived two blocks over and closer to downtown, they found Brian morosely chopping at the three-foot high wall of snow the village plows had left mounted up at the entry to the driveway.

Young Brian was pissed - he was sure those plows had pushed every inch of snow on the street right into the ends of all the driveways, maybe even ON PURPOSE. *Do they get some sort of glee out of it?* Twice he'd had to scurry out of the way as a town truck came along and pushed MORE snow into what he'd ALREADY just shoveled. So yes, he did indeed look sad, but perked up immediately when he saw four more willing hands with two snow-shovels between them. "Holy shit am

I glad to see you!" He leaned close to Tabitha for an aside: "First time ever...." Then turned to Brittany: "For real?"

"Yes, Brother Bri, for real. We'll finish this pile of white shit, you start up at the house and work down to us." Brittany got a strange sort of a smile as she fished in her jacket pocket and came out with the lighter and the pack of cigarettes she kept hidden in Tabitha's glove box.

This was a theatric that Tabitha hadn't figured out, since Brittany was the only one who used her own car. She frowned squeamishly. *Okay, stinky-breath! They're your lungs....*

Brittany lit up, stuck the cigarette firmly between her lips, and then began determined shoveling. It took a lot of extra effort to do the hard work without coughing and choking from the close proximity of the burning cigarette.

Tabitha watched skeptically, then went to help Brian. They shoveled shoulder-to-shoulder from the house back down towards the street. "I don't know what's up with your sister. It's a disgusting habit." They both stopped to watch Brittany retch with a coughing fit - she was apparently no good at mixing exercise and no-hands smoking - and then, illogically, light up another smoke.

Brittany had ulterior motives for her Samaritan visit to the village Wendell house.

The curtains up at the house parted.

The younger and by-marriage Mrs. Wendell looked out to see what kind of progress her poor son was making... *Oh! It's a mess out there! Well, Walt will be home to help him soon enough. SHOVELING is NOT women's work.* She scowled. *Oh. He HAS help.* Then her eyes flared wide as she took in the specter of her daughter, out there in the falling gloom, shoveling *with a CIGARETTE IN HER MOUTH like some blue-collar working floozy.* "WHO THE HELL DOES THAT FUCKING LITTLE TRAMP THINK SHE IS!?!"

Brittany saw the curtain drop and smiled. *Victory!* She stopped, threw away the awful cigarette with a shake of her head, and then went back to work with renewed vigor. *I don't know how those fuckers smoke and work at the same time...* Her eyes stung and her nose hurt and... *I think I'm going to barf!*

Brian came into the house a bit later, to an acid reception:

"You all have FUN out there?" His mother scowled at him - enemy by proximity.

"Yah. Brittany and her friend showed up to help!" He took in his mother's expression. "'Bout time she pulled her weight around here."

Robin ruffled her son's hair. "Thanks for all your hard work, Champ." She took a step and then turned to look towards the front window. Curtains hid the scene beyond, but it didn't matter. She could still see *the little* "Fucking harlot...." She pasted a sweet smile back on her face before continuing: "Brian, I ever catch you smoking on this property, I'll make sure you wish you were up there with her." She gave his shoulder a loving double-pat on her way by.

***

Later that snowy night, after fresh cookies and dinner, the girls sat to a game of cards with Tabitha's father.

As they learned the game of hearts, Brittany eyed the man's smoldering cigar and wondered what smoking on that would be like. *Disgusting*, she decided. The end was all wet and clamped in his mouth *like a rolled-up spoiled... vegetable.* It didn't smell any better than that, either.

Tabitha watched her friend eye the stinking brown stub in her father's mouth and then and there decided that *if Brittany takes THAT up, we are DONE. I am nofuck'nway kissing ANYBODY who carries THAT around in their mouth!* She shivered, and then pleaded to the heavens against the event.

Later, the girls settled in for a marathon night on the couch in pee-jays. Brittany was wearing some sweats borrowed from Tabitha's mother. They had textbooks out as a pretense, but MTV on the television as the evening's true activity.

Tabitha's father came through, said goodnight, paused, scratched his head as pondered the loud woman on the TeeVee, and then fled to the upstairs television and good old fashioned programming the way it was meant to be: network NFL football.

Tabitha's mother sat with the two girls for a few minutes, decided she did NOT like Cyndi Lauper, and went out to the kitchen table to fold laundry. "The woman yells too much."

Brittany got up to turn down the volume a little. She returned and snuggled up against their chaperone, the bear. "I had a friend, once. I mean, before you."

Tabitha looked over in mock shock. "Only one?"

"No, I really did. And not a bear, either. Girl named Liv, when I was about ten she moved in three or four streets down. We spent a summer running a lemonade stand together, on the green. Almost made our money back. Fresh lemons every day, and two bags of ice, that gets expensive. But it was fun. We went everywhere together." Brittany adjusted the bear, punching it down a bit.

Tabitha winced.

Brittany continued, once she was comfortable. "We were best buds for a couple of years." Brittany continued talking, but she was now twelve and walking home from school with Liv, to her own house, to work on a team-of-two project for Health Class, a pastel-colored pie chart of what and how much of each food group the two families ate that month.

***

Twelve-year-old Brittany opened the front door of her house to encounter a whirring noise: her mother pedaling furiously on the exercise bike again. She and Livvy had discussed this at length at school, just today.

Pedal, pedal, whir, whir, whir. The woman's eyes were shut with effort, Walkman headphones clamped tight over her ears, cranking for thirty miles an hour on the highways of a frenzied mind. Beta fitness- and beauty-themed workout tapes lay all over the floor of the room. A sweaty towel lay draped over the back of a nearby chair.

The girls exchanged a look.

Livvy leaned over to confide in an undertone: "I'm surprised she doesn't just do that workout on a broom...."

The two children tip-toed through to the stairs, whispering about the difference between Good Witches and Bad Witches, and then turned on each other once they were safely around the corner to cackle wildly in their best imitation of a Bad Witch. They ran up the stairs dodging a

Bad Witch's evil spells and humming what they thought was appropriate witch-music.

The whirring slowed, then stopped. Brittany's mother took the headphones off, wiped her brow with the back of her hand, and then threw the headphones across the room with zeal. They hadn't been connected to anything. *The better to hear you, my darling little SHITS!* Robin shook her head. *THAT little brat is a BAD influence and a* "BITCH." Robin's eyes squinted in scheming dark thought. "The BOTH of you...." She hopped off the bike to towel off the sweat with a faraway look in her eyes and hate on her face.

***

Sixteen-year-old Brittany sat back against the bear. "So, my mom and Liv's mom were thick as thieves at the start of it... cookouts, on the phone, shopping together, that shit. Well that sure stopped, like the next day... She must have heard us?" She shook her head, ruefully. "I think she heard us. My mom started treating Liv's mother like shit, she stopped coming around, and she started treating Livvy like shit, and eventually she stopped coming around, too, and then Livvy started hanging with some other girls..."

Tabitha sat up. "Wait. Liv MILLER?!?"

Brittany sighed. "The one and only."

"You two can't stand to even TALK to each other!"

Brittany shrugged. "Something happened. I don't know what." She held her hands open, wide, and shook her head. "Something happened. By the time I was thirteen she was gone... Thats about when the other trouble started, too. Boys - and men, sometimes - started looking at me the same way YOU do."

Tabitha blushed, and looked down at the carpet for just a second before she decided to be proud and honest and unashamed and meet her friend's gaze instead. "I don't ONLY want you for..."

"You're much more well-behaved than the boys." Brittany smiled and winked in that special way that she had.

Tabitha's mind lurched and her eyes screamed PLEASE!

"No. I'm a Guest. Anyways, my mom's kind of... Well, you've seen her in the front yard. With her, it's the milkman, the postman, and the paper boy... or the varsity jock who pumps her gas, the kid that mows the lawn next door...”

Tabitha made a face.

“Yah, I know, but it seems to be the case. Well, since I was about twelve or thirteen, when we go someplace, some of them pay more attention to ME now. They thought I was pretty. I didn’t WANT them to... It just happened.”

“You’ve got beautiful eyes. God, sometimes I think I’m just going to FALL into them...” She reached out a hand reflexively to cup Brittany’s cheek, and then dropped it back to her own lap when she realized what was happening.

“I have a headache, Dear. So anyways... It kind of came to a head when I got the modeling job. She was a little jealous of that, I think.”

“Oh, ya! I forgot about that.... I heard some things, back then. You were what, like FOURTEEN and IN THE NEWSPAPER ADS and EVERYTHING!” Tabitha beamed at the memory.

“Ah.... That’s why you’ve always been so hot for me! No, you don’t know the half of it. It's WAY worse than that!” She whispered for some reason: “I had to call Grandma for a ride home. That’s when she LOST it.”

***

Many girls in Brittany’s seventh grade were looking forward to the arrival of minor bumps and curves that would affect the boys in their midst. A lucky or unlucky few - depending on their own perspective - already had them, in various small degrees. Some were absolutely horrified by the arrival of swells and wider bottoms they had to stuff into clothing in the morning. Others were already trying to figure out how to encourage them. A few of these girls-becoming-young-women were going to be rich and famous... They were going to grow up to be MODELS!

The guidance counselor, Mister Garland to those of that general age, he did the best he could to steer them towards more practical - and likely - career tracks. Unfortunately, it was a never-ending battle with each new crop of middle-school students, one where the battlements on the opposing side were fortified by popular culture, television, and glossy new teen magazines that littered the school's cafeteria tables. He found the best course of action was to tell the delusional little girls that lots of models broke into the field when talent scouts visited college campuses:

"Oh, it happens that way ALL the time. You know, young women on the cheerleading squad, or seen around campus on the right day on their way to an ACCOUNTING class, would you believe it!" To the others, who saw through that, he suggested they buckle down on their languages. "You know, for European work. They're more likely to fly you over if they know you'll be able to drop into the culture, maybe stay a few years…" He did the best he could, and kept a scrap-book of improbable paths to modeling, all of which involved academic work and high marks. He even had a few real-life examples to trot out - several prestigious college graduates now graced the pages of the tabloids in his office. "And you know you can't play a varsity sport unless you keep your grades up… Lotta girls get recruited outta college sports…"

Rick Garland did the best he could, and some of the girls applied themselves in school a little bit harder and then continued to jabber away about how famous and beautiful and worry-free they were going to be when they grew up. Rick thought that perhaps some of these young ladies would take a LOT longer to grow up than others.

Brittany wasn't immune to the siren call of the society pages. Secretly, she too hoped to achieve momentary immortality on the pages of a glossy. She already had an idea that she was a Girl of Uncommon Beauty - that was a term the boys were passing around in the hallway, as in, "hey, she's a GUB!" She heard the term as she went by a few times, and could also tell in how a room treated her. But going through the many pages of the ads in the Sunday paper, the little booklets of color-printed pictures pushing sales on clothes, shoes, makeup, and hair-care… Brittany realized that MOST of the models were YOUNG. School-aged young. It was not something they did "when they grew up." Some of her peers - somewhere - were doing it NOW. She already read the newspaper a few times a week, so she played a hunch and started watching the classified ads in the back of the Sunday edition.

In June of her fourteenth year she saw the ad, while reading the paper at the breakfast table.

MODELS WANTED

All ages. Apply in person, 10-4 Saturday the 20th

at HENDERSON'S BOUTIQUE in the Freeway Mall, Burlington

"Mom, can we go up to that mall by the lake next Saturday?"

"SURE, Sweetie! Going shopping together would be FUN!"

"Well actually, it's something else…" Brittany handed the newspaper clipping over to her mother.

"Well!" The woman eyed her daughter speculatively. "Good catch! I've always wanted to do something like..." She looked pensive, then calculating, and then floated away in the direction of her closet.

So two weeks later Brittany and her mother went to the mall bright and early on a Saturday for a "Girl's Day Out." Robin wore her shortest dress with fine, new hose just visible over the tops of long lace-up leather boots and a tight, thin, deeply plunging sweater. She spent an hour putting on makeup and making her hair Just So.

Brittany threw on a random pair of jeans and a plaid shirt, which she tied at her midriff, and very modest underwear - a one-piece swimsuit. She knew they'd give her clothes to strut in; she'd figured that out already, even if her mother hadn't. Brittany also suspected she'd be changing behind a screen with about twenty other girls and women, so she wore what she'd be willing to be seen in. She spent a little more time on her hair, and then gave up. They'd like her and fix her hair, or they wouldn't and they'd send her home.

Mother and daughter got to the mall and found a near-riot inside. Yes, models wanted, all ages. And they were here. Four hundred women, young and old, and a few men and boys, milling about in front of and to either side of Henderson's clothing store. The shoot was taking place outside the front of the store, in a wide atrium in the mall hallway. A backdrop of fake fall foliage draped over a piece of plywood with red bricks cast into it provided the theme: a back-to-school, off-to-college shoot for fall newspaper inserts.

Brittany and her mother milled around with the other hopefuls for an hour before they were noticed. Brittany had never heard so much school-girl shrieking and giggling in one place before. Someone beckoned from a desk. A line formed, three hundred deep, as the flash-camera started clicking over at the bricks and leaves. Around noon, Brittany and her mother made it to the registration desk.

The photographer's assistant put their names on a sign-in sheet. Four-forty-four and four-forty-five p.m. "Don't go too far away, though...."

Robin milled about some more, chatted with other women, ignored her daughter, and preened whenever the photographer or his assistant were nearby.

Brittany sat on a bench with her French I textbook, alternately curling one leg up under her or the other.

Around one-thirty, someone came by and issued Brittany a large black number on a white background, much like a runner's number in a foot-race. Twenty-three. "Go right over when it's called."

Brittany shrugged, went to the bathroom, and then went right back to her homework.

An hour or so later a voice barked: "Twenty-three! Twenty-three!"

Brittany's mother suddenly appeared at her side, dragging at her arm. "Come ON! That's US, that's US!!" She just about RAN, with her daughter in tow by an elbow, over to the backdrop with the cameras on tripods and hot white lights. "HERE! HERE! Twenty-three!" She ran her fingers through her hair, and then shook her head to fluff it.

The photographer, a quick and energetic man with black hair, a black leather coat, black pants shaped to fit his legs exactly, and incongruously scuffed brown-black shoes, sighed. He scowled towards the growth that this comely young girl had just sprouted. He didn't seem to share the enthusiasm of most of his potential stars. "Name?"

"Oh, I'm Robin. It's SO nice to"

"What is HER name?" He turned away from this interloper. "What is your"

Brittany's mother cut in: "Oh, this is my daughter, Brittany." Robin let go of Brittany's arm and walked a few paces to stand in front of the brick wall. She curled a finger into the 'vine' that supported the colorful plastic foliage, thrust out a hip towards the camera, and pulled back her lips in an engaging, toothy smile that would forever remind her daughter, in the rare times that she thought of this moment, of a hungry piranha.

The Man In Black disguised rolling his eyes by reaching back to adjust one of the spotlights, then picked up a camera. He started shooting and winding the film advance on the big camera, over and over. Click, wind. Click, wind. Click, wind. A couple of times he used the flash, but mostly he didn't wait for it to charge before he clicked the next picture. "Now turn sideways, Love." It sounded like 'luff' in his sudden Continental accent. Click, wind. "Squat, if jou would." Click, wind. "Like jou are picking someczing up." Click, wind. "Merci." Click, wind. "Zhet is good. Very good. Cinque-jou."

'Five her?' Brittany, watching, scowled as she tried to compare this man's sudden mix of English and French to the Continental French she'd learned in school.... *Oh! Not, 'Five You,' he's saying 'Thank you!'*

His assistant was already leading Robin away. "Thankyou very much. We have your information...? Good, we'll call, or send proofs if we use them."

Robin stepped away from hot-lights with a royal smile.

The photographer opened the back of the camera. "Okay, you." He gestured with his finger: Stage. Now. He leaned towards his assistant, who scurried around back at his side now. "What is her name?" He wiggled two fingers: Hurry. "Brittany. Up there. No, keep the book. It fits." The accent was gone.

That was insulting. Worse, Robin watched in horror as the man put film into the empty camera. She flushed, and then scowled angrily at the scene as the Man In Black carefully took picture after picture of Brittany. She noted that he patiently waited for the flash to charge each time.

Brittany found it hard and tiring work as she stood and swooped and preened as instructed. The photographer had her pose this way and that, his disembodied voice moving behind blinding lights while issuing instructions, the flash of the camera following the voice: Move here, stand there, jump, lean, squat. "Good. Good. This is all good. Beautiful. Thankyou." He'd point. "Over there. One foot up, hand behind your hair. Good." Flash, wind, whir. "One foot up behind you, raise your other hand, can you do that? Good." Flash, wind, whir. "Good. Beautiful."

When Brittany got out of the glare of the lights and could see once more, she found that her mother was gone. *Shopping, maybe?*

The assistant came over to her. "Here's twenty bucks. Go get something to eat and then come back at five-thirty. We'll be shooting wardrobe then."

The photographer and his assistant screened about one hundred of the hopefuls that day, some of whom even got their picture taken.

Brittany found her mother at a different store, coming out with her arms full of new jeans and plaid shirts. Brittany thought that curious. *Not a look Mom usually goes for.* "Hi. I'm supposed to hang around until five, and then they're going to take pictures again."

Her mother froze in mid-step, and then came the rest of the way out of the store.

Brittany held up the twenty dollar bill and smiled brightly. "They gave us lunch money!"

"THAT is kind of inconvenient. I have to make dinner for your father and Brian."

You make them eat TeeVee dinners often enough the rest of the time... "Puh-LEAZE? I'll buy you lunch...Er, dinner?"

Her mother weighed whether having a model daughter was a social asset. It was. "Okay, if it means that much to you."

"Should we call Dad and let him know we're going to be late?"

"No. The boys will manage."

The Wendell girls went off to the food court, where Brittany wolfed down a pizza slice while her mother picked at a dry salad.

The evening shoot was a little less crazy. There were simple rope barricades up now, supported by heavy yellow plastic posts. Brittany was checked off on a clipboard and allowed in. Her mother was allowed to stand outside the rope to watch.

There was a small screened-in area behind the backdrop. The girls and boys were allowed in, one at a time, to change into outfits provided by the staff of Henderson's. They handed Brittany a short wool school-girl style skirt with heavily-folded permanent-press pleats, a package of thick navy panty-hose, ill-fitting shoes with a large buckle on top of each toe-box, and a frilly white shirt.

When she came out, there was a problem.

"Your top shows through the shirt, Miss... Wendell. Go back and get rid of the top."

Brittany whispered to a female assistant - there were more of them for the evening shoot - and was allowed to skip into Henderson's for a minute. She came back with a small and simple white bra. While some other little girl twirled and flung her hair and hammed for the camera in a similar, but much smaller outfit, Brittany went into the little impromptu dressing-room and dropped the swimsuit.

She spent two hours in front of the backdrop, off and on, in several different outfits: another skirt, their jeans and her own plaid shirt, jeans and a coat, a pleated navy skirt and plaid jacket, a plaid skirt with a navy jacket, more jeans with impractical and too-short sweaters, and once in her own one-piece swimsuit, at their request. At the end of her shoot, when she emerged from the screened-off area back in her own clothing, they gave her a bag with the various pantyhose and tights they'd dressed her in and the bra she'd needed. They also instructed Brittany to sort through what she'd worn to pick one ensemble to keep. Without too much sorting or angst she chose the Irish wool school-girl skirt and the navy-colored fitted suit jacket. Those would be out of her reach in a regular shopping trip.

***

Tabitha giggled. "I remember that blazer... and the skirt! I had you pinned up on my wall, out of the insert in the Sunday paper. You are really professional-looking... I didn't even REALIZE you were in my school until I saw you mowing lawns in it!"

"Well, that wasn't the same skirt, by then. It had gotten WAY too short - especially in back, my ass filled out." Brittany sat up. "But I liked the look." She squared her shoulders to fling the next into the light of day: "You know, my mom wasn't even THERE when I was done. The bitch DITCHED ME. TOLD me it's okay to stay late, and then BAILED once I got busy. I spent an HOUR looking around that mall for her, then I STILL didn't get it until I went to the parking lot, it's, like, DARK by then, and the car is gone." Brittany shook her head. "I mean, what the fuck?"

"Ew. Er... That's..."

"Abuse."

"What did she SAY? I mean, SOMEONE must have asked, hey, didn't you think maybe you shouldn't leave your young teenaged daughter to hitchhike eighty miles home?"

"Told them I was dawdling and it served me right to MISS my ride. Like we didn't go together. Grandma was fit to be tied. Only time I ever heard her raise her voice to my mother. She picked me up - for some reason all the phones in our house turned out to be unplugged, on accident - so Grandma got a friend to bring her up and brought me home, and then marched right up to their bedroom and started in." Brittany held her head. "Oh, what a screaming match! My dad came running down in his underwear, booked it right out of that room to check on me. He had no idea I'd been left alone up there, thought I was home. Jesus. He slept on the couch for two weeks after that. Those two couldn't stand to be in the same room for a while."

"I had no idea."

Brittany brightened. "I got a letter last summer, actually, 'come on back,' had Dad take me up this time. All the way to Montreal! One of the big nationals had a thing. They shot me in jeans for a whole day." She shrugged. "I split the two hundred bucks with my Dad, put him down as my 'Agent.' Seemed only fair. Never got any proofs back... Probably nothing ever came of it."

Tabitha looked sick. "So your mother is a serial adulterer, serial liar, serial two-year-old."

"Something like that. She's not a happy person, and I'm not happy when I'm around her."

Tabitha snuggled up against her friend. "Jesus, I'm glad you had someplace to go! You mighta turned out a stoner or something, you'd stayed there…"

Brittany smirked, and stroked Tabitha's hair absentmindedly. *If you only knew.* "I think that's enough story-time. Where are we sleeping?"

"You mean, TOGETHER?" Hope and joy sprang into the room with Tabitha's voice.

"Yah. No hanky-panky, though. I want to keep my welcome here."

Tabitha was overjoyed: *Together is still TOGETHER!*

Tabitha's parents came down in the morning to a cleared driveway, a school-closing ice-storm right on the heels of the snowstorm, and a little square of snoring forms in zipped-together sleeping bags in front of the teevee. They decided to let sleeping girls lie.

***

"Brittany, do you mind if I tell someone... about you?"

Brittany looked up from her homework. It was a frosty late-February Wednesday night and she was hard at work playing catch-up again, sitting with textbooks at the kitchen table while Grandma Wendell read in her rocker in the corner. At this point, Brittany was only doing as much as was needed to understand the concepts behind the work. Which wasn't much - she was a smart girl and being average was easy for her. The schedule was taking its toll, though. She was starting to fall down into the grading curve in her classes, which pleased her classmates and even a couple of the teachers who had vested interests in school athletics. Brittany was slipping, the bell curve becoming more uniform, and fewer Varsity athletes were in jeopardy of losing their team uniforms on account of grades. Victory for everybody, from a certain perspective, but not Brittany's. She supposed she'd no longer be 'excused' from final exams.

"Huh?"

"Do you mind if I tell someone... about you. Two." Hattie continued, carefully: "About your 'Pajama Parties' with Tabitha, I guess is how I'd put it... Do you?"

"Grandma! You mean, 'OUT' me?" Brittany looked genuinely shocked.

"Is that what they call it?"

"Yep, that IS what they call it! You didn't strike me as the type. I mean, to Out someone." Brittany laughed. "Then again, I didn't think of myself as a Lesbian until just now. I mean, I guess I MUST be if I can be Outed... Shit!" Brittany adopted the Thinker's Pose. "Maybe I should cut my hair shorter and get a nose ring and all that stuff..."

"Brittany, I never know when you're giving me a hard time, and when you're serious!"

She replied matter-of-factly: "You're not supposed to, Grandma. You're an adult. I'm a teen. I'm supposed to keep you guessing." Brittany propped her mouth against her knuckles and squinted for another moment. She looked up. "I don't suppose it will matter. Everyone was already talking about us when we were just doing homework, and they're certainly saying MORE now, and Tabitha's never hidden anything... Garden-Variety Red-Headed Lesbian, it's just who she is." Brittany paused. "I don't think it really matters, now. Everyone either knows or assumes. Who?"

"A friend. She'll be discrete, I think."

"Sure, Grandma, knock yourself out." Brittany went back to her textbook.

***

Hattie and Brittany hosted another Hockey Breakfast the next weekend. Walt dropped by on Friday evening with a trunk-load of supplies fit to feed an army, and Sylvia passed through the Hollow just in time to stop and help him carry all of it up and into the shed to be ready for the next morning. Brittany came home from work late that night to fresh pies cooling on wire racks on the counter. And another note:

NO! FOR BREAKFAST!

But Hattie had taken pity on her housemate: there was a little mini-dish of pie-filling, all cooked and cooling, with the ice-cream scoop set out prominently beside that.

Brittany smiled. And then she helped herself to the dessert: strawberry-rhubarb. *Yum!* She ignored the ice cream scoop and rooted around in the fridge until she found just the right... *Ah! Danish blue!* She grinned. "Just a little chunk...."

***

Morning came, and Brittany was just as anxious about this group meal as the first one, for some reason. She took pains to arrange herself "just so" for a nine-AM visit by twenty boys on their way to Massachusetts.

Hattie found it amusing. "Brittany, you're a waitress by trade, now. No need to get all worked up over a little company." She couldn't understand it, *the girl pacing back and forth, checking her hair in every reflective surface she passed...?*

Brittany went upstairs to get dressed in her Sunday Best at eight AM. She returned to the kitchen twenty minutes later in a knee-length grey Tweed skirt with suspenders that buttoned on to the waist. Under the suspenders she wore an un-buttoned blue oxford shirt tied at the midriff, summer-style. Brittany had a Navy blue body-stocking on under all of that. She was covered, and decent, with the bodystocking. And she knew the open, knotted shirt would keep their attention.

Hattie Wendell turned from the range top and regarded her granddaughter-slash-housemate skeptically. *Are you sure?*

Brittany met her gaze and looked back stoically, confidently, plainly.

"Okay, then." *Have it your way. She's up to something.* Hattie sighed as she turned back to the stove.

"Nothing nefarious, Grandma." She looked out the window. "Oh, good. They're here!" *Early!* The anxious, nervous teen was gone. The efficient and outgoing waitress had arrived in her place.

There was a little trouble at the door. The first hockey player had come into the door, stopped stock-still on seeing Brittany, and was rear-ended by a line of his hurrying teammates. Progress started again. The farmhouse filled with hungry young men.

The conversation was subdued this morning. They were polite, quiet, and in a hurry to eat. In addition, most of the young men were afraid to look at Brittany for some reason. A few gazes lingered, eyes rolled, faces colored over collars, and then they studiously shoveled in their food. One young man was so addled that he knocked over his orange juice. The hockey players ate up and filed out of the farmhouse in record time.

"They must have an early practice when they get there." Hattie Wendell had never seen the team dine and depart so rapidly. She looked at her granddaughter and her outfit with sudden interest as an idea hit her: "Did YOU do that?"

"You said... well last time, you said you thought I could probably handle them." She shrugged and looked down at the knot in her shirt. "I did."

Ah. "That's scary."

Brittany smiled. "But effective." And, as an added benefit, she'd certainly kept - or maybe increased - the interest of one of them.

***

Sylvia dropped by on a Sunday morning on her way back from Church, to share the bitter taste of defeat with Hattie Wendell.

"Better pull out the whiskey glasses, Hattie. It was a bad one."

"I heard. I think I need to go have a few words at the referees!" *Or at Brittany for confounding the team during their breakfast....* "Whistles go against them?"

Sylvia laughed. "No, Hattie, I was there. They earned EACH and EVERY one of those penalties. It was a loss fair and square. If that Sutton kid from Toronto hadn't scored one late in, it would have been a Shut-Out!" Sylvia held her head in her hands in despair that was only partially mocking. "What did you FEED those boys?"

"Same as always!" Hattie's brow furrowed. "Oh, crap, I guess that's the end of THAT tradition. Oh, well. It worked for twenty-three straight away games and five tournaments. Them's the shakes. Have a drink!"

Hattie poured them small, because it was only eleven-thirty on a Sunday morning, after all. The two women were tossing back the shots, the bottle on the kitchen table between them, when Brittany and Tabitha walked in.

The girls piped up in unison:

"Holy shit, Grandma!" (Brittany)

"Is that WHISKEY?!?" (Tabitha)

The two older women looked at the teens, and said loudly, primly, in unison:

"Nothing gets the bitter taste of defeat out of your mouth like a shot of whiskey!"

"Nothing takes the sting of defeat out of your mouth like a shot of whiskey!"

Then they looked at each other and laughed.

Brittany turned to Tabitha: "That's right! They lost. Hockey. These two have a tradition. I didn't realize..." She looked pointedly at the clock. "That it was a MORNING tradition! Grandma, you USED to seem so PROPER!"

"Stop giving me a hard time!" She said, more quietly, "Brittany, you may have overdone it."

Brittany put on a staged sheepish face, but said, "I doubt it."

Hattie changed the subject back, just as quickly. "Tabitha, this is Sylvia. Brittany, you remember Sylvia? She gives me a report on Away games. If they'd won, we'd be having something a little gentler."

"Nice to meet you, even under these trying circumstances." Sylvia turned her head and smiled up at Brittany. "What did you overdo?"

Her question went ignored by both parties that were privy to the waitressing at the Hockey Breakfast.

Tabitha curtsied theatrically (a strange gesture for a modern girl, but she had class, you couldn't argue that!). "Pleased to meet you, Ma'am. I hope your whiskey days end with the next game, maybe?" She looked at the glasses and shivered, and then the two girls scurried through the front room and tromped up the stairs with their bookbags.

Hattie sighed. "Well, Sylvia, I'd better hear ALL about it. How did my boys manage to screw this one up?"

"They lost fair and square, Hattie. Even before the penalties." She straightened; even in defeat there was still excitement in the game. "It all started with a missed pass that bounced off a skate and right into our own net..."

The girls came down a half hour later to raid the cookie jar. This large, earthenware crock came with the kitchen all the way back in 1870. It had provided an endless and bottomless supply of molasses and ginger cookies to at least three generations of Wendells. Before that it had probably cured pickles or held flour or sugar. Brittany had never known it to be empty- when she was little, she supposed it magic, never realizing that her grandmother always made up a fresh batch of the soft and chewy treats when she knew that the grandchildren were coming. Here and now Brittany reached into the jar furtively, trying not to clink the lid just out of childhood habit. Tabitha copied her carefully, and with a grin.

Sylvia was still there at the kitchen table with Hattie. Sylvia watched the two girls carefully as she and Hattie talked of other things. Brittany noticed and whispered something in Tabitha's ear. The two girls went to the fridge and poured some milk to go with their petite lunch. Tabitha looked back at the two older women and whispered something close in Brittany's ear. Somehow her lips brushed Brittany's neck on the way by. Twice. The two older women could see Brittany shiver. The two girls scampered out of the room in a peal of laughter, headed back upstairs for more homework.

Sylvia watched them go.

Hattie turned to Sylvia. "Can I have a little more parenting advice?"

"It's nice that they feel comfortable being themselves, here. Is this new?" Sylvia had gotten the impression - from elsewhere - that Brittany was into boys.

"Oh, no! It's kind of an occasional thing. And I think they might be a little TOO comfortable! Tabitha stays over, sometimes." Hattie sighed and shook her head. "It started innocently enough. Peejay party, then Tabitha stayed too late doing homework, then she got snowed in up here…" Hattie looked up. "Am I doing the right thing?"

Sylvia looked at her friend speculatively. "Does it BOTHER you, Hattie?"

"Heavens, NO! There's far too little love in the world to worry about who's loving who. It's just… I don't want the farmhouse to get a reputation as a bordello!"

Sylvia laced her hands under her chin and looked calmly over them at her friend. "Is Brittany exclusive? Has there been anyone else?"

I'm surprised you haven't heard. "Not up here. That I know of."

"Well, Hattie, you have some decisions to make. Soon, by the looks. You're Brittany's grandmother. But you are so much more to her, as well. What you have to decide, is, are you trying to be her friend, or her mother?" Sylvia laughed. "It's tricky with young people and same-sex affairs, isn't it?"

Hattie sighed. "I'm trying to do the Right Thing."

"I think, from what I see, that together you two probably will."

***

To complicate matters a bit, and unknown to Hattie Wendell, Tabitha wasn't the only current Romantic Interest on Brittany's mind. There was a certain hockey player who she had a cursory, skeptical, but very real interest in. She waited patiently, wondering when he'd show up at her workplace again. She also wasn't sure what to do with him if he did.

***

Now this Bruce fellow was a busy guy, what with hockey and school and the active social life that any college man is required to keep. Business school was no easy peach, and on top of that Bruce Sutton had picked up a minor: Criminal Justice Studies. He had finally figured out that he wasn't going to be some famous NHL star, wasn't going to captain some Olympic come-from-behind Dream Team. He probably wasn't even going to make Pro. Maybe a Farm Team somewhere, maybe the beer-and-peanuts two-dollar leagues, which would be alright except that he would have to find a way to support himself. He realized now that he wasn't going to do that on the ice.

Don't misunderstand - life on the ice was going great for Bruce. And his heart was still in it. He loved the feel of fresh ice under his skates. He played literally any position on the team, as necessary, and was doing a good job of it. He was consistent, dependable, even sometimes a stand-out. But Bruce Sutton was not a Miracle On Skates. He knew that too quickly, and also just in time.

***

The Academy hockey team went down to Boston Garden one night while Bruce was still a Sophomore, bussed down to watch the

Bruins play an exhibition game. One of the last before the ancient stadium was torn down, actually. The Bruins were hosting Quebec in a pre-season shakedown game. Both teams were a little rusty from a summer more-or-less off the ice, and the lineups were new. As far as Bruce was concerned, it was a scouting trip. For him. He was checking out the Bruins - he might let that team sign him up after college. Bruce was beginning to like the East Coast, and he liked the solid coverage the Bruins got in the local papers. They had a reputation, and lived up to it. Bruce had just started to get some good ice time during games at the end of his Freshman year, and so going into the early fall he felt a kinship with these older players. *I'll be out there with you in a couple of years, guys. Print me up a jersey.*

Then, in the second period, the game kicked up a notch. The hockey got fast, brutal, precise. Bruce couldn't describe it. He just knew, deep in his gut, that it was a level of hockey that he couldn't achieve now or in ten years. *If I went down the ice that fast, I'd have to loiter to catch my breath.* These guys, they went down the ice like speed-skaters in the Four-Hundred, accurate passes back and forth while full-out sprinting, and then they had enough energy left to rip off the gloves and start beating on each other over who hooked a skate first. You couldn't understand how unreal it was unless you truly knew the game. These men were ATHLETES, as well as Hockey Players.

Bruce vowed to work on cardio more, maybe add some speed runs up the local ski hill to the end of his weight-room workouts. All that muscle wouldn't do diddly for you if you were slow getting out of the gate. Doubts started to nag at his mind.

***

So Bruce picked up a Minor. His business degree seemed very exciting when he imagined running a stadium, or managing a team after his own storied career, or when he thought about running a sports agency firm. Business classes got a lot more boring when the end result he was contemplating turned out to be an eight-to-six job at some H.R. firm, or on a sales route for an encyclopedia company, or stuffed in a little cubicle on the fourth floor at Cubicles, Incorporated.

The only folks on campus that were contemplating daily excitement after graduation, as far as he could see, where the "C.J." majors: Criminal Justice Studies / Law Enforcement. Bruce's Academic

Advisor suggested - more than once - that he sign up for the Intro to Criminal Procedure course as a Sophomore Year elective. *Sure, why not?* The "studies" part of it didn't sound too exciting, but the Law Enforcement end sure did. Heck, he watched that T.V. show, "COPS," right in his dorm room. They had taped reruns on Beta and everything - his Academic Advisor freely handed out loaners to him whenever he wanted a new episode. *How cool is that?*

Between watching the Beta tapes and the coursework, Bruce realized that those Boys In Blue got some excitement out of life! *Not that different from a hockey game, really: Charging down an alley after a subject too stupid to just stop and meet the inevitable (charging down the ice after a puck to grab it before it got an "icing" call), checking and furtive hooking (those street takedowns, as officers fought an unruly subject, just looked like hockey without pads), and the car chases - who doesn't like driving fast? And to be PAID for it!*

Bruce liked the students, too. They were… different. He couldn't put a finger on it. He didn't realize that a good many of them were Veterans, at the Academy on the G.I. Bill, or that some of them were even already part- or full-time police officers. One classmate came into the lecture one day in full uniform, gun and everything, and then he realized she was working and there was probably a radio car parked outside and she was playing hooky from work - with or without sanction - to go to school. He realized these were serious people - adults. Bruce would soon turn twenty and was convinced he was becoming a grownup now, too. *Maybe like those folks.*

He hadn't written home about it, but he was now taking eighteen credits this semester, and his Advisor was suggesting a double-major and Summer School for a couple of years to catch up. The Advisor told him that both the U.S. FBI, as well as the RCMP back home in Ontario, frequently hired graduates with the combined Business-CJ major. A lot of crimes were corporate crimes, requiring a knowledge of accounting, computers, and other things touched on by a Business degree. There was a future in it, if he wanted it.

The Advisor also suggested he take one semester of French, in case he wanted to work for Interpol. French, the language of International Law Enforcement, he called it. *There's no boundary in this line of work, kid.* He told him that each case was just one more contest, kind of like the ice, only the periods were longer. Three of them: Investigation, preparation, trial. *You'll get excitement and the satisfaction of winning out of your career. I mean, if you don't decide to go Pro on the ice.* He said it with a shrug.

Bruce liked his Academic Advisor. Professor Wendell got the Big Picture.

***

Being so busy, Bruce had to be careful with his time. Fitting this new girl he wanted to chase into his schedule was going to be an extra challenge, especially since she wasn't a campus resident - or even a village resident - and he didn't have a car.... *Now how-in-the-fuck am I going to carry THAT off, eh?*

In March, he started borrowing a car once a week or so - any car he could get his hands on. Once he begged, borrowed, or coerced the use of a car, he'd take his homework over to the Smiley's ice cream counter. He usually went on a Friday night if the hockey team wasn't on the ice somewhere and Scott's car was available. He'd skip Friday and go early in the next week if he couldn't borrow a car or had a hockey conflict. Bruce would set up his books and order a pitcher of water and a dish of sherbet and do his homework for an hour, then order the cheapest dinner on the menu and do more homework for another hour. He was surprised to find that somehow it helped him to have the noise and commotion of a busy restaurant around him - he concentrated better in spite of the occasional distraction caused by proximity to Her.

When some of his assignments were done and the dinner crowd started to thin out, Bruce would ask for dessert and a coffee. He'd sip his coffee and nibble at the apple pie and mozzarella sticks (Brittany's touch, and apparently on the house) while he watched his favorite waitress at work. He didn't always get Brittany as his server, but he made sure not to ask for dessert until she was near at hand. And Bruce Sutton now knew he liked cheese with his pie. It felt right.

Just once, after several visits, Brittany came over to sit down on the stool next to him. "How long are you planning on doing this?"

"Homework? 'Til I graduate."

Brittany took a mozzarella stick from his plate, dipped it in his apple pie filling and took a theatrical bite, then two more. She made a point to triple-dip. "No. How long are you going to keep coming in here to watch me work? You're not the only one, you know." She licked her fingertip with flirty gusto and then beamed at him.

Wow. "I'd be surprised if I was... Also until I graduate, I guess."

"Well, don't get your hopes up." Brittany slid off the stool to go around the counter and wash her hands at the sink.

"I already have what I came for."

She answered from the other side of the long counter as she dried her hands on a towel. "What's that?"

"You talked to me."

Chapter Eight

Brittany and Tabitha usually did homework on Saturday afternoons if Brittany wasn't working and Tabitha wasn't babysitting for anyone. (Many of the mothers in town felt safer sending their husbands off to drive That Lesbian Girl home from babysitting, especially after all the town figured out what was going on with Trudy the Lusty Teen Serial Adulteress.)

Over the last couple of weeks, something had changed. Tabitha started becoming frustrated by her visits with Brittany. Whenever Hattie was out of the room, all she kept hearing about was: That Hockey Player this, That Hockey Player that, That Hockey Player… That Bruce guy, That Canadian one… Over and over! Brittany seemed to have endless stories about him from the farmhouse or from the diner, a new tale every week.

One Saturday afternoon Tabitha asked Hattie if she could borrow the kitchen. Hattie watched Tabitha stir up a batch of cookies heavy on rye and oatmeal and sunflower seeds. While those were in the wood-fired oven, the girl stirred together a salad with ingredients she'd brought in from her car.

Brittany was still upstairs, busy working on a week's worth of homework. She'd gotten just the tiniest bit of slack from her teachers, although no one except those involved knew that. So now she was trying to get a week ahead where she could do the work already. The only instructors who wouldn't give her the assignments ahead of time were a couple of those who ALSO coached winning Collegeville sports teams. *Strange.* She did the best she could in those by simply working through ten or twenty pages ahead in her textbooks and hoping for the best.

Hattie and Tabitha were having a fine time in the kitchen all on their own. "Alright if I borrow a couple of plastic containers with lids, Grandma Wendell?"

"Sure, dear. May I ask what's up?"

"We're going to a Contra-Dance up at the Grange. Surprise for Britt - she doesn't know yet."

"Oh! I haven't been to one of those in years! Not since the old Grange Hall downtown closed!" The memories brought a warm smile to Hattie's face.

Uh-oh. This was kind of supposed to be a COUPLE THING, not that she'd ever say that to Brittany. *Oh, well, Grandma Wendell has turned out to be a pretty easy chaperone, hasn't she?* "There's always a pot-luck beforehand. Do you want to come along? I can tell you do…"

Hattie Wendell looked at Tabitha shrewdly. "Is this a DATE?"

Tabitha grimaced. "Depends on who you ask."

"Oh dear...." Hattie looked lost in thought for a moment. "Ah! You're off the hook, Tabitha! I almost forgot - There's hockey tonight! Potsdam. We're going to KICK SOME ASS!!!" Hattie stood up and shook her fist in the air just out of habit. Then she looked around the kitchen, a little embarrassed, and sat back down. *Ooops.* She smiled across the kitchen at Tabitha. "I'd really like to go, sometime, though. If you'd take me. Would you?"

"I'd like that." Tabitha stopped for a minute, put a very thoughtful look on her face, and then a stage pout. "You KNOW people are going to TALK."

"OH! About you and me?!? I can live with that for a pot-luck and some good music!" Hattie laughed. *The girl is probably right, in this little town of ours!* "Next away-game weekend?" Hattie walked over to the calendar.

"Sure, Grandma Wendell. It's a… Plan! Actually, it's not ALWAYS on Saturday. Let's take a look." Tabitha walked over to the wall and the two of them consulted the calendar together.

The first batch of cookies were just ready to come out of the oven built into the side of the enamel and iron woodstove. Baking on a wood fire was different - as the cookies started to finish, they'd get a certain smell going in the air in the kitchen, and you knew they were done. The second batch would be harder - you'd have to time them based on how long the first ones took, plus subtract for the already-hot baking sheet. Tabitha put the pan up on the counter on a cooling rack, looked at the clock and turned to Hattie. "Thankyou. For becoming part of my family, or letting me become part of yours. Whichever. This is… nice." She put the second ancient baking sheet covered in goops of dough into the wood-fired oven and grabbed a spatula to start flipping the little round granola-like cookies from the first batch onto a plate.

It was Hattie's turn to look uncomfortable. "I hope it turns out well, Tabitha. I worry about you two. Especially you. I wouldn't want to see you get hurt." And she quickly added, "I don't think she'd ever do that on purpose. But you're both very young." *Too young to carry on an affair under this roof… I should have chased you out that first morning, but here you are, probably too young to have these worries, but you do. You're just* "too young to be this complicated, yet."

Tabitha's gaze was on her shoes when she answered in a very small voice: "I know that. I know." *But here I am.* She shrugged.

Brittany bounded into the kitchen just then, "I smell…" looked at the counter, "COOKIES!!!" And then stopped short. "Hey, why the long faces?"

Tabitha turned away for a second to compose herself, then whirled around with manic eyes. "We were talking about BOYS!"

"Right. Well, can I have a…" She reached for the cookie plate, but Tabitha slapped the reaching hand with the cookie spatula.

"OWTHATHURT!!!"

"THOSE are for LATER." Less firmly, Tabitha said, "I'd like to take you somewhere for dinner. It's a pot-luck." Tabitha gestured with the spatula to the plastic party-bowl full of salad. "With a dance afterwards."

Suddenly, Brittany looked like a deer caught in headlights.

Hattie came to the rescue. "Oh, GO! I'll catch a ride with Sylvia, or call your Dad. We spend PLENTY of time together, if that's what you're worried about."

Brittany still looked torn. She kept turning her head, and then she was playing with her hair and scowling at some unseen thing or person or problem outside of the farmhouse.

Uh-oh. Hattie sensed a disaster. *Maybe I WILL be going to a Contra-Dance tonight, after all.* It would be the first hockey game, well HOME game, that she'd missed since her husband died. *Ooof. Well, Tabitha is worth it.*

Tabitha found her voice. "WHAT?!?"

"Nothing." Brittany made her decision. "Nothing at all." She walked over and took Tabitha by the arm, elbow-in-elbow. She spun her friend carefully around the kitchen, towards the door, wearing her Happy Face. "I'd LOVE to go to a pot-luck!"

Hattie handed Tabitha the plastic containers after the girls had struggled into their boots and coats. As she watched them bustle out of the kitchen, she wondered just exactly why Brittany was so reluctant to go out. *Maybe she finally doesn't want to lead the girl on?*

***

Tabitha drove them in her father's big sedan. "My treat tonight, my car!"

Brittany stretched out a little on the big bench-style front seat - careful to keep well to the passenger side of the vehicle - and fiddled with the radio. She seemed distracted.

Tabitha filled her friend in a little, on where they were headed. "It's a dance. A Contra-Dance. That's OLD dancing, from way-back-when, in Europe or something, when the church didn't allow people to dirty-dance and Doing The Nasty was refereed by a bunch of blessed monks that told you how to do it and all that shit." She was quiet while she concentrated on cross-traffic at an intersection. "Anyway, it's really old-style dancing, like they've been doing forever, with live fiddle music. Some communities in New England, there's been contra-dancing every year for jeez, like three-hundred years or so. I know you're crazy about old-time things." She continued to jabber on about it. Tabitha seemed a little nervous. Or edgy.

A car pulled out to pass, then loitered alongside them in the wrong lane for half a mile at fifty miles an hour. The car was probably full of testosterone- and stupidity-fueled boys, likely the very same ones they had to suffer in school. It dropped back behind, then whipped around the big sedan once more on the next curve with good visibility, where they were passed for good. The exhaust left a foul-smelling plume that came through the Ford's heater vents.

Both young women shouted in unison:

"ASSHOLES!"

"ASSWIPES!"

They giggled. Like the people in the other car could actually HEAR them! They laughed again.

Brittany scooted over and changed seatbelts, sitting in the middle next to Tabitha. She could reach the radio from here without stretching. "So WHERE are we going, again?"

Tabitha gave a groan. "TO A CONTRA DANCE AT THE GRANGE! With LIVE music! What is UP with you lately, Girl?!?" She settled down. "The Grange. Up at the County Common. Some farmer's association from the old days. Ask your Grandma. It'll be like stepping back fifty or a hundred years. I know you like old-fashioned things, or else you wouldn't be doing your homework by kerosene lantern all the time... chopping firewood for your cooking, and all that shit."

"Really?" Brittany turned in her seat, and gave Tabitha a long look in the dark of the car. "You know, you're really thoughtful. I'm glad you were nice to me. In school. Whatever deep, dark, naughty thoughts prompted it! You're a cool shit!" Brittany picked up her left hand from behind Tabitha's seat and put it to her mouth. And then she mumbled, with her mouth full, "And a good cook!"

Tabitha nearly went off the road while she tried to whack Brittany with the windshield scraper-thingy. "You awful, INCONSIDERATE, UNAPPRECIATIVE, IMPATIENT… Those COOKIES are for the POT LUCK!!!"

Brittany laughed and made sure to move fully back to the passenger side of the car to stay out of reach of the windshield scraper.

Tabitha fumed outwardly for the next mile, but she was smiling on the inside. *Almost like Old Times....*

***

Dinner started promptly at six. Brittany had never seen so many Wholesome People in one place, all at the same time, except maybe at the co-op food store. She felt comfortable immediately among these easy-going and friendly people who seemed at once progressive and old-fashioned, cutting-edge with colors and tie-dye and strange hair and free clothing and conservative in their selection of a two-hundred year old social club with fiddle music and structured dancing that had not changed in hundreds of years. The normally-empty and stogey Grange Hall with its brown floors and grey walls was now a riot of color and commotion: full of women in flowing skirts of earthy colors or bright tie-died rainbow T-shirts, men in loose cotton or woolen pants and wearing suspenders and plaid shirts or real woolen Henleys. Children everywhere, active participants, not precocious but treated as full Beings.

They all ate downstairs in the cellar, where long tables and folding chairs had been set up. Brittany felt like she was at someone's very large family holiday. Everyone seemed to know each other - they asked one and all about this-and-that family member, how is so-and-so, and where is Judy tonight, how is your son off at College, and et cetera. Some of these people knew Tabitha, and asked about her family. A couple of people recognized Brittany and asked after her dad or her grandmother. No one asked after her mother.

The food lined up on a middle table was a mix heavy on vegetable dishes and cornbreads and beans and salads, but there was also a fire-filled, greasy, meaty and scrumptious chili.

Brittany tried a seafood pasta salad and got the distinct feeling that it might have been made from "Green Mountain Lobsters." *Little crayfish, cooked and frozen a few months ago when the local swimming was good?* She smiled to herself at the thought of swimming for your supper.

Tabitha turned. "What?"

"Thankyou, Tab. This is really neat. Community pot-lucks used to be a big thing in a lot of Vermont towns. And your salad is really good."

"Thanks. You can FINALLY have a COOKIE, Brittany!" She passed one over from her own plate. "Well, ANOTHER one." Tabitha took a forkful of the chili and her cheeks and forehead immediately took on the hue of her red hair. She swallowed, coughed, and switched to bites of the seafood pasta salad. "One of the really nice things Mom did for me. When she saw that I wasn't really...." She paused to take a bite, then looked around the room while she chewed on her food and her thoughts. A moment later she gestured in circles with her fork while searching for words and then continued: "...like the other girls at school. She and I had a couple of years of Friday and Saturday nights out: here, at the Unitarian church over across the river where they do movies and slideshows and poetry nights... She took me to the live theater up at the Academy and sometimes all the way down to the big college for a lecture on whales or something. Sort of a monthly circuit to introduce me to other kinds of folks."

"Wow." Brittany wore a quizzical frown. "When was that?"

"When I was, I don't know, nine or twelve. It wasn't all the time, just off and on. I think that she wanted me to know that there were other people in the world besides the jocks and wasps and gowns."

Brittany was floored. "Did she KNOW? Before you did?"

"Hmmmm. No. I knew already." She shrugged. "Mom just knew I was different. Wanted me to know that I didn't have to fit in at school to fit into the wide, wide world. It stopped when she figured I got the point. That I could be ME, whoever that was."

Brittany had stopped eating. "THAT is the SWEETEST thing I have EVER heard!"

"Well, she's not so bad..." *Not so very bad at all.* Tabitha had never questioned whether she was loved, or wanted.

Brittany went back to her squash pie, deep in thought.

The old wooden floor upstairs was kept polished to a high sheen, and everyone was firmly instructed to leave their shoes at the door.

Brittany thought it was funny to be standing in her socks with sixty other people on a Friday night. The band consisted of a fiddler, a cello player, and a woman who alternately picked on a steel guitar or played a dulcimer. A man behind a microphone "called" the dance, like a square dance, but with the difference that every person in the room partnered with every other person playing the opposite gender for a set of repeated steps during each dance set. Brittany started with her partner, Tabitha, and each of them worked their way down a line in opposite directions, dancing one set of instructions with every OTHER "partner" until they came 'round to complete the dance with the original partner again. Dancing for the wandering eye, apparently. But dancing with rigid and structured rules for steps, positions of dancers, spacing, and placement of hands. As Brittany tried to work her way up and down the room to the instructions of the caller there were helping hands, pointing fingers, polite shouts, and even pushes that came whenever she was unsure where to go next. These folks liked to keep the thing moving! Brittany got a workout - it is very physically hard work, marching to and fro to music - but she was smiling from ear-to-ear the whole evening. Sometimes she and Tabitha danced with each other, and sometimes they were far across the room, paired with other partners for a set. No one seemed too concerned about whether someone showed up with a date - or was with the date they came with - or not. And Brittany noticed that she and Tabitha were not the only women - or men - who danced together as partners, a fact which sometimes caused just a little confusion as folks in mid-step tried to figure out which form coming at them was "the female."

Tabitha leaned over as they marched forward, helped by pushes and shoves, after one such mishap: "They're used to it, they'll figure out…" Tabitha disappeared as she circled around the back of another dancer, and then came back into view to continue: "You're the Boy if you are in the right spot when they arrive."

A woman across the set merrily said, "Just watch what the other MEN do, and follow that."

Brittany laughed. "I've never been a boy before…" And did her best to follow the example of only the 'Boys,' some of who were actually women. *So confusing!* But she had about thirty iterations in which to figure it out each dance. It started to work.

Brittany had more fun that night, dancing up and down long lines, than she remembered having in ages. Her life had been all work and very little play for a few months, so swinging and marching back and forth with the crowd on this old dance floor full of apparently wholesome and unpretentious people was a very welcome change. And a new experience - Brittany hadn't even been to a school dance before.

A couple of apparently single young men with long beards and high-water workpants, maybe in their early twenties or so, came to sit near her on a couple of the breaks. Other than that, no one paid any more attention to Brittany than to anyone else in the large hall, other than being welcoming and instructive. Not at all like school or work or anywhere else she had been. Here, apparently, Brittany was nearly anonymous. She discovered that maybe she could like that.

The cold, frosty, late-winter outside air felt good when they finally left the dance at ten. The girls didn't bother with jackets, but that changed when they got into the car and sat back against the cold vinyl seat in their sweaty shirts: screams erupted. Brittany and Tabitha spilled back out the doors, arching their backs and flailing, screaming frost plumes into the air. "CO-COL-COLD!!!!"

Other people in the parking lot looked on briefly in amusement. This happened a lot in the wintertime, with new-comers. Tabitha hadn't been there in ages - she'd simply forgotten. The girls put their coats on, then got back into the car.

While the big Ford idled so the inside of the windshield would defrost, Brittany leaned over to give Tabitha a kiss on the cheek. "Thankyou, Tab. THAT was some kind of an evening." Then she slid back over to the passenger side and buckled up. "Take me home, James! Er... Tabitha!"

"Soooo... We can't go 'parking' on the way, maybe?" Tabitha looked over hopefully.

Brittany looked out the window, paused, and then gleefully replied: "Not in the snow!!"

Tabitha gestured at the wide dashboard console in front of her. "It's got good heat, and a BIG back seat!"

Brittany turned around to check. "Hmmmm. Yes, it does. I've never done anything in a car... But no." She felt a flicker of guilt: *that's not true, actually, but she doesn't need to hear about it.* She changed the subject: "I shouldn't cheat on Bruce."

Tabitha cringed, and then gritted her teeth. "But you're not even DATING this guy! He just sees you at WORK twice a week!! Brittany!" She leaned reached across the car to put her hands on each of

Brittany's shoulders, and then screamed, "YOU TWO AREN'T A COUPLE!!!"

Brittany, out of the corner of her eye, saw a fair number of the heads left in the parking lot turn towards Tabitha's Ford. *Hmmmm.* She retorted quietly. "Well, HE is certainly dating ME. And WE will be."

Tabitha didn't have anything to say to that. She put the mostly-defrosted car in drive and took Brittany home. It was a silent trip, with Tabitha frequently looking over at Brittany, a pained yet dreamy look on her face, probably thinking angst-filled and salacious thoughts about the raven-haired girl.

Brittany frequently stared out the passenger window for long periods, a dreamy look on her face, thinking about HIM.

Tabitha sighed. Often.

She dropped Brittany off at the big old farmhouse. Somehow, she had begun to feel like that was her home, sometimes. *Maybe not anymore.* Tabitha pulled off the road around the corner, just out of sight. She cried for ten minutes, and then she slowly drove all the way back to the village and her real home. *Shit.*

***

"That was really smart, Bruce." Professor Wendell nodded. *Welcome aboard, kid.* "You're not going to regret this."

His Academic Advisor had strongly suggested it, and then fast-paced both Bruce's registration and his financial paperwork: Summer school. Now they were meeting to work out the final details for classes that were just a couple of short months away.

"I'm glad you understand it's important to be strong in more than one area, academically. Not everybody gets that. But you're one of the special ones... you can handle it. Get some of your core courses out of the way now, during the summer, and then sign up for a whole shitload of electives in the Fall. Trust me, on this, Bruce. You'll be able to graduate in three years, or double-major in five, like we talked about. You know, if you decide to go ahead with law enforcement, this could really help you." Professor Wendell sat back in his chair. "Actually..." *I have a summer job all lined up for you... Now I just have to sell it:* "If you want it, I think there's a summer job in policing coming open right around here, next summer... You'll have to really get on the ball quick to get it, these things take time, a lot of time, what with background investigations and all, but...." He straightened, turned, and rotated back with a sheaf of papers. "Here it is. Job application. The State Police here use a lot of semi-civilian help on the lake and state parks during the summer. Sort of a trainee job, for folks testing the waters in law enforcement. You might find it beneficial. But like I said, you'll have to really move on it. There's a lot to do if you're at all interested: background, polygraph, the Police Academy..."

Bruce frowned and sat up straighter. "Polygraph?"

Professor Wendell waved a dismissive hand. "One of many things... Like I said, even though it's over a year away, you have to really move on this. " He paused, briefly, but continued as soon as he saw his Advisee's mouth start to form some question. "If you want it." Another pause. "You ARE interested, aren't you?" Push, push, push. The feigned rush was part of the plan. Make it seem important, he'd make it important. And they wanted to have him thoroughly vetted by next February or March, if he was the one. Ten or twelve months was a short time in the world of intensive, circumspect, cross-border pre-employment background investigations - especially since they had to hide the operation.

Bruce shrugged. Summers in Toronto no longer exactly thrilled him. SPENDING money - on schooling - instead of EARNING it over the summer, that was a problem. But schooling was a worthy expense, there happened to be some sort of amorphous aid package his Advisor thought he could get, and in the meantime the college had expedited a loan to his student account. The Registrar had mailed him a summer class enrollment schedule already, and there was this girl… Not to mention, they'd let him skate the ice right here, morning and night, as soon as they laid it down in August. "Will I be able to do that job and do next year's summer school at the same time?"

"Oh, sure. Policing is kind of a night and weekend thing. You've seen that in some of your classes - there are law officers right in there, in uniform, during the day. And this is more of a part time thing, anyway. By statute, members of the State Police Auxiliary can't work more than thirty-two hours. Cruise the lake, wave at some girls in bikinis, write some tickets for boating while intoxicated, that kind of thing. Try it next summer, if you're interested. See maybe if law enforcement might be something you want to do, later." *Soft sell now.*

Part-time job, huh? "Er… I'm Canadian. I'm not sure… Would that even WORK?"

That's why we want you. "Oh, I don't think that's a problem. You're a dual citizen, right?"

"Oh, ya!" *No shit. A summer job driving around big water on a boat…* He smiled.

Professor Wendell inspected him seriously. This next part was important. "You haven't ever voted, have you…?"

"Er… No. Not yet." *But I'm patriotic. I WILL, I swear.* He was about to open his mouth to say that...

Professor Wendell interrupted him: "Good. Don't." He leaned forward. "As a dual citizen, a citizen of two countries, you retain a lot of choices. Until you vote. Then you're driving a flagpole in the ground. Don't vote, don't register to vote, don't sign any petitions outside of college campus stuff, and you're keeping your options open. That's important, don't you think?"

Why, "Yes." It sure seemed to be, now.

"Good." Professor Wendell tapped the pile of papers with his finger. State job application, application and information for background investigation, some other paperwork. "That's the new, most important thing in your life. Get busy. Job interview is actually a testing session, a sit-down kind of like that SAT exam you took to get in here, no big deal, you're smart, it's not a pass-fail sort of thing...." He sat back. "That's next week, by the way, during my class. I'm giving you an excused absence obviously. Directions are there, on that paper on the bottom. The background information will take a while, it's about forty pages… Get right on this, Bruce." Professor Wendell stood up. "It might be real good for your future to graduate with your foot already in the door. Who knows where you'll end up?" Professor Wendell knew. Or thought he did. Actually, he was wrong, in the end.

***

Bruce hemmed and hawed for a full day.

The decision was largely made by a pair of bottomless green eyes framed in curly black hair, eyes that warmed to him as soon as he stepped in the door of Smiley's that evening. She smiled at him several time as she passed, and once he could swear that the girl winked as she grinned in his direction. He began working on the paperwork late that night, as soon as he got back to his dorm room.

**

The semester came to an end and Bruce Sutton's habits didn't change, other than now he was busy studying First Responder manuals, hazmat spill response guidebooks and a thick Constitutional Law textbook that Professor Wendell had lent him. He visited his parents for two weeks and then the Academy let him move into the Summer Dorm a couple of weeks early. Professor Wendell had pulled some strings. Campus was largely empty, there were no cars, so Bruce took up a new hobby to pair with his Brittany interest: hitch-hiking. The rainy walks in-between cars, the hot pavement, the uncertainty and long miles of late nights returning to Collegeville were worth it. The prize: Brittany's eyes, eyes that spent more and more time assessing him and sassing him as he completed the 'Special Schoolwork" assigned by Professor Wendell. Sometimes his favorite waitress took an ice-cream break on the stool next to him - proximity, but no conversation. Other times, she chatted with him whenever she passed by going this way and that around the restaurant, never actually stopping to talk, but engaging nevertheless. They started to have real conversations, briefly and sporadically. He saved money by eating but one meal a day - and that was more often than not twelve-point-six miles away, at Smileys. Twenty-five thousand, one-hundred-and-eleven steps if he didn't catch a ride. A couple of the Regulars who were used to seeing him and approved of his motives went out of their way to give him rides all the way back to campus on a couple of rainy nights. Bruce made some friends. His body leaned down - bad for hockey - and so he started eating off the Family Platter menu.

Brittany watched his efforts with growing interest and made a decision: soon.

Once, after the actual start of the Summer Session, Bruce came in with his parents. Since he was in Vermont for the summer, Mom and Dad Sutton came east to visit for a couple of days. Brittany made sure she grabbed THAT table to wait on! All three of them got served the apple pie with fried cheese appetizer, to quizzical looks from his parents. Her co-workers exchanged some looks as they watched her come and go over there. Bruce and Brittany avoided more than necessary-to-the-meal conversation by some unspoken mutual accord, and no one made introductions, but everyone had seen everyone. That felt important to both of them, now.

Brittany's co-workers exchanged whispers and speculation on nights Bruce dropped by. They could see something coming. A waitress with ties to the Academy whispered "Cottage Cheese" with a gently-teasing smile as Brittany passed in the kitchen, to snickers from the dish-boy. Brittany remained stoic. She preferred to think of herself as a Venus Flytrap sort of a girl. Sometimes the other wait-staff would change the work-load subtly when the lone college boy came into the diner, to give Those Two a minute.

Other times, as the summer wore on, Brittany just winked on her way by during busy nights, or dropped a plate of the evening's special and a side of apple pie and cheese sticks in front of him and said, "I've got the check."

Bruce took this as a very good sign. *Apparently, she wants me to keep coming around. Well, this thing next summer with the State Police will make sure that happens. If I get it.* Bruce decided not to mention it yet, until he was sure he got the job. In the meantime, he had to make it through a session of summer school and at least two more semesters of regular coursework. And of course there was hockey....

***

Paul Wendell drove his motorcycle to work sometimes, if it was good weather. The faded blue denim vest looked incongruous over the top of the formal wear he usually wore at work, but the three laughing dog heads exploding out of the embroidered center-patch on the back explained all that away.

It was amazing how many of the Topdogs wore suits or ties and jackets to work. Most people think "biker" and they picture working-class men in jeans or canvas pants: painters, welders, truck drivers, truck unloaders. That assumption couldn't be further from the truth here in this place. Bankers, business managers, small-business owners, big-business lobbyists.... Paul was not the only man cruising these highways while wearing "work" clothes under a vest that claimed they owned a piece of Quebec. Other drivers learned to give fealty and way to these vested owners of Montreal's back streets and alternate economy.

Which was a good thing.

Paul came up the Rue Sherbrooke at a pretty good clip. He was going to work early, so the traffic was pre-afternoon, pre-rush, and things were moving right along, if in fits and spurts. And then he saw that the interior billboard behind the huge, many-story glass front of the Hudson Bay Company store was changing again, and- *Becosse! It can't... Mary, Jesus, Joseph, Mother-of-God, and the Saints...*

WHAP!!

Paul rear-ended a luxury sedan stopped in a long line of traffic at a red light. He ended up on top of the trunk, seeing stars, while the motorcycle ended up UNDER the back of the car.

Ahhhh, Christ! He had lapsed into his native tongue in his double-dose of shock. Paul swatted away the helping hands, rolled off the car onto the sidewalk, got unsteadily to his feet, and took off his helmet. "Shit! No, non! I'm fine! Je suis ca va! Chu ca va!" He waved his arm angrily. "Allons!" Go!

He looked at the mess in the street - his motorcycle, the sedan riding high on top of it - and sighed. *I could have been killed.* The helmet was still in his hand - he brought it up. *Oh. That's why.* The helmet had suffered cracks and a huge flat spot. *That explains why I'm wobbly.* A man was talking in front of him, to him, gesturing wildly at the car. His car. *Oh.* The bumper and trunk of the car were wrecked - plastic and a replaceable trunk lid, mostly, but wrecked nevertheless.

A Topdog is never wrong. They are never at fault. A Topdog is never sorry. A Topdog gets into a scrape but never causes an accident.

Paul looked at the mess, at the intersection, at the stoplights, the gathered people. *Well, it's obvious that this man was stopped and I....* he shrugged and threw up his hands. *Perhaps I can buy his good graces and bury this.* "Yes, yes, we need a tow truck to help you on your merry way, I can see that!" Paul turned to get a better look at the mess that used to be his restored 1978 Milwaukee-Built.

The other driver saw the back of the vest and suddenly felt the need to produce his insurance documents. Surely they would cover the cost of fixing the nice motorcycle that now rested in pieces under his car, leaking gas onto the pavement.

Sirens filled the street.

Paul sighed. One more headache. A minor one. *No, a taxi won't do. I'm wearing the 'Dog. I have to leave this MESS in style.* He pulled his new, cumbersome-yet-suddenly-indispensable cellphone out of his pocket and used it to call the morning watchmen at a certain paper warehouse down on the Lachine Canal. "Paul. Wendell. I need a ride." Then he steeled himself for another look.

There, high up above the street and reclining out over two blocks was his sister. She was wearing this year's back-to-school fashions, but her face and cascading black curls remained the exactly the same as the last time he'd seen her. He stared, awe-struck, fixed in cement. Vibrant, full of youth, *the smile that could melt your heart.... She hasn't aged a single day!* Of course she hadn't - she'd been dead and gone for twenty-four years.

God Almighty.

***

Once busy with school, Bruce didn't hitch over as much. Too many late nights afoot interfered with wakefulness in class the next day. But he came over every time he could find a car to borrow or a ride from someone with an errand down in the Junction. He was back yet again, Tuesday night this time, for his now roughly twice-a-week study session. Brittany waited tables occasionally this evening, but managed to chat idly and briefly with Bruce quite a bit on her way by as she passed between the customers and the kitchen. No one minded on this quiet late-summer night with heat keeping people at swimming holes or home in the air conditioning. Maybe there would be a rush after the Early Show let out at the air-conditioned movie house.

Probably not. Who goes to the movies on a sweltering late-summer Tuesday night? Tips would be bad.

Brittany looked over at the ice cream counter and watched her suitor work at his notebooks. She decided it was time for a cold soda: bubbly seltzer water in pre-frozen glasses, a shot of lime flavoring, a shot of coffee syrup. She sat down on the stool next to his and set up two frosty glasses: his and hers. This time she talked during her break. "Soooooo. Even though you're a COLLEGE BOY, I'm not going to assume you're a ROCKET SCIENTIST. You notice I'm WORKING every time you show up?"

Bruce lay his pen down in the spine of his notebook. "Ya. So?"

"So maybe THAT should tell you I'm not one of those Party Girls, right? You bein' so smart an' in-" She went wide-eyed in mock awe.

"…COLLEGE an' all, maybe ya should be lookin' for some gal 's got time for parties." She returned to her native accent, squared her shoulders, and said primly: "Instead of a working girl."

"Maybe that's why I keep coming over here, eh? Although you don't look like much of a 'Working Girl' to me." Bruce looked her up and down carefully. "No. Definitely not."

Brittany cuffed him on the arm. "That's NOT what I meant." Then she thought of her car, right out there in the parking lot. She bit her lip and looked away from Bruce until the giggles passed, then carefully drew herself up and in her most serious manner said, very slowly, "I would not make ANY assumptions there, if I were you." She looked towards the door. "Customers! Bye, now!" She scurried off with an impish smile on her face that she couldn't quite morph into her service smile before she came face-to-face with the next hungry diners.

She left Bruce wondering just what the hell THAT was supposed to mean and left the customers casually wondering what the hell kind of shenanigans had been going on in there a moment prior.

Brittany stayed busy for the rest of the evening. She noticed Bruce picking up his things at the ice cream counter at about nine-thirty. She went over to say a quick goodbye: "You're so STUDIOUS! See you… Friday?"

"You never tell me when you're working...." This was new. Usually he had to chance her schedule, and if her little green hot-rod was there, he stopped. It seemed reliable enough, even a Sure Thing - she worked a lot. He opened his mouth to say, Youbet!, but Brittany was already talking.

"Well, make sure you're here." She winked. "Your competition might move in, otherwise."

We can't have that. "It's a date."

She kissed him on the cheek, right there in the restaurant, in front of the Hostess' Podium. "Good."

Bruce smirked, went wide eyed, and then started to speak, but Brittany was already headed into the dish-room. He felt himself heat up and color about the face. *Hmmm. Wow! Hmmm.*

Later, as the Smiley's staff cleaned up the dining area, Brittany approached one of her co-workers about a schedule change. "Kathy…

I'm wondering if you can take Friday night, on short notice...? It's not REALLY important, if you can't, but I have a feeling..."

Kathy looked up with a grin from the seat she was scrubbing. "Is it that guy?"

"Yes. But please keep it... I'm not sure how it's going to work out. I mean, if you can."

"I can take this Friday. I need the tips." She looked around the restaurant, which had never filled up tonight, and rolled her eyes. "Midweek sucks!"

"Good. Thanks."

***

The next evening, Brittany talked to the Manager. "Soooo... Fridays are busy, right?"

"They sure are now." Roger had just run the numbers for the last six months; up eleven percent over last year's timeframe. He might just be able to get that old set of fryolators replaced...

"A little TOO busy, maybe? For the kitchen to keep up, and the seating?"

"Well, that's how it is in the hospitality and foodservice business, Brittany. Boom and bust. You just try to become a little more efficient, get a good team together, like we have right now, so you can make hay when the sun shines, as they say." *We get that fry-o-lator upgraded, we can cycle the grease off with a drain instead of a ladle, it's quicker, and a lot less likely some poor schmuck will get burned...*

"And Monday through Wednesdays are slow."

"Yes, young lady, they are. What are you getting at?" *Oh, boy, here it comes. She's tired out from working thirty-two hours and still in school - SUMMER SCHOOL - no less, and she wants a break, so this girl wants to bail on the slow nights that NOBODY wants to work and she wants to keep her Fridays with that hundred or more in tips and wants ME to run interference with the other waitstaff for her, like I would let that happen to begin with...*

Brittany took her time, formulating her argument carefully. "Well, you've got kind of a younger crowd since I've started working here, right?"

Huh? "Ahuh." *What's she getting at?*

"And I probably brought a few of them, right?" She curtsied minutely in some fashion that accentuated her curves as she beamed at her boss with her very brightest smile.

That was a careful way to put that. Where's she going with this? "May-be…"

"Well, I'm getting a little tired out." Brittany shifted her feet.

Yep, thought so. He grimaced. *Too bad. I thought this one was going to be more of a team player.*

Brittany started swaying minutely with her hands tucked schoolgirl-style behind her back. "So I thought maybe I could have Fridays OFF, and work Monday through Thursday regular, instead. And weekends, as you need me, of course. And maybe you could let that get around a bit, with the younger crowd? Maybe that will level out the week?" The fingers of both of Brittany's hands were crossed behind her back, as she looked up all cheery-eyed.

The Manager thought about all the high-school kids that were coming around recently. Smiley's seemed to be something of a new teen hangout. With minor, yet important receipts from the ice cream and appetizer menu, and not just the ones from that Academy kid who'd become a Regular. Roger thought about all the college kids that were showing up now, mostly in small packs of young men. He could see the announcement, pasted right on the door, with a picture of her angelic face: Our Weeknight Waitstaff Team's Newest Full-Time Member. *Ya, that might do it.* "We'll see how it works. Next month?"

"Oh, maybe sooner. Kathy's got tomorrow night, she wanted the tips. And Anne, well she needs money, so she just asked for any Fridays I want to give up; good tips you know." She shrugged. "So, well… Howaboutnow?"

Okay.

So now Brittany had just given herself a little birthday present Plan-with-a-P: she'd arranged her Date Night for the next schoolyear. *A Girl has to have SOME fun, after all…. And neither Grandma nor Tabitha will ever be any wiser. As far as they know, I'm over at work!*

It is plans made on grand assumptions like this that often seem perfect at first, but usually lead sooner or later to awful disaster. Brittany's ship was about to go on the rocks in spectacular fashion, and another with it.

***

Paul Wendell obsessed about it for a week and then finally decided: *I have to know.* He called his secretary into his office and began abruptly, with a question: "You know the big Hudson's Bay Company store down on the other end of Rue Sherbrooke?"

The woman nodded. She shopped in there, as did half of urban Montreal - they were clothing merchants, slightly upscale but affordable for most. "Ouiess. Je con.... I know them."

The mandatory language laws were unfortunate, especially for the English-speakers who pre-dated the new law. New for two decades, now. A lot of business was done in a smattering of French and English and "Franglais." A third language had resulted: Quebecois.

Paul poured himself a drink and thought about taking up smoking again. He threw back his drink. "The girl in the jeans, she just went up on the big billboard. Out front. Find out who her agent is." *I HAVE to know.*

"Ca va." *My, that one certainly looks YOUNG for this business, but....* She shrugged as she went out the door and back towards her own desk. *Maybe he's looking at future talent.*

Paul was so rattled, he didn't even bother to check out his assistant's usually-interesting backside as she sashayed her way out of his office.

***

Bruce did a double-take when he stepped into the restaurant late on a Friday afternoon. There was a black-haired girl in sculpting jeans and a loose knit sweater sitting at the ice cream counter with open textbooks and a notepad, right on the chair where he usually sat. *It's HER. Now THIS is INTERESTING!*

Brittany had thought very carefully about her outfit. This was her best pair of jeans - a pair in reasonably good condition, though old, with that girdle-like cut from the mid-eighties, the ones that went all the way up to cinch around a girl's high waist, up above the hips. She'd found them at a yard-sale, leftovers from a decade when jeans were cut better for a Girl with a figure. The sweater came only to her midriff, right about the same spot the jeans came to, and under that she had on a spandex top that would be suitable for the evening's later exertions - actually, the same bodystocking she'd worn before, with a demure and same-color bra underneath it. *He'll find THAT interesting, I would think...* She heard the door at the right time, a look under her arm confirmed his shoes approaching, and she smirked to herself. *Game on.* She figured she looked pretty good from behind, sitting on that counter-stool. *A good start.* A bookbag went up on the counter beside her. She didn't turn. "Kathy?"

A uniformed waitress came over and stood on the other side of the counter, beaming a smile. "Hi. I'm not Brittany, but I'll be your Waitress this evening. Instead." She looked appraisingly at Bruce. *This is like being in a romantic movie! And the lead is HOT!*

Brittany smirked. "We get two of the usual, here?" She waggled her finger back and forth to indicate the counter in front of her and Bruce. "Thanks." She resumed doing homework.

Kathy looked across at Bruce, met his eye, and winked. *Took her long enough!* Then she went back through the door to the kitchen. *I would have jumped his bones right away, I was that age!*

Bruce tried to figure this out. *Hmmmm. Play it cool. See what happens.* He decided to keep his end of the conversation short. "Hi."

Brittany turned a page.

They each ate their slice of apple pie with fried mozzarella sticks and worked on reading from their textbooks. Brittany reached over and dipped her cheese sticks in HIS apple pie filling a few times, but other than that, she seemed absorbed in her work. She sipped coffee without even looking at the mug. When she did look up, it was to check the clock on the wall behind the counter.

Bruce started to feel confused. *Okay, shit, maybe it's a Waitress Thing this whole time and she's totally NOT interested, and I've been making an ass of myself for months, eh?* He looked around for advice hanging in the air somewhere - a thought-bubble just for him. There was none. *Shit. Damned good-looking girl, though. What do I....*

The girl looked over at the clock again.

Then he felt even more stupid. *Of course. We're FRIENDS of some sort, well, the CUSTOMER sort, and she's meeting a date here, and she's making a point of having me SEE it, since I obviously don't have a CLUE and she's just a high school kid, and oh, I could have been home watching ball games for free all summer, and I just hitch-hiked over here to watch her walk out with some other guy.*

The other waitress brought a guest check. Brittany handed her a twenty. "Thanks, Kathy."

Great. Game-ending Strike-Out. She's meeting someone. He worked to keep his expression stoic until this girl was gone with her date. *Maybe I can get a little pity-pussy with the one who winked at me... No.* He felt sick.

That very waitress looked at Bruce. "Well, stud, you're making big progress tonight! She just bought you dinner!" She smiled at Brittany and scurried to the kitchen.

Yah, that's not new. Why's she in my seat, not talking to me? Before Bruce could figure out what was going on, Brittany was off her stool and stuffing textbooks into her bookbag. "Well, come ON, pick up your shit. We've got places to be!"

Huh?

"Hello? Ya, YOU. Bruce... right?" Brittany looked at the clock again. "We've got to be somewhere in twenty minutes. You and me."

Bruce got moving. He couldn't get the sudden amused grin off his face, or the twinkle of surprise out of his eyes. *So much for playing it cool. Shit-eating-grin squared, here.* "Where, might I ask, are we going?"

"Ooooooh! So FORMAL! You'll see. Are your socks clean?"

"Huh?" He looked down. Not that he could see them under jeans and hiking shoes. "Yah. Sure."

"Come ON!" She pulled at his arm. "I'll drive."

Thank God. THAT would be awkward, Hey Baby, you want to thumb with me? Bruce then and there vowed to have a car by next week. "You are a very strange girl."

"Yes. But I have a cool car, which we need to get INTO, RIGHT NOW, and you'll like me." She smiled over her shoulder and dashed out into the summer evening heat of the parking lot.

Yes, she DID have a cool car, he'd wondered about that little hot-rod she drove, and he knew just how cool this car was once he sat in it! The lime-green super-coup was a little small, him being a big guy and all, but it was comfortable once he put the seat all the way back. Bruce was surprised: the outside was all Boy, in his mind, with turbo scoop, oversized tires, and those squiggles on the doors. The inside was clean, cozy. It smelled like Girl: strawberries, vanilla, lilac. Some sort of little stuffed pink alien with bugged-out eyes stood defiantly on the dash, feet stuck in... bubblegum.

"Nice car."

Her reply sounded exasperated, almost. "I worked for it!" There was that impish smile again.

"Does that turbo gauge really do anything?" Bruce pointed to a big round dial mounted front and center on the dash.

They were in heavy traffic now, plowing through the Saturday evening rush-to-be-somewhere hour.

Brittany turned the wheel and dodged into another lane, around a turning car, and right back into the left lane again. She had a way of checking the mirrors and blind-spots without turning her head. "No. It doesn't DO anything. It SHOWS the air pressure increase that the supercharger makes. Which TELLS me when I can really lay on the gas." She pointed at the regular, stock gauges behind the steering wheel. "I could just use the tach for the same thing, but having that there little gauge up on top tells people I'm cool." She maneuvered the car with minor twitches of the wheel and checked over her shoulder once as they zipped right and left around another turning car. "The stupid ones that can't figure it out for themselves, I mean." They came to a stoplight. "The scoop on the hood just hides the 'charger. It's too big to fit under there without a cutout over the engine."

"Did you BUILD this car?!?"

"No. I told you. I WORKED for it."

Traffic started to move again. The car glided sideways, went around two more, then glided back into the former lane, now clear ahead of traffic. It seemed like Brittany hadn't even turned the wheel.

"So… WHERE are we going?"

"On a date. Dancing, actually. School is right around the corner - timewise - and I'd really like to be going steady by then. So we're going on a date."

Oh! He scowled. *Steady? We just met!* "You go at everything like this?"

"Pretty much." She shifted up, sped up. "If it's something I want. Life is short. Gotta squeeze in as much as you can." She downshifted, caught a yellow turn arrow in an intersection, whined through, punched the gas as she straightened out the wheels, then shifted up again. When Bruce got back off his window he found his seatbelt and fastened it securely.

"I have a pre-season team workout tomorrow. Your grandmother will kill you if I get hurt before the hockey season starts." He thought of something: "I suppose I'm already a dead man just for being in the car with you?" He remembered the Hockey Breakfast eight months ago, where Brittany had been placed firmly off-limits on no uncertain terms.

"No. She won't find out. We'll be careful."

The car flew across the lane and across the road. Bruce flinched, ready to throw up his arms when they hit the trees. They sailed up a gravel driveway instead.

"We're HERE!" She turned to him with a staged, wide-eyed look of glee on her face.

Bruce saw trees. A sign:

GRANGE CENTER

Whatever that is.. A schoolhouse or really unpretentious church? "We're going to church?" *Jesus, what if she's some bible freak? Do I bail now, before my ass is stuck to a pew?*

"NO! The Grange! A dance!" She laughed. "It's a Vermont thing. Well, probably an anywhere stuck in the middle of the woods type of thing. It's fun. You'll see. We're just the TINIEST bit late, so hurry!" She parked amid twenty or so other vehicles in a crowded lot. She turned, suddenly serious: "Two things: one, no boots on the dance floor. You'll be dancing in your socks. The floor is polished. Slippery. Don't fall into anyone." She smiled, and shook her bosom in his general direction. "Except your date." She gave him a sheepish look. "It happens. Happened to me last" (she didn't mention that it was also the FIRST) "time I was here. Very embarrassing. Oh, TWO: I don't put out for College Boys. So if you're just here to get laid, well, maybe you'll have better luck with some other doe in there. But I doubt it." The look of glee came back, and she was out of the car in a flash. "COME ON! We have to HURRY!"

Brittany saw that supper was over and folks were filing up the stairs to the dance floor. *Good. Just in time.* Going to a community pot-luck on a first date would have been awkward.

But not as awkward as the next two minutes. There was a complication inside. Almost immediately. A red-headed one.

Oh, shit.

Tabitha stood stock-still, on the other side of the room, glaring at Brittany and the boy on Brittany's arm. The music hadn't started yet, unfortunately, so everyone heard it when Tabitha started muttering: "...ungrateful, two-timing little..." She had to catch her breath, and then a full-on marching band wouldn't have been enough to cover her yelling: "DOUCHBAG BITCH, CARPET-CLEANING LITTLE TRAMP, GODDAMMED MOTHERFUH!!!" She ran out of air again, and started to turn colors.

Brittany heard her grandmother's voice, right beside her elbow:

"Oh dear." With more cheer: "Hello, Brittany. Out on the town, I see?" She gave the boy a once-over look.

Brittany closed her eyes, taking a second to mentally switch gears so she could maybe *deal with this TRAIN WRECK of an evening.*

Hattie raised her voice to be heard over the bellowing coming from the red-head. "TABITHA, THIS ISN'T A NAVY DANCE! LANGUAGE DEAR! DO YOU WANT TO GO FOR A WALK AROUND THE PARKING LOT?"

Tabitha was already storming across the floor toward the exit, back to muttering a quieter string of under-her-breath curses. She didn't look in Brittany's direction again. She just disappeared out the door into the hot dusk, with Hattie exiting close behind her.

Brittany looked torn, for just one second. She shifted back and forth on her feet.

"Are we in trouble?" Bruce wasn't sure what was going on, but he WAS sure that Mrs. Hattie Wendell had just seen him arm-in-arm with her granddaughter. *Oh shit, eh?*

"No. WE aren't in any trouble. But I think I might be. Fuck!" The dirty looks on several scowling faces around her made it clear that the word had popped out her mouth out loud. "Sorry." She grabbed Bruce's hand. "Come on. Let's learn how to dance." *I'll deal with THAT later.*

"What was up with that GIRL?"

"Well, that would take a while to explain, and I'm not sure I could do it justice. The music's starting!"

Bruce had a very good time, once he figured out how to walk back and forth on the slick floor in his socks. There were a lot of women in the place, young and old, weaving and marching and spinning to the music, but Bruce had eyes for only one of them. The girl who'd just taken him back in time, to the era of fiddle-music and community dances and farmer's night and wholesome things. Just now, he was as far from hockey as he'd ever been. And it was wonderful, actually.

***

Hattie Wendell drove the two of them back to the farmhouse, piloting that big Ford along the roads and thanking heavens it wasn't dark yet. She didn't like driving anymore, especially at night.

Tabitha was crying on the other side of the car, in no shape to drive them herself. Her world had just changed in a fundamental way. Brittany was on a DATE. With a BOY. And it appeared to be sort of a STEADY THING.

When they arrived at the farmhouse, Hattie fixed Tabitha a cup of tea, let her cry some more at the kitchen table, and then sent her off to her own home in the village. "Go find yourself a nice girl. Or girls. Sow some oats. That was always the cure in my day." She took the younger girl's hand. "And don't be a stranger. You two will work it out. She's ALWAYS been your friend, Tabitha." She patted the girl on the shoulder.

Tabitha stood up, walked out to her car in a daze, got in the big empty sedan, and drifted aimlessly down the Hollow towards the village below.

***

"That was fun!" Bruce wiped the sweat off his brow with his shirt, which was temporarily off and in his hand.

They were out in the freshening night air as the dance broke up for the night after three hours of music and exertion.

"Show-off." Brittany took a long look. "Nice, though." She stretched as a way to prolong her appraisal. "The first of many fun nights." She gave him an impish look. "Get in the car."

Hmmmm. Time to test the waters, maybe? "So will I get lucky if I keep my shirt off? It's one of the tricks us College Boys use, you know." He got in the car and ran a finger along a groove in the dash in what he was sure would be a seductively suggestive manner.

"Knock yourself out. Beg, if you must... I STILL won't put out, and then I won't respect you, either." She gave him a vindictive smile. "By the way, I'm Brittany. Brittany Wendell."

He put out his hand. "Pleased to meet you. I'm Bruce. Bruce Sutton, the College Boy who is about to get his ass kicked by Mrs. Hattie Wendell. It was nice to know you, and a wonderful last night on Earth."

"I'm worth it. And only if she can catch you." Brittany started the car and then grinned over at her date. "I'd keep your skates handy, if I were you!"

"What's next?" Bruce hoped for more time with this girl, maybe a liaison of some sort before going back to his near-empty dorm. *Wait... Maybe this absolute GOUDA will come up to my room!*

She interrupted his scheming with a question asked in a merry voice: "Back to Smiley's to get your car?" They were already on the road, moving back towards the Junction and the adjoining Strip.

The night took a decidedly embarrassing, unexpected, and unpleasant turn for Bruce. "Uh... No... That's alright, eh? I, uh...." His voice went up an octave, but came down as he got it out: "I hitched my way over tonight."

Brittany grinned. "I know. I saw you get dropped off." She made a left turn through an impossibly long yellow light. "We're going to take the quick way home, and I'll drop you at the college. That's where you're staying, right?"

The ever-optimistic gigolo returned. "I would really appreciate that." *Maybe I can get her to come up. Maybe I should get a CAR? One with a big back seat? That dorm will fill up by fall....* He eyed the tiny back seat behind him.

"Don't even think about it." She reconsidered as she downshifted for a long curve onto the State Road. "Well, you can think about it. As long as you're thinking about me. But it's not going to happen. I don't-"

"I know, I know, Put Out For College Boys." *So why'd I hang around all summer, then, eh?*

"Oh, I think I'm enough to keep you coming around anyway." She became quiet. Brittany drove on through the silent night carefully and stoically. She put them up on the Interstate to stretch the car's legs a little bit and quickly found fourth gear.

Bruce liked watching his date drive. The car somehow seemed to always move in a straight line, but the little worked-over Pinto passed cars and returned to the lane, passed trucks and returned right, floated through corners in the left lane and then returned right. Brittany rarely looked over her shoulder or even in a mirror as far as he could tell, but she seemed to always know where the other traffic was. After observation and reflection, Bruce decided that Brittany was an extremely good and careful driver but that she just hid it well. Turning her head to talk was an opportunity to check a blind spot. Looking away in a mock fit of pique or to collect her thoughts, she'd file away what was coming up on the left. They were passed by faster traffic a few times, but Brittany didn't seem to mind and expended no effort to keep up. She simply set her own pace - fast - and followed it smoothly and doggedly.

Bruce recognized the exit, even in the dark. This ride was very different from his first visit to Collegeville, nearly three years before. His driver took the long plunge into the village a bit faster this time - there was a new road that was wide and comparatively straight. And, he suspected, not much fun at all for this beautiful race car driver. *I wonder what our trip down would have been like on the old road!*

Brittany stopped on the side of the street out in front of the main gate to the college. They said goodnight, made no plans to meet again, and did not exchange telephone numbers. Bruce decided not to worry, because his date DID lean over in the small car to carefully give him a wet kiss on the cheek, so quick that he didn't have time to turn his head and try to kiss her back. And now she was dumping him at the gate... but she'd be back at the diner, and so would he.

"I had a good time, Bruce. Go do some homework. Good luck with Grandma." She made shooing motions with the backs of her hands: Get out of the car.

He watched her taillights disappear up the road and sighed. *I wonder if her grandmother will read the third degree to her, or to me?* He spoke to himself and the gathering night: "I should get a car, eh?"

An unknown but familiar student passed by, going out the gate to town with a shaking head. "Yah, dude, you should. That was just embarrassing."

Chapter Nine

Tabitha and Brittany shared some classes again this year, but for some reason they weren't doing homework together anymore. Brittany even made it a point to invite her friend up to the farmhouse as they were picking up their books at the end of a study hall session. She wandered over to the red-head's desk - suddenly on the FAR side of the room - and knelt down right there beside Tabitha's desk to make sure she was heard: "Call me, I'll come get you. Anytime." Tabitha's head came up and she stared off into the distance, scowling like she'd heard a strange noise.

A frosty start to a long, strange school-year.

***

Tabitha Bayer did NOT call Brittany about maybe doing homework together on the first weekend of school. Or the second. Or the third.

She stewed alone in her room instead. She wasn't sad anymore - now she was getting angry. More and more mad, the longer she thought about it... madder, and angrier, and more mad still. Now she knew what they meant by Seeing Red. She stared at her Physics textbook and fumed. Math textbook open, unseen. British Literature anthology out in front of her, unopened, or suddenly flung across the room in a winged flutter of pages.

Her mother kept finding the girl staring off into space: books and coursework, dinner and parents unseen in front of her. She took to frequently asking, those first few weeks of her daughter's Junior schoolyear, "Tabitha, are you alright?"

"I'm fine." She'd answer with a shake of the head: I don't want to talk about it. *Just fine. My girlfriend just pitched me into a black hole.* A more intellectual part of her analyzed the problem, decided that Brittany had always been very clear that it was a one (or two, or three, then four) -time thing, she and her. *So, in light of that, the unpredictable, un-constant, un-faithful, un-reliable, ass-rag douche-bag cunt-clot of a Girl can date whomever the hell she pleases. As long as it's no longer me!* The emotional side of her was ready to push her very EX-friend into a singularity: a cosmic garbage-compactor. They were hearing about these in physics class, and Tabitha would be reading about it if she could ever focus on her schoolwork. *I'd like to watch her crush and squirm into a little dot! You don't want me? Spagettify! Take that!* The homicidal teenaged space cadet was the side running the show, at the moment.

There is a reason why 'mad' and 'crazy' are sometimes synonymous. Tabitha Bayer was close to Losing It over the raven-haired Girl.

***

Brittany took it stoically. *Whups.* She commented to her grandmother on the sudden absence of a red-head at the kitchen table: "It'll pass."

Hattie grimaced. *I think there's a little more coming than 'it will pass'....* "Be careful, there, Dear. She seems like a good friend."

Brittany shrugged. *Well, I hope it does.* She wasn't entirely engaged with the Tabitha Problem. She had a frequent visitor to the local Smiley's National Corporation franchise on her mind - one with curly dark hair, a penis that might become useful or even necessary to her life plans someday, and who increasingly seemed to mesh with her imagined 'Happily Ever After / Adulthood' picture.

***

Tabitha had a babysitting job on Monday night, three weeks into the schoolyear. That's where Tabitha cleared her head, usually. *It'll be nice to have a break and leave my problems behind for a bit....* Or so she thought, before this particular evening took a moody and dangerous turn.

This job for the Mitchells was a couple-of-times-a-month thing. Often it was great fun. The 'customer' was adorable, low-maintenance and early to bed - a darling little five-year-old who loved bedtime stories and was always asleep with an angelic smile on her face by page nine.

Fifteen minutes reading to her was the first time in five weeks that Tabitha hadn't been crying or mad.

The older brother wasn't too much trouble, either. The brother was fourteen, and technically, Tabitha wasn't there to watch him. He could come and go as he pleased, all evening. But usually he stuck around. Tabitha was pretty and fun and older and a GIRL. Why would he go anywhere else when Tabitha was over?

Tabitha put up with the attention, mostly because sometimes it was fun to have a little brother for a night, even if he thought you were Hot. And she'd started to think of nights over here at the Mitchell house as "Game Night." She even tried to have homework out of the way, sometimes, for Barry's marathon sessions with board games or dice. Lately it had been Money-Opolis and cribbage. Sometimes they played a board game called Living.

Tonight she wasn't really into it. Tabitha was resigned to her anger now: *That BITCH I used to call my FRIEND is DATING. So much for 'I'm not the dating kind of girl.' Ah-huh. Whatever.* And probably that was the end of weekends here and there up at the farmhouse, where there were always... possibilities. *Shit! Shit! That flirty little two-timing* "Shit." She didn't even know she'd said it out loud.

Barry wasn't stupid. *Tabitha is WAY On The Rag.* Usually she played a game, and if it was a board game he'd get to look down her shirt every time she reached across the table to move a piece or put down real estate. Tonight she just sat on the couch, stewing about something-or-other and being all bitchy. *I've heard about this....*

But his problems were WAY bigger than hers. "Tabitha? How about poker?"

No reply.

"Hey, Tabitha, want to play cards?"

"Mmmphhpmppmh."

Barry swore he heard growling coming from the couch. *Oh, boy.* He approached and gave her a pleading look: *I'm in a real JAM here, and* "I could use some help."

"WHAT?!?!?!?" Tabitha shook her head. "Jesus! I'm sorry. I don't MEAN to be such a bitch tonight, really. It's not you. Whadayaneed?"

Barry turned red. "You know how to play poker, right?" He shifted on his feet, standing in front of the couch like a supplicant before the older-girl throne.

Hmmmm... He WANTS something. Tabitha was already back to mad, but didn't realize she'd made the transition. "Ahuh..."

"Well, I'm going... somewhere, next weekend. And there's going to be... ah, people. A lot of people." Suddenly, he looked panicked. "Will you teach me poker so I don't end up losing, alone and naked, in front of half my class at Teeger's party?"

Ah! Tabitha's problem suddenly seemed a smidge smaller. Strip poker at fourteen! "Ahhhh, yes, that would suck." Her anger flared just as quickly as her empathy faded: *Why don't you go ask your mother, won't THAT be an interesting conversation?* She stuffed the angry thought, worked to take a calming breath, then tried to be the Professional Babysitter that she was. *Watcher of children, confidant, counselor, solver-of-problems.* "You don't know poker?"

He shook his head. "Puh-LEEEZE?"

She'd said that to Brittany, once. More than once, actually. The switch flipped - Tabitha was mad again. "Fine," *you little shit, I'll teach you and then kick your ass straight to the poorhouse. At least I won't be dangling my tiny little tits over some board game like a cow on inspection at the State Fair.* "I'll deal." She flicked her hand: go get cards. She yelled after him, "Never played strip poker before?!? Amazing!" More to tease him and shame him than anything else. Neither had she, actually. It didn't matter. Suddenly, she was feeling very superior and very, very mean.

He came sprinting back with a deck. "Uh, no… but I really wanna learn!"

Whatever. "It's easy." *Even YOU can get it.* "What are we betting?"

The thought hadn't occurred to him. He stopped in front of her, wide-eyed. "Er… Hershey's Kisses?" He'd heard that moody menstruating girls needed chocolate. His mother usually had a bag hoarded somewhere in the back of a tall cupboard for social emergencies. This qualified, he decided. *ANYTHING to mellow this red-headed witch out, tonight. Usually, she's FUN.*

Tabitha walked over and sat down at the head of the kitchen table. "Okay. Make two piles. Make mine bigger. I'm a Girl and I deserve more chocolate."

Whatever. "I'll give you everything, just teach me!" He threw down a big bulk-bag of chocolates. "Here you go."

At this point, the two teenagers had no idea just what EVERYTHING meant. They'd know soon.

"First, shuffle the deck like normal, split it and all that...." She sat back to watch him fumble with the cards. "And put those chocolates right here in front of me…" Tabitha sucked on a Kiss with relish. "Now, deal out…"

Tabitha whupped him handily. Barry was new to the game, of course, and he was also new to betting. Finally out of chocolates, with Tabitha merrily binge-eating out of her winnings, he threw in the hat. Literally. His BOSTON (Red Sox, what else was there in Boston that mattered?) cap with the big "B" front and center, his hat that was new and crisp and blue and came right from the box-office store at the stadium where he'd sat in row H seat 49 and seen a live game with Dad. Barry's prized possession. But Barry wasn't an easy loser, and he wanted to stay in the game.

"Okay," *you little bastard,* "I can take that, too."

"For half of what you haven't just eaten. That's a good hat."

"A third. It will make a nice trophy for me to wear home."

"Done." *I'll figure this out and kick your* "ASS!" He got five wildly divergent cards in his own deal.

"Watch your mouth."

They worked the cards and he folded without even seeing hers. Tabitha had a good poker face going tonight. Manic, gleeful, hostile, superior... regardless of her hand.

"Fuck." *I just lost my hat.*

"No, we're not gambling for that." *YOU have nothing to offer me.* For the first time all night, she smiled. Then she swiped Barry's - now her own - hat off the table and put it on her head.

She looked pretty cute there, sitting across the family table with HIS hat perched on her head, red and now recently bleached and pink-highlighted hair just spilling out from under along the sides of the deep dark blue hat. It didn't help his concentration, *that older absolute DISH of a Junior wearing MY HAT!* Young Barry felt some heat rise in him, in spite of his loss.

He lost his shirt, and then two socks.

"Guess you're learning the game for real, now," *you little shit!* Tabitha tipped the hat back, bonnet-style, thought for a moment, took it off, shook her mop of hair, then used her two hands to put some curl in the rim. She put it back on, changed her mind and took it off to torture the brim back to somewhat straight.

Barry flinched.

Tabitha put Barry's hat back on her head, brim low and level, military style. "You'd better do a lot better than that up at Teeger's or everyone will be seeing your pecker." She reached forward and patted him on the arm, cruelly, because she knew that with his shirt off in front of her, any touch would make him fizz like a shaken soda. "Don't worry. You won't be the only one. And it's just a pecker. They're all the same." She wondered about that, idly, as she popped another piece of chocolate into her mouth. *Are they?*

Barry blushed. But he REALLY wanted that hat back, before she ruined it further. He started to concentrate, and played better. Some chocolate started to move back across the table. Then his shirt and socks.

Tabitha wanted to keep the trophy hat. *It's MINE now!* She rather liked her new prop. She lost all the remaining chocolate, then a sock, then the other sock, then bet her jeans. She decided her jeans were safer, since the two of them were sitting at a table. She made Barry turn around while she wiggled out of them, and then tossed them up on top of the chocolate he'd just put in the middle.

"You can turn back around now." *I am SO going to get those back. And then I'm going to get YOURS,* "You little shit." *And I'm keeping MY hat.* She snugged it down. "Fits nice!" She beamed at him out from under the brim, just to tease him.

Tabitha played on without her pants, but then Barry bet and lost his, and even though he'd won his shirt back, he'd never put it on. The strangest thing seemed to be happening, and Tabitha didn't really notice, but no one was bothering to put any clothes back ON. They just kept betting and winning and losing, and they weren't even taking clothing out of the middle of the table anymore, just keeping close mental track instead.

Tabitha's bra came off and she didn't think much on it. *The little gawker always has his nose half in the front of my shirts anyway.* He'd probably seen what he was seeing already. She tried to hold the cards just about at the right level to preserve some mystery.

Barry watched furtively and briefly while she took off the holy of holies - *A GIRL'S BRA!* - and then realized he was about to see *EVEN MORE THAN THAT!!!* He avoided looking anywhere but at his cards while he tried to figure out if it was worth pissing her off, and possibly ending the night, by studying the new real estate displayed across the table.

And that's how pile grew in the middle of the kitchen table until they were both down to their underwear bottoms.

Tabitha decided to take a break. She got up and walked aimlessly around the kitchen, on display and not caring. "You can look. You might as well." *No one else is, anymore.* She stopped short, and turned to face him.

Barry trembled like a leaf, sitting there at the kitchen table in his underpants, one leg bouncing up and down with nervous, excited energy as he watched the unattainable wiggle and sway around his kitchen. Breasts. Butt-cheeks and hips in too-thin underwear. *The school's LESBIAN, the BABYSITTER, TABITHA! With her clothing off, RIGHT THERE.*

Hmmm. "Never seen anyone naked, before?" She watched him coolly. *Fizzing like a shaken soda, that boy....*

Barry, wide-eyed, shook his head. *Not in a million - well, fourteen - years.* It didn't help him that THIS was the girl he'd been crushing on for a year.

"Do you want to kiss me?" She gave him a flirty, pouty little purse of her lips.

Ahuh. You bet. Right now. He was out of the chair and straining at the seams of his underwear in front of her in a heartbeat. He didn't know what to do next - how do you start a kiss?

She held out her arms: Step here. "Kiss me, Barry." She leaned up into his face. *Take THAT, you Bitch!*

Barry stepped forward. It was awkward... something was in the way of this new experience. He was trying not to poke against her stomach with it, then she kissed him again with some heat behind it - actually it was anger, but Barry didn't know that. Suddenly, Barry didn't care if she was impaled through and through.

Tabitha leaned back, but kept her arms around his neck as she scrutinized him with unreadable eyes.

Barry assumed it was over. His face broke out into a moony grin. *My first kiss. She kissed me twice! My first naked girl. My first boner ever in front of anyone else. I think it's still poking her right in the stomach, I wonder if I should back up?* Instead he leaned forward, hoping for maybe one more AMAZING experience with this girl's lips.

He got the surprise of his life, instead.

"Wait." Tabitha backed up a step, hooked her underwear down and used her arms to help as she hopped her bare bottom backwards, up onto the Mitchell family chopping block, still wearing a slightly knocked-askew Boston Red Sox cap. "Kiss me again, Barry. Kiss me and fuck me." *TWO can be loose around this town, Brittany Wendell!*

And then she angry-humped herself, and maybe Brittany, with the boy's body.

It's not TOO awful, she thought clinically, at one point when her mind was detached for a moment. At least he didn't have scratchy hair all over his face or smell of beer (Tabitha's frequent assumptions about unlikely Boy Sex). But it wasn't sweet or romantic or tender, or any of the other things it should have been and often isn't. Tabitha's only emotion, when she was feeling anything, was anger. Barry was eager. Angry and eager made a bad combination for anything but hard and fast love.

Afterwards, when Tabitha had come back to her senses (and Barry lay insensate on the couch, the scene of their second crime), she suddenly became terrified that little five-year-old Olivia had come down for a drink of juice or something and seen her older brother splitting open - literally, to Tabitha's surprise - the babysitter on the kitchen counter. *How could you be so fucking stupid, Girl?!?* Tabitha tip-toed up the stairs and creeped into the bedroom to check on the little one. She found the child wrapped up in her Scooby blanket, just as Tabitha had left her three hours ago. *Good.* It never occurred to her what she would say if the child woke up and saw her at the door naked - Tabitha wasn't thinking very clearly this evening.

The relief made Tabitha giddy. She went down to the fridge and was just putting together a sandwich when she noticed the mess:

Roast beef... wow, this is really rare. She rooted around in a shelf lower down, oblivious to the fact that she was standing in someone else's kitchen naked as a jaybird. After-glow does that sometimes. *Do they have...* she rooted in a shelf lower down and found a bag of Swiss cheese slices. *Oh, good, they have whole wheat bread.* She straightened up to set it out on the counter and... *OH! That's disgusting. Did WE do....* She leaned in. *Messy!* Tabitha curiously scrutinized the various co-mingled fluids coagulating on the chopping block and then decided to make her sandwich on a different counter. *I'll have to clean that-* "SHIT!!"

Car lights in the driveway!

Tabitha sprinted through the kitchen in her bareness, scooping up clothing and socks and underwear on the way by. She vaulted onto a nearly-comatose Barry on the couch in the living room and placed her finger in front of her lips. "SSHSHHSSSSHHH!!!!! Put this fuckin' shit on, NOW!" She looked over her shoulder at the front door. "Your parents!" She was already busy stuffing herself into her own clothes as fast as she could go. "And this NEVER happened. I hear about this in school and I'll hunt you down and cut off your pecker. I MEAN IT. HURRY!!!"

Tabitha and Barry made it to the kitchen table, more or less fully-dressed, and sat back down at the card game. Tabitha reached across the table to stuff a chocolate kiss in his mouth. "You weren't bad, you know. I think. Game-face, now, Barry!" She smiled at him and put the blue hat snugly on his head. "You never speak of this again, and I'll love you for EVER. Think about that. HI, MISSES MITCHELL! DID YOU GUYS HAVE A GOOD MEETING?"

The Mitchells were one-half of the schoolboard in this small town.

"We were trying to figure out how to get you kids some of those new computer..." Anne Mitchell stopped short and gave Tabitha a quizzical look.

Tabitha looked down. *Uh-oh.* She turned around in her chair real quick, and when she came back around to face them, her shirt was buttoned. "You little SHIT!" She smiled and slapped Barry's arm.

Barry looked like a deer caught in headlights.

Tabitha resembled a tomato with bright pink hair, but she was all charm and smiles. "I'm SO sorry. I had a boy over, I sent him home when Barry got back. You know how they ARE." She whirled Barry. "Jesus, good thing I had a BRA on. You could have TOLD me!"

Phillip Mitchell was thinking, *Why would ANY fourteen year old boy remind a girl to button up? Hmmmmm. That lucky little shit played poker for -* he scowled at the table *- ah, CHOCOLATES, all the while sitting across from that girl with her shirt open the whole time. Stuff of dreams when I was that age.... Ooo, boy.* Something wasn't adding up, but the meeting had been long and fractious, it was late, and he was never going to get the whole story out of these kids anyway. The boy in question was probably somewhere in the house right now, shitting his pants and stuffed in a closet until he could make his escape. *Hmmmmph.*

Mrs. Mitchel looked confused. "But Tabitha, you're the LAST girl I thought would have... But you don't LIKE boys!"

Gee, "I guess the whole town DOES know. Well, everyone's got to try something NEW now and again, right?" Tabitha looked straight at Barry. "PLEASE don't say anything. I wouldn't want it to get around. It was a ONE TIME thing. It'll NEVER happen again, I promise."

Mr. Mitchell went over to the fridge. "Do whatever you want, Tabitha. Just please do it somewhere else where Barry isn't going to walk in on... whatever you were doing." A schoolboard meeting pre-empted supper, and he was hungry. As he put his hand on the door to open the fridge, Phillip Mitchell noticed the chopping block. It was right next to the fridge. He did a little double-take and was just turning his head to really frown at the surface....

Tabitha's color suddenly drained as she leaped out of the chair to intervene. She streaked past the man to deal with THAT problem before he figured it all out. "Oh! Be ready in JUST a MINUTE. Made a couple of sandwiches, got some cleaning up to do!"

Mr. Mitchell shooed his son out of the room for some help with the recycling in the garage. "I need a hand out here, Bud." He stole a furtive look over at the chopping block as he left the room.

Tabitha did a little wiping up with paper towels, then rummaged around under the sink and finally found some strong cleaner that she didn't think would poison the Mitchells. She gave a last look for HAIRS or something stupid like that and then put away the bread and mayo from her abandoned sandwich and thanked her lucky stars that she'd gotten to cleaning in time... *Maybe?* Good thing MISSES Mitchell hadn't seen it. Tabitha had a gut feeling that the woman would KNOW. *Yuk. So that's why my crotch stings so!* Well, at least she had visible evidence of her wounds, now. *Thanks, Brittany, look at the mess you've made.* She was no longer crying by the time Anne Mitchell came down from checking on Olivia.

"Thank goodness she's a heavy sleeper, huh?" Mrs. Mitchell stopped short.

Tabitha wiped her nose with the heel of her hand.

Mrs. Mitchell rushed over and put her arms around Tabitha. "Feel a little bit topsy-turvy right now?"

Tabitha hugged back, she wasn't sure why. *You have no idea.* She nodded against Mrs. Mitchell's bosom while more tears spilled out.

"Try to spend the whole night with him next time. It helps." She patted the girl's back. "This WAS your first time, right?"

Tabitha nodded, and smeared snot all over Mrs. Mitchell's sweater. She reached up and tried to wipe it off, and then realized that she was more or less pawing the woman's boob. She jumped back, tears still streaming. "Sorry!" And then started laughing, snot and tears flying from her face.

Mrs. Mitchell had a good laugh, too, as she walked across the kitchen to get a handful of Kleenex for them. "That's the first time I've ever been pawed-over by a woman. Don't tell Phil! This will be OUR little secret..."

One of many, tonight, apparently. "It's a nice boob." Tabitha was drying up.

Mrs. Mitchell changed the subject. She WAS on the schoolboard, after all. "Soooo. Does this happen often? Boys? Or girls... coming over while we're out?"

"No. First time. Usually Barry and I play cards or Monopoly or have a tee-vee date." *Whups. Getting a little close to the New Truth.* "I've never had ANYONE over... before."

"Well, I used to do that, on occasion. Don't tell Phil. I think maybe you should set a strict schedule with Barry, though." She looked over reflexively at the kitchen counter with its built-in hardwood cutting board. "Throw him out and tell him not to come back until a certain time. Nine-O'clock would be fine. He's a fourteen year old boy. He's got places to go." *And I think he's spending entirely too much time circling around you, when you're here.* "Will you do that, next time?"

You bet. But there "Won't be a next time."

"Well, that's up to you. Just TRY not to let the kids see anything."

Mr. Mitchell and Barry were coming in the door from the garage, fresh from make-work and some discussion. Barry was trying to keep a wide smile off his face. It wasn't working.

Mr. Mitchell went back out to start the car again, to take their Sitter home.

Mrs. Mitchell scrutinized her son carefully. "Don't laugh, Barry. Someday we'll come home and catch YOU in here with your zipper down and someone on your lap." She added, more sternly: "And it better not be 'til you are twenty-one or you're grounded until you finish law school. Now scoot. It's a school-night."

Mr. Mitchell drove Tabitha home in a very awkward silence. Finally: "Do Barry and I need to have a talk, did he SEE any of that?"

"Nnnnn-oo. You don't need to give him The Talk," *he did quite fine all on his own.* "Thanks for covering on the ahhh…" *Nevermind.*

"Are you alright?"

Jesus. Tabitha started to tear up. *Not again.* She steeled herself. *No, I am definitely NOT alright. But I'm a lot better just because everyone keeps asking. And NOT alright has nothing to do with what your son and I did on your kitchen counter.* "That was nice of you to ask. I'm very sorry. I'm fine."

"You have nothing to be sorry for. Just try to use better judgement. Anne… is strict. If she sees you as a bad influence…" He sighed. "I'm a little disappointed, myself."

That makes two of us. "I might have been led astray by stupidity. I'm REALLY sorry."

Mr. Mitchell sighed. "It happens all over the world. Just, well, could you keep a cork in it when you're sitting? You have a responsibility when you're watching a child." *Really bad choice of words, Phil.* He winced.

Tabitha didn't even notice. "I'm really sorry."

He knew he didn't have the full story. *This girl seems pretty meek... almost upset, but then again...* she'd been caught with her clothes all askew. "Are you SURE you're alright?"

"Ya. I'm fine." She knew she didn't SOUND fine. *Fuck it.* "My girlfriend hooked up with a boy." Tabitha started crying again. Mister Mitchell received the honor of being the first person to hear about it since Grandma Wendell saw it happen. She relayed the story briefly, between tears. "I wanted to see... WHY. I was angry. I'm really sorry about the..." *bloody MESS I left at your house. Two messes. Jesus.*

"And how much did Barry see when he walked in on you?"

Shit. THINK, girl! "Probably more than he should have. I'm sure he's a changed boy." *There. That covers just about anything the boy might say.* And it was the truth. All the way. That seemed important.

Mr. Mitchell drove with one hand while rubbing his stubbled chin with the other, deep in thought. He looked grim.

"I'm SORRY, I really am." *You have no idea. Stupid, stupid, stupid, STUPID,* "STUPID!!"

"Take it easy on yourself. He's fourteen. Would've been an issue soon enough. Are you SURE you're alright?"

Fine. I'm just FINE. My girlfriend left me and I just raped your - very willing - fourteen year old and "I'm fine." Tabitha wondered if it was illegal to have sex with someone you were babysitting. She'd never considered that before, mostly because it was a ludicrous idea. *Hmmmm.* She also wondered if word would get around up at Teeger's place next week. *In two weeks, will I be fighting off every underaged boy in the school, or will I be completing my Junior year from jail? Do they send you to jail for hooking up with a fourteen year old boy?*

Somehow, they had arrived in Tabitha's parent's driveway. *Oh. I can get out of the car now.* "Thankyou." She unbuckled her seatbelt. "Sorry." She opened her door. "I'm really, really STUPID" *and going to*

JAIL! She slammed the door, flinched, and then as she turned to flee she yelled a snotty "SORRY!" about the door. Tabitha turned towards the house and then wiped her nose on the back of her arm. *Oh, now I've got to pull it together, my parents are still downstairs. Great.*

Phillip Mitchell waited through these histrionics and then backed out onto the highway. *Teens go through a rough patch... maybe our children don't need to see that.* He decided that maybe they'd find a younger sitter. *That way...* "What the hell are you thinking, Phil?" Sure, just hire the boy a girl his own age to sit his sister, and they might as well be hiring him a concubine. *Jesus, they'd sit there on the couch unsupervised all night and nature would take its course and his little boy would be a DAD at fifteen! Better keep Tabitha, and give her another good talking-to about not having any FRIENDS over.* He drove away lost in thought about what a fourteen year old boy, his boy, might get up to with a receptive female, and what kind of complications that might have on his kid's college career.

Tabitha loitered in her yard, smoking a cigarette filched from her father's car, quite aware that it was one more stupid decision in a night full of them, and banging her forehead with the heel of her hand. Her life felt suddenly very complicated, and very threatened by her own rash decision-making. It wasn't ALL bad though. Tonight's regret and shame wasn't as strong as the hurt she'd been feeling for weeks. She did FEEL better, even if her crotch and her conscience both burned and throbbed to high heaven from the pounding she'd given that little boy. *Shit.* She laughed, and started crying again. This time over the loss of the boy, to whom she obviously would never return. *What the fuck is WRONG with me?!?*

Tabitha's mother got it only half right as she gave her suddenly-standoffish and quiet daughter a gentle smile and a one-armed hug on the way up to bed. She'd heard some things around town. She shook her head. *That Brittany Wendell.... And now she's smoking.* "Need to tell me about it?"

Her daughter's eyes went wild and wide. *NOFUCKIN'WAY!* Tabitha's head shivered back and forth in a rapid no, *no, NO, NO, not in a million years, NO!!*

She'll talk about it when she's ready.

Tabitha would go almost three quarters of a year before she could finally talk to her mother about all THAT!

***

Tabitha didn't babysit for those folks again. They didn't call and she didn't check in to see why. Let sleeping dogs lie, so-to-speak. She and the boy passed in the hallways at school, on a daily basis, and Tabitha grimaced inwardly every time. Barry had special but carefully hidden smiles for her on a couple of occasions, but she was relieved that he didn't show up with flowers or candy hearts or big plans for Winter Ball. After a week, Tabitha stopped worrying about a Scene. No rumors ever reached her ears, either - no stares after weekend parties, no strange looks in the hallway, no finger-pointing, no gaggle of pubescent boys lining up to request favors, and no police knocking at her door. That one had Tabitha especially worried.

She found a note in her locker once, a few weeks later, pushed in through the vents at the top:

MISS YOU AT CARDS

That was the extent of Barry's communications about their little tryst... other than those secret smiles that, if seen, could just be interpreted as a Freshman boy going all moony over an unachievable Junior. Barry was apparently a Good Shit, and careful with his mouth. Tabitha breathed a sigh of relief as Barry turned fifteen. They were only a year apart now, not so inappropriate... *I can leave that little mess right behind!* Except she couldn't - around every corner, she expected to find a detective in a suit, judgmental parents, angry parents, a shaming priest. *Stupid, stupid, stupid!!*

Tabitha breathed a second sigh of relief, but also felt a little guilt, when the boy started noticing other females in the school - girls his own age. He didn't seem to notice her anymore at all. *Good. Best he gets his mind off me.*

Later, Barry would actively avoid her.

***

Brittany went to a couple of the Friday-night hockey games with her grandmother, who was surprised to have her granddaughter's company at the rink - usually, the girl was circling around Tabitha. Little brother Brian even sat through a game with them once, arriving with his father in tow, too. The family matriarch was overjoyed: nearly the whole family together at the rink! Hattie had to call in a couple of favors to get tickets - they were a hot item back in those days when the Academy team was skating on a streak. The two youngest Wendells managed not to tease or kill each other for the entire game. The family was growing up.

Brittany and Bruce were still dating, though not frequently. He was busy with college and hockey and she was busy with high school and work. He showed up at the restaurant a little less, but often enough to signal his continued interest. On the Friday evenings that he wasn't playing hockey and Brittany wasn't working, they had a date. They made it work. There was interest and intrigue on his part. He wasn't quite sure what SHE was playing at.

Dates were up in the 'Big City on the Shore,' as Brittany called it, ninety miles away. They didn't want to be seen by any of the local folks.

Brittany liked the anonymity because she didn't want to change her reputation until she was Sure.

Bruce didn't want to get killed by an elderly female hockey fan. He'd already escaped that fate once.

***

Paul Wendell was stuck in traffic again, in his car this time, two intersections down from that giant storefront where his dead sister lorded over the street, lounging in a pair of SQUIGGLE! jeans and a decidedly this-year's-fashion sweater (*I don't ever remember her owning a bare-midriff top, and she would have been run out of the house if they'd caught her in something like that...*). The young woman's image reclined behind glass, her form stretched out over two blocks and two stories high. *Suzy!* Her long black curls cascaded down to street level in the window by the main entrance. Paul shuddered. *The hair that wound around that tractor shaft and took her life....*

He started taking a different way into work the next day.

***

The City of Burlington is actually a small downtown - not even as big as any neighborhood of Montreal - parked on the western coast of Vermont, a former harbor town that was once the lumber export capital of the New World. Lumber wharves dominated the waterfront up into World War Two, then oil tanks sprouted and grew and spread up and down the bay, and now the tiny metropolis produced college students and sailboat slips.

Burlington, to Bruce, felt like a little section in a back corner of Toronto. It was a good place for a date - lots to see and do that was different from the surroundings in Collegeville, much of it open until late in the night. He sometimes missed the urban bustle of Human Civilization - he'd been further out in the sticks, but never for whole SEMESTERS at a time!

Vermont's "City on the Lake" was also far away from Complications - convenient for both of them: Brittany still hoped for some sort of reconciliation with Tabitha, her best and only friend, though the girl continued to give her a cold shoulder in school. Bruce didn't want to get thrown off the hockey team - the coaches might just make good on their threat. You never knew.

Bruce asked about the redhead, again, once, when they were in Brittany's car on the way back South from the little city: "So what was up with that GIRL, the one your grandmother left with, eh?"

"Like I said: THAT would take more explaining than I care to do. She was having a bad day." And apparently STILL is. Tabitha held her nose in the air whenever Brittany was in the area, still.

Bruce didn't push it. He liked this girl. She was full of surprises! Like their second date, on a rare Thursday night when she wasn't working.

***

Brittany took Bruce up to the pedestrian-only shopping and dining street in the Big City during the pre-Holiday season between Halloween and Thanksgiving. Bruce would soon be going home to Canada and Real Cities for a week, and then head out on the road on a tour with the Academy hockey team for another two weeks. Brittany decided to show this cosmopolitan boy from the Outside World a bit of the city life right nearby.

The street she brought him to was called Church Street because it was headed by an ancient steepled brick building that had served the city for close to two-hundred years. City Hall anchored the other end. Five blocks of brick pavement stones linked the two, lined by mini-malls and boutiques, restaurants and bookstores. Brittany decided to be a big spender that night. She wanted to show this College Boy the world! She chose take-out: paper cups full of hot tomato soup and heavy, foil-wrapped squares containing sandwiches of melted Swiss cheese and a three-quarter inch thick layer of turkey on made-that-day sourdough bread. She had them sit on a park bench that was at the head of the street, so she could admire the people and bustle and lights.

She grinned at him. "Best restaurant seat in town." She talked around a mouthful of hot sandwich, venting steam into the frosty air like some dragon.

"Really? My ass is cold."

"Mmmmmhuuummm. If you can survive the hockey bench, ON WHICH YOU SPEND SO MUCH TIME, BY THE WAY, you can survive this."

"Ouch." He sipped from his soup cup. "So how did a Country Lass like yourself end up finding this thriving metropolis?"

"Hmmmm. THAT story is short enough." She paused to sample her own soup. "There was this boy." She gave a sideways smirk. "Funny how so many stories start like that: 'There was this boy.' A nice boy. I slept with him, well, not really SLEEPING, in water actually, but you get the idea…" She sat up straight, tipped her head back, and put the back of her wrist up against her forehead. She let her mouth droop open and her eyes roll back in her head as she briefly rocked her pelvis on the cold bench.

Bruce watched, transfixed, his own jaw slack. He almost dropped his soup. When he recovered, she was already nibbling on her sandwich again, looking all innocent. He narrowed his eyes. "YOU are NOT exactly what you SEEM, are you?"

She chewed for a moment. "…And after that he couldn't stop thinking about me. He kept pestering me for more, actually. A RELATIONSHIP, he called it. So eventually, months later, I caved, and let him take me on a date. He brought me here. We had dinner over there." She pointed to a glassed-in seating section at a fancy and expensive-looking bistro, where most of the diners were in some version of formal wear.

Bruce thought that those people probably were WARM, and their dinner wasn't ICING OVER during conversation.

She continued, and pointed down the street. "…And we had dessert right in the back of that car you rode in. WAY too cramped. Especially on a full stomach." Brittany looked sideways at her date. "Don't tell anyone. I SWORE him to SECRECY. As far as anyone else knows, it was a one-shot deal. So-to-speak."

Bruce grinned, and repeated himself: "You are NOT at ALL what you seem." Then he got a calculating look. "And you DO put out…"

"Oh, he wasn't a College Boy. That's the rule, you know."

Bruce looked at his shoes. "Oh." *Krap.*

"Are you POUTING?!?" Brittany put down her soup, grabbed his chin, and shook it side-to-side. "Poor, poor Brucie! Hmmmm. Scratchy. Oh, well."

"No, Brittany, not pouting. I'm THINKING. Mentally reviewing my little black book to see who on campus might later tonight take pity on a poor bloke who's dating one really great girl and sleeping with several other less great but more available ones. Whose parent-figures AREN'T homicidal, by the way."

"My grandmother isn't a parent-figure. I'm sort of Out On My Own, now. Think of her more as a REALLY protective roommate." Brittany patted his knee. "Lets get coffee."

They walked down the brightly-lit street through throngs of people until Brittany steered them into a shop. "Dessert! It's not the back of my car, but it will have to do. Crumpets - they're not too bad - THAT way." She pointed to a glass case. "The world's best hot chocolate - the sign says so - this way." She headed towards the expresso bar for hot chocolate. "As you can see, I'm a very big spender. Only the best for an eligible stud-muffin like you, Bruce. I have to keep your mind off those College Girls. At least while you're out on the town with me."

Bruce wondered to himself if that was permission to run around on her.

"No. I'm just being pragmatic."

"You're scary."

"You've said that before. Yet, you keep coming back."

They sat down. Bruce had a dark, thick coffee and a croissant. Brittany stirred her cocoa, trying to cool it down and blend the frothy, creamy top into the drink. She took a very careful sip from the top and came up with a moustache. She wiped her upper lip with a finger, which then got a theatrical bath in her mouth. "MMmmmm, good!" She winked.

Bruce sat there, watching her lick her own finger, transfixed. His mind went to all sorts of places that were quite natural for a Young Buck in rut, but he had the good sense not to voice any of his thoughts.

Brittany took another sip and licked the foam off her lips. *Well, he passed that test. Not a moron. Good.* "Soooo… This is our second date, right?"

"Unless you count all those study dinners."

Brittany thought about that. "Well, then we should count those two hockey games I went to. I NEVER go to those things!" She'd been to a couple of Tabitha's, before, but THAT was different.

"How about the hockey breakfast?"

"No way. There were about six of you there I was trying to choose between."

"When did you make up your mind?"

When you were watching my eyes instead of my tits, like the rest of them. "Did you watch my ass when my back was turned?"

Yes. Of course. Every time I could. "Just now?"

"No. At the breakfast."

"Maybe sometimes. It's a very nice ass, Brittany. The finest, really."

"Thankyou." *Well, I did bring it up. I'll let it slide.* Brittany didn't want to hold him to an unachievable standard, after all.

"You didn't answer my question." He waited.

She never would, apparently. "Call me Bri. My friends call me Britt, but YOU can call me Bri. Brie, like the cheese. One thing on the outside, but inside all creamy and yummy and delicious. Goes with just about anything. Spreadable, under the right circumstances. Bri."

She'd left Bruce speechless again. He completely forgot about his question. Finally, he stuck out his hand. "Bri. I like that. Still Bruce. I suppose you could call me Brew?"

"We'll stick with Bruce." She shook his hand confidently, forcefully, palm-to-palm. "So, Bruce. Do you want to get out of here?" She drew a squiggly line on the top of his thigh with a finger.

He tried to play it cool, but his whole body was immediately thrilled.

"Normally, I'd make you suffer through eight or ten more dates, but I'm in a hurry in life." She grabbed his hand and hopped off her coffee-shop stool. "Let's get a hotel room." She had to tug at him, as he was rooted with surprise, but she got him moving towards the door. "If I ever hear about ANY of this, that's the END. Understand?" Her standard dictum, though he didn't know it.

Bruce's mouth was too thick with shock and excitement to say anything, so he just nodded vigorously and followed her. That would have to do for an answer. He'd expected to be more cool about it, but she had a way of making the world turn upside down. On the way to Brittany's souped-up Pinto, he managed to tell her that he had hockey practice and classes in the morning.

"And I've got HIGH SCHOOL! We'll get an early wake-up call. Say, four. That puts us back in town by six, even if we drag our feet a little. That work?" She gave him a coquettish look over her shoulder as she led him through the milling students and diners and shoppers on the street.

Oh ya. That works.

She patted the hood of the little green car as she crossed in front of it to get back in. "Don't worry... won't be any cops out that time of morning. We'll make good time!"

Hmmmm. Something there unsettled him, he wasn't sure what, but *ya, it would be lucky to make that trip quick, eh?*

Poor Bruce Sutton didn't know what hit him, that night.

They ended up at a budget motor inn a few miles down a major road out of town.

Brittany paid and then set out to make him forget all about those College Girls, in her own unique way. She dropped her coat as soon as they were inside the room, then her jeans, and then took her sweater off over her head. Under that, just a very slinky and tiny little slip. "Go ahead, undress. Leave your undies on the bottom. You can put your hands anywhere they want to land, but keep your prick in your shorts or we take the quick way home." Then she got into the bed, held the covers open for him, and waited.

Bruce moved to take his coat off.

"Hurry up! It's a school-night and it's late!"

"You are SO strange."

"But not so strange that you won't climb into bed with me!"

"No, not that strange. And you are also very pretty, and very, very... intriguing." He walked over to the bed and made a point to kiss her chastely on the lips. "Am I to seduce you?"

She let him linger, briefly, then turned her head, and he finished with a sucking kiss on her cheek instead instead of where he'd intended it as she replied: "No. You are to sleep." She patted the sheets next to her again. "Old New England tradition. Bundling. Come on. If you can sleep next to me, you can have me for good."

Really? She's assuming an awful lot, eh?

"Yes. But you'll learn I'm usually right." Brittany looked him over with a critical eye while he took off most of his clothes, and then scooted to one side so he could get into the bed. "Nice erection."

"Thankyou for noticing." Bruce had bedded plenty of ladies in his time, and some who were not so lady-like. This felt different. Bigger. He was climbing into bed, apparently to SLEEP, with this very curvy and unique young woman. He wondered if he'd be ABLE to sleep. "Will you-"

"No." Brittany let him get settled, and then backed up against him. Something was in the way. She wiggled, and found way to accommodate the protrusion. "Mmmmmmm. This is nice. No taking advantage of me once I'm asleep."

Which she was, soon. Burning the candle at both ends had tired Brittany out.

Bruce lay behind his date for quite some time. Confused, lustful, excited, gleeful, his arms around her, one hand copping a feel on a conveniently-located breast, his crotch throbbing against her very soft and round and inviting bottom through two layers of fabric, worrying about how he would ever get to sleep. He fell asleep wondering whether he was going to forget all about those other girls, or look one up real quick as soon as they got back to town. He still hadn't even properly kissed her, *and here I am poking against her backside IN BED....*

***

Then he woke up, and they were still curled together, the room telephone ringing insistently and no time had passed because they were still tangled exactly as they just had been when he'd felt her relax into sleep.

Brittany reached out to the night-stand, made the noise go away with a quick lift and drop of the handset, and then sat up to stretch alluringly.

Wow. Bruce smirked. *I had my hand on that boob under that sheer nighty. All night... wow.*

Brittany let him look for a beat too long to let it be entirely decent, smirked, and then jumped out of the bed. "Okay! Lets hit the shower, Sunshine. We've got fifteen minutes to clear out of here."

All business in the morning, apparently. *Just as well.* He was due at the rink at exactly six AM. It would NOT do to be late to even the informal practice, EVER. He was realizing that this would probably be the last hockey he would ever play, here at the Academy, and being benched for even a single game for irresponsible conduct would cost him a significant portion of his career.

There was a problem in the shower: a staring problem.

"Just pretend it's the locker room." She looked sideways. "You hockey players don't oo-oogle each other, do you?"

Bruce eyed Brittany's soapy breasts, so near to him in these close confines that they were pressing and swelling against him as she spun this way and that in the water. "THAT is different." *God, this girl is absolutely...* Bruce shook his head reflexively, then flinched in pleasure. Other parts were rubbing accidentally, too. He thought he might burst.

"Not different in this context. We're not having sex. We're having a shower. And no, you won't explode... you just WANT to."

"Hmmm.... This is still WAY more enjoyable. And frustrating. Soap, please."

"Oh? Do you want me to leave?" She reached for the shower curtain.

"Of course not. I just want to bitch."

"You'd miss practice."

"There is that."

Bruce was in and out of the shower in five minutes, even though there was a naked girl in there with him. He wouldn't have thought it possible, before now.

Brittany was out of the shower, dried, dressed and styled before he was even finished drying off.

"How do you do that?"

"A busy Working Girl has to turn it over quick!" She smiled coquettishly and wiggled her bare midriff.

Bruce squinted as he contemplated her, then shook his head and threw on yesterday's clothes.

Brittany treated them to a nice big breakfast with all the trimmings at a diner adjacent to the Interstate highway. She sat down next to him and announced, "We have twenty-five minutes. It's early, so the kitchen will be quick. You'll have at least five minutes to eat." She slid over until their butts were touching.

A waitress brought menus, but Brittany gave a dismissive wave of her hand. "Don't need those! Tall stack, eggs however twice, bacon. Cram it all onto one plate, if you can. BIG order of home-fries on the side, put legs on those. Coffees and two tall O-jays, and can we get the Florida-O to go, too?"

The waitress smirked. "Sure thing, Sweetie. Would your husband like anything?"

Who knows what she saw, that waitress. Something that was between them, that morning? But she saw it, and it was on her mind, and it just came out that way. They just looked married, in that moment. Comfortable. Intimately loving. Unconditionally loving. Calmly loving. Can you be pronounced Man and Wife under God by a stranger, inadvertently? Perhaps Brittany and Bruce would find out.

If Hattie didn't kill him first.

Time started moving again.

Their waitress saw Brittany's left hand on the table, ringless. *Oooops!* The embarrassed smile made it to her eyes.

"Maybe someday." Brittany patted the top of her date's hand. "We ARE together, though. We're SHARING that plate." Brittany's other hand found Bruce's under the table. She gave his hand a playful squeeze, and then kept it in hers.

Bruce sat there, wondering to himself, *Now why on Earth did the waitress just say THAT?*

The unknown waitress turned on her heel to go to the kitchen.

Brittany leaned over towards Bruce's face and put her lips against his ear in a manner that she was sure would thrill and tease him. "Did YOU put her up to that?"

Bruce didn't whisper. The subtleties of the moment were lost on him. "What are you talking about?!? I just got IN here." This whole adventure was all just a little too strange and... ROMANTIC for his taste.

Brittany snickered. *Typical boy. The M-word scares him. As it rightly should.* Marriage. Husband. Wife. Words that sixteen- and twenty-something-year-olds probably didn't really understand until later. *That WAS a little strange, though. I'm in a hurry in life, yes, but not THAT much of a hurry!*

Brittany and Bruce stayed quiet for a time. Bruce fiddled with a sugar packet as he furtively drank in the beauty next to him. Their coffee came. The waitress retreated quickly. Brittany stirred cream into her coffee, lost in thought. They were still thinking about it.

They both said, at the same time:

"That was weird."

"That was strange, eh?"

They laughed and looked at each other and laughed and looked at each other with unfamiliar speculation and then were quiet again until their food came.

The waitress was relieved that their smiles were back. *That was awkward! Awkward doesn't bring much for tips.* She held out the plate and the Styrofoam box of home-fries. "Right in the middle, then?"

"Yep. Thanks."

Bruce grinned. He felt something. He did not know what it was. Her leg against his? Sharing food off the same plate? Together at this early hour? The way she'd looked when she'd sat up and stretched next to him in the bed this morning? The way she calmly and firmly handled her car, her schedule, him, their date?

"Romeo! A boy has to have his fuel. Eat up! You have eight minutes." She leaned over conspiratorially. "And don't worry - THEY don't know we're wearing the same clothes that we had on yesterday."

They both giggled. Her moods were infectious.

Bruce misinterpreted his feeling. He was young. It was understandable, given his position. "So… Bri. Under exactly WHAT conditions are you spreadable, eh?"

Brittany put down her fork. "You'll see."

Oh, will I? He brightened even more, straightened up a bit, and got some gusto to his dining. He realized she was still holding his hand. He'd never held hands with a girl before...

Brittany finished two more mouthfuls of potato wedges slathered in ketchup before she continued. "Someday."

Bruce's shoulders slumped.

Brittany grinned, and let go of his hand to poke him in the ribs.

Bruce took a sip of water.

They say that water molecules are attracted to one another, minutely, but inevitably. One by one the molecules in a glass of water exert a force that can overcome even gravity, sticking to each other until they rise in a pipette or curl up minutely around the edge of a glass. That is also why a swimmer can wade or even dive into the cold and clinging embrace of a pool on a hot day, but a person who falls uncontrolled into water from a great height, even into the gentlest of waters, will be crushed upon impact, smashed on the tight and irrevocable bond that each molecule of water has for another. The human body is made up mostly of water, eighty-five percent or more. We are sentient, walking bags of water. And this morning, Bruce's water started to feel a force for Brittany's, and Brittany's for his. Their waters yearned to be together. It was a force so tiny, so imperceptible, that they could not have told you when it began to happen. But the effects of the sum of the molecules were strong, and in the end, inevitable.

Perhaps their waitress was a diviner, spending her weekends using a forked willow rod to lead well-drilling crews towards aqueous ground, and on one early Friday morning divining the growing attraction between Brittany's molecules and Bruce's instead.

Bruce ate the last of his breakfast in the car on the way back into the hills on the Interstate as his driver breezed them south at one-and-one-half times the speed limit. He thanked his lucky stars they didn't have snow to contend with, and blessed Brittany's foresight for having the to-go container already delivered with their breakfast.

Brittany dropped him off behind his dorm, on a service road out of sight of the rest of the Academy campus. Today was one of those few days when she felt like her car was just a tiny bit too conspicuous. She rolled down her window as he went around the front of the car. "Bye, Brucie." She raised her voice: "Remember: NO ONE knows about this. And the LONGER no one knows, the more likely it will keep happening." She shrugged and pouted, there behind the wheel, all in a single expression. "IF you're interested."

Bruce stood outside the driver's door of the car and resisted the urge to lean down to kiss that strawberry-colored mouth. It was an especially frosty November morning, maybe five below.

Their breath swirled and mixed, hers floating up out of the car, his hanging in a cloud around his head that slowly sank towards the car on this bitter and windless morning. Their waters were already mixing, out there, in the air.

"You're not the one that has to worry. Does your grandmother own a gun?"

"Yup. Several. All us folks out in the sticks have a couple around, I guess. For young bucks that won't stay out of the fresh crops." Brittany started the engine. She winked, rolled up the window, and then zoomed away.

The warm car exhaust cut through their mixing breath momentarily, and then the fog came together again in its wake, and swirled and mixed and lingered as the door to the basement of the dormitory opened and shut.

Brittany had to wait for an ambulance when she arrived back at the Tee with the main road. Its siren made her think of her grandmother, all alone up there in the Hollow. I hope she was alright last night....

***

Tabitha woke to the sound of a siren, bolted up out of bed, and peeked around the curtain to see if the police car - it had to be a police car - was pulling up out front of her parent's house.

The siren wailed and moved on and faded.

Stupid, stupid, stupid! How could I have been so "STUPID!"

***

"BRITTANY WENDELL, YOU ARE GROUNDED!"

Whups. "Good morning, Grammy."

"I know you come home LATE sometimes, but this isn't LATE, it's the NEXT DAY!"

Brittany Wendell arrived home to a housemate-slash-grandmother who was worked-up and tired-out.

The woman had been up, waiting, ever since she'd gotten out of bed to go to the bathroom at one, only to realize that Brittany's car still wasn't back in the driveway. She'd spent the rest of the night in the rocking chair at the back of the kitchen, wondering whether the phone would ring or if she'd have to place that first, dreaded call. *'Have you seen Brittany?'*

"Grandma, I'm SORRY! I didn't want to wake you in the middle of..."

"Well, I'd certainly rather get a phone call and then be asleep ten minutes later, NOT worried, than wake up and find you MISSING and then BE AWAKE ALL THE REST OF THE NIGHT wondering if you're ALRIGHT or IN A CAR WRECK SOMEWHERE or IN TROUBLE!"

Crap. Crap, crap, crap. "I'm SORRY, Grandma. Look, I need to do a few things and get to school before I'm late. Can you yell at me when I get home tonight after work, or follow me and yell while I get ready?" Brittany edged towards the back stairs.

Hattie shooed her granddaughter off with a dismissive wave. The girl returned in five minutes in a different outfit.

Brittany's grandmother started back in: "Well, you don't look hung over and your hair looks like it's seen a shower. That leaves two options: Boy or girl." She had a thought. "Or with you, I suppose it could mean Boy AND Girl."

Brittany's voice came out of the fridge. "Wow, Grandma, that was unusually unkind of you." She was packing a lunch. "No pie?"

"Call it lack of sleep. I'm sorry, yes, that was inappropriate. No pie left, dear. So?"

"Not what you think, Grandma. A late night in the Big City, so I got a hotel room. No one got lucky." *Yet.*

Hattie looked at her granddaughter skeptically, then sighed. *Be careful with this one, Hattie. You've lost one before.* "It's kind of hard to Ground a girl who's always at work, home studying, or at school. Don't make me worry, Brittany. CALL. You already have more freedom than anyone should expect at your age. And you usually don't abuse it. But you DID abuse me. Tell me when you're not coming home, even if you don't find out until the middle of the night." She went over to the other side of the kitchen and cupped her granddaughter's face in her palm. "I'd like to know you're safe."

"I'm sorry, Grandma."

"And do you REALLY think you should be out all night on a school-night, with all that you're doing already?"

"No, Grandma. That's why I got the hotel room."

There wasn't much that Hattie could say to that.

Later that week, Hattie Wendell would have the phone company man - who would turn out to be a woman, to Hattie's chagrin and then delight - up to wire a service to the upstairs of the house. Hattie would sigh when she looked at the new telephone on her nightstand: plastic, pushbuttons. She'd frown. *Well, it will have to do.*

***

Bruce laced up his skates in the locker room, out of breath. He was just a couple of minutes late. He'd had to sprint down to the rink with his hockey bag over his shoulder, trying not to slip on the early-season snow and slush. He was glad it was DOWN to the rink instead of

UP. Everyone else was out on the ice already, running through personal warm-ups before the coaching staff came in.

Curtis, the Team Captain, poked his head back in. "Ah. There you are!" He inspected his teammate closely. "Late night, huh?"

"Sort of."

"So, Brucie, how's that little cherry Gouda?" He gave a lecherous grin.

How does he know? Bruce didn't look up from his task. "Complicated. And she's a Br... hell of a wheel." *If you only knew the half of it.*

Curtis considered that as he watched Bruce labor to cinch up his laces. "Well, I bet she's not going to have the wax on much longer!" He was fishing for information. What he really meant, was: Have you taken her, yet? But it was unseemly to ask. "Hear you were gone all night, Studly."

Bruce did not know how to even begin to explain it. He didn't really want to try. How do you explain the hold that a suddenly chaste and unaccommodating sixteen-year-old can have over you? How do you get rid of it? *Go find somebody the right age who puts her legs in the air on request, that's how. That woman from Montreal....* He finally finished his laces to his satisfaction. Now he could skate. He threw on the rest of his pads, his practice jersey, picked up his helmet and stick. On his way out of the locker room, he leaned over close to his Captain. "Look. I don't want to get killed this year. Just between you and me, YES, I was with her. No, I have NOT penetrated her." He rolled his eyes at Curtis's skeptical look. "For real, NO. I don't want to talk about it." He shook his head. "Anybody else asks, I was was poking some Swiss over in another dorm. We gotta keep this low-key or the coaches and the grandma are all going to be fighting over who gets to whack me. And the girl probably has a father, too." He hadn't actually considered that before. His Academic Advisor's name was Professor Wendell... He shook his head. *No way. Maybe a distant uncle.* "Save my ass and don't bring her up again."

"Sure, Bruce! Don't want nobody gettin' his hand caught in the cheese case! I gotchorback, Studley Do-Right!"

I sure hope you do...

***

Brittany made it to school on time, but not early enough to catch a certain redhead before class. She really wanted to talk with the girl. Alone. There were so many new things to discuss! Brittany frowned. NOT that she'd want to hear them. Running to chat with Tabitha was turning out to be a hard habit to break.

Instead, she didn't see Tabitha until Biology. It was icy at their worktable, as it had been for ten weeks. They did as much of their work as they could independently, communicated shared tasks succinctly and professionally, and then went their separate ways when the bell rang. It looked like it was going to go that way for the rest of the winter. It can be a cold, cruel season.

***

"Well?" Paul paced anxiously in front of his assistant's desk. He'd made the mistake of falling into habit and taking his usual route to work today.

She looked up from her ledger and shrugged. "Allo au tu."

The woman could be informal. Her boss was banging her three or four times a month, he bought half her clothes - including this curve-hugging silk skirt-and-jacket ensemble - and they had dinner before work at least twice a week. "Comment ca v-"

He forgot his language in his frustration: "So who is she?"

Huh? The woman had already forgotten about her boss's intertest in that far-too-young poster-girl down at the Hudson's store. She gave her boss a blank look.

"La fille!" The girl! "On the storefront billboard!" He shook arms held wide and high, arms that embraced the troubling vignette that he couldn't get out of his head. "The girl at Hudsons!"

"Oh." *You can't be serious about her.* The woman's head shook. *We've never employed...* "I thought - "

Paul stabbed the front of her desk with an angry finger. "Call over there and FIND OUT WHERE THEY GOT HER. Which agency. Call them and find out WHO she IS and WHERE she CAME FROM." He poked the desk again, quickly, firmly. "Today."

***

Brittany tried to reconcile with Tabitha one more time, just after Thanksgiving. The first snow had arrived, socked them in with nearly a foot on the ground for most of a week, and then melted away in a rainstorm into slushy puddles in the streets that froze hard when the temperatures dropped into the below-zeros. Then the temperature rose again and they got more rain to freeze on top of the grey landscape. A bleak way to start a long winter.

Brittany looked forward for a different sort of a thaw. She tried to follow Tabitha after class, to see if they could talk. They couldn't.

Tabitha turned around, saw Brittany there behind her, looked pensive for a moment of frozen time, and then walked right out the front door of the school and down the street in her T-shirt and shorts. She probably didn't go to far, as it was only forty-some degrees out. But Tabitha had made her point.

Brittany hurried off to her locker and spent a few minutes there, dabbing her eyes with Kleenex. No one paid any attention.

The next day after Bio, Tabitha waited and watched from the top of the stairs at the end of the hallway. Surely Brittany would come by on her way up the stairs to her next class, and if they both ditched, they'd be able to talk.

A few minutes later, Brittany was at her locker, in a funk. She'd been waiting outside Tabitha's next class, hoping to hear the girl say SOMETHING, ANYTHING. *Just TALK to me, Tabitha!* But Tabitha was a no-show at her scheduled class. *Shit.* So now Brittany was late, and crying, and really confused. "I can't fucking take this anymore!" *And apparently I'm not going to keep it together at school. It's friggin' getting worse instead of better!* The raven-haired girl slammed her locker and hurried down the hallway towards the Office Section.

Tabitha saw Brittany's feet disappear in the opposite direction. She waited a minute and then sighed a heavy sigh. *Son of a* "Bitch!" She shook her short red and fading pink locks, stood up, hugged her books to her chest, and hurried off to class. Shrug. *Maybe I can try to sneak in late.*

Brittany arrived at the office a mess. "I really need fifteen minutes," she said, between sobs and hiccups, as she pointed to the stack of blank late-slips. Brittany got something else at the office: a cigarette.

The secretary looked a little dubious about that second request, *but the girl is a wreck*, so she reached into her purse and took out a little clutch that held a pack of cigarettes and a lighter. She handed them over reluctantly. "I want these back in fourteen minutes." She looked around the office furtively. "You get caught, you don't know where they came from."

Brittany grabbed the clutch and ran out the door, tears still streaming. She went around the corner to sit down on a five-gallon salt bucket placed conveniently on the backside of a hedge. She lit one of the cigarettes and smoked and cried and thought about Tabitha. She hadn't expected THIS. Brittany was BURSTING with news and she couldn't tell anyone, especially not the person she MOST wanted to tell, who was NOT talking to her, and was also probably the person who most DIDN'T want to hear it.

Rick Garland happened to be returning from an appointment downtown and as he walked up the front steps of the school building he was surprised to see a plume of smoke rising out of the bushes around the corner from the front door. *Hmmm.* He knew class was in session, just by the way the school was quiet. He checked his watch anyway. *Yep, the bell rang eight minutes ago. A double strike! Good. It's time these little Cretans had an example, there had been far too much of...* "Brittany Wendell?!"

She still had a wet-looking ball of tissue in one hand, along with a Carolina Slim cigarette In Menthol For Fresh Flavor in the other. Brittany's tears were mostly stopped now. "Yup, that's me, Sheriff." She wiped her nose with the back of a hand. "How do I post bail?"

Not what he expected. Not WHO he expected. He recognized the plaid clutch, too. *No shit. Well, she must have been one hell of a train wreck when she got to the office...* "Bad day?"

"Started great. Humpphflph!" She laughed and snot came out of her nose. She wiped with her wrist, then wiped her eyes with her fingers. "It went in the toilet shortly after that."

"Do you need to talk about it?"

Her reply came out high-pitched. "Yaaaah." She was about to ball again. *Talking is exactly what I need to do, but the problem is YOU aren't* "The person I need to talk to...SHE isn't in the mood." Brittany lapsed into dripping silence.

Rick waited.

Brittany didn't say anything more. She just stuck the cigarette - short, now - in her mouth and smoked defiantly.

He held out his hand.

Brittany put the lighter back in the clutch and put that in his hand. She kept the cigarette that was in her mouth.

Rick left her there, behind the bush, weeping and nursing a cigarette that was fast burning down to the filter.

He went into the building, entered the front office with a flourish, and held up the clutch. The secretary looked up at her plaid-covered pack of smokes, returning in the wrong hands. "Oh dear."

"Forget something? I don't know whether to suspend HER or YOU." He chuckled. Then he raised his eyebrows and tipped his head in a question: *Do you know what's going on?*

The secretary had a pretty good idea. Tabitha had been down in the dumps lately. *Now this. Maybe Brittany'd gone crawling back to Tabitha and the girl has given her the cold shoulder?* "No. It'll probably work itself out, though."

"Yah. It probably will." He turned to leave, but paused halfway out the door of the office. "So when do you want to take your suspension?"

"Very funny."

***

Robin Wendell got a phone call late on a Thursday morning as she was breezing out the door to her Social Obligation Of The Day. Her hurry might have explained her increasingly acid tone, or maybe it was something else.

"Hello?" Robin started with a cheery greeting, and then the phone call went South.

"Allo. Is this the Walter Wendell Agency?"

"Huh?" Something about that title made Robin's hackles come up. *That fucker think he's jetting off to some jungle island to play spy again?* "Who are you?"

"Mon nom est... is Katerine, I am calling from Montreal, and I am wondering about one of your models... we only have nom de... we only have the young woman's working name: Brittany."

Robin squinted. "There's no one here by that name."

Crash!

She'd hung up the phone handset so hard she'd ripped the base right off the wall.

Katerine heard the minor explosion as a thump and a rip of static before the call went dead. *No one there by that name... Do I have the wrong agency?* The woman scowled. *Not very professional phone manners. The Help down there must be new.*

***

"Well, I found the girl's agency, but they've lost track of her...."

Paul Wendell's head whipped around. "Lost track?!"

Katerine shrugged. "That's what the woman from Walter Wendell said."

Paul's eyes went wide. *It CAN'T be!* "Katerina, call... never mind." He shook his head to clear it. "I'll be out on the floor."

He looks like he's seen an apparition. What's gotten into Paul lately? I haven't felt his breath on my cleavage for two weeks, now! Not even dinner! She was forming an idea that meshed with her view of events and her boss's sudden infatuation with an over-sized Poster Child just down the street: *I'm about to be replaced by a younger model!* Katerine sighed, crumpled up her brief notes on this too-young little poster-girl, and threw the whole mess in the trash. *Well, tit for tat.* Katerine decided she'd better start looking for work elsewhere. *Age and allure, that IS how I took that man from his wife....*

Paul was out at the bar, pointing at a bottle of aged Scotch normally reserved for very special customers. *The worst of news calls for a shot of the best.*

***

Tabitha took her father's big car and drove over to Smiley's on a cold, damp winter night in early December. She parked in a lot that seemed to resemble a lake - although the temperature was well below freezing, somehow dirty, dark water flowed in rivulets down both sides of the cross-road and the parking lot was more of a moonlight-dappled pond.... The big Ford made a bow-wave as it nosed down into the parking area. *Strange weather for winter*, but it wasn't even Christmas yet, and in a few weeks it would be snow three feet deep instead of water. Tabitha parked where she could keep her feet dry and dodged puddles and rivulets all the way to the front door of the diner. What she could see from the foyer, between the inner and outer doors, stopped her in her tracks.

Brittany worked behind the ice cream counter, and at this moment leaned over it with her elbows resting on either side of someone's dinner plate. Close. She was looking into a man's face, a dreamy expression in her eyes. From the back, it was hard to tell, but Tabitha thought it was probably the same guy from the Grange. *Shit*. Tabitha turned and looked around. *No one coming* - the lot was nearly empty. No cars with headlights to sweep her with illumination through the glass doors. The foyer was dark. No one could really see her. She waited and watched.

The man-boy's shoulders were shaking. He was younger than she had first thought. *It has to be the same one*. Brittany laughed. *He must be laughing, too*. Brittany had just opened a... textbook? It was on the counter, beside the plate, and she was stabbing a page with her finger. Then she whirled and went back to work. The boy - *no, he looks more like a man, but I'm SURE it's the same one from the Grange* - was doing homework there at the counter. *Aaahhh. Makes sense... college guy*. Brittany waited on customers and ignored him. He looked in Brittany's direction periodically, following her with his head as she engaged the customers or carried trays. Tabitha couldn't see very far into the restaurant, so Brittany often disappeared from view, but Tabitha could tell where she was by watching this fellow's gaze. He turned fully sideways, face visible in profile. The New Interest looked content, appraising, peaceful. Loving. Brittany went back to the ice cream counter - on the customer side this time - and had a brief word with her beau. He beamed over his shoulder at her, a hand holding his place in the book, the other holding hers....

Oh, shit. What to do, what to do, what to do... Tabitha paced back and forth minutely, shifting weight from one foot to the other and back, her stomach in knots. *To go in or go home...?*

"Your best friend get the Boy?"

Tabitha jerked from the startle. She hadn't heard the woman come into the foyer. She didn't turn, but just replied to the foyer in general: "Something like that, I guess."

"It happens. It's hard." The voice was aged, though the woman now at her side seemed hardly older than Tabitha. The woman nodded her head slowly up and down in affirmation. "What you have to do is decide who you want there. In two or five or ten years time? Who are you going to be writing to about those big things in life? Who is going to come over to see the new baby?" She put her hand on Tabitha's shoulder as they both peered through the glass into the brightly-lit scene on the other side. "Choose well." And then the woman opened the inner door and stepped into Smiley's. Tabitha slipped out the other door, back into the night....

Tabitha greeted morning fitfully, confused to find herself in her bed. She'd gone for a long drive and fallen asleep in the big sedan on the side of a dark road, the windows open against a sudden change of weather - summer heat - and the din of spring peepers, those little lustful whistling frogs, cheeping so loud it made her ears ring. For some reason, while sleeping in the car, she'd had bad dreams about that woman from the foyer at Smiley's....

Tabitha slapped her alarm clock on the bookcase beside her bed and those frogs stopped chirping. *Oh... another dream.* She came fully awake, looked around her bedroom, frowned, considered for a moment, and then- *Oh, SHIT!!!* Tabitha let out a brief and muffled scream, scrambled out of bed, tangled her legs in the covers, almost tripped, caught herself on a chair, and looked at the calendar: DECEMBER. "Nofuckinway." *SHIT!!! September twenty-seventh... October... well, I was stressed, so of course I didn't....* Tabitha looked over at the corner, at the bureau, at the bottom drawer where she kept her red and black granny undies. No. Fucking. Way. "Well, I am totally FUCKED!" She nearly shrieked out the last word.

Her mother, downstairs, wondered what all the caterwauling was about. *Oh, well. She's a teenager. It will pass or she'll ask for help.*

Upstairs, Tabitha giggled, snorted, then choked back a sob. *No need to cry, girl*, "S'not happening." *NO. FUCKING. WAY. IS. THAT. HAPPENING. December...* Tabitha looked at the other drawer, the one where her jeans stayed folded and ready and NOT FITTING lately.

Well, of course. You're a growing TEENAGER. Growing, alright! "NO FUCKING WAY!"

Outside her door, Tabitha's passing mother said, "Well good morning to you, Tabitha! Language!"

Tabitha didn't even notice. She was mentally counting days in September, forwards and back, forwards and back.

***

Brittany asked for a Monday night off ("for a school thing") and went by Tabitha's most regular babysitting job. She knocked on the door and was startled when a young girl with smeared lipstick opened it.

"Well, I've got Monday nights, now. Have for, like, jeez, like TWO MONTHS! Like, try her house?" The girl snickered after she closed the door. *Maybe that's why Tabitha isn't getting the Mitchell's business anymore, this Brittany dropping by for a little bit of Tabitha....* The new Sitter went back to the couch and her paid date with Barry.

Barry was still hanging around the house when the sitter was there, but he made it a point to vamoose before his parents got home. He didn't want them to realize he had any sort of growing interest in the girl. He'd return ten minutes after they did, acting like he'd been out all night. Frankly, he was hoping they'd join another board or two, so he could wrestle on that couch more than once a week…

Right now, as this younger, new-and-improved sitter sat back down on the couch, Barry wanted to know who'd been at the door.

"That Brittany girl. She, like, dripped by to see Tabitha!"

They both laughed at her joke, and then they went back to the business at hand.

Brittany got back in her car, steeled herself, and drove across town and up through the gently falling snow to the farmhouse. Snowflakes swirled in the dark road behind the car, and then once again settled to the pavement.

***

Tabitha thought it through for a few more days and then realized that she now had a big, dark, scary secret, one that she held all to herself like a big rock in the pit of her stomach. A very adult secret. *Well, I'll be an adult by the time this is through!* She sighed. She felt very alone. The person she wanted to tell wasn't available. She didn't really have any other friends... not THAT kind of friend, at any rate. *Barry?* She snorted. *Hardly! THAT would lead to disaster!*

Grief and dread radiated out from the rock in her stomach. There was one other person to whom Tabitha usually went, someone safe and wise and comforting, someone older and experienced in this kind of problem, *she will surely hold my hand through all of this... no.* The consequences of sharing this Secret were unknown and the repercussions, if the information got into the wrong hands... those terrible possible events were un-thinkable. Tabitha unconsciously pulled her sweater tight around herself. *Mommy, I'm scared.*

***

They saw each other for the first time in two weeks at Plant Biology on the second Monday in January. It was no longer frosty, but it was uncomfortable and business-like and pained. They were still lab partners. They were still not talking. Neither one of them knew how to start. So much to say, so many hurt feelings, yet so much history! And such divergent needs, at this point, apparently. But, regardless, they needed to talk, and one of them needed to start the conversation.

The bell rang instead.

Brittany and Tabitha went their separate ways.

Chapter Ten

It finally happened by accident, in the grocery store right in the middle of the Mill Village, on a dreary winter Friday afternoon in the third week of January.

They were both in the feminine products aisle, each looking at a different set of shelves. Brittany, wandering in to scrutinize the tampon selection, didn't notice her (apparently) ex-friend. Tabitha stood staring vacantly and wearily in the general direction of the opposite shelf without really seeing anything. She certainly didn't see Brittany... Tabitha wasn't noticing much of anything at all these days. She was facing the diaper selection, of all things.

Brittany noticed first. "Hi." She shifted a foot so she was facing Tabitha.

"Oh!" Pause. "Hi." Surprise, and then a dead hello.

"Miss you." Brittany reached out, imperceptibly.

Tabitha was mad today. Or still mad. She was having a Very Bad Day and Brittany's emotional needs were a VERY small concern to her at the moment. Her own emotions were vacillating wildly up and down, back and forth. "Not enough to ditch Romeo." She'd still wasn't sure she'd driven over to the diner that night, *was it all a dream?* But she knew anyways, *every little awful bit of it!*

"I cry over you. Is that enough?"

I don't really give a shit WHO you cry over. Well, maybe if you were crying over that GUY, 'cause he was a skeeze, and you came crying to me.... Her eyes narrowed under the unruly pink and red mop of hair. "Why?"

"Why do I cry?" Brittany put her hands on her hips. This was hard, and Tabitha wasn't HELPING. "DUH! My Best Friend is pissed at me because... BECAUSE..." Brittany gave up. She couldn't really say it. She teared up instead.

"JESUS, you really ARE crying over me! Whatthefuck, girl?!? If you're so fucking broken up over it, then WHY are you with HIM, instead of..." Tabitha leaned in close and whispered in a hiss, all squinty-eyed in her sudden rage: "Me?" Tabitha's hands were on her hips now, too.

Squaring off.

It would have been nice if those two had noticed their own physical cues and then realized they needed to take it down a notch. Instead, other folks in the store noticed it for them. Shoppers avoided that aisle, but many of them loitered in the general area to see what was going to happen. These two were NEWS, and it looked like they were going to maybe MAKE SOME MORE today! The rude were hoping to see mayonnaise jars and ketchup flying. Sorry, folks, wrong aisle for that! The polite were hoping for a reconciliation, and didn't want to intrude, on the chance that things would get left unsaid if there were too many people around. Some of those IN THE KNOW were hoping for a reconciliation and then a steamy SCENE, right there in the grocery store, with dropped packages and kissing and groping and faces arched to the sky in erotic bliss... Most of the ones hoping for that were male.

Brittany did a good job of keeping her composure, but she was having a hard time. This was NOT how their First Conversation In Forever was supposed to play out. She backed up a step, uncertain.

Tabitha, who was working up a good head of steam that she just couldn't seem to let go of, leaned in towards Brittany and quietly asked, "Are you Out?"

"Huh?" *Out of what? Things to say? No. Tampons. Yah. That's why I'm here.* She scowled in confusion, almost laughed.

Thank goodness, the moment was broken!

Unfortunately, it takes two to break a moment when two are involved. Tabitha gestured to the two ends of the aisle. "Do all these people, here, know that you and I sleep... USED to sleep together?"

Brittany looked around. "I don't think they'd be watching if they didn't. Who the fuck cares?"

Tabitha grabbed Brittany and kissed her hard on the mouth. "THAT's for MISSING me." And then she pushed Brittany away and slapped her in the face. WHAP!!

Brittany's face stung, and everything flashed red, but she didn't fall back. Instead, she stood rooted in shock and turned her face back towards an unexpectedly violent fr-

"THAT's for sneaking around behind my back and letting me SEE it. That HURT!" Tabitha pulled her ex-friend back in towards her, forcefully, and gave her a hug. "THAT's one of the things that I've missed." Tabitha pushed Brittany away again and -

"HEY!" Brittany knew what was coming this time and threw up an arm. It was the wrong one and did not protect her other cheek.

WHAP!!! Tabitha slapped Brittany, just as hard and fast as she could pull it off, on the other cheek.

Brittany saw stars.

Tabitha reared back her head and let loose before Brittany even straightened back up: "and THAT'S FOR BEING A CHEATING LITTLE BABY-DYKE BITCH!!!" Tabitha turned and stormed out of the store in tears.

Brittany took a moment to recover. She was too shocked to cry, but she did get MAD. *NOBODY fuckin' HITS Brittany Wendell!* She got a certain look on her face, like the clouds passing over the sun right before a windy downpour that would keep the roof company and the tree-removal services busy for a few weeks, and then Brittany Wendell marched towards the front of the store with her fists clenched and her groceries abandoned on the floor in aisle three.

Folks had a lot to say about that!

"Uh-oh!"

"Here we go!"

Someone let out a few short barks.

"Oh shit!"

"Oh, NO!"

"Cat fight! Better call animal control!"

"Oh dear, shouldn't somebody stop them?"

"Bitch-fest in the parking lot! Tickets three dollars!"

Well, you really COULD have sold tickets to be in the parking lot THIS afternoon, that is for sure true.

Brittany didn't hear any of the comments. She wasn't entirely aware of her surroundings anymore, apparently. She knocked over poor little Mrs. Allen on her way through the register line. The other folks got out of the way when they saw the black-haired girl with the dark look headed through, but poor Mrs. Allen, with her aluminum cane, couldn't get out of the way fast enough. Shaking her head - and her cane - as she lay on the glossy linoleum floor just inside the door, she repeated over and over, "Well! I never! Well! I never! Well. Such behavior! Well!" She kept repeating it even as bystanders and a cashier helped her back to her feet.

Brittany stomped in place and then stormed out of the automatic door, never taking her eyes off Tabitha's car, once it was in view. Storming through an automatic door is kind of hard to do, since you have to wait for it, but Brittany pulled it off - she was THAT mad.

She found Tabitha crying behind the wheel of her father's big Ford in the parking lot. Brittany banged on the side window with her palm. BANG BANG BANG BANG "HEY!" BANG! You in there! BANG! BANG! "How DARE you slap me, you CHERRY LITTLE BITCH!!!" She was screeching now: "NOBODY fucking slaps me, 'Specially not some little UN-STRETCHED PEACH-POP like YOU!"

Tabitha got back out of the car like she was shot out of it - the door nearly came off the hinges, bounced, and almost knocked a growling Tabitha back into the car. "Goddamnedfuckin'piece'a..." She fought the door out of the way and then rounded on her black-haired nemesis. "WELL FUCK YOU! So poked full of holes by now, you're a colander!"

Careful, girls, it's getting awfully personal… There were some people gathering out front of the store, waiting to see how the storm broke. Not that the two friends squaring off noticed it.

"You already HAD YOUR SHOT and it SUCKED!" Brittany gave Tabitha an evil smile and a steamy, come-hither scrunch of her nose. *Top that, Bitch!*

"Then WHY do you always COME BACK for MORE, you WHORING little wanna-be BABY-DYKE?!" Tabitha took a menacing step. She really WAS having a hard time with emotional regulation lately.

"You WISH you had my fuckin' action, it's not MY fault I'm ALL YOU CAN GET in this town, you little piece of red-topped carpet-cleaning shit!"

Quite a crowd was gathering now, and someone in the store was this minute on the phone to the cops. Public Decency was at risk, you know. The store manager was next in line to use the phone - insurance requirements and lawsuits, company policy and all that. It was obvious to everyone that these two girls were going to Go At It, right there on the cold ground, and -

It was like a football game, when the snap comes: they both went forward as if someone had yelled HIKE! But it was far more bloody. A combined six-hundred and seventy-two pounds of padded linemen coming together couldn't have made a collision that explosive. WHUMP! Slaps and then fists and then the dark-haired one got a handful of short red hair and she was holding the other girl's head down and in place so that her fist could keep going and going and going at that face… The red-head was giving her all, too, though, and Brittany was getting a thumping as Tabitha kept punching up and up, blindly, and about every third or fourth punch connected with the underside of the bigger girl's chin. And then they were on the pavement, rolling and growling and snarling and screaming and flailing away and it really DID sound like a couple of cats and for just a moment Tabitha was on top of Brittany's neck, and then the pile reversed end-over-end and the back of Tabitha's head hit the pavement with a THORK! that everyone could HEAR and they thought for sure it was over and someone was DEAD, but no, that redhead just kept swinging, even from the ground and OH BOY! the crowd was really getting their money's worth and cars were stopping on the main street and…

Burt, the Police Chief, got called out by the Highway Foreman's secretary, over the Town Radio: "Go on up to the store, there's a melee and Fred's worked-up enough to stammer, frankly the man sounds panicked, and the County's got two calls on it, too, and oh, while you're in the neighborhood, we're getting calls about, ah, something is stopping traffic on Main Street..."

Now Burt was an old-school law officer, kind of conservative and not given to putting up with anything strange, college-town or not. When the call came in, he threw his coffee and pastry in the gutter and hoofed it over to the car as quickly as his sixty-two years and his swinging late-midlife tire would let him. *Folks never call about this shit. Fight, schmite.* Fred, the manager, had called from the store, and you couldn't really rattle Fred, and the dispatcher/secretary said on the radio call that he sounded EXCITED, and that MEANT something.

Fred was charged up, alright, but it wasn't THAT kind of excited! Why, he'd bought CABLE at fifty-five dollars a month just so he could watch this kind of kinky shit, and here it was, LIVE and IN COLOR! (Black hair versus redhead! His money was on the red-head, boy she was pissed!) and it's *RIGHT HERE IN THIS PARKING LOT, WHOOOHOOOOOOO!!!!* He'd called the town offices out of a sense of civic duty, and once he hung up the phone, his job was DONE and Fred was now a legitimate SPECTATOR!

Burt started up his personal-slash-patrol car, parked right there on the sidewalk out front of Mrs. Folsom's Bakery like it usually was for half of every morning, his beloved deep-blue 1984 Ford Crown Victoria with a spotlight on the side and two bubble-lamps in the back window that would make the whole car strobe blue and the dual H-pipes exhaust on a no-emissions-control package that only the cops could get, and it had a hundred and ten on the clock now, and it was just getting broken in and the ride was smoother every month... That car would do a buck-thirty if he really stood on it....

Burt turned on those rotating bubble-lights, waited a second for traffic to scatter, then pulled off the sidewalk and into the busy ring-road around the Mill Village Common, where he promptly made all of twenty miles an hour. *Yes, these assholes are getting out of the way, but they're taking their sweet time doing it!* He chanced a rolling stop at the main road - he really couldn't see shit with all the flashing blue glare off the INSIDE of the frosty windshield. *Fucking car wonta-even had time to thaw out by the time I....*

Bruce was driving by the store, and he stopped, too, distracted from forward progress up Main Street by *some sort of something going on in that parking lot and it looks - Holy SHIT! That's Brittany... and that angry little redhead from the Grange, and they're going at it Full Throttle, right there in the parking lot!* The only thing that seemed to be missing were a bunch of hairy, beer-drinking bikers standing around taking bets on the action. It looked like a fight on the ice, except... *worse. Much worse.* Bruce was shocked at the violence. He was about to abandon his new used car right in the road and go over there when he saw the blue lights behind him. *Well that solves THAT problem.* Bruce decided to keep going.

So Burt rolled up on East Street right in front of the store's single-row parking lot and the first thing he sees is a crowd, and right at the front of it is Fred, the store manager: cheering, swinging and jumping just like he's ringside at the heavyweight championship. *Complainant shaken up? No. Gleeful? Definitely!*

Burt left the car haphazardly in the middle of the road, straddling both narrow lanes, and pushed his way through the assembled crowd. "Jesus Christ wouldya let me in here, GO HOME, ALLAYA! NOTHIN' TA SEE HERE NOW WOULDJA... Oh." *Well, there IS something to see, alright...* Not the kind of fight he'd been expecting. Burt watched, transfixed. Holy shit! *That little red-head dyke, she's got the other one - the Wendell girl, isn't she? - in a headlock, and by Jesus she MEANS it!* They squirmed and growled as the little red-head kept grinding the other girl's head into the mat right there on the cold, wet, salty pavement. *Ow! These two girls are tryin'ta KILL each other!* Burt was still trying to figure out exactly how the hell he was going to grab onto them without putting his hands somewhere too soft...

And then they rolled right up on his polished black boots, still going at it. He actually stepped back, had to. The girls were both on the ground, looking up, when they saw the Royal blue stripe on the black pants and the silhouette of the campaign hat against the sky.

The two girls reacted together:

"Holy shit!"

"Oh, FUCK!"

They were up and running like frightened deer across the lot, across Main Street, through a puddle of slush and over a snowbank and around the back of the old, falling-down community stable, out of sight.

Burt certainly couldn't get out of the gate as quickly as those girls had disappeared, why he couldn't have shot a bullet that would have kept up with those two as they raced away! That foot pursuit was a lost cause before it started. Besides - they'd run off TOGETHER, hadn't they?

"It's all over, folks, they're probably back there makin' up, now just go on back to your... whatever."

Fred bounced over, still panting and out of breath and hoarse from all his yelling. "WELL?!? What are you going to DO to them? Don't you have to CATCH them?!?" The man's eyes were bugged out to the point of medical concern.

Burt hitched up his ever-sagging belt and wondered if an eyeball actually COULD ever fall out of its socket... "Catch them? Whyenthehellwould I do THAT? I know who they are. Did they damage anything?"

"But don't you have to ARREST them?!?"

"Whythehell would I do that? They're not fightin' NOW, are they? They're RUNNIN'! I wish my own kid's 'd show me that much respect!"

Fred nearly shook with something between rage and avid glee: "BUT YOU'VE GOT TO ARREST THEM!!!"

The crowd now had a different sort of a show to watch. Boy, Fred's eyes sure did look wild!

"Fred!" He grabbed the man's arm. *Standthefuckstill and talk sense!* "Did they BREAK anything?"

"Aahhhh... Besides each other, you mean?"

"Ya. Shirley said you were rattled. Whadtheybreak in the store?"

"You... Ah... Nothing, I guess. But it was a hell of a fight, wasn't it!?! I thought someone was gonna get KILLED and didjyaSEE how that redhead got UP ON TOP and - YOU'VE GOT TO CATCH THEM AND FRISK THEM AND ARREST THEM!!!!" Fred had turned purple, with the bugged-out eyes even further out of his head, and unseemly amounts of spittle collected at the corners of his mouth.

Burt replied quietly. *Man's already cranked-up enough.* "I'm sure you'd like to see that. Fred: Go take a cold shower, and then get back to work." He waved his arm in the general direction of the girl's flight: "They're probably having a laugh and sharing a root beer right about now."

Actually, they were still running. Brittany and Tabitha just about fell down a steep, snowy bank below the back side of the stable, went into the river, and then ran splashing and tripping along the icy edge like a couple of convicts on break-out. They kept going until they came to a familiar ravine behind Tabitha's house. They didn't stop, they just left the river and hoofed it up the hill, heavy-footed and shivering already, alternately pushing each other out of the way in an every-woman-for-herself frenzy or pushing the other forward from below when the leader slipped on the narrow, nearly vertical, snow-covered summer-only path up the muddy and icy gully. When they topped the ravine and got to a piece of semi-bare, straw-grey, frozen lawn at the base of the big leafless maple in Tabitha's back yard they collapsed together in a heap. Here was a place where they'd spent a lot of time in happier days and better weather.

"Shit!"

Both at once:

"Fuck me!"

"Eff'n Christmas!"

"Fu-uuuuck!"

They started laughing and giggling and crying and laughing again, then Brittany's head ended up in Tabitha's lap and Tabitha looked down at- "DID I DO THAT TO YOU?!?"

A bloody mess covered Brittany's forehead, making it hard to see just how bad it was underneath. Her bottom lip was fat and bleeding. A piece of skin was missing on the side of her chin, and that gaping divot was bleeding freely.

Tabitha hadn't fared much better. The face Brittany looked up at had a right eye already swollen mostly shut and Tabitha's nose bled freely over her jacket, still. Both of them were wet almost to the knees from their flight through the river, and they were covered with mud.

"Probably no worse than you." Brittany laughed. "You look like I feel! Ww-w-we've gotta get cleaned up and I've gotta g-g-g-gget back to mmm-mm-m-mmm-my ccc-cc-cccc-ccc-car." Brittany suddenly started to shiver.

Shock and hypothermia are a bad and sudden combination, especially for those on the lam.

Tabitha slowly stood up - that took some doing, she was stiff and sore already and there was some sort of ringing in her ears that wouldn't go away and she had the beginnings of a splitting headache.... She held her hand out to her sometimes-friend. She knew one thing: *I need to warm up, QUICK! Bad Things could happen...* "L..LL-LL-Let's hit the showers, ff-fff-ffighters!" She helped Brittany up off the cold ground and tried to control the chattering of her own teeth.

Brittany stood there, her teeth clicking and clacking, too, scowled as best as she was able with swollen and frozen face, and then sighed. "Why th-th-th-the hell n-nn-not."

They walked to the back door of Tabitha's house hand-in-hand.

Tabitha started: "I'm s-s-s-sorry ab-bb-bb-bout your face." But only gave so much ground. "Y-y-y-you're still a cheat'n bitch."

"I was n-n-n-never YOUR bitch to begin with. I'm sorry about-t-y-y-y-your n-n-n-nn-nnose..." It's hard to carry on any sort of conversation with convulsive shivers going on. Brittany sure was glad they were approaching a warm house!

An hour, two hot cocoas, one shower, and two towels later, they were at least warm, presentable and peaceful. Brittany wore some of Tabitha's mother's clothes, which sort-of fit, enough for the moment. The clothes from the fight were spinning in the dryer. The jackets were probably ruined, but were on the backs of chairs over furnace vents. The girls sat sprawled on a sofa, Tabitha's legs resting in Brittany's lap. A tinsel-covered Christmas tree still standing sentinel across the room refereed them.

Brittany held a homemade ice-pack to her forehead: a one-pound bag of sliced green beans. "Can we NOT do that again? I HURT!" Brittany winced as she shifted the green beans over a little.

Tabitha looked in a hand-mirror and winced. "Brittany Wendell, you gave me a black eye! Yes! Er...NO, let's NOT do that again, girl!"

Tabitha's mother came in the front door just then. "Oh! Brittany! It's nice to..." She looked both of the girls up and down. "I see you two made up. Good." The woman turned on her heel and fled from the room in haste. "Eiyiyiyi."

The young women heard that, but they hurt to much to giggle. And they were both still a little mad.

Tabitha tipped the mirror and tried to figure out how to suck in her lip a little on one side, so it wouldn't look fat. "You're still a whore."

Brittany dabbed at the blood on her forehead with a wet washcloth. "You're sort of right, I suppose. Fuckin A-Hole, oowwww! THAT GODDAMN HURTS!!!!" She opened her eyes again, recovered, and said, "You're still a cherry piece of shit."

Tabitha was very still for a moment. Then she replied very quietly: "THAT may not be entirely true anymore."

"Oh?" Brittany looked up with wide eyes. "Oh!"

Tabitha put the mirror down. "I really HAVE missed you. And you've missed... a bunch. Stuff." *Yes, I got stuffed.* She sighed, and grimaced. "We have a lot to talk about."

Brittany moved Tabitha's feet and stood up. "Apparently, we do." *Wow!* "You wanna come up to the house?"

"I do. You have NO IDEA how much we have to talk about, really." Tabitha looked furtively toward the other reaches of the house, where her mother's sharp ears might be hiding.

Brittany got the hint. She started putting on her still-wet jacket. "Yes, I suppose we do. But first I have to get my car. I'll be back in ten-"

"DON'T LEAVE!" Tabitha reached out with wide-eyed alarm. I'll go WITH you!" There was no way Tabitha was letting Brittany out of this house alone, now they were talking. She was afraid that reconciliation might come undone once Brittany had even a few moments to lick her wounds.

"Alright." Brittany thought for a second. "Grab your backpack and some peejays." Brittany shrugged. "Just in case."

The corner of Tabitha's mouth went up, in spite of herself. Habit, maybe.

"NO slinky stuff! I'm not putting out for anyone that beats me up!" Brittany wanted some ground rules down early.

Tabitha stage-moped up the stairs to get her things. She was actually glad that Brittany had ruled out any hanky-panky. The neighbors, a married couple, fought loudly and frequently. They also frequently made up and then fucked into all hours of the night afterwards, also loudly. Tabitha heard them - both times - several times a month. She found it disgusting.

She was back down in a long minute and then she and Brittany were off to get the Pinto. They took side streets and slunk through backyard lanes and along hedges and sprinted across the main road like squirrels.

"Oh, thank God, the cops are gone!" Brittany had half expected to find her car towed or staked-out or being dusted for fingerprints. As she eyed her car and the general area for surveillance, she asked, "What do we do with YOUR car?"

"Leave it. My Dad will get it, if I ask nice."

Brittany shrugged. Problem solved. The two girls ran across the smaller street, both dove in through the passenger door, scrambled to straighten out their limbs and torsos so they were properly arranged with Brittany in the driver's seat, and then wiggled around to find and fasten seat belts. It probably would have been quicker if they'd each just walked to the proper door, got in, and started the car normally, but neither one of them was a seasoned criminal yet. Baby steps, for both of them, at this point. Brittany backed up, nearly over the sidewalk on the other side of the small street, cut the wheel sharp, and got them the hell out of there. As they burst out onto Main Street, the engine's RPM's were up enough for the supercharger to take over and the tires let out a loud screech before Brittany got off the gas a little. She managed to get it straightened back out as she let off to get it into third. It wasn't the first time she'd squealed the tires, but it was the first time she'd laid a guilt-strip on the road. For the first time in her life, she actually FELT like a criminal.

Burt wasn't born yesterday, you know. He was simply waiting in the first driveway on the road up through the Hollow. The little green Pinto went flying by and then -

"OH SHIT, there's BLUE LIGHTS behind us!" Brittany grinned and rolled her eyes in surrender.

Tabitha looked back and actually screamed: "EeeeeEEEEEEEKK!!!!!"

The girls had never been in THAT kind of trouble before, and might have been just a little over-dramatic. Tabitha might have had some OTHER reasons to be afraid of law enforcement professionals, of course.

Brittany gave Tabitha a funny look as she pulled over to the side of the road, and a warning: "We're not pullin' any Dukes-of-Hazard shit, here. He WON'T arrest us for a dust-up." She rolled her eyes. "Probably just wants to get a good look at the two dykes who were duking it out." *I hope.* Brittany looked in the mirror. The same guy as before, old and a giant pot-belly, climbing out of the big sedan on the shoulder right behind them. She looked back at her passenger again. "WILL YOU STOP PISSING YOUR PANTS! You're freaking me out!"

Tabitha, white and trembling, nodded. "'K-k-kay."

"JESUS, girl, it's" Brittany lowered her voice because the cop was adjacent to the car now. "no big deal." She rolled the crank to lower her window.

"Ma'am, it certainly IS a Big Deal. Please shut off your engine and take the keys out of the ignition."

Oh KRAP! Now Brittany, too, was shitting her pants. Well, no, only figuratively, but she did suddenly have a case of the farts, and didn't feel very well. NOT how she expected today to GO. She held the keys out the window, towards the cop.

Burt gestured dismissively towards the interior of the car with the back of his gun hand. "Top of the dash is fine." He watched the girl's shaking hand deposit the keys up on the vinyl, next to a big round pressure gauge that probably obstructed her view and was definitely a two-point ticket under State rules. His head shook reflexively. *Kids.* He backed up to keep safely out of reach, just out of good habit, and stooped down a bit to look in the driver's window, across at the other girl. *Ow!* He couldn't hide his wince. He scrutinized them silently for a moment. *These two good and fucked each other up! Look like a couple of prize-fighters come out of a motorcycle crash....* "You two plan on doin' this often?"

Very quietly, Brittany said, "No?"

Tabitha, staring straight ahead, shook her head meekly.

"Good. You two watch too much TeeVee. Don't run from the law. Bad habit that'll fuck you up." Burt didn't normally talk that way, but he was good with kids. (Well, all but his own.) He knew how to make them listen up.

"Yes, sir." (Brittany)

Yessir, sir." (Tabitha)

Good. They're paying attention. "You two all made up?"

Well, that was kind of obvious, they were IN the car TOGETHER, but no one in that Pinto was going to be smart-mouthing right now.

"Uh-huh. Yessir." (Brittany)

Nod, nod, nod. (Tabitha)

Jesus, "You two look like shit. You better get some ice on that eye, Pronto, there, missy." He stood back up and looked down at Brittany. "Aren't you that Model Girl all the other ones bitch about?"

Brittany smiled ruefully. "Yep. That's me." She smiled a stage smile, all teeth, up at the police officer. *Ow.* Her face hurt. *Dammit!* She grimaced.

"You gotta keep that forehead and chin WET dearie, long time... least a week or two. Put Vaseline or first-aid cream or cow teat balm or some shit like that on it, be generous, and then put a bandage on it and KEEP it there, every day." He leaned down to take another close look. "Ow. Go the two weeks. Maybe three." He stood back up. "You'll look like a Goddamn fuckin' moron, but you'll keep your good looks, won't need but a dab-a makeup ta cuv-rit, back in-da newspaper and catalogue pictures fer sure." He put his hands on his hips. "This happened anywhere else but your hometown, you'd both get a ticket for misdemeanor assault - Mutual Affray, they call it. Goes to court no matter who started it. Someone gets hurt, might become a Felony." He frowned, and bent back down so both girls could see him. The redhead still looked straight ahead, at nothing. *Why, she's pale as all hell where her face isn't fucked up....* He put some venom in his voice: "The two prize-fighters ever SLEPT together..." He paused for just the briefest of seconds, "Then it becomes DOMESTIC ASSAULT which is an immediate Felony and ruined lives and A RECORD, no matter whether somebody gets a scratch or everybody's smilin' an' all kissy afterward or not. You FOLLOWIN' me?" *There. Scare the piss outta these two and maybe this shit won't happen again downtown in broad daylight. They sure look like scrappers, though!* He could see that they got it, all four eyes saucer-wide. *Good.*

Both girls looked straight forward in the ensuing silence, wide-eyed, slowly nodding.

"Good. Good. I'm your Police Chief, Burt Robinson. I'm pretty sure who YOU two are, but why don't we be all introduced, friendly and proper like?" He stooped down even further, and stuck his head nearly in the window, then backed up a step when he realized he was Too Close.

Brittany put out her hand, tentatively. "Brittany Wendell. Pleased?" She looked skeptical about that last part.

He ignored her outstretched hand. "Yep. Pleasedtameetchatoo. You, miss?"

"Aahhhh... Tabitha? Tabitha Bayer. I'm REALLY sorry."

"Tell her that. Nicetameetcha." Burt stepped back, looked the car up and down one end to the other, dramatically, and frowned. "Off the record: I got in a bit of a chase with this car right at the end of the summer..."

Brittany sunk down in her seat minutely.

"And I never quite caught up. Lost it somewhere up off the end of the Hollow. That YOU, or the Frey boy, drivin' it then?"

No one spoke.

Burt sighed. "I said OFF THE RECORD. I said it, I meant it."

Brittany sank down further, almost below the window opening. "Mmeeeee?"

"Thought so. Miss Wendell: You scared the shit outta me. I was SURE you were gonta wreck. Live to twenty, girl. You see blue-lights a'hindya, pull the hell over." He turned on his heel and started walking back to his car.

Brittany and Tabitha waited in suspended animation until the siren chirped behind them.

Brittany looked in the mirror. The flashing lights were off. The cop sat behind the wheel of his car, making shoo-ing motions with the backs of his down-turned hands. Go, get. Brittany reached up, grabbed the keys, and started the Pinto hot-rod. She noticed Tabitha, her hands steepled in front of her in prayer, whispering thanks to the roof of the car. Once they were back on the pavement and speeding up, Brittany reached over and patted Tabitha on the thigh. "RELAX, girlfriend! We're off the hook!"

Tabitha's mouth grimaced to one side, her eyes pivoting to the other, towards Brittany. "MAY-be." She sat in the seat worrying over the effects a fight and hypothermia might have on her body.

Wow. Tabitha had gotten kind of strange in two-plus short months.

***

"Tabitha!!" Hattie Wendell shuffled over towards the porch door. "It's nice to see... Oh, dear." She put her hand out carefully, with her fingers under Brittany's chin and gently turned her granddaughter's face back and forth. "You two made up, didn't you?" She turned to examine Tabitha's eye. "Oooo. Rather roughly, apparently."

Brittany thought that Tabitha looked awfully cute in that moment, fresh in from the cold, with her short red hair all poking out from under a ski hat, all tousled and still wet from their shower, her swollen eye frozen in a angry red-purple wink. Tabitha was doing that funny thing with her mouth and remaining eye going in separate directions again. Brittany watched her grandmother examine her friend, then she leaned over, took her friends battered face in her own hands, looked into Tabitha's one good eye, and answered her grandmother: "Yes, we did."

They piled the rest of the way into the kitchen to take off hats and coats and boots.

Grandma Wendell made a few clucking noises, and gave an "Oh, my..." when she saw the backs of the coats. "Had a grounder, I see..."

Brittany took Tabitha's hand. "It's nice to have you back. I HAVE missed you." She gave her friend a chaste but meaningful kiss on the lips and looked into her one open eye. "You feel like part of my family that's been missing. Grandma, can she-"

"If she doesn't mind leftovers." Grandma couldn't figure out whether to smirk or wince. *That's probably about where things stand.* "And not much of them, at that. You should have called. I could have started a roast or something...." She grimaced. "You're not going to start back in here, are you?"

Brittany and Tabitha shook their heads grimly, ruefully, and finished getting out of their winter things. It was a slow process. They were sore.

Tabitha looked up from the unraveling laces of her boot: "Leftovers in this kitchen beats gourmet anywhere else in the world." She turned her head to look sideways up at Brittany. "This feels like home as much as the other place. Shit, how did we get this fu- funny thing going on between us?"

"Let's go talk about exactly that." Brittany put a damp dish-towel on her face, and held out a cold bag of frozen peas from the past summer's garden to Tabitha. "Some peas for dinner, Grandma? They're thawing…" She eyed her grandmother. "We have a LOT of catching up to do. Mind if we don't help get dinner ready? Other than thawing vegetables?"

"Leftovers, dear, nothing to it anyways! We'll make up some peas after your face feels better, Tabitha, dear. Oooof. You two go on." She gave them the same shoo-ing away gesture that the cop had.

Tabitha winced.

They settled in Brittany's bedroom. Tabitha lay sideways on the bed, holding the peas too her still-swelling eye.

Brittany sat on the floor and dabbed an age-old local balm recipe on her forehead and chin: a mixture of calendula flowers, pie-crust shortening, and beeswax. The recipe had been passed down in the Wendell family for generations, right along with the farmhouse - a lot of cuts, burns, and scrapes on a farm. She grabbed some more goop out of the jar for a scrape on her cheek: "Per the doctor's - uh, Police Chief's orders!"

Tabitha flinched just watching. "Ow. Sorry."

Brittany, ever- businesslike: "So. What are we gonna do?"

Silence. The bedroom stayed that way until Grandma Wendell called them to supper.

Uh-oh.

On the way to the table Tabitha threw the bag of peas into the refrigerator. She turned towards Brittany's grandmother and lit up with a puffy and one-eyed smile. "Shepard's pie! You call that LEFTOVERS? Yum!" She hugged Hattie. "Thankyou."

"It seemed easy enough to do with what I had." A good way to stretch leftovers, actually. The problem was how to cook it quickly. She had furtively nuked it for fifteen minutes before she put it in the wood-fired range to a finish, as a way to speed things up.

The exhausted prize-fighters perked up while eating the second-day potato, corn, and beef mixture. The two girls talked of school and work and schoolmates and gradually things started to feel familiar. Hattie mostly kept quiet. Eventually they nearly forgot her, as she'd hoped they would. They had something to settle, those two.

After eating, while they helped clear the table, Brittany tried again. Working on The Problem here, in this kitchen, just felt right. "So, Tab... What are we going to do?"

Tabitha halted in mid-step, carrying a stack of three plates towards the sink. She looked at the floor. "Just like it was?" She looked up to check the reaction.

Brittany shook her head. "'Lots changed."

Tabitha agreed, very quickly and quietly: "Yes, it has." She put the plates on the counter next to the sink and walked over to whisper something in Brittany's ear.

Brittany's eyes got VERY wide Her breathing stopped. "Holy sh..." Finally: "What the..." *HOW the...* "fucking HELL!?! You SURE?!?"

Tabitha's bottom lip curled downward as she nodded curtly. Her eyes were suddenly wet.

Brittany jumped back, as she grabbed Tabitha's upper arms. "Holy fuckin' SHIT, Girl! You have GOT to TELL me about THAT!" She leaned in close, inquisitive. "WHO?!?"

Tabitha shook her head in regret. A habit, now. Tears were openly running down her swollen, temporarily-ruined face. Tabitha leaned in and whispered in Brittany's ear again.

"ABSOLUTELY NOT!!! He's like, a CHILD! How did you get him to put down his TONKA TRUCKS and CRAYONS long enough!?! Are you fucking KIDDING ME?!?" Brittany held Tabitha at arm's length again, shook her head with a startle, and then looked down at the girl's shirt-front with curious and skeptical eyes.

"I was MAD. And I wanted to see what you... What it was LIKE."

Hattie, who was working at the sink, had gotten very still. *Oh, dear.* All SORTS of alarm bells were going off in her head.

Brittany looked very closely at her friend's face, her one good eye. "Well?!?" She raised an eyebrow.

"Anyone older would be WAY too scratchy and...." She shrugged. "Not my thing. DAMMIT! The FIRST TIME I try something NEW I get totally FUCKED!!!!" Her grief and rage caused her to be nearly screaming as she stamped her foot.

They had both totally forgotten about Grandma Wendell, who was holding her breath and trying very hard to be invisible. It was the girl's kitchen, for the moment. Hattie felt she couldn't even be decent and move to a doorway, for fear that they would notice her.

"When?"

Tabitha said it plaintively, sadly, resignedly: "June. I... ahh... checked again a couple of days ago." She scrunched up her mouth in distaste. Her voice broke in a screech as she yelled, "It turned FUCKIN' BLUE AGAIN!" Tabitha started wailing: "Oh, Brittany, I'M GONNA HAVE A BABY!!" And she went to pieces right there, her body turned to liquid and she flowed down the front of a surprised and unprepared Brittany and onto the floor in a thump, sobbing and screaming in a way she hadn't since she was sixteen months old, the most recent time she'd had a problem so big and a vocabulary so woefully inadequate to articulate her pain and worry.

Brittany, standing over her friend, and Grandma Wendell, over at the sink, shared the briefest of looks for a micro-second, and then Brittany dropped to the floor behind her friend, rocking her back and forth in loving and enveloping arms, holding, rocking, holding, soothing, while Tabitha cried herself out.

Hattie sat down heavily in the nearest chair, there at the table.

Brittany called in sick to work that evening, the first time she had done that, by the way.

Hattie watched the girls go off to bed - *probably sharing one* - at eight. She didn't say anything. The worst that could happen HAD, and it was not a night for poor Tabitha to be alone. The old woman remained in the kitchen over a tepid cup of tea, shaking her head and trying to read the future.

Tabitha lay weeping in Brittany's arms until she finally exhausted herself into a dry-eyed sleep sometime after ten.

Brittany lay awake long afterwards, looking down at the cute and pretty and beautiful and precious living person in her embrace, a living thing that was now TWO. *Shit.* She was very confused.

That was when she started forgetting him.

***

Bruce showed up at Smiley's in his brand-new (to him) battered old sedan that he'd just purchased for six hundred dollars, eager to show Brittany his new investment and expecting to take her out to a midnight screening of some just-come-out Cops versus Bikers movie at the small campus theater. He'd arranged it before hand, gotten the key to the auditorium from a buddy, and had it all carefully planned out, right down to the popcorn-cart loaded and ready to plug in. They'd have the theater to themselves, since it was late. Who knew what kind of mischief they might get up to in that dark theater!

Huh. No Brittany at Smiley's.

Kathy sauntered over looking surprised. "She called in sick, poor girl. I figured YOU'D be over there, feeding her chicken soup or something!"

Bruce left, puzzled and a little hurt. Of course, he didn't have a phone number (just the dorm-phone at the end of the hallway, one payphone number for everyone). *She could have left a message for me at the diner, at least.* He frowned. No, he wasn't going to call the farmhouse at night. Or ever. Bruce wanted to live to see twenty-two - too many close close calls there already!

***

The girls came down early, lured into the kitchen once again by the smell of bacon and coffee. Just like old times. Hattie Wendell had left the swinging door to the front room and upstairs open so the smell would get up there to them. *Best not to lay around in your troubles.*

They both looked awful, physically. Like car-wreck survivors, or something. Hattie winced again, and pulled more peas out of the freezer as Tabitha went by. "It might help, still..." *Going to be eating a lot of those this week... maybe I should make Pea Pie....* She looked in a cupboard to see if she had canned salmon.

Tabitha was mostly back together, just a little bit mopey. Resigned, now. She had told someone. It was real.

Brittany wanted to firm up one concern, once she was sitting at that old kitchen table where perhaps generations of Wendell problems had been aired and solved. "So what are you going to DO?"

"I don't know." *Oh. OH!* Tabitha shuddered at some thought. "Oh, Brittany, I already TOLD you: I'm going to have... a baby. Oh, I am SO screwed!!!" Tabitha clenched her fists and looked beyond the ceiling to the Heavens.

Hattie Wendell gave a silent prayer of thanks - the alternative didn't bear contemplating, but she'd been worried - and then she set toast and bacon down in front of the girl. "That's how it usually happens, Tabitha. Who is the father?"

Brittany cut in. "You do NOT want to know, Grandma. It's not even legal." She shuddered. "Babies making babies."

"Oh, dear." Hattie frowned. "Shame on you!"

"I know, I KNOW! I WAS MAD!! I wasn't in my right mind." Tabitha squirmed in her chair - a physical manifestation of her mental state. "Shit. What am I gonna DOOOOO?!? I can't say it was the Immaculate Conception, I don't even go to CHURCH, and if people start thinking about it... I don't want to give birth in jail or reform school or whatever they do to sixteen-year-old girls who seduce younger boys."

Hattie turned around from the kitchen range. "Tabitha! Good gracious! Are you going to tell him?"

"I was MAD and I was trying something NEW in a non-threatening environment!!! No. I'm not going to tell him. And I hope he doesn't figure it out. I don't see any reason to saddle a ninth-grader with fatherhood."

"Oh, dear... That's wise, I think." Hattie paused. "I thought you said you didn't need The Talk."

"I didn't... exactly PLAN it."

Hattie Wendell could be hard when she thought the occasion deserved it. "No one ever does. That's no excuse for a little care. You have a WOMB, Tabitha, with a mind of its own."

"I KNOW that! Now."

Brittany sat very still through this exchange.

The kitchen became silent for a moment.

Very quietly, Brittany said, "You could tell people I'm the father." She smiled and continued with more conviction: "They'd get so busy thinking about THAT, they'd forget all about... the boy."

Brittany's grandmother looked over. "Are you sure you want to do that?"

"Why not? We're already the talk of the town. And in a way I AM. It's sort of my fault." Brittany looked at Tabitha. "If you hadn't seen... The Boy. At the Grange. I'm really, REALLY sorry, Tabitha. That was a STUPID place to go. I fathered the EVENTS that led up to it, sort of.... There!"

Hattie persisted: "I see where you're going with this, Dear, but being a father is a lot of responsibility. Tabitha, here," She laid her gentle hand on top of the now-mostly-reverted-to-red mop of hair and gave it a loving pat. "...is going to need a lot of help from the father. Who is it really, by the way?" She could be persistent.

"You DON'T want to know. And I don't think anyone should." Brittany lowered her voice. "Tabitha was a very BAD girl."

"I was MAD Goddammit! I wasn't thinking clearly and I was just ANGRY all the time and then I just got this FEELING and I wanted to fuck the first thing I saw. It made me feel better. For about a minute." Tabitha scowled down at the floor.

Grandma Wendell chuckled ruefully. "Oh dear, I just should have given you two the talk. Shame on me. Tabitha, you were OVULATING. Sometimes that happens. Your body led you exactly where it wanted to go. It CAN happen the very first time, and often DOES. Have you told your parents?"

Tabitha shook her head. She was tearing up again.

Brittany scooted away from the breakfast table and patted her leg. Tabitha hopped out of her chair, sat on Brittany's lap and buried her face in the other young woman's curly black hair.

Hattie Wendell sat down in Tabitha's now-vacant chair and started patting the girl's shoulder. "It will be ALRIGHT. It will be a BLESSING."

Brittany's hair started waving rhythmically - Tabitha was shaking her head back and forth in it, No! No! No!

"It will be a HARD blessing, but it will be wonderful. You'll see. You will be a YOUNG parent, and full of LIFE, and someday you'll be a young grandparent, still able to throw a football and whack a puck across the ice. It's NOT the END of your life, it's the BEGINNING of life." She still rubbed Tabitha's back, while the young woman shook with sobs. "And your parents will be fine... Didn't you say that your mother's biggest worry was that her little Girl-loving daughter would never give her grandchildren? Well, you've solved that."

Tabitha couldn't be consoled. The lump in Brittany's hair said a muffled, "But not NOW!" The last word became a screech as she sobbed again.

"They'll be fine. You'll see. They'll yell and scream for a day or two, just like you are now, and then they'll think it's the best thing that ever happened." Grandma Wendell sure hoped that was actually the case.

Brittany turned and kissed the most conveniently close part of the distraught person sitting on her lap, which happened to be an armpit. It didn't matter. "I really DO want to be the father. I DO love you, you know. Just not the way you want me to."

The red-haired head buried in Brittany's black cascade of curls started sobbing even harder.

***

Brittany gave Tabitha a ride back to the village shortly before noon, on her way to work. Tabitha wanted to hash some things out on the way down the Hollow Road.

"Brittany, where does this leave US?"

"Same as before? It worked."

"But you're DATING now! You still ARE, aren't you? That Bruce guy you couldn't shut up about?"

"And you're carrying around SOMEONE ELSE'S unborn child!"

Not much to say to that. Tabitha looked down, and then asked, very quietly: "You really want me to tell everyone you are the father?" She couldn't look up to meet Brittany's eye.

"Well, sure. Ya, why not?" Brittany smirked.

"This is SERIOUS, Britt!" Tabitha looked up now, sternly. "Are you going to BE THERE for me?"

"Of course. I know what you're asking. I will."

"I will, too. There. You're a father. Too bad we don't have a witness. Now, HOW in the HELL are you going to be in TWO PLACES, well THREE since you work so much, at once?!?" Tabitha was on the verge of tears again. Frustration. Helplessness. Loss. "And WHAT are you going to do when I want MORE from you than you're willing to GIVE to me, because you're with HIM?"

They came to the stop-sign at the bottom of the Hollow Road. Right to Tabitha's. Left to work. Brittany shut the car off, there at the intersection. "You got plans today?"

"Besides going home and moping about and trying to screw up the courage to talk to my mom? Nothing."

"You've got your books with you?" Tabitha was a reader. Brittany smiled inwardly. *Won't THIS be a switch!*

"What?!? Yah. So?"

"Come to work. Read your book. I'll buy you dinner. If you get bored you can steal my car and go home, just don't forget to pick me up later?"

"Really?"

"Really." Brittany started the car back up and turned left.

"What about HIM?"

"Yes, he comes in sometimes. He brings his schoolwork. He's partial to cheese sticks and apple pie. Says it reminds him of breakfast at the farmhouse. You know, when the team is up there. Yes, you two might end up eating dinner together while I work. Can you handle that?"

"Who are you going to go HOME with?"

"Nobody. I'll have him drive you home - he's a gentleman, don't worry - and I'll finally have the bed to myself! Actually, it's not like that. He and I don't... I told him I don't put out for College Boys."

Tabitha turned in her seat to get a good look at Brittany. "You went on at the mouth about him like that for MONTHS, you're actually DATING this guy, and you haven't even SLEPT with him?!"

Brittany started blushing. "Well, I didn't say THAT. We've slept together. Once. But nothing happened."

Tabitha was confused. "What?! WHY?" This went against just about everything she knew - well, thought she knew - about her friend.

Brittany continued: "I wanted to see if we're comfortable. Him and me. Without THAT."

"Were you?" Tabitha glared. "Comfortable?" She and Brittany fell asleep together all the time. They were Best Friends AND lovers. It was easy.

"Best sleep of my life."

Tabitha was crushed. Very quietly, she asked, "What about with me?"

"Well, girl, we've never spent the night together without making hanky-panky half of it, have we? And last night doesn't count. I was up half the night..." *worrying*. "Thinking." Brittany suddenly brightened. "We should try it sometime." Brittany winked. "If you can keep your hands off me."

Tabitha was still about two statements back in the conversation. "So this College Boy isn't... trying to get a piece?"

"Oh, he's TRYING! Less, lately. I think he's got something on the side. And I guess you're going to be MY something on the side. If you can deal with that." Brittany looked over at her friend, driving peripherally while she waited with raised eyebrows. Well?

"So let me get this straight: You two are DATING each other and FUCKING someone else? BOTH of you?" Tabitha found that idea incredible. Especially from Brittany, who up until this point had seemed to Tabitha like the Queen of quick and easy sex. Me, this boy, me, that boy, me again, another boy... "You are one fucked up Frieda." She said it almost in disgust.

"Well, I'm pretty sure HE has something on the side. I don't. Yet." Brittany was still waiting.

"If that's really what's going on, you two are perfect for each other." She sighed. "You're strange, Britt."

"That's what he says."

Tabitha panicked about two stoplights away, when she could see the big Smiley's face looming above the used car lots. "Brittany, you called in SICK last night, now you're showing up with BANDAGES all over your face and I've got a FAT LIP and one hell of a SHINER, what are they going to THINK and are you going to be in TROUBLE?!?"

"Oh, shit!" There was nothing to do at this point but make the turn, since they were there already. "You can chicken out and take the car back home, if you want. I say we just roll right in there together and park you at the counter and we'll see what happens. It's the first time I've bailed. It'll be okay…"

"You say so…"

Brittany parked and went around to hold Tabitha's door open.

"Game face, Tab."

"Face is too fucked up for that, thank you very much."

Smiley's was already busy. They got a lot of curious looks, and then everyone went back to what they were doing.

The Manager came forward and wanted a word with Brittany. She pointed at the ice cream counter and gave Tabitha a gentle push towards a stool. "Go over there and get some reading done." She winked.

Roger didn't miss that. "Come on back to the office, for a minute, Brittany." He closed the door behind them. He started talking as he turned away from the door, before he even crossed the room to sit down behind his desk. "I'll save you the story, though I'd find it fascinating, I'm sure." He sat. "You going to do this often?"

"Nope." Ooops. *He's got the whole thing.* "First and last time, I think."

"Good, because I waited tables half the night last night, and nobody tips a guy for shit, especially an OLD GUY, and the dish-room staff live on their cut of the tips, you know that. We have to be RELIABLE here, Brittany. I had somewhere else to be, actually, but instead I was HERE." *Hustling my ass for salary and* "...forking over two-dollar tips to my dishroom guys."

"I'm sorry. And I mean that."

"We won't have THIS particular conversation twice. You have everyone's number. If you're really sick, find a cover. Don't just call the restaurant."

"Yessir. Not sick much." She felt sick now, though.

"Good." Message received. Roger leaned back and relaxed. "Now: What did you do to your... What the hell happened to you? You two get in a car wreck on a wild night out or something?" *Sure looks like it.*

Brittany's eyes went wide. *Uh-oh. So maybe not. She steeled herself. Great, I've got to throw us under the bus. Here goes!* "Off the record?"

Oh, boy. He paused. "Sure." *He wasn't so sure, now.*

"REALLY off the record."

Uh-oh. He couldn't imagine where this was going. *Car wreck while running from the police? Fight at a party? Nod, nod.* "Let's have it." Now he NEEDED to know, officially. *Something is up....*

"We had a little tiff and I was bleeding a little too much to come to work and she was a wreck 'cause, well, she just... Nevermind. It won't happen again in a million years. I've got bills to pay, just like everyone else here." *More, now.*

They all say that. He actually believed Brittany, though. *Wait...* "Are you telling me that YOU TWO did this to each other?"

"Ayup."

"Then WHY is she HERE?"

"She's my best friend."

Oh. That makes sense. His jaw worked, but no words came out. Finally: "Bad judgement, Miss Wendell. I can't have any fighting here, or any domestics, or any hard feelings, or any soap operas. I've been giving you too much latitude around here, I'm afraid. She needs to leave."

Actually, Roger, and Brittany too, would be involved in a hell of a fight in the parking lot in a couple of years, and Brittany would bring up this evening's stern warning as the ambulance medics dabbed blood off their faces and checked their pupils and removed the other victims. She and Roger would laugh, as much as their injuries would let them, giddy with shock, relief and exhaustion, but it would be Morgue Humor -

inappropriate. It would not be a merry situation, that night far into the future.

Back here in the now Brittany stood up and put her hand on the doorknob. *Okay, goodbye, we're out of here, have a nice night waiting tables.* She breathed deep. Instead, she said, "Okay. She's gone. I'm going to go out there all smiley and talk with her for a sec so there's not a scene, is that alright?"

"Make it quick." He wasn't giving an inch. *Time to make sure she knows who is in charge*, although the 'not a scene' part sounded like a very good idea.

"Yes, Dad." *That always gets him.* She saw the corners of his mouth twitch. She opened the door the rest of the way, put on a bright smile and went over to the ice cream bar. She leaned in close beside her friend, and said very quietly: "Hey, girl, you're getting thrown out for kicking the shit out of their best waitress. No, no, it's OKAY. Here," She took some money out of a clutch from her little purse. "Here's forty bucks. Here's my keys. Go to that seedy motel right out back and get a room. Leave the car in front and the light on, so I know which one. I'll knock after work."

Tabitha scowled. "A room?"

"You two will be even. Go watch TeeVee. Read. I'll be over." She gave Tabitha a peck on the cheek and scurried off into the kitchen.

Tabitha stood, shell-shocked, feeling sucker-punched. There was some sort of manager-guy standing right there with his hands behind his back, obviously waiting for her to leave. *Shit. Whatafuckinday. Week. Month.* Tabitha rolled her eyes at the man and slipped out the door with her backpack containing overnight things and 1950's English tragic romance novels. *So I'm spending the night in a hotel room with Neville Shute. Who knew!*

Brittany came back out of the kitchen, putting on an apron. The kitchen staff, once they'd seen her face, had given her the benefit of the doubt. Somebody with that many bandages on must have been out for plastic surgery. Brittany strolled up to the manager and smiled. "I nearly walked out."

"I know. That would have been prideful and very stupid."

"I know."

A family came in. Brittany went to work.

Over the course of the evening five customers actually had the backbone to ask just what exactly had happened to her face. The rest of the customers just stared.

"This? THIS?" She pointed to her forehead or chin. "You should see the OTHER guy! Would you like fries with that?" Or, "He didn't SEEM that big, when I decided to steal his lunch.... Small, medium, or large shake with that?"

Brittany knocked at the motel door at ten-fifty p.m. "They let me split a couple of minutes early. I said I had a hot date waiting next door. Hungry?" She held out two Styrofoam boxes.

"Starving. Get your ass in here, this place gives me the creeps!"

"Well, ya, it's not as nice as the place I took Bruce, but it'll do. You two have both gotten me into a hotel room, now."

Tabitha glared, but then grabbed a box and sat on the bed. "VERY funny." She popped open the box and found a take-out order consisting of foodservice-quality pickles and two scoops of vanilla ice cream. "NOT funny." She held out the styro container. "This one's yours. What's in the other one?"

Brittany smiled. "A turkey Smiley-Melt and fries. I already ate. Sorry you had to wait. I'll put your dessert outside to keep cold."

"Don't bother. I'm not THAT pregnant yet." Tabitha looked around the room. "You have a strange idea of a date." Tabitha liked the farmhouse a lot more.

"Don't say I didn't try." Brittany looked at the room phone and hoped local calls were free. "We've got some calls to make. Why don't we do this the RIGHT way: You call your house and tell your parents that you're spending the night with me up at the farmhouse. I'll call Grandma and tell her I'm spending the night down in the village, at your house." She held out the phone.

"YOU are a hoot." Tabitha took the phone and dialed her own number. Her mother answered. "Hi, Mom. No, nothing... I'm not going to be home. No, actually I AM with her but NO, we're spending the night in sin at a sleezy hotel." Pause. "Really." Pause. "Over on the Strip, behind Smiley's." Pause. "Yah, that one." Pause. "We've already checked in." Pause. "No, I don't know what she's up to." Pause. "Yah, I'm sure. See you tomorrow morning." Pause. "Yah, you too... Bye." She hung up the phone, and turned to grin at Brittany:

"There! I'm getting her primed and ready for when I announce that you got me pregnant!"

Brittany took the phone. "Good idea." She dialed the farmhouse. "Hi, Grandma! Remember, you said I should call you if…" Pause. "Yep. Hotel." Pause. "Yes, but there I can't have a parade of boys and girls coming in and out at all hours, so I'll make less money…" Pause. "We will. All of us." Pause. "Thanks, Grandma, you too." She hung up.

"There. Done. Eat up."

Brittany watched late-night TeeVee while Tabitha ate. They sat side-by-side on the bed, knees touching, comfortable. Tabitha was asleep halfway through her sandwich. Brittany woke her back up, helped her sleepy friend undress, and tucked her into the bed. Brittany hopped in the shower for five minutes and then flopped in behind the sleeping-again Tabitha's form and put her arms around her. Tabitha stirred briefly, scooted up closer to the warm embrace behind her, and folded a leg around Brittany's. Brittany lay awake, thinking. For a long, long time.

***

Tabitha went home in a couple of days. She spent Sunday morning watching cartoons in the front room at her parent's house. She hadn't done that in years. She stayed in front of the tee-vee as noon-time programming took her to the savannahs of Africa. Early afternoon brought black-and-white re-runs of Sci-Fi adventures across the galaxy on a lost and wandering planet. She sat, staring vacantly, through a war movie. Boxing. She paid more attention to that, because every time her mind wandered, she'd see herself and Brittany on the TV, going at it in the ring with the big gloves on, instead of the two men who were really in the bout. *Pregnancy makes you hallucinate?*

She woke up to a gentle shake. Her mother was there. The windows were dark. Evening.

Her mother bent over her. "You stayed up a little too late partying the other night?" She smiled, but her mouth frowned at the corners. Concern. "You're awfully young to be starting down that road, don't you think?"

You have no idea. "It's not what you think. I'm sick" *to my stomach over being pregnant* "and not up to much today."

"Well, no, you don't look WELL. Maybe you shouldn't stay out so late?"

"Ya. Prob'ly not."

Her mother started to leave the room. She stopped in the doorway and looked back over her shoulder. "You could have her over here, you know, instead of running around to hotel rooms. We'll just say it's a pee-jay party and leave it at that, okay? We're pretty used to her, here, now." She giggled - not a sound she usually made - and continued her thought: "It's not like you're going to get pregnant or anything!"

Tabitha winced.

Her mother came back. "Are you SURE you're alright?" She peered down, close into Tabitha's face, concerned.

Tabitha met her mother's eyes with the one she could see out of. Her other eye was still swollen shut. "I'm fine, Mom." *Just Mourning Sickness.* "Thanks." *Mourning the life I imagined: Next schoolyear as a carefree Senior. Going to Junior Prom in a hot little dress and dancing with all the boys that will, just once. Summer jobs as a camp counselor... I was going to be the first girl player on a Men's Varsity college hockey team, dammit! I was going to meet girls. And women. I was Going Places. Dammit! I'm going to be barefoot and tied to a fucking CRIB by a LEASH!*

Now would be the time to say it. She was mad enough to. Just say it. Mom, something unexpected has happened. Mom, I really screwed up. Mom, I got In The Way. Mom, sit down. Mommy, I'm scared. Mom, can I keep it?

She never did say anything that evening, not when her mother came in to watch Sixty Minutes, not when both her parents sat down on the couch to catch the Sunday Night Movie at eight, not the next morning, not the next evening, not the next weekend.

***

Traffic and business seemed to conspire to put Paul Wendell in front of that larger-than-life display of his long-gone sister on a weekly basis.

Finally, the man couldn't take it anymore.

He called up the Night Office at a certain paper warehouse and made a request: "I need to borrow one of your Watchers. Personal business."

He hung up the phone and dialed a different number, also known by heart. "Ahh! Allo! Michaud! It's been a long time, no? I have a job for a private investigator, a real one, licensed in Vermont."

He felt better already. *At least I'll know.*

***

Tabitha's father noticed the shift in his daughter, and simply asked her mother about it. "She okay?"

"Something's up. Still Girl Trouble, maybe?"

The man rolled his eyes. *My daughter the hockey player* (that was okay) *and butch beaver-eater* (NOT so okay, but what are ya gonna do about Kids These Days), *all broken up over a girl!* But he put his hand on Tabitha's head while on his way back to the couch with a snack and he tousled her hair. "Kid." That's all he said, all he could say, and all he needed to say in the context of their relationship. *Maybe she'll meet a nice Boy.*

Tabitha stared at the TV and ignored the lingering Christmas decorations in the living room and broaching Valentine's day ads on network programming. She sighed. *I suppose I'll have to put a train around a Christmas tree in a few years.* She pondered The Problem. The Communication Problem. Somehow, every time Tabitha thought of the conversation she would have with her Mother, she suddenly pictured herself flat on her back in a doctor's office, her legs up in stirrups, a medical shop-vac pushed up between her legs - *in THERE. No!No!No!NO!NO!NO!*

Another evening, on the same couch, Tabitha woke from a stupor to jingle bells chir-chirring on the TeeVee. Some post-Christmas-season shopping ad. *WAY too cheery!* She looked around the living room, still sparkling with strands of Christmas lights that hadn't been taken down yet (her mother mistakenly thought the festive atmosphere might help her daughter's mood). "Happy Fucking New Year."

Her father opened his mouth to tell her to watch her language. His wife put a restraining hand on his arm and shook her head before he got a sound out.

Tabitha went up to bed clutching a ginger-ale halfway through the movie, sick to her stomach with grief and worry.

***

Bruce didn't consider himself a possessive guy, so he wasn't too troubled by Brittany's many commitments - known and unknown - at first. She was a working high-school student, he was a College Boy, a double-major, as well as a hockey player. So she'd missed a date...it was during her school vacation, so she should have been plenty free, and they'd agreed on it in advance.... And now he was back from New Year's school break and hockey tourneys and she was STILL scarce. But since he wasn't insecure, so *WHERE THE HELL WERE YOU FOR OUR PRE-ARRANGED DATE?* became: "Been busy?"

Brittany had just finished her shift at Smiley's and was coming out of the bathroom/locker-room.

The other employees didn't bother to chase Bruce out the door with the last of the customers anymore. They knew he'd go when Brittany did, sometimes after helping her wipe down tables if they were in a rush to get somewhere.

Roger had even put Bruce to work for cash this evening, for an after-theater rush that took the local Smiley's management (Roger) by surprise. "No one knows about this, but I'm in a real pinch tonight, and you DO seem to be part of the Smiley's family, don't you?" So Bruce put away his books and spend the night at the fry-o-lators and pots-and-pans sink, much to Brittany's amusement and approval. *Good, he's not afraid of a little work, and he inspires the confidence of Roger, too.* She nodded her head. *He's real.*

Bruce was less sure. She was still running out every night after their "date" at her workplace, with nary a minute in the parking lot.

On this evening, Brittany walked over and gave Bruce a warm kiss on the mouth. "Busy? Yep. You wouldn't believe." She ducked down a little as he helped her put on her coat. "Thankyou. Missed you, Brucie, over Christmas. Can't WAIT 'til summer, I know this great little ice-cream place that's open 'til MIDNIGHT, then we can have a REAL DATE after work!"

Versus two minutes in the parking lot. Bruce's attention was starting to wander. Again, he wondered about his infatuation with this girl of the green eyes. He couldn't figure out what he wanted, but he knew it was more than hurried minutes after work.

She grabbed his hand and they started walking to their cars. She imagined picking him up at his dorm regularly, now, on her way to Smileys.

They were in different places.

He was wondering if she was worth the effort. *We HAD a date... one you missed.* "A date... I TRIED, Bri. I had a movie all set up after work..." *Maybe she's got something on the side?*

"I KNOW." She stamped her foot as she walked, but didn't realize it. "I'm SORRY!"

He noticed. *WHAT is UP with this girl?* "Look: Could you at least call and leave a message at the dorm if you're going to bail? Or leave a message here?" He gestured out his arm at the giant Smiley's sign. "That's fair, eh?"

***

They were still talking about it after closing on the next night he visited. They picked up almost where they'd left off the previous night.

She'd called his dorm, as requested, but to arrange to pick him up. Bruce was pleasantly surprised and still game... for now. They left the restaurant and headed to the little green hot-rod at ten minutes after eleven, after wiping down tables, doing the floors, tidying up the counter, and getting the on-table ketchup bottles and napkin dispensers ready for the breakfast shift in seven short hours. Bruce had rolled up his sleeves as usual. The other waitstaff made up an extra bucket of soapy water for their new "helper."

Bruce felt like he was on the verge of accidentally picking up a job in the restaurant business. *Is she worth all this?*

Brittany opened the passenger door, closed it after him, then went around to her driver's door. *Ever the gentleman... Er, lady.* She replied to last week's argument as she got in: "Yes. You were right. And what I should have been doing. Calling, I mean." *I need to get an extension up to my bedroom, Pronto!* Of course, up there in the Hollow, it was still all Party Lines, so EVERYONE would know when she or he was bailing on a date, and THAT wasn't so good… Because everyone would know about the date in the first place. For some reason, Brittany still wanted to keep her moves private.

"And WHY can't I call YOU?" A grin spread across his face. "I looked up your number, well, your Grandma's, in the phone book…"

"You KNOW why you can't call." She started the car. "My grandmother would have BOTH our asses, College Boy." She kissed him, then put the car in gear and drove out onto the road. "I'm much too young to die."

Her grandmother was right, and he was bad news for her future, but his waters were pulling at hers, ever more forcefully, as they drove over snowy roads back towards Collegeville. Those rising tides pulled them towards their first fight.

Brittany could feel it. She changed the subject.

"You wanted to know what happened before Christmas. To my face." The bandages were still on, but smaller. She was following the Chief's prescription to the letter and then adding a couple of weeks to the instructions. She figured cops knew about fights.

Bruce had a pretty good idea what had happened, he'd seen them in the parking lot, but he was curious to hear what she'd say about it.

"I got in a fight, pretty much got my ass kicked by the smaller kid, but I got in a few licks of my own." There, that ought to change the subject.

"You and that redhead don't like each other very much, do you?"

Ooooops. News travels fast. "We have our moments."

"Will you come up to my dorm room?"

Whoah. "I'll have to think about that. A lot of prying eyes." *Grandma would kill me, and Dad might FIND me!* Walter Wendell was known to prowl the dorms at night sometimes. All the Academy staff did, on a rotation. *Wouldn't THAT be awkward! I'd be back home in the village with a lock on the bedroom door before I got my mouth open to say 'Hi Dad…'* She could sense the boy getting tense again. She looked over. "Bruce, I'd like that. It's… complicated." She sighed. "It's risky."

The car was quiet for a long time, until they were idling at the back of his dorm. Brittany looked over his shoulder as she went to kiss him and saw a pool table, right there in the basement. Salvation. She leaned in further, and whispered wetly in his ear: "Let's start with the BASEMENT of your dorm. I want to play pool."

So the lovebirds finally had another real date. Playing pool in the basement. Because all work and no play, while a good winnowing tactic, makes for a boring love story - especially for the boy in it. He still wasn't in it for the long term. Brittany was, but Bruce didn't know that. The Moment-with-a-capital-M at breakfast in the city was long passed for him.

Now billiards can be a very intimate game, what with a low table and frequent leaning and bending and various awkward angles at which the body ends up to make banked shots. Brittany wasn't very good at pool, but she WAS good at leaning and bending, so she put on quite a show in her tight, high-waisted jeans and clinging after-work sweater. She was a good-looking girl.

Bruce had started to entertain thoughts of finding greener pastures. This whole homework-and-dinner thing got boring, at some point. But now, after an hour of playing pool with Brittany, Bruce was once again entranced, for a little while at least. At twelve-thirty, Brittany threw the pool cue on the table, hopped up on a nearby washing machine, and said, "Okay, Brucie, now I'll live up to my new nickname. A little. Come over here and stand between my legs and kiss me, you big College-Boy stud!"

"YOU are a TEASE."

"Yes, but you'll keep coming back for more." She wrapped her legs around him to make sure he stayed put.

Yes, he decided, *yes I will.*

At one in the morning, Brittany left in a cloud of hot breath and car exhaust. She'd managed to keep her pants on. But *OH, I WANTED him!!* She could just FEEL her skin reaching for his, yearning to be against his hard muscles. She let conjugal thoughts rule for just a moment, now that it was safe, and growled out loud.

She didn't know that it was their waters calling, molecules of one reaching for the molecules of another. Two hydrogens and an oxygen, swirling, stretching atomic forces, forever trying to ensnare another molecule into their orbit, times a million squared molecules in the body.

Bruce went up a flight of stairs, out the front door of the dorm, and across the street to see if anyone was still awake over in one of the other dorms. Maybe somebody would take pity on him. *That Cynthia chick over in Paine Hall certainly seems accommodating...* His molecules were hotter, swirling faster, and less prone to settle down. But he knew he would keep going back to that diner, maybe until the end of his days. He shook his head, and then did a strange new thing: he stopped, turned around, and went back to his own square of brick.

***

Bruce was away the next two weekends, including Friday nights. Away games frequently competed for his attention.

Hattie Wendell wasn't fit company, because her Boys were on a losing streak. It would be whiskey on Sunday again, she feared.

Tabitha had Brittany's full attention. They did homework at the kitchen table in the farmhouse on a Saturday morning in late February. Brittany had gone down to the village for groceries and came back with milk, flour, bacon, yogurt, and a red-head, too. Hattie was glad enough to have company to cook for. Company distracted her from bad hockey.

"What time do you have to go over to work, Brittany?"

"Leave at two or so."

"You two going to want some lunch, then?"

"MMmmmm." (Brittany)

"You bet!" (Tabitha)

"I'll make some stew. No morning sickness yet, Tabitha?"

Tabitha looked up, with her pencil eraser at the corner of her mouth. "Well, sort of... Sometimes I don't eat breakfast, now. That seems to make it better. But I'm not throwing up, if that's what you mean!"

"Ah, you're one of the lucky ones! You're staring to get the glow, now, you know."

Brittany put down her own pencil and looked across the wide, polished maple boards of the table at her friend. Really looked, with new eyes. Tabitha certainly was! Glowing. *She looks absolutely BEAUTIFUL.* Suddenly Brittany wanted to jump her friend's bones right there at the big kitchen table. *Ah, Grandma, could you 'scuze us for forty minutes or so…* "You DO look pretty good right now, Tab. Wow. I thought you were doing more makeup to cover your eye. It isn't even that green under it any more. I'd…" *jump your bones right here.*

Tabitha blushed at all the attention.

Grandma Wendell explained: "The lucky ones get a real feeling of well-being from motherhood. Well, at least from being with-child. Good for the baby, too, I expect." She stopped chopping walnuts and apples and went over to the table to put a hand on Tabitha's head. "Feeling a wee bit better about all this, these days?"

"Yup. Haven't cried in about two weeks. Just feel… better. Can't help it." Tabitha stood up to go pour a cup of tea from the ever-boiling kettle on the wood-fired range. She knew her way around the kitchen now. "Baby, meh. Wonder if a stroller will fit through the classroom doors? Thinking of getting a big yellow smiley-face shirt to put on when I get fat." She shrugged, pondered the innards of a cabinet, and selected Earl Grey. "Weird thoughts, but happy."

"Have you told your folks?" Hattie knew the answer before she asked.

"WE'RE NOT GOING THERE." The happy glow was replaced by fierce determination.

Hattie chuckled, looked over at her granddaughter, and said, "I'd sure take that as a NO, wouldn't you?"

Brittany picked up her pencil and went back to work. "That's what it sounds like to me!" She worked on her notes, while at the same time asking, "You going to wait until they see the bump?"

"Something like that. Maybe longer." Tabitha sat back down at her homework. End of conversation.

"Make sure you tell them BEFORE you deliver, or they'll think you're just babysitting a very young customer for a really long time." Brittany giggled.

"DROP IT." Tabitha growled from between the pages of her textbook.

"Yes, Ma'am." Brittany bit her lip in mirth. Tabitha HATED Ma'am, and now that she would be a mother, she would be hearing it a lot.

Hattie went to stir the stew at the range-top. "Oh dear."

A bit later, as the three of them ate a nice lunch of celery-carrot-apple-venison-walnut stew and drop-biscuits, Tabitha realized there were some things she needed to know. She asked a few questions over lunch: "So how much am I supposed to eat, here, Grandma Wendell? Like a horse, for two, or like a bird, so I don't end up all big and bloaty?"

"I always just ate the same as I had been, maybe a little less as I got big. I was a very active girl, and when I got big and shut up in the house I ate less, because I was doing less. It was hard. Sometimes I didn't want to eat at all, and sometimes I wanted to eat everything in the kitchen and then make some more. I think it helps not to add too much weight, along with all the other changes to your body. But you don't want to starve your child, either. Just keep things normal, if you can, by force of will."

"Will it hurt? As I stretch out?"

"It's gradual. Your back will hurt to high heaven, though." A thought occurred to Hattie: "Have you been to a doctor?"

Tabitha paled.

"No, huh?" Grandma Wendell turned to Brittany. "Well, you're the father. Do the right thing and bring her to the doctor. She's young. She should go. Soon." She went back to stirring a pot of bubbling corn gruel that would go into pudding later.

Brittany put down her yellow Number Two-and-One-Half pencil again. "Can you tell, yet?"

Tabitha smiled a wet sort of smile. "I think I can. I'm poofy down there, but it's hard in the middle. Like on your period. But all the time. And I'm definitely stretching even my new jeans a little."

Tabitha and Brittany had taken a trip down to the Junction to shop for stretch-jeans for the expecting mother, one and two sizes larger than usual.

Tabitha tugged at the waistline of the latest pair of jeans - unbuttoned - to get more room, and then pulled her shirt down over the problem. "New clothes for me, soon, I think." She pondered. "I've never really been the rah-rah type, but I think school-themed sweats are in my future soon. Trouble when I bend over." She grinned. "And - 'Scuze me Grandma Wendell - and I'm... HORNY. Like... I feel something down there and I want MORE. I don't know. I can't describe it. But I'm definitely swelling out a bump, and..." She frowned. "Thirsting for someone to make the next one?" She looked down at the womb that was suddenly running her life. "This is some weird shit."

Brittany was coming up out of her chair. "Can I feel?"

"Sure." Tabitha took off her sweater as she stood up.

Hattie Wendell had another sudden thought. "Tabitha, you're not still playing hockey, are you?" She was afraid of the answer.

"No, Ma'am. Too much chance of a fall." Tabitha's hand went instinctively to a spot just below her belly-button, a spot that sloped in now, because now her belly was ahead of the rest of her just a tiny bit. Tabitha probably didn't even know she'd put a hand there.

Hattie and her granddaughter shared a look and raised eyebrows. *Cupping her belly like a mother... she'll start to show soon, extra clothes and jackets or not.*

Brittany, out of sight behind Tabitha, nodded, already feeling the plump hardness of a perfect ball shape that was new.

Wow. THAT one giving up hockey. "That must have been hard, Dear." Hattie couldn't remember a winter where that red-headed tomboy hadn't been out on the ice roughing it up with the boys, or more often, skating through and under and around them. "Giving up the ice."

Tabitha stood proudly as Brittany explored. "Not as hard as regret would be." She added, hurriedly, "I mean, I don't WANT a baby. But since I'm... I can't explain it."

Brittany, from behind, suggested, "You've had your cry and now you're getting on with it and don't want to have all that grief for nothing." She measured Tabitha's new waist with her hands, nodded, and went back to exploring with a frown.

Hattie remembered other such days in this kitchen, quiet and intimate and private. Her twelve-years-gone husband. Many decades ago, a first child, lost just days after birth. The stab of fear that hit, fainter and faded now, but hitting still, as she remembered Paul in her belly. Phillip. Walter. And then Suzy, gone twenty-some years now. Their father placing a curious hand on her oven, just for a moment, here and there and always in private. *Being felt up is so much more... PUBLIC now. What strange changes to the world.*

Brittany stood behind her friend and ran her hands gently up and down the young woman's belly. She went lower. Then higher.

Brittany's eyes got big. "YOU are DEFINITELY different!" She went around front to give Tabitha a hug, then held her at arm's length. "Tabitha! You're going to have a BABY!" Brittany smiled from ear-to-ear and then burst into tears.

Hattie turned, shaking a wooden spoon in her hand. "Don't get TOO excited, girl! ONE of you at a time is quite enough. And make sure you take her to see a doctor. I mean it! You wanted first pregnancies to be monitored, even in the old days." She shook the spoon again. "A lot can happen." Hattie looked pointedly at Brittany. "Make her go. Please."

Brittany shrugged. *I'll try.* She looked up at the clock. "I've got to get ready for work. Come up with me."

The girls left the kitchen.

Hattie stirred the remains of the stew pensively. A little while later she heard water running in the tub. Splashing. Giggling. Those girls. Well, at least she didn't have to worry over whether she should go up there and put a stop to it. *Someone is already pregnant.*

"Come to work?" Brittany lay up against the end of the tub, holding Tabitha's womb with one hand and working over the suds in the short, red hair in front of her with the fingers of the other hand. Tabitha being pregnant was making Brittany feel very… affectionate. "GOD, I love this!"

NOT something either of them had expected.

Tabitha certainly didn't mind, though! "Maybe I should have got knocked up a year ago, then all this BOY STUFF wouldn't have happened!" She frowned and switched topics: "So I can get thrown out again?"

"Well, neither one of us LOOKS like we've been in a fight anymore. If that happens, take my car home. Come back and get me at ten-thirty or so."

Tabitha looked back over her shoulder, mouth open, eyes still shut because of the shampoo. Brittany leaned forward, over Tabitha's back, and kissed the edge of those upturned lips for a moment.

Aaahhhh! "I've missed this." Tabitha pulled away, smiled, and turned back forward. "Stay in town tonight?" She rubbed at soap running down into her still-closed eyes. "Rinse me."

Brittany pushed her friend down into the water between her legs.

Tabitha came back up. "Spspsppspppppppththhheeeewww!" She wiped suds off her face with the back of her hand. "Even got a fancy-dancy modern shower there and everything! Although... I really do like this!"

Brittany giggled. "I'll bet you do. Alright. What about your folks?"

"Mom's figured us out. She said I should have you to the house, instead of wasting money on a hotel room. She likes you. Anyways, like I said... We have to prime them for taking it at face value that YOU are the father!"

"True..." Brittany pondered this. "Alright. Let's switch. Time to do my hair."

When they were settled in the tub again, and Tabitha was running her fingers through the sudsy black hair in front of her, Brittany steeled herself and spoke: "I'm still seeing him."

Tabitha's fingers paused. "I know."

"I don't want you to get hurt."

"I know."

Tabitha shoved her friend under the water for a little rinse, and debated holding there for just a little too long. *I've heard about that*: Sometimes pregnancy made a woman homicidal.

***

Tabitha did homework at the ice cream bar while Brittany waited tables. The visit was uneventful, other than a few curious looks from regular customers who were used to seeing Bruce there.

And then there was Roger, the manager. He came out front at one point, saw Tabitha there, and he looked curious, alright. Maybe a little angry.

Tabitha's head retreated down into the high neck of her hoodie as she made a turtle-like effort to disappear. Retreat failing, she colored and focused on her schoolwork with renewed and business-like effort.

Roger turned and looked pointedly at Brittany.

Brittany shrugged, as much as she was able to while holding a tray full of Smiley Specials. She kept working.

Roger retreated to his office, where he looked to the ceiling, threw up his hands and shook his head.

Later in the evening, as they passed in the wide corridor to the kitchen, Roger eyed Brittany on his way by. "This is a switch."

Brittany smiled an enigmatic smile, but didn't say anything. *If you only knew.*

***

The girls called in sick to school on a Monday a couple of weeks later.

They spent the Sunday night before that nervous morning at the farmhouse - Grandma Wendell was more than happy to help them along in this particular chore. That following morning, when they should have been in school, Brittany instead drove them an hour north into the next county. More privacy there. Fewer nosey maybe-neighbors and distant relatives.

The appointment started well, and in good company - a lot of young mothers in the waiting room at this small hospital. Some of the women had little children in tow, and there was nobody in the room that either Brittany or Tabitha recognized.

Tabitha endured forty minutes of anxious waiting.

Brittany flip-flopped between mild amusement and fascination with their errand and their surroundings. She couldn't figure out why her friend was so WORKED UP over a simple doctor's visit. She did her best to console, rubbing Tabitha's back with her hand while she looked right and left at the other mothers, parents who were tending to children on laps or at feet. She wondered what that would be like.

Tabitha kept imagining a gothic-looking torture device in the middle of a room, with waiting straps and a tray of sharp knives close beside.

The examination room they were eventually led to did have a table in the middle of it, but there were no black iron stirrups and no surgical instruments at the ready. Tabitha's quivering ebbed, a little. The Prep-Nurse took her blood pressure - twice - frowned, took her other vitals, and then pulled the door shut as she left the two young women in the room. "Doctor Senesac will be just a few minutes…"

After a wait that seemed interminable to Tabitha, the door opened. A business-like, middle-aged doctor came flitting into the room. Tabitha scrutinized the yellow lab coat, long black hair twisted into a messy bun, and high heels with little yellow bows on them. *She doesn't SEEM like a killer….*

Doctor Senesac walked by the heavy swiveling doctor's chair and sat down on the visitor chair next to the desk. "Hello, I'm Doctor Senesac. Rebecca." She leaned forward, put her elbows on her knees, and looked up expectantly at the two girls. *There's a story of some kind here, and not the usual one… I can see it already.*

Brittany and Tabitha sat side-by-side on the examination table with its paper cover, the two girls leaning in together for support, one of them pale and glowing and the other patting her friend's hand and looking very serious. They remained mute - Tabitha was scared speechless and Brittany, uncharacteristically, didn't know what to say.

Hmmm. "So what's going on? Cash visit for a gyno exam. We don't normally do two at once, but okay, who's first?"

Tabitha remained unmoved.

Brittany decided to just say it. *Everything will be easier afterwards.* "My friend here… Was told she should see a Gyno. She's…" She felt Tabitha shrink beneath her encompassing, comforting arm.

"Oh! That's easy enough!" The woman stood up, twirled in a swirl of yellow fabric, and reached down into a drawer. She came up holding a pair of stirrups that she dropped into slots in the end of the table.

"NOOOOOooooo!!!"

Tabitha was already trying to scoot backwards off the end of the table and Brittany was off it and onto her feet, right there beside her distressed friend, trying to comfort her somehow. It wasn't working.

The woman in yellow came over to Tabitha's other side. "What is it, Sweetie? You're SAFE here. No one's going to hurt you." She looked across Tabitha at Brittany while she asked, "What are you so scared of?"

Tabitha buried her head in Brittany's front. She put out a trembling hand and pointed blindly towards the end of the examination table. "I don't WANT an ABORTION!"

Doctor Senesac got it. Right away. *Some jackass old cod of a school nurse has shown that fucking abortion film in the girls-only sex-ed class*, the one where you see a woman's feet writhing in the stirrups as she is "butchered" in the most graphic way possible. *They must have used two gallons of cow's blood on the sheet between the woman's legs.* A propaganda film from another time. *And they're still showing the fucking thing in school!* The yellow dress swished and fanned as Doctor Senesac hurried to draw the black iron stirrups back out of the slots. The design hadn't changed since the thirties, she was sure. *Perfect prop for that film.* She dropped them noisily in a drawer and slammed it shut. She picked up the phone on the desk. "Yes, Hi. Push everything off two. That? Cancel it, the woman's a… She'll reschedule, trust me. Thanks." She went over to Tabitha, who was crying on the paper sheet. "They're gone. You're safe here." She hopped backwards up onto the exam table beside Tabitha, then put her arm around her. "When you can, why don't you tell me about it."

Brittany looked up. "She's in... pregnant." Her breath caught. She'd just had a light-bulb. "Is THAT why you won't tell your Mom?"

The little mop of hair in her arms nodded up and down.

Ah.

Doctor Senesac's eyes went wide. *Oh! There's the story! That poor girl!* She rubbed and patted the poor young woman's back. *Part of it…. Time to get to work on that part I can help with.*

Tabitha calmed down, eventually. The doctor was careful, gentle, and slow. She took the blood pressure again. Did a routine physical and history exam. Did a more careful and focused exam related to the pregnancy. Everything was fine. Rebecca thought Tabitha was somewhere around eighteen or twenty weeks, now, "But it sounds like you'd know better exactly how far along you are…" *Wow, she doesn't look it, yet….* She tested Tabitha for a spectrum of STD's, just in case, although it was "Not likely, from the sounds of it, but you never know, and you should catch it early." The doctor in the yellow dress and bows gave them a bunch of pamphlets to read through, and then a gentle lecture: "I would STRONGLY encourage you to have a talk with your parents, but that's up to you. When you get to twenty-four weeks, that's six months, you're home-free, if you really want to go about it this way, if they haven't figured it out already. NOBODY around here does third trimester abortions. But you should really talk with your parents long before that." She frowned. "Do you have an adult, one who's had babies, who you feel comfortable talking with?"

Brittany spoke up. "My grandmother. Tabitha practically lives up there with us, weekends."

"Good. You're going to need her. Tell your own mother as soon as you can. You're going to need her, too. She might take it better than you think. Come back in four weeks. That puts you at six months." *Hopefully, you and your mother have had a little talk by then.* "We'll see you monthly, or even every two weeks, after that. You're young and this is a first pregnancy." She was also somewhat worried about Tabitha's small stature and shape. Physically, the girl wasn't as far along as she'd like. "CALL or COME BACK if you have any questions or problems. Okay?"

Tabitha nodded. She was still being kind of quiet today. *A lot to think about, this bun in the oven.* And she had a life to protect.

Doctor Senesac turned to Brittany. "Thankyou for bringing her down. Take good care of her." She gave Tabitha a hug and a supportive "I'm so happy for you!" and then sent them on their way.

Tabitha left the appointment feeling just the tiniest bit calmer, but suddenly shell-shocked by all the new information she had. And still worried. *I only have to hide this for a month or four now....*

Chapter Eleven

For the rest of that winter, Bruce and Brittany played pool at least once a week after their improvised dinner dates at Smiley's. The games were shorter, as Brittany's long hours were starting to catch up with her. But the table-top contests were fun and flirty and she was keeping his attention. There was one other thing - there was ALWAYS kissing on that washing machine afterwards. Brittany didn't think she could wait much longer. *Having a pregnant friend is DEFINITELY making me horny as a spring-time frog!* Brittany was learning some new things about herself, courtesy of Tabitha's condition.

She ditched school one afternoon in the late winter, so she could visit Doctor Senesac, just to make sure there wouldn't be TWO of them pregnant. *Just in case I lose my head.*

***

Three hours to the north, in a much busier and more cosmopolitan place, a Secretary-slash-Personal-Assistant stuck her head into her boss's office. "Someone from the Prentice Agency on the line for you... an investigator?"

Paul Wendell waved his hand as if at a fly. *I'll get to it in a minute.* That man would stay on hold for a customer from this organization. (Actually, though he wouldn't admit it to himself, it was dread that caused the wait. He needed a moment to steel himself.)

"...And Fidelity Labrador Bank is on line three?" The woman raised her hem to a flirty level and twirled a full circle as she said, "It's something about the new cash machine out in front, I think." *He's not even looking at me.* She'd picked the short wool skirt and a tight sweater that Paul used to really like - clothing that she worked really hard to stay in shape to wear. *I used to have that man's undivided attention when I was on his tables half the night...*

"Tell Fidelity I'll call them this afternoon. I've got to take this other call right now."

"Oh - " The assistant shook her head and stuck her blonde curls back around the corner again. "Your daughter stopped by."

"Yes, yes." He waved his hand again. "She's up on a school break."

His sometimes-mistress smirked and her dimples pulled deep as her eyes flared in merriment. "She asked for an application."

"WHAT?!" Paul Wendell's chair screeched on the floor. This woman had his exclusive focus now. "She..." *No.* "What did you say?"

The woman shrugged and pointed at the phone blinking away on Paul's massive mahogany and Verde Antique serpentine desktop. "She wants a job."

Paul waved away the figurative fly again. "A job? Here!?" He closed his eyes and shook his head. *She can't be serious. She wants another four years at some OTHER school* (Cynthia had a degree from McGill and most of another one from that military school in Vermont that happened to be located in his very hometown) *and she thinks I won't pay for it* (he couldn't, not anymore, she'd used up that cash cow) *and so she's putting the screws to me to make sure she gets what she wants.... Where NOW?* Paul contemplated the complications of a commercial loan from an actual bank, the normal way that parents paid for a too-expensive college. "She probably wants to see some OTHER country for four years." He waved his hand dismissively again. "Put her off." He turned to the blinking phone and sighed. He was afraid he already knew the answer the phone would provide. *My problems seemed to be multiplying.*

***

It had to happen eventually. Tabitha went to work with Brittany, and Bruce just happened to show up that same Wednesday night. Bearing roses. Valentine's Day evening, after all.

Whups. Forgot about that! Shit. Brittany sighed inwardly. *Too effin' busy!* She shrugged and put on a wide smile. *This will be interesting!* She rushed over, met him at the door with a kiss on the cheek, and seated him right there at the dessert counter next to Tabitha. "Bruce, Tabitha. Tabitha, Bruce." She whirled away and went back to work out on the busy floor. Everyone stopping by for a quick dinner before their movie-date made for two busy rushes at Smiley's. Brittany wouldn't have very much time for these two tonight. *Maybe it's for the best.*

Bruce scowled briefly in confusion. *Isn't this the little bitchy one that keeps getting pissed off whenever Brittany comes around?* He turned sideways to get her full measure. *A tiny little thing, but angry!* "You're the same one from the Grange, right?" It just popped out. He hadn't realized he'd said it until...

Tabitha answered curtly: "Yep." She was having a hard time. *The competition.* Here and in the flesh. She thought of just hopping off the stool and ripping off her bulky sweatshirt. *Your Brittany did THIS to me, after a fashion, and she's MINE now!* Instead, she went back to her homework, stewing and ignoring him.

"You certainly are moody. Pleased to meet you. I think." He dug out a textbook: CRIMINAL PROCEDURE.

Tabitha looked down at her belly, hidden under the big green hoodie, and cringed.

Brittany swooped by a while later to dump a large platter unceremoniously on the counter between them. Mozzarella sticks, apple pie (two slices) with ice cream on top, and pickles on the side. She turned to the side and kissed Tabitha on the ear, then to the other side to give Bruce's ear a nibble.

Bruce recovered from his thrill - that girl could pull his testicles up to his neck sometimes - and frowned. *That was weird. What the fuck?* Brittany was already gone.

Tabitha cracked the tiniest of smiles. *That BITCH! Fuck'n pickles and ice cream again, she keeps working it in!* They WERE good. Crunch. Brittany kept a stash of real cured-in-the-jar pickles back there somewhere in one of the commercial refrigerators.

Bruce grabbed a mozzarella stick, used a fork to peel the ice cream and top crust off a slice of pie, and dipped his fried cheese into the pie filling. He pushed the pile of vanilla ice cream over towards the redhead's side of the plate.

They studied and grazed for a while, silent.

Finally, Tabitha spoke: "You Canadians are strange. I've never seen anyone do that with deep-fried cheese before."

"I don't think it's a Canadian thing. It's the closest she can get me to pie and cheese, like at the farmhouse, eh? I don't know why I dip it."

"Freudian."

"Huh?"

"You want to dip HER, but you can't so in your frustration you dip a stick into the nearest pie you can find."

Ouch. "Well, if you say so. Are you two friends?"

"Yep."

"Then why were you beating the" he leaned in close, over the platter, and hissed quietly, "SHIT out of each other downtown a couple of months ago?"

A voice, right behind them: "Yes, why were we?" Brittany stood there, looking at Tabitha, awaiting an answer.

Tabitha didn't seem to be able to remember. "Probably over a boy or something stupid like that."

Brittany put two coffees down on the counter and scurried away to the kitchen.

Roger called her into his office as she went by. "Got a sec, Brittany?" He shut the door. "Kitchen's got your orders, right?"

Uh-oh.

He sat back down, leaned back until the chair was sure to dump him, and put his hands behind his head. "Why do I feel like there's a volcano simmering out there at the ice cream counter?"

Well, he does work with people. A lot. Brittany met his eye and then started laughing. "You KNOW, don't you?" *The whole damn shebang, he's finally got it now!*

"I know you're playing with fire."

"Tell me about it. You don't know the HALF of it." She sat down in the cheap metal folding chair by the door and leaned forward. "Can I TRUST you?"

Roger stayed quiet, an amused and patient expression on his face. *Let's hear it.*

"She's pregnant. You're like the fourth person to know."

"Yours?" He said it straight-faced, but he couldn't keep the sparkle out of his eyes, or his voice.

"As a matter of fact, yes, mine." Brittany groaned. "What the fuck am I going to DO?"

"You want it both ways." Roger sat forward.

"Yep."

"Can't no one have it both ways, Brittany. The train going down two tracks ALWAYS derails. Have fun while it lasts, but please, don't let me come out of here and see a brawl at the ice cream counter. You're a good kid. You just got the bandages off from last time. I'd hate to fire you over trouble."

"Yep." *I'd hate that, too.*

"Good luck." He got up to open the door. "My lips are sealed."

He followed Brittany out front. He was worried he'd see a hockey player with a fist-full of red hair and broken china all over, with customers scrambling for the exit....

Roger needn't have worried. They were both sitting at the counter, stoically doing homework, his from college with slightly thicker and denser textbooks, hers from high school with the thinner and well-illustrated textbooks with larger print. Each reached blindly for nearby coffee cups and munchies from the plate. Roger watched for a moment. *Not showing yet, but then again, she's bundled up. Pickles and ice cream... her request, or Brittany's joke?* He saw the redhead turn and regard the boy with expressionless eyes. Roger shrugged and went on to other matters. *They aren't killing each other yet.* Maybe the young man would turn out to be a polygamist and it would work out for the three of them. *Hmph! Hardly likely!*

Brittany visited both of them one more time, to take away the plate. Other than that she left them there together, to their own devices. *Sink or swim!*

At quarter to eleven she hopped up on a stool next to Bruce. "Would you mind taking Tabitha home?"

"What? Sure. I..." He turned. "Where do you live?"

"In the village. About four blocks from your dorm, I think." Tabitha wasn't icy to him anymore, at least.

They both asked the question at the same time:

"Where are YOU going?" (Bruce)

"What about YOU?" (Tabitha)

"Me?" Brittany smiled sweetly. "I'm going home and going to bed. These late nights are killing me. See you in school, tomorrow, Tab." With that, she was gone - out the door and into the night.

Tabitha and Bruce still had to pick up their books. They went uncomfortably out the door and into the parking lot together a few minutes later.

Tabitha stopped and looked around. "Which car?"

The rust-bucket with the "Ontario plates." Bruce was still self-conscious about his bargain-basement used car, purchased on a quick trip home with Scotty, and bought specifically for trips over to this diner.

"Oh. Makes sense." *Whups.*

"You don't have to be nervous. I don't bite, and I don't Put Out, either."

Tabitha laughed - a little longer and heartier than the idle remark deserved, perhaps. *If you only knew.* "Oh, I am SO relieved." She climbed into the rusty old sedan. *In three or four months you'd be counting back the weeks, trying to figure out how you'd become a father so quickly!* She grinned. "This is strange."

"I'll say, eh? But she's a strange girl, so we should expect it."

"You got that right..."

The car had to warm up to defrost the windshield. It was a big old engine, loose and slow to warm, so they had time to talk.

Tabitha referenced one of his now-packed-up textbooks: "CRIMINAL PROCEDURE. You going to be a lawyer?"

"I used to think I was going to be a hockey player. Or a businessman. Now I think I'll probably be a cop. Break up fights in parking lots, that kind of thing."

"Very funny." Tabitha was warming up to him. *He SEEMS nice.*

"Were you two fighting over who gets ME?"

Tabitha laughed hysterically, a prolonged storm of mirth that left her holding her belly. When she could speak again, she tried to be honest: "Well, we were fighting over you, yes, after a fashion. But don't read too much into it, you'll get it all wrong."

The car was finally showing some heat around the bottom edges of the windshield. Bruce pulled out of the parking lot. He looked sideways at Tabitha as he drove. "I really like her, you know. What little I know about her. Your friend is one-of-a-kind."

"THAT I know. And she really likes you a lot. More than you know." *Or she'd never have dumped ME for YOU.*

"Really?" Bruce's chest swelled under his jacket. "Sometimes I can't tell WHAT is going on in that head of hers."

"That's a common problem."

***

Brittany waited eagerly at their shared lab bench in the Biology room the next morning.

Tabitha came through the door, her face all soft and radiant and her NHL sweatshirt - an XL-boy's, over a puffy hoodie - hanging almost to her knees, like a skirt. "I think I've invented a new style." She pulled up the bottom edge of the sweatshirt and flashed Brittany a view of her hips. "Leggings. Stretchy. Very comfortable."

Brittany gave her friend a thumbs-up. "That will cover... STYLE ISSUES for quite some time." She changed subjects quickly, because she was eager to know: "So? Whadyathink?"

"I think you like living dangerously." Tabitha scowled, but her eyes were merry.

"Someone else said that, recently. Not him. So, did the ride home go okay?"

Tabitha smirked. "He's a real gentleman, eh?"

"He can't help it, he's Canadian." Brittany leaned in. "Did he try to put any moves on you at all?"

"No. But I sure wanted to put some on HIM. I don't even LIKE boys, and I thought he was FINE. I see why you're having a hard time." Tabitha put her bookbag up on the table and pulled out her notebook. She sat down, opened the notebook, and said, primly: "Don't leave me alone around him again. I'm…" She leaned in, dropped her voice and made it sound husky to continue: "In A Way and horny as all hell and I might jump his bones just for the heck of it." She sat back up straight. "They say you can't dent a baby until the third trimester."

"TABITHA!" Brittany was genuinely shocked. By a lot of things she'd just heard.

The whole class turned around to look at them. The teacher, already up at the blackboard, gave Brittany Wendell his sternest stare.

Brittany pulled out her own notebook and hissed, "Don't you DARE."

***

A week later, Tabitha and Bruce met at the ice cream counter again.

Brittany had picked up Bruce on her way to work, and then Tabitha came into Smileys not long after he got settled.

Whups! Brittany winced.

Roger watched with some amount of dismay as Brittany put the money into the register and ring up two "specials" for the counter. He watched for a beat longer than was polite, then made a decision to move on to more pressing things. On his way by Brittany, Roger asked, "How big is this harem of yours?" And later: "Are we going to have to make the counter longer?" He smiled, though. The ice cream counter rarely filled up on a weekday evening, *and the two who seem to frequent it aren't killing each other. Yet.*

Tabitha and Bruce did schoolwork and Brittany waited tables. It was a slow night, early in the week, but Brittany avoided her suitors by keeping busy with spot-cleaning and being extra-engaging with the few customers that came through.

Brittany, purse already over her shoulder, settled the matter of after-work company and transportation at the front door, quite simply: "Have a nice drive, you two!" And then she was gone, out into the night, by herself.

Roger looked on in amusement.

On the way home, Bruce sat back on the big bench seat in Tabitha's car and wondered exactly what was going on. *Is Bri having her friend screen me? Test me?* The corners of his mouth went up... *SHARE me?* The redhead was being quiet tonight. He turned sideways to face his driver. "Do you fight with ALL your friends, eh?"

"No…" *What friends?* Tabitha had a little case of the self-pities going on, which is why she'd stalked Brittany to the diner. "Just her."

"HHmmmmmmmm." He scowled. *Something to think about there, eh?*

***

Over the next few weeks, Tabitha was up at the farmhouse as much as she was at home. Brittany had cut her work schedule back - she was off on Fridays and Wednesdays, too, and was picking up afternoon and evening weekend shifts where they were available. She was trying to keep some balance between Now and Future, as best she could. Bruce knew she was off on Fridays. Tabitha knew she was off on Wednesdays. Nobody knew everything except her. Each of her friends had an evening all their own, and one or two they had to share. At some point in there, Brittany realized she didn't have an evening of her own. *Well, I don't really need to....*

Hattie Wendell got used to having an overnight guest sometimes mid-week or Saturday night, and almost always on Sunday evening. She had given up on any sort of propriety or appearances. Soon enough there would be much more to talk about than Those Two nearly living here together, and about a minute after that their lives would take very different turns! Brittany off to college in a year and a half or so, Tabitha to motherhood and playgrounds and pre-schools and Reading Day at the library.

Sylvia dropped by frequently and regardless of the hockey schedule. She watched the bustling and growing household with amusement. Sylvia was of the opinion that times were more open-minded, and as long as their grades didn't suffer, maybe the two young women were setting a good example, committed relationships and all that.

If you only knew! Hattie had some suspicions and once again thanked her lucky stars that Brittany hadn't developed this close type of overnight relationship with a boy. THAT would have been much more sticky, and she would have had to put down her foot. Early.

Brittany and Tabitha often sat side-by-side in the front room, doing homework by lantern-light, Brittany with her hand extended and resting on Tabitha's stomach. Brittany was apparently waiting for the first kicks.

Tabitha was suddenly getting bigger by leaps and bounds. Her swelling was now protruding - round like a ball and pushing her belly-button straight out in front. She'd taken to wearing loose men's oxfords with the tails un-tucked, big bulky wool sweaters, and she'd also swiped her father's heavy woolen hunting jacket to wear over all of that.

Hattie worried that by Spring, the girl would be suffering heatstroke. "Shouldn't you say something to your folks, now, maybe…?"

Tabitha shrugged. "They'll figure it out in about three more months. No sense in hurrying it."

Brittany teased her about the clothing, sometimes. "You little plaid woodchuck! Next you'll be barefoot and toothless and forget how to read."

"THAT isn't funny!" Sometimes Tabitha had a quick retort: "And you'll be wearing greasy wife-beater T-shirts and watching football on the teevee and, oh, by the way, passing out CIGARS in June!"

Brittany continued to take her friend into the upstairs bathroom sometimes, to give her a nice long soak-and-scrub in the tub. It helped take the pressure off the poor girl's back, and it was hard for her to reach all the way down to wash anything below her knees by herself. Brittany loved to lounge on her bed after these baths, with her head in Tabitha's lap - nestled up against the young woman's womb. There was a little life in there! *Sometime any minute I'm going to feel it MOVE!*

Brittany started to think about motherhood. A lot.

Her grandmother could see it. "Now don't you go getting any ideas. And WHY are your BREASTS filling out all of a sudden, Brittany?" She scowled with her hands on her hips and watched as Brittany bent to put a plate of beans and ham in front of Tabitha. Hattie's eyes narrowed as she appraised the young woman's shirt-front while it swayed back and forth before she straightened back up. "Don't tell me YOU'VE got a bun in the oven, too?"

"Don't worry, Grandma. I'm on the Pill. It does that." She looked down. "Fringe benefit for the boys, I suppose…"

"That's a relief. I think." She thought for a moment, and skeptically regarded the two young women in the kitchen with her. "Or maybe not." She looked at Brittany and saw… *something is different.* "But your plans have changed, haven't they?"

"Yes, they have. Completely." *I'm so horny I could jump… a College Boy.* She brightened. "And I've got ALL SORTS of ideas!" She beamed at her grandmother.

"I was afraid of that. Don't get carried away. You have another whole year of school ahead of you."

Yes, there is that to think about….

***

Tabitha signed up for the GED exam coming at the end of March. "I just don't think I can leave a two-month-old, even with my parents, and-"

"Will they know it's yours?" Brittany ducked Tabitha's gentle swat.

"…Go off to school like nothing's changed."

"EVERYTHING's changed."

"Yup. I want to nurse around the clock, and rock him or her in a rocker, and read stories, play catch…" She looked down. "I'm done with school. For a long time, I think." She sighed.

"And you'll be a GREAT mom!" Brittany did her best. Every once in a while, her friend got a case of scared. "Don't you want to know what color blankets to buy?"

Tabitha shook her head. She didn't know the sex of the baby. Brittany did, she'd been there at the sonogram. Tabitha asked to hear about everything health-wise, but not that. She wanted to find out the conventional way, in three months. Brittany worked hard not to accidentally drop hints.

"So, you pass the GED and drop out, just like that?"

"I'm not sure. I'm going to see if they'll let me go to graduation. Maybe this year, with Frey and Trudy's class. For my parents, so they can see me walk the stage. No sense doing it next year, when I've already been out of school." Tabitha shrugged. "I used to babysit for the Mitchells. I have some sway with the schoolboard."

"I think they'll see your point. It happened in THEIR kitchen, after all." Brittany waited to duck.

Tabitha didn't take the bait. "It's not like I'm asking for a diploma. I ought to have my GED in-hand before June, so I can just wave it at the schoolboard and ask to walk. They let that Old Guy get his GED and gown up to walk across the stage last year…"

"He left school to go to World War Two. His son is the PRINCIPAL. I think that's different." Brittany smirked. "You want company across that stage?"

Tabitha whirled, and grimaced and said "Oooof." Once she recovered: "Really? But you CAN'T. You've got a year to go…"

Brittany put on her Game Face. This was practice for an argument she would soon make in a more important venue. "So what am I taking for classes next year? Advanced Placement English. A.P. Math - calculus. A.P. Chemistry, then A.P. Physics. A.P. History." She gathered herself to get it right. "Tabitha, these are all classes that they've ginned up to keep me in school! The College-Prep kids, next year they're taking THE SAME CLASSES that we're sitting THIS YEAR. Then they'll graduate and go off to college. We're ALREADY taking half our classes with the Seniors. Why am I going to stick around? And why are they going to throw an A.P. class for two or three kids?" She leaned in close and said, conspiratorially, "I can take college classes at the Academy for free. Dad teaches there, remember? Or I can just ENROLL. For that matter, I can get free tuition at ANY of the schools in this state, because he teaches there. So why am I going to loiter around the town school system? It doesn't make sense!"

Tabitha frowned. "So you're going to take the GED test, too?"

"No, Girl. I want my diploma. I've taken all the classes that meet the minimum requirement to get it, AND I have all the classes that colleges want to see for Admissions requirements. I checked. Any class I take at school next year, I can apply against college credit. Spend an extra year in high school to spend one less year in college?" She shuddered. "Ick! How about spend an extra year in college and get out of the high school early!"

Tabitha looked dreamy for a moment. "That's a really wonderful idea." She held out her arm. "I'd LOVE to march up to the stage with you. If they'd let us." She dropped her arm and frowned. "They'll never let you."

"We'll see. Next schoolboard meeting, I'm showing up with my transcripts, admissions requirements lists for every school in the state, and my winning smile."

Tabitha looked unsure. "Didn't you have to play a SPORT, too, or something? Show you're a Team Player and patriotic to the institution and all that shit?"

Brittany frowned. "I worked. Worked my ass off, actually." *Restaurants are a team sport.* "That will have to do."

***

Bruce finally lured Brittany up to his dorm room in late March.

Or maybe she lured him.

It was a rare night that she wasn't working and he wasn't off playing hockey somewhere.

He'd convinced her that the coaches wouldn't kill him if they got caught. The team was winning again, thanks in large part to some hustles that one of their Defensemen - Bruce, actually - had made.

Brittany had convinced herself and then Bruce that her grandmother would never find out what was REALLY going on, since the woman would just assume Brittany was at work or staying in the Village with Tabitha. (Bruce didn't know what Staying At Tabitha's meant, and Brittany wasn't going to tell him, not quite yet... *that's a bit of a Side Issue for later*.)

So two of them headed back to Collegeville in Brittany's car after the usual evening at Smiley's.

She made it clear to Bruce, in the car, on the way: "Playing pool in the basement all hours is ONE THING. Going UPSTAIRS is ENTIRELY ANOTHER. We CANNOT be seen." She did not specify WHY. She supposed he'd figure it out eventually - *maybe someday when he meets his Academic Advisor at the wedding?* As they passed the road up to the Hollow, Brittany began to feel all abuzz with excitement and... something new. She turned the car onto the campus, drove up behind Hanover Hall, and tried to keep her cool as she and Bruce stoically parked the car like this happened every night. *Why does this feel so different?* She knew why. She planned to jump his bones.

HE didn't know that yet. Bruce had high hopes that "going upstairs" might LEAD to bedding - and actually humping - this increasingly intriguing and sexy girl, but for now, he was under the assumption that proximity to his bed was a promising and figurative first step in a long and perhaps multi-night game of seduction.

They passed right by the basement laundry-slash-rec room and headed around a cement corner into a nearby stairwell.

Bruce went up the stairs first, peeked into his third-floor hallway, and motioned: Coast is clear.

Brittany hustled her way up the stairs. She did NOT want witnesses. *Wouldn't that be JUST PEACHY if Professor Wendell made some sort of rounds this evening, or overheard gossip about 'that Wendell chick' as he was exiting one of his lectures?*

Brittany joined Bruce at the fire door and peered into the long hallway. Late evening. Every door closed. Nobody around. "Go unlock your door. I'll wait and come a-running." She kissed him on the mouth. "Go!"

Whatever. Melodramatic sneaky-stuff. Bruce sauntered down the hallway to his door, opened it, and checked: no roommate. *Good. THAT would spook her! Hopefully Curtis is off prowling town for the night....* He pointed: In.

Brittany came haul-assing down the linoleum, slap-slap-slap-slap went her shoes, she skittered past the door, lunged out and threw a hand to catch the doorframe, jerked to a stop, dove into Bruce and his doorway and landed right on top of him there in the middle of the room. She looked over her shoulder briefly to kick the door shut with her foot, then let go of herself. She'd waited long enough! Brittany nearly attacked him.

Kissing became frantic. Bodies twisted. Some clothes were torn off by greedy hands. Growling, surprise, laughing, guttural sounds, half-words, haste, grunting, relief.

Their waters mixed.

Their coupling was perhaps more thorough than Bruce had been hoping for. Only sometime later did he realize he'd never put on a condom. Brittany had not stopped him. He'd not stopped himself. He had a drawer FULL of the things right next to the bed. "Uh... Brittany?" They were still coupled. He looked down between them. Sweat pooled on their stomachs: his, hers, *Ours*.

"Forget something, Stud? Me, too." Whups! Brittany giggled. "Remember what I said about commitments? Landing me in the sack... er, on the floor, is no small thing." In more ways than one, apparently. "Shit." She frowned. *I hope THIS College Boy doesn't HAVE anything. Time for another trip to Tabitha's Gyno, I guess I WILL make it that double appointment... dammit!*

Bruce misinterpreted her expression of worry. He would spend the next few months fretting and keeping close track of Brittany's waistline. Every time she over-ate, swelled for her period, or had a little unrelieved gas, he would be sure his future was ruined.... and then in July he would get the surprise of his life!

But that was later.

***

Brittany wanted to come by again the next night. This visit was a little less frantic. She looked around the dorm room curiously as Bruce shut the door. "Hmmm. So THIS is how a College Boy lives. It's cleaner than I expected."

Bruce stood up proudly, chest out. "We're not ALL slobs." He and his roommate had spent the better part of the day, in-between classes, cleaning and hauling accumulated refuse out, just in case this girl ever dropped by again. So far, he'd kept Curtis in-the-dark about what a

VISIT entailed - his roommate, off on some all-night tom-catting of his own, didn't know that the girl had SPENT THE NIGHT. And quite NAKED, too.

Brittany sniffed. "Smells so piney fresh!" Like cleaner... a few things have changed in here since last night!

Bruce wondered if she knew, and was teasing him.

She did - she remembered how it had looked twelve hours ago. *Different, for sure. Good. He made an effort for me, and at least he knows HOW to tidy up.* "You should have used a little less cleaner. Then I wouldn't have known you just scrubbed the shit out of this place in honor of my visit. Why didn't you do that the first time?" Brittany looked left. "Nice couch." It took up most of one wall, in-between desks crammed into corners. Brittany flopped down on it, on her stomach.

Bruce saw that round, heart-shaped ass on his couch and suddenly his pulse doubled. "I didn't know you were coming." And she'd surprised him by coming back so soon, *but at least I got the place ready this time!*

Brittany looked back over her shoulder at him, followed Bruce's eyes to her bottom, and sat up. "Come over here." She patted the sofa beside her, and he sat. She kissed him on the mouth and then looked into his eyes. "I'm a serious girl, you know that, right?"

"I've figured that out."

"I want to live in that farmhouse and fill it with babies. Children. Like it used to be."

Bruce's breathing stopped. *Whoah, now!* Then he wondered if he'd already maybe had a hand in doing just that, just last night. *Shit.*

Brittany misunderstood the look on his face and clarified: "Not right now, but someday."

Inwardly, Bruce cringed. What every College Boy dreaded: *Sticky Cottage Cheese!* The worst kind. *Then why have I been hanging around like a love-struck puppy for six months? Maybe I've got a hand in giving her the wrong idea...*

"I'm not a love-her-and-leave-her kind of a girl, not for you College Boys. Everything I'm doing now, I'm doing for my future." She leaned over and kissed his mouth for a long time. Then she pulled back and scrutinized his face. "Including you."

"I'm a Junior in college and I'm from a million miles away and I have NO IDEA what my future will bring, eh?"

"Maybe your future brought ME." She kissed him - possessively this time instead of passionately. "If I thought you were going to stick around, I'd probably put out frequently, you know."

"You play quite a game." *I've been stalking you for, what? Six months? Eight months?*

She answered his un-spoken question: "Thirteen months and a day. Don't be surprised if we end up married someday. This is your warning." Actually, Brittany thought that probably the waitress's slip-up had been warning enough for them both. *That woman could see it already, even back then.* She waited.

Bruce waited. He'd never had a girl hint at long-term before. He wasn't sure what to say. Finally: "Does that mean I get to spread the Brie again?"

Brittany smiled, and batted her eyelashes. *Oh, I hope so.* "Is your roommate coming back?" *Silly boy, he thinks he's seducing ME!* Somehow, the top buttons on Brittany's shirt had come undone. There was DEPTH in there, and rising swells on each side of the deep. She made sure to breath heavily. *The old heaving bosom trick should do it...*

Bruce tore his gaze away to rummage in a desk drawer. "Not if I stick this here red piece of tape to the outside of the door."

"Get busy."

When he got back into the room, she was already in the bed, her jeans and button-up in a messy pile on the couch where she'd been sitting. Brittany growled: "Come here. Kiss me. RIGHT NOW." *I can't stand to wait another minute, now that I'm here!* Parts of her that were involved in procreation were running the show once again....

Their waters were going to be contained by a condom this time. Bruce didn't want any sticky cottage-cheese-got-pregnant problems. *If it's not too late already....* He turned and his eyes got wide. *Holy shit, that girl is beautiful! And now naked....* Bruce suddenly decided that Sticky and Cottage and room-fuls of wailing snot-nosed babies were all inconsequential and possibly worthy complications. At least for the desperate moment.

Afterwards, Brittany eased around and spooned with her new lover for a time and then decided she had a call to make. *This man is comfy.*

I'm going to STAY. Her fears at being Found Out evaporated in the afterglow. "I've got to use the phone." She put on one of Bruce's long plaid shirts and calmly walked barefoot down to the end of the hall, where the floor's telephone hung on the wall.

Bruce was now the one panicking. He shut the door to the room and hoped that if she was caught in the hallway, he could remain anonymous. *Maybe she'll just walk out like that and hop in her car and GO and I won't have to face a mad coach and a homicidal grandmother....*

Brittany dialed and was relieved her grandmother had put a phone in upstairs, and also was used to Brittany calling from Tabitha's house. "Hi, Grandma... Yes... Ya, I'm staying in the village tonight." *Well, it isn't a total lie*, and the woman didn't ask for specifics, *thank God*. "That's right. See you tomorrow night at eleven or so, or the next morning." She looked speculatively up the hallway towards door three-zero-nine. "Sorry I'm so busy." The woman was telling her to live while she could. Nice. "Thanks, Grandma. Goodnight." Brittany hung up the phone, pranced down the hall, dropped the shirt, and snuggled back in with her lover. She sat up on one elbow suddenly - "Oh... You should take the tape off the door. Poor boy has to sleep sometime, I imagine."

Bruce rolled towards her. "He's probably found some other place to go."

"What if I'm the only girl on the whole campus who is Putting Out tonight?"

"Good point." *Not likely, but you never know*.... Bruce climbed over her, got out of bed, opened the door eight inches, and ripped the strip of electrical tape off the door. He held it up as he closed the door. "Happy?"

"Yes. I can't stand the thought of someone having to sleep on a dirty floor for me. Well, anyone except for your regular lover."

Bruce tried not to flinch. *So she knows*.

"Of course." She shrugged *If he only knew!* She smirked. *TWO can be devious! Speaking of devious...* "Does anyone ever pull the tape off?"

Bruce DID flinch. "Never! It's considered the worst kind of treachery."

"Especially if it's your roommate's girlfriend or little sister in the bed with you, or the Hot Girl from the other dorm, stuff like that?" Brittany turned at him and grinned. "I'm wise to your tom-catting ways, College Boy."

"Well, yes it can get kind of ...sticky." Bruce gave her a long kiss. "But I think we're safe in this situation."

You DO realize my FATHER is your Academic Advisor, don't you? They hadn't actually discussed it, but Brittany had figured it out fairly easily, so Bruce MUST know. "I can think of some ways this could get rather sticky in a hurry." She snuggled up against him again.

Bruce mis-interpreted, and immediately thought of their recent, first, hasty, un-protected sex and probable pregnancy again: *Great, just great. Fatherhood before graduation. Won't Mom and Dad be proud!*

Brittany found Just The Right Spot to put her backside, one that caused Bruce to tense into her reflexively. *There, that must be about right...* "Do Academic Advisors ever patrol the halls at night?" She felt his returning erection wither, and then she didn't feel it at all.

"He IS your father, isn't he?" HE was Professor Wendell, Bruce's Advisor, and also instructor in one of his classes now.

"Yup. One mis-step and we're screwed. He's even more dangerous than Grandma. She's only killed once." Brittany was only half-kidding. "We're just going to keep this low-key for a bit."

Jesus, and she was out at the PHONE! He'd just seen Professor Wendell patrolling the hallways... what, five days ago? His eyes went wide. *I didn't wear a condom last time!* His face screwed up in the picture of horror. *Just great. I just impregnated - maybe - the daughter of a college official who I happen to interact with every day. I wonder if he'll kill me or make me part of the family?*

"I told you we might end up married..." Brittany grinned in the dark. "Unless he never finds out."

"Not in a million years. VERY low-key. Yes, Ma'am."

The door opened, on cue.

Bruce's hockey team Captain, Curtis, came into the room, flipped on the overhead light, and closed the door.

Brittany dove down deep under the spread-out sleeping bag Bruce was using as a bed-cover.

"Oh, shit, sorry!" Curtis backed towards the door. "You should have put out the tape!"

"No, it's fine." Bruce shielded his eyes from the bright light suddenly intruding. "We're ahhh… sleeping."

Brittany recognized the voice from the hockey breakfasts. She was a pragmatic Girl without shame. "We were not!" She poked her head out into the light, but carefully kept the makeshift comforter pinned to the rest of her. "We were having wild, carnal, messy sex. Messier than planned, sometimes. But we're done now."

Curtis took a moment of stunned silence to recover himself. "In the DORM, Brucie?! You sonofabitch, you ARE gonna get yourself killed!" He pointed at Brittany. "You're her granddaughter!"

"Well, everybody is SOMEBODY's granddaughter. YOU…" Brittany carefully pulled a naked arm out from under cover and pointed at Curtis. "are sworn to secrecy. There are people on this campus that I'm more afraid of than Grandma." She gave Bruce, lying next to her still, a prim kiss on the lips. "And YOU are sworn to be careful. Duck if you see my grandmother coming. Or my father."

Curtis pondered for a stunned moment and then turned on a desk lamp. He reached back to the doorway to kill the overhead light and then made a show of averting his eyes as he turned back to the room. "I ah… gotta grab some stuff."

Brittany rolled over to face the wall and snuggled her backside back up against Bruce. "Why don't you go to bed, Curtis. I don't bite." She giggled. "And I'll bet this isn't the first time this room has slept three…" She reached a finger around and poked her lover in the side.

Now how the hell does she know about THAT?! Bruce lay awake for quite a while. He didn't know whether to be embarrassed to be walked in on, or proud of his catch. But he DID know she was full of surprises.

A small, sleepy voice came out from under his arm: "You ain't seen nothin' yet."

***

Brittany arranged coverage at the diner, informed Bruce and Tabitha so that neither of them would waste a trip, and prepared to face the school board. Tabitha wanted to come along, but Brittany squelched that idea. She didn't want the board to think her motivations were purely social. They weren't.

Brittany got a little surprise when she got to the meeting. Her BOSS, of all people, was on the schoolboard! *I didn't know he lived here!* NOW she knew why he was gone for a few hours on a weeknight every second and fourth weeks of the month. *Schoolboard?! When did that happen? Oh, shit. Will it matter?*

There was a lot riding on it, so she was nervous, at first, before she got her back up. "So that basic problem is, I could spend another year in the Collegeville's Public School System, accumulating credits towards graduation with classes that waive freshman year college course requirements. OR, I can spend next year actually AT a college, accumulating COLLEGE CREDITS towards a degree that I will have at twenty or twenty-one, or even possibly double-major, say in History AND Education, and graduate with my cohort with TWO degrees and no later than most people graduate with one." She had to stop to take a breath. "If you look at my paystubs from this year, and my transcripts from the last three years, you can see that I can probably pull off a double-major in four years." She stood by her folding chair, waiting, projecting confidence, and worrying no less than if she was arguing her own fate in a court of law. Brittany did NOT want to spend another year at high school. She was ready to move on with life.

"Miss Wendell, aren't you scheduled to take a selection of Advanced Placement courses over the next two semesters?" That question came Mr. Mitchell. Brittany realized, suddenly, that she was intimately connected to every member of the schoolboard in the strangest of coincidences. *An episode of THIS IS YOUR LIFE, here?* It somewhat unsettled her.

"Yes, ah, yes, that is ah... yes, the SCHOOL'S plan, but ah... many, no MOST, most of my classmates will graduate next year? Upon completion of the aahhh... very same courses that I am completing THIS year? If these courses that I will complete by June make my classmates, ahh, all eligible for college enrollment, why do I have to wait?" She took a breath and squared herself away by force of will. "It seems... frivolous."

Mrs. Mitchell frowned from down at the other end of folding tables. "Brittany, why don't you want to go to high school next year? That's what this is really about, isn't it?"

Mr. Mitchell added: "You could take these Aay-Pee classes and apply for college credit once you've completed them with adequate grades, and skip some college classes."

"I want to take these classes AT college. If I take them at the public school, I will be, ahhh... like a transfer student! I mean, come second year of college. I want to start as a Freshman, take the same classes as my... cohort, and spend my four years as a member of the college community, then... matriculate out into the working world." She thought the big, professional-sounding words were important. She was also talking a line of shit. She had OTHER plans, part of a different Plan altogether, but these folks didn't need to know that.

Roger raised his index finger off the folding table that served as his desk. "Miss Wendell, state again, succinctly, your reason for wanting to ditch a year of high school." He looked serious. More stern than she ever saw him at work.

Will he ask awkward questions? This one wasn't, but what was next? Brittany took a breath. "I'm in a hurry in life. I want to get out into the world and do my thing now, while I'm hungry for it. Before I get tied down by... complications." She saw Roger's eyebrows go up minutely.

So did her dad's. *Just exactly WHAT kind of complications might interfere with college, young lady?* Being a member of the schoolboard was going to be extra-informative tonight, apparently. So far, he hadn't asked any questions. He assumed that Brittany thought he'd be a pushover. Dad can I move out. Check. Dad, can I run off to college early? Check? He supposed they'd already had that talk... She had mentioned living with his mother and commuting to school every day. He didn't think she'd meant COLLEGE school, but maybe he hadn't been paying enough attention... *I suppose I have to recuse myself anyway. So I'll stay quiet for the moment.*

Roger didn't ask for clarification on complications, and Brittany breathed a sigh of relief. He was the one who knew the most about them anyway. His questions could have revealed more than her answers. The next question caught her off guard, though.

Mr. Mitchell asked, "So basically, you're asking us to sign off to the State Board of Education that you've completed school, even though you haven't technically done that, because school is too easy for you and you've gotten yourself ahead?"

Ooof. Think! Brittany colored. "I never said that. I worked HARD. Ask my grandmother. If I'm not at work, I'm probably at the kitchen table doing homework."

Heads turned towards Hattie Wendell, in a chair back by the door. Tonight's "audience" consisted of three, plus a camera-man from the local cable news service, actually run by the student news club at the Academy. Hattie nodded. "At work or hitting the books" *or in a hotel room or in the village humping an already pregnant teenager or romping around town God knows where screwing who knows for who-knows-what. She's probably made the rounds in those dorms, too?* "She's got drive, I'll give her that..."

Roger spoke up again. It wasn't a question. "Her grades haven't gone down too much, and she's been with me since last year, and she's up to thirty hours a week now. That's actually quite impressive." He turned to Schoolboard Member Wendell. "Does she NEED to work that much? She's gone down a whole letter grade. Only to B's, mind you but..."

Brittany's dad shrugged. He didn't realize she was working so much. "She seems to have a plan." He caught a break and no one was looking when he rolled his eyes.

"That's right. I have a plan. And if you'll agree that I've completed the coursework that the school requires for graduation of THE REST of my classmates, why can't I just bump up the year a bit and get a head start on what's next?"

Mrs. Mitchell demurred. "It's not that simple, Brittany. You have to complete a certain number of high school credits to qualify for a diploma. It's state law. We can't just willy-nilly sign you off."

Schoolboard member Wendell spread his hands. "It's not really our call, Brittany." He nodded his head, a glum expression on his face. "It was a really good idea, though." *Important to be supportive*, he thought.

Brittany stormed out in a barely-disguised huff.

* * *

Brittany was a busy Girl. She divided her time three ways, spending some nights down in the village with Tabitha, a few at the dorm, and just a few more at the farmhouse. The red-head visited the farmhouse with her. The boy did not.

When Brittany was there at the ancestral home with its apple trees and wide porch and cozy kitchen, she could see her babies frolicking around the house. It made her womb ache. But she took her birth control religiously, and she was making the College Boy wear condoms now that she had her head on straight.

The nights that Tabitha got her company, Brittany spent a lot of time exploring that rapidly-changing, red-headed body: the bigger curves, the visibly protruding basketball shape that was filling her skin and stretching it, the breasts that were now growing wide and heavy. Brittany couldn't get enough of that bulging baby-belly. Sometimes on what she called 'Tabitha Nights,' Hattie would go into the front room to find the pregnant red-head sitting on the couch with Brittany sitting between her feet, leaning her ear into the big belly above her.

Tabitha kept getting bigger.

Brittany spent more time with the Young Mother. Thoughts of the boy began to become sporadic.

***

The weather was warming up, imperceptibly at first, but then there was a rain and the snow down in town ran away into the surging ditches, overrunning brooks and filling angry brown rivers. The patch of south-facing lawn on Mrs. Hackett's place started greening up one day when the sun was out. On another afternoon it was sixty degrees by two o'clock. Everyone knew that Mrs. Hackett's crocuses would be up soon, even if they got buried in one more snow. Clothes changed: lighter jackets; quilt-lined flannel and canvas shirts replaced by all-season plaid button-ups. The optimistic braved the ever-variable spring weather in shorts, even if the wind still had a bite to it.

There was even a day up in the cold Hollow when Brittany shoveled back snowbanks at the farmhouse wearing a bikini in order to work on her early-season tan. It was sixty-seven degrees in the sun and thirty-five in the shade back behind the barn where she was dumping the snow. Going back and forth with the full and empty shovel while wearing tall rubber boots and four little black triangles on strings felt like running back and forth between a sauna and a cold brook.

Brittany's grandmother pulled back a sheer and wispy 19th-century black lace curtain, looked out the parlor window, and thought that maybe her granddaughter had forgotten to put on clothes before she went out to shovel. *My, how pregnancy has that poor Girl addled!* She shook her head and let the curtain drop. *Probably going to addle a few drivers today, too, if she's not careful!*

Tabitha lounged in the sun in a chair parked on hard snow in the middle of the front lawn and watched her friend carry the snow back and forth. Tabitha wore sweatpants pulled up to the knee and a sleeveless tee shirt. She looked like a kid sitting with a basketball on her lap. She covered up in haste every time she heard a vehicle coming along the road.

Brittany stopped her shoveling to watch Tabitha scramble into the jacket, and then un-scramble when she realized it was the oversized brown delivery truck. Brittany stuck the shovel in the receding snowbank. "You look cute in it, but it's not going to work anymore."

Tabitha looked pot-bellied, even in size XL winter wool.

The UPS driver almost went off the road. He hardly noticed the red-head with the baby-bump, but the young woman shoveling SNOW while wearing mud-boots and a too-small BIKINI was a bit much, even for a seasoned delivery driver who thought he'd seen it all.

***

Bruce missed Brittany. He realized it was dangerous and also irresponsible to liaison overnight too often, but he LIKED sleeping with her. She was a good screw - the best, actually, in his self-described widely experienced opinion - and she fit just right as he drifted off to sleep. She had a cute and very tiny little snore sometimes, just enough so that now he missed it when she wasn't there. *Uh-oh.* He wasn't making the rounds at the other dorms anymore, and those words, 'we might be married someday' kept echoing in his head. *Oh shit. Stupid little girl…* Except she WASN'T a little girl. She was a hard-charging, hard-working, very serious seventeen-year-old who appeared to be stalking him for children. *If I haven't already provided that accidentally on the first night... Shit! What's going to happen NEXT year, when she's graduating school and I'm graduating college, and we're going our separate ways?* For the first time in his life, the future WORRIED him. And one other thing... he kept remembering their morning-after breakfast, and hearing the waitress: What would your husband like? And he would FEEL something when he remembered that. Something new. *What the hell is THIS, eh?*

***

One Friday afternoon after school, Brittany followed Tabitha home and they did their schoolwork at the kitchen table at Tabitha's house.

Brittany wasn't planning to head back to the farmhouse later, on this evening. She had a Plan going:

Grandma Wendell was over at the rink right now, watching a late-season game, probably cussing out the referees. She'd gone to the game along with her friend Sylvia and a new hockey fan: Walter Wendell, who had begun to take an interest in his employer's hockey program. Grandma Wendell would catch a ride home with Sylvia, thinking that Brittany was staying down in the village with Tabitha. Tabitha would think that Brittany was headed up to the farmhouse. Brittany's dad would remain entirely in the dark and hopefully NOT go on rounds through the dorms on his way home. Brittany would take a detour just a short way down the road and have another night with Bruce. Complicated, but achievable.

The only three people who knew everything were Brittany, Bruce, and Curtis. *Well, that's not true... those two think Tab is a peejay party.* She dismissed that problem as irrelevant. Tabitha SUSPECTED, of course, because she knew Brittany was still seeing him, and she also knew Brittany was On The Pill. Grandma Wendell knew Brittany was On The Pill, but didn't know that it was because she'd settled on One Boy and wasn't always as particularly careful as she should be. Hopefully her father didn't have the least clue about ANY of what was going on. The situation was contained, in Brittany's estimation.

But she looked over and saw something that WASN'T contained. Tabitha, sweating her face wet in the increasing spring heat, wearing a hoodie sweatshirt and a hunting jacket while sitting as close to the kitchen table as she could get, which wasn't very close. And the bottom of the jacket was unbuttoned now, because she simply couldn't get it closed over the basketball popping out of her midsection. Brittany sighed in frustration and shoved her chair back. "It's TIME, don't you think? You're going to get heatstroke."

Tabitha knew exactly what time had come. "Noooooooooooo!!" She clutched the jacket around her. Sometimes a secret becomes a bad habit.

"It'll be FINE." Brittany grabbed her friend by the hand and dragged her, protesting all the way, out into the living room. Tabitha's mother was in there, busy at ironing laundry in front of the television.

"Oh, hi! You two finally taking a break from all that homework? Honey, can you BELIEVE that you two are going to be SENIORS next year? Time flies... Oh." She looked back and forth between the two girls and then shut off the iron and pushed the switch on the teevee with the toe of her shoe. It went dark. The room was silent for a moment. She took a breath, and then: "There. You finally ready to talk?"

"TABITHA HERE has some news..."

"Britt, you are SUCH a bitch and I'm going to grind your face into the first parking lot I see. Again."

"Fine, fine, just TELL her and then I'll drive us over to the store..."

Tabitha rolled her eyes. "FINE! Mom, you'd better sit down."

"Well, yes." She was struggling to meet her daughter's eye. She was distracted by the popped-open buttons on her husband's hunting coat. *I'll have to fix those....*

"And please STAY sitting, because you're going to yell, and I can't take that right now, so I might have to leave until you've gotten it all out." Tabitha wrung her hands together.

"Okay..." Mrs. Bayer sat down on the couch, leaned forward, and found herself at approximately eye-level with her daughter's... bump. She tried not to stare at it.

Brittany elbowed Tabitha in the arm.

"ALRIGHT GODDAMIT!!" Tabitha put on a bright, cheery, wide stage-smile. "Mom, I'm pregnant. I'm going to have a baby. I'm going to be a mother." Tabitha deflated and took an unconscious step back.

"Well of course you are! You weren't wearing that old coat to be fashionable, that's for sure!" She looked up at her daughter and smiled. "Tabitha, you haven't asked for tampons in months. I'm really glad you finally told me, though." She stood up and gave her much-shorter daughter a hug. "Oh, I'm sorry, I'm supposed to be sitting!" She let go of Tabitha and stepped back to get a good look at her.

Tabitha promptly fell sideways into the seat on the couch that her mother had just vacated, either from shock or from heat, none of the three was sure.

Brittany teared up and smirked at the same time. "See! I TOLD you it would be okay!"

Tabitha's mother asked The Question. "Who is the father? I mean, I didn't think…" She gave Brittany an appraising head-to-toe survey.

Brittany stepped forward. "I am." Her tone said something.

Tabitha's mother sat back down, rather abruptly, next to her daughter. "I see. That bad, huh?"

Brittany nodded vigorously, wide-eyed. "Don't even go there, please, Ma'am."

"Tabitha, did anyone HURT you?"

Tabitha sniffled. "Nothing like that. I was just stupid. Once. You don't want to know. I can't tell you."

"Ohhh-kayyy! But I don't think I'm going to be able to sell that to your father. Nice try, Brittany."

Brittany persisted: "Well, that's what I'm telling everyone."

"I thought you had a boyfriend over at the college…"

Brittany stamped her foot. "I HATE this town! Alright, yes, I have a boyfriend. But I'm going to be the father."

Tabitha's mother's eyebrows went up. "You'll be busy! That's a serious commitment. If you're serious."

"I am." Brittany scowled. "I'm ALREADY busy. You have no idea."

"Oh, I think I'm getting the picture. You do like a fast pace, don't you?" She turned her head. "Tabitha, how are you with that?"

"Confused." She said it stoically and pragmatically. That was the least of her problems right now. Brittany had done a remarkable job of Being There just recently.

"Yes, I would imagine." *She's kicking that can down the road, apparently....* "Well, I see you've been to the doctor?"

Tabitha went wide-eyed. "How... We paid cash. How did you...?"

"It was right on last month's insurance statement. Lab Services, pre-term ultrasound. Boy or Girl?"

Brittany smacked her own forehead. "Crap!" *I can't believe I didn't think of that!* "I'll tell you later. She doesn't want to know."

"Oh! A surprise, then! That's very old-fashioned, but not unusual... Makes it hard to decorate a baby-room, though... Honey, why didn't you tell me? I've been worried about you, you know, though I WAS glad to see you were getting checkups."

"I thought you'd be mad." Tabitha looked embarrassed, sad, and happy all at once.

"Well, I was at first. I got over it."

"I thought you'd pester me about who the father is."

"I think your own father still might. Get your story straight, my Virgin Daughter. He's going to have questions when he gets home."

Tabitha put her arms around her mother. "Thanks, Mom."

"Are you alright?"

"Yah." *I am now.*

***

Tabitha's father wasn't quite so easy.

Brittany stayed to supper and was happy to be there for that conversation. *Just in case of complications.*

Brittany being Brittany, she might possibly have created more of them, instead....

Just after Tabitha's father got home from work, when they were done setting the table, Brittany took Tabitha aside in the kitchen and whispered in her ear: "Let ME handle this one. Trust me." She pulled Tabitha's jacket off over the reluctant girl's shoulders, kissed her on the lips as she folded the jacket over her own arm, and looked her in the eyes. *It will be okay.*

Tabitha nodded *Yes*, but looked a lot less sure than that. Frankly, she looked panicked.

Her mother walked by with a steaming pan of potatoes. She gave Tabitha a pat on the shoulder and a surreptitious thumbs-up: *You can do it, Girl.*

Tabitha's father sat at the head of the table, reading the newspaper. His cigarette dangled from his lips, a thin curl of smoke wisping up from the end. He turned a page.

Brittany sat down at one side of the table. She scooted her chair out a little more and patted her leg: *Here.* Pat, pat. Tabitha sat down on her friend's lap, as instructed, and put her arm around Brittany's neck.

"OOOOF!" Brittany grunted. "You're getting HEAVY, Girl!"

Tabitha's father put down the paper and frowned at the girls. "No rough-housing at the dinner table." The paper went back up.

"Dad, that was so, like, TEN years ago! Can Brittany and I talk to you about something more... adult?"

The paper went back down. Mr. Bayer's eyebrows went up. There was something about his little girl's expression that made him uneasy, her looking at him expectantly like that. He couldn't put a finger on it, but... *Jesus, she IS getting fat!* He hadn't seen her in a T-shirt in MONTHS and now... "Oh shit."

Brittany smiled. "You did good, Tab. Run! Run as fast as you can waddle, while I explain it all to him!"

Tabitha scurried, er... SWAYED, she was to that point, out to the kitchen and the safety of her mother's skirts.

The cigarette fell out into his lap as Tabitha's father watched his daughter peek back around the corner. The little girl was all breasts and belly. *She looks just like my wife did when...* "You've got to be KIDDING me." He turned to Brittany, then back to the kitchen where his wife and Tabitha were both now peering around the corner of a doorway. "But I thought you two were Lesbians or something..." His chair scraped back as he stood up. "How the HELL did THIS happen???" His cheeks were getting that purple color...

Brittany knew she had to tread very carefully, but unfortunately it wasn't in her nature. She put on a big smile. "The usual way. Almost seven months along. You've got two more months, give or take, to get your mind around it."

"Who's the father?"

"I HATE THAT QUESTION!!" Tabitha, protesting from the kitchen.

Brittany's smile faded. She was very direct. "You don't want to know the answer to that question, and you don't"

"NOW YOU WAIT JUST A MINUTE YOUNG LADY, I'M TABITHA'S FATHER AND I WA"

Suddenly, Tabitha's mother was there at the table, laying a restraining hand on her husband's arm. "You'd better let her finish."

Pause. "Oh shit."

Brittany continued: "You don't want to know, and you don't want to go digging or getting other people thinking about it. Trust me. It would be VERY BAD for Tabitha. It might come out anyways, and if it does… It will be bad." *Like breast-feeding during visits at JAIL bad!* "The LESS you know, the BETTER. If anyone asks, I'm the father."

The man looked at her, struck incredulous. *This wild little girl, telling ME how it is…* He looked at his daughter and his head shook, though he didn't know it. Then his head swiveled to his daughter's wild little friend and his eyes narrowed. He started to open his mouth-

Brittany tried again: "That's how we're leaving it. It's really for the best if people make their own assumptions and don't start asking questions."

I'll deal with THAT bad influence later…. Mister Bayer rounded towards the kitchen and his daughter, and began yelling at the form just visible at the edge of the doorway. "Jesus CHRIST, girl, WHAT DID YOU DO?!? WHAT were you THINKING?!?"

"Well, she was a wreck for weeks afterward, is that enough?"

He didn't hear the noise coming from the interloper's mouth. "WHAT ABOUT COLLEGE, TABITHA, WHAT ABOUT THAT?!?"

Brittany took that question, too, as any responsible young man might. "That depends on her, and you, and a lot of things that haven't happened yet. Don't rule it out." She couldn't help herself - she didn't

like authority figures, especially ones that were yelling at her pregnant friend. "She's having a baby, not cutting off her head."

Tabitha's father went wide-eyed. "YOU'RE A BAD INFLUENCE AND A SMART-MOUTH!" He turned to move towards this disrespectful little upstart in his kitchen, his temple pulsing and his eyes suddenly screwing into hostile slits.

Oh shit. "Yes, I probably am. I'm sorry about that part." Brittany began backing towards the kitchen in time with Mr. Bayer's steps. "TABITHA, TIME TO GO! OUT TO THE CAR, NOW, GIRL!" Brittany turned and ran for the kitchen.

The wrath behind her was slow, but building steam.

Mrs. Bayer held out two backpacks. She caressed Tabitha's hair and gave her a gentle push towards the door and escape. She frowned as Brittany went by, handed off the young woman's backpack, and asked, "Could that have gone better, maybe?"

"Sorry! He's madder at me than her, that will work!"

The girls scooted out the door, but they could hear the thunderstorm behind them:

"NOT SO FAST, I'M GONNA HAVE A WORD WITH YOU YOUNG LADY! WE'RE GONNA RUN YOU TO A CLINIC AND THEY'RE GONNA FIX THIS THING AND THEN WE'RE GONNA HAVE A LITTLE MORE DISCIPLINE AROUND-"

His bellowing was cut off by the sound of a slap.

The girls made a clean getaway in a screech of tires.

***

Tabitha spent the evening crying in Brittany's arms in her bedroom at the farmhouse. Brittany excused herself to make one phone call, from the upstairs extension, to have a message passed on and - hopefully - finally written on the dry-erase board on the door at Bruce's room:

Tell Curtis I won't be by tonight.

Regrets! - The Girl

She thought that sufficiently opaque so that nobody would be any wiser for overhearing or reading it. She hoped Bruce would get it... he was probably at an after-game party.

The next morning during breakfast, Hattie Wendell mentioned that Easter was coming up. "Next Sunday, dears! Tabitha, you're practically part of the family now, you're welcome to stay for dinner. Around one, I should think. Your father will miss you and will be begging for you to come back home after that, I imagine."

"Oh, fuh...." Brittany felt suddenly sick. "You don't think she should go home."

Hattie shook her head. "No, just rub salt in the wound at this point." She patted Tabitha on the shoulder. "Give him a chance to get his mind around what's really important, I think. I'm sure he loves you. It's just a bit of a shock."

***

Tabitha did stay the whole week up at the Wendell place, as it turned out.

She checked in with her mother a few times while Mr. Bayer was at work and found that the weather had not improved.

"Oh, he's carrying on a bit, at the moment. He's angry that you hid it from us, he's angry that you're pregnant, he's angry that it's too late to... Well, he's not thinking very clearly."

"Oh."

"Stay up there, for now."

"Are YOU okay? There are more bedrooms up here, you know..."

"Tabitha! How sweet of you! No, I'm fine. He can be difficult to live with, when he gets like this, but someone needs to make his dinners for him."

Tabitha discussed these calls with Brittany, and they decided that Tabitha's insistence on hiding her pregnancy had probably saved a life. They had a good cry together over the almosts and nearlies of that awful, horrible, terrible prospect.

***

Bert, the Collegeville Constable and Chief of the Mill Village Police Department, stopped up on Tuesday night.

His imposing form cast a long shadow into the kitchen from his place in the open doorway. He didn't really want to come in - *my luck, their luck, I'll prob'bly catch the two young ladies drinking beer or somesuch shit.* Hattie Wendell was well-known for anti-social tendencies when she didn't agree with whatever the norm of the moment was. He held his big hat in his hands as he explained his predicament (the crown probably would have scraped the low ceiling, had he kept it on). "Hattie, Tabitha's father sent me up here to bring her home. She's not emancipated, so I kind of HAVE to..."

Tabitha came around the corner from the parlor, wearing a bright-yellow and slightly too-small T-shirt. She and Brittany had just last night finished it, using a laundry marker to make a big, perky smiley-face on the front, right where Tabitha's belly was biggest. She was startled to see a policeman standing just inside the kitchen door, but stood herself proudly on display in the middle of the kitchen, her heart racing. *No hiding it now, I wonder if he's here about the boy?*

Bert looked past Hattie, giving Tabitha the once-over. "Oh. 'Splains that."

Hattie stepped further back out of the way. "Why don't you sit down for a cup of coffee and some cookies, Bert." She threw a hand at the table. Brittany was off at work, so it was just Hattie, Bert and now Tabitha. Hattie thought it was possibly better this way. *That girl has a way of tweaking people up, sometimes.* "Ginger-molasses, this week...."

Bert didn't sit, but he did come the rest of the way into the kitchen and stood there with his hat twirling slowly in his hands in front of him.

Tabitha sat at - or rather, near - the table and helped herself to a ginger cookie from the plate in the middle. It might be the last cookie she got from this kitchen for quite some time. "They're good!" She could hardly swallow in her terror. Tears threatened in the corners of her eyes. *So much here I will miss....*

"You just tell him?" Bert spun the hat. "Your Dad sent me up."

Oh. Oh! That! Please let it be THAT! "Didn't go so well, Mister Policeman. You here to... take me back?"

"Bert. Call me Bert. Shit, your as much an adult as I am, now... Not anymore." His merry eyes danced over her. "Brittany do that to yeh?"

Tabitha felt a flicker of fear again. "In a manner of speaking, yes. She's the father."

The mirth left Bert's face as he became serious: "That what you told your Dad?"

Tabitha nodded and looked sad.

"'Splains a whole lot. Why don't you stay up here a few more days 'til he cools down? I'll go and have a talk with him, tell him he's bein' a shit." His head shook, unconsciously, apparently. "Damn." The man turned towards the door and then had an afterthought: "Call if ya need help ta the hospital." The police department had a four wheel drive that could handle mud season and frost heaves. The ambulance service didn't. Bert had a feeling the girl might be spending a LONG time up here.

The kitchen door closed with a soft thud and then they heard the thum-thump-thump of stiff-soled boots retreating down the three porch steps.

Tabitha stood frozen, waiting for the other shoe to drop. Waiting for the policeman to turn around and come back into the kitchen: *oh, I forgot one other thing, Tabitha, you're under arrest for forceable incest of a baby-sitting customer, put your hands behind your back and say your goodbyes....*

"That went well." Hattie watched Bert back his car out onto the road, and then shut the big kitchen door. "I thought I might be arrested for harboring a fugitive!"

Tabitha snapped out of it. She looked furtively at her belly. "You still might, I suppose..."

"Still worried about that, are you?"

"Not 'til I saw the police in the kitchen."

"Why don't you tell me who it is, and then I can tell you that you shouldn't worry so much?"

"Nice try. Brittany is the father."

"Tabitha, what are you going to say at the hospital? There's a birth certificate, you know. 'My Girlfriend' probably isn't going to fly when the attending physician is filling in the blanks."

Oh... shit.

***

Hattie had a secondary motive for having Tabitha around on Easter. The rest of the Wendell family was coming up from the village. They were going to try it again, unfortunately. Hattie didn't think it would go any better this time around. Brittany might need a shoulder to lean on.

Easter morning was warm and sunny and breezy. A fair-sized part of the lawn peeked out amongst the piles of snow, and even up here the crocus patch was sprouting up at the base of the old maple. The road thawed out mid-morning, and by noon a passing motorist was stuck, buried to the tops of the wheels, right in front of the farmhouse where the pavement ended. Sylvia. How convenient.

She came up the steps and as Hattie was already opening the door for her, Sylvia lamented, "I KNEW I shouldn't have taken this way back home! Always thaws out early, right there where it faces the morning sun... Hattie, can I use your phone?" She seemed a bit red about the face, apparently embarrassed that she'd managed to get a four-wheel-drive truck - jacked up, no less - stuck right in front of Hattie's house.

"Sure, Sylvia, come right in..." She looked out in the road briefly... "Oh dear! How on Earth did you do THAT?" Hattie took her coat and settled her friend by the in-line dialer on the antique phone.

There was a brief cacophony in the kitchen while Sylvia dialed the garage to see if she could get pulled out:

"Hello, Silvia!" (Brittany, over at the range, stirring a large pan of gravy)

"Hello!" (Tabitha, facing the sink, stretching forward to wash some accumulated cookware)

"Can you stay to Easter dinner?" (Hattie Wendell, expecting the answer to be No, but it couldn't hurt to ask, could it?)

Sylvia grinned from ear to ear. "Thankyou, Hattie, I think I might. It certainly smells good in here! I was on-call this morning, and all the kids have been placed, so actually, I'm all alone up there today... I was going to gin up a dinner for one." She paused, listening to the phone.

"Oh, good! No need for you to cook. Walt can pull you out with the old tractor, I think it will make it through the lane, and then you can drive on home once the sun drops behind the hill. It should freeze back up pretty quickly after sunset, I should think. You can bring some leftovers for Hank.""

Well, "I guess I'll have to, thankyou." Sylvia put the phone handset back on the wooden box. "Phone is off the hook at the garage, I guess I'm not the only fool stuck out on a back road, or maybe Hayden doesn't want to leave his own Sunday dinner." She smiled ruefully. "I'm lucky Hank's not waiting on me..." She frowned. "He's at both jobs, today."

"Oh, dear. Well, we always have room for one more! I'll make sure to send you with some leftovers." Hattie paused. "What will Hank do?"

"Oh, he'll find someone's Easter dinner to crash. Someone closer to the County Offices, I would imagine." Sylvia got a brief look of indigestion.

Just then a car came gingerly up the bumpy pavement from town. Walt stopped to disgorge his passengers right there on the road, in the middle of the pavement, and then parked on the side of the road up close to a softening snowbank, with two wheels still on the blacktop and two on still-frozen ground in the shade, so that he could back out onto the safety of a hard road. Everyone had to walk the last fifty yards to the farmhouse, but it was better than walking all the way back to town if the car got stuck.

Grey skies and light, spitting snow blew in with the rest of the Wendell family. Probably following her mother around, thought Brittany. She and Tabitha traded places.

Walt and Brian bounded up the steps, followed by Robin, who wore impossible-for-the-season heels under her skirt. By the time she made it through the mud and up the stone steps to the porch, Walt and Brian were already taking off their coats in the kitchen.

Walt grinned. "Sylvia, that's some parking job!"

Brian said, "I didn't even know you could get a four-wheel-drive STUCK, not anywhere!"

Sylvia shrugged. "Well, it's certainly hung up now! Hi."

Just then, Robin came into the kitchen. She stopped short, and her eyes narrowed. "Sylvia."

"Oh, hello, Robin. Sorry to crash. I seem to be parked, for a little while. How are you?"

Quiet, that's how she was. She looked at Hattie, her husband, and Brittany.

Brittany held out an arm. "Hi, Mom, let me take your coat." *What awful, muddy shoes the woman is wearing. I'll just let her keep those.*

Robin thought she'd been set up.

But she wasn't the only one in for a surprise. Tabitha turned with spoon in hand, and several in the room did a double-take.

Now that it was out, Tabitha was into wearing tight, bright T-shirts that went well with her unmanageable red hair. She had a heavy bowl in one hand, and a spoon in the other. "Hello! Yes, I've gained some weight. It's the cooking up here!"

Sylvia collected herself first. She smiled. "Nice to see you again, Tabitha."

Walt had seen her at a schoolboard meeting, but she'd still been under sweatshirts there.

Brian had heard and seen some things around school, so he wasn't surprised, but her figure was still shocking to him.

Robin, well this was the first she'd heard of it, and she was trying to figure out why everyone was acting so… NORMAL.

Grandma Wendell quickly and efficiently set about putting everyone to work in the kitchen. "There's plenty left to do!"

Brittany came up beside Tabitha a few minutes later and kissed her on the cheek. "You're doing very well. No shame, Girl!"

Tabitha held up the wooden spoon like a talisman and repeated, "No shame!"

Robin worked at the counter beside Hattie and was trying, ineffectively, to seed grapes for the fruit salad. Hattie leaned over behind her helper-of-the-moment and nodded her head towards the young couple in the kitchen as said to Sylvia, "I shouldn't have left those two alone together!"

Three of the other four women in the room laughed.

Brittany's mother couldn't hide a brief expression of distaste. *So this is YOUR fault, too, then... I KNEW it.*

Sylvia continued to grin, but also looked puzzled.

Hattie shook her head. No. *Not here, not now.*

Robin continued to stew. *Hang around here long enough and EVERYONE gets pregnant!* Robin knew THAT well enough. The knife drew blood - she'd cut her finger instead of a grape. "FUCK!" Robin went to the sink in a suddenly silent kitchen.

The day passed. Robin didn't bleed to death. Folks caught up. Dinner was a fine and fun affair. Robin, knowing that Sylvia worked for the Department of Social Welfare, was on her best behavior on the outside and seething on the inside.

Walt thought maybe it was good practice, having someone else around like this. He was thanking his lucky stars. He wasn't planning on towing out that woman's truck until the last possible moment. *Why ruin a good day?*

Brittany sat in the parlor with her dad after dinner. "It's mine, Dad, for all intents and purposes. For a while. Let's just say I had a direct hand in its conception. Accidentally."

Walt raised his eyebrow. "I find that hard to believe, but I suppose miracles do happen. How are her parents taking it?"

"Mrs. Bayer? She thinks it's a great gift, 'cause now her grandchildren problem is solved. Mr. Bayer? He's still trying to work his head around it."

Me, too. Same age, best friend... "I'm glad it wasn't you."

"What if I wasn't far behind?"

"Jesus, I hope not!" Walter looked his daughter over discreetly but carefully. "Aren't you a little young?"

Brittany pointed back into the kitchen. "Same age as her. Haven't you noticed how I'm kind of on fast-forward, here, with life? It won't be long, Dad."

"Brittany, having a child is a serious and expensive and time-consuming adventure that is best saved for... another time." He sat back and scowled at his daughter: "Didn't I just hear you tell the school board that you're planning a busy college career?!"

Brittany waved that away. "I'm about to find out ALL about having a child. In about two months."

"Learn well. And don't drop any hints to your mother!"

"I don't think so. As a matter of fact, I think I hear her yelling at someone now?"

Yes, there was a commotion in the kitchen... Brittany heard the word "hippie" and something about a "want-to-be commune" and "drag my daughter" and something about a "GODAWFUL MESS!" *Uh-oh.*

Both Walter and Brittany bolted from the parlor couch.

Brittany's mother stood at the sink with an apron on (and still in those horrible fancy high-heel shoes full of mud, she was too vain to take them off, apparently), but she was facing away from the dishes, and shaking her finger at Tabitha. She clammed up and went back to washing porcelain plates as soon as her husband came into view.

Walt ran his hands through his hair (a frustration cue that was becoming increasingly common, these days) and decided he'd better get the truck unstuck, just in case anyone had to go home in a hurry (probably them). He disappeared out to the barn.

Brittany's little brother Brian was fascinated by Tabitha's bulging belly. He kept staring at it every time he came in with another stack of dishes from the table. Brittany and Tabitha passed wordless communication and followed him out to the nearly-cleaned-up dining room.

Brittany started. "Don't be getting any ideas. This is not a Freebie."

Tabitha took over. "Don't be getting any OTHER ideas, either. This is going to SUCK. Wait 'til your thirty." She took the boy's hand and put it on her belly. As she moved it slowly around, the back of the boy's hand brushed the underside of a breast.

He turned scarlet.

"Don't worry about it. It's just a breast. They get in the way a lot. That's where the baby's going to get her food, so they got bigger." She moved his hand down to the bottom of her fundus and back up to the middle. "All the way down there. Imagine trying to tie your shoes in the morning."

Robin walked into the room, with Sylvia and Hattie right on her heels. "WHA - I don't BELIEVE this!!"

Tabitha and the boy froze.

Sylvia laughed. "Well, I see someone in the Wendell family is going to be an Oh-Bee-Gee-Why-Enn! You should be proud - he'll be rich and VERY comfortable around women!" The dining room filled with laughter.

Tabitha leaned in close to Brian. "It's okay. Scoot along now, before your mom sees your woody." It was an entirely normal reaction. She straightened up and beamed. "Nothing to be ashamed of."

Brittany's mother had put up with enough. She grabbed her coat and Walt's keys and sprinted out the kitchen door and down the stone stairs in a bitter huff.

They heard the Wendell family car start and do an eight-point turn on the pavement before it screamed down the road towards the village.

"I hope she doesn't go off the road...."

"I hope they find medication for that."

"Brittany Wendell! That was an awful thing to say! But you're probably right."

***

The tractor got stuck in the yard.

They all had a good laugh about that, and then Walt set to trying to start the old bulldozer that his father had once used in the sugarbush for springtime sap collection, so many years ago. First Walter took the battery out of Sylvia's truck and swapped it into the tray under the seat of the crawler. Then he had to bleed the fuel line and put some new kero from the farmhouse lamps into the bowl. The rusty old machine started after a short half hour of work. Brittany and Tabitha both helped (watched, actually) because they thought they might have to do it sometime. The three of them emerged from the shed victorious, with Brittany driving the crawler, steering with two tall levers on either side of the hard seat. Walt and Tabitha followed behind on foot in the path the dozer blade was making.

Brittany got the rusty, clankety old machine out onto the road and to within twenty feet of the truck. She put the gearshift in neutral, remembered to drop the blade, and hopped off. "You'd better do it from here, Dad." She had to yell. It was a very loud machine.

Walt thanked his lucky stars they hadn't thrown a track across the lawn. The machine hadn't moved since last time someone got stuck, probably back when his father was still alive.... He'd have to be extra careful on the hard surface of the highway, as the ancient and un-greased track-tensioners snapped and creaked while he turned the machine. "OKAY!! WHEN I GIVE YOU THE THUMBS-UP..." He showed Brittany the motion. He was practically bellowing in her face, but he wasn't sure she could hear over the roar. "UP! UP! DRAG THAT CABLE OVER TO THE TRUCK AND HOOK IT AROUND SOMETHING STOUT - THAT BALL HITCH WON'T WORK, TRY THE AXLE... AXLE WOULD BE FINE!! WHEN I SCOOT MY HANDS, LIKE THIS..." He motioned again, and continued: "THAT MEANS VAMOOSE! IF THE CABLE LETS GO, YOU DON'T WANT TO BE ANYWHERE NEAR IT!!" *And lets hope it doesn't come winging all the way back here to the seat...* He decided to keep it short - that would help with the lift and was less cable to hit him in the back of the head of it snapped...it was a really old cable. "DON'T GET STUCK, THAT CABLE HAS A LOT OF SHARP ENDS!"

Brittany nodded.

Walt worked the crawler around in the road until the back, where the winch was, faced the sinking truck from about four feet away.

Brittany took hold of the cable and dragged with all her might to unspool it out enough so she could get it to the truck. She lost a boot in the mud. "Fuck!!" Nobody heard her, the bulldozer was too loud. She dropped the cable, heaved her boot out of the mud with both hands and managed to get it back onto a still-clean sock without losing her balance. A little more tugging, some cursing, and one stick from the sharp frayed ends of cable and then she got the heavy, rusty cable looped around the ball hitch. Next, she hooked it underneath something on the bumper so it would hopefully stay put.

Walt grimaced. *Yah, she couldn't hear me.* "AXLE!" He pointed. "AXLE!!"

How the fuck am I gonna do THAT?!? Axle's all the way "UNDER! UNDER!!" Brittany pointed. "IN THE MUD!"

Walt couldn't hear her, but could see her mouth moving, and followed her pointing finger. *Oh.* He tossed his hands in the air. *I guess you could swim... maybe not.*

Brittany re-wrapped the cable around the tow-hitch, and then hooked it onto the short chain that dangled there beside it. *There.* She turned to her dad and shrugged. *Best I can do.*

Shit. Walt prayed he wouldn't rip off the poor woman's bumper and gave wild swings of his arm.

Brittany got well back.

Walt put some tension on it to lift the truck, set the brake on the winch, put the crawler in gear, and ever so slowly took the slack out. The wire creaked. The crawler slowed, loaded down, and then the truck bucked and began to rise out of the mud.

They could hear the sucking sound even over the whirPOPwhir-POPwhirPOP-whirPOPwhir of the crawler engine. Walt dragged the truck all the way out onto the pavement, then Brittany ran up to the cab of the now-rolling-free truck and pushed down on the parking brake so that it wouldn't run into the back of the crawler. Her dad stopped pulling. Mission Accomplished. Brittany surveyed the remains of the incident and decided, yes, as long as a bumper didn't pull off or an axle stay behind in the mud, she could probably pull off a rescue like this by herself, should the need arise.

Walt thanked his lucky stars that the bumper was still on the truck, then wound up the wire around the winch and put the dozer away in the shed. He restored the battery into Sylvia's pickup while everyone else returned to cleaning up in the kitchen. *I guess I'd better buy a battery and have Brittany start this thing a few times every year.* Maybe if she regularly plowed out the lane, that would be enough to keep it charged and keep a path open to the road....

While Walt figured on how to keep things in better working order around a long-abandoned farm, Brian went around inside the house with a broom, cleaning up piles of mud left by a pair of high-heels. Sylvia helped Brittany and Tabitha wash and dry dishes and serving bowls. Hattie made up a big box full of wide-mouth jars crammed with leftover corn gravy, ham, sweet potatoes, pea pie, Jell-o salad, and carrots. Sylvia got a whole maple-sugar-and-squash pie all to herself, to share with Hank whenever he finally made it home.

"Oh, I think this might be gone before he sees it! You snooze, you loose! You SURE you want to give away this whole thing, Hattie?"

"Oh, don't worry. I've got two willing helpers, we'll gin up two more before you're even home. And I've got one to send home with the boys, don't you worry. Pecan, Walt's favorite!"

Walt arrived back in the kitchen as all this was happening, through the shed door from the back, and tried to hide the fact that he was eyeing that squash pie that his mother had just given Sylvia. He really wanted that maple-squash pie. *Oh, well.* He thought about watching his own car leave without him. That meant only one thing. "How bad was it?"

Everyone knew to what he was referring.

"Not too bad." Hattie was being generous.

"Anyone have to throw her out?"

"No. She left on her own." Hattie shook her head. "Right after she saw Tabitha, here, helping your curious son feel up her belly."

Walt sighed. *Yes, it was probably harmless, but way too… Bohemian, yes that was the word for it, for my wife.* That explains that. *Not really such a big thing, but* "Yes, that would probably do it." He turned. "Sylvia… Which way are you going home, and do you have room in that truck for hitchhikers, two in number?"

"Dad, I can-"

Sylvia interrupted Walt's daughter: "Yes, I've got room! Going through the village anyways, this time, I think. Better road. The next house I get stuck out front of might not have a dozer in the shed!" She held out her arms. "I can get you two home. In exchange for a box of leftovers." She grinned.

"Sounds fair. When you're ready. No rush."

Sylvia had seen Walt eyeing the maple-squash pie. She had a sudden inspiration. She grinned, pulled the pie-carrier out of the box, and set it on the table. "What's the rush? Why don't we all sit down to some pie, first?"

Walt couldn't believe his luck.

She winked. "I told you Hank would never see it!"

***

Tabitha went home that night.

"It's time." Hattie loved the girl's company, but she did have a family down in the village. "Your father will be ready."

Brittany dropped her off on her own way to work at Smiley's. Easter night would be slow, but somebody had to be there, because they had to be open.

Tabitha's father HAD missed her. He was still mad, but he was careful to try to hide it.

Tabitha made a half-hearted effort to do homework in front of SIXTY MINUTES. She was back to heavy sweatshirts. She didn't want to throw her condition in his face. Mr. Bayer was sitting in his stuffed chair, absorbed. Or so she thought.

He finally spoke: "Are you a wild girl?"

"No, Dad, I am an about-to-be-a-mother-girl. That's VERY different. I'm about to be the as-opposite-of-wild as you can POSSIBLY imagine."

He pointed lazily toward the general direction of her bulging womb.

"It was just ONE time, just ONE. I made a mistake. Which I regretted almost immediately. BEFORE I found out I was pregnant. I'm a one-woman kind of girl, otherwise."

Her father chuckled, in spite of himself. "You did solve one problem, didn't you?"

"ACCIDENTALLY, but yes. No more worries about where the grandkids are going to come from!" She gently patted her belly, then thrilled into a smile as she felt a little tickle, like gas. A kick. "One of them's right here." She scooted up onto the arm of the big chair, beside him.

Her father put out his cigarette and waved the smoke away with his hand. "Bad for the baby. I'll smoke outdoors now. Did that when YOU were on the way, too."

Tabitha hugged her Dad.

***

"Zhey seem to be a couple, and quite committed!" The watcher - a man known to some as Demond - raised an eyebrow. "Zhe other one is... she quickens with child!"

Paul Wendell shrugged stoically. "So she's living there too?"

"Oui, yes, zhe both of zhem."

"You're sure they live there?"

"All week I have watched. Zhe black-haired one comes and goes, to work, zhe red-head stays and learns to cook. Zhey should open a bakery. On a wood fire, no less!" Actually, the man known to others only as 'The Demon' had enjoyed this little project - a trip down to play voyeur at the Wendell farmhouse was like going back in time. He shrugged. "One big 'appy family!"

Still on the wood range. Paul nodded. *That sounds like Mom.* A flicker of sadness passed through him, nostalgia maybe. "She's well?"

The Demon knew a man's homesickness, from another life perhaps, and understood the question. He put a hand on Paul's shoulder. "She is fine. Probably not as you remember 'er, she is grey and stooped et... elle est... wrinkle." He quickly shook his head. "But not frail. 'Perky,' you would call it, certainment." He leaned in and made sure he caught this man's eye. "She still splits her own kindling. Elle fait bon vivre!" He smiled as he straightened back up. "She is surrounded by a beautiful family on zhe American holiday."

Paul's inquiry sounded almost timid: "What's the girl call her?"

The Demon smiled gently, warmly. He could feel the man's pain - he too had left home a long, long time ago, never to look back. "She calls her 'Grandma,' as did zhe red-headed child-with-child." *This poor man, tough getting family news vicariously....* "Zhey are most certainly family now." He gestured at his pictures, spread out there on the heavy desk in the quiet management office of a busy strip club that was a world away from the quaint farmhouse. "Zhere is another thing you should know...." How to phrase it. "Zhe red-head with child... she called zhe black-haired fille, she called her 'zhe father.' I think that zhey are married, zhose two, as married as two young women with a child on zhe way can possibly be." *It's kind of tender, actually, once I got over the shock!* And anyone could see it - "Zhose two lovers, zhey will grow old together, I am sure of it!"

Paul was momentarily speechless. *Wow. Mom's changed! She'd have never put up with that when...* He frowned. *Well how do I know that?* He eyed a bottle of Scotch over in the corner, then shook his head. *No. That's been too much my comfort lately. I need a clear head.* A sudden thought occurred: "Any idea who's the donor?"

The Demon grinned. "A young man circles zhem both, but never around your mother's house. Zhey are very... familiar with each other. But he has his own iron in zhe other fires, as we would say." The biker's mirth caused a brief and uncharacteristic giggle, which he quickly swallowed so as not to burden the poor man to whom he was reporting.

Ah. He nodded.

"Do you wish to know more?" Actually there was a LOT more to disclose... but the man had not asked for a report on his own daughter. *Little Cynthia appears to be QUITE involved in this story, as a side-dish, but neither she, nor her father, appear to know it.* The Demon-man grinned in delight.

Paul Wendell shook his head. *I get the picture. Enough of it, anyway.* "Thankyou." He gestured at the pile of black-and-white pictures, some of which were false-color: infrared film. "These will trouble me to no end if I keep them."

"I will save you zhat nuisance." The Demon scooped the collage of the life that Paul had missed into a manila envelope and left the office shaking his head. *Poor man. Better to leave the past in your wake.*

The three dog heads on the back of the departing man's denim vest laughed at Paul Wendell as they receded. He sighed. *I wonder how it would have turned had I stayed?*

His assistant stuck her head around the door-frame. "Paul, your daughter's here for you."

Paul's head shook in a rapid tremor of disbelief. "HERE?" He had some difficulty shifting gears. *Oh. Her.* "NOW?" It was business hours. *She will see things no young lady should!*

"Yes." She frowned. *The little upstart is* "Sitting in my chair, at this moment." *And I would like you to DO SOMETHING with her so as to get her out of it!*

Paul sighed. Resigned, now: "Send her in, let's see what she wants." *It's not like she doesn't see enough of me at home this week....* He frowned. *I'll have to make a rule: no visiting at the club.* His head shook. *She should know that already!*

Cynthia Wendell Dituscano came bouncing into her father's office, all trussed up in fancy - and slightly racy - clothing. "Daddy!"

She looks like one of the employees.... He shuddered. *Maybe it's the style, now. I can't criticize her dress, it would be damaging.* "Daughter!" He stood up. "How pleasant to see you! How can I be of service to you today?" *And how can I keep you from ever setting foot in this establishment again?*

Outside, Demond Du Normande stepped out onto the street behind the club and began to absolutely howl with laughter. "A magnifique! Ho-ho-HO! Je suis amusee!" *I cannot believe how... CONVOLUTEE this family is! They could not have set this up better if they'd TRIED to make cinema!* The outlaw biker regarded the manila folder in his hand. *This has all the makings of a what do they call it... CLUSTER-FUCK!* He brayed anew on incorporating this new phrase into his musing. *Yes, that's it perfectly!* This man referred to by most as "The Demon" walked away towards other business shaking his head over it. *It is good the poor man didn't press. His heart would have stopped.*

The Demon cackled all the way to a dark and forbidding basement bar around the corner, one where he kept a small office in the back. The pictures would go into his file cabinets - everything did.

CHAPTER TWELVE

Brittany and Bruce celebrated a reconciliation in his dorm room on the following Tuesday night, right after she got out of work. He'd just gotten back to school from a week away: four tournament games and then three days in Toronto with his parents. Brittany fell into his dorm room at just before midnight, throwing her bookbag down and pouncing on him before the door was even quite closed. They were no longer exactly keeping it secret. Half the dorm knew that Bruce and Curtis had a TOWNIE in there at night, sometimes. All sorts of WILD STORIES flew round about THAT! A new cheese was christened, in honor of the situation: Sandwich Gouda. Ripe, yummy, spreadable at the right temperature, and good on either loaf: rye bread or white. There were persistent and ugly rumors that Sandwich Gouda was even served with both breads at the same time on occasion: one slice of each on either side.

Brittany shut out the square of bright light by closing the door and turned with an angry smirk that Bruce couldn't see. "Your classmates think I'm screwing both of you." She'd heard the new term enough times in the hallway to figure it out. She shed her clothes and hopped into the bed to revel in skin-on-skin contact and the feel of making his body DO things.

"You are actually SLEEPING with both of us, eh?" Bruce grinned at her, there beside him in the dark.

Brittany spoke primly: "A matter of context, I think." She wondered if her dad had heard about this yet. *Probably not. He'd have one or the other of us locked up.* Her eyebrow went up. *Maybe all three of us... Curtis just for knowing.*

They had the room to themselves this night. Curtis was gone half the time, actually. He'd found a Townie of his own: one who lived in a small apartment over her parent's garage. The girl had that privacy and she also had a new - and fatherless - baby that was increasingly becoming a major interest in Curtis's life.

Trudy Jones had taken to parenting like a duck to water. Regardless of her new responsibilities and the massive change to her life, she still wanted a man there on occasion. Curtis was happy to comply, and didn't seem to mind sharing her with a demanding ten-month-old. He actually genuinely liked this girl, even with the distraction of parenting. Curtis said she called him her "Come And Go Man." Lately, it seemed to have become Come and Stay.

Angry wives around the county breathed a sigh of relief. That *CONCUBINE* was ensnared - twice over. Errant husbands would be less likely to find willing temptation.

As Brittany and Bruce lay in bed about six blocks up from Trudy and Curtis on this steamy springtime night, a gentle, on-again-off-again breeze brought warm puffs of air from deep out of the southern Midwest where it was already planting season. Heat, fecundity, promise rode on the air. After mixing their waters - or as close as the frightened couple was willing to come to it - Brittany and Bruce sat in the open dorm window with the lights out and watched campus life go by in the night. Another couple was conducting a similar post-Easter-break reconciliation in a well-lit room in the dormitory across the street. Below them, a taxi occasionally came and went. Students filed towards the dorms on sidewalks, in groups of two's and three's, mostly coming home from the library, which closed at midnight.

Silence. The sounds of campus were temporarily carried away by a stirring of the wind.

The breeze shifted.

She screamed: "PEEPERS!!!"

Brittany's exclamation was so loud that a startled Bruce nearly fell out the window. Landing on the pavement three stories below would have hurt. A lot. Landing there naked as a jaybird would have hurt MORE. He grabbed her tighter, grabbed the window-frame, and turned his head once he felt sufficiently braced. "Whatthefuck, eh?"

She started talking gibberish again: "PEEPERS! I HEAR PEEPERS!!"

Bruce wasn't from the area; He had no idea just how much the local residents valued the signs that told of the end of another long, grey, icy, bitter, awful, filled-with-shoveling winter.

"The frogs, you mean?"

"PEEPERS! Spring peepers!" She vaulted off the windowsill, thankfully TOWARDS the room (Bruce wasn't really sure which way she was going to go, she was so excited), and began pulling on clothing. "Come ON!"

Okay. Whatever, eh? Bruce dutifully pulled on his clothes and sneakers. "Going somewhere, are we?"

"You'll see! Shit. I've got to call Grandma."

Bruce followed as she bolted out of the room and stopped at the hallway phone adjacent to the stairwell. "Hi, Grandma. I'm SO sorry. Time got past me again. Yes, staying down here in the village." She listened. "Yes." Pause. "Goodnight." She hung up the phone and turned to Bruce to grab his hand. She was already dragging him down the stairwell. "Thank GOD she has a phone upstairs by the bed, or this wouldn't work. I really AM away too much. You have GOT to see this!"

They arrived at the bottom of the stairwell hand-in-hand, bursting out of the crash-door and into the warm night. Brittany dragged her lover on and on through the streets, turning this way and that, until they were down at the old abandoned depot by the railroad tracks. She turned and led Bruce off the street and onto the crunching stone ballast of the track. The rail-tops gleamed whenever the clouds parted way for the moon. Brittany slowed to a walk on the tracks - it was too easy to trip. The frogs were louder.

They stopped where the railroad grade cut through a swamp. There was snow all over, still, on the hills, in bright patches that seemed to move here and there in the night, but the swamp was mostly free of it. The night was suddenly still, as if the frogs had never been.

"Don't worry. They'll be back."

He wasn't worried. His beautiful girl was going nuts over the sound of slimy green things waking up for spring. *Big Deal.*

Brittany held very still. Bruce humored her.

One by one, they started again. Peep. Peep, peep. Peep. Peep. Peep, peep. Peep. Peep, peep, peep, peep. The chirps were loud, but no louder than the whistle of a bird. Within a minute the increasing noise hurt Bruce's ears. Hundreds, maybe THOUSANDS of frogs all chirping at once, all overlapping into a din that made his ears hum.

Brittany was yelling. "You feel that? Your ears?"

Bruce felt it in his feet, too. *Bad.* He grabbed Brittany and pulled her off her feet, over the embankment.

A wall of light that had been hidden by the curve passed over their heads.

Brittany marveled at the moving metal wall of din just above them. *WOW! Train. Fast.*

Then it was gone. The peepers were silent.

Bruce felt suddenly older. "Let's go." He pulled Brittany carefully up to the edge of the track.

"Wow! Forgot about that!" She looked back at the swamp as they started walking. "I've been here every year since I was eight and snuck out the first time, to find the peepers." She tripped on a railroad tie, regained her footing just as the moon disappeared behind clouds, and clung to Bruce to remain upright as she stubbed her toe again. She hardly noticed. "I caught one once, when I was ten. Got wet from head to toe. Got busted, too. Wet shoes made too much noise going up the stairs. First of many showdowns at home. They're brown, I think. Grounded for two weeks. Hard to tell in the dark. They have a little splotchy EX on their back." She chattered along as they made their way along the gravel and stones and back towards the village and light. "TINY things, hard to imagine they make that much noise. I'm here the first night they're out. Every year." She stopped. "And now you've been, too. You're taking part in my history." She kissed his cheek.

Doesn't take long for this girl to get strange... are they ALL like this, here? He was maturing, so he knew not to voice his thoughts.

They walked hand-in-hand, in silence, for a while. The moon came out, and stayed out. They turned onto village streets again.

"Bruce?"

"Yah, Bri?"

"Be there for the rest of my history?" She stopped, turned. "Maybe you will, and maybe you won't, but I'm offering myself to you. If you stay here, in this town. If you work hard." *You seem serious enough.* "I want to fill that farmhouse, the one where you've been to breakfast, I want to fill it with children. Bring life back to it, every day, not just holidays and hockey breakfasts. Make a family."

Bruce remained quiet. *This is the SECOND time she's brought that up!* He worked very hard in that moment to avoid rolling his eyes. *What was it with these little townie girls and their whole I-want-to-grow-up-and-get-married fixation?* At the same time, he had just a flicker of... something. That Something New he only felt around, or when he thought of, her: Brittany. He even thought of her on the increasingly-rare evenings when he visited Cynthia, just for old-times sake. He was too young to realize what that was.

"Bruce?" She grabbed his hand and started leading him back to the dorm.

"Mmmmm?"

"Do you want me a lot?"

Bruce thought about the frogs. Twenty thousand little male frogs getting laid out there in the swamp - or trying to. "Cheep! Cheep! Cheep!"

Brittany giggled and stopped to kiss him in a quiet spot on the street. She pulled back and looked into his eyes, there under the moon and surrounded by the sounds of a Spring night. "Do you want me enough to marry me?"

What a silly girl. "The MAN is supposed to ask. Actually, I think..." *I DO. Suddenly I can't IMAGINE keeping that kind of company with anyone but you, but* "You're still in high school, and I'm only halfway through college. Of course I do." He frowned. "Why don't you graduate high school first, though..." *She's YOUNG.* He'd never thought that before. He had another frightening thought. "Are you still on the pill?"

"Of course. Things can move awfully fast around here, though." She winked.

"What's THAT supposed to mean?" With sudden clarity, he realized he had been chasing this girl for her tail, while she had been wagging her tail for a future husband. And his reluctance didn't seem to put her off. *Uh-oh.*

By way of an answer, Brittany just said, "Well, don't say I didn't warn you." She grabbed his hand and went skipping off towards the dorm, dragging him behind. Tabitha's pregnancy was driving Brittany batty. She knew it, but couldn't do anything to stop it.

***

Bruce woke up before she did. He was still wrapped around her sleeping form - they hadn't moved an inch all night. He smiled. And then he buried his nose in that curly black hair and lay there in his bed, thinking: *Is this what EVERY morning could be like?*

Brittany missed school that day, and there was a minor scandal around Hanover Hall because SOMEONE had a TOWN GIRL in their room ALL DAY. That was a violation of the rules of etiquette, not to mention military order, and suggested a SERIOUS pairing.

Bruce was just trying it out, for a lark. *What would it be like if SHE lived where I live?* He'd never thought about that before....

Sometime later in the morning Brittany woke, went out on the campus for coffee and a bagel (wondering what she'd say if she ran into her dad), and then came back to do her Junior-year high-school homework in the dorm room. Bruce, and sometimes Curtis, came and went while Brittany remained. She stayed until mid-afternoon, when she had to go up to the farmhouse to get changed for her shift at Smiley's.

She left Bruce with a lot to think about. The room seemed changed somehow.

Fortunately, Curtis was cool, and played down the rumors. "Nah, he just tired her out all night, and he's too much of a gentleman to kick her out the door 'till she's recovered."

Across the grassy quad, Cynthia fumed in the news - heard repeatedly via the rumor mill - and vowed to do two things: *fermez moi castor, ca vient de s'eteindre* - shut that boy off for good - and figure out what the hell had gone wrong that her allure couldn't keep that prick's interest! *Osti de Crisse! T'es faite a l'os! Merde! I'll keep the next one so interested, his tongue will fall out!*

***

Bruce called his folks a couple of nights later.

He had a superficial conversation with both parents, and then talked with his father a little more.

"Dad. There's this girl...."

Only one?! Boy, he's changed! His parents were well-acquainted - and uncomfortable - with their only child's tom-catting habits, even back in school. *Funny he slows down when he gets to college!* His son wasn't saying anything, so his father voiced his thoughts: "Got caught in the catnip, did you?"

"Something like that."

I wonder if we'll be meeting a grandbaby next time we see him? "How do you feel about that?"

"How did you KNOW?"

Oh! He's REALLY serious! The man's eyebrows went up.

His wife, across the kitchen, regarded the husband and the phone with narrowed eyes. *Caught? Feel? Is my boy getting DISTRACTED by something... someone?* She began eavesdropping with open and concerned abandon, torn between visions of daughter-in-law visits and dreams of her son's successes in life. These were mutually-exclusive pictures.

The elder male Sutton made eye contact with his wife as he answered the question. "We... I met someone right. Special, and right. It wasn't quite the right time, but we made it the right time. She was worth it."

Oh. "I..."

Silence.

"Is that why you've been kind of scarce?" They'd started to feel shut out, this last year.

"I may stay out here a while."

That was the understatement of his life.

***

"So?" Brittany waited in eager anticipation.

"Oh, I won't get the score for a month." Tabitha shrugged the tips of her shoulders. "But I'm sure I passed. And the schoolboard is going to let me walk."

Brittany jumped up and hugged her friend from behind, jumping with glee.

Tabitha stayed right where she was. Getting out of a chair was too much work these days. She tipped her head back against Brittany's breast and smiled up at the chin and cascade of black hair. "I get to graduate."

Hattie looked up from the cutting board, where she was rolling out crust for a savory meat pie. "Tabitha, that's wonderful news. I'm so happy for you." She cast a wary eye at the beach-ball pushing against her farmhouse table. "I hope you make it that far." She laughed.

Tabitha smiled serenely. "In the oven, or in my arms, me and Theodore are walking the stage." Tabitha put her hand on her belly on the word THEODORE.

Brittany jumped back. "Tab... You..."

She laughed. "I got curious. I asked my mom. She might have twisted my arm a little..."

Hattie came over and cupped Tabitha's head. "It's only a little over a month away, I think it's probably time you knew. Time to buy blankets and such." She went back to the crust on the counter. "It's a nice name, Theodore."

"I think so. Ted for short, the nickname. It has a nice ring." Tabitha grinned from ear to ear.

Hattie stiffened. She said, very quietly to herself, "Oh dear." She continued rolling out the pie, but her shoulders shook with mirth.

Brittany came around to Tabitha's side to face her. "I'm glad. THAT was a HARD secret to keep!" She dropped to her knees and put her mouth up close to Tabitha's belly. "Hello, Teddy! Hello in there!"

"Ooooff!" Tabitha's cheeks blew out. "He heard you!"

Brittany also suddenly got a strange look on her face as a thought occurred.

From across the kitchen, in a quavering voice, Hattie asked, "Tabitha, what is THEO-dore's MIDDLE name?" She suspected she already knew the general gist of the answer.

Tabitha sat up primly, and elevated her chin as she proudly replied, "Edward... Theodore Edward."

Brittany's eyes got wide. "TABITHA! NO! YOU CAN'T!"

"I certainly CAN and I AM. Sometime in the near future I will introduce to the world mister Ted E. Bayer." She beamed.

"He's going to hate you." Brittany slumped into a chair.

When Hattie stopped laughing, she suggested a solution to Brittany: "Well, you're the father. Do the right thing. Marry the girl and make Teddy there a Wendell."

Brittany was on the cusp of saying, I might just have to, but then thought better of it. *Tab might take me up on it here and now and then I'd be stuck a cheating wench.* A flicker of guilt passed through her.

Tabitha sat in righteous resolve. "I think it's a fine name for a boy."

***

Brittany called her Dad a few evenings later.

"Hi, ya, it's me. Get this. Ted E. Bayer." Pause. "That's right." She shook her head at the phone. "Nothing I can do. Vermont's not a marry state, yet, for People Like Us." Pause. "Thanks, Dad. We may take you up on that, if Grandma and I can convince her. She's pretty set on it. That was sweet of you." Pause.

Her dad had just offered to fly them to California - a state where they COULD marry - to save Theodore E. from the Bayer last name.

Walter Wendell had surreptitious reasons for arranging his daughter's easy marriage to Tabitha: he'd heard rumors about "that Wendell girl" who might be staying in one of the dorms sometimes. THAT situation made him uneasy for all SORTS of reasons. *Especially if it's true and it's the wrong dorm, the wrong floor, the wrong room, the wrong young man.... What are the odds?*

"Well, actually, Dad, I'm calling about something else."

"Oh?"

"I'd skip the schoolboard meeting this week, if I were you."

"Really." He sighed. "Is it going to get contentious?"

"There might be a little gentle arm-twisting."

Oh shit. Won't this be interesting.

***

Brittany drove an hour south to Springfield to sit for the GED on a warm Saturday morning, then hauled-ass back north to make it to work in time. She thanked her lucky stars that Michael Frey had built the car well, and also that no Troopers seemed to take an interest in the little green bullet that worked its way northwards against the timeclock.

***

She attended the schoolboard meeting the following week.

"It's nice to see you again, Miss Wendell. How can we help you this time?" Mr. Mitchell looked sideways and for the first time really thought about the absence of schoolboard member Wendell. *Hmmmm.*

"Good evening. I just sat for the GED. I expect that I scored adequately to receive my paper, and I'd like to graduate with this year's class as a result."

Frowns. They'd just been through this with... Tabitha Bayer.

Roger smirked. He could see where she was going with it. He nodded when no one else except Brittany was looking, although with one eyebrow raised. He shook his head and sighed an exasperated sort of sigh when the other board members had him in their peripheral vision. Actually, Roger wasn't sure if it was a good idea... *but she seems to be running her own show.*

Mrs. Mitchell finally filled the frustrated silence: "Why don't you just finish school?"

Brittany changed the subject: "You recently let another student, someone with fewer completed advanced courses, I might add, let THAT person skip into this graduating class. Or so I hear."

Mr. Mitchell responded sternly, as any adult should to this wildly preposterous idea. "THAT situation is different. Miss Bayer is pregnant. She'll be managing a newborn next schoolyear." He looked around to his board for support. Heads were nodding.

"I can get that way. Rather quickly. Might even be time to be working on the second one.... I'd be quite occupied by the time graduation rolled around next year...." Brittany smiled her most charming smile.

Roger shook his head minutely. *Bad move, young lady....*

Mr. Mitchell looked angry. "You're unbelievable! You can't just SKIP a schoolyear, Miss Wendell." He pushed back from the folding table to confer with his colleagues. He sat back down in a minute. "Miss Wendell, most colleges REQUIRE a high-school diploma. We would be remiss to just let someone of your caliber just waltz out of here without finishing school."

Brittany dug around in her purse and came out with an envelope. "I've been accepted at college already. Early acceptance program at the Academy. They want the brightest minds committed by the end of their Junior year in high school, that's fairly common. I'm one of them."

Roger cut in: "Brittany... Miss Wendell, I believe that early acceptance is CONTINGENT on finishing high school. Correct?" He felt bad, bursting her bubble.

Brittany sighed. "I'm sure going to enjoy motherhood."

Roger grimaced. Mr. and Mrs. Mitchell frowned. They huddled, heads together again.

Mrs. Mitchell spoke for the group: "The answer is NO. If it was up to me, I'd shoo you out the door and into a cap and gown right now" *just to get rid of you.* "But it's not up to me. The STATE sets these rules."

Brittany persisted. "Thankyou, but all I want to do is WALK. A GED will do fine."

Roger shook his head. "Actually, Brittany, it won't. You never know what's coming at you in life. Get that high school diploma. It means something."

Mrs. Mitchell had a parting comment: "And don't go getting yourself In A Condition. We made ONE exception, and I'm already regretting it." She shook her finger. "You're a very strong-willed, but mis-directed girl. Please don't abuse our time again."

Brittany stood, and said, in an extra-crisp voice usually reserved for especially troublesome customers, "Thank-You-VeryMuch."

She wasn't done, though.

**

Not a great deal changed between Brittany and Bruce, or so they thought. But everything changed, because they were past courting.

Bruce forgot Cynthia's phone number for good (he never knew he'd been Shut Off, much to Cynthia's growing frustration).

Brittany became a little scarce around Tabitha's house.

Brittany and Bruce fell into being a couple, mostly in secret, but in full view of the diner and the residents of the third floor of his dorm. She dropped by to pick him up more often. He didn't come to the restaurant as much anymore, but when he did, Bruce was received as Brittany's family. There were quick looks and nods from and between the other employees. The regular customers knew their routine, and might come in the door telling Brittany she'd better get pie and cheese ready, her customer was pulling into the lot. Those that had come to know them looked on at Young Love and smiled their best wishes upon them.

Bruce disappeared for a few weeks here and there when school and the last of the year's hockey games took him away. Some intensive course for a job in the upcoming summer took him away for three weeks, too. Then he was busy catching up: Final projects, in which he had to really excel to get average grades in some of his classes due to his recent prolonged absences.

Brittany understood the pressures and commitments of college life - she was busy enough with high school and waitressing and Tabitha's ever-bigger baby bump. By way of being involved in his life, Brittany went to a couple of Bruce's last home games, where she sat near middle ice with her grandmother and Sylvia.

Bruce tried hard to put on an extra-vigorous show on the ice, to impress his lady-love up there in the stands next to that boisterous old Wendell woman. He took too many chances, was a little too aggressive, and ended up making an unintended impression on the referees several times - with trips to the penalty box. He tried harder to ignore the black-haired beauty up in Section Seven.

***

At the very last hockey game, Brittany's dad even joined them, much to everyone's delight. Walter Wendell was often elsewhere on Game Night, but being a Professor at the school, he made sure to fly his department's colors at the rink a couple of times a year, and recently a bit more than that. He sat right between his mother and his daughter and was amused to compare the wildly divergent styles of cheering on his left and right: his mother, shaking her fist, yelling mild curses, frequently standing to boo the referees; Brittany, standing only when the rest of the crowd stood, demurely yelling encouragement at the home team and veiled put-downs at the opposing bench.

Hattie was delighted to see Walt at another game and glad to have the girl's company, too. Brittany hadn't been around much lately, even to sleep. What a pleasure to have them both here! *That girl has something going on somewhere*, Hattie was sure of it. Some recent weeks she was gone overnight more than half the time. Hattie was concerned, of course. *No schoolgirl should be working nearly full time and tramping around town overnight on the other nights.* She shook her head. *She's not with Tabitha. THAT little girl - well, not so little now - wouldn't be HALF as grumpy as she was, every time she visited the farmhouse, if Brittany was spending nights down there* with her pregnant friend. Hattie wondered what boy or boys her dear lusty and pragmatic granddaughter was victimizing this time. She really hoped the young woman wasn't turning into a harlot, but she hadn't ever known her to have any sort of long-term relationship with anyone but Tabitha. *And there's certainly no stopping her now, not unless I put a lock on her door, let the air out of her tires, and arrange for her to lose her job!*

It never occurred to Hattie that the terms of Brittany's current romantic relationship might finally be the conventional ones, but possibly turned on their head, and much more serious than schoolgirl dating games: love, marriage, children. Bruce had come quietly and carefully chasing Brittany. She had responded by assessing this boy and then, once he passed muster, she had started a very earnest pursuit of him. And now they were courting for real. How the tables had turned!

It DID occur to Hattie that her granddaughter's interest in the game seemed unusually focused. It seemed like every time player number Twenty-Two left the ice, her granddaughter's head turned to follow him to the bench. Hattie watched more closely. Back on the ice. *Yes, so is Brittany's interest.*

A face-off.

A little dust-up on the ice. Whistles.

Hattie Wendell had to give the referees a piece of her mind. *They saw that COMPLETELY wrong, the* "DUNCES CAN'T EVEN SPOT A HOOK WHEN IT'S IN THEIR OWN SKATE! GET YOUR EYES CHECKED YOU MORONS!" She sat back down.

Not too many seats away, Sylvian grinned.

Walt tucked his neck down into his sweater collar. *I'm not seeing this, I don't know her, I should have sat with Ed.* He looked around furtively to see how many people were staring - he was sure they were.

Sylvia caught Walt's gaze with a twinkle in her own eye, and she shrugged. *She hasn't jumped out onto the ice. Yet.*

Brittany didn't really notice her grandmother's antics. It looked like Bruce might have a little skate-limp on his way off the ice, unnecessary referees on either side of him like he was a felon casing his escape or something… *oh, I hope he's alright.*

Number Twenty-Two to the penalty box.

Hattie watched her granddaughter's interest suddenly centering almost entirely on the hole. *Hmmm. Number Twenty-Two.* And as Hattie scrutinized her granddaughter, she realized that someone else was watching her, too. *Number Twenty-Two, from the penalty box, watching… Brittany.* Hattie shook her head. That wasn't going to be good for Bruce's hockey. *He needs to pay attention to what's happening on the ice, even from the Hole! Tsk, tsk.*

Someone else noticed Brittany's distraction. Walther Wendell grimaced. *I hope this isn't what it looks like. That boy is going to become complicated.* He sighed. *Figures it would end up like that, though.* Walt's eyebrow went up and down ruefully as he considered the possible futures. His evening was ruined, now, and maybe his daughter's life, too, but he would be careful not to show it.

Hattie thought back to last Fall. *The folk dance at the Grange... hmmm. Maybe Brittany HAS settled down after all!* She shrugged minutely. *The girl could do worse.* Maybe the young man would convince her to slow down her wild ways and... *Well, maybe ONE toddler at a time is enough, for now.* Hattie thought about the threats she'd made at that Hockey Breakfast after Brittany had moved up to the farmhouse. She suppressed a grin. *Poor boy must be scared half out of his mind, no wonder they're keeping it a secret!*

Now Hattie could watch the game in earnest, again.

Walt lay awake down in the village later that night, frequently striking a Thinker's Pose as he tossed and turned on the pillows, wondering how to get his dear but willful daughter out from under this heavy twist of a spiteful and darkly comedic fate. *Dammit!*

Chapter Thirteen

A Wider Orbit....

"Tabitha and Brittany

Sitt'n in a tree

Kay-eye-ess-ess-eye-en-gee!

First comes love

Then comes marriage

Then comes Teddy in a baby carriage!"

Giggles in the school's long hallway. A whistle.

"Gee, Tab, we've got our very own personal cheerleading squad. Isn't that nice." Brittany took it stoically.

Easy for her. She's not the one who's pregnant. "Fuck you all." Tabitha continued calmly and primly: "May your birth control measures fail miserably when you're with your most skenky, desperate hump."

An stern, older voice emerged behind the girls. "Tabitha, that was disgusting and not very nice and NOT AT ALL lady-like."

"Yes, Mrs. Hatcher, I'm sorry Mrs. Hatcher."

No you're not. You're pregnant and moody and a bad influence on the rest of them. Mrs. Hatcher sighed and ducked into her classroom. *It was so much more… PROPER when the ones In That Way were shipped off to prepare for motherhood somewhere PRIVATE, with others of their own situation.* She pushed into her classroom and put on a bright smile, wondering which of these engaging young women would be next to fall for the old line.

Brittany giggled. When Mrs. Hatcher was out of earshot she said, "Woman probably went after her husband every night with the cast iron frying pan when SHE was pregnant."

Both girls laughed musically and walked arm-in-arm to their next classes amidst a cacophony of cat-calls, whistles, and hoots, some of which echoed a common and useful-to-the-girls refrain: "Brittany, you should have put on a rubber!"

There was also one random lusty yell from a brother of the builder of a green hot-rod: "Hey, Brittany, did you fuck my brother with that dick?!" (He didn't like his older-now-graduated brother very much.) That comment made this Frey boy the hero of the day, both for its vulgarity and for its originality.

Brittany and Tabitha also passed one now-fifteen-year-old boy in the hallway, one who blushed crimson as they went by, but kept his mouth shut and eyes forward, just as he had been instructed. *Good Boy.*

Tabitha was done with the tricks: sweatshirts, coats, sweat-pants, out-of-season jackets, and finally her father's jackets. She'd kept it up in school for about two weeks after she told her parents the Big News, and then gave up. Let the world know. Today she wore a size Two-XL tie-dye T-shirt tied in a knot below her bump and a loose, frilly skirt with a waistband that dove way down under the global protrusion that preceded her around every corner. Tabitha had returned to her old self.

Brittany couldn't get enough of her friend, and one spot in particular. She was forever coming up behind the bulging girl, putting her arms around her and sneaking a hand under the clothing to hold the bottom of the sloshing aquarium, just over and now ending IN the girl's curly-hairs. She would do that for ten minutes at a time, sometimes, when they were up at the farmhouse.

Tabitha had taken to swatting Brittany away when they were in school. It was embarrassing, and was going to get them In Trouble. "STOPPIT, BRIT! JESUS!!" Tabitha twisted around, away from Brittany's groping hands, and backed up to her locker so that she was safe for a moment. "You'd think you like me BETTER pregnant!"

"Oh, I think I do. If I was a boy, I'd definitely fuck you. Right now."

Tabitha looked skeptical, but smiled, in spite of herself. "Really? Right here in school?"

"Youbetcha. We'd find an empty room SOMEWHERE in this place... Maybe under the bleachers. I've heard that's the usual spot."

"Well, I'm horny as a toad these days." She grabbed Brittany's hand. A challenge. "Lead the way." Something about the hormones coursing through her body made Tabitha just TINGLE down there, all the time. It was counter-intuitive - she was already knocked up. *What's the point?* But sometimes she sure wanted someone to SCRATCH that tingle!

"I said, IF I was a BOY." Brittany gave her friend a kiss on the cheek and turned to open her own locker.

"Teasing bitch." Tabitha put on her best for-show pout.

The other kids in school were used to the couple, now, so random acts of affection no longer caused a commotion around them, other than the cat-calls. The teasing was different, and some of it was possibly even meant to be friendly, but sometimes the line between friendly teasing and awful hazing was very blurred.

Generally, it was the boys who were the worst.

Tabitha's female classmates were quieter. Children can be very cruel, but teenaged females who are sexually active are also very scared, if they are not stupid or totally moony as a cow over some boy or other. It - the baby-bump - could happen to any one of them. The initial teasing and gossiping had been tempered by concern and curiosity most of all, and also the CUTE-factor. Tabitha was beautiful, and even more so now that she was a mother-to-be... she just radiated vibrancy and well-being from her every pore. She wore it well, and it fit with the mis-guided stereotypical image that her classmates had of lesbians and hippies (considered one-in-the-same), however untrue that picture might be.

Within a few weeks, her classmates couldn't imagine Tabitha any other way than nearing full-term, waddling between classes, and wearing a bulging, stretched-out T-shirt.

The boys were a little harder. They were still jealous that Tabitha had landed one of the most desired young women in the school. Tabitha got her, instead of one - or many - of them. A few young men were a little confused and they teased and stared and gossiped more than any of the girls ever did, convention notwithstanding. Gradually, they too came to accept Brittany and Tabitha as a couple.

Near Prom Time the couple's picture went in as a last-minute addition to the yearbook. Just a random picture in the hallway, Brittany with her arm around Tabitha, faced towards the camera but casting a sidelong glance at the baby-bump below and beside her. A picture that could have been taken any one of many days, with Tabitha's left hand up on top of her bump, smiling angelically at the picture-taker. Neither girl remembered the picture until they saw it in the yearbook - an ambush of both them and the Yearbook Advisor. Page Twenty-Seven, in the Superlatives: 'Couple Most likely To Wed.' When asked about it, Brittany had no comment. Tabitha hoped so, but was under no illusion that she'd be that lucky.

***

"Come to a party? It's off-campus." Bruce waited, but Brittany wasn't saying yes. He persisted: "Toga. You know, sheets and Romans and all that. It'll be fun, eh?"

"Do you think that's a good idea? Kind of dangerous… Coaches, Grandma…"

"I kind of doubt your Grandma goes to toga parties." Bruce smiled his most boyish, innocent smile. "I like living dangerously."

"It's your funeral." Brittany looked grim. Serious.

"Cheer up. You'll have fun."

Okay, fine! Brittany was feeling contrary for some reason, this evening. *More fun than you can imagine, Brucie!*

***

Brittany spent the late afternoon and suppertime hanging with a lonely, pregnant young woman at a house in the village. There were some problems with Tabitha, who was ever-larger, but strangely enough, also starving for affection. And a little grumpy about both.

"Puh-LEASE, girl?" Tabitha was displaying bedroom eyes for Brittany again this evening. She sensed she was in a competition, and suddenly she didn't want to lose at this late stage in the game. Sex? No! Cuddling, back-rubs, affection, love? Tabitha was starving for those. And she couldn't imagine anyone providing those very important sacraments except one black-haired, green-eyed girl that STILL curled her toes and sped her heart, nearing full-term or not.

"NOOOOO! You had your chance!" Brittany pushed the pregnant red-head gently away. "That's disgusting, Tab. I squeeze you too hard and you'll deliver RIGHT HERE."

"But I'm so HOT and DESPERATE, I could screw a BOY right now!" Not really. Mostly she wanted to lay back in the tub at the farmhouse and feel Brittany wash her hair and feet.

Tabitha wanted LOVE and AFFECTION. Intimacy, attention, love and sex: those are sometimes hard concepts for a young person to fully understand until later.

Brittany sized her friend up at arm's length. "You want a boy? Then go DO that!" Brittany gave her friend a grin. "It worked for you once before!" An empty threat that Brittany wasn't going to worry over.

Tabitha sulked, crossed her arms over her now-getting-in-the-way-of-everything lap and bosom. "Too hairy. The legal ones I mean. Boobs." She sized up Brittany. "I want BOOBS! YOU ARE SUCH A…" Tabitha tried to think of a dirty word. "FRIEND!!!"

"Exactly. And that's just how it is now."

"Don't you want to FEEL the baby?"

"Yes, actually, I do. But last time I did that when you were... lonely, and we somehow ended up in bed together. Sorry, Babe." Brittany got up and crossed to the door. She caressed Tabitha's cheek on the way. "Call me when you aren't in the way of being... how you are. You're too dangerous right now. I've got to go home."

Tabitha got up and belly-ran to the door. "I'll call Grandma and let her know you're on the way!"

Brittany looked back and yelled as she got into the Pinto. "Thanksalot. You're a bitch, you know!"

"You're a cheat!"

"Yeah, I am. But I'm not carrying around someone else's child!"

"I HATE you!"

The green Pinto was already driving off. Tabitha could be all spit and fury on her bad days - Brittany was glad she had someplace to go, and someone else to hang with.

***

Brittany met Bruce at the back of the dorm.

"Hi, Brucie!" Brittany jumped out of the car and bounced over to him, floating impossibly between bounds, graceful as ever. "Still think this is a good idea?"

"It'll be fine."

You say so....

They started walking, arm-in-arm, up the sidewalk towards the village. Whenever a car and its bright, secret-spilling headlights approached, Brittany steered Bruce into a dark yard, where they kissed and licked and tugged at earlobes with teeth and caressed necklines with the smooth, soft, wet inner skin of lips until the bright danger was past. They meandered and ambled, furtive like animals, ever further from the campus and ever closer to music and noise and yelling. The couple turned left at one corner, right at another. Now they followed music, commotion, yells diagonally across town: right, left, right, left, right until they came to an overflowing porch filled with... Romans and Ceasars and scantily-clad women trailing tiny pieces of sheet across a shoulder or a thigh.

Someone passed in the street, already in a drunken stumble. He whirled, started to trip on his sheet, miraculously recovered, and raised his plastic beer-stein. The curly-haired Roman yelled out to Bruce in a booming, deep voice: "Hail to the Gladiator of the Hockey Arena, to his great attip... att-p... aptipude... SHIT! Skill with a stick!!!" The sheet-draped Senator turned to Brittany and raised his beer. "And to his merry bride-to-be, Receiver of the Stick, soon to be wed under the eyes of God and All!" He toasted even higher, still walking forward and looking backwards. Then tripped. And fell. The beer remained upright, and half full. All was well. The Roman got up laughing, inspected his drink, drained it, and ran up to the porch.

"Did YOU put him up to that?" Brittany stood on the sidewalk in front of Bruce, her hands on her hips, a look of mock fierceness on her face.

Bruce held up his hands in peace. "I had NOTHING to do with that. He was drunk."

"Who was it?"

"I have no idea." THAT was his Left Wing. *Who is going to get his ass kicked once he's sober. BRIDE-TO-BE?!? What the fuck?* Bruce took Brittany's hand. "This is going to seem a bit strange to you. It's a College-Boy party. There are going to be some new and maybe shocking things. Things that College Boys and Girls do that maybe you kids from the sticks haven't seen yet. Especially you young'uns."

"Was that a TALK?" *Did he just give me a TALKING-TO?!?* "Brucie, that was SO SWEET! I'll try not to be too awfully shocked. If I get scared, can I hold you?" She smiled playfully, let go of his hand, and ran into the party. Up onto the porch and right through the front door and into the throng of sheet-clad bodies.

Holy shit! I hope she's okay in there.... Bruce hurried in after her, but a sudden flood of people coming out got in his way.

Brittany inserted herself deep into the house and then scrutinized the party for HER evening's entertainment. She scored right away.

When Bruce found her, after fighting his way through the crowded house for about ten minutes, Brittany was sitting on a couch.

She was holding a flat cigarette paper and a baggie on her lap, one on one leg, one on the other. She was just opening the baggie.

"Whoah, there, girlie! Let me show you how to…" He bent, reached over to the lamp table beside the couch and grabbed a cigarette paper out of the package at Brittany's elbow. "You crease it like this and then you..." He looked up from his hands to discovered that somehow, Brittany was already holding a cigarette-perfect joint to her ruby-red lips and puffing on a nearby odor-control candle. "Shit."

Brittany responded in a tight voice. "Maybe us Just Kids out in the sticks...." She blew a long cloud of smoke out. "...Could teach you

College Boys a thing or two? Here." She waved her fingers. "Give me that paper, I'll roll another one."

"Can't. Party-time comes AFTER hockey. Your grandmother really WOULD kill me, and the coaches would DEFINITELY throw my ass off the team."

"What about Cupid there, out front, in the Toga?"

"Who?"

"Your Wing. He was drunk-as-a-skunk."

"THAT I can do. But this... Wait...where did you learn to do THAT!?" He gestured at the near-perfect roll in her hand. "You're like, TWELVE YEARS OLD, you shouldn't even KNOW WHAT THAT IS yet, eh?"

"Never judge a book by its cover. Let me tell you a story, College-Man." She took another deep pull, went wide-eyed, snorted smoke out her nose, and then blew a perfectly-formed smoke ring at her surprised date. "Siddown, Brucie." She patted the couch. "It started when..."

***

It started one evening not long after her fourteenth birthday party. Brittany and Robin Wendell were arguing, as usual.

"Brittany, it REALLY is EMBARRASSING when I invite your friends over and you don't even give them the TIME OF DAY!" The woman was sitting on the foot of her bed, one hand on the covers over Brittany's foot, acting all COMMISSERATING, like the conversation was to help Brittany.

"They're NOT MY FRIENDS. They're your friends' daughters. There's a DIFFERENCE."

"Well, they're your classmates. You should try to get along."

"I don't WANT to get along, they HATE me!"

"Well, if you weren't such a SNOB to everybody, maybe you would HAVE some friends. It's really awful when I have to beg people to bring their kids over so you can have a birthday."

Mom, you are such a bitch. "You want me to have friends?"

"Of COURSE, dear! That's all I want is for you to be HAPPY!" *And normal. Jesus, girl, you're a NERD or something!*

"Well, fine, Mom. Next week I'll have friends. Lots of them." *Take that.*

"Well sweetie! That's WONDERFUL!" *And how are you going to pull THAT off, after spending fourteen years being such a little stuck-up PRINCESS?* Brittany's mother was all smiles, but there was a calculating look in her eyes. She stood up and clapped her hands together, *Yippee!* "I'll take you ALL out to ICE CREAM and the MOVIES - I suppose we'll have to rent a van!" Her mother ran out of the room with a false manic- gleeful look on her face.

You wait, you bitch. Brittany had some work of her own she had to do, RIGHT NOW.

She waited 'til her mother was occupied down in her Fitness Room. The whir-whir-whir of the bike told her that her mother would be off in her own world.

Brittany put on one of her birthday presents and then covered it with a pink oxford, which she tied shut in front of her with a knot at the tails. She looked down. *Slutty. Good. Blue-jeans last year....* she rooted around in a drawer, found scissors, and began cutting denim. "Shorts this year!" She held them up and out, nodded, and put them on. She raided her baby-sitting and lawn-mowing money, then hopped on her little one-speed bike with its yellow banana seat and tall handlebars. She spun off in the direction of Mill Village's downtown. The warm spring air felt liberating, and angry pedaling made the intermittent streetlights of the village flash by faster and faster, even if her lungs burned.

She checked behind the church, first. It's funny, really. All manner of bad behavior happened back there. Illegal, immoral, ill-advised. Brittany was hoping for at least two of the three. But no one was there.

She tried at the path to the footbridge, behind the long-abandoned stone-cutting sheds. No luck.

Finally, she leaned her little childhood bicycle against the falling-down boards at the outdoor rink from long ago - an empty, silent and nearly forgotten wasteland of plywood and weeds, now that the college had converted the stables into a fancy indoor rink. Brittany carefully stuck her head down into the changing hut, which was bent and crooked and at an unlikely angle, but still standing for some inexplicable reason.

Paydirt! Brittany stifled a victorious grin.

Three of her schoolmates, two from a class one year ahead and one from a couple of years behind, lazed in the little falling-in shack, sitting in a dreary circle. They looked up as one, broken from their all-absorbing task: sitting around a flickering candle, bitching about their world and sharing a cigarette.

"Whoah!"

"Get lost... Brittany?"

"The library's THAT way, har, har, haw!"

They weren't happy to see her, of course - she didn't fit with their crowd. Dyed hair, spiked hair, shaved here and there, leather if they could afford it, black cotton if they couldn't. Goth, punk, metal, pierced... they were whatever pissed off parents, police, and priests in the moment. Brittany, however shunned and alone and different, still represented the wannabees and the Beautiful People and the Joneses. The little den became quiet. Their little slice of heathen descended back into boredom when Brittany sat down on a wall-mount bench. The three children had acid thoughts that they kept to themselves:

Nerdy-girl wants to hang out.

Whatever.

Ignore it and maybe it will go away.

Brittany looked back and forth. She didn't THINK they'd rob her. She reached into her black, lacy birthday-present's cups (the two boys were suddenly no longer bored) and took out two folds of cash (the girl was suddenly interested). "I can tell you hoodlums aren't holding, or you'd be smoking it right now. I want to get high. Where can we get some REALLY GOOD weed around here?" Brittany was careful to be specific. *I don't want to get stuck in front of some sort of powder or something scary like a needle.* Her PLAN involved being in control, not acting chicken-shit the first time somebody showed her something new.

Now Sean, Trista, and Kevin had just been complaining about just how JONESIN' they all were, and how it really SUCKED that nobody had a DIME for even the cheapest street-weed. Here comes this proper-pretty little girl flashing TWO thick WADS of fives and tens, looking to hook up. Fortune favors the fuck-up!

"Wait here with Trista." Sean reached over to grab a fold of cash.

Brittany pulled her hand towards her bosom and held on tight.

Sean copped a feel as he tried to grab the money.

Brittany pretended it hadn't happened. She had bigger fish to fry. "Nofuckinway. Hook ME up and I'll share like I'm the Easter Bunny. Walk with that cash and I'll never see you again." Brittany pushed the money deep back into her age-inappropriate birthday present.

"Paranoid bitch, isn't she?" Sean looked around at his little brother. "Whadaya say, Kev? Should we hook her up?"

"Come ON!!" Trista was pissed. "What if she's, like, a COP or something?!?"

Brittany, Sean, and Kevin all turned, hands on hips, and stared down at Trista, who was still sitting on a bench. She shrank under the three withering scowls.

"Yeah, Trista. Like the CHILD-police, a special NARC UNIT they set up just to catch freaks like us. Whatever. Come on. I know just where to go. Up on quarry street."

***

"Girl out there wants to meet you." Sean pointed out the window.

Frankie looked down into the parking lot and saw a hot little piece of ass drooped over a frilly little girl's bike, looking bored and maybe angry. She was right under a security light. She was wearing a lacy teddy that disappeared into fresh cut-offs. *Great. Another jail-bait wants to fuck-trade for some dope. Do these little assholes think it grew on TREES?* Frankie had to PAY for shit to grow this stuff, like ELECTRICITY for the grow-lights, Miracle-Grow, potting soil... *Fuckit. She DOES look FINE, whoever she is... and not one of these used-up little Goth stoners!* He thought about the bed, what he'd have to move to get some room for a little party.... *What the hell.* "Show her up."

Brittany climbed the long stairs on the outside of the building, headed into an attic apartment in the seedy, Layabout-Larry section of town. With her three new friends. *If you could see me now, Mom!* That thought brought the gleeful smile she needed to her nervous face.

A guy with missing teeth and groping eyes leered at her from the top of the stairs.

Brittany's step hitched. *Jesus, I'm flat as a board here, still playing with crayons and dolls, and this guy's falling over himself.... Ick!* She resisted the impulse to put an arm over her collarbone and finished climbing the stairs.

"Where'd they dig YOU up? Ain't seen y' around nowhere…" *Jesus, she looks like the Prom Queen or something!* He handed a bottle of beer to Kevin. "Why don't you three go have a beer down at the quarry. Your friend will see you in about…" He sized Brittany up and down. "An hour or two."

Brittany's three new friends hung their heads and started down the stairs, hopes for high times dashed, at least for the present.

"Kev! Wait!" *Not so fast. You are NOT leaving me ALONE with this guy! Icky!!!* Brittany worked very hard to keep the stoic look on her face. "Hang on." She turned and dug in her bodice again. "How much will this get us?"

Frankie's eyes got big. *These little shits finally have MONEY! Good.* Frankie had bills to pay. Like three months back rent for this leaky-roofed hole. He took the cash. Counted it. *Fives and tens. Good. That's a very good start.* His eyebrows went up. *Eighty bucks. Very good.* "Wait here."

Frankie went and rummaged in a room out of sight. He came back with a Ziploc sandwich bag with a sprinkle of something along the bottom. "Grow-light Gold, man! I make the best stuff in town, girlie!"

Sean and Trista scowled at Frankie. Trista kept her mouth shut while Sean tried to figure out how to play it. They could side on Frankie, and then ask for a cut later. Which he might or might not give. Or they could side on this Brittany chick, and make a friend. *A friend who has another tit and maybe another handful of cash for another day, maybe even more after that?* He couldn't spell his own name in school - or that's what he wanted his teachers to think - but in the business of GETTING FUCKED UP he was as shrewd and calculating as anyone with an MBA.

Sean turned to Brittany. "Make him give you half the cash back, or ask for more than a mini-plate special." *Now to keep things smooth all around.* "His stuff's GOOD, it's got a lot of pollen in it, that's why it looks kind-a gold, see, 'cause of the flowers, and that's what you want, but it's not worth THAT much. It IS the best around town, though."

Frankie was already headed back out of sight down the hall, grumbling and sputtering.

Brittany looked over at Sean. Thanks, she mouthed.

He looked at his shoe, and blushed a little.

Trista slapped the back of Sean's head - hard. Whap!

Frankie came back into the front room. The baggie had gotten bigger - it was almost a third full. He held it out to Sean. "Happy, Mister Better Business Bureau?" He tossed the baggie across the room at Brittany. "He's right. Best stuff around, girlie." He brightened. "Hey, you guys can HANG if you want! TeeVee is on later, we can make popcorn and shit..." Frankie looked over at Brittany. A little too hopefully.

Not on your life. You're about thirty, you look like you don't work, and your place smells like a skunk with rotten shoes. Brittany turned on her heel dismissively. "'Nother time, I expect."

Her new best friends followed her - or her new stash - down the stairs to her bicycle. They got petulant looks on their faces when she grabbed the handlebars and threw a leg up over to get on. *There goes that.*

Brittany turned. "Where to?"

The smiles came back.

"Let's show her the quarry."

Brittany had been to the quarry before, but the daytime quarry and the quarry of the dark of night weren't at all the same. She liked how the orange light from the fire flickered on the dark black walls of stone, how the noise of town was swallowed up by the high piles of shattered stone around them, how the black hole beside them echoed back the higher-pitched and louder-spoken parts of a conversation.

She choked and coughed and nearly died on her first puff, but she got the hang of it by the third time their stinky little pipe came around to her.

"The cops come, throw the pipe, but throw it somewhere we can FIND it later, they're hard to get."

"Not much will happen the first time, no one ever really gets fucked up the first time. It has to build up or some shit like that."

"You'll be really fucked up, but you won't know it. We'll be able to tell, though."

"Hold it in, like this…" Sean was turning blue. Cough. Giggle. "For as long as you can. It'll work better."

"Don't hold it in too long, you're not used to it, you'll cough it all out."

Brittany got all this contrary advice and much more during that night. She DID feel it, because not much had been funny to her lately, and now EVERYTHING was funny. The hard rock ramparts clattered and rustled with echoes - fragments of words and thoughts. The dope made each syllable and echo profound, funny and creepy, comforting - all at once. BIGGER, too, as the stone walls retreated off into the night. They were sitting in black space, and she thought she was going to CRAP HER SHORTS she was laughing so hard, and she had NO IDEA why!

After they had been there ten or twenty minutes, Trista stood up and said, "I have to go. It's, like, three A-period M-period, and I've got to be home when my mom gets up at five or I'll be in the shitter!"

This brought a fresh round of nose-giggles out of Brittany, because: *There is NO FUCKIN WAY it is already THREE. You are full of CRAP, I KNOW it's got to be like, TEN.* It just seemed too improbable that ANYBODY's mother would allow her to come in ANY TIME after ten. Brittany knew she'd be locked out of the house and then grounded forever if she showed up a minute later than that. Then there was the image of Trista in the shitter... that brought a fresh fit of laughing as she got a sudden picture of Trista, up-side down in the toilet, with her legs waving wildly in the air.

Trista was standing right beside her now. The girl leaned down close, her hand brushing the front of Brittany's teddy as she leaned in to kiss Brittany on the cheek. "Hmmmm. Soft. Thanks for sharing." Trista stood back up. "Ah, Brittany? Maybe you shouldn't ride the bike tonight?" Trista looked worried.

"Good idea!" Sean's face broke into a wide smile as inspiration fell on him. He reached over to help Brittany up, but his eyes were on the bicycle as he pulled her to her feet. "You have to get used to our

Wicked Ways. Designated Rider and all that." He pointed: "Kevin, hop on the bike."

Brittany's three new best friends deposited her at the Wendell home not too very long before the birds started their first morning notes. They left her sitting on the doorstep, musing on how the hell she was going to get in without waking her parents. She saw that Kevin was still riding the bike - her bike - as the three hoodlums disappeared down the block under streetlights that would soon go out for the day. *Oh, well. The price of friends.* Brittany searched the pockets of her cutoffs. *Shit! My bag of dope is gone. Guess this was a one-time experiment in Friends. Oh, well.* Brittany had a sudden thought. She peeked inside her bodice. Not in the left cup. She turned her head. Not in the right cup. *Shit. Friends are expensive, apparently.*

Her dad found her asleep on the doorstep, leaning against the door, when he opened it to get the morning paper.

Brittany was grounded for two weeks.

***

She found them at the quarry. "Hi."

"Heyayay! Brittany's back!" Trista looked sufficiently fake-happy.

"Whereyabeen, Brittany?" Sean was all cheery, too. Like they'd been waiting for her, here, all this time.

Right.

Kevin was sufficiently disinterested in Brittany's arrival to suggest that he was probably the most straight-forward of her new friends.

Brittany addressed him: "Grounded. Did you have fun with my dope and my money while I was gone?"

Non-committal grunts.

"I want my bike back."

Sean spoke up again. "What bike?"

"The bike YOU rode away from my house, the one you probably already sold when the MONEY you" she looked at Trista "lifted off me ran out."

Kevin made a great show of carefully searching his cranium. "I don't remember a bike."

"Fine. Me and my money will go find some new smoking buddies." Brittany turned on her heel.

"Wait…" Trista got up. "It MIGHT be over at Hathaways's place. In their yard sale. Sort of a consignment… thing."

Kevin reached up and slapped Trista on the ass. Hard.

"OWfuckerthatHURT!" Trista stomped her foot down dangerously close to Kevin's crotch.

"How much did he get for it?" Brittany addressed her new Better Friend. "For real."

Trista scurried away from Kevin. "Twenty."

Brittany gestured towards the path back down to the village. "Well, Trista, let's go yard-sale shopping and then let's go find some dope."

Brittany bought her bicycle back for thirty-five dollars. She didn't see the point in claiming it was hers. *It's mine now.* She'd paid for it. *Again. At least it's not trashed.* They'd taken good care of it, hoping to maximize its value when they converted it into cash or dope. The Hathaways had a perpetual covered yard sale - it was actually in the garage - all summer. Her bike hadn't even gotten rained on.

"So, Trista, where can we get some dope?"

* * *

Frankie wasn't happy to see them. "AGAIN?" You kids have been going through reefer like it's… fuckin' ay… fuckin' CEREAL or somethin'!" He stepped out onto the landing at the top of the stairs. "Look, this shit takes time to grow and cultivate. I rush it, and I end up with junk ain't no better than roadside rope, and that's free. I'm diggin' into my own PRIVATE STASH here to keep you kids loopy, and I've run into the BOTTOM of the BARREL, dig?"

Trista looked genuinely bummed out - a real affect snuck through her lifeless, disinterested mask.

"Hey, don't take it so hard. You kids have been fucked up twenty-three hours a day for what, like, TWO WEEKS straight? Maybe it's time to SLOW DOWN a little bit." He giggled. *Good parenting advice... wow, these could be my own kids someday!* Something in that thought unnerved him just a tiny bit, but he couldn't put his finger on it, so he let it go. "Fuck off, Little Rascals."

Brittany put her hands on her hips and leaned out from behind Trista. "So where DO we go?"

"I really don't give a shit. Somewhere else besides my doorstep. And don't come back for a month, children." Frankie stepped into his apartment and slammed the door. *Just as well. They've been coming around too much, and somebody in the way of a parent or a cop is going to get wise to this little grow-house.* He scowled at his empty and messy living room. *Those kids are taking advantage of my generosity. And my green thumb. Fuckum.*

Brittany turned to Trista. "Well?"

"I kind of know these GUYS..."

Those guys didn't have any, either. Or said they didn't. But they might be able to find some if the girls would stick around for a while.

Those girls didn't. Brittany steered them out as fast as she could arrange it. The guys were about thirty. They had bad teeth and a worse 'apartment' in the back of a house trailer that Brittany hoped to never SEE, let alone set foot in, again.

Just as they got outside, one of Those Guys stumbled out to the metal front doorstep and handed Trista a dirty scrap of paper. "Might work. You two ladies get some, bring it by. We'll all have a party. We've got WINE." He giggled and went back inside.

Brittany waited a beat and then turned to Trista, who was tucking the scrap of paper in her front pocket. "OOOOh, he's got WINE!" She gave the younger girl a stage smile and big wide eyes. "I think if we came back with some dope, we could GET LAID!"

Trista looked thoughtful. "I don't think we'd HAVE to come with dope..." She also looked way to serious.

"So... should we call that number?"

Trista shrugged and made a non-committal noise. "Those guys have wine...." She eyed the just-closed door. The closest way to haze your brain was the best way, apparently.

Brittany shivered and gave up. "Trista? You want a beer?"

"Huh? Ya!"

"Come over to my house. I can get us a couple of beers. Fuckin' WINE, what the HELL?" Brittany shook her head with stage emphasis. She picked up her bike off the lawn in front of the trailer and started pushing it back towards the village.

Trista started going on and on and ON at the mouth about all the different kinds of beer she'd tried.

Brittany thought the girl sounded full of shit.

***

Back at her house, Brittany raided the fridge and found a brand-new six-pack of Coors. She took three.

"Won't they NOTICE?"

Brittany smiled. "I hope they do. Let's go out back."

Brittany and Trista sat out back under a big maple, drinking beer, burping, and giggling. It wasn't Brittany's first taste of beer, but it was the first time she'd helped herself.

Trista was a mess five or six sips into the second can, and kept making sour faces.

"You don't really like it, do you?"

"Naaa... 'Sallright. I'fe drunk a LOD of Cures."

Ya. Right. "You can have another one if you give me that piece of paper with the phone number...."

Brittany got grounded for a week when her mother got home and found her and some other girl passed out in the backyard with a litter of empty beer-cans around the two of them.

She got grounded for an ADDITIONAL week when her dad came home and found his sixpack of Coors gone. He remained calm but firm. "That's stealing Brittany. You didn't ask. And what's up with this sudden interest in BEER? You're about... several years TOO YOUNG for that kind of behavior."

Brittany did have that piece of paper with the phone number, though.

***

"Where the fuck'd you get this nummer?" The gruff and gravely voice on the phone didn't sound happy to be hearing from her, or maybe anyone.

"A couple of guys."

"Bitch, there's like, a hundred THOUSAND guys in this fuckin' state. Got ta be A LITTLE MORE SPECIFIC."

Brittany was glad she was on the phone, and not in the same room with the man. Whoever and wherever he was. She'd gotten the town from the area code and prefix on the phone number, through information. Coos County, New Hampshire. She'd looked on a map. *Somewhere up in the boondocks way north of anywhere. How the heck could some guy from up in the middle of the Northwoods hook her up with dope? Weird. Oh, shit!* She furtively turned away from the street as her dad's car went by the telephone booth.

"WELL, speak da fuck up!" Whoever he was, he was impatient.

"A couple of guys in Collegeville, Mill Village... I don't even know their names. I'm sorry."

Silence. Then: "YoubetchoreASS you're sorry, bitch! No one's supposed to call this nummer."

Brittany thought hard. "Well, they told me someone at this number was pretty good with getting... THINGS for people."

"What da fuck." *She SOUNDS cute. Maybe it's worth the trip, just to see who this musical little voice is.* "Ya. Maybe. Sometimes."

Brittany poured the sugar into her voice. "Well, could NOW be one of those times? Maybe?" She used an expression she'd picked up from her new friends. "We're JONES'N down here, WHOLE town's out of weed and"

"JESUSCHRISTAMIGHTY! Don't SAY it, girlie! Not on da fuckin' phone, bitch!"

"Sorry."

"Fine. That's a long way, so you better be buyin' in BULK, hear me?"

"How much is that?"

"Bring five."

"Baggies? Dollars? Five what?"

"Five hunnert ya dumb cunt! And ya sound STUPID, so I'd better say it: NO CHECKS! Five hunnert CASH, lady."

Brittany had to put down the phone for a second. *HOLY SHIT! This is SOME KIND of phone number!* "Ya. Sure. Got it. When and where?"

"Mill Village end of Collegeville, you said, right?" He didn't wait for confirmation. "Meetcha up near da 'spressway exit. There's a little dirt road just down da hill, take a drive on it t' a pull-off about a mile back in on da road, right in da woods...."

"Ahhh, I don't know about that. I'm biking right now, and I'm not sure I'm going to make it up that hill..." *And I wouldn't meet you in the woods to save my own life!*

"Lost your license, huh?" *That involves Pigs, and Pigs are trouble, so that means SHE is maybe trouble. But sure sounds sweet.... What to do, what to do, five hunnret says I'll get to do YOU....* "You want it right down in the middle of Main Street in broad daylight?" *As if.*

"Something like that would be great."

Jesus, what a stupid cunt. "Tellyawhat, cutie. There's a little turnaround at the bottom of da big hill on that road from town up to da inte'state. Just after da old mansion. You know where I am?"

Brittany knew exactly where the old mansion was. "Yes. I can get there." *Oh, crappola! THAT place STILL gives me the CREEPS!* (There was a story there, and now there would be one more!) Her hair stood up just thinking about going back there.... *I hope he doesn't want to go IN the-*

"Thursday morning, Missy. Don't be late."

How exactly can you be late to a WHOLE MORNING? "Got it."

"Good." Errol wondered if she'd be able to round up the whole five. *She sounds new at this.* He had a sudden inspiration. "Honey? Bring a backpack." *There. Good deed done.* Not to mention saving his own skin if somebody drove by when the bitch was trying to pedal back to town with a half-pound mini-bale balanced on her ten-speed. He dropped the phone in the cradle.

And that was how Brittany Wendell came to meet Errol Sweet, a man who should have been totally out of her social and geographic orbit.

***

He got to the pull-off first. He'd made good time, but he was freezing his ass off. Next time, if there WAS a next time, he was going to drive down in a CAR. He'd just put the finishing touches on his pieced-together Harley, and *the trip is good shake-down run, but it's cold as a motherfuck'n witch's TIT today!* Sixty-five miles on a motorcycle was a LONG trip on a frosty Vermont morning, sunny summer day or not.

He looked up.

Here came this *absolute PHILLY of a girl on a little bicycle, an absolute Grade A HOTTIE of a thing*, all languid and leggy in that awkward early-teenaged way. *And here she is, that cherry little voice, coming to me and ON DISPLAY* as she pedaled up the road.... Thought left his mind as he stared, open-mouthed, predator-eyed and momentarily dumb. *This can't be... well maybe... no shit!* She rode straight up to him and hopped off the kiddy-bike. He was speechless. *She can't be a minute over fifteen, if that! Fortune favors! Now THIS little slip-'n-slide thing is worth the trip!*

This must be him? Jesus, what if it's NOT! "Ah... Er... Meh...." Brittany suddenly felt sick. "You got something for me?" *Icky. Icky, icky, icky!* All SORTS of alarm bells she didn't even know she HAD were going off! Brittany, who'd been fourteen for all of two months now, wondered if she'd see fifteen. *But I might have LOTS of friends, Mom, if I survive this!*

Oh ya, baby, I got something for you. Right here. He felt that little tickle somewhere behind his waterworks. "Ya. Let's see some cash, little girl."

"Let's see some dope, little man."

He almost slapped her. Instead, he counted to twenty. THAT was a trick he'd learned from his many daughters, the bitches.

The weird little man had a big, pointy beard and a pot-belly. Brittany hadn't MEANT to call him little. But that's what he was: almost elf-like - he was even shorter that SHE was. She'd never seen anyone wearing a plaid hunting jacket while riding a motorcycle. *Such a strange little man.* She scowled. *Hello?* She resisted the urge to wave a hand in front of his eyes. At first he had been checking her out like she was some sort of new flavor of candy. *Yuck.* Now he was frozen in suspended animation, and slowly turning red. *You-hoo? Are you having stroke or something?* He seemed to come to some sort of recovery: his color returned to normal, what little of it could be seen around the hair and beard and plaid.

The hairy man looked up and down the road, then waggled a finger at her. "Don't you fuck'n MOVE. I'll be right back." Then he hopped on his big motorcycle, kicked it over with an Olympic-style effort, and blasted down the road in a whirl of dust and thunder.

What the hey?

Errol went about a mile. No police cars. He'd wondered if he'd see about twenty parked at the farm at the bottom end of the road. He checked the out-of-business restaurant just up from the intersection. Lot empty. He turned around, went flying back up the hill at seventy, passed the scowling little girl, then drove up the intersecting dirt road a half mile or so. No cop-cars. He returned to the pull-off and *the little piece of candy* waiting for him there.

Brittany was over some of her initial fear and now was mostly experiencing a strong feeling of distaste. "Did you have a nice ride?" *This guy is as spastic as some of the boys in my seventh-grade classes!* She was trying to buy something, carrying around WAY TOO MUCH money, and he was suddenly joy-riding back and forth on his motorcycle. "Can we get this over with?"

What a mouthy little cunt. He'd slap some sense - and some manners - into her if they ever hooked up. *When.* He savored that thought before replying, "I had to make sure it wasn't a setup. I don't know you from a road-kill turd. Now, whadayaafter, again?"

"Pot."

"L'see the money."

Brittany sighed. Resigned. And started digging in a pocket of the backpack.

Good. She's actually got it!

"Here you go. In fifties. I told the bank I was buying one of those mountain-bikes."

Dumb cunt 's gonna get us both in trouble. "Never BUYING. They're gonna expect to SEE IT, see you ON it. LOOKING. Got to have the money 'cause yer SHOPPING. Yer LOOKING for one of those... whatever. Think ahead, girlie!" He took the cash. Counted it. "Good. Good." He handed back some of it, pocketed the rest. "Gettin'taknowya money." He gestured to the money Brittany was now holding. "There's two-fifty there. Bring another two-fifty just like it tomorrow, and we'll do business."

"That's seven-hundred and fifty dollars!" Brittany was sure smart enough to know that no sandwich baggie full of weed was worth a year's baby-sitting money.

"No, that's two-fifty gettin' ta know ya money and five-hunnert tradin' money. Cost of doin' business, girlie. Cost of gettin' to know ME." He leered and beamed at her like he was wearing his best Sunday suit.

Good God, I think he thinks I should be... INTERESTED? Yuu-uuuck! Brittany wanted to vomit. She shivered instead. *Creepy!* She gave the man a clipped "Fine." She didn't sound like she meant it. "Tomorrow. Same place?"

"Yes," *you dumb little bitch,* "same place."

He kicked over his bike and roared off.

***

Brittany had to hit her savings hard. She had two large plastic candy-jars full of spare change and ones and tens and twenties, money that had been pocket-change at one time and was squirreled away for ice cream trips and days at the fair and other things that never came to pass when you didn't have friends. *Well now I have friends, just like Mom wanted, and my friends don't want to go to the ice cream window... they want to get high. Se be it.*

***

Brittany pedaled past the old falling-down mansion on her one-speed bike one more time that next morning.

The man was there at the pull-off just around the corner, waiting in a beat-up old car. He tried to offer her a ride, "cruising," as he called it.

The hair stood up on the back of Brittany's neck. Suddenly she saw child abduction, white slavery, bare feet, and maternity clothes in her future. Dirty children of various ages clinging at her skirts. She backed up a little bit and declined. "No" *fucking WAY I would ever get into a car with YOU*, "thanks." She dug in her pants pockets for two wads of cash. The teller at the bank had been so happy to help Brittany convert to big jars full of coins and small bills into fifty-dollar bills that actually fit in a pocket. *If she only knew!* "Got to get right back...."

"Yer not very adventurous, are you? Gotta learn to be a FUN girl!" He pulled a gallon-sized freezer-bag out from under the seat of his car and handed it over.

"Shit!" Brittany's eyes were big as saucers. *Howinthehell am I EVER going to get rid of that much dope?*

"Well don't just STARE! It's what you came fer, right? Well then TUCK IT THE FUCK AWAY in yer BACKPACK before some rubber-necking ASSHOLE goes by on the road and SEES US with this shit!"

His fists flexed - a cue that Brittany, in her inexperience, missed.

"JESUS - they make them stupid today or what?!?"

Yeah. Fuck you, too, little man. "Sure thing." She put her backpack on and started to straddle her bike.

Errol decided to get all sweet. It took a few deep breaths. *Maybe I can still get some from this tasty little cunt..* "You want ta burn one up for a minute afore you go pedalin' down da road, Missy?" He bared his blackened and rotting teeth at her in a wolfish smile.

She almost jumped back out of reflex. As it was she got all tangled up in the bike and fell INTO him and that hairy face full of *WORMY TEETH* and *SOUR BREATH*... She gagged as he caught her, his face so close that his beard was tickling her nose. "Can't!" She said it tightly. She tried to talk through her teeth and NOT BREATHE. "Got somewhere to BE!" *Please, God, GET ME OUT OF HERE!* She sprang up out of his clutching, groping hands, onto her bike, and was already pedaling for her life in one fluid jump. *Can't this fuck'n thing go any faster?!?*

"CALL ANYTIME YOU WANT MORE, MISSY! ANY TIME AT ALL!" *Little philly is going like it was a race. Must really actually have some place to be!* He savored the feel of her in his hands and wondered if he'd be able to get her clothes off with or without a fuss. *No matter either way. I wish she'd fallen right da fuck int'r the back seat!*

Errol took the envelope of cash off the seat, caressed the open end of it with his tongue, and threw it into the glove box. She'd call again, and he'd get more than money next time. He shook his head. *If I had one of their VESTS, that would get me a little respect-fuck from this philly, for sure! Buncha Canuck puss-wads!*

***

Members of the Topdogs Motorcycle Club were required by club mandate to turn their denim vests '"Dogs-In" before any premeditated criminal activity. The TOPDOGS were a gentlemen's organization, a social club, a group of like-minded motorcycle aficionados. The TOPDOGS were NOT members of a criminal organization ruled by Organized Crime. Thus, whenever a member was in the middle of criminal activity, he WASN'T a Topdog. Period.

Topdog vests turned with the regularity of the tide - but they always stayed on, whichever side faced in or out.

Errol Sweet showed up to a drug deal in a pastorale town in Vermont in a red-and-black-checked wool-plaid hunting jacket because he hadn't been given any parts of the club colors. *I got ta ride half-a-hunnret miles on a motorcycle in a fuckid HUNTIN' JACKET 'cause the fuckin' Topdogs assholes wouldn't even give me a tiny little support patch ta wear on a vest!* A constant source of gnawing worry and slight: no snarling dog patches for Errol, let alone actually issuing him the embroidered banner strips that proudly shouted "TOPDOGS - QUEBEC," or Errol's secret wish, "TOPDOGS - VERMONT." (He'd be Club President of that chapter, being the first, he was sure.) Instead, he was going to wear that plaid jacket on their 'Dog business EVERY FUCK'N DAY until he shamed them into issuing him one of the famed and coveted denim vests, even if the cuss-ed thing was fuck'n BLANK. *But they sure as hell ought to at least put a tiny little support patch and a Topdogs banner on it, for all the shit I pull for them!*

The Topdogs Motorcycle Club, Quebec Chapter, would never issue any part of the uniform - that's what it was - to Errol Sweet.

Stickers for his bike? Sure. He'd done a passable job of cobbling together a sweet machine, and they handed out those vinyl adhesive Topdog images like candy, so sure, Errol had a three-headed dog snarling angrily from each side of his bike's gas tank. The pro football teams handed out all manner of merchandise - that didn't make you a football player. And they really did hand out TOPDOGS-themed stuff all over - coffee cups, bandanas, calendars, even Tee-shirts (though somehow, whenever Errol came around, they were "out," even if he could see a box full of the shit right in front of him).

But the REAL stuff - members-only? Errol would often SEE it, often STARE at it covetously, and sometimes FEAR it, but he'd never get to wear it. The club found Errol Sweet very useful, but they also didn't like him: he was ill-mannered, un-washed, ugly, frequently loudly opinionated, and almost always wrong.

And one other thing: not a one of the Topdogs would EVER leave that asshole alone with any of their children.

***

"HOLY SHIT GIRL, where did you get all that SHIT!?!"

"Fuck me!"

"GODDAMMIT, GIRL, that's like, WHOAH!"

Brittany couldn't tell whether they were happy or angry. She COULD tell that her new little group of FRIENDS hadn't seen that much before. Hands kept reaching for the super-size Zip-loc baggie. She was careful to keep it out of reach. "So what should I DO with it?"

"SMOKE IT!!!" Times three. At least they were unanimous on that.

"Sooo… I hate to tell y'all, but I have a lot of money tied up in this little bag. More than I planned."

She wasn't sure they were paying attention. Trista was bouncing up and down on her toes with her hands clasped together, like she was waiting for a parade clown to throw candy. The boys were eyeing the bag and whispering to each other. Reflexively licking their chops. *Bad sign there... like wolves and I'm the the girl in the woods. .*

She started in again, louder. "Look, kiddos, I'm going to have to CHARGE you for this stuff, this time, cause it isn't free to ME, you know what I mean?"

Faces fell.

She was thinking in a rush. *This is going WAY AHEAD of The Plan. Mom's going to LOVE this (not really I'll be grounded for life, that's IF she doesn't turn me over to the cops on the spot, well jail WOULD get me away from her)! Maybe that makes it a good idea.* Brittany started talking very slowly, working it out as she went. "HOW MUCH do you pay for a joint?"

The boys squinted suspiciously.

Trista asked, "You mean all rolled up and ready to go?"

"Yeah. All rolled up. Don't lowball me, 'cause I'm going to check with Frankie. And not just him. Others, too. How much?"

Kevin was eager to show how much he knew. "Ten or fifteen bucks, right, that's how much you paid for those" WHAP!

Trista gave Kevin a very hostile look. But what stopped Kevin was the whack he got in the back of the head from Sean. It was hard enough to set him forward on his feet. He shut his mouth in a tight thin line, regained his balance, and scowled over his shoulder at Sean. The quarry was quiet.

"Do you know any people that would BUY a few joints?" *THIS will get me friends! Won't Mommy be happy!* Her eyes flared in a crazy smile that scared her new social group out of outright robbery.

They hadn't dealt with crazy much, but they knew it when they saw it.

Silence for a minute.

Sean spoke this time. "A few."

"Okay. Here's how it's going to work." *THINK, BRITTANY!* "Ahhh, I'm going to give you dope, all rolled up..." *Added value product, just like they taught us in Home Ec...* "Ahhh, how about for five bucks a joint. I know you shits are tight for money, but that discount ought to help you out, right?"

Faces around the quarry brightened up. Christmas had arrived.

"You guys ought to be able to find five bucks SOMEWHERE." *Like maybe by selling two for ten or fifteen and coming back for*

"More… When you need more, you, ahhh…" THINK! "Oh! You chalk that mailbox on the corner by my house. You know what I mean?"

Blank looks.

"You have a Beta-player at any of your houses?"

"Yaaaaa." Trista did not see where this was going.

"Rent a spy movie. That one that came out a couple years ago?"

Sean nodded. He was starting to smile.

"Watch that. We're going super-secret here. When you need more, chalk the mailbox by my house. I'll meet you here at… four-thirty the next afternoon. We'll trade." She thought again. "If you want a BUNCH, chalk the mailbox twice. NO ONE CALLS MY HOUSE. You can drop by," (*Mom will just LOVE that, my perfectly un-perfect new friends and all will just THRILL her.*) "if you want, but NO BUSINESS there. And if it GETS BACK TO ME that I'm involved in ANY of this, the party stops. Immediately and forever. You guys are my Front." She'd learned that word recently. "Understand?"

Three smiling heads shaking yes. Anyone can find five bucks. And then they were going to be IN THE MONEY. And even more important to these focused young minds: IN THE SMOKE!!

***

So that's how Brittany got some friends (which her mother DID NOT approve of), how she learned to roll a tight joint (which her recently ex-State Police dad WAS NOT going to find out about), and how she got started in the drug trade (which neither parent, or anyone else other than her three new Best Friends would ever know about).

Night after night she sat up late in her room with rolling papers. She got pretty good at it after the first week. She figured she had to get at least one-hundred and fifty smokes out of that bag to break even. She was very careful. She breathed a sigh of relief when school started again in the fall and she had one third of the bag left at the one-hundredth joint. She started rolling smaller, tighter. She was getting to be an expert.

Her new friends were starting to go through it a lot faster now. She suspected that they were taking their low-priced goods on the road, as it were, to neighboring towns. There just weren't a lot of dopers around Collegeville, as far as she knew. Whatever. They were getting their smokes and coming up with money for more. Fair enough. She never thought about the police. It was just pot.

She should have thought it through.

In those days, kids still WHISPERED about pot. Getting caught could mean anything: the Deputy might take it and smoke it himself, the parent might flush it down the toilet, the local cop might Send You Up and you could finish school in the Woodside Juvenile Detention Facility. Back then, it was ILLEGAL AS HELL, and you could RUIN your life legally, even if you didn't become a full-out habitual Stoner with your life in a ruined haze of poor choices and bad cravings, just like the school warned you about.

***

Walter Wendell got the surprise of his life when he noticed a chalked mailbox - *WAY too obvious!* - right there on his street. He'd years-ago stopped looking for such signs, but he was trained to observe them, by his government no less, and the simple yellow mark screamed at him the first day he saw it.

Well, it IS a military town, after a fashion... but HERE? A SPY at a private ROTC academy? If we're penetrated, just exactly what secrets are they... oh, no a PLANT. He sat at his desk, ostensibly to grade papers, but his mind was on that mailbox. *So they stick someone here, push them through the ROTC system, and then they become an officer in the military? WHO is THEY? The Chinese? Wouldn't a student be vetted? He scowled. Do I CALL someone? Ya, won't that just sound crazy: Agent Walter Wendell, twenty years out of it, suddenly has a hot tip from middle-of-nowhere-ville! Shit.* He forcibly pushed the mailbox and its yellow stripe out of his mind and concentrated on the task in front of him: educating young minds.

***

It's hard to cover up the smell of a pound of really good marijuana. THAT was a problem, right away.

"Brittany, what is that SMELL in your room? Is your laundry basket getting sour?" Her mother was standing outside her room with an empty laundry basket. Hint, hint.

Brittany's younger brother hammed it up from his room across the hall. "Eeeewww! Moldy crotch-juice! Bee, you should WASH!"

Brittany resisted the urge to walk across the hall and slap him across the face with one of his fungoidal athletic socks.

Brittany's mother was so sweet to THE BROTHER. "Brian, you be glad YOU don't have a vagina. She can't help it."

Gee, thanks, Mom.

Her mother held out the laundry basket.

Think fast. "Won't work, Mom. A skunk sprayed in my room."

That brought her brother, wild-eyed with excitement, to his bedroom door.

Her mother stuck her head past Brittany's door-jamb and peered around the corners of the room for a skunk. *That won't do. Not at all!* Having some sort of wildlife incident in your daughter's room was NOT, and never would be, a social asset.

Brittany back-pedaled. "Uh, I mean, a skunk sprayed my CLOTHES. ME. I washed them already. It almost worked." *Think.* "I didn't even know they still smelled. I can't smell it anymore. Used to it, you know." Which she was. She'd had no idea that they could smell the dope out in the hallway. *I'll have to put a window-fan on when I'm rolling.*

Her brother was making the most out of this new wealth of information. "Sis stinks SO BAD she doesn't even know when she's been sprayed by a SKUNK!"

"Shut the fuck up, Brian."

"BRITTANY! You watch your MOUTH! I don't like what you're learning from your new, ah, FRIENDS." She said it with as much distaste as she could muster. "Try to avoid skunks in the future, dear. No boy wants to date a stinky girl." She turned and went downstairs, but left the laundry basket.

Brittany searched her mind for some way to get back at the insensitive nag who called herself 'mother.' *I hate you!* She really DID hate her mother. But the feeling was mutual, so she had absolutely none of the guilt that so many other teens feel. This may have saved her. She decided the fallout of her current Plan - known and unknown - would have to do.

Brother Brian wasn't through. "She'll never get a date anyways! Stinky when she's skunked, stinky when she's not. Especially now that she's BLEEDING ALL THE TIME!!!" He slammed his door.

Brian had been especially delighted to find out that Brittany had started menstruating, and to have it all explained to him by his mother while his sister suffered away in earshot. *Like it was any of his BUSINESS.* Like he didn't know. *Little fuckers were laughing about PERIODS every day in school by the time they were twelve.* He'd kept it all straight-faced and serious and concerned the whole time Mom was explaining it to him, "Well, remember when our dog came into heat? Well, Brittany's coming into heat now, every month…" *BITCH!!!* And then as soon as Mom was out of earshot, Brian had started in. "Brittany's going to be pulling herself around with her arms, dragging her bleeding ass on the carpet…" Blah, blah, blah. The worst thing was, the mother of the two children let him CARRY ON like that, ALL THE TIME. "Oh, it's new and unfamiliar to him and that's how he's dealing with it." *BITCH!!! NOTHING about ME should be FAMILIAR to that little ASSWIPE!*

Standing there in her room, fuming about all that, it occurred to Brittany that she could bleed her underwear red every month. *There! Deal with that, Mommy!* She shook her head. *Bad Plan.* She could see the fallout from that already - *I'll be doing my own laundry.*

Brittany looked at the empty laundry basket. *So I guess she wants me to clean my room? Why am I thinking about this? I have HOMEWORK and ROLLING to do. A schoolgirl with friends and dope is a busy girl!*

***

She had to call for more dope halfway through September.

This time, the guy on the phone said, "Well, that's a long way down there. Bring a thousand."

Holy dogshit almighty what the frig have I got myself into!

She had it, though. Barely. She'd got one-hundred and sixty-seven joints out of that bag - finally using a graduated plastic iced-tea scoop to carefully measure each one. One hundred and sixty-seven at five dollars a pop. She had the passbook to her small savings account. Brittany tried not think about where this was going. She DID think about how much her ever-growing circle of friends was pissing off her mom. *THAT is something to treasure. New friends just dropping by ALL THE TIME, now!*

***

Her dad talked to her about it one night.

"Brittany, can I come in?" She looked up from her homework with a look of... *panic? Interesting.*

"Sure, Dad. Uh... Sit on the bed." Brittany's other chair had a shoebox sitting on it at the moment. A shoebox full of dope and rolling papers. She'd taken a break from rolling... her fingers were tired.

"Howyadoin, kid?"

"Tired. Having school and a social life and all that American Dream stuff isn't all it's cracked up to be."

"Keeping too many late hours?"

"What? ME? I'm a KID! We're full of boundless energy, ready for anything day or night, sleep optional seven days a week!" She gave him a wide-eyed and manic smile.

"Maybe you ought to slow it down a bit."

"So many friends, so many social commitments, so little time until college!"

"Actually, your mother and I are a little worried about that. Your friends."

"You mean SHE's worried and YOU came to talk to me about it."

She's always been a smart girl. "Maybe something like that."

"Well, Dad, can I speak honestly? Like I would to a friend, a REAL one, not those hooligans I've been bringing around? TRUTHFULLY?" She waited.

He kind of smiled at that. *Hooligans. Well, she has THAT right, at least.* "Yah, Brittany. Anything goes." Now he waited.

"She's a bitch."

His face clouded. Not what he thought they were talking about.

"No. I mean it. To me. You know, when I was TWELVE, and I hit a hundred and five pounds, she told me how HAPPY she was for me, because now I could STAY at that weight so I could get MARRIED? She bought me a DIET PLAN!"

Walter frowned. He didn't know about that.

"And it's just gotten worse..." Brittany balled her fists. "I think she's already got him picked out. Some boy she wants to hump that will increase her social status when I'm married to him!"

Walt wanted to rebuke her for that one, but she had a look about her, so he let it go. *And it's probably true.* He cringed. *So the kids can see it.*

"And she's CONSTANTLY criticizing me just because I don't have any friends." Sob. "Well, was." Sniffle. "Now I have friends, and that pisses her off too." Wet giggle.

Walt reached around and found a nearby box of Kleenex for her. "Well, it might be your CHOICE of friends…"

"BUT SHE WANTS ME TO BE FRIENDS WITH HER BITCHY LITTLE SOCIAL BLUE-BLOOD WANNA-BE CLUB OR SOMETHING!!! I HATE THEM! THEY HATE ME!"

"Okay, okay." He gave the 'Settle Down' gesture with his hands. "Soooo… She wants to pick who you should be friends with?"

"YES!!!"

"Don't yell at me, I'm listening."

"I'M SORRY! Sorry. You know, the very girls in school that I get along with LEAST are the ones she needs me to be friends with. She likes them so much, why doesn't SHE go out to Smiley's with them!"

"So the Goth wannabes and… what did you call them, 'Hooligans' that you've been bringing by, are they who you get along with best?" He hoped that wasn't the case, but he had to ask.

"Of course not, they're a bunch of dead-enders and then some. But they are FRIENDS, and that's what Mommy wanted!" Brittany flipped her dad another manic smile.

Walt wasn't quite sure what she was trying to accomplish, but he had a pretty good idea that something unexpected was going to come of it, at least for Brittany.

"Well, I'm here if you need me. Be careful, Britt. Revenge friends, that whole thing can turn around and bite you in the ass." He patted her head carefully and left the room.

You have no idea, Dad.

Actually, he did have an idea... *That girl has some absolutely QUALITY dope in here, and quite a bit of it by the absolute REEK of her room.* He closed the door heavy with worry. *We'll all be lucky if she doesn't end up in jail. Now what am I going to do about THIS?*

Walter Wendell went to take a look in the phone book.

***

In a fit of pique, she tried it, but the Laundry Plan backfired. Brittany was getting a little stressed, this whole dope thing was just GETTING OUT OF HAND, and she was bleeding to no end on account of it.

Her dear mother showed up at her bedroom door with the laundry basket and the WASHBOARD, of all things, to suddenly change the rules: "Time for SOMEONE to learn how to do laundry. You have skills to learn if you're going to keep a good husband, Brittany!"

Brittany seethed, and followed her mother down to the utility sink. *Bitch, bitch, BITCH!*

***

Former U.S. Army Special Forces and three-letter agency officer Walter Wendell staked out the mailbox off and on for a while after he saw the chalk marks coming and going with ever more frequency. He thought he'd been caught when suddenly there were SIX broad slash-marks across the blue metal box, but no, the next week there they were again in one's and two's. *What the hell is going on?!* After two weeks of casually but carefully watching, he got his answer: kids! They seemed mildly familiar, even. From Collegeville, certainly. He caught two of them chalking the box on a Thursday evening, one playing look-out and one standing with his back to the box, hands behind him, chalk in one of his hands. *They're taking this super-secret stuff seriously!* He was relieved to discover that the kids in his town were apparently reading spy-novels now. Tricks of state-craft and trade-craft meant to prevent and start wars were now being employed to arrange teenaged... *whatever they're up to.*

He faded back into the shadows.

Relieved to find that his beloved Academy was safe from prying, spying foreign government eyes, Walter turned his thoughts to more pressing problems: his increasingly dopey daughter and the exciting prospect of his new side job serving on a new anti-organized crime task force. He gave the mailbox one more thought and then forgot about it: *Good thing I didn't make any phone calls... I woulda looked like a grade-A asshole!*

***

By spring it was *just REALLY GETTING OUT OF HAND.* Brittany stood at the turn-off by the bridge with two other people, MEN, that she DIDN'T KNOW, waiting for the ugly, hairy little elf-man to complete this latest "package deal."

The other two, a worn-out looking twenty-something in torn and dirty clothes and a ski-bum kind of guy, had arrived in separate cars from separate directions. Brittany had just watched FIVE THOUSAND dollars change hands: The TWO THOUSAND that she had just handed over (*God HELP me what have I gotten myself into!*) and fifteen hundred from each of the other bozos.

The little man put the money on top of his car and reached down to rummage in the back seat. He brought up three shopping bags, looked at them, thought about it, and threw one of them back on the floor. He turned and handed one of the bags to Brittany. He threw the other bag to Brittany's brand-new "Business Associates" as he'd called them.

The street-bum looked into the bag, looked at the ski-bum, and then looked over at the little man in plaid. "What gives? I thought we were each getting a bag?"

"Well I thought youtwo'ud EACH have some REAL money. A thousand don't get ya shit. You know that!"

The ski-bum hung his head and stammered: "Well, it's like, just that, well DUDE, it's like dope has just got REAL easy to find down there all-a-the sudden, man. DEMAND is OFF 'cause everywhere ya turn around, SOMEONE has already got just a FISTFULL of JOINTS."

Brittany decided she did not need to be party to this particular business conversation. "Well, see you all. I've got to go home and smoke this!" She threw the bag in her backpack and hopped on her new tricked-out mountain-bike, complete with studded winter tires.

"Wait just a minute, there, missy!" The little plaid woodchuck strutted over to her. "Don't-cha-think maybe I should know how ta get a-hold-of-ya, in case of something comes up? Maybe we could, ah, get together. Again. More often."

"Oooh. My boyfriend would kick my ASS if anyone started calling. I'm dumping him next week, though. I'll get back to you on that." She winked with both eyes and a scrunched-up nose.

Errol leaned in for a kiss on that pretty little face. He got air.

Brittany was already down the road twenty feet, wheels turning, peddling for all she was worth to escape that piano-keyboard mouth full of composting teeth.

"What's her name?" The ski-bum had both business and personal reasons for asking. That pretty little girl had just purchased one HELL of a LOT of dope.

Errol turned. "HowthefuckshouldIknow? She won't say TWO FUCKIN' WORDS IN A ROW to me. Scittish little thing." He shook his head. He was really missing an opportunity there, with that one.

Street-bum wanted some information, but he had to be careful how he went about getting it. Errol wasn't a fool. "Nice pussy on that one, I'll bet."

"Yeah…" Errol's eyes got all dreamy. "Nice tight one, somewhere under there. Can't wait for summer!" *Be nice to suggest a little swim in that brook* right under the bridge, come hot weather.

"When she start coming around?"

"Oh, last summer sometime."

The other two traded a look. "We'll be seeing you, Errol."

"Call any time."

***

Brittany was careful. She DID NOT want any of these people to know where she lived. Ever. She parked her bottom on the steps of the old empty school with a blue windbreaker zipped up over her yellow jacket, a different-colored ski-hat on, and her hair all tucked up. Her bike was secreted out back behind the building and her backpack was between her knees with the back of it - the black side - facing towards the road. There were lots of houses within shouting distance. Two small children who she remotely kind of knew were playing on the swing-set, with their mother keeping a frequent eye on them from the trailer next door. Brittany Wendell was incognito and safe, more or less.

She watched a car drive back and forth on the road. The blue charger. The two bum-fucks were cruising around together, passing about every five minutes, trying to find her. Great. They didn't give her a second look on any of six passes. Eventually, the blue Charger headed back up the hill towards the interstate.

Brittany grabbed her backpack. *Time to go, and FAST!*

***

Two miles away and three years later, Bruce Sutton gave Brittany a wide-eyed scowl. "Holy SHIT, girl!" It wasn't funny anymore, even with the burned-down nub of the joint re-lit between them. "So it got pretty scary." Bruce sat back, regarding Brittany Wendell in a new light. *This girl is NOT who I thought she was....* The party had gotten louder around them, but neither noticed.

Brittany was still holding the joint. "OhmyGod, YES!" She doubled over, coughing with laughter. *I can't believe I just TOLD HIM all this shit!*

"Are you still the county's biggest dope dealer?" Bruce worried about what was next. Good time to get the truth out of her. *Got to make a decision.*

"No! I got out of it. Cops showed up at my house!"

Bruce grimaced. *Great. I'm dating a felon.* "That must have been interesting."

Brittany laughed, coughed, and slapped her knee. She was three sheets to the wind. "That's JUST what my DAD said!" She smiled up at Bruce, more composed now. "Timing is everything. I had about a sandwich baggie left. Chump change in the shoebox. I'd just been to the bank. Cop thought my little friends who ratted me out were probably trying to pin it on me so they could duck out of it themselves. Didn't believe a pretty little straight-A right-side-of-the-tracks girl like me could be supplying half the county. Took my shoebox, gave me a stern lecture, shook my parent's hands, and that's the last I heard of it, mostly, other than Mom yelling."

Bruce looked relieved.

***

Actually, her dad DID come talk to her, afterwards.

Walter Wendell knocked on the doorframe while Brittany was doing homework.

Brittany's mother's new rule: Open bedroom door. No hiding anything nefarious. A teen felon was NOT a social asset!

"Come on in, Dad."

"That was scary and interesting."

"Yes, that was, wasn't it." No shame, no apologies, no cowering. A minute shrug of her shoulders instead.

He didn't know whether she was hiding in her schoolwork, or just getting on with life, but he was glad to see it. His little girl, sitting at her desk in her room, highlighting passages in a textbook. A lot better than sitting on the other side of vertical steel bars at visiting time at the women's correctional institution, or where-ever she might have been sent if it had gone some other way.

He seemed to want to just watch her, so Brittany returned to her homework. *Just as well. I've been neglecting it.* Playing at being a Stoner had taken her down a whole letter-grade.

Actually, Walter Wendell had been the one to arrange the visit by the Constable, but he'd make sure Brittany never found that out. Scare her, get rid of it, be done with it, and if it turned out to be a mess, Bert could follow it back down the tree to the root. Walt had even arranged the timing, and therefore the amount of money and dope in the box. *Better we call, and when it looks right, than someone else does when there's a whole shitload of cash in there....* His first visit to the shoebox in Brittany's room had been eye-opening and mildly worrying. Walter had, since then, been making frequent visits to Brittany's room when the rest of the family was out of the way. *So, my wild little almost-daughter...* "Are you going to scare us like that often?"

"Probably not."

"It was risky. You could be in a lot more trouble."

"I know."

"You owe anybody?"

God, no! THEY owe ME! She smiled. *But I'll never see it.*

The smile unnerved him. Walter repeated his question: "Do you OWE anybody? For what you were dealing out of the shoebox?"

Brittany pushed her chair back from the desk. *Well, he WAS a cop for a while....* She turned to face him and then settled down with her elbows on her knees. "Are you asking a question or are you trying to tell me what you think happened?"

That was a little more direct - and precocious - than he was prepared for, and his tone said it for him: "What DID happen, Brittany?"

"Easiest way to get friends quick. Always have dope. It got kind of... out of control, there, at the end."

His eyebrow went up. "So you ARE all done, right?"

"I think now would be a good time to be out of it."

That's good to hear. "That's right. You could wind up somewhere you don't want to be."

Brittany thought of the last deal, with THREE skanky men she didn't know standing on the side of the road, looking at her ass. *You have NO idea.* "I know, Dad."

"I hope so." He frowned even more. "So how bad did you hit your savings?"

"Not too bad. I've got about twenty-five hundred more in there now than when I started." She saw his face and quickly added: "Don't tell Mom. She'd make me donate it to charity or something."

Walt was struck speechless for a minute. Finally: "YOU are SCARY. You SURE some Mafia outfit isn't going to come up here looking for you?"

"All set, Dad. Don't owe anybody a DIME, and they don't even have my phone number."

"The police found you." He knew how, but he wanted to leave her unsettled by the experience.

"Yeah, they did. It'll be okay, though."

Walt didn't look so certain. He retreated into the hallway, stopped, and turned back. "PLEASE don't make me regret not grounding you for the rest of your natural life."

"Yes, Dad." She went back to her homework.

***

Bruce looked shell-shocked, almost sick. Brittany leered at him, a giggly scowl on her face. "What?!"

"It's just kind of the funniest thing, actually, Brie..." He hadn't told her yet. *I go off to the police academy in two weeks - I'm going to be an Auxiliary Trooper this summer!* "Maybe now isn't the time." He eyed the messy haze of her eyes.

"WHAT?" Brittany looked at the stub in her hand, out again. She re-lit it from the candle, burning the ends of her fingers.

"Nothing." He waved the thought away. *Well, I'm not a police officer YET. But Jesus,* "I'm dating a dope dealer, eh?"

"REFORMED, Brucie. It was a one-time thing. How about ONE MORE TIME for the both of us, before we're grownups, just for old times sake?" Brittany took a big drag off the stub of a joint, coughed, and held it. She blew the smoke in his face, gazed at him with dangerous and challenging eyes that he'd never seen before, and then kissed him wetly on the mouth.

Oh. Bruce felt all sorts of unexpected temptation pulling at his middle. He frowned in discomfort as he contemplated something that just a minute ago had seemed like a really bad idea.

Brittany's slightly-askew and challenging eyes toyed with his resolve.

Just one more time, sure, why not?

CHAPTER FOURTEEN

The prom at Mill Village High was held outdoors, under a full moon. A first- and last-time thing (too many couples wandering off under the bushes in hard-to-chaperone areas for the school administration to repeat that romantic mistake).

Tabitha and Brittany went together, of course.

Almost every boy in their class - as well as some of the Seniors and a few enterprising Sophomores - cut in to dance with Tabitha, who was big as a house by then and in a custom bridal gown cut to fit over her belly. She had come up with the idea as a way to have a little fun going along with the yearbook, and also so she could have a few wedding-reception-style memories with the "father" of her child. And maybe just to tweak Brittany's tail a bit. She'd kept her dress secret until her date stopped the little green car in front of the house in town to pick up her friend.

The boys had hatched a plan to keep Tabitha and Brittany apart, so they could all each have a dance with that fox of a (*too bad*) Lesbian with the dark black curls and the plum-colored dress that technically met the dress-code but was fitted closer than an Olympic bathing suit. There was also the matter of those eyes: the arresting green eyes that caused a young man to become confused over whether he wanted to stare at her figure or her eyes until she was already twirling away in the arms of the next boy.

Tabitha never sat idle - a few young women danced with her "just so I can say I tried it," as if her sexual orientation made it any different whether they danced with her or twirled and swirled and gyrated with other young women who were friends and classmates. Quite a few boys danced with Tabitha, either so their buddies could have a spin with Brittany, or out of genuine interest. Some of the young men got a little woody out of dancing with "that pregnant one," especially on the slow songs, though none of them would admit to it. Tabitha was amused by all the attention, and even felt a little complimented by it, so she didn't raise a fuss, though she did whisper a few times: "Don't hold me so close. You'll poke the baby's eye out."

Jeffrey sought Brittany's hand for a dance, for old-times' sake. As they danced slow and close to a fast song - Brittany's little gift to the Nice Boy who'd shown her the ropes - he thanked his lucky stars that HE wasn't the father of the child those two hippie chicks were about to share. When news of Tabitha's pregnancy broke, the poor boy had been certain that the whole Swimming Hole incident had simply been Brittany stalking him for the very same Lesbian Love Child that the redhead was now carrying around in her wedding-dress-covered belly. When Brittany eventually peeled away to accommodate another classmate, Jeffrey went outside into the moonlight with a sudden case of the shakes. Fatherhood - not even simply as anonymous Sperm Donor - was NOT on his high school to-do Bucket List. Eventually, his panic attack was over and memories of the NICE parts of that hot autumn afternoon took over, as they will in a young person.

Jeffrey eyed the moonlit bushes and then, suddenly inspired, went back inside and sought out a Nice Girl who he knew was On The Pill and soon Going Off To College. He made a Proposal of sorts, once he was able to arrange a private moment.

Liv told him to go fuck himself. *You should have come knocking when you had your chance!* Livvy did have her sights set on Jeffrey once upon a time, but then he'd somehow talked Brittany Wendell into going 'swimming' and that was the end of that. *I'm not playing seconds to that girl! Then, now, or EVER!*

Late in the night, but not too late, Brittany Wendell and Tabitha Bayer shut off the boys and enjoyed their own prom for a while. While trying to slow-dance to a popular new song: "Constant Craving" by K. D.

Lang. (Tabitha had skipped up to the DJ to request that one), Tabitha whispered into Brittany's ear for a few seconds.

"Sure." After all, first and last Prom happens only once and a girl should get her wish.

They spun and kissed outside in the light of the full moon, slightly bent at the waist to accommodate their new family member, father (close enough) and mother of the new life between them.

Too soon, another song came on. George Michael: "Careless Whispers." Brittany's request.

Tabitha remembered that there was a boy in Brittany's life, on and off, but always present between them. She stepped back, and looked down at her belly. "Are you going to tell him, or leave me?"

"I don't know WHAT I'm going to do." Brittany frowned. "I'm very confused."

The night was over.

Brittany drove them to Tabitha's house. Tabitha's mother and father were still up, and wanted more pictures. Tabitha's mom thought this might be the only time she ever saw her daughter in a wedding dress... they put the camera away quickly, though. Tabitha's parents could tell there was Trouble.

Tabitha and Brittany went up to Tabitha's room to hash things out, or try to. Tabitha also needed help getting out of her dress. But she was angry, and saying angry words.

Brittany cried quietly while she went behind her friend and reached up to start on the long zipper on the back of the white dress. "I wish I could marry two people."

Tabitha stiffened when she heard those words from behind her. Half of that was the words she most wanted to hear. "Well, you've got to MAKE UP YOUR MIND, don't you?" *Take that, Bitch.* Tabitha had grown tired of chasing some girl who was all moony over a boy who was more and more frequently never around. Tired of hearing about him. Tired of waiting. Tired of playing Standby Second.

Brittany had the zipper about halfway down when she thought about how many other places in town this was probably happening, and how many fathers were probably waiting on their toes to chase boys out of girl's bedrooms before the dress hit the floor. A strange tradition, letting the young man unzip his date at the end of it, and then interrupting coitus before it even began…. Old New England 'Bundling' gone modern. Brittany had a feeling SHE wasn't going to get chased anywhere… she kissed Tabitha's back between the open zipper sides.

Tabitha wasn't expecting it. Her mood changed in a second. "Oh, dear God, girl, you are SO unFAIR!!" She looked down at herself in the wedding dress as a tongue went up and down her back. *OhmyGod.*

A muffled voice from behind her. "You know, Tab, this here unzipping is pretty romantic…"

Tabitha turned to look her friend in the eye. "Old time's sake?"

Brittany felt her pulse quicken. *What the hell.* "Old times sake." She nodded.

They carefully - owing to Tabitha's condition - reclined onto the bed as Brittany kissed and nibbled. Sometime later, Brittany's purple-black dress peeled off - there was no zipper, it was a stretchy pull-down - and Tabitha's dress came the rest of the way off revealing… Maternity lace, ordered from the same wedding shop. With the full moon outside, Tabitha began a calculated play keep Brittany's interest - one complicated by discomfort, a very UN-flexible and UN-athletic body, and a third little person in the room. Intimacy instead of randy sex: the two young women lay with bodies twined and cuddled hugged and caressed and smiled and cried and talked of and reveled in all that had happened and all that was yet to pass between them, however it worked out in the end.

Brittany kind of knew what her friend was up to… but she didn't care. She had a serious case of romance-on-the-brain, multiplied by proximity to a hot, pregnant… *friend?* She frowned, unseen, and then pushed the confusing thoughts out of her head. She whispered close into the girl's ear: "I guess I'll spend the night." *God, it feels so GOOD to be with her! Hugging in bed is like, WAY better when it's the right form….*

She didn't really think that one through.

Tabitha's father paced downstairs. Brittany's car was on the street, the passenger door still open. Twenty minutes passed. He looked over at his wife. "It's nearly midnight. I should chase her out of there."

His wife laughed. "Oh, that's a hoot! WHY? They spend half the nights together lately… Our little girl's ALREADY knocked up, for goodness gracious!"

Tabitha's father still hadn't made the paradigm shift. "I just don't think she should be up there all night with a date… If that girl was a boy, I'd sure have to chase her out. It's PROM night."

Tabitha's mother walked over and put her arms around her husband to stop his pacing. "I'm not even sure we SHOULD chase out a boy, at this point, if it was the father." *And those two, they're wed by circumstance and that big belly, I think.* She stood on tiptoe. "Relax." She kissed his cheek affectionately. "Let them have their… argument... and let them settle whatever it is, and let them make up. Let them have their night." She stepped back and gestured to the folded-up crib now waiting behind the couch. "T's going to be pretty busy in the not-too-distant-future. This may be the only party she gets." She winked at her husband. "Remember what WE did last time we ended up down the hall from honeymooners?"

He did. The couple had been anonymous and loud and young and in a room just down the hotel hallway, and had kept them up half the night - until they got their own ideas. He stood there for ten seconds considering that. "Why am I suddenly such a prude just because it's Prom Night?" *Christ, those two are gonna end up swimming in babies up in that farmhouse like a couple of hippies, but...* Suddenly, that didn't seem like such a bad ending for his daughter. He brightened. "I'll be right back." He went out front with idea of parking Brittany's car off the street. He'd already secretly been hoping for a chance to get behind the wheel of this little hot rod which had been manufactured the year he graduated from high school - *now's my chance? Awww, shit!* He couldn't find the keys, so he closed the door and locked it up right there on the curb. Tabitha's father went into his garage and found a reflective traffic cone that he couldn't remember how he'd acquired. He put that behind the bumper, about ten feet back. *Be a shame to come out in the morning and find a dent in that nice little custom sports car.* He looked at the side, at that pink (grey, now, in the dark) squiggle. *Hmmmm. What we did... that sounds like a damn good idea.* He hurried back into the house.

His wife had cream sherry and two glasses laid out. She'd turned lights down, put on silk, and now waited demurely on the couch for her husband of twenty years. When the door opened, she stood and let the silk fall open as it would. "Come here, husband."

***

Brittany and Tabitha had to be slow and careful and more intimate than overtly sexual. There was a third little person in the room, after all. It felt good, though, bodies together without clothing or concern. Brittany still couldn't get enough of exploring that tummy, somewhat to Tabitha's impatience. Sometimes the tummy explored back - Teddy was kicking a lot, now.

"Oooof!!" She slapped away Brittany's hands in mock consternation. "You just want to make love to my tummy!" Tabitha wanted her to want more... Tabitha still couldn't - and wouldn't ever - get enough of Brittany's smell, feel, touch, eyes, hair...

"Well, I have to get my fill now... you won't be like this forever." *It's driving me wild.* "I want one."

"Take it. It's yours!" Tabitha looked down at her engorged, beach-ball like, tight-stretched abdomen. "You sure? Trust me, it SUCKS!" She yawned. *I can't WAIT to* "get this PARASITE out of me!"

Brittany bent and crooned over the belly: "She doesn't mean it, little Teddy-in-there! She loves you and I love you and-" She felt Teddy kick again. "OH! I want one!"

"Girl, my Condition is driving you batshit CRAZY!" Tabitha put a tiny hand on her fundus, so far over the top and back down under that she could no longer see it. "You'll change your mind first day you're sloshing around in the heat." She grimaced as she tried to get comfortable on the mattress. "Or when your back starts to hurt all the time."

"Yes. Probably." Brittany rolled over and looked her friend in the eye: "Thankyou. For sharing this." Brittany sat up. "Roll." She patted the mattress. "I'll work you over until you're asleep." Brittany Wendell, Massage Therapist to the pregnant! *Could I make a career of this? I'd LIKE to!* Brittany started to knead with her fingers. She'd been doing it for a while, so she knew where she had to be gentle and where she could really put her back into it.

"Wow. WOW! You DO love me!"

"Yes." Brittany nodded, unconsciously, unseen. "I probably do."

***

They both woke sometime after one, spooned together there on Tabitha's childhood bed. A young woman had stirred in her sleep and woken the other, probably.

Brittany smiled. She knew right away.

Tabitha picked up her head and took a second to make out the sounds. Then her eyes got real wide. She squealed: "EEeeeeeeewwW!!" She buried her head in a comforter-covered pillow (they were still on TOP of the bed) and folded the cushion around her ears. She let out a muffled "yuck."

Brittany started giggling. She leaned down and whispered in Tabitha's pillow: "Well, I guess the girl's father isn't going to come up and chase her date out of the room." She kissed the back of Tabitha's neck. "Good thing. It'd take FOREVER to get back into that dress…"

In the adjacent room the parents stopped what they were doing when they heard one of the girls yell "EEeeeewwWW!!" The older couple looked at each other; one smirked, one grimaced.

Mrs. Bayer put a hand on her husband's arm: Wait. "Tabitha is going to have a baby. Her girlfriend is with her. They're married, or married enough. Our little girl grew up."

Tabitha's father flinched, then sighed, and then said what they were both thinking: "Well, I guess somebody Got There!" He flinched again. He had a hard time wrapping his mind around being in the same house as his daughter *while she was… They're just CHILDREN!* He smiled in spite of himself. One of those children was about to give him a grandchild.

"I know it's strange. Take it for the blessing it is." Mrs. Bayer batted her eyes up at Mr. Bayer. "You're not going to let her be the ONLY one, are you, Dear?"

I guess not! "Seems to me, you were too moody for ANYTHING at that stage…" He said it with a smile - he was teasing her. It was also true.

Hmmph. "Well, I'm NOT moody NOW." She winked. *Come hither, Husband.*

***

Bruce noted Brittany's increasing absences and chuckled to himself, because he was nearly giddy with a secret.

He and Brittany still hadn't talked about the summer; it was a slightly uncomfortable subject, the prospect of their separation.

Brittany was afraid that Bruce would find summer romance somewhere Away (probably back in Toronto), and have lost interest by the time he returned in the Fall. She didn't THINK that would come to pass, but this was the first boy in her life that made her just a little bit insecure. THIS ONE mattered. She WANTED him. Right between her legs, donating children to her imagined adulthood, where she was convinced she could keep him interested and participating in the picture of their future that she'd drawn. She mis-identified that flicker of hope, fear and jealousy as love. A lot of young folks make that mistake.

Bruce was afraid to get pinned down on his plans, at first, and worried that Brittany would demand monogamy over long distance and weeks. By January, he didn't care if she wanted fidelity - his Academic Advisor's plan seemed like a good idea. He'd have to have a miracle to pull it off, but by March he had his miracle, and by April he was making preparations. Right before the end of the Spring college semester, Bruce departed for the two-week, part-time course at the Vermont Police Academy. His Advisor had made it sound like a long-shot, but amazingly Bruce had slid right into that summer policing job right here in Vermont! He was BURSTING to tell Brittany, but he figured it would be more fun to walk into Smiley's in his Auxiliary Trooper uniform - with a gun on his hip and everything! One evening in the early summer he'd show up to give his lover a happy surprise and inform her that he'd be right nearby. He couldn't WAIT to see the look on her face.

It never occurred to him that there might be somebody else in the picture by then. Actually, it was Bruce who got the surprise, and his shock came at the very beginning of July. But that was later.

***

Tabitha was up at the farmhouse again for a quiet late-spring Sunday afternoon of homework and cookies. Only a couple of weeks left until Graduation. Well, technically, Tabitha wasn't graduating. But she WAS walking with that GED. She thought the timing had worked out pretty well: she was due one week AFTER commencement. "I'll walk the stage big as a house. In front of the whole town." She turned to

Brittany and smiled. "I just wish you could be up there with me, to share my shame…" She grinned wider.

Hattie looked over to gauge the young woman's mood, and saw that she had spoken with mirth. *Good. No sense worrying about your reputation when you'll be seen pushing a stroller soon enough.* "Oh, that reminds me, Tabitha. I know it's a bit old-fashioned, but there's a stroller out back that you could use, if you need one. It's roomy. They were, in the old days…"

"That's really nice. Thankyou." Tabitha shuddered. She'd already looked at it, in the shed. The rubber wheels were mouse-chewed, the blue and white canvas top was shredded, the whole thing was rusty, and frankly, even when it was new it must have looked like something out of a Victorian horror movie. "My mom is VERY into this. She hasn't had a baby to take care of in seventeen years. Mom's taking me out to get a stroller and a car-seat. Next week, actually."

"Okay, well, it's there if you need it. Or around here, in the yard." Hattie did hope that the baby would make it up, once in a while. She couldn't quite tell what was going to end up of THOSE TWO. One minute it seemed like they'd be living up here together, and then next Brittany would be scarce and Tabitha would be in a funk. "Feel free to bring him up to visit."

Tabitha's eyes narrowed. Brittany suddenly found her homework entrancing.

A few minutes later Brittany pushed back from the table. "So… about Graduation. Actually, I have news." She dug around in her bookbag. "Mister Garland seems to have my back…" She came up with a letter in her hand. She opened it up, and read, paraphrasing: "Took A.P. English in eighth grade, credits, blah, blah, blah… It turns out, if you count the classes that I sat with the older kids when I was in seventh and eighth grade, I have enough credits to graduate." She grinned. "Tab, I'm going to be there on the stage with you!"

Tabitha screamed, immediately started crying, and then suddenly shouted, "OWGODDAMMIT!"

Hattie admonished her, for the ump-teenth time: "Watch your language, he can hear you."

Brittany shook her head. *Silly girl, you should know better!* "Don't get excited, the baby will kick."

Tabitha blew air in and out and said, "He just DID! Oooof!" Then she kept crying as Brittany came over and hugged her from the side.

Hattie wanted to know: "So, Brittany, you're actually attending Commencement to get a diploma?"

"Yep." She stepped back from Tabitha. "All growed up and about to be a father" She grinned at Tabitha. "And headed to college - commuter student - in the Fall." *Oh. OH!* "Grandma, can I still LIVE here?" The thought had never occurred to her to ask.

"Why OF COURSE, dear, this is your HOME!" Hattie cast an appraising glance at Tabitha, thought about a certain hockey player, and wondered just how many people would be living in the farmhouse in the Fall. She sighed. *So complicated, this girl.*

Things settled down after hugs, and the young women went back to their schoolwork. Hattie went back to baking cookies and pies for the next week. The wood-fired oven made the kitchen nearly unbearable in the May heat - they had the doors propped wide open. Occasionally a bird swooped under the porch, in through the door, and onto the plate of cookies in the middle of the table.

Brittany gentle and half-heartedly swatted at them like houseflies. She didn't much mind SHARING, but these little what-ever-they-were sometimes POOPED on the cookies, and that was a show-stopper! *I suppose I'll be learning a lot more about poop in a few weeks....* She glanced over at Tabitha. *That life in that belly is going to be here soon. She made a person!*

Tabitha looked up, noticed the scrutiny, and smiled sweetly.

Hattie looked on, nearly broken-hearted for the not-quite-couple. *I wonder if Tabitha knows about the boy? They need to work it out soon, or it will confuse the child!*

Brittany returned to studying World History. Tabitha struggled with some especially difficult Chemistry, not that it mattered with her GED in-hand, but she didn't want to be known as a slacker. By mutual accord the girls were NOT doing their Biology homework: a lab project on the human reproductive organs.

Brittany looked pointedly at Tabitha's bulging mid-section. "Whadayathink, Tab? We can skip the Advanced Bio?" She turned to Grandma. "Reproductive System. I think by bringing a living demonstration into the classroom every day, we have gained an adequate understanding of that particular subject."

Tabitha didn't look up from her work. "Alright, I'm doing my own little personal lab project, so what's YOUR excuse?" She was in another grumpy phase for a few minutes. It switched back and forth a lot with her, right now.

Brittany thought for a moment. "I was there to watch!"

Hattie stopped chopping carrots and turned her head to look over her spectacles at her granddaughter.

"I MEAN FOR THE WHOLE PREGNANCY! Grandma, get your mind out of the gutter." Brittany thought for a moment. "We've both got a pretty good understanding about... The other."

Hattie Wendell thought she should get something on the record: "I THOUGHT I heard you two say you DIDN'T need The Talk, LAST TIME. Just short of a year before YOU, Tabitha, got PREGNANT. Maybe you should DO that biology homework?"

The girls didn't have anything to say to that, so they shrugged and went silently back to their textbooks.

Supper was simple: Beans and pork and pie, all cooked in the wood-fired range. Carrots left over from last summer, that Hattie had just dug out of the thawed and warming ground in the garden. Brittany remarked on how good it was to have wood-fire-baked beans, and how she appreciated her grandmother slaving away over the hot range in the sweltering kitchen in the ever-warmer weather. The two girls attacked the fresh carrots (first fresh produce of the season!) for dessert, instead of the scrumptious-looking apple pie made from preserves put up last fall. The carrots, carefully covered with straw right where they grew five months ago, had firmed up nicely. They were sweet and crisp and they tasted like summer.

Tabitha struggled out of her chair and waddled over to the kitchen sink to help with the dishes. She had to stand so far back that she could hardly reach the faucet. That big belly again. "Oh, I can't wait 'till he's OUT!!" But she was smiling. "Oooof!" Her smile disappeared.

Hattie smiled. "He doesn't like doing dishes. Walt was like that. You have to reach, it puts pressure on him. Brittany, come here and give your... whatever... a rest. She's the mother of your love-child, you should do the dishes for her."

"Yes, Ma'am." Brittany was absorbed with her thoughts, and started in on the dishes in auto-pilot.

Brittany's grandmother put her arm around Tabitha. "I have something to show you." She put her finger to her lips as she carefully steered Tabitha around the kitchen. She opened a cabinet door and moved an antique tin labeled 'BEANS.' Behind were four cans of store-brand baked beans. Hattie put the tin back. She gently moved Tabitha over to the spice cabinet, where she pointed to bottles of allspice and ground brown mustard. She moved and pointed to a ceramic crockpot: Brown sugar. She pointed to the braided onions hanging in the doorway to the shed. She guided Tabitha to the fridge, opened the door, and picked up a little bottle to hand to Tabitha: LIQUID SMOKE. Hattie put the bottle back, shook her head, and after a wary glance at Brittany over at the sink, said, "She doesn't know. It just gets too hot in this kitchen in the summer. I can't take it in my old age..." She leaned in close to Tabitha's ear. "In general, I start a low fire right before she gets home. I just can't bear to tell her." She guided Tabitha out the doorway into the shed and lifted up a cardboard box to expose a new-looking microwave, the cord running up to a new all-weather outlet there in the shed. "You're sworn to secrecy. Welcome to the family."

Tabitha got over her shock relatively quickly, and returned to the kitchen with a grin. *Family!* She joined Brittany at the sink, but then said, "Oooof."

Brittany was still lost in her own world. She was thinking about Bruce, and wondering what their reconciliation would be like in the fall. *I never even said a proper goodbye!* One week he just stopped showing up at Smiley's in the evening, and she realized that she'd taken his twice-weekly visits for granted, and that the college year was OVER, and he was probably going back to Ontario for the summer soon, and she didn't have his phone number and he didn't have hers. *Shit. I'd better drop by his dorm room and trade numbers, just as soon as things slow down here with Tabitha...* The station-wagon full of children, the dog, the house, the picket fence... all of that was at risk. She was surprised to discover that she didn't have a handle on something in her life, especially THIS. *Him.*

Hattie watched Tabitha stretch and reach for a minute and then shooed her away. "It won't be long, now, Dear. You'd better just rest."

"Three more weeks, at most! I can't wait! I can't even tie my own shoes anymore, it's AWFUL!"

Brittany came back to the moment, back to the farmhouse kitchen. She grabbed her friend's hand. "And it's WONDERFUL. You look beautiful tonight, you know that?" *I think I could jump your bones right now.*

Hattie turned to regard the couple, and especially her granddaughter, skeptically.

The young women didn't notice.

"I'm a WHALE! I'VE GOT A WHOLE FRIGGIN AQUARIUM SLOSHING AROUND IN THEREOOOOOOOFFF!!!" Tabitha winced. Shouting made the baby kick.

"Watch your language in front of the baby, Dear." Yet again, Hattie Wendell gently chided Tabitha: "He can hear you. And it's a good habit to get into, for when they start talking."

Brittany dismissed her troubling thoughts and started leading her friend towards the front of the house. "Start a bath, Tab. I'll help Grandma with the rest of the dishes and then I'll be right up." *I can't wait to bathe that Girl...*

Tabitha's scowl became cheery around the edges and then her face broke into a wide, angelic, cloud-parting grin. A bath always took the pressure off her back for a little while, and seemed to sooth little Teddy inside, too. She thumped off towards the front stairs and the bathroom at the top of them. *A bath with Brittany is even BETTER.*

Grandma Wendell stepped sideways to make room for Brittany at the sink. "Best thing they ever did, Paul and your Grandfather. Ripping out the bedroom and putting in a more-or-less waterproof floor and a bathroom. I don't think she'd fit in a washtub. She staying the night?"

That was the most Brittany had ever heard said about her Uncle. "Yeah, I think so... that okay?" She shifted. "When did he leave?"

Right before you were born, dear. "Of course, but check with Tabitha's folks, 'cause they may want to share her too." Hattie thought it would be cruel to keep the only child's pregnancy from a set of future grandparents. "Before you were born."

"Is he dead?"

"He's dead to us. Maybe." Hattie shrugged. "Just a memory, now." She patted the top of the raven-colored curls. "Go. I'll get the rest of these."

"She's uncomfortable all the time, now. Got to wipe that awful frown off her face for a little while. Not good for the baby, her moods. I'll give her a good scrubbing." Brittany shrugged. "Probably a month since she's washed her feet."

"That's very sweet of you."

Brittany looked down. She wanted to ask something, but couldn't quite bring her self to do it. That was the first time in seventeen years that she'd heard the word 'Paul" come out of her grandmother's mouth. Instead, she said, "I'm trying to be a good father."

"Ahuh." Hattie gave her granddaughter a penetrating look. "How's that going?"

"Nobody seems to be asking around anymore. Everyone thinks we're a couple and the baby just happened. Quite contrary to recent lessons in the Biology classroom… No one came up with any ideas and they just sort of forgot about it." Brittany started drying another plate. She wanted to talk some more. "Tabitha has a lot of new friends, now. The girls are curious, want to feel her belly, hear about what it's like. That kind of thing."

"The real father?"

"Oh, who knows. They've given up on guessing. A certain boy DID eventually stop in the hall and ask to feel her belly, though." Brittany grinned.

"Oh?" That was more than Hattie Wendell had heard about the father since that first day when Tabitha came by the farmhouse, crying and pregnant. "What happened of that?"

"Tabitha took him into the Girl's bathroom and gave him Privileges for a minute."

"Huh?"

"She ran his hands over her body and let him feel all the changes. She let him feel the baby move around. Stuff like that."

"Oh! But won't people figure out he's the father?"

Brittany giggled. "No one will figure ANYTHING out! A teacher caught them."

Hattie put her hand to her mouth. *Oh no!*

"They both have detention, and he's a celebrity. He told his friends he'd always wanted to make out with a pregnant chick, she told everyone she was having a hormonal lust moment and took the first set of arms that came by. No one will think twice about it." She shrugged. "He's safe. Tab's safe. They're too busy gossiping about what Tabitha and I do in the dark to wonder about the biological father."

They were silent and still at the sink for a moment.

Brittany's heart hammered for some strange reason. "Grandma... can she stay a little more often?"

Thought so... "You mean, live here?" Hattie smiled at the thought. "As a housemate, or bath partner?"

"Does it matter?" For some reason, Brittany felt a strange sort of melancholy flicker through her at the thought of NOT having Tabitha close by. She did not correctly identify it.

"As I said, just be kind to her parents. This may be the only grandchild their only child has. Maybe you should... time-share, I think they call it." *I wonder if you'll timeshare the boy, too, when he comes back around?*

"Yes. Of course." *I just want her to be wherever I am.* Then her eyes popped wide open as she came to a strange and certain truth: "I... I think maybe... I might... I love her. I mean, like..." *ROMANTICALLY.* She didn't have the words for it - that one didn't seem BIG enough. Brittany held her hands out and open in a strange sort of half-grope, half-shrug.

Yes, I'm quite sure you do. "Will you be giving up boys, then?" Brittany's grandmother didn't mean to be cruel, she was simply teasing in her own pragmatic way. She got an immediate reaction, and she was saddened by it.

Brittany went wide-eyed and the girl's head twitched unconsciously left and right. *Someone's missing.* "I... Oh."

Forgot about him again, did you? "Better figure that out, Granddaughter."

The dishes were all done. Brittany scurried off to the upstairs bathroom in a confused state, leaving her grandmother to sit in the kitchen and ponder this strange girl who seemed to be in love with one person and dating another. *I wonder if that college student knows about Tabitha? Maybe it was just a school-year thing?*

Tabitha was just getting into the tub when Brittany arrived upstairs. "Mmmmmmmm. I love this old tub. I wish we had a tub at MY house!"

This IS your house, you're here as much as I am now. "You come up here and take a bath any time you want, Tabitha."

"It won't matter in a couple of weeks. It just feels so NICE to take the WEIGHT off right now!" Tabitha lay back, shut her eyes, and breathed deep.

Brittany found a fresh washcloth and started soaping up her friend, one limb at a time. "Just lay there and get scrubbed, girl. You're not supposed to exert yourself."

Oh, God it feels good to be pampered... "Thanks, Brit. Aren't you afraid I'll get worked up?"

"You're too big to catch me now. You waddle too slow. Get worked up, I don't care. I'll outrun you!" Brittany gave her friend a kiss on the lips and a wink.

Tabitha teared up a little, maybe with unbridled joy, maybe with sadness for what never would truly be. She groaned. "This is nice." She leaned further into her friend. *I've missed you.* "You love me, too. Like, LOVE me love me."

"Yes, Tabitha. I believe I do." Brittany sounded defeated. "But I WANT him. I just HAVE to HAVE him."

Tabitha smiled and cried as she held up a leg out of the water so that Brittany could scrub it. "Some day you'll get him out of your system and be done with it."

Brittany stopped scrubbing, the washcloth suspended in mid-air above a knee as she peered into the future. "I don't think so. It's gone too far."

Tabitha didn't know what to say to that.

Brittany resumed gentle, loving scrubbing.

Tabitha lay back with her eyes shut. Eventually, she asked, "Well, just Be There for Teddy."

"I will."

***

Paul Wendell had a meeting with that investigator from down in the states in just a few minutes, but he had a major complication to deal with first. "You WHAT?!"

"I got a job, Daddy!" Cynthia was all smiles. "Here!" She frowned. "Oh... Mom threw me out. Can I move into my room in your house, or should I get a different place...?" She put a finger to her bottom lip.

Paul shook his head. To him it looked far to familiar, that pose - like the come-ons he paid his girls to display every twelve minutes at twelve tables. Five times an hour times twelve tables equals sixty dances an hour times twenty dollars plus drinks... it was easier to digress into the math. "Cynthia, I absolutely CANNOT have you working here!" He shook his head. "It is simply NOT possible." He shuddered. "Not proper." *Nor is her dress... her breasts look like they may tear free of that shirt at the slightest change of the barometer.* "Not suitable!" *I wonder if I should give her my coat?*

Cynthia put on her best crestfallen look and eyed the door. "Well, there are plenty of other clubs on this row..." Her face brightened. "Or perhaps one a few streets back!" Cheaper, darker clubs where the clientele might occasionally go home with the entertainment, or visa-versa.

Paul Wendell recoiled in horror. "Zut! No! No, no, no! You would not be suitable for that work! Here or there!"

His daughter wiggled her shoulders and scrunched up her nose at him. "Oh, I think I can be VERY suitable!"

Her father closed his eyes against the horror and the show of what he should not see and sighed. "But Cynthia, dear sweet Cynthia, you are my DAUGHTER. Ma fille...." His head shook again. "I cannot see you in your birthday suit every day.... it's not right." Not to mention he'd never be able to look a certain Mister Dituscano in the eye again. His ex-wife's father was not a man to disappoint lightly. Paul opened his hands in supplication, PLEASE!, then quickly dropped them when he realized that it could be perceived as suggestive of groping the poorly-clad bosom in front of him. He shook his head rapidly to clear it. "No."

Pretense and mirth dropped from Cynthia's face. "Daddy, EVERYBODY in here is SOMEONE's daughter." She gestured out towards the floor and the naked and semi-naked women strutting around out there. She raised an eyebrow. *See?*

Paul felt sudden horror as the first of many sudden and mildly disturbing epiphanies hit him.

Enlightenment, Papa! "Who better to run the club? THAT is what I want to do. Someday. I have my art degree, and now I have my business degree. I want to go into the business of selling art, Daddy." She swept her hand out towards the strip-show to demonstrate exactly what kind of art that would be. "I want to sit in that chair right there - yours - someday." She put the sweet back into her face. "So whether I do that here, or somewhere else on the street, I'm going to go into the business. WHERE I do it is up to you." She tipped her head and raised an eyebrow.

Paul was at a loss for words. He held his head and then finally looked up. "You have no idea what you're getting into."

"THAT, mon pere, is why I want to WORK here for a bit." She theatrically turned over a hand and left her index finger pointing at the floor under her feet. "Ici!" She took two steps and sat on the edge of his desk, her hip coming just a little too close to his nose.

A move that last year he would not have noticed, and now it made him recoil in terror. Context is everything. *What a terrible year!* He held his hands up in the air over his head, half trying to shake some sense out of Fate, half like a lizard at a run. His brain was trying to escape.

Cynthia's face softened in empathy, but her tone remained jovial, almost harsh. *Poor Daddy.* "You pigs run these women like they're livestock." Her eyes flared and then narrowed. "I want to run them like ART. Treasures. We all ARE you know." She swiveled on the polished surface to look down at her father. "Someday, I WILL run this place. Or one like it."

She noticed his discomfort, grinned, and hopped off her father's desk to languidly frame herself in the door. "I've got the body for it." She swept her fingertips up and down in the general direction of her artful assets. "The question is, do I do it here," she pointed down at the floor beneath her feet again "or out there?" She swept her arm out towards the front, the neighborhood, the streets.

"Cynthia, it does not matter where you debase yourself. And..." He cast about wildly. "Your mother will KILL me!"

His daughter shrugged. "I'm a grown woman."

Paul buried his eyes in his palms. *This MUST be a bad dream.* "You have two degrees..."

"Yes. And I plan to use them, right here on this street." She straightened up archly. "I think that a WOMAN should be running things here." She looked out to the show-floor again. "It's a woman's business, run by a bunch of pigs."

Paul went wide-eyed in fright. He shook his hands at her, palm-down. *Pipe down! Quiet down!*

"Oh, don't worry, Daddy! We all talk that way in the back."

I can't have heard right. "What were you doing back there?"

"Working, Papa! I was here all night last night!" She smiled wide. "I made almost two hundred in tips!" She became serious again. "Eighty percent of your employees are women. It should be run by a woman. This business is ABOUT women."

She was wrong about that, but she wouldn't truly understand that for several years, yet.

Here or there. Here or there. She'll do it, you know she will. Here or there.... her father sighed. Beaten. "Call me Paul." *I'm being punished. That's it. I walked out on my family and now I'm being punished. But wait...* "You're my daughter. I wanted more for you." He nodded. "That's why I stayed here." He opened his hands. "All this... so I could have more for you."

"Well thankyou, Daddy, but you've got exactly what I want." She whirled and strutted out to the show-floor, across it, and towards the dressing - well, UN-dressing - rooms at the back.

Paul thought he might be sick.

One of the waitresses came into his office in her barely-there service outfit. She wanted to ask a question. He answered without ever looking directly in her direction.

Paul Wendell was afraid to look at his own help, now.

***

Tabitha delivered on the eleventh day of June.

Her water broke as she was standing in line to sit down on one of fifty-four hard metal folding chairs lined up in the front rows at Commencement. The school Principal, being a good administrator, was ready for any contingency. He had the lucky couple's GED and diploma laid out separately, just in case. Brittany and Tabitha received their parchment in a hasty, ten-second ceremony at the back of the ambulance, right before the medics closed the doors: "Here you go, ladies. You'll need these in life. Good luck!"

The remaining high school graduates sent them off with a cheer as the school band struck up an impromptu, un-practiced, and not-altogether-pleasing rendition of the Wedding March.

Rick Garland suspected that was just where those two were headed. He'd even come to approve, lately. *That Wendell Girl can always go back to school when she comes to her senses, later.* He turned to the Principal: *Guess that* "turned out alright, didn't it?"

The combined Mill Village and Collegeville School District Principal smiled almost giddily. "I'm sure glad the ambulance got her right out of here before it got messy!" Nothing could ruin a Graduation Ceremony like the noisy and bloody spectacle of a delivery....

***

Tabitha became frightened almost immediately. She held Brittany's hand in a death-grip as the ambulance bounced and swayed across the grass toward the gates and the road that would take them on a twenty-two minute ride to the hospital. She grabbed her friend's upper arm with a rictus claw as another spasm seized her. Tabitha's desperate grip would leave Brittany black-and-blue for a week. The contraction passed and Tabitha tried to sit up against the restraining safety belts holding her to the stretcher. Wide-eyed, full-on panic invaded the red-headed teen: "GET THIS THING OUT OF ME!"

The attending medic grinned and cringed at the same time. It was going awfully fast - contractions a mere two minutes apart, already. "That's the idea, ma'am. Just lay back, concentrate on breathing like I said, and let nature take its course. You may feel like you need to poop - don't, that's a sign that the baby is-"

"I don't WANT to have a baby. Please." Her head shook back and forth in frantic denial and then paused as her whole body tensed. "GET IT OU-OOOOoooOOOOOoooOFFFF!!" Tabitha's demand ended in a panting scream.

Brittany suddenly thought motherhood didn't look so hot. Frankly, she was frightened, too, and starting to cry. "It's okay, we're on the way to the hosp-"

"YOU AWFUL GODDAMNED BITCH, THIS IS YOUR FUCKING F--aaaawwwoooOOOOOOFFFF!" Tabitha relaxed suddenly, took a deep breath, smiled, and then went wide-eyed in fear as the next contraction hit her. "BITCH!!!!!"

Jesus, this is going fast... the medic was torn. He really wanted to deliver a baby, but he also didn't want to screw it up. *What if there are Complications? Best case: she delivers right there as we're backing into the E.R., and any problems come up, I can just hand her off to-*

"AAAAAAAaaaOOOOOOooooooOOOFFF!!" Tabitha strained up against the restraints again. "Brittany." She shook her head back and forth vigorously. "I don't want to be pregnant. Make it go away. I don- AAAhhoooo.... OOOOOooooo.... OOOaaaAAAH!!" Pant, pant, pant. "Brittany, I don't know about this..." Her head shook back and forth. "I really, really don't know about this!"

Brittany wasn't so sure anymore, either.

The medic eyed the cabinet where they kept the pillows and blankets. *Maybe I should get ready for-*

"BRITTANY! OOOoooofff," puff, "oooff," puff, "oooOOOOOFFFgoddammit!" Tabitha's hand shot out to grab Brittany's arm again. "I REALLY don't want to... can I not do this?" Puff, puff, puff, puff. Meekly, weakly, high-pitched: "I've changed my mind."

Well a little late for THAT, sweetie! The medic put a folded-up white hospital blanket between and under the woman's legs. A catcher's mitt... just in case. *Jeez, this is going fast.* "When did you say your water broke?"

Brittany answered the medic's question, since Tabitha had seized up in pain again. "Ten minutes ago, while we were in line..."

"Okay, listen..." He knelt right at Tabitha's head and waited for her pain to subside enough that she was sensate. "You've got to work on your breathing. Slow, deep, steady, don't hold it, and let your body do the work." *Complications?* "Did your Gyno tell you the position of the baby recently?"

Brittany nodded vigorously and yelled over screams from Tabitha: "HEAD DOWN! Flipped ABOUT THREE WEEKS ago."

The medic breathed a sigh of relief and then shuddered as the redheaded mother screeched. He stuck his head forward into the little hole that passed into the cab of the ambulance. "Grand old time back here..."

They both heard yelling from the box, and ignored it.

"Motherfuh... Brit, you bitch, you get-oooOOOFFFF!! Get down here and do this for meEEEAAARRGH!!"

The driver shrugged. They were in a long line of weekend traffic heading to shopping, with lots of stopping for turning cars and merging lanes, and nobody seemed to Give A Shit about an ambulance with it's lights flashing. "Smooth ride, at least...."

The medic rolled his eyes and pulled his attention back to this very young mother in the middle of accomplishing her first delivery. *I should have picked driving today.*

Brittany knelt at her friend's raving head and tried to comfort the poor girl as the mop of red and pink hair tossed back and forth in time with her screams. Screams which came closer and closer together.

The medic was busy down there where all the action was about to happen, and didn't have much time to reassure them - things were moving awfully fast with this tiny and bloated young woman as she went wide-eyed with pain and fear, tensed, and then yelled regrets, all in a repeating cycle. It seemed it would be a close race to get to the Emergency Room, let alone the Delivery Ward.

At one point, Brittany turned and leaned her head into the small cutout between the patient box and the driver's cab to ask a quiet but exasperated question: "Can't this fuck'n thing go any faster?" *A hospital room and real doctors seems like a really good idea.*

The woman driving the ambulance ignored the freaked-out girl. *You should have attended her birthing classes, sweetie! Then you'd know what was coming!*

In the end, the emerging infant decided where he'd be born. There was some concern when he arrived in the ambulance about three blocks from the E.R.... Tabitha had DEFINATELY wanted the comforts of the hospital, once she realized what birthing actually entailed. There was nothing comforting about delivering in the back of a cramped and lurching ambulance. Six pounds, two ounces and popping out within twenty-three minutes after the water broke, the infant was small, like his mother. Once he was cleaned up by the hospital staff, Theodore Edward

Bayer was pink-nosed, red-cheeked, and wrinkle-fore-headed. He alternated between angry purple and pale white, squirming, crying, and protesting this new world around him, just like he was supposed to be.

***

The major task of any day soon became keeping him quiet. Theodore was a screamer.

Tabitha took him to the hospital several times, just to make sure. They looked for signs of incipient pre-natal infections, colic, allergies, unusual blood-work, or any of a host of other problems. The Pediatric Nurse Practitioner smiled as she delivered the news, and thanked her lucky stars that her own kids had been relatively good natured compared to this one. "Nope, healthy as a horse. Some of them are just like that - really strong lungs! Very vocal and very clingy. Get yourself a sling, carry him around all the time, then see what happens."

So Tabitha did just that, and Brittany helped, and it worked well that Theodore had two mothers, because he kept both of them very busy indeed. Brittany missed two days of work, was back waiting tables the third day after the delivery, and thanked her lucky stars she had a job and thus a break from the ever-stronger screaming.

Tabitha discovered that she couldn't sleep when Brittany was on Mother Duty, even with ear-plugs in. The minute Teddy started to wail, even if she was passed out with exhaustion, her breasts would start to go all on their own, and then eventually the cold and wet mess of her shirt would wake her up if the running milk didn't. Her own mother bought her a pump and together the three of them soon declared the device a gift from God. Teddy continued to wail, though, even after feedings.

***

There was an informal christening, in Tabitha's yard, on Theodore's seventh day, a beautiful clean-aired summer morning full of sun and promise. The Bayer home and yard were decorated with blue balloons and ribbons so that the new addition could be presented to the entire community as they stopped by the house in two's and three's.

Brittany's mother even stopped by, briefly, and dropped off a very thoughtful gift: Brittany's old baby 'onesie,' washed and brushed and carefully folded. "I know it's the wrong color, but I don't think he'll care if you don't show any pictures around when he's older." She turned to Brittany. "I disagree with almost everything you've done so far in life, but this turned out okay, didn't it?" Then the woman spun on her heel and left.

Brian and Brittany looked at each other, mouths agape.

Brian carefully shrugged his shoulders. He was sitting in the rocker, doing baby-duty at the moment. Teddy was actually quiet, for the time being. "She has her moments."

The Mitchells dropped by - the couple on the school board who used to sometimes employ Tabitha to watch their pre-school-aged daughter. They were surprised to find their fifteen-year-old son already there, paying his respects to the new mother and babe in the shaded back yard of the Bayer home. Barry wanted to see the family baby-sitter's new infant, apparently.

Mrs. Mitchell talked with Tabitha for a bit, held the baby, and then remarked, "Barry was a screamer, too. We never figured out why. It passed when he was eight months, then came back with a vengeance when he was two." She looked the baby over and then gave Tabitha a bit of advice: "Be ready. I think it's good that there are two of you. You'll need the respite."

Uh-oh. Tabitha, Brittany and Barry shared a look.

The Mitchells left a generous gift - several month's worth of diapers coupons, all stacked and stapled with the most recent on the bottom, and an open account at the store, with the heading on the slip stating, "baby things."

Mr. Mitchell held out his arm. "Come on, Barry. Let's get you home. You'll have one of your own soon enough the way you're carrying on."

Tabitha colored and looked at a nearby tree root until they were gone from the back yard.

Brittany went over and sat next to the new mother and whispered, "SO busted."

Tabitha looked up, put on a brave face, and said, "Yep. I deserved that." Regret crossed her face, only briefly, and then she looked over at her new son and steeled her nerve. She then and there vowed to use ALL of the coupons, but to buy only one box of diapers on the account, ever.

"But they were very nice to you. Considering." Brittany cradled the back of her friend's head. "Let it go. There's nothing you can do."

"Yep." Tabitha shook it off and went to sit in the rocker to hold her new baby. "How's my little Ted E. Bayer?"

The assembled family and friends groaned out loud.

***

The next few weeks passed in a whirlwind. Theodore's crying just got louder and lustier and more frequent. The two young women started to get tired. Not long after that, Tabitha's parents started to get a little tired, too, so the young couple moved things up to the farmhouse for a little bit, where Hattie Wendell got to share in the noise and labors. But that's the raising of a newborn, which is lucky if it's full of more joys than sorrows and mostly it's hard work. Brittany worked full-time at Smiley's, coming home to take over from Tabitha and then fall into bed in a room with a baby and a tired New Mother and hope they all got a LITTLE sleep over the course of the night. 'Home' was wherever little Teddy was, whether it be Tabitha's house in the village or up at the farmhouse, and he split his time about equally. The only time little Teddy settled down seemed to be when he was WITH someone, so they began taking turns sleeping in a chair with Theodore sitting in the sling. It was the only thing they could think to do.

***

Paul Wendell's headaches didn't cease. He watched - or avoided watching - his daughter work (depending on her state of undress) and noted how she flirted with the customers and seemed perfectly at ease in the environment. He wondered where he'd gone wrong. He had never let her set foot within a hundred yards of this street, let alone IN the establishment. *I have failed as a father.* And then he realized that he employed fifty-seven other women who also pranced and flirted, disrobed and displayed. Another epiphany hit and his headaches increased.

One more little thing troubled him.

He hadn't thought about it - the baby - her - for years. He'd picked up and left town as soon as he found out... *what else could I do? I already HAD a family going up here!* The only reason he was still at the farm for half the year was because he knew his father needed the help. Especially after Suzy was gone.... His new Brothers and Masters approved of his family commitment - they respected the fact that he wanted to ease his old man's last years on the farm after Suzy died. Then that little Summer Wench he kept had gotten pregnant - *I suppose that is, in some measure, MY fault too* - and so he had to flee.

A man cannot serve two masters, and unknown to everyone up in the Hollow, Paul Wendell was already a married man. Married to a girl he'd seen every summer for six years at a two-week camp on Miles Pond, an exciting and exotic girl who came and departed on the back of a motorcycle each time. Then one year he realized that they were eighteen and they'd not be back to a kid's summer camp, so on that last day he'd asked her to marry him and the next summer they met right there and were married at the chapel. *I suppose we're held up as a shining example of camper history and lore.* His eyebrows went up. *I hope not!* They'd suffered a bitter divorce after only nine years together. He supposed he was lucky to keep his life.

He'd taken one look at his - now reportedly pregnant - summer fuck-piece, there in the farmhouse kitchen with his parents and her father and he'd realized that any sort of future with her would be a twice-over living Hell. Paul had walked out to the car and flown back to the wife, child, and Topdogs family that he truly loved and owed. No looking back, either. Until now.

Because Paul Wendell was convinced of one thing: that black-haired girl draped over the storefront just three kilometers away, the girl raised by his mother there at the farm... she was Robin's daughter. *My daughter.*

***

Mrs. Mitchell dropped by the house in the village again, one day when Tabitha's mother happened to be out. She wanted to check on little Theodore and see how Tabitha was getting along. She watched Tabitha fuss and nurse and fawn over the infant for a little while, and then said, out of the blue, "I'm a Mandatory Reporter, you know. Because of my job."

"I know." A tear dribbled down Tabitha's cheek.

"You're good with him."

"Thanks. How did you know?"

"Well, we kind of caught you two in the act, didn't we? I mean, once we got over the denial..."

"I'm sorry. I'm not a harlot." She looked down at the infant cradled to her. "Well, maybe I am."

"You've been very careful."

"Wish I'd been MORE careful, or maybe MORE smart, earlier." Tabitha wiped a tear from the end of her nose with her free hand.

Mrs. Mitchell snorted. "No you don't. There's no need for tears. He's a beautiful baby. Fourteen-year-old girls get pregnant sometimes, often by an older boy. This time, the shoe is on the other foot. Yes, we're mad. But you have exactly what you want, don't you?" She gave Tabitha a shrewd look.

"I didn't do it on purpose."

"No, I don't think you did." She cupped the back of Tabitha's head and looked her in the eye. "Be good to him. We're going to ask Barry to stay away. Don't take it personally." She kissed Teddy on the top of his head. "I've been thinking. Try a hat. I still think it was an ear infection, with Barry. He's always got troubles with earaches, even now." She reached into her bag and pulled out a parcel. "Maybe it will help. I washed it already, it can go right on." *I want a photo album. Just in case this is the only Grandchild I ever have. But I can't ask. I can't use that word.* "Try it, if you'd like."

"Thankyou. Yes, of course." Tabitha opened up the little brown bag and spread the hat out over Theodore's little nearly bald head. "That makes sense. Thankyou very much."

Mrs. Mitchell sighed, and sat down. "May I?" This was more complicated than she wanted to acknowledge. "I saw the birth certificate. FATHER UNKNOWN. Are you applying for welfare?"

Tabitha's eyes went wide with surprise. "Oh, no. My parents, Grandma Wendell... And Brittany is actually working full-time." She shook her head. "I'd never do that. Too many questions. We don't need to. Teddy and I will be fine. They'd want to know, wouldn't they?"

Yes, I would have to dig into that. Mrs. Mitchell was the state functionary who would do the digging. "That's why I'm here, actually." *And if I ask the question, I'm part of a conspiracy.* She could cite the state law, Title and Section, that she was already violating. She blurted the next, impulsively: "I could go to jail, you know. Because I figured it out."

"I was afraid of sirens right up until... I panicked when I heard the ambulance coming, at Graduation. I thought they'd finally caught up with me. I'm sorry. I really fu... made a mistake." She snuggled the baby close. "I'm still worried."

"Don't. You'd go on the sex offender registry. You wouldn't be able to teach, or have unsupervised contact with children - other than your own. Two teenagers... It would be unsavory, and it would follow you, probably, maybe, but it wouldn't ruin your life. Stop worrying and get on with motherhood."

"We still really haven't said it, have we?"

Mrs. Mitchell answered sternly: "No. And we shouldn't." *I CANNOT know.* "I have STRONG suspicions, but that's it. If I KNOW, and I don't report for investigation, I will go to jail. I've already talked with a lawyer." *There, you know a lot more than I planned to tell you.*

"I'm sorry."

"I know. I have to go. Keep a low profile. Except with Brittany. You did good, there, actually." *And please move to another state if you're going to apply for welfare, I'd like to spend my mid-life at home,* "Thankyou." She smiled. "I hope that thing with the Wendell girl works out for you."

"Brittany?" Tabitha smiled. "You know, I think that's going to work out, no matter how it works out. She runs around a bit, but she makes a good second mother in spite of it."

Mrs. Mitchell smiled. "I'd heard that about her. I'm glad you know. You take care." And then she let herself out the door with a prayer.

I wonder if I should just turn the whole mess over to my supervisor. She felt sick. *I can't imagine how THAT would go: Sylvia, I fucked up!*

***

A short week later, Hattie Wendell and Brittany went over an extra-large shopping list for the up-coming weekend.

"Make sure you pick up BOTH kinds of hotdogs. I don't know what those folks usually eat. And get the BIG package of hamburger…" Hattie looked up from the list they were huddled over and surveyed the kitchen. *What am I missing?*

"They eat about the same as we do, Grandma, except they don't have garden vegetables." Brittany patted her grandmother on the arm. "It will be fine. They're nice people. Just like you."

Tabitha's parents were coming up to the farmhouse to share in the Wendell family Fourth-of-July celebration. Tabitha's own surviving grandmothers (both of them) had moved down to Florida and gotten a condo together. They were too far away to get together on holidays by any other means than a piles of pictures and a phone call, which would be placed from the farmhouse this year. The Wendells and Bayers were family, of sorts, now.

Hattie was nervous as all heck about it. She wanted these new visitors to have a good time. *It's almost like hosting the in-laws…*

The phone rang. Brittany went to get it. "Oh! Hi, Dad." Brittany listened for a minute, and her face got very serious. "I see." Then she brightened. "Well, that makes it easier, I guess. I'll cancel the State Trooper." Blah, blah, blah. Her facial expressions changed several times. "Okay. Then we'll see you and that worm of a brother of mine. Sorry!" She smiled. "Yes, it will be a nice family gathering. I can't WAIT for you to see Teddy again! He's gotten so much BIGGER, already! And he has HAIR!" She smiled with glee, and listened some more. "Yes, still crying all the time, still healthy as a horse. Tab says he's drinking her dry." Listen, listen. Her face brightened. "Formula? Sure, we'll try it, if it's okay with Tab… That's nice of you." Pause. "Okay. Good. Bye, Dad." She hung up the antique phone.

"Well, what's new with your father? They're still coming alright?"

"Ahhh… HE is coming. BRIAN is coming."

"Oh dear."

"Maybe it's better."

"Maybe it is. Too bad, though."

Brittany's dad had told her that her mother had "some other place to be" on the Fourth. Whatever that meant. It probably really was for the best. The kind of fireworks that happened whenever that woman was around her daughter weren't going to be welcome, even on Independence Day. That's why Brittany was living at the farmhouse.

Hattie suddenly seemed relaxed about the upcoming gathering - the twinkle came back into her eye. "You know, I think we're all going to have a very nice time." She looked up at Brittany, and waited until she caught her granddaughter's gaze. "Why don't you invite that Bruce fellow. The hockey player. I heard he's staying here this summer, got some sort of local job. Have him over, he could probably use some place to go for the holiday. I think you know him."

Hattie wasn't a meddler. She actually thought she was doing her granddaughter a favor of sorts....

Brittany stood there, frozen, not saying anything, her thoughts and her heart racing. *Oh! Bruce. Bruce! It's been WEEKS. Does she KNOW? Is this a HOCKEY thing, or a HAVE THE BOY OVER TO MEET THE FAMILY, AND OH, ALSO YOUR BABY AND GIRLFRIEND thing?* Brittany's mind whirled, trying to figure this out. And wondering how to get hold of him.

"Well, don't just stand there. Give him a call. Something tells me you know how to get ahold of the boy."

"Sure, Grandma... He's been kind of hard to get in touch with, lately, though." *Jesus, I think I plumb forgot about him. Wait - he got a JOB here? Holy shit, it's JULY and we haven't even TALKED. Wait - HOW did GRANDMA know he's working HERE this summer... I don't even know that...* Brittany turned and opened her mouth to ask the question, but didn't know where to start.

My, she's got a funny look on her face.... Hattie shooed her granddaughter away with the backs of her hands. Go. "Invite him up. If you want to." *Poor addled girl. She's gotten herself too busy to juggle two lovers, a baby, and a job. Go figure.*

***

Brittany dropped by Bruce's dorm on the way to the grocery store. He was gone. EVERYONE was gone. College was out for the summer. The whole dorm was empty and under renovations. Brittany slapped her forehead, standing there in front of her car, flummoxed, looking at the full-to-overflowing dumpsters and the empty windows. *Boy am I a fuckup.* She'd just assumed he be right there for her to pick up with when things slowed down with the new baby...

Brittany snuck in through a ground-floor window that had been knocked out for the construction and went up to his room. Well, what USED to be his room. No notes. No cryptic message scrawled on the wall by the door. Nothing. Furniture gone. New paint, floor freshly waxed. Capped wires dangling from the ceiling where the overhead light used to be. Room sterile, empty, and Bruce erased. Like he had never been there.

This is my fault. I told him never to call the farmhouse. They'd been busy. She'd always called him. On the dorm phone. From work. Or he dropped by. Hit or miss. Well, she'd gone and gotten distracted and then she'd missed. In the biggest way. *Shit. Now he's GONE. The house, the station wagon, the dog, the white picket fuck'n fence, the KIDS!!! Holy fuck'n SHIT!! I LIKED that sonofabitch!* She stamped her foot as angry tears threatened. Brittany wasn't used to defeat, or mistakes.

The mad yowl echoed through the the empty hallways and could even be heard out in the vacant Quad between the Academy buildings.

"FUCKINGODDAMNEDESTIDIOT!!!!"

Brittany surveyed the empty and sterile room and tried to square what she was seeing with the time she'd actually spent in the room. Then she tried to plan, envision, imagine some sort of continued lives for her and for Bruce - twin futures that would somehow intersect. She couldn't. *Well... I guess THIS is the end of THAT!*

THE END

Or is it? Want to follow the rest of their adventures?

ANOTHER BOOK IS ON THE WAY!

STAY TUNED!

FOR BRUCE

Bruce Sutton

June 12, 1972 - 1997 (est.)

Thankyou for purchasing this Self-Published book!

I'd like to know what you thought of this tale...

and other readers would like to hear your thoughts!

I'd be grateful if you'd review or rate *BEFORE, a Novel* by J. Kilburn. You can find the book on **Goodreads** and ***Readers' Favorite***. Feel free to post a review to your own favorite blog or fiction fan-site... it's your suggestions that help other readers find their next literary adventure!

Want to read more about Bruce Sutton?

Want to read more by writer J. Kilburn?

Introducing the TOPDOGS Motorcycle Club of Quebec! *Heaven's Door, a Novel* is a lurid, dark, and daring plunge into a big-city Organized Crime underworld. Set in Vermont and Montreal. Meet the characters cast as the "Bad Guys" in the Heaven's Door saga.

visit www.topdogsnovel.com or see it at your favorite Online Bookseller

WHAT READERS HAVE SAID about writer J. Kilburn's previous work:

HEAVEN'S DOOR, a Novel

"A six-hour reading marathon - I couldn't put it down!" - P.S.

"Authentic... J. Kilburn, where did you do your time?!" - E.S.

"*Heaven's Door* by J. Kilburn comes in swinging and rarely stops."
- *Self-Publishing Review*

"*Heaven's Door* is a heart-stopping tale of good versus evil." - *InD'tale Magazine*

"Wild storytelling is part of this novel's raucous, dangerous power." - *Self-Publishing Review*

"The world here is rich and full of compelling characters, but I can't help but feel like we skimmed over the top of too many of them." - *Independent Book Review*

Readers wanted to know more about the characters from

Heaven's Door, a Novel... well, here they are in *BEFORE* !

The Author:

J. Kilburn's narrative style has been compared to those of Joyce Carol Oates, Virginia Wolfe, D.H. Lawrence, Hunter S. Thompson, and Nell Zink. His subjects and almost cinematic descriptions of setting have earned his work comparison to movies and television shows like *Sons of Anarchy*, *Tin Star*, *Twin Peaks*, and *Thelma and Louise*. Prior to **Heaven's Door, a Novel** and **BEFORE**, Kilburn's other published work was a feature-length investigative news article that got the whole page in his community newspaper.

Kilburn lives a quiet and private life on the shore of America's sixth Great Lake. He has lived and worked in Vermont, Massachusetts, Illinois, and Minnesota. During these travels, Kilburn has dabbled in law enforcement, private security, emergency medicine, truck driving, and horse-logging. Other occupations have included at-risk youth mentor, big-city process server, park ranger, and industrial wastewater treatment operator. Along the way, he's pedaled to 14,000 feet above sea-level in a major bicycle race, been marooned overnight on a deserted island, ridden a motorcycle from Chicago to Thunder Bay, and hiked Vermont's highest peaks to watch sunsets on both the longest and coldest days of the year. He currently maintains plastics processing machinery for a major manufacturing company. When not at work he and his wife enjoy life around a little urban farm complete with greenhouse, garden, and mini-barn. Their current flock is composed of four chickens and a cat named Sierra Feral.

From the Author

I never intended to write a Coming-of-Age book; that idea was the furthest thing from my mind as these characters started to take form on a sun-dappled lined yellow legal pad. With a shade-tree as a ceiling and mown grass as a desk, I was beginning Character Development for my next book when events started to spiral out of control.

One of the reviews of my last book had called my characters "intriguing," but wished for more of the back-story about them. So as I sat under that tree by the lake, I started fleshing out a the main character - a man who looses his life while serving the Greater Good. I turned back the clock and started with a boy. I gave him family, class-mates, friends and eventually romance. I spent some time with the love interest, and fleshed-out her community and family as well. Somewhere in there, those characters took the pen from my hands and began writing their own story. They surprised me with plot twists I never imagined. They invited other characters into the plot, thickened and sweetened it, and stirred up some trouble of their own making.

I sat back and watched with fascination and amusement as a story took shape - not the one I'd been writing. These characters took the stage, threw out the script, and performed their own play. At one point (900 pages of draft), I realized that I had a new book, one that was complete and stand-alone. I revised, inserted a few tidbits here and there to unify some common themes, re-read and edited the hell out of it, and now it is in your hands.

J. Kilburn